Privacy

Interrupted

Privacy

Interrupted

PAULIE J. JOHNSON

THE REGENCY
PUBLISHERS

ISBN: 978-1-958517-39-0   (PB)
ISBN: 978-1-958517-40-6   (HB)
ISBN: 978-1-958517-38-3   (E-book)

Some characters and events in this book are fictitious and products of the author's imagination. Any similarity to real persons, living or dead, is coincidental and not intended by the author.

Book Ordering Information

The Regency Publishers, International
7 Bell Yard London WO2A2JR

info@theregencypublishers.com
www.theregencypublishers.international
+44 20 8133 0466

Printed in the United States of America

FOREWARD

A young boy loses his twin brother at the age of ten, and two years later, he loses his mother to cancer. He overcomes many mental disorders that developed from having a photographic memory and uses his beliefs to guide his life. He had problems talking to people, so he withdrew to a life of seclusion.

A judge intervened, and through the Judge, he met a Senator that recognized his capabilities, and a rocky relationship followed for the rest of their lives.

The damage came to him when he saved a girl from death. He didn't have the skills to talk to people, and he had to fight a battle that he knew nothing about; it was a battle of love. The problem he had was the girl that he saved was the Senator's daughter that he knew, but she didn't know him. His life was kept secret from her for a purpose.

To complicate matters, he lived his life of seclusion in the mountains and worked his thoughts out by working on other projects that he had.

The girl he saved was a prisoner of the weather, he couldn't help her back to safety, and he knew that him being around her would only cause her discomfort.

She was injured and required attention, which meant he had to remain nearby. She didn't have anyone but the man that saved her life, so she was at his mercy, and he was at hers.

Neither one of them expected what was to unfold.

CHAPTER ONE

I arose from my bedroll, long before the dawn had broken. I opened my door and saw nothing but the white snow that had been keeping me enclosed for most of the day before. I learned from experience that even though the snow wasn't a bother, it was the dampness it possessed that allowed the cold to penetrate a person's clothing, even for those that were prepared.

I slipped on my bearskin parka and prepared myself for the day to come, and firewood was at the top of my list. When I walked out of my little place, I was greeted from the beginning of the rise of the sun, and I forced myself to stop to watch it. That was the only time a person could see what it looked like. When the rays were above the mountains, no one could look directly into it without being blinded.

I looked over at my sled and then walked to it, laid my guns down on the tarp, and prepared myself for the trip. After attaching my sled harness to my shoulders, I leaned forward and began my little walk.

Fortunately, I chose my home place correctly. The walk of the slope of ascent was always the hardest part; it was mostly all uphill. The incline wasn't so much the problem, but by the time I added the mix of the environment together, it made each day a different day. I looked up and began my calculations. I looked at the distance I had to travel along with the incline, and with it, I had to figure in the softness of the snow; it was harder to walk when you labored every step, and then I had to add the heavy clothing and the pulling of the sled, and even the snowshoes. In summer, it was only an hour's walk away for me. To someone not accustomed to my location, it would have taken them three hours; the elevation and the other factors would have been too strenuous without having to stop and rest every fifteen to twenty minutes. But this was the beginning of winter, and after minutes of calculating, I had my arrival time to reach my destination around noon. Given that, nothing stopped me. The downhill was the easy part, the weight of the firewood didn't need much work from me other than guiding the sled, and even then, I had to restrain the sled from exceeding my speed. I found out the hard way that sometimes you have to load a sled full of firewood two or three times, and you also have to repair a broken sled about that many times too.

I took a short fifteen-minute break to ensure I didn't have company and then resumed walking.

I soon saw the wood from a distance that I was after. The summer before, I had chopped up some fallen trees, and I took full advantage of the bounty that they had to offer.

I stopped and rested before I began my work and scanned my surroundings for unwelcome guests.

Off in the distance, I heard the first sounds of people that I hadn't heard since my visit to get my supplies; it was the sound of a snowmobile straining to achieve what it was asked to do.

I stood up and began my work, loading the firewood on my sled, and gave my trespassers no further attention.

I had my sled half full when I heard the engine topping a hill beyond a ridge. I stopped my work and listened as it came to a stop just over from where I was.

I looked up at the top of the ridge and saw a tall figure walk towards the cliff and look down. Another figure walked up, and soon the person that was looking down turned to meet that person and was struck in the face with a fist. I watched that person fall and graze a rock that jutted out from the cliff. The figure that struck that person calmly walked over and took a look down. I reached for my rifle, but I was too late. I heard the engine start and listened to the sound of the snowmobile as it grew feint.

I headed immediately over to where the person fell. The person's front was concealed in the snow; I didn't expect to see who I saw when I pulled it out.

By the time I had gotten to her, she was blue in the face. That only meant one thing, she wasn't breathing. I swept her mouth of the snow, tried to clear all I could out of her nose, and began giving her breaths to revive her. I then went and began thrusting to her abdomen and went back to giving her breaths. Then shifted back to her abdomen and gave her hard forward thrusts to pump her lungs. I switched back to breathing for her. It wasn't the right way to give CPR, but I had no other choice.

The sound of air being gasped into her lungs brought me my relief. I drug her over to my sled. I had to put her down to dump the wood I had stacked onto it. I picked her up and placed her on it, and took off my coat and covered her as best as I could, her legs dangled over the sled, and I had to let them drag in the snow.

She needed medical attention, and I was the only one who could give it to her; she was a mess.

It was the next night before she awoke from my bedroll.

I was sitting in a corner I used for my work area, and I heard her stirring around. I put some more wood into my little wood stove to help take the chill out of the air and give off a little flicker of light.

"Where am I?" She asked as she stuck her head out of my bedroll.

"I'll answer all your questions in due time." I said to her, "You've been out since yesterday; I know you have to use the bathroom to relieve yourself." "There's an outhouse to your right when you go out the door."

She tried to move, but she was in pain.

I got up to assist her, and she immediately became frightened as I grew close; I expected as much.

I stopped, knelt on one knee, and spoke softly in hopes that I could use my voice to calm her fears. "You've got a twelve-inch gash in your butt; I had to sew you up, you're lucky it wasn't your head, or you more than likely wouldn't have survived the fall." "Now, as I said, I know you have to go relieve yourself." "That's what brought you out of your unconscious state," I said once again, putting softness in my voice.

I put on my snowshoes and then walked over to help her up from where she lay.

"Take it slow and easy; the pain that you feel now is nothing compared to the pain you'll feel when you start healing." "You'll feel worse before you'll feel better," I told her.

I helped her get up on her feet and walked with her as she put her arm around my neck and used me for her support. She nursed the soreness she had in her butt and tried to put as little weight as she could on it. I helped place her in my sled and told her to lean over on her other hip so that the trip wasn't painful.

"How far is it?" She asked me.

"It's not far." "With the soft snow, you can't walk without sinking up to your crotch on every step, and in the shape you're in, that's just not an option." "I only have one pair of snowshoes, so I have to carry you to my sled." "You'll find that the seat inside the outhouse is covered with some bear fur; the skin of the butt isn't any match for anything that freezes quickly." "You get to enjoy a luxury that I had to find out the hard way." "You have a pain in your butt, and so did I," I said to her.

We soon reached the outhouse, and I helped her into the shack.

"Are you going to stand outside?" She had nervousness in her voice.

"No, ma'am, I'll be giving you your privacy." "I'll be a ways away, and when you need me, just call out." I shut the door and walked off, and then I stood and looked up and watched the sky on a clear night. The wind was silent, and the snow was heavy. I was soon interrupted by the young lady calling.

I walked over, and she opened the door. I helped ease her back down on my sled and then began pulling her back to my little place and helped get her back in my bedroll.

I put some more wood into my stove and raised the temperature of my little place a few more degrees.

"Now," I began, "I have to know what you remember before we got to this point." "If I say anything, you might believe what I said, and that won't achieve anything." "So I have to hear from you what you remember."

5

"My husband and I were taking a ride to Cooper's Bluff from the ski resort." "We were having a good time, and then we stopped." "I looked down from the top to see what everything looked like and." She stopped and looked up at me and began crying.

There was nothing I could do for her. I walked back to the corner I had been sitting in doing some work and started where I had left off. She cried for a long time before she eased her tears.

"How long have you been married?" I asked her.

"This was our fourth anniversary." She stated in what sounded like a sad voice.

"Have you had fights in the past?" I asked her.

"I don't know what happened." She said as she started crying once again. I held my silence.

"Who are you?" She asked me as she tried to catch her breath.

"My name is Smith," I told her.

"What else?" She asked.

"That's it, just Smith." "My father was drunk and named my twin brother both Smith and me." "No first name, no middle name, just Smith, the both of us."

Then it was her that went silent. I knew she had questions, but she didn't know where to begin. It was my turn.

"You said that you and your husband were taking a ride to Cooper's Bluff." "That's twenty miles east of the ski resort." "You landed at the base of Miller's Ridge." "We're thirty miles west of that resort."

"Has he ever come here before, without you?" I asked her.

"About four or five months ago, he said he wanted to look around." She replied.

"Did he come with friends of his?" I continued in my questioning.

"No, it was supposed to be a short trip to check out the resort." "What are you getting at?" She asked me. She sounded curious that I was asking her questions.

"There aren't any four-wheelers at the resort; the reason for that is, it's only open in the winter; he brought one with him, didn't he?"

"Yeah, how did you know?" She had a voice of surprise to her.

"The road is only accessible in summer; spring is unpredictable because when the snow melts, it saturates the road with water, and it becomes undrivable." "In the fall, due to the elevation, the road freezes, and anyone that drives on it finds themselves sliding off of it into the bottom of the ravine." "So, it's closed for all seasons except summer." "That was the only time your husband could have come." "There's a train that transports everything that the resort needs, supplies, people, everything comes in and goes out using that train." "That's how you got here," I said, looking down at the pad that I had on my lap.

"I don't understand?" She said, sounding confused.

I took a deep breath, exhaled, and lit a small candle next to me for light. After I did, I opened the pages on my pad and began drawing a quick sketch.

"What are you doing?" She said as she sat up on her elbow a little to watch me.

"It's said that a picture is worth a thousand words; if you can give me a few moments, I think you'll have a clearer understanding." After I finished, I handed it over to her and put the candle beside her.

"This is me." She remarked, "I remember that dress, and I remember that necklace." "I still have that." She said, looking over at me, "I was about twelve then; who are you, and how did you know about this?"

"You were eleven, not twelve." "You were at a birthday party for a congressman that your father had ties with." "The party was supposed to be for his daughter, but it was for the congressman to get endorsements from those that he invited." "Their endorsements meant financial contributions to him." "You were wearing a blue dress, with lace around the collar, and you were standing a good foot or better above the rest of the kids." "I could see you didn't like being there, and you looked like you felt awkward."

"Were you one of the kids?" She asked me with less fear of me than she had had earlier.

"I was with the Judge." "I made the pizzas you ate," I told her.

"You're kidding me?" She said in awe.

"No, I was fifteen." "That was the day I met your father, and that was the day that I saw you."

"But, that was what?" "Thirteen years ago." She said, "How come I never heard of you?"

"Because after I met your father, I was taken away by him." I responded to her question, "But, we'll go over some of that later." "When I saw you fall, by the time I made it over, you weren't breathing." "There are two deaths, a biological death, and a clinical death; either way, when you're born in this world, you poop, and when you die, you poop; that's why you've got my long johns on, in case you're wondering." "I wear three pairs, and I have three other pairs." "I wash my bottom pair and put on another pair to wear." "That's changed now; you're wearing my other three pairs." "Anyway, back to my story." "Out here, I couldn't perform CPR on you." "You're in an area where you would have suffered a great deal of pain." "To accomplish CPR the right way, you have to compress the diaphragm about two inches or further to reach your heart to do any good." "If I did that, chances are I would have broken one or two of your ribs, and if I did, I could have punctured one or both of your lungs." "That meant to revive you, I didn't know if I was going to be successful, and I had no way of knowing if you suffered any internal injuries from the fall." "I had to make a decision, and I didn't have time." "When I got to you, you were head first in the snow, and you were buried up to your knees." "You're lucky; we had two days of soft snow." "Had it have been a blizzard instead of a light snow, you would have felt the snow like the rocks that lay at its bottom, and if you had fallen two feet deeper, you probably would have broken your neck, so you had a lot of luck on your side if you can look at it that way." "So, if your abdomen is sore, I hope it's from my thrusts I gave you to force your lungs to react and not from damage that was done to any vital organs." "If I had to choose between the two, I wouldn't have been able to watch you suffer the pain that you would have gone through; you would have died a slow and miserable death." "I don't want to frighten you, but there's a possibility that this may not be over with." "When I pulled you out, you had snow in your mouth and nose." "I did my best to clear the snow from your mouth and nose to give you mouth to mouth, I might have forced some snow into your lungs, and that gives me a fear that you could get pneumonia."

"People will search for me." She stated to me.

"Ma'am, I'm sure they will, but they're searching for you fifty miles away from where you're supposed to be." "They won't look here." "I asked you if you had any fights with your husband, and you answered that you didn't know what happened." "First off, he had to park somewhere on that road and ride an ATV in." "Something's not adding up." "Did you hear him specifically say to anyone else about you and him taking a ride to Cooper's Bluff?" I asked her.

"Yeah, he told all of our friends we'd be back later."

"But did you hear him say that he was going to Cooper's Bluff, or are you assuming that he told your friends?" I asked her the same question once again.

"Yes, he told everyone."

"Tell me exactly, word for word, what he said," I told her.

"He told everyone that we were taking a ride over to Cooper's Bluff." She sounded miffed.

"Then you have to ask yourself this question, why are you fifty miles from where you're supposed to be in this condition if he didn't plan this?" "You're a retired senator's daughter, I would assume, you have a life insurance policy, correct?"

"Yes"

"Were you two having money problems?" I asked her.

"No, my husband is an attorney; he works for a law firm." She answered.

"How much is your life insurance?" I asked her.

"It's for five million." She said to me.

"Five million huh, and I assume it's set up under a simple will, you die, he gets everything, and if he dies, you get everything, am I wrong?" I asked her.

"Yeah, that's the way he wanted it." "He said no one needs complicated, drawn-out lists of who gets what; everything is simple, this way."

"Yes, ma'am, that's the way it turned out too." "Within a few days, they won't be looking for you anymore; you'll be considered to have become a victim of the cold." "Those clothes you were wearing would have made sure of it." "After a month, they'll assume the animals have taken care of your remains, and they would have been right." "You'll not be found." "That was his plan." "He came here riding on a four-wheeler for one purpose; he knew he had to stash a can of gas to get him back." "He wouldn't have enough gas to get him back to the resort on a snowmobile, he did all that riding to throw suspicion away from him, and he knew he couldn't make it back without more fuel." "He planned this out." "Because of the outcome, I have suspicions that he may have behaved like he was in love with you from the start to make others believe he did." "The day you married him was the day he started to carry out his act of your murder." "That's what doesn't add up, he had to have a plan, and I believe he had this on his mind before he met you." "He was looking for someone with your status." "To get a large sum of insurance on someone, you can't be just anybody." "He not only gets a cool five million, but he's a playboy all over again, with no one the wiser." "Did he have an affair?" I asked her.

"No"

"Are you sure?" "Did he take trips for his client's sake and stay gone a few days now and then," I stated.

"It was his job." She quickly asserted her answer.

"I'm sure it was, but he made one mistake; you didn't die." "The problem that you have now is that you're snowed in." "There's no way out, and once winter sets in, you become a prisoner, not by me, but by winter." "The nights can freeze a human in less than twenty minutes." "My sleeping bag is good for forty below." "If I try to get you back, and a storm blows in, we'll be trapped." "Not from the cold, but the snow; its weight will be enough to crush us." "Add the condition you're in and what normally takes me a week to reach that resort without snow, and the fact that I would be towing you all the way, means roughly it would take me a month or more." "Jane, I want you to listen to me; you're not in any danger as long as you're with me." "If you try and leave from here when I'm gone, I'll not be able to follow you if it's snowing when I get back, your tracks will be covered up, and if I do find you, I'll remove my long johns." "I'll need them; you won't." "I wouldn't be able to bury you." "This ground is frozen, and the wolves or cougars or bears

9

will make quick work of you." "If you leave, your husband's plan will succeed even though you survived the fall."

"You called me Jane." She stated, surprised.

"That's your name," I said to her.

"Yeah, but it sounds strange coming from a man that I've never seen, yet alone know." She responded.

"Are you hungry?" I asked her.

"Are you a wanted man?" She said, ignoring my question.

"I guess I would answer that yes, and no." "Did I break the law?" "No, I'm not a criminal." "Do I have enemies?" "Yes, I do." "Now, are you hungry, I've got some biscuits working out in my oven, and I've got some sausage I can fry up?"

I didn't expect her to answer, and I got up without it, got my pan out, put it on top of my fireplace, and had some pan sausage frying. I put them aside, went outside, brushed the coals away from my Dutch oven with a lid I used to cook, and took the top off it. The aroma of the biscuits filled my little house. I put some sausage on a biscuit and asked her if she wanted some butter to go along with it.

"Where do you get butter?" She asked with curiosity.

"I make it." "If you overbeat whipping cream, it passes the whipped cream stage and becomes butter." "Or you can let it sit in a refrigerator for a couple of months, and it becomes butter without whipping it." "I can't do that here; the whipping cream freezes, so I take out five quarts of whipping cream from my shed and let it thaw and do it the old fashion way by churning it." "Or, instead of butter, I have preserves, if you like." "Or, you can have both the butter and preserves," I said to her.

"Did you make those too?" She asked.

"Yes"

"What are you doing out here?" She asked me, "We rode for a long way, and I didn't see anything except snow and trees."

"That's a long story, and it brings back memories that I don't want to bring back right now and to see you has done that." I said to her.

I got up from where I was sitting and began to leave.

"Where are you going?" She asked.

"I have issues, and I need to work on them." "The snow and the moon give me light to work by, so I'm able to take advantage of it; besides, you don't need me around anymore."

"Aren't you going to eat?" She asked.

"I'm not hungry," I told her.

"Did I say something wrong to you?" She asked me.

"Jane, there's a lot of things you don't know about me." "Your father does." "When you get home, and you're alone with him, you can ask him what he knows about me." "I made you some clothes while you were out." I said, changing the subject, "These two pieces are for your legs." I showed them to her and how to put them on. "I couldn't make you a one-piece suit, so I had to make two leg pieces." "They're bear skin, with fur, so they'll keep you warm." "Both of them have moccasins sewn in at the bottom; they're made out of beaver hides so that they will resist the dampness of the snow." "Plus, the rocks won't hurt your feet when you start to be able to get around." "You have on one pair of socks; that's for a purpose." "You sweat with two pairs and moisture freezes; you'll end up with frostbite." I leaned over and picked up another garment. "These are like a pair of shorts." I held them up to my front to show her. "You put the leg pieces on first and tie them by wrapping the leather around your leg and tie it in a square knot." "That way, they won't slip down as you walk." "Do you know how to tie a square knot?" I asked her. "No"

"Okay, first tie a granny knot, like this." I showed her how, "Next, you tie a reverse granny knot." I also showed her, "This way, you can tie and untie the knot without problems." "You'll know if you tied two granny knots instead of a square knot, I'll have to cut the leather." "The knot binds and gets tighter." "You can try as hard as you can to untie it, but you always end up having to cut the leather." "Pull the shorts over the top of the legs with the legging tied." "Then tie the shorts the same way." "That way, you have a double tie strap to assure that the leggings won't start falling as you walk, and the waist has an expandable cord sewn inside to where all you have to do is hook the hooks together; for a belt." "The coat was a different story." "It wasn't as difficult, and I made it parka style like mine so you can pull the hood over your head to protect your ears from the wind." "It's also made of bear fur." "The fur will provide you with warmth, and its length should reach down to your knees." "It's all warm, but it won't protect you from this environment very long if you become caught out in it."

"Smith," she said as I turned to walk out the door.

I turned to confront her.

"You didn't tell me how you remembered that party?" She stated.

"I have a photographic memory," I said and then turned and left.

After taking care of the girl, I started chopping the wood I had gone back and got.

I chopped the pieces all night long.

Morning came, and I began working on some of my other projects. I stopped when I heard the door opening, and when I walked around to the front, I saw her.

I walked over to her, helped her to my thinking quarters, and left her till she called for me. I placed her back into the sled and stopped at the cabin.

I was going to help her in when she asked me what I was doing last night, "I heard a lot of noise." She told me.

"We need wood to stay warm by and cook by, so I chop wood to think, and I stay busy doing other things."

"Like what?" She asked me.

"I'll show you." I pulled her around to the side of my building, and she looked surprised.

"I'm making some totem poles for the resort."

"How many?" She asked.

"About a dozen or so, I look, and when I find the right size tree, I cut it down and drag the pole back and chip the bark from the tree and begin my sculpture." "Each one is different; none of them is the same."

"They're beautiful." She said with a surprised look on her face.

I noticed her beginning to shake.

"You shouldn't have come out here without being dressed for it." "I told you those long johns aren't going to keep you warm." When I leaned over to pick her up to take her in, I could tell that she felt warm. "You've got a temperature." "Do you have pain in your chest when you breathe?" I asked her as I put her back inside the bedroll.

"No, I just feel sore." She replied.

"That's probably from the stomach thrust I had to give you." I reached over and grabbed some blankets from where they sat in a corner, covered her up with them, and then zipped the sleeping bag closed. I went outside and gathered some wood and piled it over next to my wood stove.

I then went back outside and returned with a frozen chicken. I took another Dutch oven and turned it upside down on top of my woodstove and filled the Dutch oven that had I cooked my biscuits in with snow and placed it on top of the Dutch oven that I turned upside down so it would melt the snow into water and placed the chicken on top of the snow so when the snow melted into water, it wouldn't cook the frozen chicken. My mission was to allow the water to warm and thaw the chicken before cooking it.

I then sat down in my corner and began working on some things I was involved with.

From the glow of the fire inside the woodstove, I could see that the girl was shaking wildly and put two more blankets on her. I took off my clothes, left my long johns on, unzipped the zipper to the sleeping bag, and got in.

I felt her lift the blankets she had on her, and she reached out her hand and pulled herself to me. Soon she lifted the tops of her long johns and then lifted the back of mine and squeezed me hard.

Then she rolled me over the other way and did the same; she needed me to give her all the heat I could give her.

I got up several times that day and put more wood on the fire and more snow in the pot for the chicken. She received me each time with arms begging for my body heat when I got into my bedroll.

We were tightly bound together, and she rolled around trying to find comfort in her ailing from her soreness from the gash she received on her butt and the fever she had.

Late that night, I tended to my fire and the chicken. The young lady stuck her head out of the sleeping bag.

"What time is it?" She asked.

"About three, maybe four in the morning, I don't know." "I don't need a watch or a clock," I informed her.

"I've been out that long?" She asked.

"Yes, ma'am."

"What are you doing?" She stated to me.

"I'm making some chicken corn meal soup." "It'll make you feel better," I stated to her.

"I don't have an appetite." She uttered.

"I know." I said to her, "Jane, your husband's name is "Russell" isn't it?"

"Yes, how did you know?"

"You called me Russell a couple of times in your sleep."

"Smith, are you through doing what you're doing? I want to talk to you?"

I moved the pot over from the direct heat and bent down on my knees to listen to her.

"No, I need you in the bed." She said to me.

I got in, and she pulled me into her body.

"You act as you've never been with a woman." She stated.

"I haven't," I told her.

"How long have you been here?" She asked.

"Almost eleven years." "I came here two years after I met your father." I relayed to her, "My father was in the military, and I have never seen him." "My mother had an issue, and he left us when I was young." "She got assisted living pay, and we lived in an old hunter's shack back in the woods." "We lived on a place they called a nine-mile road." "They called it that because at the end where we lived was nine miles to the road." "Come rain; there was no way in and no way out." "I told you that my mother had an issue" "I did the cooking for us." "The dirt road turned to clay and stopped anyone from driving on it when it was wet." "It was guaranteed that if anyone tried, they would be rewarded by getting stuck." "If we didn't have what we needed, we did without." "My brother and I would do a lot of hiking and fishing from the creek and building our fires." "I'd tell him stories that I had read, and we lived the life of the pirates, or whatever we wanted to be."

"How come you never said anything about me, you know, my size?" She asked.

"How tall are you?" I asked her.

"Six eleven."

"Then, if you were a man, you would say seven, maybe even seven one or even seven two or seven foot three." "Men lie; they always want to be taller, but you're not, you're a woman, so you say I'm six eleven." "It sounds shorter than saying seven feet." "So, you're not six eleven even; you're six eleven plus." "If you say six eleven and a half, people think seven-foot, because they round it off, and even at six eleven, they still think seven feet." "I bet you don't even own one pair of high heels." I said to her, "And I'm sure you've heard all of the terms like how's the weather up there, or be careful of low flying planes, but you could tell me what I haven't read about, I bet you've heard them all." "I would imagine everyone would ask you what team you played on in school." "Being tall, a person automatically assumes you played basketball." "But what they don't see is the little girl inside of you, the little girl that would love to dance with someone her size and I would imagine that there weren't many requests to do so." "The boys got laughed at if they did." "I've been around, and if you were a boy, the girls would be hanging all over you; it's tough, though, when you're the tallest girl in the school." "Everyone can spot you out in a crowd." "Jane, I see a love-starved girl that fell in love with a man that showed her affection." "Was he the first person to do that?"

"Yes"

"I was living in a lie too." I told her, "When I was young, my brother and I were the results of that lie." "I was on my way to pick my brother up from school one day." "I was home schooled, and he had to go to a special school; I was ten then." "When I started walking down the road, I saw that someone had been in a wreck." "The police told me to keep going." "I felt sorry for whoever it was; that car was twisted every which way." "When I got to the school, they said my father had picked my brother up already." "I told them no, he wasn't supposed to, but he did." "I was walking back to our house when the Chief of Police stopped and asked me where I was going." "I told him, home." "He said, what's your name, son?" "I told him, Smith." "I saw the expression on his face changed, and I knew something was wrong." "He said, get in, Smith, I'll give you a ride." "Jane, I found out that there was going to be a court-martial for my father for being drunk on duty the next day." "They were going to kick him out of the military." "He picked up my brother, and when they crashed, my father died immediately, and my brother, my twin brother, was on life support for three days." "When they crashed, his head hit

14

the windshield, and part of his skull was pushed into his brain." "I watched the doctors come and talk to my mother, but it didn't do much good." "Due to her issue, she didn't have any understanding of what was going on." "I later found out that my father had bought a bottle before he picked up my brother." "The bottle was almost empty, and he was drunk when he went off the road and hit a tree." "He was traveling at a high rate of speed, and there weren't any brake marks." "But, since he was in the military, they buried him." "We didn't have any money, so they burned my brother."

This time it was me that she grabbed hold of. My tears exploded from my eyes.

Like her, it took me a long time to regain my composure; I got out of her arms that fought me from doing so and began picking the meat from the bones of the chicken and putting it back in the broth.

I went on to say, as my tears flowed. "Half of me died that day." "I no longer went hiking, or fishing, or pretending to be anyone, other than who I was anymore." "I read every day, and I learned many things." "I escaped from my life that way." I wiped my tears from my eyes with my sleeves and continued, "To graduate, I had to write an essay, and it had to be witnessed by a representative of their choosing." "I was twelve, and my degree was based on certification as to whether it was me that turned in the material and not someone else." "I carried my typewriter to the school, and when I entered, there were a lot of people staring at me." "I asked where the Counselor was that I needed and was directed to where his office was." "When I entered, a man looked at me real funny." "I told him that I was sent here to see a person by the name of Holmes, and if he could show me where he was at, I would appreciate it." "I was talking to him." "I showed him my papers, and he then recalled my name because I just had one name." "He said"." I'm sorry son; I wasn't expecting to see you." "I didn't see any need to say anything to him, and then he looked at me, and gave me an assignment." "I asked him if they had paper for my typewriter." "I didn't have any." "That was the first time I ever saw a computer in my life, I read about them but I never actually saw one." "He said, we don't use typewriters anymore, we use computers." "Then, he asked, do you know anything about computers, and I told him no, I didn't have one." "I then asked him." "Do you have a book on this computer?" "He was treating me like a young child and soon handed me the book." "I started reading, and thirty minutes later, I was typing faster than I could type on my old typewriter." "He came in later and told me it was time for me to take a break, and I told him, not now, I'll take one later." "He left and returned at lunch." "I told him not now, I'll eat later." "He returned with a sandwich and some milk, and then left." "He came back in the next time and stopped me from writing more." I said as my tears began flowing again, and then I caught myself, and went on "He grabbed hold of me and made me stop to eat." "I couldn't." "I had things that were inside of me that had to come out." "When he left, I went back to my work, and left the half eaten sandwich on the paper plate." "Later, it was time to go home, and I asked him if I could take some paper with me, for my typewriter, and he asked me why." "I looked up at him, and told him that I wasn't through." "He gave me my paper and I left." "The next day, I arrived and handed him the paper that he gave me." "What's this, he asked me." "I told him, I didn't get to write down everything that I wanted to say yesterday, so I went home and worked on it there." "I then said I didn't have enough paper, so I used the back to write more." "I told him that I numbered the pages so that he wouldn't have problems from where I had left off yesterday." "I then went in and continued from where I had left off from on the paper that I took home." "It was later when I heard a commotion outside of the room and went to see what was happening." "A program was damaged when the secretary kicked the cord out of the socket and shut the computer down and the computer wouldn't reboot when she plugged it back in." "I walked over and removed the back panel and took out the hard drive and took off the top." "I took a small extension cord and cut the end that you plugged in the wall socket and wired it to a piece of small metal, to where I could reestablish the circuit." I reinstalled it and plugged it back in and I rebooted it." "I typed in the code to reprogram it and it came back up without a problem, and then went back in and continued in writing my essay." "After a few minutes the counselor came in, that time he didn't treat me like a kid." "He asked me what I did, and I told him that if someone builds something, then when it breaks down, someone has to fix it." "They have books to teach those people how to fix the problems that they have." "I done what the book said for me to do, only I didn't do it exactly the way it was said, I bypassed some of the circuitry and fused all them together." "He didn't understand what I was telling him, and after a few minutes he started scratching his head and just walked out." "When I left that day, he gave me a whole unopened package of typewriter paper, and like before, I turned it in the next day." "On the third day, I went to the school and then left for home with another package of paper in hand." "I worked long into the night and finished." "I arose to tell my mother I was going and when I went into her room." "I saw her eyes had a blank and hazy look to them." "Her hands were cold, and her face was white." I brushed more tears from my eyes, and fought myself to continue "It was raining hard that morning." "I walked into the police station soaking wet with mud creeping up to my knees on my pants, and they had to use heavy equipment to come down that road and get my momma." "They burned her like my brother." "She had leukemia, and I didn't know." "She didn't go in for treatments, and on that day the second half of me died." "I didn't have anything left in me."

I stopped talking, for it was difficult for me to go on.

I made some slurry with the cornmeal and poured it into the broth slowly, along with the chicken I had picked, while stirring the pot. My goal was to make sure it wasn't too thin or too thick. When the cornmeal was cooked, I gave her a mug full and told her to take a few sips. "You need strength to fight this fever." "They say feed a cold, starve a fever." "That may be, but out here, there aren't any rules." "We either live, or we die."

She soon handed me my mug back; it was empty; I refilled it, and she ate that too.

I sat everything aside to take care of everything later and sat down in my corner.

"Smith," she said to me, "would you come to lay down with me."

I eased in the bedroll, and she pulled me to her. "You're hot." She said to me.

"Jane, when my mother died, the Chief came and took me away, and some people put me in another home." "I left that place, and when they came back and got me, they put me somewhere else, and I left again." "That night in the silence, the wind was still, and the sound traveled for miles." "I heard them coming for me as they turned to come down the road I lived on, and I waited for them on my porch." "The Chief brought another man with him, and this other man had a son; he looked like my brother." "That's when I found out why my brother looked the way he did; he had Down's syndrome." "That's why he went to school, and I didn't." "I never saw my brother the way other people saw him; to me, he was my brother, and I loved him." "The man began talking to me, and I ignored him and talked directly to his son." "I asked him if he liked camping and hiking and roasting hot dogs over an open fire." "I saw his smile, and that told me all that I needed to know." "I went inside my house and got my brother's pistol belt with his canteen attached to it and had him try it on."

"He had the biggest smile on him from ear to ear," I said to him. "The next time you come out here, we'll take a hike, and we'll explore the world that stands before us." "The man introduced himself as Judge Harper." "Then he said, son, I'm sorry, but you can't stay here by yourself; you have to have a guardian." "I looked over at him and said." "Then your son can stay here and live with me." "I can take care of him, and he can take care of me; he's old enough." "He gave me a strange look, and he didn't expect the answer I gave." "He was against what I had in mind and was getting ready to make a ruling right then and there." "Sir, I said to him, in all due respect to your position, you'll not be able to keep me where I don't want to be." "If I can't be here, then the next time you come here, I'll not be waiting for you like I did this time." "He sat down on the stairs and put his hands to his face and sat there for a long time rubbing it with his hands." "Smith, he said, Holmes gave the Chief the essay you were writing and told us what you did to the computer, he read it and brought it to me, and after I read it, and listened to what the Chief had to say." "I agree with the consensus of the Counselor and the Chief that we're dealing with a delicate situation." "The Counselor contacted the Chief because you didn't come back." "We told him why." "Son, he said, he called me and said that he and his wife wanted to foster you." "I finished that essay that night my momma died, I told him." "I have it in my room." "I got up and went and got the paper and handed it to him, and told him; I'd appreciate it if you are seen to it that it got into Mister Holmes hands, and sir, tell him I thank him, but I can't live away from my home." "He stood and asked me if I would come home with him for the night." "I politely told him no, and he used his son to his advantage." "I left to go with him." "For someone who didn't have an appetite, I'd hate to see it when you did," I told her, trying to get off of the subject.

"Turn around and face me; I want to see what you look like." She stated to me.

I rolled over, and she had some words for me.

"Jane, I can tell by your eyes that you have words to the effect of an apology, and if you want to say something in that way, I'd rather not hear it." "You were in a situation that you found yourself to be in that anyone would have been frightened." I said to her, "I don't shave; I don't have any reason to." "I'm scroungy looking, and my hair is all matted. I don't need to brush it here."

"That's not what I was going to say; well, I was going to say that, but differently, but not like you put it." She said.

"All right," I told her, "I'll stay silent and let you find the words you want to say, but be careful. I don't want to hear words of thank you mentioned; I do not need it." "If the situation had been reversed, you would have done the same for me."

"You make it tough on someone; you know that?" She commented, "Okay." "I was going to say the cornmeal soup hit the spot."

"You were hungry, that's all," I said to her.

She quickly put her hand over my mouth.

"Let me finish." She stated, "I woke up not knowing anything that happened, and you were right; I was scared." "But you did a strange thing; you went outside and left me alone." "You worked and went about your business as usual." "I needed help; I hurt, and you gave me that help." "You'd be over in that corner right now, sitting if I didn't ask you to lay down with me." "Smith,

I still have a fever, and it makes me feel cold; if I call out my husband's name again, I don't want you to think that I'm looking at him when I see you, I erased him from my life, he's history now."

"When you leave, I'll be history too." I told her, "This is my home, it's only a twelve by twelve rock building, but it's my home." "I've lived here eleven years; I was seventeen when I found it." "A mail lady accidentally dropped a Christmas card off in our mail, and it had a picture of deer feeding out in the meadow with snow, like it is now, and in the background, there was a cabin with smoke coming out of its chimney." "One day, I came upon this spot and camped right outside of where we're at now." "I looked up, and the moon was full, and I saw movement from the corner of my eye." "I reached for my guns fearing that it was a bear, and the meadow looked like that Christmas card; it was full of deer." "I guess that's why I picked this spot here." I said to her, "But, I have known no woman, and I seek none." "It's hard for me to sleep, and I work on projects to keep me busy." "So, if you expect nothing from me, then we can live our lives in harmony." "I don't wish to have interaction with anyone; I don't do well around people."

"I wasn't asking you to love me." "Is that what you were thinking?" She stated to me. "I'm not even divorced yet, and you already think I'm on the prowl looking for someone to love?"

"See, that's one of the problems I have; I don't understand how to talk to a woman without saying things that come out wrong." I expressed, "I tried to tell people what I saw, and I could tell people didn't like me being around them."

"Look, forget it, let's just drop the subject." She said. She took off the top of her long johns, did the same to me, and held onto me tight. Her body was hot, and our bodies were wet with sweat; she opened the zipper of the sleeping bag a small way to let the heat escape and allow the cool air to enter now and then so that she could breathe.

The next morning, I went and got another chicken out of the shed.

"Now, what are you doing?" She asked me.

"I'm boiling another chicken." "It's good for what ails you." I told her, "Your immune system is under attack, and I need to help your body fight off its enemy."

"Are you making more cornmeal soup?" She asked me.

"No, I'm making chicken stuffed fried jalapeno peppers." "When you were sleeping, I noticed that you've got congestion building up in your lungs." "When I listened to you breathing, I heard the sounds of strider on each breath, and the jalapenos help you to breathe easier by opening up your nasal passages." "The chicken will let the medicine go down; If not for the chicken, the jalapenos would be too hot to eat by themselves." "I have two ways to apply this, one is orally, and two, I can touch a little to your nose, and you'll have instant relief." "But, it also burns, so we'll try the chicken first."

"Well, put the chicken on, and come back to bed, and put it on slow." She ordered me, "Every time you get out and back in, I get hot and cold."

When I got back into bed with her, she took my hand and put it underneath her long johns and over her wound that I had sewn up. She had pain there. She made a sound of pleasure, and I laid my head down, and we were entwined, and that's when she raised her head slightly and kissed me.

She pulled back from me. "You're not participating." She said.

"I don't know what you want of me; I don't know what I'm supposed to do." "Am I Russell?" I asked.

"No, you're Smith; Russell is gone and forgotten; Russell will never be brought up in a conversation when we speak anymore, okay?" "If I have to live with a man that reminds me of a man that tried to kill me, then we'll not have pleasant conversations." She said to me with a voice that had anger for her husband, "Can we at least agree that Russell is no longer in my life?" "That was determined by me when you brought me to my senses." "Now, I don't know how long you intend on keeping me here, and as long as I'm here, there are rules we have to live by."

"Jane, you're not a captive of mine, here."

"Shhh, you're talking when you're supposed to be listening." She said to me, "Rule number one; I'm a woman, and you're a man; you're going to have to get over me kissing you." "This was supposed to be a celebration of my fourth anniversary, and I should feel miserable, well I am, but I'm not talking about me being sick." "I'm talking about when I kissed you; it felt good." "I was married for four years, and what's his name never seemed to kiss me with feelings." "You don't either, but I understand the reasons why you don't." "There are reasons for everything, I guess." "Number two, you have a hot body, and up here, I need a hot body to sleep; I have a fever, you know." "You even said I might get pneumonia, and now you say I'm getting congested." "Number three; I can change any rule at any time." "That's my right as a woman." "Now, the first thing I want to know is how did you do that?" She said to me.

"I'm not with an understanding," I told her.

"It was only a couple of days ago I found myself in a strange man's bedroll, and now, I'm in your arms with your hand on my butt feeling the best I've ever felt in my life." She stated to me.

"What does it feel like?" I asked her.

"What?"

"Feeling the best you've ever felt." "When you met your husband, didn't he make you feel like the best you ever felt?" I asked her.

"I thought that we agreed my husband would never be mentioned in our conversation again." "You've already broken one of my rules." "Smith, I did love my husband, but it's not that hard for me to stop loving someone that tried to kill me."

"I was thinking that when you leave, I was wondering how long it would take for you to feel like that with someone else." "Jane, I have a wall that stands between me and the world that exists through your eyes," I spoke of my feelings.

"Why is it that I find myself having a great deal of difficulty when I talk to you," she injected her feeling "my feelings for you make me want to hold you and never let you get up out of this bed and be separated from me again." "Smith, I'm not supposed to feel like this, but I can't explain it." "I thought a man loved me, but I found out he didn't."

"Does love work that quick?" I asked her.

"Smith, tell me something; when you look at me, what do you see?" She questioned me.

"I see a girl eleven years old, and she's not happy; she's wearing a necklace with the name of Buttercup secured onto a ring on her bracelet."

"That's what my father calls me." She said, jerking back.

"I know." "I got to stay in my house." "The Judge would bring his son over, and we'd go exploring the creek like I did when I was with my brother the boy or should I say the man." "His mental capacity would never develop past being twelve years old." "Imagine being twelve years old all of your life," I said to her.

"The Judge's wife brought him over one day and was going to prepare us a dinner out of the food she had brought." "She brought a cookbook to try and cook something she wanted to learn how to make to take as a side dish to a church social." "I looked at it and told her she was doing it wrong, and I stepped in to show her how the book was telling her how to make it." "I ended up making six dishes that evening." "She left with them, and the next thing I know, some of the ladies from the church would come to my house and ask me if I could show them what they were doing wrong." "Soon, I was helping a lot of them, and they fed me well." "You use a formula when baking, and you have to use precise measurements." "They weren't." "I stayed there at my house till I was fifteen, and that's when the Judge came by to ask me if I would go with him to the party for a congressman's daughter." "I guess that maybe he thought that me doing the cooking of the pizzas for the kids would be good for the congressman's political future, but it didn't turn out to be that way." "I didn't know you would be there, and I didn't know anything about you before that time." "I asked the Judge if he planned on supporting the congressman." "He pulled his car over and parked it on the side of the road and put his flashers on." "He then turned to me and said." "Smith, a lot of men think they are smart, and there's very few that he knew that was smart." "I know when something is on your mind." "Do you want to tell me something?" "He asked me." "I told him that the congressman is going to lose this election, and he's only going to get thirty-eight percent of the votes." "He knows this, and all he wants is the money that he'll raise to put away in his cash fund." "I then looked at him and told him he's using you for his political gain" "and then told him that he was embezzling funds from the government, and if you support him, you'll be supporting the hangman to pull your lever." "The Judge told me that I was making some powerful accusations, and I told him to take me to his office, and I'll show him his proof." "Later that evening was when I met your father." "The Judge contacted him, and I showed him where the congressman's money trail was." "He wanted to know how I accessed the files." "I never told him, and he forgot it." "When we went to the party, I saw you, and that's where I saw you wearing your necklace." "It hung just above the neckline of your dress." "People forget passwords that they set up and when I saw the name Buttercup on the bracelet." "I knew I had the password I needed to read about your father's activities." "Your father didn't endorse the congressman, and neither did the Judge; he lost his reelection bid and got thirty-eight percent of the votes, as I said." "And your father was the man that exposed his businesses and stripped him from doing any business with any businesses that worked with the government." "He later was arrested for misappropriating campaign funds and accepting bribes." "I felt sorry for his wife and children; they had to endure the shame he brought on them." "That hurt me knowing that I hurt them." I said to her, "There was a newspaperman that was there that caught your father's attention to me." "The man had been drinking strongly." "I didn't like the way he acted around those kids." "I guess I saw my father in him." "He said something, and I sounded off; my comments surprised both the Judge and your father." "They didn't expect to hear the words that came from my mouth." "I verbally opposed him and protested by an unsolicited expression of my opinion and told him that he was a biased newspaperman, and he misquoted those that he liked and also those that he didn't like." "I told him that he was using his paper to manipulate the people into thinking his thoughts and not the view of the people and that his kind of paper was pure propaganda and the people don't want to read it." "I blasted him by telling him in front of everyone that if he weren't filing for bankruptcy, he would be soon." "The Judge left the party and took me home early; we never talked on the ride back." "That night when your father took you home, he came back and got me, and it was that night he took me away from my home." "I later found out that there was a man there that gave him a tip that my statements were accurate." "When he came and got me, he took me to a place with guards, and that's where I found out that he was given a tip." "I walked over to where the computers were, and I accessed the paper's computers and found out that three days before the party, the newspaper had filed for bankruptcy; it was disclosed publicly one week later." "I left the place he brought me to, and it took me three days to walk back home." "He was like the Chief, he came and got me, and I left again." "The last time I left, they had me under restricted security; I escaped and came back home." "I was walking on the road and smelled smoke; when I got closer to my home, the smoke I smelled was my home; it burned." "I never found out if someone sought revenge or if a bunch of kids was out looking for a good time." "But I sat there crying." "Your father drove up and sat with me." "I told him my momma and my brother were in there; they burned them twice." "He took me in his arms and said, Smith, I want you to know from the bottom of my heart that I didn't know about this." "When he took me back again, I accessed his files." "It wasn't hard, he never changed Buttercup for his password, and I sent for him." "When he walked in, I asked him to have a seat, and when he sat down, I told him." "I know why you brought me here; I accessed your files." "I told him you're not going to win this election unless you make a change; the people have a bitter taste in their mouth right now, I informed him." "If you lose, this project is going to be disbanded." "I won't work with others, I informed him." "He sat down, and we talked." "I handed him a letter that I printed by hand and told him to read every word that was printed and repeat every word to the press, exactly the way I wrote it."

"What happened?" She asked.

"You should know; he's your father," I told her.

"He switched to being an independent, and he won the election." She stated to me.

"Do you remember what he said in his speech?" I asked her.

"He made a lot of speeches." She said.

"He's known in his circle as Jack "the Hammer" Morgan for his tough talks, and in other circles, he's also known as Jack "the Ripper" Morgan, for his same tough talk for his Jackass attitude, and he was stubborn as a mule, you might say that he was adamant in his ways." "He got that name because he told the people in his speech that he couldn't serve the people any longer, justly." "Under one party, he was under criticism for opposing certain bills, and he thought that the best way to serve the people was to run as an independent." "He stated that when a good plan is planned, he wanted to listen, and it didn't matter to him who presented it." "That way, he had the freedom to accept only the good for the people and not be compelled to accept a bill just because his party wanted it." "He then told them that not all bills that are passed are good; he didn't want to be a part of those bills that he opposed, for the good of the people." "He then said, my name is Jack Morgan; I'm running as an independent; if you want someone else for the job, vote for someone else." "The rest is history, your father won, and here I am, taking care of his little Buttercup for him."

"How come he never told me about you?" She asked me.

"Information about me is restricted." "When you go home, your father won't answer any questions you pose about me."

"Why?" She asked

"That's restricted information," I told her.

"So you think of me as an eleven-year-old girl then?"

"No, I think of you, as a lady that landed in a place that has a man lying next to her that she feels fond of." "You're the first girl I've ever laid next to, and I've never felt a girl's skin against my skin."

"Then what's the problem here, with us?" She asked.

"The problem is I can't talk about myself to you or anyone else." "As I said, here, I live inside my world." "Outside this area, I'm not the person I am here."

"So, you're the real prisoner here then?" She commented.

"No, I choose this place, I need my privacy, and it seems the only place I can find it is here, that is until my privacy was interrupted," I stated.

"Do you have some kind of disorder or something?" Her voice had hostility in its deliverance.

"You might say that I have many assessments of my problems," I responded to her.

"Like what?" She said to me with a little less anger than she used earlier.

"Like, for one thing, I can't talk about myself."

"Smith, I'm getting this feeling that you're fighting me, I'm going to be here a long time, and I can't keep getting answers like that's restricted information." "If you're not a criminal, you can give me a little hint." She said with a little edginess.

"Okay, let's try this one." "On one of the trips I took with your father, he was having a hard time dealing with a dignitary." "I looked over and noticed the man's son." "I walked over and talked to him and went back to be with your father." "I stopped the man and began speaking to him in his language, and your father quickly looked at me." "I told your father to leave me; I'm needed to work here for a while." "He didn't like that, but the king won, and I stayed and worked with his son." "When your father came back to pick me up, he had relations shored up, and the king became an ally, and your father got the airbase that he wanted."

"What was wrong with his son, or is that restricted information too?" She said.

24

"No, his son had dyslexia." "I worked with him and told him what he was experiencing and helped him to learn how to overcome his boundaries, now he's the king of that country, and he's still an ally."

"My father didn't know you could speak their language?" She asked.

"There were a lot of things your father didn't know about me and still doesn't know about me." "He was in on some tests that they were giving me, and they flashed numbers on a screen, and I copied down the numbers."

"They then flashed twenty numbers consisting of ten numbers each; then they gave me twenty numbers consisting of twenty numbers each; then they went crazy, they tried fifty numbers, and after I finished the fiftieth number, they wanted more tests." "They used PI." "PI has an infinite number that keeps on going and going." "After three hundred numbers and two hours later, that's when they found out that I had a photographic memory." "I have seen an advertisement in a book, and I came here."

I put some more snow in the pot where I was cooking my chicken. When I finished, the girl opened up the bedroll for me to get back in, and she quickly pulled me to her. Her temperature was starting to go higher again, and she was starting to shake.

She rolled over a little and let out a painful moan; she had leaned a little too far and touched the wound she had received. She took my hand, placed it over it, and then let out a sigh; she easily rolled over to where my hand was under her, protecting her wound.

Two times that night, she opened the bedroll and stuck her head out to breathe, and each time she zipped it back up and tried to use my body to warm hers. She shook badly that night, and I was beginning to become concerned.

Her pain was bad in her butt, and she rolled over to lie on top of me.

That morning, she was sleeping better; her fever had broken, at least for the time being.

I got up and deboned the chicken and started slicing my peppers lengthways and removing the seeds. I hand squeezed the chicken, broke it up into small pieces, and went and got some cracker meal and cheese from my storeroom. I diced the cheese, stuck a cubed piece inside a portion of the chicken, and formed the portion into the pepper to look like an egg.

I dredged the stuffed peppers in the cracker meal and into some eggs that I took out of a bag that had been previously cracked. It came from a restaurant where all they had to do was put it in boiling water, and they had scrambled eggs for a buffet. After dipping the pepper into the eggs, I dropped it into the cracker meal. When I completed the batch of stuffed peppers, I got some oil, poured it into a pot, and waited for the oil to get hot. I dropped in the first batch and let them cook to a golden brown. I was almost through cooking when the girl awoke.

"Are you hungry?" I asked her.

"My head is all stuffy." She said.

"I know, and I'm going to fix that," I responded to her.

"Here, try one of these; I said, handing her a stuffed pepper."

"I'm not hungry."

"It's not for hunger; it's medicine for your stuffy head." I explained, "Now eat."

"She took a bite and then started fanning her mouth." "It's hot."

"I know your forehead will be sweating, and you'll be able to breathe, trust me." "Take another bite."

"Water, she said, give me some water."

"I went outside and put some snow in a cup, and she took a bite of the snow to cool her mouth."

"This stuff is hot."

I handed her some cloth.

"What's this for?" She asked me.

"You'll see," I told her.

I ate a few, and she watched me. She grew bold and asked for another one. This time she ate it with the fervor of delight. But she still ate her ice to cool her mouth from burning. Her complaints stopped after she finished eating her ninth one.

She looked over at me.

"Use the rag," I told her as I handed her another pepper.

"That evening, her nose was raw from blowing it." "That's when her coughing started."

"Jane, you don't have a fever with a cold." "They'll come a time when your coughing can't be stopped; you'll feel like you have to let it go." "When that time comes, let it go." "It's your body's way of rejecting foreign agents inside your lungs." "You have fluid that's building up; it's phlegm, and when it comes out, you'll start to heal." "But, you won't get better until you get worse."

"You mean I have to go through more of this?" "Why didn't you just let me die?" She said to me.

CHAPTER TWO

The girl's temperature started getting hotter, and she began to go in and out of a state of delirium. I arose from beside her and began putting the skins I had made on her. I put some skins on my sled to cushion her ride and sat her down on the sleigh.

When she opened her eyes, she stared at me with a confused state of mind, and then she fell back asleep in my arms.

I washed her face and hair, and when she opened her eyes, she saw me as myself.

"Hello," I said to her and added, "You look tired." She responded with a hard and prolonged cough.

"Drink some water," I told her.

She began looking around.

"Where am I?"

"I call this place healing waters," I told her as I cupped my hand and captured water so she would drink. I talked to her as she took a sip. "I found this place while out scouting one day." "The snow was coming down, and I saw a mist rising out of the rocks." "It took a good three weeks of my time, but the reward justified my actions." "I knew from the mist that came from the rocks that there was an underground spring here." "You, my dear lady, are sitting in the same waters that some of our early ancestors sat in." "Look on the walls over there." I nodded the direction with my head. The fire I had, gave off a glimmer of light. "Can you read cave paintings?" I asked her. I didn't wait for her to answer, "That first painting to the right; that was the first painting, it tells of an attack, and how they escaped with their lives and they had to leave the dead behind." "There was a slaughter." "Their god was the moon." "See the moon's face; it's looking down on the people." "It's not a happy face, so they believed that their lives were changed because of his anger with them." "The next painting, that's next to it, depicts their arrival here." "They used the waters to sit in like we're doing now, the water is warm, and it made their body feel good." "If you notice, one of the people has an arm that's slightly bent." "That's not from the formation that he painted." "Somebody in the tribe had a broken arm." "They bathed here, ate here, and slept here." "Notice the picture above that picture."

"I don't see anything except what looks like a cloud." The girl said.

"Exactly, they didn't either, but they believed that something was responsible for their good fortune, they didn't come here by accident, they believed something guided them, or so they thought, the cloud is the mist I saw when I found this place." "They had to have passed this way in the winter." "I never saw the mist any other time, except in the winter." "That next one tells me of the successful hunts and births of their children, along with the deaths of the elderly." "You and I would have been old people then, but they show people bent over and walking with the rest." "That means they were a close group and took care of their family." "If you pay attention to the one to the left of the other one, you'll notice that there are more people than there were before." "They thrived and prospered here." "Now, take a look at the next one; there are changes in the way it's drawn; look at the others, can you see the difference?" "Whoever was the storyteller died, and another took his place." "Whoever it was, had the same thing that all painters have, an identity." "A style that no one else had; these people were from around the tenth century or earlier," I told her.

"How can you tell?" She asked.

"They were hunters, not farmers." "None of the pictures show tools of any kind, only weapons." "Before Columbus came and discovered America, there were others that came here and traded." "History books only tell of America after we landed on Plymouth Rock." "These people only lived by the four seasons, and according to that picture over there to the top left, they died mostly in the winter from starvation." "I can only hypothesize that these people were nomadic till they found this place, and in their travels, they encountered hostility." "Their god, the moon, gives me that suspicion; it meant they slept under the stars and was always ready to move." "The last one, at the lower left, is a grave marker." "This is where they all died." "When I found this place, I removed a load of rocks as big as boulders." "There was a rockslide, and it sealed their fate." "None of them escaped." "Their god, the moon, is angry above them; they believed he did this for them worshipping another god, the god of the mist."

"How can you see that?" She asked.

"A lot of thinking and a lot more thinking, and one day it comes upon you." "Miller's Cliff is like that because that part of the mountain dropped down, there had to be an earthquake, and I think that earthquake that caused Miller's Cliff to be formed was also the same earthquake that sealed the fate of these people."

"It's a code, nothing more; everything is a code." "Genetics, a code." "Defects occur sometimes, and dominant genes overrule what is believed." I told her, "Our bodies are affected by abnormalities in those codes." "But Jane, life doesn't always work the way it's supposed to." "Sometimes, a dominant gene decides your height, the color of your eyes, and the color of your hair." "So, genetics is overridden by a dominant gene, and the genetics that makes up the dominant gene is now passed onto the genetics of the girl or the man that is born." "It's a form of adaption to a climate sometimes." "Mother Nature has a way of dealing with a short supply of males in all species, or the reverse, the female," I said to her. "In every species, a shortage of one or the other will have a boom in the shortage, low male population, more male births, low female population, and more female births."

"Everything in time is a code; that code has the option to change at any given time." "This earth is changing as we speak, not drastically but ever so slowly, but we don't see it because what happens to the earth takes millions, if not billions of years, to notice the changes that were made." "Ten thousand years is just a second on the clock to the earth." "These mountains; they were formed by continents breaking away and traveling to where it meets now; right here where we sit, billions of years ago." "This place here; one time, two continents collided and met each other, and the battle began, two opposing forces pushing until one continent yielded and slid under the other continent, and these mountains were born." "Back then, you probably would have been boiled if you sat here." "Time is a code; this code of time destroys everything." "This earth; is like all other living things, and all things must die, even the earth." "It's a dying planet, and man is an organism that feeds off of this dying planet as insects feed off of a carcass." "But, for now, it still has life, and therefore, so do we." "We live in a perfect time, and we believe the sun will always come up tomorrow." "It doesn't matter one way or the other." "None of us will be alive to question why it didn't." "Man won't be able to live in environments that aren't perfect for him to exist." "This environment is perfect right now, but one little bobble and all chaos unravel."

"The climate was ideal during the times of the dinosaurs for them to exist." "Back then, there were twenty-hour days, not eight to ten like today, and when the moon orbited the earth, its gravitational pull pulled at the earth until it tore apart." "Air wasn't suitable for man; he couldn't survive unless he had lungs twenty times the size that he has now." "Methane, ethane, hydrogen sulfide, carbon dioxide, and other gases were given off by volcanic action." "This was great for plants of all kinds and all sizes, and they prospered." "This earth had herds and herds of herbivores; that's plant-eaters," I said to her.

"I know what that means." She commented, "But go ahead."

I then continued, "A lot of species that lived then were wiped out." "Man believes a meteorite hit the earth and caused all the plants to die, and in turn, the dinosaurs that fed off of the plant-eaters died because they didn't have any food and they turned on themselves." "The codes don't support those beliefs." "There are too many variables that remain a question." "Areas that show evidence are only confirmations of what happened to that area; it's not the whole story, just a fraction of it." "One day, when I'm dead, someone will come here and discover this place, and healing waters will be turned into a park." "They'll see this place as a gold mine." "They won't tell the truth when they tell the story of the paintings on the walls." "To them, the sun will always come up tomorrow; they don't look beyond today to see tomorrow."

"You know that cliff you looked down from?" I asked her.

"How can I forget it?" She said as she gently rubbed her butt.

"That's miller's cliff." "A man by the name of Eric Miller was mapping territory in the early eighteen hundreds." "He camped up close to the top, and he arose one morning ready to set out on his expedition." "The story goes that when the sun hit the cliff, he saw gold." "He inspected it and convinced others that he had found a whole mountain of gold." "They, in turn, invested and bought almost three hundred thousand acres at fifteen cents an acre." "That doesn't sound like much, but, back then, fifteen cents was worth something; besides, this land wasn't habitable." "Vegetables don't grow here; the season is too short." "That was just the start." "The cost of mining and the cost of travel and transporting their tools weighed heavy on the investors." "The ore was mined, and then they found out their fate; they had invested in fool's gold." "Rumor spread that Eric Miller is buried at the bottom of that cliff." "That isn't true; Eric Miller was killed by claim jumpers." "They got involved when he came into town, there was a shootout with him and some other men at the assayer's office, and they buried him in his hometown where his family lived." "He died before the mining started." "The assayer never got the ore to be examined, and the investors lost a fortune." "All this land around here has names from the people that came across it and claimed it for themselves one way or another." "Cooper's Bluff; it was just that." "He won it on a bluff in cards." "Or so the story goes." "It's not easy to verify everything you hear or read." "I say that because I never could find out what Cooper covered the bet with; it certainly wasn't gold." "Or was it?" "See, Eric Miller and Cooper were partners in their early years." "The ore that Miller brought to the assayers was real gold, Alexander Cooper was mining it, and Cooper set up Miller to be killed." "Cooper got away with the gold and with the murder of Eric Miller." "They both schemed to defraud their investors." "Cooper got away with it." "The investors lost everything, and Eric Miller lost his life." "This is a big country; back then, you could go anywhere and tell everyone a name you called yourself and go someplace else and call your name something else, and no one doubted you." "What were they going to do, investigate?" "Cooper and Miller were the only ones that knew where the gold was, but they couldn't afford the men or the tools and wagons to do the job, so they stole two teams of mules with wagons." "Miller didn't have any idea that he was being double-crossed."

"How do you know this?" "That happened a hundred years ago." She said.

"It was two hundred and six, to be exact, and I don't know that these things I say are true, but when pieces don't fit in a puzzle, you can't force another piece to fit." "You have to keep looking until the piece of the puzzle looks like it fits, and then you try to place it in the right spot." "When you find that right piece, the others begin to become easier to place, and soon a form in the shape of a picture gives the viewer a better idea of where the other pieces go." I told her, "Jane, back then, you couldn't hire anyone; no man could be trusted."

She shook her head back and forth and asked out of the blue. "Okay." "Mister know it all, then how come this water is so warm?"

"You want to know, or are you being facetious?" I said to her.

"I want to know what you know." She said, smiling. "Right now, I'm learning a lot of things about you."

"There's an underground spring that's traveling close to a hot zone, and it's heated before it comes out." I told her, "I've taken temperature samples every month since I've been here." "Right now, the water temperature is one hundred and two degrees even." "When I first found it, the temperature was a hundred and two-point two." "So the water is cooling down at two-tenths of a degree per decade or so, give or take a tenth of a degree." "I can't be certain; I'd have to take samples every hundred years for ten thousand years to give you a correct answer to my theory." "It may stay a hundred and two for fifty more years; I haven't had enough time to study all I need to study." "In several hundred million years, all of these mountains will be worn away by the weather, and they'll look like big hills and not like the mountains that they are today." "I believe these mountains are dead, the plates underneath us, or continents aren't fighting each other anymore." "You asked what I thought, and that's what I think," I said to her. I changed the subject. "This is where I brought you when I got to you, I had to clean you up, and I couldn't do it in a washtub or the river; the water would have had an impact on you." "Your clothes are under that rock if you want to sew them up and wear them." I moved the rock under in the water to show her, and she told me to throw them nasty things away. "Now, do you see what I meant when I said you were dead?" I said to her.

"Smith, you didn't finish what you were saying."

"About what?"

"You know the dinosaurs?" "What happened to them?"

"Jane, I'm like all the others; I merely have an opinion, and living in today's world, my opinion doesn't mean anything to anyone."

"I'm listening." She said.

"Well, that's a battle that's being fought as we speak and long before we were born, and I'm sure a hundred years from now, someone will write an article explaining his theory and get a grant to explore it." "What does it matter what I think." "All those people with ideas and theories and belief's have doctorate degrees, and they all have different views other than mine." "How can you have so many people that have doctorates disagreeing with each other?" "That only tells me that if one is right, then all the others are wrong." "But they have a degree just the same." "If they gave a degree in common sense, then very few of those people that have a degree would have that degree that they have." "Not all educated people are smart." "They bought it; all it took was the right amount of money that was needed." "But, that's not what you asked." "You asked what I believed." "When you look up at the full moon on a clear night, what do you see?" I answered for her because she didn't understand what I was asking. "You see craters and pockets where something powerful hit it, right?" "Some scientists believe the moon came from the earth after a powerful source crashed into it, and thus the earth wasn't anything more than a pile of dust." "What facts that took place thousands of billions of years ago are buried at the level that the earth was born, and no man can go there, no tools can reach the beginning of time, and the proof is always needed to sway those with a different opinion." "Right now, the moon is escaping the gravitational pull of the earth at one and a half inches per year." "No one knows how long the moon remained in orbit around the earth until it started to escape the earth's gravitational pull." "Some scientists believe that our planet collided with another planet that eventually formed the earth." "They give periods of all this happening." "No one possesses this knowledge." "It is said that the earth began cooling off when plant life appeared." "It is said that the earliest plant life was a type of algae and this plant caused the earth to cool down." "By cooling off, I mean the earth was encased in ice for over three hundred million years, or so it is said by some scientist." "Once again" "no one possesses that knowledge." "Nothing was alive." "No species existed on the earth" "Some scientists believe it was molten lava at the time before the earth began cooling down and water was nonexistent then, and no one and I mean no one can tell anyone about anything, about how the earth was formed and evolved." "There wasn't an ozone layer to keep harmful ultraviolet rays of the sun from entering our atmosphere, so there was no life that existed, and there wasn't any oxygen." "Back then, you were looking at extreme temperatures." "Our Earth was a violent planet." "Supposedly after the earth began cooling down." "Allegedly after those three hundred million years, the sun began warming the earth." "Moisture condensed and formed rain." "If there wasn't any water, then how was it that it rained." "Trees that had grown fell, and since there weren't any organisms that fed off of the dying trees, they eventually turned into coal after fires." "Once again, man believes that organisms developed in the oceans and hundreds of millions of years, organisms began to exist on land and once again plant life was born." "Single-cell organisms evolved into the carnivores and herbivores." "Of course, there were a lot of animals that became extinct from not being able to adapt." "This is where the moon enters." "Those that believe that the moon was formed after the explosion of two planets colliding and forming into the earth also believe that the earth is six billion years old." "Man believed that Earth was flat at one time." "Man does not know the knowledge that he thinks he has; he only has speculation." "He can only determine what species existed in a certain period." "A lot of species existed, but a man can't tell of those species unless a species has been found." "Mother Nature destroyed many remnants of those species." "Hundreds of millions of years ago isn't enough time to verify how old this earth is because if two planets collided and formed into one planet, then I have to ask how long did it take to develop into one planet." "It is possible that the moon's gravitational pull caused a lot of damage to the earth." "It was so close that we had twenty-hour days, and the moon's gravitational pull was a lot stronger then." "That had to take hundreds of millions of years; dinosaurs didn't exist then." "The scientists that have a theory that a meteorite caused the dust to cover the earth and destroy plant life aren't using science to portray what happened." "Once again, man doesn't have the knowledge they need, they claim fact, but speculation has formed an assumption." "There were meteorites; the moon is riddled with proof of meteors hitting it." "But what caused the meteors to shower the earth and the moon?" "There is an answer." "In economics, what affects one country affects others." "So goes space." "This earth was close enough to encounter a catastrophic event, a nova of a nearby planet." "Just like there was a nova of this planet, or so the scientist state." "There are asteroid belts throughout our solar systems." "Asteroids aren't formed except from a planet that went nova." "Did these asteroids come from our planet?" "The earth was impacted by shock waves that killed off a lot of species, but not all of them." "We have species that evolved today that looked different when they existed then." "This shock wave interfered with the codes that the earth lived under." "The code changed, and so did the earth." "I believe that the moon was so close that it ripped the earth apart and caused the earth to have a mega explosion knocking the moon out of our orbit." "The Mariana Strait is thirty-eight thousand feet deep, and you can put Mount Everest in it, and the top of Mount Everest will still be three thousand feet below water." "All deserts were once oceans that were hundreds of feet deep." "These deserts have fossils of crustations that's three hundred feet above those deserts." "I believe those deserts had to drain to the lowest point when that explosion occurred." "The Mariana Strait." "Had it not of done so, the earth would have split." "There are fissures at the bottom of the Mariana Strait that emit temperatures of over twelve hundred degrees, and life exists at the bottom of the Marian Strait." "Scientists once believed that no organism could survive a temperature that hot, but they found themselves to be wrong." "The moon is one hundred and eighty thousand miles from earth, yet it affects our tides." "In ten years, the moon is going to have a natural anomaly, a wobble, and when that happens." "The oceans are going to rise and flood a large portion that man calls home today along the coast." "He's helpless to avoid it." "What people don't understand about climate change is that climate change has changed thousands of times since the beginning of Earth." "Man is ignorant; they only live for a short period, and man will become extinct faster than any species that lived on earth." "Right now, everyone is waiting on the next wobble; they can't defend themselves from tornadoes, earthquakes, volcanoes, tsunamis, or any manmade disaster." "We're talking about something man cannot defend himself from; that's the unknown." "If man were around when the dinosaurs were alive and were as smart as he thinks he is today, he would know more than he thinks he knows." "I said that climate change has occurred many times." "Think of Atlantis." "it's buried hundreds of feet below the ocean." I told her, "I'm boring you, aren't I?" I said to her. "I do that." "I get to ranting and raving, and the next thing I know."

"Smith, finish what you were saying." She interrupted me.

"I was just going to say that the earth is controlled by the moon as well as the sun, and without the moon, the earth's axis will act as a top." "The moon is a part of our life; it's necessary for our survival." "When the moon slips further and further away, the forces of nature will alter." "Man cannot adapt, so I say we live in a perfect time." "One day, the earth will hiccup, and the man won't have anywhere to run." "The earth is doomed to returning to the planet it was before the dinosaurs existed, and man is helpless to stop it from happening." "What affects one universe, affects us, what affects our universe, affects others." "It's nothing more than a domino effect." "Maybe one day, in a couple of billion years or less, the moon that gave us our stability will collide with another planet and give that planet life in another solar system."

"You have serious trouble talking to people, don't you?" She stated.

I smiled at her. "I'm sorry, I'm not used to talking to people, and I guess I let myself get carried away, and then the next thing I know, I'm going on like a fool."

"Smith, I heard what you said, and I listened real good; you are a thinker, and I happen to agree with what you believe." "It sounds good, and who's to say that's not the way it happened?"

"It's just an opinion," I said to her. "And opinions don't mean anything unless you have proof, and until then, it's disputable." "There's only one opinion that counts, and that's the person you talk to." "He or she doesn't care what you think."

She began coughing, and then she was coughing and unable to stop.

"You have to keep coughing," I told her, "you have to force yourself to bring up the phlegm." "You're fighting it, keep coughing; you have to bring it up." "Come on, come on," I said, trying to coax her. "That's it," I told her.

"Smith"

"Don't fight it; keep coughing." "Your body is doing what it's supposed to do," I said to her.

The next thing I knew, she was calling out Ralph's name. She had turned away from me, and I put my arms around her stomach, and each time she called for Ralph, I squeezed her tightly, forcing her to expel everything. I washed her face after and gave her some water to wash her mouth out.

I scooped up some sand from the bottom of the warm creek and told her to take a finger full and use the sand to brush her teeth; I showed her how by doing mine.

She then did the same, and I scooped up water and rinsed my mouth out. She also followed my lead and did the same.

"Do you feel better now?" I asked her.

"I can breathe." She said.

"It's not over yet." I told her, "You'll still have a fever, and you'll be going through all of this again." "Last night, when I put my hand over the cut you have, I felt the heat around it." "These waters are warm, and the flow cleanses the wound." "Those people that lived here, those pictures tell me the reason why they lived here."

"What did you see?" She asked.

"You," I told her.

"What's that supposed to mean?" She stated.

"Well, these people believed that these waters held healing powers, I bring you here, and you feel better, so maybe there is something to the fact that these are healing waters." "A man of education would argue, though." I told her, "After all, man believed there was a fountain of youth."

This time, it was her that smiled.

"So, we're in a dilemma," I said to her "like all the scientists that have theories, some would say that yes, these waters do have certain powers, and some would seek other sources for its remedies." "There isn't such a thing as waters that heal." "But those that say that either isn't sick or they don't understand the power of the brain." "They let the stomach tell them they're hungry, they let their nose tell them they're hungry, and they let their eyes see more than the stomach can hold." "The brain is wasted to the addicted, no matter the drug," I stated to her.

"What do you think?" She asked me. "Is there healing waters somewhere out there?"

"I think it feels warm, and it sure beats that washtub." "Jane, can I be honest with you without offending you?" I asked her.

"What kind of question is that?" She answered.

I hesitated before I began, "You called me a know-it-all." "That's one of the reasons I'm here; I don't like being around people."

"You've never really sat down with anybody and talked, have you?" She said.

"I talked to your dad, and I talked to the Judge."

"No, Smith, I'm talking about talking with a girl, a young woman."

"I've never been around any." "I've always been busy," I replied to her statement.

"Doing what?" She asked.

"Well, my totem poles, and while I'm working on my poles, I think about other projects as well."

"What other projects?"

"That's restricted information, and then I work on my wallets and purses and other leather goods to sell at the resort."

"Wait a minute." She interrupted me, "You said you work with leather too?"

"Well, I haven't had a chance in the last few days, I've been indisposed, and I haven't been able to do much of anything lately," I told her.

"No, really, you do leatherwork?" She asked again.

"Yes, those clothes I made for you; I used lace that I use for tying in the inserts for the wallets and the purses." "I can't use thread." "I've got ten cowhides underneath my bedroll." "I cut the leather and use my tools to draw a scene." "When I take you back, I'll give you one of your choices if you want one."

"Please don't tell me that you used lace for my stitches." She said, sounding concerned.

"No, you'd be surprised how strong the fishing line can be, and you can get it in a large spool, too," I told her.

"Smith, I'm sorry I called you that, you know, a know-it-all, you know what I was called at school?" "I was nicknamed the stork." "My yearbook has got the stork in parentheses below my name."

"Kids don't realize that they can hurt kids by words alone." I told her, "Kids have a way of wanting to play by teasing." "It's harmless, but they leave lasting impressions on what they say." "They don't realize that until someone makes a comment that hurts them, then what was funny isn't funny anymore." "That's a part of growing up everyone went through." "I didn't go to school, so I never talked to other kids." "I guess I was fortunate in that respect. I wouldn't have been able to stay there." "So we came from different upbringings, and we experienced different forms of pains." "Deep inside your heart, you hide a lot of those emotional insecurities, and they can never be released; you contain them." "There's no one to tell them to, trust isn't something you give to just anyone, and so far, you haven't found anyone that you trust; you only thought you did," I said to her.

"Smith, you asked me if my husband told my friends where we were going." "They weren't my friends; they were his." She said.

"How much money do you have?" She asked.

"Why do you ask that?"

"Because no one I know that has money lives like this." She answered.

"I have all I need." "I didn't have any money when I was a young boy, I never had a television set, and we never had a radio." "I read and told stories to my brother by a fire, and I was happy." "When I see that fire next to us, and I hold you in my arms like I am now, I thought of my brother." "You're the only person that's been here beside your father and me."

"I told you when I found this place, I stayed." "There are one hundred and fifty-seven thousand acres between here and the resort." "My corporation owns that one hundred and fifty-seven thousand acres and the ski resort." "I don't pay taxes on anything; it's all the corporation's money, and the Corporation is a charity corporation." "Your father is a lobbyist for my corporation."

"You, being the senator's daughter, were given a package; it was taken care of by your father." Am I wrong?"

"No, I thought it was because my father was an influential man." "You seem to have caught me off guard here." She said.

"Like father like daughter," I told her.

"What's that supposed to mean?" She fired back.

"Your father told me the same thing." "He wasn't prepared for me, and I caught him off guard."

"Is that why you won't talk about you and him?" She asked.

"No, there are things that your father and I participated in, and my identity was kept top secret." "Your father learned that after spending a little time with me." "I treated him as an outsider." "I couldn't let him in." I told her, "He came to me one night while I was in my room reading." "He closed the door behind him and sat down in a chair and asked me, what's going on." "I, in turn, asked him, whose side was he on?" "He asked me what I meant by that, and I said to be of one party and not listen to the other party is promoting a one-party government, and that we were halfway there." "We have governments like that already; it's called the communist party and the socialist party." "Then I asked him, which party does he lean his support to?" "His answer to me was that he supported both parties." "I told him you can't support both parties; you can only support one party and oppose the other party." "There isn't any bill that's a good bill, that's half right and half wrong." "Someone is affected more than others." "Then I asked him again, whose side was he on; which party did he lean his support to?" "He didn't answer me then, so I went back to reading my book." "He said while I was reading that he supported the people." "I looked up and told him; you know they have a people's party too, along with a Whig party and a green party and a tea party, and an independent party." "I went over to my computer and started working." "I asked him to come over to have a look." "Do you know this man?" I said to him." "Sure, he's on one of my committees, he said." "I did a little more searching, and then he got interested in what I was doing." "His deposits he made in his bank came from sources that I traced to prominent individuals that were going to make a lot of money if a bill was passed." "I showed him a document that stated that his vote was going to be a favorable vote." I looked up at him and asked him again, "whose side are you on?" "He looked at me about the way you're looking at me now, and then he answered, I support the people's rights." "I turned around and emptied the congressman's bank account and donated all of his money to a charitable organization in his name." "I gave all of his money he had away." "Can you imagine his look of surprise when he found out?" "Your father had a look of his own." "I opened up another man's computer, and again I turned around and asked your father if he knew him." "He didn't answer me that time." "I once again asked him, whose side are you on, and he once again replied, I support the people's rights." "I turned around and donated his bank account to another charitable organization, in his name." "Then I told your father that I knew what he wanted from me, and I wouldn't do what he wanted." "I deleted my files from all records." "I was nothing more than his guest then." "That's when your father came back to me and said that he underestimated me." "I asked him once again, and then I told him this will be the final time that I ask him." "Whose side are you on?" "He was silent." "I told him he could speak; I disabled the bugs that they had in my room." "All they could hear was a loud ringing." "I told him." "He asked me what I wanted." "I told him I needed a lab, where I could do my work in privacy, and he asked me if I knew what I was doing." "I walked back over to my computer and typed in a code, and a blackout occurred, I shut down the whole compound, and as I stood there in the dark, I told him, I hope you backed up all your information on those computers, but you don't need them anymore, no power, no computers." "I went back and sat on my bed, and he heard my voice." "I deliver my messages to those that can hear what I have to say, those that don't listen, I don't waste my time trying to persuade them." "I then told him." "I'm tired, and these people are wasting my time, I won't build what they want me to build, and I don't like people around me watching me while I work" "He began lecturing me on how my work was an important project." "I stopped him and then told him." "You have an agent working in these perimeters; did you know that?" "No, he said, I didn't." "Then, I told him." "Everything that's going on here has been jeopardized." "I just infected a virus into every computer that feeds on this facility." "You don't have to worry about anything anymore." "Problem solved."

"What happened then?" She asked.

"Their facility was destroyed when I destroyed the information that they collected." "It would have taken them ten years to regain what they lost."

"Your father and I became better friends, and I traveled with him to a lot of places." "Jane, I never trusted anyone, not even your father, and he knew that." "In a business, you have to have people that are behind you to succeed." "In my business, I can't have anyone behind me, and that meant that your father had to stand beside me or get out of my way."

"What happened to that agent?" She asked.

"He was killed." I said to her, "Is that why you tell me when I ask you questions that I'm asking restricted information?"

"Yes."

"Does it have anything to do with the government?" She questioned.

"Yes," I said.

"I don't understand?" She stated.

"Well, that country and the other countries that stole that information now have fourteen satellites in orbit that's under my control." "He delivered a package for me, and that package can be opened whenever I need to." "I send it a message, and it only obeys my command." "No one can identify my code; I padlocked it." "You might think of it as a gun that's pointed at you; only if you fire it, it hits the person that fires it."

"Do you trust me?" She asked me.

"No"

"How can you say that?" She said

"Did you trust your husband?" I asked her.

"You broke my rule again, Smith." "Please don't mention him again." "Now, why don't you trust me?"

"Trust is a relationship that takes a long time to build; you started trusting me when I showed you the picture I drew of you when I first met you." "Without that picture, I don't think you would be friendly with me now." "I've talked to you and said more to you than I've ever spoken in my entire life, to anyone, even your father." "I don't like being around people." "I want to leave and work on my projects."

"Smith, do I make you want to leave and work?"

"No, I slept a few hours; when you were shaking and holding me, I fell asleep." I then looked into her eyes. "Jane, in what I do, my destiny is written that I might not come back." "I'm called a problem solver."

"Do you kill people?" She asked.

"I destroy what man builds to destroy." "Man today uses computers for everything that is done technologically." "Satellites, missiles, submarines, telephone's, nuclear plants, refineries, even trains, you name it." "They all operate on codes that give the computers their commands." "I merely destroy the codes and activate a death sentence." "I dissolve and kill communications." "Have you ever been to a store where they lost power?" I asked her. "Their progress is stalled, cameras can't operate, and thieves can do what they do best; there's no surveillance." "Money can't change hands, cash registers don't work, and scanners can't scan." "Large places call for backup generators; if they don't work, then nothing works." "Communication is broken, and no one does anything." "Managers of companies are afraid to make decisions unless they can get permission." "Militaries are the same way, break communication, and no one knows what to do without orders." "I kill people that kill people."

"You know," she said, "when I woke up in your room, I couldn't see anything, and everything was really, really dark." "A lot of things raced through my mind, but this wasn't one of them."

"Your father will feel relieved when you talk to him then." I said, "He always thought he neglected his family." "That's why I told him when I found this place that I needed someone on the inside, a lobbyist." "It gave him his freedom." "Besides the perks were better, his daughter got a free all-expenses-paid to stay at the resort."

She began kissing me again. She stopped and looked at me. "Rule number one."

I smiled, and she started in again. This time when she stopped, she took my cheeks in one hand, squeezed them, and kissed me again. Then she took both hands, pushed the sides of my mouth together, and kissed me again.

She stopped and started shaking her head back and forth. "This isn't working; I'm not getting any reaction from you at all." She said.

I took a deep breath. "Jane, when you first kissed someone, did you know what to do?"

"But, you're a man." She said.

"I may be a man, but I know nothing of what you know." "I've never been around people long."

"Smith, when we lay together, and our bodies touch, don't you feel something inside?" You don't have some kind of a yearning, or a desire, or anything?" She said.

"Did you sleep with a boy on your first kiss?" I asked her.

"This is our second kiss." She said, "And that's restricted information."

"Jane, I can't live outside of my world." "I feel friction."

"Then, I'll live here." She argued.

"You living here is like me living out there, you can't do it." "I'd have you wanting to find a way to leave in a few hours." "My talking to myself would drive you crazy."

"I've already been here for three days, and I find myself wanting to live with you forever, so I've already passed the time frame that you said I wouldn't make it to." She asserted, "Why do you talk to yourself, anyway?"

"Have you ever played chess?" I asked.

"No"

"Checkers then," I said.

"Yeah"

"Well, to win at checkers, you devise a plan, a strategy, you need to know ahead of time what moves your opponent should make, if the checker isn't moved that's supposed to be moved, then you're dealing with a person that doesn't have much in cranial capacity, a Napoleonic mind drives him." "By moving the wrong checker, he either doesn't know how to play checkers, or he's undermining his opponent to find out what his next move is."

Do you hear voices too?" She asked.

"Not anymore," I said to her.

"How long do you do this?" "You know, doing what you're doing, talking to yourself." She asked.

"I have a little problem there." "I don't think of one thing, or two things, or three things; I think of a lot of things at the same time while I work." "When I can't sleep, I work for days, and I work nights; I think better that way." "But, I think out loud when I think; it helps me to weigh my arguments." "Most people read an article and put it down and say; I learned something that I didn't know." "I read that article and read the story behind the story because that's the real story." "We don't call a lie a lie; we now call it a diluted expression of freedom of speech." "Slander and libel don't mean anything to people who take oaths; all guilty criminals claim innocence in court, or they plead the Fifth Amendment, so no one has to answer anything." "Listen to a presidential debate; you can openly lie and slander an opponent about anything you say." "So now, in our justice system, what used to be termed innocent until proven guilty, no longer applies." "Get a letter from the IRS and tell them their wrong; you'll have to prove your innocence in court; all they have to do is make an accusation." "We signed a constitution, and when it was signed, that's the only time that everyone there agreed with what it said." "It was signed a little over two hundred years ago, and since then, we've had over two hundred amendments to the constitution, and now today, half of the people disagree with what the other half thinks." "That's how misinformation is spread by misquoting the truth." "Are you ready to go, now?" I asked her. I knew I was starting to vent my feelings.

"Not really." She said.

"Okay," I replied and held my tongue.

"You don't like the government much, do you?" She said.

"You aren't listening to what I'm saying; no one does." "That's why I have a problem." "That's why I am the way I am." I said to her, "I can't convince those that think otherwise, and trying to do so would be futile." "When you have corruption in a corporation, you file for bankruptcy to do damage control."

"One person isn't a major damage to a business; it costs, but to have two people involved, then they're able to do damage at twice the cost." "More, and the corporation suffers losses." "No more business for that business; it was brought down internally." "Benedict Arnold was real close to being the father of our country," I said to her. "There are a lot of areas in our government that need damage control." "We've lost our businesses and labor force to other countries." "Jane, we have many people that are betraying this country, and they are lawmakers from both parties." "I don't like that; it upsets me." "But, people read their paper and read only the things that they want to hear." "When they put it down, they say, I learned something." "I don't like to hear news media promoting biased opinions; they dilute the freedom of speech." "I don't like to see what was said, deleted, and I don't like to hear, what I meant to say, and I don't like to see one person receiving praise and negative words spoken about the other in every column, every day." "History repeats itself over and over and over and over."

She pulled off her top and put the rock over it, and then she did the same to me and put my shirt under the rock. She then gently and easily straddled my lap and pulled herself to me.

"What do you feel, Smith?"

"Afraid"

"Put your arms around me, and hug me." She said to me.

When I did, she said, "Now, what do you feel?"

"Scared"

She began kissing me on my neck and my shoulders.

"Now, what do you feel?"

"Like I'm trespassing on private property."

She sat up and looked at me. "How deep do I have to go to reach that fifteen-year-old boy that saw me and remembered everything I wore and what I looked like just by looking at me for thirty seconds; when most men can't remember what you wore the day before?"

"Jane, this was what you were frightened about when you woke up in my bedroll."

"Okay." "Now it's my turn." She said, "Smith look at me, all of me," she said, sitting up, "am I attractive to you?"

"Yes"

"Then, we need to practice on rule number one, a lot, and I'm going to see to it that you get real good at it; I think that's why I'm here." "But, there's a price for my lessons." "You have a corporation, and you pay for my perks, you said." "I want more; you can afford it." "I want you to show me that I'm attracted to me." "When I kiss you, I want to be kissed back." "It doesn't have to be perfect, I'll teach you the way I want to be kissed, and if you don't get it right the first time, then we'll kiss again, and then if you don't get it right, the next time, then we'll keep on kissing until you do." "Do you argue against that?" She asked me.

"Jane, you're not listening." "You can't fall in love with someone like me; I can't live with anyone."

"Then we've got all winter to work on rule number one." She said, smiling her smile. "What happened after you told my dad what you wanted?" She said as she pulled herself back to lean against my chest and laid her head on my shoulders.

"He got it for me." "He's done a lot for me." "He built my lab, and he built that resort, and he got me the land I asked for."

"How did you do that?" She asked.

"Checkers," I told her. "Until the game is over, there's always going to be a move; when it's over, you have a winner, and you have a loser." "Your father didn't find out about me until after seventeen satellites had been launched and were put in orbit." "All of them are under my control." "They did a mission to remove my works, and the satellite is nothing more than a piece of junk metal floating around in space now." "Do you know how much it cost to put a satellite in orbit and then go up again and try to repair it, and after that, it doesn't work?" "Well, the price you hear quoted isn't an accurate quote." "But, people believe what they hear and read, and then they say, man, I learned something today."

"Now, are you ready to go?" I asked.

"Yes," she said.

"Smith, are you afraid of a woman because you think that you might conceive a child like your brother?"

"I had those thoughts many, many, many times before." "I never could understand why my brother was born like he was, and I was born like me." "But that's not a problem; I'll never be with someone."

I helped her out of the creek, removed our tops from under the rock, and put them over a line I had strung out to dry the clothes that I washed.

I took off the bottom of my long johns, leaving me bare-skinned, and heard the girl behind me. I turned around to see her looking at me.

"You need some sun; those legs give off a glare." Then she said, "Give me a hand and help me get out of mine."

"Give me a minute and let me get dressed," I told her.

"Smith, these bottoms are cold." She said.

I went and helped her undress, and now she too was bare-skinned; I then saw her smile. She grabbed me and said; rule number one, and she pulled me to her and started kissing me again. Then I heard her comment, "Smith, I can feel something that tells me that you're beginning to feel my kisses."

"Jane, you know you should take up the game of chess; I think you would be an opponent worthy of any adversary." "You weren't cold, were you?"

"Shhh, you're talking again." I put more wood on the fire, and we practiced on rule number one for a long time. She then eased up and got her coat and limped back over to me, and straddled my lap, and put the coat over the top of us, covering us up, and she began teaching me how she liked to be kissed again.

The day turned into night, and she fell asleep while lying on my chest. Several times her coughing found herself in the creek; she was beginning to rid herself of the fluids in her lungs. I took the opportunity to load the fire with more wood. After rinsing out her mouth, she returned to the warmth that my body gave her. She would position herself on my lap and lay her body on my chest, she was hot with temperature, and she found my heat to have relief from the cold that she felt.

She also had trouble sleeping that night, and twice she woke up and easily lifted her head to look at me. She tried not to disturb me from my sleep, but I wasn't asleep. When her eyes met mine, she smiled and kissed me.

"Are you having a problem, now?" She asked.

I put my arms around her.

"Yes," I told her.

"I'll give you a penny for your thoughts." She said.

"I was wondering why you have this affection towards me, and now I find myself caught off guard." "You were in love with."

"Smith," she stopped me from continuing, "don't mention him." She said determinately.

"Okay." "You were in love with a man for a long time, so you must have thought of him as a soul mate." "I was wondering when the time came."

"Smith, are you talking about us now?" She once again stopped me from saying what I wanted to say.

"Jane, I never knew if my father was ever in love with my mother, and there's a part of my life I don't have the answers that I'm looking for." "The pieces to the puzzle were never in the box." "Your mother and father had arguments and fights," "I remember one time your father came to stay with me for three days." "I knew he wasn't there for me." "Do you have a memory of this?" I asked her.

"Smith, everybody has buttons that are pushed." "It's healthy for a relationship; it shows that no matter what happens, you still want to be with that person." "When you both can hold each other and kiss, it's a way of saying, I missed you, and it's like falling in love with that person all over again."

"I read where sometimes a kiss doesn't mean anything." I told her, "I got a picture of the author and studied her." "I understood what she meant when I saw her picture." "It's not that way with me; I can't fight, and I want to leave." "I don't know how to talk to people." "You said so yourself, I'm a know-it-all, so I'm not around people long without finding myself coming back here." "I know my outcome." "I lost my brother, and I lost my mother." "I'll lose you too when you leave, and I."

She began kissing me again to stop me from talking, and she only stopped kissing me to wipe the tears from my eyes. She pulled one side of her golden hair behind her ear and then said. "So, you do have a love for me?"

"I've never been in love," I said.

"Do you love sleeping with me?" She said.

"What is love?" I answered slowly.

"Do you like holding me?" She asked.

"Yes," I said with the same slowness.

"Do you like my lips touching yours, as much as I love kissing you?" She said, smiling.

"Yes"

"Then Smith, I'll take that kind of love, and I'll be satisfied with that." "Now, I can see you're thinking about something else." She said. "And I think I know how to work this out." I looked at her. "You need to work to think, and I don't like it when you're not with me." "So, from now on, when you're outside working, I'll be there with you." "I'll do my best to keep up with you to go wherever you go." "But my butt can't take a walk right now; I won't be able to keep up with you." "Do you have any disagreement with anything I said so far?" She asked.

"No"

"Then we've reached a milestone here" "we've agreed on an arrangement, and that means that we're making progress." "Now, there's something else that I want to find out, and now is the best time to bring it up." She said to me.

"Do you love me?" She asked.

"Jane, you don't know what you're letting yourself get involved in." "I told you that I've never been in love, so that's a question that I never knew I would be asked." "But all I can say about your question is, I never met someone that was able to penetrate my defenses that I set up to protect my world, the way you have." "If I had seen you at the resort while I was getting my supplies, I would have looked to see what you grew up to be, but I wouldn't have interfered with your life in any way." "You never would have heard from me." "But, all that put aside, you've got me trapped beneath you, naked, and you ask me if I love you." "So, I ask myself, is this love?" "Then, I say, she gives me all she can to show me that she has feelings for me." "But I don't return the attention that she gives me; I've never had emotions as I have with you." "I ask myself, being the person that I am, I ask, does she really want to be with me, or will she fade away?"

"You don't trust anyone, do you"? She stated to me.

"I don't like people who lie to me," I told her, "And I meet many that use it whenever they speak." "If I say I love you, I'd mean it." "But, if you ever told me a lie, I wouldn't mean it anymore, and I'm afraid we're not in a good love." "If you studied any psychology in school, you would know that the first thing you don't do is get involved with someone that has issues," I told her.

"Like you, for instance?" She said, "Smith, I know you have a problem, and I did study psychology, but I know what the cure for your problem is." "You need me because you are a lonely man, and I need you because I was lied to." "I'm like you in that respect; that's why it wasn't that hard for me to put what's his name behind me." "And I, too, would be lonely without you." "I know it's only been three days, but being in your arms right now, I feel the strangest I've ever felt." "Now, I'll never lie to you, and I'll never betray you." "No one's ever made me feel like you make me feel." "Not even ole what's his face." "Can you tell me that you love me?" She said.

I looked into her eyes, and I could see redness; she was going to cry, no matter what my answer was.

"Jane, I was confused when you said you were in love with me." "I was honest with you." "I never knew what love meant." "You've taught me things that I've never learned." "I get a strange feeling when you hold me." "If being in love means that you want me to be with you as your mother and father, then I have to say, yes." "I told you that I don't know what to do or what to say." "I honestly meant what I said, and you should listen to me; I'm not a good man to be with."

"You are a very sensitive man; you know that?" She stated to me, "You need some powerful medicine." And then she kissed me for a long, long time.

She stopped and looked at me.

"You asked me if my husband went on trips for his clients." "Do you think I was being cheated on?" She asked.

"Did I hit a sore spot when I mentioned it, or did you have suspicions already"? "Maybe we should let this be," I told her.

"No, I want to hear what you think." She said.

"Jane, something doesn't add up." "Five million is a lot of money; he knows that amount will bring an investigation." "But without a body, nothing can be proved." "But you said he works for a law firm, your father is a retired senator, so I imagine his law firm pays him well." "Five million isn't much when you talk money to a successful law firm." "Assuming, that is, that your father used them in his business."

"He did, many times." She said.

"Then, we're talking in the tens of millions in legal compensation, am I correct?" I asked.

"Yes"

"Jane, your husband could have been set up for a kill." "If your husband was having an affair, I believe the person he was having an affair with is pregnant." "I think that maybe he was desperate, and with you gone, no one would have any clue." "When you go home, you might discover this." "I'm not saying any of this is true, but it enters my mind," I told her.

"You can't stop, can you?" "I mean, you're always thinking about things that don't matter." "What you just said does matter, it hit home, but it tells me that you're always thinking." "This code you see, tell me what you see." She asked.

"Checker's," I told her. "There's never a question that doesn't have an answer." "That answer to the question has been erased, and speculation is all that remains." "This speculation opens avenues to explore a thought or a theory." "Man grew up with the idea that the earth was flat, and anybody sailing close would fall off the earth." "There were sea monsters that were told of and ships with men lost at sea from attacks from these monsters." "Today, these types of stories are ridiculed and laughed at." "But that was centuries of years ago." "Whale boats were aplenty, and smaller boats were sent out to capture their prey." "Giant squid is alive and doing well deep in oceans; they are known to attack Sperm whales for defense." "Who's to say that a small boat wasn't attacked by creatures that exist today, and the stories that were told were true, only time changed the way some of them were told, and the truth became part of the untruth, to make a story sound better." "I see a code here, and it leans more to one side than it does to the other." "Did your husband make trips to one city or more?"

"More"

"Did your husband set up this vacation?" I asked her.

"Yes" "Why?" She asked quickly.

"I'm thinking that he could have been involved in being blackmailed." "I told you, I don't read an article and listen to what is said; I read an article and read the story behind a story." "Here, we may have a story, but there may be a story behind this story." I told her, "You'll find that answer out when the due time comes; don't be surprised if there's a story behind this story." "For every action performed by man, there is a man with a reason." "You'll learn more of what that reason was when you leave here." "After all, he did try to kill you."

"When you're with me, do you do this kind of thinking all the time?" She asked.

"I try not to," I told her.

"See, Smith, that's what love is all about." "Love is not being afraid to say things like that." "Besides, what you say, makes me think of things like that too." "You know things like why did he want to kill me."

"What do you think about it?" I asked.

"Rule number one." She then began kissing me for a long, long time, and we fell back asleep.

During the night, we awoke and put on our clothes. I pulled her over to the shack, and she quickly hobbled over to the bedroll and got undressed, and covered herself up.

"Come on, slowpoke; I need a heater; I should have made you get in first." She said, shivering.

When I got in, she rolled me over to be face to face with her.

"Now, Smith, this is where you take me in your arms and hold me with feelings." "I may act like I'm trying to get away from you, and I may make sounds that may make you think that you're hurting me." "You're not; my fever makes me want more heat, and Smith, I'm starting to get a feeling that you do have feelings for me." She said as she spoke softly to me and began practicing her rules.

She awoke that morning and spoke to me.

"I can feel you. Are you having a problem, now?" She asked.

"Yes"

She rolled over on me and used her sleeves to wipe my eyes.

She adjusted herself to form to our body's difference and arched her back so that her head lay down on my chest.

"Your heart's beating fast." She said. "Did you have a dream?"

"No"

"Were you thinking about your mother and brother?"

"No, I was thinking about you," I told her.

"Why does that make you upset?"

"You've broken my code, and no one's been able to do that." "I never let anyone in, and you did it without trying to."

"So, why are you upset?" She asked.

"Jane, I didn't want this to happen."

"Smith, I thought we were doing well here?"

"That's not it; one day, your father will come home and tell you I won't be coming back."

"Don't talk like that." She said to me.

"Jane, it's the truth." "I never intended for you to react to me the way you did." "I showed you that picture of yourself when you were at the party to calm you of the fear you had of me." "It worked, but I didn't expect what happened to happen."

"I just want you to know that when that day comes, I want you to be prepared."

"Smith, you said you work when you get like this, get up, and go to work, go out and cut down your trees, work on your leather, make your totem poles, cut up the firewood, do whatever you do when you get like this, don't let me stop you from doing anything, I'm just here for the winter, remember?" She was upset.

She unzipped the bedroll and gently pushed on my back to urge me to get up and get dressed.

I did so, gathered my guns, and went outside. I took a small stroll and stopped. I went over to a tree, began cutting some branches, brought them back to my cabin, then sat the branches down, went into my work shed, and got the tools I needed.

I built a small fire outside, sat down, and began my work when I heard the door open. The girl looked around and saw me.

She shouted, "Smith, I'm sorry."

I looked over at her and returned to my work.

Soon I heard the door open again and saw her with her warm skin on. I got up, walked over to her, and told her to sit in the sled. I waited, and then I pulled her over to the fire where I was at. I went and rolled a section of wood that I was going to chop up to make firewood, but its purpose was given amnesty; I needed it to sit on.

"What are you doing?" She asked.

"I'm making you some snowshoes." "Being cooped up in that cabin makes you edgy, and I don't like being around you when you're edgy." "I'm going to be gone a while, and you'll need to go to the outhouse now and then." "I'm making you these snowshoes so you can walk without difficulty."

"Why are you leaving me?"

"It's better this way." "I told you I have problems, and you being here has brought me complications that I don't know how to deal with."

"Smith, we're dealing with them now." "You have to talk to me." "We have to talk to each other, and I have a problem too." "In case you don't know, women are cursed, and I'm about to start my cycle, and I don't have any sanitary napkins to wear." She tightened her hands into a fist and pressed her lips tight.

I put my work down in my lap and looked at her.

"Smith, you don't know how nasty a person feels walking around wet."

I stood and placed my work aside and pulled her back to the cabin. I helped her up and told her to lie down on the bedroll. I reached under it and felt around and pulled out one of my skins and told her to lift her butt, and I slid the skin underneath her.

I cut out a pattern and then folded it over her like a diaper, slid the skin underneath, and tied a square knot that the leg pieces offered as a belt.

"How's that feel?" I asked her.

"What is it?"

"It's an outdoorsman's sanitary napkin," I told her. I then untied it, removed it from her, took some of the skin, sewed the sides and the back in the diaper-looking panties, pushed the rest of the skins inside the liner, and sewed it up.

I put it back on her and then asked her how it felt.

"Uncomfortable," she said.

"Well, at least, I won't have to remember you by the long johns you left behind." I told her, "Put these on when you start, and we'll clean them when we take our bath at healing waters." "I'll start making you some more, right now, so you'll always feel clean and fresh."

"Smith, I'm sorry for the way I acted." "I didn't mean for what I said to come out the way I said it."

"It's all right; it had to be said and dealt with." I related my thought to her.

"That's another thing we need to talk about." She stated, "I don't want you to bring up things like that again." "When you do, it's like telling me that you love me, but you have reservations against loving me." "It scares me, and I get a strong feeling that you're fighting me." "When you do, I hurt, and when you hurt, I hurt." "So don't hurt me anymore by talking to me like that." "Is that understood?" She said to me.

I didn't answer her.

"Smith, I need an answer from you."

"I'll never mention it again," I told her.

"Now," she spoke with a purpose, "I looked back at the cabin from the fire outside." "Why does the top look like that?"

"When you first awoke from the bedroll, you slumped down to keep from hitting your head on any low objects, it was dark, and you naturally assumed that my cabin was like all other places that people live." "Stand up for a moment," I told her.

I then told her to lift her hands into the air when she did. When she did, I asked her what she felt.

"Nothing," she said.

"You don't have to crouch here; you can stand and not be bothered." "When I found you and assessed you to see if you had any broken bones." "I noticed two scars on your forehead." "They were from ceiling fans, weren't they?"

"Yes," She said slowly.

"Jane, ceiling fans normally hang one foot from the ceiling, on an eight-foot ceiling that leaves seven feet."

"So that's what this is about." She said, "Smith, I'm seven foot one; I lied to you about my size."

"I know, that's why I told you that I didn't think we were in a good love." "Smith"

"Jane, I understand; you don't need to answer; I know." "It's something you had to live with all of your life." "When you started noticing what other people said and did by staring at you and teasing with you about your size,

52

they didn't realize what they were doing to you emotionally." "I bet there were a lot of times you cried in bed going to sleep." "I say so because I have problems of my own."

"Does that mean you're not leaving me?" She asked.

"Oh no, I'm leaving, I have work to do, I have to build snowshoes for you to be able to walk in, and I have to gather firewood, and I have to do my work." "But right now, let me show you why you don't have to worry about bumping your head," I said.

I walked outside, untied a tarp over my cabin, took it off, and walked back inside.

"It's beautiful," she said. "Where did you get it?"

"I had it made and brought it here and built an A-frame to hoist it onto the top to make my roof."

"Here," I moved a ladder I had and put it next to the wall, "climb up and take a look outside."

After a few steps, she stopped. "This is amazing."

"I wanted to watch the stars at night and see if I could see any animals; the snow is like a light at night." I told her, "The moon helps me to think, and I enjoy gazing up at the stars." "I saw some pictures of a zoo that people have seen the animals from inside a dome." "I thought that it would be good to have as a solar panel in winter." "It turned out; I use it for the same purpose as those people did that used it in the zoo."

"Late at night, on a full moon, I watch deer, and bears, and wolves, and other animals that inhabit this area."

"Do they bother you?" She asked.

"At first they did; the smell of food made them curious." "I built a fire and made camp." "One night, I awoke to a pack of wolves attacking my horse; I shot four of the wolves and made gloves out of them, and ended up shooting my horse." "I had to chop up my horse to pull the carcass away; I didn't need bears to go along with the wolves." "I kept wood on the rest of the remains to burn the scent of blood."

"I had one gun then, and now I have three." "Those bear skins that you're wearing were from bears that didn't go the other way when I was around, they stalked me to healing waters, and I shot them at the entrance."

"I have two thirty-thirties because I can fire them quickly, and I have an elephant gun for close range." "I don't kill any animals unless I'm on their menu." "The elephant gun dispatches an elephant, so when the bullet strikes a bear, I mean to kill it, and I do so without prejudice because he's trying to kill me."

"What am I wearing now?" She asked.

"The gloves I made from the wolves, but under the circumstances, a man has to resort to unorthodox changes that he encounters."

"You're talking about me, aren't you?" She attacked my comment.

"You can always take them off and walk around naked." "Of course, you'll be limited to walking inside my cabin; it's too cold out there for a nudist," I told her.

"Oh!" "you have a humor side to you." "You're a funny man." "Smith don't leave me alone by myself here." She then added.

"You don't have anything to fear here," I reassured her.

"That's not it, I want to be with you, and I want to go where you go." "I want to watch you as you work; I want to see what you do here, in your world, before I dropped in on you."

"Was that pun intended?" I asked her.

She smiled.

"Oh!" "You're a clever girl; you used a counter-attack and moved a checker that I didn't expect you to move."

"Smith, you're a brilliant man." "I can't compete with you when it comes to just about anything, but I do find myself having an advantage when it comes to talking to you, and I also find myself having the same disadvantage when it comes to talking to you." "You are a very, very sensitive man, and I find I can easily offend you when I say the wrong thing to you." "I need a promise from you." She said to me, "I need you to tell me that you won't leave me here, alone, for anything." "Smith, I lied to you about my height, but that was before I said I never would." "I didn't realize at the time that that one simple little lie would upset you the way it did, but I'm sorry, and I'll never, never, ever, ever say anything that's a lie to you again; no matter how small it seems to me, I see it means a lot more to you, and I'm sorry for that, and Smith you'll never hear me apologize for lying to you again, I won't have too, I'll never do it." "When we talked about my size, you knew I was lying, and you let me tell my lie to you, and you never said anything about it." "At the time, I didn't realize I was being sized up for what I said, and I'm not talking about my height, but in my defense, I never met a man that could put little pieces together the way you can." "I did have problems growing up, and you were right when you asked about my husband being the first man that paid me any attention." "You were also right when you mentioned about me wishing someone was my size to dance with." "But Smith, I never got that wish, and I needed someone to love me, and I got cheated in that department." "I've tried my best to find an answer to why I feel so drawn to you, but try as hard as I can; I can't find an answer." "All I know is that I have an empty feeling without you." "So, please, Smith, forgive me."

"Do you say those things to all the men you meet that have a skylight?" I said to her.

She stepped down slowly and gingerly from the ladder and took me in her arms. "You're the first man I've known with a skylight, and it makes me want to lay with you and watch the stars." "You know how to treat a girl; you know that?"

She bent down and started kissing me, and then we found ourselves on the bedroll. She was giving me more lessons on how she wanted to be kissed.

That night the stars were bright, and the sky was clear. I put wood into my stove, and its glow gave off shadows on the wall. I watched them as they danced about effortlessly.

I got up, pulled my ladder over, and stepped up to view the land outside. Moments later, I called for Jane to take a look, and I got down, and she stepped up to see what I was looking at.

"I can see four of them." She said.

I climbed up the ladder behind her.

"Look over to your left by the trees; there's three more," I stated. "They're older and wiser; they use the trees as cover." "The deer in the open are young yearlings; they haven't the wisdom of the older deer, so caution is overlooked." "If anything would attack, it would come from below the meadow." "You can see the smoke that comes from my stove; it's blowing away from them."

"What are they doing?" She asked.

"The winter is harsh on all animals here; many die from starvation or an injury." "The sick, the weak, the old, the young, nothing escapes the jaws of death here." "It's highly unlikely that any of these animals will die of old age." "They live the life of the hunter and the hunted, and when the hunter is injured, he dies the same fate as those he hunted." "I plant oats up on that ridge, come fall, deer are numerous during the harvest." They fatten themselves up to survive." "I spend a long time at night where you're at watching them."

I stepped down from the ladder.

"You know where to bring a girl on a date, don't you?" She chuckled.

"I've never been on a date," I told her.

She looked down at me from the ladder. "So, I'm your first date?"

"Everything about you is my first." "When you kissed me, which was my first kiss." "When you laid down next to me, which was the first time I've ever felt a girl's skin." "I talked to women, church ladies, the judge's wife, but I never talked to a girl, so I'm ignorant in this field." "You were wrong; you're smarter than me in areas that I don't have any knowledge of."

"Smith, you have a way of seducing a girl with the way you talk." She said as she was getting down from the ladder.

"You're safe with me," I told her.

"Smith, I don't think you understand what I'm saying." "You aren't safe with me." She grabbed me, and then she pulled me down to lie down on my bedroll with her. She rolled over on top of me, bit me on my ear gently, and whispered. "I'll be gentle."

I stirred the next morning, and she pulled me over, and I rested on top of her; she gave me a tight squeeze. "If you're leaving me, I won't let you go." She stated.

"I was going to fix breakfast, and I was going to thaw out a rib roast for supper." "I have a feel-good day, and when I have a feel-good day, I like to reward myself by cooking something I like." "How do you like your prime rib, rare or rare?" I asked her.

"Pink," she said.

"Rare it is then," I told her.

"Smith, I wish I could have met you earlier."

"You did, remember, you were eleven," I remarked.

"Yes, and if you had talked to me then the way you talk to me now, I would be an eleven-year-old girl with a serious crush on you, and Smith, I love you."

I bent down and kissed her the way she liked to be kissed, and then I raised my head and spoke to her

"That was the only way I could make you feel that I love you too." "Nothing else would have told you that, except that kiss."

"You're a dangerous man." She laughed. "But, you're a better cook, and I'm going to take full advantage of this feel-good day you're having."

I smiled at her. "It's the skylight, right?"

She smiled back at me. "Ditto." She replied. I got up and went to my storage room, brought back a rib roast that I had cut up and frozen for my winter supplies, and set it aside to thaw. The heat from the woodstove allowed the meat to thaw at room temperature. I prepared to cook us some breakfast when the girl spoke.

"Smith," Jane said, "forget about breakfast and let's sleep in late; I'm really tired."

I looked over at her and saw a smile. "You don't have sleeping on your mind," I told her.

She pretended to yawn and smiled at me again. I eased into bed, and she covered me with her body and showered me with kisses.

That afternoon, I relit my fire out in my fire pit, and I adjusted my coals to allow the heat to cook my rib roast slow. I then went into my storage room and took two potatoes from a plastic garbage can, washed them, and then wrapped them up in some aluminum foil, and I also sat them down in the coals of the fire. I tended to them periodically, turning them to cook evenly.

The girl came out of the cabin, and I helped her over to the fire where I was working on her snowshoes while I cooked.

She watched me as I worked.

I looked over at her and saw her watching me.

"I cut some green branches, and I spliced the big end and the small end." "See this tool; it's a hand-cranked drill." "I turn the handle, and the drill bit turns, and soon, voila, we have two holes and two limbs that are now one."

"We take a piece of wire, poke it through the holes and tie them by twisting it tight." "Then we secure it better by wrapping more wire around where we cut the hole, we want strength, and movement will tear the limbs." "Now, we bend the other spliced ends together, and we tie the wire the same way." I showed her, "We now have almost a perfect circle." "Now, we drill holes about every inch or so, and we do it all the way around." After I finished, I showed her.

"See this line here?" I told her. "This is the same fishing line that I used for your stitches, I run the line in and out of the holes, and then I cross them and cross them again, and tie it off with the branches in between to soften the weight as you walk." I showed her the finished product. "See if you can stand on it," I told her.

After she tested it, I did the other the same way. I then fashioned straps that held the snowshoes from flopping up and down as she walked. I put them on her and asked her to walk around and give them a test. She still nursed her sore butt by not putting weight on it.

She did as I asked.

"Stomp down on the snow with your good leg," I said, and when she did, she looked over at me.

"Now, you can go anywhere and do anything I do." "If you have pain, we'll stop and rest; I'll put a little snow on the wound and numb the pain." "But, don't worry; I have enough to do around here to last a week or two." "By then, you won't be suffering from the pain you are now."

I walked over, turned the potatoes, and looked at my rib roast.

"How did you learn to cook like that?"

"All recipes are alike; put this in, or take this out." "It's more of a preference thing." I told her, "With baking, formulas are used, and you can't take this out or put that in; everything has to be precise, or whatever you cook will end up in a disaster." "A stove can be simple; all you have to do is put a pot on top of the coals and let your food cook." "All you have to do is adjust the temperature to your desire." "An oven can be just as simple; the coals are placed far enough apart so that you can put your pot in the middle and let the heat radiate to the pot, only you have to put a lid on the pot and add some coals around the pot and on top of the lid." "That's how I cooked those biscuits we ate." "I use a Dutch oven when I cook like this." "A little monitoring, and soon you can sit back and smell the aroma that the food gives off, and that lets me know, whether I'm cooking too slow, too fast, or just right." "You have to be careful, though; bears and wolves can smell food miles away." "You get a funny feeling watching animals watching you."

"Take a deep breath," I told her. "What do you think?"

"It smells good."

"You're getting hungry, aren't you?" I said to her, "I just put it on." "Jane, do you remember the pizza you ate at that party?" I asked her.

"I didn't like pizza's much." She said.

"So, to you, a pizza is a pizza then." I stated, "Back then, you had dislikes in the food that you ate." "You ate only the things you liked and didn't eat anything that had something on it that you didn't like, right?"

"Yes, pretty much." She said.

"What about now? Do you eat the foods you didn't eat when you were young?"

"Yes, and sometimes I can't get enough of it."

"I did too, except with me, I didn't like certain foods because they disagreed with my digestive system." "I told you, I had enemies; they're pan sausage, tomato sauce, and eggs." "I love them all, but they give me digestion problems all day long." "That's one reason, I eat one meal a day, and that's after dark." "I get lazy, and I don't want to work on anything physical after I eat."

I got up and started walking to my storage unit and came back with a couple of cans of mushrooms. I got a pot and poured them in and sat them on the coals to cook in its juices.

"You do a lot of cooking for one person." She said.

"Well, it depends on how you look at it." "If you hadn't been here, I would be eating rib roast for three or four days, then I would be eating beef tips with rice for a few more, or steak fajitas, whatever, I would be eating beef; until it was gone."

"I'm fortunate to have you here, dining with me." "I get tired of eating leftovers every day until it's gone, and judging by the way you put away that cornmeal soup and stuffed peppers." "I won't be eating leftovers much anymore."

"Hey!" "That isn't nice to say." She scolded me.

"I'm teasing, and I shouldn't," I told her. "Besides, a rule of thumb is to be proportionately correct, you take the width of the hips and length of your legs, and they should be the same." "Jane, you don't have a problem there." "What's the length of your pants"? I asked her.

"I wear size forty-two in men's jeans." "I can't find my size in women's clothing." She stated.

"And your hips?" I asked.

"They're thirty-six's."

"You don't just shop anywhere, do you?" I said to her.

"No, I have to special order all my pants, and I wear men's tee shirts and sweatshirts. I just can't find pants that length." She said.

"Hold on a minute," I said to her and went inside my cabin and brought out two pairs of old pants that I had holes in one and the other was a pair I wore regularly. I cut the one with holes at the knees and began sewing them to the pair of jeans I had extra at the bottom. All I was doing was sewing the pieces I had cut off onto the jeans to make them longer. Soon, I was through with my sewing. "Try these on," I told her.

She took off the leggings I had made for her, and then she pulled down the shorts I had made. She then pulled up the pants to her waist and buttoned them.

"How do they feel?" I asked.

"I feel like a human able to walk around without all those skins tied onto me."

"Are they tight around the waist?" I asked her.

"I'm wearing that thing you made me earlier." She said.

I unbuttoned her pants. "How's that?" I asked her.

"That's better." She said.

"All right then, I have some thirty-eight's that I wear over my long johns; they'll feel better on you."

I got up, flipped over the potatoes, stirred the mushrooms, and looked at my rib roast. I walked inside my cabin, got a meat thermometer, and inserted it into the meat. It read an internal temperature of a hundred and forty degrees, and I took the pot off from the fire and took it inside the cabin and came back outside and squeezed the potatoes; they were done. So I also took them inside.

Before I did, I told Jane that she could come to fix her potato if she was ready.

I soon prepared it the way she asked me; she liked hers heavy on the butter. I walked outside and got the mushrooms, and I scooped some up for her, put some on my plate, and sat the rest on the woodstove.

I then prepared my potato, opened the lid on the pot, and started slicing her off a piece of the rib roast.

She didn't need encouragement to eat; she didn't know where to begin.

"You want some horseradish sauce with that?" I asked her.

"You're kidding, right?"

I chuckled and went into my storeroom and brought her some back.

"Smith, you're going to laugh at me." "I thought when I woke up here that I wouldn't be eating much." "I had the belief that I was going to have to survive on nothing but wild game." Her grin told me that she was happy she was wrong.

"Come winter," I began, "I can pack in frozen foods, come spring, I smoke most of my meat, or cure it in salt, the smoked meat is all right, but the meat cured in salt has to be boiled to remove the saltiness." I tried can goods, but, after that spring, I went back to smoking or curing the meat in salt." "I'm not much of a canned food eater, and I cooked a lot of my foods and vacuum-packed them to where all I had to do was put them in boiling water and make a pan of biscuits or cornbread or some rolls, or buns." "But you can only bring in so much on a wagon."

"Those church ladies that I helped cook for gave me all kinds of recipe books to read, and they liked what they learned, and I was never without food. They made special trips to see that I was fed." "There were times when I was taken over to their houses, and I used their stoves and ovens." "Their husbands welcomed me warmly, and they enjoyed my visits."

"I can remember every recipe," I told her.

"This is delicious; the meat is perfect, not bloody, and not grey, but pink." She remarked, "Do you know how hard it is to get a steak cooked the way you want it?" She asked.

"Meat has a carry over cooking; if you take it off at a certain temperature, it continues to cook until it reaches the hottest it's going to get, and then it starts to cool down; that's called resting the meat." "As it cools down, it creates a vacuum and draws the juices back into the meat." "You said you wanted the meat pink; I had to take the rib roast off at around a hundred and forty degrees for the meat not to have blood."

"I don't care how you do it; I like it." She said.

"Then the next time you eat a rib roast, you'll think of this moment in time." I told her, "Today is a day of building memories." I said to her.

"Smith, the next time I eat rib roast, you're going to cook it, and I'll be eating it with you."

I got up and cut her another piece of meat from the roast and put it on her plate.

"That's enough." She complained.

"You need your strength, we've got a long winter ahead, and this weather burns a lot more calories than you think." She didn't complain anymore.

She sat her plate aside and patted her stomach. "What's for dessert?" She asked, laughing.

"I can make you an apple or a peach crisp if you like?" "It's really simple to do."

"I was kidding; I'm stuffed to the gills." She laughed. "Let's take a walk; I feel miserable now."

"Are you sure that you're up to it?" I asked her.

"There's so much to see that's I've not gotten to see." "If I start hurting, I'll stop." She implored.

"Get in the sleigh, and I'll pull you around." "That way, you won't tire out," I told her.

She looked around to get a better view of her surroundings, something that she didn't get much time to do.

"What's that over there?" She asked.

I smiled at her. "That's ole blue; I brought her here the year after I found this place." "She can cook the best barbeque a man ever sunk his teeth into." "She makes the best-smoked chicken, and her ribs turn out to where a man without teeth can eat it, the bone pulls out leaving nothing but the meat." "Put a brisket on her, with the fat side up and cook her on low heat, for twenty-four hours and, you'll hurt yourself from eating too much." "But, cooking it is only half the secret."

"You got my attention." She said.

"I can't tell you, that's restricted information. I chuckled.

"Is that where you do your leatherwork at, over there?" She pointed to the workshop I built.

"Yeah, it's a small place, but I don't need more than a stool and a counter to work on." "You want to take a look?" I asked her.

"That's what I'm here for." She said.

We walked into the little shed, and she looked around. "What are these?"

"My tools, I use them for engraving designs and pictures on the leather." "Here, let me show you."

"I take a piece of leather." "I've got eight of them cut out already and dampen a rag with snow to get the leather wet; it's easier to cut that way." I said to her, "You draw an outline of the picture you want with the scalpel, like this, and then take this tool here and tap it with this small mallet." I began to draw a picture of a big buck with large antlers jumping over a fallen tree and then using the beveling tool to highlight the deer. "Then you have to tamp down the outline of him with this tool, like this, to give him a three-dimensional look." "Add some trees." I dampened the leather once again and continued, "Now add a few bushes with this tool and do the same with that tool to give a three-dimensional look like I did the deer, and just like that, you create a scene of beauty." "One thing about doing leatherwork, time passes quickly." "You put it aside, and the next time you look at it, you dampen the leather, and soon something else is added to the picture on the wallet." "It's the same with the purses." "People buy leather wallets and purses for one thing; they last a long, long time." "You have to be careful, though; you get carried away and find yourself working in here too long when you should be out doing other things." "Beautiful weather requires you to do outdoor work, and miserable weather offers you the availability to work on the things that require indoor activity." "Leatherwork is one of the miserable weather activities." She looked around at my completed works. "Do you see anything you like?" I asked her.

"What do I need them for?" "I'm not going anywhere, anytime soon." She shot back.

"What's up there?" She pointed in the direction that she wanted me to see. "That's where I found you." "At the top of that slope is Miller's Ridge."

"You mean I fell from up there?" She seemed surprised. "Now I know what you meant when you told me that I'm lucky."

"Yeah, he must have knocked you out, your body was slumped over, and when you hit the rock, it made you turn end over end."

"Can we go there?" She asked.

"It's a good way up there; you might not be in the best of shape for the trip right now," I told her.

"I want to see where I fell from." She urged me.

"Let me get a gun, and we'll set off and see how far you make it," I said to her.

She was breathing heavy about two hundred yards, and we stopped to rest.

"You want to go back and give it a try another day again?" I said to her.

"No, I want to see." "Besides, you're the one that's doing all the work." She replied.

We set out, and once again, we stopped a little ways from where we began.

"The air's a lot thinner up here." I told her, "You can't do as much up here as what you can do down in the city." "You tire out quickly, and your body's energy puts a strain on your strength." "We've got all day, and there's no hurry to be anywhere, so don't push yourself too hard." "I found out the best way to achieve a goal is to pace myself, and sometimes I have to alter my pace," I told her, trying my best to explain without telling her that I didn't think she was in the best shape.

It was in the afternoon when we arrived at the place where she had landed. I helped her up from my sleigh and showed her where she had been and how deep she sank when she hit the snow.

"Your legs were the only things sticking out, I pulled you out, and you weren't breathing; that's when I gave you breaths and abdominal thrusts when you revived, I put you on my sled and took you back to healing waters, the rest is history," I told her.

"I don't see how I survived the fall." She said.

"You had luck on your side."

She turned around and looked to the back of her.

"When I was looking down below, I saw this place, and I thought it was the most beautiful place I had ever been to." "I turned around to tell my husband that I wanted this to be our special place." "That's when I saw his fist coming at my face." "I couldn't get out of the way, and now, I'm here, and I'm with you, in my special place, with the man I want to be with." She stated.

"Jane"

"Smith, no excuses, when I saw the look on his face when he hit me, he didn't love me, he never did, I know that now." "You were right, and you were right all along."

I put my head down towards the ground and gave her time to collect her thoughts. When I looked back at her, I caught movement above me. I quickly took the gun from my shoulder and shot the cat leaping from a ledge above us from my hip. I fired once and had my gun cocked and fired again, and then I jumped in front of the girl. The cougar hit me high on my shoulder, and we fell backward, tumbling down the bank in the snow.

I got to my feet quickly and had my knife pulled, ready for another attack. I saw the cat dead, and I plopped down on my knees in the snow.

The young girl came to my side as quickly as she could.

"He was going to kill me." She said as she knelt to me.

"Yes," I said as I fell backward with my head looking up to the sky.

"What's the matter, Smith? You're scaring me?"

"Open my coat and tell me how bad he got me?" I said to her.

She moved fast, and soon I saw her crying.

"Did he get in my abdomen?" I asked her.

"No, he clawed you from your chest to your bottom rib." "I can see bones, Smith." She said as tears flowed down her eyes.

I smiled and looked up at her. "Jane, listen to me." "This is important." "When it comes a time, the sun rises in the east." "That's where the resort is; you'll come to a road, and when you do." "Go up." "Take my guns and walk in that direction." I smiled at her once again, and I lost my thoughts.

I opened my eyes, and I couldn't see; I felt my chest easily, and then I knew what I felt. I tried to get up and make it to the door, and I felt the girl fighting me.

"I have to go outside," I told her. I knelt in the snow on my knees and fell face-first into it.

I felt her trying to help me up. "Jane, I have to relieve myself; leave me."

She did the work for me and then helped me back to the bedroll. This time, I was burning up with a fever, and she was trying to provide me with her warmth.

I saw a blur and smiled. "Momma, where's my brother; I want to see my brother?"

"Smith, Smith, it's me, Jane," I heard her voice.

"Jane, I'm sorry."

"Smith, you have to help me; I can't carry you."

"You have to let me die." "I want to go home to be with my brother." "I want to see my brother."

"Smith, please, please, you have to help me." I heard her begging me.

63

I tried to stand and walk, but she did most of the work. I felt warmth, and I felt her cradling me in her arms and rocking and singing a song, I heard her crying as she sang, and then I fell back into oblivion.

When I opened my eyes again, I saw the young girl crying with her face in my chest.

"Jane." She lifted her head and looked at me quickly. "Jane, I thought I was going to die and not have anyone that loved me." "I don't have that worry anymore." "I'm going to die a happy man."

"Smith, we're at healing waters; you can't die; this place won't let you die." She began crying as she talked. "You said that it has powers that no other waters have." "Remember the story you told me of the people that came here."

I smiled at her, and I once again lost my thoughts.

I awoke back in my bedroll and felt the warmth of the girl's body.

I tried to get up, and the girl again restrained me.

"Jane, I need ice to kill the pain; it hurts badly." "Let me go."

I felt her helping me up, and I fell into the snow. She tried to get me up, and I told her no, I needed the cold. "I'm hot, I have to fight my temperature, or I'll have seizures."

"Smith, I don't know what to do?"

"Jane, you've done all you can do." "I told you, you would have done the same for me."

I awoke to the smell of meat.

I felt my head lift and a warm liquid dripping down my mouth. I sipped a little and then a little more. Then I felt the girl getting into the bedroll with me and covering me up with the blankets I used for her.

"Jane"

"I'm here, Smith." She said.

"I saw my momma."

"Yes, Smith." She said softly.

"Jane," I said, crying, "I wanted my brother to be there." "But, he wasn't." "I never got to see him."

"Smith," she started crying, "I saw your brother, and he said that you couldn't be with him yet." "He told me to tell you he loved you and that he would be waiting for you, but you couldn't come right now; it wasn't your time."

I was crying uncontrollably. "I wanted to see him." "I wanted to see him." "I miss him, real bad."

"I know Smith, but when I saw him, he had on his pistol belt, and he was wearing his canteen, and he told me to tell you he was going to fight pirates and outlaws." "Smith, he told me that he was awful proud of you." Then I heard her burst into tears again, and then I didn't hear anything anymore.

CHAPTER THREE

I felt my head raised, and water was trying to go down my throat. I took a small sip, looked up, and saw bright lights shining down on me.

Smith, Smith, Smith, I heard a voice repeating my name. "Smith, can you hear me?"

"Who is it?" I said groggily.

"It's me, Jack." "Smith, wake up." I felt someone shaking my arm easily. I slowly opened my eyes and saw a blurred face. "Jack, Jane's husband?"

He stopped me in mid-sentence. "Smith, we have important matters to discuss, so try to snap out of it." "Jane's outside waiting on you; she hasn't been asleep since you've arrived."

"Jack, her husband, tried to kill her," I said to him.

"Smith, he never returned." "We thought they were lost, and we never found a trace." "Jane and I had a long time to talk while you were out." He said to me.

"He's still up there then," I said. "Did you tell her that?"

"Yes"

"Jack, she says she loves me."

"Smith, we all need someone, and you're not any different."

"Can I see her?" I asked him.

He stood and walked outside, and soon the door burst open, and Jane came running towards me, with tears in her eyes.

"What happened?" I asked her.

"Smith, you were rambling and fighting me." "I heard the sounds of a helicopter, and then I saw my dad and another man enter the cabin, and we came here."

"Where am I?" I asked.

"Smith, they wouldn't tell me."

"Oh!" "Then I know," I said.

"What do you know, Smith?" She asked.

"I'm needed, or I'd be dead." "Your father wouldn't have come for me otherwise; I told you I had secrets; your father was the only person that knew where I was at." "Do you know how hard it is not to tell someone that asks you a question, and you have to tell them that you can't answer what they ask of you?" I informed her.

A tall, lanky man walked into the room and stood in front of my bed.

"You're not supposed to be here, Mister President," I told him. "This is a restricted area."

"Mister Smith, Jack called me up and asked for an interview." He said.

"Sir, are any of your people in here?" I said, still fighting my drowsiness.

"I've got three men." He said.

"I'm sorry, but you'll have to tell them to leave," I told him.

"Smith"

"Mister President, no one is allowed in here. If you want them around you, then you can leave with them." "Jack will fill me in on what you want."

He turned to his men and ordered them to leave.

"Sir," I heard one of the men comment.

"Do you always let your subordinates argue with you when you give them an order?" I asked him.

He looked over at the man and nodded his head for them to leave.

"Smith, they're gone," Jack said.

"Computer initiate sleep activation and send in James and Ruby," I commanded, and soon I was being attended to.

"Ease me up a little bit, James." I said to him, and when he did, I asked him, "What do I look like?"

"Sir, they mutilated you." He expressed.

"Do what you got to do." I stated, "Now, sir, you've got other things to attend to, so why am I here?" I was firm in my language.

"We've got a problem." "We intercepted a letter." He replied and then commented, "We can take care of this later." I could assume that he saw James working on me.

"Do you have it with you?" I asked him.

"It's in my briefcase." He said, and then he got up to get it for me.

Ruby brushed him back with her arm, began looking the briefcase over, and then backed away.

"Sorry, sir, you have your people, and I have mine." "Before you and I continue in what you came here for, you have to swear an oath." I told him, "Otherwise, this meeting will never take place." "I'm sure Jack informed you of that before you came here," I said to him.

"I don't think I understand." He answered.

"It's a simple oath," I told him. "I don't do business with liars, and when I look at a man, I know what I'm looking at, so I need you to swear to me that you won't ever lie to me." "Be careful in what you say," I told him. "I'm sure you've heard that it's usually the first impression you get that's the correct one."

"Smith, you have my word as a man." He said.

I reached out my hand and took his.

"A handshake is all that's needed between two men," I told him. "It used to mean something years ago, and it still does to me," I said to him.

"Smith," He said, taking my hand and putting his other hand on top of my hand that I was shaking his other hand with. "You're every bit of the man that Jack told me you were." "I give me my word, and I'll take it with me to my grave."

"You have a light grip, sir." I told him, "And you choose your words carefully." "Sir, there's one other thing." "When your men got on the elevator, they were gassed; they won't remember what happened for the past three days, so don't be answering any questions." "They know my location, and they know what I look like; I can't allow that," I told him.

"Smith, can I ask you a question?" He followed.

"Sir, I would have drugged you too and not have thought twice about it." I gave him my warning.

"Jack was right." "He told me to be cautious around you, and you've shown me what he was preparing me for, only he didn't tell me how cautious I should be." "I'm a man of my word." He stated to me.

"You can hand me that letter now." I told him, "Ruby has seen to it that it's not a threat; she won't stop you."

When he handed it to me, I didn't bother reading it; to me, it meant nothing. I scanned the letter as I held it up into the light and then asked Ruby to get me a sheet of onion paper and a pencil.

"You and I both know I'm not here, except for a reason; what is that reason?" I said to him.

"There's going to be a launch; no one would have a concern, except it's been reported to be carrying a nuclear warhead." He replied and then stated, "We can't take a chance on this."

"Who is it?" I asked him.

"He calls himself the Messiah." He said.

"Sir, it's a threat, nothing more." I told him, "No country will tolerate any country to launch an armed missile and detonate a nuclear warhead; it's bad business for everyone."

"We know that, but if the launch succeeds, other countries are threatening action." He stated.

"So, he'd be opening Pandora's box." I exclaimed, "Pull up a chair over here, Sir, and let me show you something."

"Smith, we can take care of this later." He once again reiterated, "Don't worry, Sir "James knows what he's doing." "We do it now." "I don't want you back here again."

I looked up into the light with the letter with my good arm so that I could see through it again.

"Look at the letter Sir." I gave it to him and told him to hold it up into the light for me,

I once again showed it to the President "If you notice, you'll see that every fifth letter is slightly written deeper into the paper." "And it's slightly spaced a little further away than the rest of the letters?" "Those are our key letters." "Now watch." I put the sheet of onion paper over the letter with one hand and started rubbing gently with the pencil sideways; I was darkening the whole onion paper to cover the letter.

"It's encrypted, Sir." After I finished, I showed him the paper with the key letters darkened. "She's a double agent, sir." "Her family is being held hostage; the simple fact is that your people have her figured wrong, she's an ally, and you have a traitor that works for the Messiah." "She gave me his name, sir." "He's special agent Gilmore." "If you take him in, the Messiah will know some things up and kill her family." "If these men you have are supposed to be your best men, I'd be worried." "When is the launch supposed to take place?"

"All finished, Sir," James stated.

"That'll be all," I told him.

"Now, when is the launch supposed to take place." I again asked him.

"Our sources tell us in three months." He said.

"Then, I don't have time to waste; your sources are wrong." I told him, "We're looking at six weeks."

"Smitty, you're not in any condition to act." He said.

"Sir, they know she's a double agent." "She says that they're going to execute her and her family, and if that happens, every double agent will have reservations on what they do, you'll lose the trust that every double agent we have in every country if we don't do anything to stop him." "What do you want me to do? Sit back and let it happen?" "If I don't act, the ramifications could interfere with ongoing missions, and every single one of our agents could be in jeopardy, and you know that." "If these people are executed, we lose important prospects, but if we are successful, it will fortify decisions made because we will show them that we'll give them the security they need." "Death doesn't mean much to too many people when working with beliefs, but to put their family in harm's way is a whole different matter?" "You know I have to go get her and her family out, and I have a launch that needs to be destroyed." "You knew that when you entered this room, or you'd be somewhere else." "Sir, I want all correspondence to the agent to cease." "They'll not torture her or her family if she doesn't receive communication." "Sir, failure to initiate contact with her will give me the time I need to plan and orchestrate my objective." "We have to give them the impression that we believe she is working for them." "They'll be double thinking of what's going on between them and us, and during their confused state of mind, I'll attack the weak link of the chain."

"You want commandoes readied?" He asked.

"No sir, I want Jack as a political envoy" "we need to establish a diplomatic plea to ask our adversary to reconsider his plans." "Nothing will be accomplished, but I need his attention involved on something else." "I have to buy time, he's bluffing, and he knows it; as long as he can carry on in his performance, I can buy my time." I said to him, "Other than that; I have all the commando's I'll need." "Don't worry; no one will suspect that you had anything to do with this." "You can't afford that, and you know it, as I do." "What do you have in mind?" He asked me.

"Sir, have you ever been bitten by a mosquito?" I asked him.

"I don't quite follow you." He said.

"Sir, there are many ways to kill a missile." "Have you ever thought about what insects live on a mosquito, and what insect lives on that insect of that mosquito?" I asked him.

He smiled at me and stood up from the chair he was sitting in. "Smith, I had my reservations when Jack came and talked to me, and I'm going to leave here without them." He stated to me.

"Sir, I need you to keep everyone calm, and I think you already know that you're going to be up against some tough resistance." "Mister President, I forbid you to mention my name or anything about me to anyone outside of this room." "I'm sure that was one of the many items that Jack briefed you on about me as well as whom you would be dealing with."

"I understand." He said.

He turned and began walking out with Ruby by his side. Jane came running over to be next to me. She looked down at my chest and pulled the dressing up so that she could see.

"It's amazing what that Doctor did to you." She stated.

I looked at her father. If I have to kiss someone's butt, then I'm going to choose the butt that I have to kiss." I told him, "I'm glad to have you back, sir." I said to him.

"You were right, Smith," Jane said. "My father got the FBI involved, and my husband was being blackmailed."

"Is there a child involved?" I asked her.

"Yes" "She's pregnant."

"Jane, a woman that's been betrayed, feels anger for the woman that allowed her husband to become friendly with her." "You have that right to be angry." "She knew exactly what she was doing, and she succeeded." "But, there's a child involved, and that child is caught in the middle." "That child is going to grow up knowing who the father was and will more than likely associate this situation as for it being conceived, to blackmail your husband."

"What do you want me to do?" She asked.

"Did your husband have life insurance in the same amount?"

"Yes"

"Then I want you to listen to what I have to say, and this will be your decision alone." "I want to set up an account in a trust fund with my corporation." "When the baby turns twenty-five, the baby can collect it." "I'd like for you to let the baby live a life without hate and anger from you; it wasn't the baby that put you at the bottom of Miller's Cliff." "Let the baby have it." "You don't need it." "When the child is twenty-five, give it an explanation of what happened, and hopefully, the truth will provide that child an answer." "In this situation, there isn't a right way to approach what has happened; sometimes, we don't have any control over how a life is played out." "The baby could grow up with issues like me, and one day, I may have to pay him or her a visit and talk." "Do you have objections?" I asked her.

"No, I'll do whatever you say." She said.

"Now, Jack back to you, he wants commercial time, he wants the media involved, that's the purpose of the threat of the launch." "So we have to give him all the attention he can handle." "Keep him on the news and in the papers."

"Smith, you're not ready."

"No, I'm not now, but I will be." "Now, where is your wife?" I asked.

"Home, when I got the call, I came to get you, and that's when I found out my daughter was alive, and you saved her, not once but twice."

"Have you told her mother yet?" I asked him.

"No, I haven't had a chance." "You were in the operating room for ten hours, and that's when my daughter and I had a lengthy conversation about you."

"Then you need to call her, and tell her where you're at, and tell her that her daughter has been found safe; she deserves that." "A heart that has been broken is healed immediately when it receives good news," I told him. I looked over at Jane. "You need to spend time with your mother and tell her how much you missed her." "She's not going to want to be apart from you again; she thought she lost you, and now she finds out she didn't." "James, I'm going to need a haircut and a shave," I commanded.

"Yes, sir." He replied as he left the room to get his clippers and straight razor.

"Smith, I don't want to leave here," Jane said.

"Jack, call your wife and tell her to come here; she won't resist your commands." "The mention of Jane being alive and her being here will assure that."

He left, and Jane and I were alone.

James walked in, laid my head down, and cut off my hair.

I gave a command to my computer to initiate the launch of my surveillance cameras, and twelve screens displayed our surroundings.

"Where are we?" She asked.

"I told you that your father got me my lab." "I also told you that he got me a hundred and fifty-seven thousand acres of land and built me a ski resort." "Well, that resort was built to cover what was underneath it, my lab." "When you meet your mother, you won't be away from me, but your mother will see what I see." I exclaimed, "Your father is going to be busy, and he's not going to be able to spend time with her for a little while." "I have a narrow window in which to carry out my assignment." "Your father knew why I told him to contact his wife and tell her to come here." "Your father works under my command, and your mother is going to be alone for a while." "When this is over, she'll have a better understanding of why this was done to her." "Jane, I can't count on speculation." "I don't have any guarantees on when he plans to execute his captors; the only guarantee I have is that he will." "That means I won't have much time to be with you either." "I couldn't find the words to say to tell you that being with someone like me would have its drawbacks." "I tried so many ways, and you kept silencing my words." "So, this was what I was trying to tell you; I don't have a life." "You and your mother will have private rooms here, in my lab, and when your father is here, they can be together as if they were home."

"Is this what you meant when you told me you weren't the same person outside of where you found me?" She asked.

"Yes"

"Then where's your room?" She said.

"I don't have one; I didn't need it." "When I work, I don't sleep much, and if I do, it's usually because I sat down and dozed off in my chair."

"Where's my room?" She asked.

"You can choose anyone you want," I told her.

"Smith, when you get tired, don't fall asleep in a chair; come to bed with me so I can sleep." "I can't sleep without you." "I've fallen in love with you, and my parents will have to deal with me sleeping with you anyway they have to, but I can't go to sleep without you." She said. "Smith, we were doing so good back at the cabin, and I wish we were still there."

"Sir, I'm going to need you to be still," James said as he lathered up my face and began shaving me. Jane bent forward to watch my face transform from a man with a beard and long stringy hair into a man that didn't resemble anything like the man she saw at the cabin.

James wiped my face and left.

"I heard you haven't had any sleep since I came here," I told her as she sat staring at my face. "Hand me three of those pain pills in that bottle; they'll help me sleep." She did as I asked, and she took three of them also.

I started to get up and was slow in doing so. Jane helped me to a room and undressed me. She slowly eased me down into bed, got undressed, and slid under the covers to be with me. After she did, she gently put her arm over my waist and kissed me.

"I wish it was cold like back at the cabin." She said. "You're body heat was warm to me."

"Jane, all you have to do is say out loud, computer, lower the room temperature to sixty degrees or whatever temperature you want," I told her.

"You're kidding me?"

"No, just tell the computer what you want, and you'll get it," I told her.

"Computer," she said, "Lower the temperature in the room to fifty degrees, please."

Within minutes, she squeezed me, and then she ordered the computer to raise the temperature to sixty degrees.

"I feel strange sleeping next to you without all that hair." "Smith, you're a very handsome man." She said. "And no, I'm not using psychology on you." She said, giggling, "There is something that I need to know, though." She said.

"What is it?" I asked her.

"I want to know how someone like you can love someone like me." She whispered.

"Are you talking about your height here?" I stated.

"That's got something to do with it." She then added, "Along with a lot more things I want to ask, but I can't think of anything right now." "This isn't easy for me to take all of this in."

"I tried to tell you," I said to her. "Jane, I don't know how to talk to people without saying what I feel and feeling what I say." "People found me to be disturbing and annoying." "I don't see what you see; I can't see through your eyes; I can only guess." "But what I see looking from my eyes is I see a girl that cares for me, and I've never cared for anyone like her in my life, so I have pieces of a puzzle where I can't find any pieces that fit, and I find myself confused." "When we first met, you had no way of knowing anything about me." "I know you didn't expect any of this, and I certainly didn't." "You know I had issues that I struggle with, and yet you fought my thoughts then, and you still fight my thoughts now."

"Smith, I'm in love with you." She answered.

"Then there's the answer to your question; I love you because you love me," I said to her.

"Smith, who are those people?"

"What people?" I asked her.

"Those people that were in there taking care of you earlier." She answered.

"You mean James and Ruby?" I said.

"Yeah, them."

"Computer; send James and Ruby in here, please," I ordered.

A couple of minutes went by when we were in front of them.

"James, this is Jane, Ruby, this is Jane," I said to them.

"Glad to make your acquaintance, ma'am," James said.

Ruby curtsied and replied graciously, and Jane bowed her head to acknowledge them.

"James and Ruby, I would like for you to take Jane under your charge." "Protect her at all times, and show her respect; she's got my heart in her mind." Ruby began crying, and Jane grabbed the top blanket and covered herself, then got up and held Ruby. "Jane, lay back down, please." I told her, "Ruby," I commanded her, "remove all your clothes for me." I said to her.

"Smith, is something wrong with you?" Jane said.

"Ruby, please do as I ask," I ordered. After she got through, Jane was in shock and sat up and looked at her. "She has latex for skin, and she lacks a woman's features, but she's programmed to listen and learn." "This is a female prototype." "I call her Ruby." "Her emotions are easily tilted, as you just witnessed." "The female prototypes are programmed like that of a predator; it sensed your weakness and found a way to befriend you." "Her language capabilities are at the control of her program, so when she hears the words she knows the language," "and she" "my prototype" "can change into any ethnic group it chooses."

"Ruby, please take off your face," I commanded.

When she did, Jane got back in bed with me and didn't want to see what she was looking at; she was trying to hide behind me. "The eyes are lubricated with a saline solution that discolors them to resemble redness from the veins." "Go ahead and touch her," I said to Jane.

"No, I did already."

"You can get dressed now, Ruby," I said.

"James here is the same way; he's a prototype too." "I can have him take off his clothes if you want."

"No, no, I think I've seen plenty already." She had a scared voice to her.

"You can leave us now," I commanded them.

When they went out the door, Jane looked at me surprised.

"Smith, this is not what I expected." She said as she laid her head down on my arm. "This is oh so not real." "It's like a scene in a science fiction movie, but this is way too real." She said, trying to sort out what she was confronted with.

The pills soon began affecting us both, and we slept till the next morning when her mother arrived.

A knock came at our door, and soon the girl's father came in with his wife. She saw her daughter in bed with me and looked somewhat bewildered.

"What's going on here?" She asked with a smitten voice.

"Honey," Jack said, "There's been a problem." "Sit down, and let me say something." He said as he pulled up a chair for her. When she sat down, Jack began explaining, "I would like for you to meet Smith." "Smith, this is my wife, Ellen."

"Ma'am," I nodded my head to her.

"Ellen, Smith, and I worked together for thirteen years now; I met him when he was fifteen."

"When I traveled to other countries as a liaison, Smith went with me." "He worked while I worked." "I was a frontman, and it was Smith that did the real work." "Something has come up to where we were called back into action." "There are lives at stake here, and our government can't get involved."

"But, that doesn't explain this." She said, referring to her daughter in bed with me.

"Dad, it's okay, mom; we need to take a walk. I need you to see what this place looks like; we're going to be staying here awhile."

"What, have you been brainwashed?"

"Mom, I'll explain as best as I can," she said to her, "but we need to take a walk." "So I need for the both of you to get out so I can get dressed."

We watched as they left, and when they walked out, Jane jumped up out of bed and put on her clothes as I lay in bed. She stopped after fluffing her hair, looked back down at me, and bent over to kiss me. "You are better looking today than what you looked like yesterday." She said as she stroked my hair, "I love you." She said when she stood up and opened the door to leave

Later, Jack sat in a chair while I fell back to sleep when they returned.

"I don't know what to think of this," Ellen stated, waking me as she opened the door without knocking.

"Ma'am, I didn't know what to think either when things happened the way they did," I said to her as I lay my head back down on my pillow.

"My daughter said you drew a picture of her at eleven when she went to a birthday party."

"Yes, ma'am." "That's where I met your husband," I told her.

"How can a person do that; you know, remember everything?" She asked.

"Ma'am, there isn't a person out there in the world that's walking around that doesn't have a problem, and at the moment, I seem to be yours."

"Where was I at?" She asked me.

"I don't know, ma'am; all I know is you weren't there." "I wasn't concerned with your business." "But being that it was a birthday party for a daughter of a congressman, I can only assume there was friction between you and the congressman's wife, or you would have been there with your daughter along with the rest of the women."

She smiled and stated, "I always thought she was an uppity snit that behaved like a real."

"Mom, that's enough." Her daughter said.

"Well, she wanted everyone to know that her husband was a powerful man."
"When he lost his reelection bid, I was really happy; he got what he deserved."

"Yes, ma'am, he did," I told her. "Your husband made sure of that."

"I hear that I'm a prisoner of yours, is that true?" She said as she stuck her nose up in the air.

"Yes, and no, it all depends on whether you find happiness here or you find it to be something else," I responded.

"Is my daughter a prisoner too?"

"No"

"Why?" She asked.

"Because she's found her happiness here, she doesn't want to leave, and if you seek the answer to the question you just asked, it should be proposed to your daughter and not me."

"So, you're going to use restraint on me if I choose to leave?" She said.

"Momma"

"That's alright, Jane; your mother is playing checkers." I told her, "Ma'am, these quarters are yours to use at your disposal." "When this is over, you can leave and enjoy the life you had before you came here." "To mention anything about me will ultimately bring harm to your husband and your daughter; this you will have to learn." "Your husband knew this, and he never acted out of his duties as an ambassador; he did so to protect you and your daughter." "You were under guard where ever you went and whatever you did outside your house."

"By who?" She said.

"They were friends of mine," I said to her. "It was easier for your husband to work when he didn't worry about you." "You were always safe."

"You mean you had someone spying on me?" She said sarcastically.

"That's interpretation; I prefer the word protecting compared to spying." I stated, "Ma'am, your husband is going to be away for a while." "He'll return now and then to give me his reports." "You'll have your privacy, and I'll have mine." "I'll not interfere with anything you wish to do," I said to her.

"What if I say no?" She replied.

"You won't." "You're not that kind of a person." "Your daughter chooses to be here, and your husband is here." "Your place is with them; you won't give me any problems," I told her.

"My daughter told me about what happened, and she also told me you were a brilliant man, but I didn't know just how brilliant you were until now, so how long am I to be kept here against my will?"

"Ma'am, time is against us," I stated.

"That's not an answer." She said.

"Momma"

I interrupted Jane again, "Ma'am, you weren't listening."

"Honey," Jack said, "Smith knows what's been asked of him."

Then Jane's mother looked at her husband. "Is this what you were doing when we started arguing?"

"Yes," he said.

Then she looked at me. "I thought he was seeing another woman, it turns out, he was with a young man," "and all this time, I thought it was me; I thought that I was dull and boring." "I'm not a socialite, you know, but in his business, I pretended to be." "I had to behave in a manner of sophistication; I hated all of those dinners and after-dinner meetings and smiling at all the people that thought they were above the rest of the others." "I felt a load being lifted off of me when he retired, and I didn't have to go to those dinners and other functions that they had to entertain kings and other dignitaries when they visited." "I thought everyone, even the visitors, wore plastic expressions on their faces, and I guess I was too." "Now, after all this time, I find out what I thought was happening wasn't happening at all." She looked up at her husband. "I must have made it difficult for you." "I'm sorry, Jack, I was wrong."

"Well, ma'am, you weren't entirely wrong." I said to her, "Computer send for Misses Ellen Morgan, please."

She looked at me strangely when I said those words, and when my prototype came walking in looking like her, she fainted. The prototype caught her before she hit the floor and held her in its arms. "Put her in Jack's bed," I commanded.

"Jack, would you mind making us a pot of coffee." "I haven't had a good cup of coffee since I left." Jane helped me get out of bed and get dressed when he left.

"Which one of those prototypes would be in here helping you?" She asked.

"You're jealous of an android?" I asked her.

"Smith, they don't look anything like a robot, and now that you mentioned it, it did walk and talk and act the same way that my mother does."

We made our way slowly into the kitchen. Jack poured me a cup of coffee, and I took a sip.

Ellen came out of her room later and sat at the table with her eyes fixed on me, and she looked back at her husband. "So, how long have you been a spy?" She asked him.

"Ma'am, he isn't a spy; he's an operator." I interrupted, "I drafted him; I used him; he didn't use me." "Your husband gave me information without his knowledge, and I used that information to secure all quadrants of my existence." "Your husband joined me when I showed him that there were traitors in our government." "He chose the right path, or he would have been standing in front of me, and I would have had to move him out of the way, the same as I did to others." "That day, he earned my trust; before then, he was like anyone else I meet, I don't trust anyone."

"You met your other half, your alter ego." "Ma'am, Jack was always in the line of fire, he needed protection, and the best way to do it was to send in a prototype, a humanoid surrogate, you, or should I say a mechanical humanoid twin that is capable of reacting in milliseconds." "It would have killed to save Jack." "So when you said that a lot of those people looked plastic to you, think of how you looked to them," I told her.

She looked at her husband and asked him. "How long are you going to be staying?"

"Ma'am, are you sure you're talking to the real Jack; the prototype would tell you the same thing," I said.

"Careful, Ellen; he can pick your brain," Jack said.

"Computer; could you send Jack in for me."

A few minutes later, she was greeted. "Hello Ellen, I didn't expect you to be up and about so soon." "We've got some talking to do." He said.

She jumped up and backed away from the chair, staring at both of them.

"You can go back now, James; you're not needed any longer," I said to him.

"Yes, sir, the Jack that was sitting down and talking to Ellen said before he left." She fainted again.

"Oh, my God." Jane said, "This is so really not happening."

Jack walked over, turned on the water faucet, put a little bit in his hand, and bent down to sprinkle a little water on her face. When she came to, she looked over at me, confused.

"I wasn't going to put Jack in harm's way either." I told her, "Ma'am, sometimes I get confused myself." I said to her.

"Careful, Ellen; he can pick your brain." Jack said, "And I have to leave tonight."

"How did you know I asked that?" She said, turning to look up at him.

"I had to know what was said up to the minute of a switch." He told her, "Smith put an implant inside my ear, and that way I can hear everything the prototype hears."

"Ma'am, are you sure you're talking to the real Jack?" I said to her, and she immediately looked at Jack and then back at me.

"Oh lord, this is getting way too spooky," Jane said.

"Would someone please tell me what in the hell is going on, and are you the real Jack, she said to Jack?"

"Ellen, Smith doesn't build his prototypes anatomically correct." "There's only one way to tell whether you're talking to me or his prototype, and I'm not pulling my pants down in front of my daughter." He told her.

Ellen looked down at Jack's zipper, and Jane told her not to even think about it.

"Smith, I'm not going to be surprised like that again, am I?" She asked.

"No, ma'am, I had a point to make, and I made it, and I choose a direct approach over an indirect one."

"One more thing, did I kiss that thing at the depot?" She asked.

"Yes, ma'am," I answered her.

"Can I take the bandage off of you; I want to look at your chest?" She asked me.

"I can call James to remove the dressing," I told her.

"Don't worry; I'll be gentle." She said.

I saw Jane's face look straight down at the floor and began smiling a big smile.

I saw the expression on the lady's face. "My daughter said you stepped in front of her, or it would have been her."

"That's enough of that." I told her, "I know what you're leading to, and I don't have time for it." "The cat looked malnourished, and Jane looked like an animal to him." "He was only doing what all cats do for survival, kill and eat their prey."

"I didn't pack enough clothes for three days, let alone three months." She said.

"That's not going to be a problem," I told her.

"I'm sorry, but my daughter told me not to lose my control." "But, I find you to be a very rude man."

"Ma'am, I don't apologize for my actions, but that's a matter of interpretation; I have my difficulties, the same as everyone else." "I just find it a waste of time communicating with people; they don't listen to what I say, and I can tell when they have their mind on something else." "Ma'am, you mentioned clothes earlier." "You have a wardrobe in the storage room, and it contains everything from lounge dresses to evening gowns." "Take a look, and you may find it to be to your liking." "Computer; send Ruby in, please," I ordered.

We waited, and soon we were being poured another cup of coffee.

"Ruby, Jane, and Ellen need some clothes to make them feel comfortable."

Yes, Sir, she said, and my screens displayed the fashions modeled in the catalogs.

"Ellen, Jane, please tell Ruby what you want," I told them.

"I can't function without information," Ruby said to them.

Both of them looked over at me.

"You have to tell her what kind of fashion you like." I said, "She's here to serve you." "Just tell her what you want her to do, just like you were talking to a sales clerk at a department store." "Computer; display fashions from Paris," I ordered. The screens came on, and clothes were flashing on the screens. "See how it's done." "You tell the computer to go on to the next page and so on and so on." "Tomorrow, you'll have everything you ordered waiting for you, and Ruby can alter your clothes any way you choose." "Computer; display rodeo attire." I said, "See, how easy it is, you just give a verbal command, and Ruby will make you what you want." I said once again, "Computer; show Ellen and Jane in the clothing that they're looking at now."

Ellen wasn't a fan of western attire and quickly told the computer to change the screen to casual wear. She started to catch on and soon both she and Jane were shopping.

"Where were you when I needed you?" Jane said, looking over at me wearing a smile.

I took some pain pills and left them looking at themselves dressed in different clothes criticizing how they looked.

I walked around my track when the girl's mother walked up behind me.

"You know it's two in the morning?" She said to me.

"No, I got to walking and thinking, and the next thing I know, I lost my way." "You can't sleep either, I see," I said.

"No, when Jack left, he told me to stay out of your way, but it seems that's the only time I can be alone with you." She answered.

"So you want to talk then?" "Well, ask away," I told her as I walked.

"Why did you build those things?" She asked.

"Let's be analytical and not coy around." I related to her. "You find anger with me because I don't have problems in speaking what I have to say." "You had issues pretending to be someone you weren't." "In what Jack did, he needed someone that didn't have those issues." "Jack was a politician, and you didn't like talking politics, so neither one of you could find too much to say to each other." "So when Jack needed to hear a controversial argument without me here, he talked to James." "I made Ruby so that Jack always had ways of finding out information from women." "They tell me a lot by the way they act."

"Did he ever?" I stopped her before she continued.

"Ellen, you're talking about a machine; it's nothing more than a humanoid, a robot, an android, a prototype, and it listens." "I say that because it's nothing more than a computer that's built to resemble that of a human." "When he was at home with you, he never talked about his job; he was at home." "This is where he came to when he had to work, and when he was here, he vented his anger." "He had to travel, and your alter ego did what you didn't like to do." "Jack liked his work, and you liked not being around him when he did." "You and he got along better after I gave him someone that he could talk to." "You could care less about what person gets elected." "Jack was nothing more than a pawn, but he knew how important his role was." "You didn't like talking about politics, and Jack needed to know the decisions he made were the right ones, and talking to James or Ruby was like talking to me; I programmed them."

"My daughter told me that you were difficult to have a conversation with." She stated. "What were you thinking about when I walked up?" She asked me. "Or is that some kind of secret stuff."

"Ma'am, I was thinking about how time passes by." "We seem to rush to get to where we're going, and we seem to rush to do everything we can in the short time we have." "Our stomach tells our brain it's hungry, so we rush to eat to satisfy that hunger." "We rush to grow up, and that means we're in a rush to die." "I see you have a little grey at the roots of your hair next to your ear that's been dyed." "I don't think you're happy with the way you look, ma'am." "Now, if you think that's rude of me, then I apologize; I can only say what I feel." "I can't articulate; you and I are similar; I don't like politics either."

"Why?" She asked.

"Ma'am, in areas of unfamiliar territories, man has very little faith in what they don't believe in." "You didn't." "James and Ruby prove that to you." "I don't think you would be able to follow me," I told her.

"Give me a try, and let me decide that." She challenged me.

I turned around to look at her. "Are you familiar with Nostradamus?" I asked her.

"I heard of him, but what brought him into the conversation?" She questioned me.

"I guess that's the part on whether you can understand what I'm thinking." "No one does, so don't feel uneasy." "Nostradamus was a prophet that lived in the early sixteenth century; his predictions have been a topic of conversation ever since he wrote his findings." "I'm not interested in his prophecies, but he predicted many of our military and civilian transportation that we use today, and he did all of this before any kind of machinery of this nature was even thought about." "He had to do his work under the cloak of secrecy, all someone had to do in those days was make a claim of you practicing sorcery, and you would be burned at stake or thrown in a river with a big rock tied around your feet, or have your head chopped off with an ax, and all it took was an accusation from anyone for all this to happen." "The Wright brothers were in a race along with other innovative inventors to build the first airplane; it only flew for a short distance, but it proved that man could fly." "Later in time, a plane was used as surveillance on his enemies, it was used for that purpose because it couldn't carry armory, and technology was to come." "These planes encountered enemy planes, and one day a pilot took out his pistol and fired it by hand at a pilot that was harassing him by flying beside him." "This brought in the age of trying to put weapons on airplanes, and a machine gun was installed and thus the invention of synchronized firing through the propeller was born." "Mistakes were made, and inventions were born from those mistakes." "A lot of people died trying to prove someone was right." "Today, look at our weapons." "All inventions to provide man with a better living eventually end up being tested for its use in war."

"If it weren't for the Chinese, we Americans wouldn't know anything about gun powder."

"What are you getting at?" She asked.

"Our ancestors were pioneers in developing weapons of death, and they didn't have the knowledge that they were doing so at that time." "All they knew was that if you hit a man with a rock, you stopped him, and the stone ax was given a new purpose." "Benjamin Franklin also saw machinery to be used in war; he was an inventor." "He wasn't in politics for his ideals; he owned a printing press, and he wanted a contract with the government." "What people don't know was that Benjamin Franklin was known for his sexual orgies that he put on." "You don't see that in a history book." "Strange as it may sound, that's where James and Ruby entered into my mind." "I was obsessed and gave all my hours trying to figure out every option." "It came to me one day while I was chopping wood for my stove." "Build them like humans." "I sketched out my prototypes and ended up with James and Ruby."

"Their bodies are pure titanium steel from the arteries to the veins and muscles and bones." "Each one is outfitted with hydraulic reservoirs that are designed in the chest cavity; much like our heart and each android are capable of lifting to one thousand pounds." "They don't need weapons; they can kill any man with one swing of their fists." "Nostradamus studied alchemy, and the Wright brothers used theory." "I work with chemistry, entomology, microbiology, and radioactive genetic DNA, atomic and subatomic matter, and I work with antimatter, as well as other areas that will bring me success." "I only work these areas for one reason; there are others out there that are working in these areas too, and they're not doing it for the betterment of mankind." "Material that falls in the wrong hands doesn't make for a good relationship with a country." "Ma'am, we're a warring nation, we've declared war on crime, war on poverty, war on hunger, war on drugs, and we keep getting beat in every war we declare."

"War is a prosperous business for those with companies profiting from war." "Just like Benjamin Franklin did it." "You don't like talking politics; it anger's you." "I find that you and Jack make for a strange pair." "It's said that opposites attract, and I concur with that statement." I said to her, "Today, we live in a threat of a division of our country." "Half of the people believe one thing, and half of the people believe the opposite; when it tilts to one side, the democracy of this country will be threatened." "We'll end up becoming a socialist country." "Many people will die." "Ma'am, if you travel to another state, you'll find that that state is a state that is under the control of a one-party rule." "The civil war was fought because the south was going to secede from the union; North Carolina fired on Fort Sumner in eighteen sixty-one to declare that." "The union couldn't allow that; the south had the ports and the commodities that the north needed, not to mention the revenue from taxes that would have been lost." "The people were told something else, and they believed what they were told." "History books don't print the whole truth, just bits and pieces that fit properly; after all, people believe what they're told." "When did you find out that there wasn't an Easter bunny or a Santa Claus?" I asked her.

"Is this the way you talked to my husband?" She sounded shocked.

"I told you, I didn't trust your husband; he and I didn't speak about anything I was working with." "He didn't have any knowledge of what was going on at the time, and it was better that way."

"So, how did you and he finally start doing this?" She asked.

"One night, he came and was talking to a man, and I eased dropped in on him." "I planted bugs everywhere, and I knew everything that was going on." "I then sent a message to all the computers in use at the facility, for all information to be relayed to my computers."

"I took a man out without his knowledge, and he was upset with me."

"What did the guy do?" Ellen asked.

"He used an inferior component, I say inferior because he sabotaged it; it failed and destroyed his work, leaving no evidence." "The cost of the time he wasted was priceless, but what cost were the five people that were killed in an accident testing his work." "He created a flaw to sell it later; it was doomed when he conceived the idea of selling it." "I sent for your husband, and we talked." "I told him, I don't trust you, and I don't trust anyone here." "He wanted me to explain to him, much like you are now." I told her, "I showed him my work, and he was interested in it." "He was going to call another man in to examine my work." "I rolled it up and set fire to it and told him; no one sees anything I do." "I design and build and test my prototypes; no one looks over my shoulder." "I then left him, and he came to my room later, and we had a pleasant talk; that's when your husband started to know me better, but when he turned to leave, I told him I wanted it to be made clear to him." "Jack, I enjoyed our talk, but for the record, I still don't trust you on anything."

"What happened to that man?" She asked.

"He's no longer with us," I told her.

"Did you kill him?"

"No, he's serving five life sentences in prison; he'll never see the light of day again; your husband saved his life." I told her, "He wanted to handle him his way."

"Then what happened?" She asked.

"One day, your husband was going to a country to try and calm a situation; he wasn't going to be successful, and he knew it, there was only one way to defuse his problem." "To make the story short, I went with him, and the dictator of that country was assassinated while we visited." "Turmoil erupted, and a new leader was installed later." "On our return, we talked." "Jack was quiet for a long period, and when he did speak, he asked me if I knew anything about what happened." "I told him, by killing one man, thousands of lives will be spared, and then he asked me if I had anything to do with the assassination." "I looked over at him and told him that I installed a camera with a paper sniper round at the top of his palace." "The camera was sighted in at three hundred yards and was accurate at one-quarter of an inch." "I knew he was going to give a speech to his people because I had accessed his itinerary." "Jack was going to be killed as soon as he stepped up to the podium." "When I stepped on my heel, my target went down, and no one heard a shot." "I told him, yes, and then he asked me how I did it, and I told him." "I then added, in case you're wondering." "The paper bullet shattered his temple and blew up internally." "I told him, the same thing that I'm telling you, there was only one way to defuse that situation; he didn't speak to me for the rest of the trip."

"You mean you killed a man at fifteen?" She said.

"Would you rather have had me let them kill your husband? Would that have made you feel better? If so, you and I wouldn't be having this conversation now?" "I killed him because your husband was set up for an assassination." "It was rigged to make it look like it was a rebel's rebellion." "I only had two decisions to question." "Do what's right or do what's wrong." "Have you ever done anything you thought was wrong?" I asked her.

"I'm thinking that maybe I've been doing a lot of wrong things lately." She said.

"Ma'am, your husband chose a long time ago to do what he thought was the right thing to do, and it cost him dearly." "He had to keep his life a secret from you for a reason, and that reason was me, so if you want to blame him for doing what he had to do, then it's me you should be angry at."

"What happened to the person that took over that man's rule that you killed." She asked.

"I gave him a message telling him I killed his predecessor, and I'll kill him too." "It was time for a leader to lead his people to a better government, and if he were not that leader, I would pay him a visit, and his country would be installing a new leader." "I told him he can't trust anyone, not even his own family." "Power is a drug, it went to his head, and that country now has another leader." "He received the same message I sent to the other ones." "He's still in power, and he's a good leader." "I told you, your husband wasn't using me; it was I that was using him." "That's when he didn't give me my orders anymore, he took them from me, and he's been taking orders from me ever since." "All machinery can only function as long as nothing interferes with it." "I simply cut off whatever supplies the machinery that I target by overloading its components, and the result is I render whatever is operating inoperative." "One small tiny piece of abrasive material can destroy millions of dollars of equipment that's in good condition." "A diamond is priceless, especially on what I use it for." I told her, "Have you ever really watched the bees as they pollinated plants and flowers." "It's not what you see that attracts them; it's what you don't see?" "Humans only pay attention to what is noticeable." "The plants give off ultraviolet light, and that's what attracts insects to it." "Spray an artificial attractant onto an engine, and insects can cause destruction." "Ma'am, when it comes to you and Jack, if you think I did wrong for doing what I thought was right." I can only offer you an apology." "But I stand by my decision."

"How can you switch a conversation around like that, and what makes you say that?" She asked.

"Your husband started coming to me when the Secret Service, and CIA, and the FBI, all gave him a visit." "I sent a message to all leaders to leave him alone; he was off-limits and not to be touched."

"What happened?" She asked.

"Ma'am, no one questions the President of the United States."

"You got the president to tell them that?"

"No, but they believed the message they got was." "That's when you're husband was convinced." "Good soldiers never question their leader; they only take commands." "You don't have to be smart in the military; all you have to do is outrank the person you give orders to." "Those that question their leaders are never promoted." "Military is a lot like a corporation; you don't anger the boss." "Your husband was speechless knowing that I controlled our leaders, and they followed my orders." "I never told him again that I didn't trust him." "He never said a word to anyone; you can testify to that."

"Smith, I'm worried about you." She said.

"Ma'am, I told you I can't talk to people." "You have a little bit of me in you." I told her, "You don't like talking to people about politics, and in what I do, politics are involved." "So, like Jack, you repel his conversations, and you find it difficult to have one with me."

"Smith, my daughter went to private school, and on her prom night, she didn't go; no one asked her out." She cried that night, and I couldn't do anything to make her feel better, and I feel the same way with you, helpless." "Her husband had me suspicious from the start." "I thought he was using her for his advancement in being a lawyer, and he was." "I couldn't tell her that either; she found someone that showed interest in her, and she was happy." "Then all of this happened" "Smith, I don't really know how to say this, but my daughter is a lot happier now than when she was with Russell." "I was wrong in what I thought about my husband, and I'm happy to find out that I was wrong, and I feel like I have so much to make up for." "But, I did miss my husband when he was gone, and I was happy when he was home." "I caught up on my sleep because my security was lying next to me." "My daughter is insecure; she found out that her past didn't have any meaning; she needs to catch up on her sleep." "She says she loves you, and she says you said you love her." "Smith, go get some sleep so my daughter can get some sleep; she's in love with you." She calmly said to me and simultaneously helped me to my room.

"Ma'am, I need my pills." She left and brought me back the bottle with some water.

She took my hand and gently touched the side of my face with her hand. "Thank you for bringing my daughter back to me." "She's all I got, and Smith, if it means anything at all to you, I don't have the same feelings about you the way I did about her husband, you I like, him I didn't." "Now, get some rest and tackle whatever you need to do tomorrow."

"I can see where your daughter gets her fire from," I told her.

She gave me a little smile "Smith, you're a man that has very strong convictions from what my daughter tells me, and from what I hear you say, you don't quibble or mince words when you talk." "I am frightened of you." "I don't know what to expect from you." "And I don't like it when a man can look at me and can tell me what I'm thinking." "It bothers me."

"Ma'am, imagine yourself waking up in a small one-room shack, lying in my bedroll with my hair hanging down past my shoulders all matted up, and then put a stringy beard on my face." "That's what Jane saw me as when she first opened her eyes." "She was scared, and she didn't know what to expect from me, but she listened." "Can you draw that picture of me meeting her face to face in your mind?" I said to her.

She then turned and walked into her room, and I opened the door to mine to see that the light was still on. I turned it off, pulled my clothes off, took a shower, and got into the bed easily so that I wouldn't wake the girl. It didn't matter; she was like a spider in her web. She felt the slightest touch of the bed and eased herself over to lie next to me. I turned over and wrapped my arm over her, and she wrapped me up with her body, and we both fell to sleep.

I awoke to Jane being gone, and when I got up from my bed, I noticed a pair of shorts lying on a table in the room. I put them on and then opened the door and walked out.

I walked towards my spa and saw the ladies sitting in the warm water, and when I walked up to them, I entered and sat next to Jane.

"We took a walk around, and this place is huge." Ellen stated, "You've got a kitchen, a gym, a swimming pool, a spa, and all kinds of equipment that I don't even know what they are, and there's a whole library full of books." "Smith, you couldn't have read all of those books."

"Each of those books is written by people that have questions, it's a way to voice their suspicions to other people's findings, and they write those books to either counter someone's thoughts or to elevate their standings in what they believe." "Some of them are questionable, and some of them aren't." "They want to impress people with a theory, but ask them what direction the sun comes up, or ask them which pole is magnetic, and they couldn't answer any of them." "So, some of the books I question." I then looked at them. "The sun comes up in the east, and the South Pole is the magnetic pole, not the north." "But some people believe that will change soon."

"What do you think?" Ellen asked.

"Well, that doesn't matter." I told her, "To me, everyone that has an opinion on a matter thinks that their opinion is the only one that matters." "I think you ask questions to try and befriend me." "I had a lot of doctors that did that." "They didn't like it when I corrected them."

"A lot of those books are about secret government tests that were conducted." "We Americans are angered to hear that heinous acts were performed by our government, on our people, so we cast doubt, and then we say that can't be true." "I'm sorry to disappoint you, Ellen, but we do; we aren't any different from the enemy we fight, an enemy never acknowledges torture, and neither do we." "You live in a different world than I do." "And because of that, you and I struggle." "Your husband had to have a place that was secret for me." "I found what I was looking for, and he built me my lab in this wilderness." "It's ninety-two thousand square feet, and I disguised it by making this place into a ski resort to cover my tracks." "No one suspects an organization to exist within an organization," I told her.

"So this place is secret then?" Ellen said, "My husband never told me of these things."

"Ma'am, there's a lot of things that you don't know about your husband, you didn't care for what he had to do, you didn't like to attend dinners, and you didn't like the people that gave false expressions." "I'm like that too, but your husband had to." "The money I got from those people gave most of them the expressions they wore."

"Take a break and rest," she said to me.

"I'm all right, ma'am."

"Smith, do as I say, and don't give me any trouble, you're not in any condition to fight me, and besides, we need to talk." She said assertively, "You have to relax and let your body heal."

"My mother can be a little controlling sometimes," Jane said when I looked at her.

"Jane, your mother is finding things out that she's upset with herself for." "She's your mother, and she wants to be a good mother. To her, it's a tough job, and it's one of those questions that you pose to yourself, she can't find an answer to that question, and she's bothered by it." I said, looking over at Ellen.

Ellen left and soon returned with my bottle of pills and a glass of water.

I took a few of the pills and then swallowed them and drank some water that she gave me. I didn't do it other than for one reason; she was tending to me in a fashion that I found to be as if that was her way of showing me that she was trying to find a way to let me know she was there for me. She just didn't understand everything she needed to know; she hadn't been with me that long.

"Is that right, Momma?" "Are you frightened that you haven't been a good mother?" Jane asked her.

"Smith told me last night that we were always in a hurry to do whatever it is that we need to do." "I had a hard time sleeping." "He opened my eyes, and I realized that he was telling me that you're no longer my little girl." "He was right; you grew up on me way too fast." She said.

Jane took her hand and gave the water a little stir and smiled at me when she glanced at me.

"Let me guess, a hundred and two-point two?" She said, smiling.

"Okay, what's going on?" Her mother said.

Jane answered her by telling her that it was restricted information; she recalled healing waters.

"Ma'am," I said to her, "It's like reading a book, and you didn't start at the beginning; you started reading it in the middle, so you don't know how the book began."

"Do you have a fear of people?" She looked at me and said bluntly.

"In the medical field, they have a name for that; it's called Anthropophobia." "They also have a name for a lot of other things that I was diagnosed to have wrong with me." "It depends on what doctor you go to and what that doctor thinks, much like what you think, Ma'am." "When it comes to the brain, doctors are knowledgeable in only one-tenth of one percent of what goes on in there." "Let's say I ask you if you can tell me what man will look like in one hundred years." "What would you tell me?" I asked her.

"I don't know." She said.

"Then take a look backward in time a hundred years." "How many wars have we been involved in?" I asked her, "Then go back a hundred years before those hundred years." "How many wars were we involved in?" "Ellen, you can go back in time until we landed on Plymouth Rock, and you'll find that we've been at war since we landed here." "That's a lot of people dead, and they never passed along their name." "War is where you can get away with murder." "If someone doesn't like someone, shoot them in the back, and problem solved." "It's happened in every war we've had." "It doesn't take much for people that are trained to kill, to kill for reasons of their own." "It's hard to fight a war when you don't know who the enemy is or what he looks like." "He could be sitting in the foxhole with you." "Man in his quest has succeeded in building the ultimate weapon that will end all wars." "I won't be around to see it come to pass, or maybe I will, but Ma'am, you should know me as a pessimist; it only takes one man to destroy the world, and the wheels have been set in motion as we speak."

"Did you say these things to those doctors?" She asked.

"Yes, ma'am, and all of them had a fascination with their key, their watch's, and their pens." "So if you need to see a doctor, then one day that doctor will be the person that's going to tell you you're going to die." "All doctors I saw gave me pills to take." "When I asked them what were they for?" "I would get an opinion on a diagnosis, I never went back to see any of them, and I never took their pills." "Ma'am, there are people everywhere that have to be dealt with." "According to psychologists, every man and woman at some point in their life has contemplated suicide." "It's not the contemplation of killing themselves that they ponder, it's the thought of how would they do it, and they have pills that can help you do that too." "What point does a person reach before that person carries out the attempt?" "Then ask yourself if someone is going to commit suicide, does that person fear taking other people's lives." "That's happened too." "If you read a paper, or watch the news, you'll see it every day; domestic violence is an omen of the things to come, our government is a lot like the people I send a message to; they aren't listening very well to what the people are telling them, and soon, our problems will escalate, the people are becoming angry." "I can only fight an enemy if I know who he is, and today no one knows anyone that lives next door to them anymore." "That's a fear of people; that's Anthropophobia." "So, do you know everyone that lives in your neighborhood?" I asked her, "I like the world where I live." "There's peace, and there aren't any people there so that I can work, and I can think, I don't read any papers or watch television." "I know what's going on without having to read about it or see it." "I had my privacy there, and I had my privacy here." "I don't have that anymore." "Jane came, and my life changed, I can't live here, and I can't ask Jane to live with me."

"I thought we put an end to that discussion earlier?" Jane interrupted me. "We've been over this before," I said to her.

"That's right, and I told you then, my place is with you, Smith. You've got problems, and I've got problems." "One of the problems we both have is you've got to learn how to live with me; I'm going to be with you." "So, you're going to have to do a lot of work to figure out how you and I can get along." "That means you'll be working on totem poles and doing leatherwork, and you'll be doing all of this because I'm going to be helping you." "I told you, I know what your problem is, and I'm going to change that." "Do you wish to waste your time and speak all those words of wisdom you have on someone that's not listening to you?" She said, sounding a lot like her mother, "Now, I need reassurance again; you've brought up something that makes me wonder if you're playing checkers with me." "Do you love me?" She asked me blankly in front of her mother, and her mother turned to me.

"Yes, I do," I said.

"Then it's settled; we need to put an end to that subject. I don't want it mentioned or brought up again." She said to me. "Momma Smith likes to live in a life of solitude. I can't live without him, so that means I'm going to be living with him." "It's a lengthy explanation, and we'll have a long time to talk about it, but now isn't the time." She told her.

I got out of the hot tub and stepped on the treadmill. I looked at Ellen.

"You can't lose twenty pounds," I told her, "and you know it." "What did you do in school, swim?"

"Oooh!" "I'm impressed." "You have a keen eye of perception." She said.

"That scar you have on your knee isn't from swimming; you got that from another sport." I told her, "It was more physical than swimming, so you took up swimming for the rehabilitation of that injury."

She chuckled. "You don't miss a thing, do you?" "It cost us our championship, and I had to have knee surgery, and it put an end to my athletic career." "I worked out and went out for the team." "I swam in three meets, and I guess I wasn't good enough." She stated to me.

"Ma'am, there are people that play games, and there are people that play games to win." "You played against someone; whether it was a coach or the player herself that was in the game to win, you were a target as soon as the game began." "If the girl that took you out didn't succeed, someone else would have." "Less than one-tenth of one percent of all athletic players make it to the majors, injuries force all the ones that are good out and the ones that aren't any good, well, they never had a chance anyway; so, they were living in a dream." "Good players are hit the hardest, and cheap shots are always going to be what ruins a good player." "Games are not played to play; they are played to win." "You found that out the hard way." "Do you blame the coach or the player?" I asked her.

"I blamed both of them." She said.

"Ma'am, I'm sure you knew the consequences each time you suited up." I expressed to her.

"Everybody knew that they could get hurt." She said.

"Yes, ma'am." "Ma'am, did any of the girls on your team lose their temper and let a cheap shot end the athletic career of a girl on the other team?"

"Yes"

"Did you play to play, or did you play to win?" I asked her.

"I played to win." She said.

"Yes, ma'am, and you played in a sport against someone else that played to win too, only they were willing to go one step further." "Ma'am, a cheap shot doesn't go unrecognized." "The girl that took you out, put a target on her." "Word gets around, and she became known to other teams for what she did to you." I increased the speed on the treadmill, and Ellen warned me not to push myself. I returned her comment, "Did they tell you that when you got out of surgery, don't push yourself?" "Or did they tell you to sit on your tuff and wait to heal?" "Judging by your figure, you exercise daily, so I assume it's because Jack is gone most of the time, and you need something to do to release a vent from being in the house by yourself; boredom is a drug, it makes you restless."

"Smith, I told you last night that you tell me a lot of things that frighten me, and you're starting to frighten me again." "I don't like it when a man can look at me and tell me what I do when I'm alone." "And Smith" "she got her leg broken."

I went silent and sped up my machine. Ellen got out of the hot tub, walked over to where I was walking, and turned the treadmill down.

"You might be smart, but you had better start listening to me." "I've been through all of this before, and I've suffered by not listening." "Today you walk, tomorrow you walk, the next day you increase the regiment, and when those stitches are out, we work harder, but right now, we don't want to push ourselves." She then walked back, stepped down in the hot tub, and sat down.

I looked down at her daughter, and she didn't know what to say.

"Ma'am, you can leave if you like." I told her, "You can go skiing, or you can go for a walk, or you can leave and go home; I don't care." "I didn't bring you here to hold you captive." "Jack wanted to work with me on this exercise, and I thought you being here would make him feel better knowing you were with Jane, and he would be able to have a clear mind while he works." "You'll have protection like before." "I don't have time to recuperate slowly."

"I push myself because if I don't feel the pain, then I'm not pushing myself hard enough."

"Smith," Jane said as she was about to comment.

"It's all right, Jane; I told you I'm not the same person outside of my world, and I'm okay here." "If your mother chooses to leave, then I was wrong about her." "She won't speak to anybody about anything she sees, and she knows it."

"Smith, you're doing that thing to me again." Ellen said."Do you always get what you want?"

"Ma'am, I'm looking at a lady right now that's gotten everything she's wanted," I said to her.

"What is it you want of me?" She asked.

"Nothing, you're a guest, and you can leave whenever you get ready. It's my fault, and I know that." I left them and went to the pool to try and exercise the top muscles of my chest.

Time went by, and I saw Ellen walking towards me. She dove into the pool, swam over to the steps, and sat down on the bottom step.

"Look," she began, "this is all new to me; I never knew anything like this existed." "You don't act or talk like normal men, and sometimes I get to wondering if I might be talking to one of those things you built." "I don't know what to believe anymore."

"You talked to Jane, didn't you?" "That's why she's not with you," I told her.

"Smith, you're doing that thing again." "My daughter said you're not a man to go up against; you'll leave and never speak to me again." "That's not what I want." "I know something is up, but I don't know what it is." "But I do know you're a man that doesn't listen to anyone." "None of those books in that library taught you anything, did they?"

"Ma'am, first off, there's a man out there that's going to kill a lot of people." "Innocent people." "Men, women, and children." "He would chop off your head in front of all of his people and show it live on the news." "He's sick." "And another thing, those books were written by college-educated people that read other books that college-educated people wrote." "I learned the most about life from reading children's books; they had morals in their stories." "And some of those books in there were written by people who had nothing more than an opinion; not all of them are factual." "I haven't read any of them that shared the same opinion as mine." I told her, "What do I do, write a book like them and disclose my theory; there are thousands that would contradict me?" "It doesn't matter; I'll tell you the same thing as I told your daughter." "The earth will die." "We live in a perfect time, but some people think that's about to change." "That is if you were to take the time and read those books in my library," I told her.

"How do you find time to read them?" She asked.

"I'm a speed reader." "I read the left side of the page with my left eye and the right side of the page with my right eye."

"That's amazing." She said.

I got out of the pool and pulled the bandage off. Ellen came up to me, and I took a bottle and asked her to open it for me.

When she gave it back, I took a swab and applied the salve over my wound.

"Here, let me do that." She grabbed the bottle from me. "What is this stuff? It stinks?"

"It's anesthetic glue; it seals my cuts and keeps air out of my wound," I told her.

"Smith, you make my daughter happy. I don't want her thinking that you and I are fighting." Her statement had a sadness to it "I'm not perfect, and sometimes I say things before I think." "She told me to be careful in what I say around you, and I'm not used to someone like you."

"Ma'am, if you treated her husband the way you treat me, do you think she would be where she's at now?"

"I don't know." She said.

"But you thought about it, didn't you?" "You're her mother, and you have certain rights as her mother." "I told you earlier; it's not you; it's me." "So to blame you for the person I am would be unjust," I said to her. I cut some bandages and taped them to my side. "I guess you said your goodbyes to Jack when he left."

"It was hard to see him go." "I thought all of that was behind us." She said.

"Ma'am, he's an envoy." "James and Ruby went with him, and they are programmed to speak and understand all languages, but they reply in English." "Their mission is to retrieve any information that might be helpful to me, and I need to see what I'm up against." "I need to know how many soldiers I'll be up against, and I need to know where the compounds are located, along with surrounding terrain that I can use to travel undetected; everything is known to me before I leave this place." "Jack knows what I need to see." "It's taken me sixteen years to get to where I'm at today." "I lost my world when I was twelve. I didn't have any more life in me." I told her, "When I was sitting at my campsite, back at my place, I noticed for the first time in my life that as I sat there, there wasn't anything on my mind." "Then it struck me." "To achieve a goal is to reach above all others and accomplish what you set out to do." "Jane reinforced my direction and showed me that I needed to put the most effort in following through on my commitment."

"Smith, sooner or later, you're going to have to stop talking in riddles and open up to me and tell me what's going on." She said.

"Ma'am, my brother was the only person that I ever talked to, and he's dead." "I read stories to him by the campfire." "My mother was mentally insane." "I couldn't find any records to find out if she was insane before my father met her or if she went insane later." "You seem to know a little about how people act when they have a psychological disorder." I said to her, "Can a person go insane like someone snapping their fingers?"

"Smith, I'm sorry." She remarked.

"Ma'am, I haven't found anyone that can tell me my answer." "So far, I've only talked to people that were sane but pretended to be insane, and I've talked to people that were supposed to be insane but said they were sane." "I asked myself that question almost every day of my life." "I found it to be one of those questions that don't have an answer, but I bet if you look inside my library, you'll find a book that someone has written and gave an opinion of that question," I informed her.

She was speechless for a time, and she then told me that she didn't know how to answer me.

"You can go back and tell Jane that you've had your talk with me and patched things up between us." I stated to her, "She didn't have the answers she needed to know, just like you don't."

"Smith, my daughter was pretty stern when she warned me not to lie to you." "So, I'll give it my best shot." "When I came here, I was happy that my husband called and said my daughter was alive, there were all kinds of thoughts racing through my mind, and my life was exactly like you said, filled with issues of my own." "I've spent time here with my daughter, and she's pretty adamant about being with you, but she's worried."

I turned my head away from her and said to her, "There aren't guarantees in life; tomorrow is always taken for granted, but not by me." "Ma'am, look at me, you can see what Jane can't, I am only one life; I may be able to save tens of thousands of lives, which one is more important?"

"You don't like me, do you?" She said.

"Ma'am, I see you, and I see your daughter." "One of them has fallen in love with me, and the other one cares for me, but she's frightened of me." "I didn't want that to happen, Jack knew this, and we never spoke of you and Jane in our conversations for those reasons." "Business had to remain business; we couldn't afford to be distracted." "I'd like for you to do me a favor, though," I asked her.

"What?" She quickly responded.

"Don't ever ask Jack about what I'm going to do; his allegiance is sworn to me." "If you ask him, he'll lie to you, and then you'll find out why I don't like anyone to lie to me, see I'll never put trust in that individual again, it's been lost, and it'll never return." "So ma'am, please don't ask, or you'll find out how much a lie hurts." "It will hurt you for the rest of your life together, and your marriage will not be whole anymore." "I'll be responsible for that too. I brought you here, and we talked, and I whetted your curiosity." "Do you love Jack enough to find out if what I say is the truth?" "Or do you love Jack enough to never mention this conversation to him unless I'm dead, and if that happens, I won't care anyway," I said to her?

The lady went into her room, and I was alone, and my privacy was uninvaded. When she came back out, I was in my weapons hall. She entered the room and looked around, and then she asked.

"Does this place have significance?" She said.

"To know about these weapons is useful." "But, it's not often that they are available for your use." "Most of these weapons are a collection of simple farming tools, in the day they were used, revolts erupted, and all those farming tools became a weapon to kill." "I train to understand that all objects can be used as a weapon." "A chair can ward off an attack, or it can crush the neck." "A broom can deliver the same blows to kill; a cane can do the same thing." "A pair of shoes with the strings tied together thrown at a running man's feet can stop a man long enough to end his life." "The objective is not to put yourself in that situation in the first place, but, sometimes, you can't avoid a confrontation."

"Like me, huh?" She spoke.

"No, ma'am, not like you." "You worry that your husband might be in danger; now that you find out he's not the man you thought he was." "He has diplomatic immunity; he can't be touched, especially when James and Ruby are with him." "His job is to get me information, and I do the rest." "No one has any suspicions that he has involvement, and he's not there when I act." "But everything has to go according to a plan, and sometimes plans don't go the way it was planned," I confessed.

"What happens if it doesn't work out then?" She asked.

"Then, it depends on how many men I'm facing; Samson would have been killed if the soldiers had guns before he got to swing one blow with the jaw bone of an ass." "But you don't fight enemy's guards with guns," I said while attempting to go through my exercises, nursing my chest. "You don't want to alert suspicion of your presence by noise; if you do, you lose the advantage of the element of surprise." "You have to take them out silently." "Create confusion, and when they divert their attention, you do what you went there for." "A blow dart dipped in poison to the throat, a rap behind the neck with a staff, or a knife that slices the throat, and someone who gets paid a dollar a day get killed." I stopped my exercises and looked at her. "I need a purpose in all of this." "What do people honestly hope to accomplish?" "A suicidal maniac is capable of killing millions of people; it's been proven time and time again." "Man cannot stop those that want weapons of mass destruction, especially when someone out there is willing to sell it to them for the price they demand." "All countries build weapons to sell to other countries, it only matters whose side you're on, and with some, it doesn't matter." "It's like an oil spill in an ocean; what good is it going to do to clean the beaches when the oil is still flowing." "Nothing is accomplished, except a waste of time, but the people have to be appeased, and so news media's cover the concern that the company that worked without fear of what if, destroys their livelihood." "Then when it happens, they'll say why and watch as fingers are pointed; Ellen that too has been witnessed." "We have too much government of the government and not enough government of the government." "Why wash a car? Why don't people just go ahead and wax it, mud and all? It's the same difference." "It's always the same." "Money buys someone, somewhere, a little power, and it goes to his head." I stopped and slowed my breathing down and looked at Ellen. "I let myself wander again, didn't I?"

I turned and walked away and began my walk around the track. When I got to where I started, Ellen met me and walked with me.

"Smith, how long will it take for you to learn to trust me?" She asked me.

"You have my trust; you've tried to penetrate my shield; Jane was able to do that." "You showed concern by bringing me my pills and water, and you walked with me to bring out my thoughts aloud." "I bet you did that with Jane too when she was young; walk with her and get her to talking." "It worked with her, and you thought it would work with me."

"Smith, don't do that." "I feel like I'm afraid to say anything because you know within a few seconds what I want, and that bothers me."

"No, ma'am, what bothers you is wondering if Jack has already lied to you." "Trust is something you don't give to someone; they have to earn it." "I'll give you a little test." I told her, "Let's just say that you tell someone something and that someone goes and tells what you said to someone else." "Would you say anything to that person when you talk to that person knowing it would be repeated?"

"No, I wouldn't talk to them anymore." She said.

"Yes, ma'am, and if you found out that Jack has lied to you, you would feel the same way, betrayed." "But ma'am, there is another side to the question." "What if I wanted a rumor started? Who would be the best person to go to?" I said, looking at her.

"The person you talked to that told other people." She responded.

"Yes, ma'am, sometimes opportunity delivers itself in strange ways."

I walked over to my cabinet drawer and pulled out a small pair of my scissors and a pair of alligator clips.

"What are you doing?" She said as I was reaching for some rubbing alcohol.

"I'm going to take these stitches out," I said.

"Smith, you are such a pain in the butt." "It's not time yet." She had a tone of anger.

I sat down, wiped my glue off with the alcohol, and clipped the first of the stitches.

"Give me that; I don't know which one of us is more bull-headed." She commented.

She went and took some ice out of the freezer to put it on my chest.

"Ma'am, you don't need that," I informed her.

"Smith, you've got over a hundred stitches in you."

"I'll be alright," I said as I laid down on the couch in my control room. She started clipping the stitches and quickly began jerking them out. When she spoke, it was to tell me that she was through.

I went and got the glue I had used earlier and was beginning to put it on, and Ellen grabbed it out of my hand and started doing it for me.

"What are you doing?" I asked her.

"I'm trying to see what my daughter sees in you, and I want to know what attracts her to you." "Do you know what attracted me to Jack?" She asked me.

"No, ma'am."

"He was easy for me to talk to." "I really felt uncomfortable being around him, and he knew it." "He played a trick on me, and I'll never forgive him for what he did." She started laughing. "That man got a pair of handcuffs and cuffed one to his hand and cuffed the other one to mine, and he wouldn't give me the key to unlocking the cuffs." "He made me walk around with him, and he took me to a diner where he liked to go, and when he reached for someone's hand, mine would follow." "Well, they would see the cuffs, and he told them that I was in his protective custody." "I didn't speak to him for a week." "A knock came at my door one morning, and flowers were delivered to me." "The note in it said." "I'm sorry, I thought I had the right person cuffed to my wrist, but I must have made a mistake, and I apologize to you." "After I read the note a dozen times, I don't really remember too much except driving down the road to his office." "I walked past his secretary, and she was trying to stop me." "When I walked in, he was in a meeting, and I looked him in the eye and asked him straight out." "Are we two a pair, I said?" "He looked at me dumbfounded and then got serious with me and said I want to be." "I told him in front of everyone there, then you be at my house after work, and we'll set our rules." "You should have seen those men's faces when I said that to him." She began laughing from remembering that period in time. "I left, and we've been together ever since that day." She concluded. "There, all finished." "Smith, I didn't mean to sound the way I did earlier." "I'm concerned about you for my daughter's sake; a person that doesn't rest is doing more harm to his body than good."

"I'll tell you what," I told her. "I'll do as you ask, but only if you go and lie down to sleep too." "You look tired, and you're not a good trainer when you're trying to keep up with the one that you're trying to train." "Jack won't be gone long; he's putting information out to get information." "He'll be here in a few days, and he'll stay for a few days, and then he'll be gone again." "Ellen, all those thoughts you had of him were my fault, not his." "I want you to remember that when you have thoughts in your mind of the past." "But there's something I want you to think about before you go to sleep." "It's not easy doing what he does and having to leave you behind." "It was rough on him, and I didn't want him back in." "I think he came and got me because he couldn't stop; he was worried about me the same way as you and Jane." "I'm telling you this because I would like you to be more supportive and not have curiosity when he isn't home at a certain time, or he has to fly away quickly, or he gets a phone call from someone." "You know who he is and what he is if you and he are having bad times." "I'll know, and I'll leave him out of my plans."

"You mean; you didn't want him here?"

"No, ma'am, I didn't."

"Why not?"

"Well, let's just say that we parted company because we suffered from irreconcilable differences." "Now, he's back here, and he's working with me again." "There's been one minor difference; this time, his wife and daughter are with me." "So, if you don't mind, when we meet later, tell me what I should do about this." "If you haven't noticed, Jack's put on a few pounds since I saw him last," I said to her as I left.

I went into my room and then pulled off my shorts and eased into the bed. I put a towel over my chest and put a heating pad on it to increase the circulation of my blood to that area. Jane rolled over and gave me a kiss.

"Where you been, handsome?" She asked.

"Doing what you sent your mother to me for, she doesn't like me talking to her, but she's worried that she'll lose you to me, and that has her bothered."

"What are we going to do?" She asked.

"Jane, why did you have to fall in love with me?" I stated to her, looking for her excuse.

"I was hoping it was a mutual feeling." She said, "I keep asking you for reassurance that you really do love me." "I have a fear that I'll wake up and you'll be gone." "Smith, I get this feeling that you love me, but you're not in love with me."

"I can't lose anyone else in my life," I told her. "It seems as if people that commit themselves don't stay committed anymore." "There's always a reason why, and I feel that I'm not any different; I don't want to lose anyone else."

"Is this going to be a long speech?" She asked, "Because I'm really tired, you chose to leave me in the middle of the night, and I know you have things on your mind." "So lie still and let me hold you, so I can sleep." She once again gave me a kiss and molded her body to mine. We were both tired, and sleep came to us quickly.

I arose later, and just like the day before, the girl was already up. I picked up the heating pad that I set aside in the night and put it on the top of the dresser.

"Afternoon," Ellen said when I poured myself a cup of coffee. "Have a seat; we need to talk." "We were doing our women thing, and since we're going to be here for a while, we came to realize that we can't help you if you don't let us know what to do."

I took a sip of my coffee. "I work alone; that way, I don't have to worry about blowing up anybody except myself."

I took my cup of coffee, walked to the wall, and commanded my computer to open my doors to my command post. I heard the chairs sliding back, and the ladies were standing next to me to watch the wall lift and reveal the computer that I gave orders to.

"Computer; show me the data from quadrant three-sector three, four, and five." I got up to look at my screens closer.

"Computer; retrieve data three months back from today." As I was doing the same to the pictures I received, I watched as the ladies entered and sat on my couch. Then I walked back and put the pictures up I had seen before.

I smiled and turned to look at the women with a surprised look on their faces.

"Are you okay?" Ellen asked.

"Tell me what you see," I told her.

I put the pictures up, and then I replaced them. Then I put the pictures up again. "Did you see it?" I asked her.

"See what?" She asked.

"Computer; zoom in three hundred percent."

"Look again closely." I put them back up, and then I put the next pictures up and then the next. "Did you see it?"

"I don't know what I'm looking for?" She said.

"Look in these sets of pictures." I showed them. "Now, look at this set; what do you see?"

"I still don't know what you're asking of me." She said, shaking her head back and forth.

"See this little piece right here." "That's the top outline of a truck in the back of the building; they have two sets of generators; you can see one set over here." I showed her. "The ones under the steel canopy here are their backups." "The truck is unloading fuel for the generators." I walked over and stared at one of the buildings and then looked at the others. "That's what I thought," I said out loud. I turned and faced them again. "He's a masochist, and he enjoys delivering his pain; this man likes to torture his captives." "This building here is his torture chamber." "I can be polite and give you a different interpretation and call it his interrogation room." "But a rose by any other name is still a rose." I said to them, "If someone was being held hostage in their quarters, I would have my information." I told her and then returned my attention back to my pictures. "One more twist," I said.

"Smith, I don't know about Jane, but you're going to have to help me out here," Ellen said.

I turned and looked at them both and told them. "This is going to get ugly."

"You can't keep talking and leaving us out of your thoughts as if we're not here." She said, demanding her answer.

"I've said too much." I walked away, and the woman shouted for me to stop. "Smith, I'm tired of being left out of what's been going on in my life behind my back." "I need to know what's going on." Ellen was commanding in her response.

I stopped and bowed my head down, and I then said without turning around. "This isn't one mission; it's compounded."

I left them and began my walk around my track; I was soon joined by both Jane and Ellen. They were silent while I walked, and they didn't want to interfere with my thoughts.

"Ellen, Jack didn't like going anyplace without you, and that's why I built Ruby." "I couldn't use him unless you were on board." "You had to know what he was doing, or his cover would have been in jeopardy." "A wife that is hostile with a husband gives signals off to other people, and flags appear." "No one suspects anyone that has a wife beside him and laughing as if nothing is out of the ordinary; your job was to keep the women away from their husbands." "Jack can perform better, while you or should I say Ruby was performing." "Ruby downloads all conversations and all visual information into my mainframe." "I listen to all conversations and watch how they act, and in return, they tell me if they know what I want to know." "You asked me what you had to do to gain my trust." I said to her, "You've got it; now it's up to you to show me I didn't make a mistake." "For the record, I didn't want you here either, but Jane came into the picture, and not having you here would have been a torture that no mother would have been able to endure." "Jack is without the feelings he had before we all met." "He no longer has to lead a double life that he led."

"When I was brought here, it was Jack that came and got me; he was the only man that knew where I was." "He didn't expect to find Jane there." "He had the same feelings that you had; you both feared the worst." "She was deceived and wound up fifty miles from where she was supposed to be." "Jane was brought here, and not having you around would have been too stressing for her, not to mention your husband." "Both of them would have had to keep silent about her being alive." "Jack wouldn't have been able to go home without Jane; it would have destroyed your marriage." "As I said, there were unforeseen circumstances involved, and I had to make a decision."

"So I've been a real pain in the butt then; what happens now?" She asked.

"Nothing, I have to work out and plan my strategy, and I'll know more as the days go by." "I only hope he gives me time, or this mission will cost me the lives of my cargo, two adults and two children." "I was given a window of three months; that's when they think the launch is scheduled." "I think he's lying." "I have to catch him off guard and hopefully get in, and get out with his captives, and do all of this without his knowledge; it sounds simple enough." "You made a mistake when you asked me what you could do to gain my trust." I told her, "If I tell you something, I'll have my answer, so think before you give me that answer."

She looked at me and asked me what I needed.

"If I tell you something and tell you not to tell Jack, would you tell him what I said if he asked you, or would you tell him a lie?" I looked at her seriously.

She found it difficult to answer.

I followed through with my meaning. "I don't like people that lie to me, Jane knows this, and your husband knows this." "If you ever lie to me, I'll never have any relations with you again." "Your husband had to do this for me, so think how much it hurts to look at your wife and not tell the truth about where you were if she asked." "Things have changed, and now you and Jane are involved." "I don't lie to people I know." "Now, you have to ask the question, have you ever been lied to?" I asked her, "Now, I ask you one more time, and this time you know what the outcome will be." "Would you tell Jack a lie if I asked you to?" I said to her slowly.

"Yes"

"Why?" I asked her.

"Because I think you have split multiple personalities, and I can't figure out who I'm talking to half of the time." She said quickly.

I smiled at her. "That was the diagnosis of one of the doctors I saw." "Which one of those persons do you see that that doctor saw when he looked at me?" "And ma'am, remember, you've given me the same oath that your husband gave me thirteen years ago." "He swore to me his allegiance that he would never lie to me, and to me, that means everything."

"You have a mean streak to you; you know that?" She said, "I don't like the way you talk to me; you get me all confused, and I can't think straight."

"Ellen, can you be loyal to your husband and to me?"

She looked at me and then headed towards her room without giving me an answer.

"My mother isn't mad at you." Jane said, "She's like me when I first met you." "I thought you talked in riddles a lot." "I know you better now."

"Jane, your mother, is happy for you, and right now, she's happy." "For a long time, she's been the matriarch of her family, and now she fears I can change that." "Your mother is the first woman that has ever challenged me, and you are the first girl to do that." "You ran into difficulties with me, and you accepted me for who I am, and then you embraced me with your passion." "For the first time in my life, I feel as if I've found someone I can be with." "The Judge and his family, they wanted me, but that wasn't my home." "The Chief of Police tried all he could to help me; I was mostly trouble to him, and they too wanted me to share their home with them, but that wasn't my home either." "Your father tried his best to deal with me, but I never wanted anyone's devotion." "I lost those feelings some time ago." "I've analyzed and assessed what my diagnosis is, and I owe it all to you."

"Me, how?" She asked, surprised.

"You said I was lonely, and you were going to change that." "I read a lot of books, but I never could understand the theories behind some of the beliefs I read about. I realized why I was paralyzed and void of feelings when I saw you." "Jane, a lot of those books were describing what it felt like to be happy." "I never could grasp the feeling that they were trying to relay to me, and I grew up without any of those feelings." "When I look at you, I see someone that has deep feelings for me, and now I understand a lot of things that I didn't before."

"Smith, let me stop you for a moment." "The problem I have is, is with you, and the problem you have is, is with me." "That's not to say that you and I aren't going to have a difference of opinions, that's being human, everyone does, but I think what you're trying to say is that you feel better when you're with me, instead of being alone, am I right?"

"Yes"

"Now, the problem you have with me is, I like being with you all the time, but I know you, and you need your time alone." "I'm willing to give you all the time you need, I won't interfere, and when you're ready to be with me, I would prefer you came to be with me and not think about something else while you're talking to me." "Can you do that?" She asked.

"I can't stop," I told her.

"Okay, then we know that's one of the problems that we'll have to work on." She said. "Now, what are we going to do about my parents?"

"Your mother is of her own free will."

"Are you going to tell her that?" She responded.

"No," I said.

"And what about me?"

"You, I don't see as a problem." "You don't play checkers very well, so I have to let you think that you're playing me while I'm playing you, and you've been playing a game with me for a while now."

"Am I winning?" She asked.

"So far, you been able to take all my men, and you haven't lost any," I told her.

"Do you concede the game then?" She chided me and then put her arm around my neck. "Smith, what you just said to me was the reassurance that I needed from you."

"No, it was me that received the reassurance that I needed from you," I told her.

"See there, you just said I love you again, you might not have used those words exactly, but you said it plain as day." She said and continued, "I was told one time; that it only takes a woman seconds to know if a man is worth spending time with." "That first night when I came to, you helped me up, and then you left." "I sat up thinking about you and wondering about that picture you drew; you didn't act like the man I thought you were." "You had that mystery to you." "I couldn't see your face in the dim light, and when I was able to see it, I still couldn't see you behind all that hair." "There were all kinds of questions going through my mind, and you never came back, and then when you did, you got in bed to help break my fever." "Smith, that's when I knew that I was beginning to have feelings for you, why I don't know, now let's get back to my problem." "I'm a woman that needs a lot of reassurance, so I hope you understand that sometimes I wish you could find time for me." "But Smith, I only want you with me and not with the problems you think about." "I'm a selfish person when it comes to you; I'm like a giddy little girl with her first crush on a guy, and I like you to show your affection for me; a kiss can go a long way with me." "These things that I'm telling you don't come from a book, and I don't know if I'm able to reach down inside that brain of yours and grab your hand to keep you from falling, and that's got me worried." "You know you aren't the only one that has issues here." "When you kissed me, that was the second kiss that I was ever kissed." "The first kiss doesn't count; he didn't really love me, so you're the first man that's ever kissed me that kissed me for real." "I had cooties, you know, so no one wanted to touch me." "I digressed and withdrew." "I guess I have my mother's side when it comes to socializing." "It was hard with my husband to go anywhere and not have people staring at you as you walked in and had to duck under a door or having to stoop down to look in the mirror." "You think you have problems going someplace? Take a real good look at me; I do too." "So, I want you to understand something that I have to say." "I know what you do is above my understanding; being the daughter of a senator, I naturally took political science classes, but I let my husband tell me what to do, so that should tell you that I only took the classes because I was expected too." "I felt bad when you talked to me about my husband, but when I found out what you told me turned out to be the truth, that made me feel even worse." "Smith, he lied to me, for four years, he was lying to me." "You aren't anything like Russell was at all, and Smith, my role in life has changed; when you sat and talked with me, I never had anyone that ever really did that, well except for my mother." She said.

"You've never said these things to anyone, have you, not even your mother?" I replied to her comment.

"No, I couldn't. I didn't know that was in me until now." "But Smith, I'm glad I said it."

"Jane, you've given me private thoughts that can only be heard by me; they weren't meant for other ears." "That's trust." "To give someone trust is a special gift that isn't shared by anyone, except that person you shared it with." "Do you feel better now?" I asked her.

She gave me a smile. "When I'm with you, I always feel great."

"Good then, I have diagnosed and assessed you're ailment, and since we both suffer from a common but curable condition, I find that you suffer from loneliness, the same as I." I told her and then proceeded with my lecture, "I can change that; look at you, and I see that eleven-year-old girl that wanted to fit in with all the rest of the kids." "I knew you were going to have problems when you grew up, but I had problems of my own to deal with." "I made something a couple of years ago, and I was going to test them out when the right time came." "I guess that may be the right time could be now." "Give me a few minutes, and I'll be back," I said to her.

I left, and when I returned, I saw her mouth take on a huge smile.

"Are they prototypes too?" She asked.

"Yeah, they're spring-loaded, and I have air shocks to absorb the landing," I told her.

"How do you make them look like you're really that tall?"

"My prosthetics are molded to fit my feet like a ballerina that dances on her toes." "Add a pair of long pants and a long shirt, and voila."

"You know, you're one weird dude, but I mean that in a genius way." She said.

"Jane, I was wondering if you, well, I mean, I was."

"Smith, spit it out; you're stammering." "You've never had problems saying what you think." She said.

"Jane, I don't know how to dance, and I was wondering if you could teach me how?"

"Smith, I don't either, so we would both be learning together." She stated.

"I could watch a video," I told her.

"Smith, some girls get flowers to show them that they're special; this is way beyond special to me." "For the first time in my life, someone is looking at me eye to eye, without me sitting down in a chair." "Let's put on some music and test those new legs of yours." She said, "Computer, initiate music to slow dance by." She commanded.

I took her in my arms, and she held me tight. We moved together, and she had her lips pressed to mine during the whole song. We danced through the night.

CHAPTER FOUR

I was awake early the next morning peeling shrimp when I heard a door open, and I soon saw it was the girl's mother walking towards me.

"What are you doing up?" She asked me as she poured herself a cup of coffee.

"I like to rest when I work hard, and the only way I can achieve this is to commit a sin." I told her, "I have a lust for the taste of desire, and my lust must be satisfied." "I'm peeling this shrimp for tonight." "I'm going to sauté them in butter, and I've got chicken breasts that I'll roast and a link of sausage that I'll cut up and cook with some onions, and celery, and bell peppers, all served on a bed of linguini."

"That sounds like a lot of work to me; you need some help?" She asked.

"No, ma'am, I work when I work." "I cook to rest and relax." "But, I still work when I cook."

"Smith, I'm worried; you've been pushing yourself too hard?" She said, sounding as if she wanted to have a conversation with me. By her expression, I saw that she wanted us to be friendlier towards each other. She knew that I knew, so I knew it was difficult for her to be there.

"I'm tender in all my muscles in my chest, and I feel every move I make." I said to her, "If I keep taking those pills, I can't concentrate; they make me lose focus, so I designed a chest overlay to shield me from any blows."

I pulled out a quart of whipping cream from the refrigerator. "Do you know what whipped cream is?" I asked her.

"Sure, it's a topping for pies and stuff." She responded.

"Yes, ma'am, whipping cream is a cream that incorporates air to give it its texture." "Before, it was just cream, but when it was whipped, the air that was incorporated as it whipped was what gave it consistency." "Rubber works the same way, and when you whip the rubber with a small amount of liquid Plexiglas and some bonding resins, then you have a lightweight shield, pliable, yet resistant." "It was around four thousand years ago when the army's marched with protective gear designed to stop arrows and lances from killing them." "This primitive protection was used by the gladiators for over eight hundred years A. D." "They were limited on the blows that they could yield." "The weight alone with the armor tired out the weak." "Today, they are worthless; a bullet wouldn't have any problem penetrating the armor and killing the human inside." "I'll know soon enough if I'm on the right track or if I need to take another course of direction," I told her while cleaning the shrimp.

"Smith, you're talking about something that I have no idea what you're talking about." She commented and then stated, "It's not easy for me to follow you sometimes. I ask a question, and the next thing I know, you're talking about three different things."

"I'm sorry; I'm not used to explaining what I do." "I was just trying to be involved in a conversation without dominating it." "I've got a prototype cooling down now, I can't wait and not think, so I clean my shrimp and do my thinking, and two chores are done at the same time." "Now, I have three, talking to you and cleaning my shrimp and thinking about my plans."

She took another sip of her coffee as I finished cleaning my shrimp.

"Smith, I was wrong for what I said." "You were talking about me, weren't you?"

"Ma'am"?

"I'm a controlling person, and I catch myself sounding bossy; I dominate our conversations." She said, "I think when Jack's home, I begin to get on his nerves." "Smith, I tried hard not to lose my temper, but I always seemed to test his limits."

"Maybe things will be different for you now." I told her, "You know where he's going while he's away, and you know where he's at, and you know where he's coming to when he comes back." "Ellen, you shouldn't feel bad when you talk about yourself that way. I told you that I'm the person that's responsible for your anger."

"No, Smith, it's me, I snap." She replied.

"Ma'am, you're tired; you've been tired since you came here." "It's been clear to me that this lifestyle you're in isn't received well." "When you found out that Jane was lost and feared dead, you hurt from crying, and what little sleep you got, you woke up, and the crying started all over again." "Ellen, I hadn't seen you get as agitated as you describe yourself, so that makes me believe that there's a possibility that you started venting your frustrations out on Jack when Jane got married." "You lost your baby girl, and you were helpless." I tried to explain her situation.

"What am I going to do, Smith?"

"Do you want to go back home?" I asked her.

"It's not the same anymore." She answered, "Both of us sat around the Christmas tree every Christmas and watched as Jane popped some popcorn and wrapped it around the tree." "By the time she was ten, she was cutting out her own ornaments with construction paper and a pair of scissors and trimming the top of our tree without a ladder." "I've still got them packed away for that special day." She gave me notice.

"Ma'am, are you an overprotective mother?"

"I didn't think I was, but now I'm starting to think differently."

"Maybe that's because you're with Jane again," I told her.

"Smith, she's entitled to live her own life. I didn't think that Russell was right for her, so I wasn't ready to let her go."

"Yes, ma'am, maybe now you know how your parents felt when Jack married you and took you away."

"I never saw it that way." She said.

"Ma'am, Jane needs you now more than she's ever needed you," I told her.

I began working on another project, and as she watched, she asked, "Now, what are you doing?"

"Making yeast rolls." "Have you ever made yeast rolls?" I asked her.

"No, I'm not a cook." "Jack was gone most of the time, and I didn't cook for myself." She responded.

When I turned to face her, I gave her a smile. "Then, it's time you learned how to make yeast rolls, and then you'll know how to do it for the rest of your life."

"Come here; I'll show you." She hesitated for a moment. "Get up from the chair, and let's do this together."

When she stood next to me, I began, "First off, the key to memorization is to formulate a trigger to remember." "I call these rolls the rule of eight; that's because there are eight steps and eight ingredients involved."

"First off, a baker's scale is exactly like a recipe scale, except different forms of measurements are utilized." "For example, one tablespoon of water is one half of an ounce; two tablespoons is one ounce." "One cup is equal to eight ounces that mean sixteen tablespoons are in a cup." "Two cups equals one pint that means sixteen ounces and thirty-two tablespoons in a pint." "Two pints equals one quart, and that equals thirty-two ounces; four cups to a quart means sixty-four tablespoons." "You're in luck, though; I have a scale, so as we work on our formula, begin to imagine if you didn't have a scale, how would you be able to complete you're objective?" "Let's say you were like me and on an assignment if these rolls don't turn out the way you want them to." "Then the mission will be a failure."

"I don't like the way that sounded." She said.

I smiled at her and then instructed her on what to do next. "First, we need ten ounces of warm water to blossom one ounce of yeast." I handed her a small plastic cup and told her to place it on the scales." "See, you have a fraction of weight showing on the scales; we zero the weight out by adjusting the knob to zero." "Each container you put on a scale needs to be zeroed out." "Now, pour the yeast in until it reads one ounce; that's step one." When she finished, I handed her another container and told her to do the same. She zeroed the scales, and I told her that we needed ten ounces of warm water.

I ran the water and felt it with my fingers and told her to do the same. "If you can feel warmth, the water is ready." I caught some in another bowl and told her to pour the ten ounces in the plastic container on the scales. When she did, I informed her. "Baking isn't a recipe; it's a formula; formulas that aren't followed are not going to yield what you wish to achieve." "Formula's have to be exact; now pour the yeast into the warm water." "You can tell if the water is too hot or not hot enough because the yeast won't bloom, or you can use a thermometer and take the guesswork out; this is step two." I told her, "So, you now have step one completed, and step two completed, the ten ounces of warm water and the one ounce of yeast blooming, and that brings us to step three." "Take our mixing bowl from our mixer, place it on our scales and zero it out." I watched as she did as I asked, "Take this cup and scoop out some bread flour out of the package and measure twenty-two ounces, which would be what if you didn't have a scale?" I asked her.

She thought for a moment but was a little slow in thinking, so I gave her a little assistance.

"You should automatically know that twenty-two ounces are doubled when thinking of tablespoons, and since two tablespoons are equal to one ounce, we can either measure it out one tablespoon at a time or by the cup." "Now, how many ounces were in a cup?" I said to her.

Eight, she answered.

"And how many tablespoons are they in one cup?"

"Sixteen." She said.

"So, what is the answer to the question?" I said to her.

"Three cups is twenty-four ounces, so we need less than three cups, so that's two cups and six ounces and six ounces is, we need two and three-quarter cups." She said with a big smile of assuredness.

"Okay, pour in one cup, and let's check it and see," I told her as I took a spoon and leveled off the flour at the top of the measuring cup and let it fall back into the package.

She looked at me after she saw the scale reading eight ounces.

"Now pour in another cup, and let's see what we have." After she finished, she immediately filled the cup to three-quarters full and began sprinkling it in to see that the measurement was true.

"Now, that's step three, and for step four, we need one-half ounce of salt."

"That's one tablespoon." She said. I gave her a smile and proceeded with my instructions.

"Yeah, but we have a scale, so we're looking for point five," I told her as I did the same to the salt as I did the flour. When she looked at me, I instructed her that in weight, you have a level weight.

"Ma'am, people use different measurements, and they aren't accurate measurements." "Some people scoop flour and end up with a cup and a half." "The same in salt or sugar, a tablespoon is scooped, and the result is twice the amount that was asked for," I explained.

"Two ounces of sugar for step five, and for step six, one ounce of this dried milk powder," I said, giving her enough time to keep up with me. "Then step seven is four ounces of butter that's been softened, and step eight is two ounces of eggs." "In case you want to know?" I told her. "One large egg equals two ounces."

"We place the contents back on our mixer and lock it down, and then we take our water with our yeast and begin to incorporate the mixture on low speed," I said to her.

"Now, see how the dough is formed and showing you that no flower remains dry." "That tells us that we're now ready to knead the dough by putting it on the second speed and let it work for ten minutes." "This is where we find out if we need to add flour or a little water," I told her.

I turned off the machine put it on second speed, and then turned it back on.

"Why did you do that?" She asked.

"What?"

"You turned the mixer off and then back on." She said.

"That's because if you change gears while it's running, you'll strip the gears." "They're not designed to shift speeds while engaged in service, the gears strip." "That's something that the manufacturers don't want people to know. They are designed for a certain price," I told her.

"I didn't know that." "Jane and I used to make cookies; I thought the dough was too thick."

"So you've had it happen to you, huh?" I said.

"Three times, I thought the mixers were cheaply made." She replied.

"See the sides of the dough wanting to cling to the pot; watch this." I took my hand, grabbed a pinch of flour, and sprayed it with my fingers by tossing it gently in the mixture. It let the dough become smooth and satiny, and it no longer wanted to cling to the bowl. I looked at her. "That's what we want to achieve; see how the dough pulls away from the pot and not cling to it; we have achieved perfection." "Now, we wait," I said.

The minutes passed, and I turned off the mixture and poured it out on the counter.

"You can make hamburger buns, or poor boy buns, hot dog buns, twists, knots, or whatever you need in the way of bread by this one formula."

"Now, three ounces is a nice size roll or a medium hamburger bun or a hot dog bun." "One and a half ounces are just right for the rolls that we wish to achieve." "So cut off some dough and zero the scale and place it on top to weigh." "We want all of our rolls to be the same size." "That's called portioning," I said. When she got the weight she wanted, my next step was to show her what I wanted by doing the first roll as an example. With my good arm, I rolled the dough into a ball and placed it on a sheet pan. "Take some dough and roll the dough while pushing down on the table." When she finished, I instructed her to place it on the sheet pan and give it enough space so that each roll could rise without touching the other.

"Now, we do the rest the same way, and we let it rise for about an hour or so." Soon we had the rolls in the oven to allow them to rise at room temperature.

"Now we wait," I said. "Was that hard for you?"

"No, actually, it was really simple." "I thought it was more difficult than that." She responded.

"Smith, my daughter told me never to argue with you." "But, I don't know anything about you, and my daughter has chosen you for her knight in shining armor." "I want to have a relationship with my son-in-law."

"Son-in-law?" I looked at her and said.

"As long as you and my daughter are together, you'll always be my son-in-law." "I don't care if you're married, or if you two just live together, to me, you'll still be my son-in-law."

"And how does Jack feel about this?" I asked her.

"The subject was never brought up between us." "This is how I feel, and the matter between you and him is up to you and him." "All that I know is that I want the man that my daughter loves to like being with me and not fighting with me." "Jane told me to leave you alone, and I don't want that." "I want to be able to walk around, and when we part, I won't have doubts that I'm leaving you and her with regrets of me coming here." "Smith, I don't want to be a distant mother to my daughter." "When I open my mouth, I put my foot in it. I know that maybe I'm doing that right now, but I don't know what to call you."

"I was coming here to get my supplies one time," I said to her. "I stopped up on the mountain and looked down into the valley below." "I watched the train that brought you here; come and go." "I sat up there and listened to the whistle as it came in and as it left." "There wasn't a reason to blow it, but it gave the people that were riding it a little taste of what it was like to live back in the eighteen hundreds." "I've got one hundred and sixty-four sketches of the way people looked like back then that's hanging up on the walls inside the cars." "Ma'am, I took a ride on that train and watched the people as they looked at the pictures." "I noticed that kids only paid attention to what the kids back then looked like; they weren't interested in the adults." "I thought for a long time that night." "To me, I saw that train as the train of life and death." "Some of those people would never make it back here again; this would be their first and last time for them, and to some of them, it was the train of life." "People getting married and spending their honeymoons here and babies being conceived." "This place has a place for the young." "When they come as kids, they remember, and they come back as adults." "You want to call me a name," I said. "You're like the rest; you want me to be a member of a family." "What good does it do to have a photographic memory and not have any memories of my father and mother ever being together?" "There weren't any pictures of them to be had." "I searched and done all kinds of background checks, but I never got any answers to the question I asked." "I listened, and I heard the train's whistle again," I told her. "I wondered to myself, how many of those people that got married and conceived a child stayed married and watched their babies grow to be young adults." "I researched and found that seventy-six percent of people that get married, get divorced, and of those seventy-six percent, ninety-two percent of them remarried, and of those ninety-two percent, forty-three percent of them divorced and of those forty-three percent, eighty-six percent of them remarried." "You can't go by those figures exclusively, people die, and the statistics are affected." "I wondered for a long time why what happened to change the way people feel about each other? When did your marriage begin to wobble?" I asked her, "When Jack came in, you went to be with him, but you didn't kiss him as Jane kissed me." "So you don't respond to him with the same feelings you had when you first became united," I said to her.

"Smith, I've known Jack for a little over twenty-seven years." "Jack and I love each other, but we get the same feelings when we kiss. We don't need to claw each other and behave like a couple of young kids." "Jane is young, and I think she feels alive being with you." "Jack and I are from the old school, and we like to keep our lives private, and as far as people getting divorced, it's better that they do. No one should stay married for the children's sake." "The children would be the ones that would get hurt." "Smith, I can't talk to you. I say the wrong things all the time." "I've never run into someone quite like you, and when I talked to my daughter, she said you were very uh." She paused some and then proceeded. "She said you were sensitive, and I'm beginning to learn just how sensitive you are." "I have feelings too, except I have to vent mine somehow." "And, I can't be that way with you. You walk away and divert your attention on whatever catches your thoughts." "When I was walking and letting off steam before we went to bed, I heard the music, and I looked over to see you dancing with my daughter." "I stopped, and tears came to my eyes." "I looked and saw you both dancing cheek to cheek." "That has never happened." "My husband told me that one of the problems you had was an acute obsessive disorder, and you can't help yourself." "I just want you to know that I don't want to be one of those people that a son-in-law can't tolerate."

"And you couldn't sleep because you thought that I saw you that way?" I said to her.

"That's pretty much it." She said to me, "But there's one other thing, I don't like being called ma'am by you, it sounds like I'm an old hag, and you don't accept me, I prefer Ellen."

"I need to go to my lab." "I'll be back before the rolls are ready," I told her.

"Can I come?" She asked.

"If you wish," I said.

"Ellen, I don't want others to know me or know of me." "I can travel and go anywhere and be anybody I want to be." "Your husband understood this and never mentioned my name to you or anyone he knew, business or otherwise." "That was done for a purpose." "Do you understand what I'm saying?"

"Yeah, when in public, I'm not supposed to tell anyone you're my son-in-law or to go further. I'm not supposed to act like I even know you."

"Now, as far as what you wish to call me in private, that can be your decision." I told her, "I prefer smith."

"This place where you live," she asked "is there room for me?"

"No, I'll have to build you one; my cabin is a twelve by twelve rock shack. I only built mine big enough to house one person."

"And, when you come back here?" She asked me with the same shyness.

"I can build you a unit to live in, or you can be here with Jane and me, and Jack, but I'm sorry, I can't call someone else mother." "Did we get the things you wanted to get cleared up, cleared up yet?" I asked her.

"No, I still don't know how to talk to you; I get scared when I do." She said.

"Ellen, I've been protected from others since I was twelve, and before that, I never met very many people, especially children." "I have difficulty talking to people the same as you have difficulty talking to me."

I gave instructions for my doors to be opened to my lab. When we walked in, I watched as the lady looked around at my machinery.

"What are all these things?" She asked.

"That's a lathe over there, and those over in the corner are pressers where I build my models, and over there, I pointed to her, is where we're headed." "I built a mold and combined the resins and the rubber together to see if my theory was correct," I said to her.

I unlatched the top of my mold and removed it, revealing an overlay that I had made, and pulled it over my chest. I held it at the bottom with one hand and struck the center with the other. It had a resemblance to a thin life preserver that wasn't inflated.

I looked around and saw a pry bar and told Ellen to strike me in the chest.

"No, I can't do that. I might miss." She told me.

"Ellen, there's a lot of things I don't want to do, but I have to know where I stand." "Now take this bar and strike my chest with it or I'll go wake Jane up and tell her to do it."

"Smith, please."

I smiled at her and said to her, "I wouldn't be asking you to if I thought it wouldn't shield me, you know that."

She reared back and struck me with a force that I didn't expect, and I went tumbling backward. She came running over to me crying and tried to pick me up, but she wasn't strong enough.

I looked up at her and smiled. "I didn't feel a thing." "It works," I told her.

"You scared me half to death; don't ever do that to me again." She said with a shaky voice.

"Ellen, do you know what this means?"

She answered with a no.

I removed my overlay and then told her, "This means it's time to go and cook the rolls." I said, smiling at her.

When the oven door opened, Ellen was set aback at seeing them. "We preheat the oven to four hundred degrees and cook them for around ten minutes or so; it depends on the heating source," I told her. When the buzzer went off, I gave her the honor of putting the pan in, and we waited till the tops were a golden color; and I also gave her the honor of taking them out after they were done. "The best part is reserved for last." I said as I gave her one with some butter that I put inside, "Now, we test to see if our mission was accomplished or was it a failure." I told her.

She took a bite of it and then started her moaning, "I haven't eaten these for a long time." Then she stopped and looked at me. "My husband used to bring me home yeast rolls, just like these." "He said he always stopped off at a special bakery." "You cooked those rolls, didn't you?"

"Yes, ma'am."

"And what about those other foods he brought home? Did you cook those too?"

"Yes, ma'am."

She took another roll and put some butter on it also, "I need a second opinion." She said. "Do you like to cook, huh?"

"Now, that's a story in itself." I told her, "One day, I was working on one of my projects, and I got a strong urge to have a bacon, lettuce, and tomato sandwich." "The only cooking part was the bacon, but I always thought cooking helped to remove my stress. I feed the body food for fuel only, and tonight I feed the body for a reward of success." "Today is a feel-good day; I'll rest, and tomorrow, I'll work twice as hard to rebuild my body back to the strength that I had before the accident." "But food never had a taste to me." "That was the part that I couldn't understand." "Why did I crave a BLT?" I said to her to bring home a point.

I got up and bid her a good night.

"So you're going back to bed?" She asked.

"I have pain, you gave me quite a wallop back there, and I didn't expect to be knocked backward." "Did you happen to play softball too?" I asked her and then let her know that I was playing with her by giving her a smile.

"See, that's what I'm talking about." "I don't know how to take you." She commented.

"If you stop trying to understand who I am, then you'll find out who you are; to know me is to know yourself." "Do you know who you are?" I asked her, "Good night, Ellen, and don't eat all the rolls up trying to answer your questions, they're addicted to the weak, and they go directly to the hips."

I smiled at her, walked to my room, and shut the door behind me as I entered. Like the night before, I eased into bed, and the young girl pulled herself over to me.

"Was my mother awake?"

"Yes, she came in about three," I said.

"Smith, that's my mother."

"I know, she's entitled to be who she is, your mother, and I fully understand your mother; she wants to be mine too," I told her.

"Did she talk about you and me that way?" She asked.

"I thought all mothers did that, and father's too, and Jane, I can tell by the way you squeeze me, you're not tired of me yet."

"Is anything on your mind right now besides me?" She asked.

"You said I'm not allowed to bring my thoughts in when I'm with you."

"Smith, the first time we slept together, you were restless; you tossed and turned and woke up all the time." "I could feel you, but I didn't want to let you know." "You were pretty much a stranger then, at least to me; I didn't know you." "But, there was something about you that I couldn't explain." "The third night, you never woke up once, and you never rolled around and moved like you were fighting something anymore." "I couldn't go back to sleep; I did what I didn't expect to do; I put my arm over you and held you, I didn't want to, but when I did, I didn't want to let you go." "And Smith, I think whether you want me or not, you need me, and you need me because you can relax when you're in my arms, and I think because out of everyone in this world, you can only trust me." "I think you know that." "Being tall does have certain advantages, you know." "I do my own thinking when I turn over when you're not in bed." "Smith, I remember you telling me that you never had anyone hold you in their arms, and that night when I did that, I think that I made you nervous." "You're not restless anymore, and Smith, I know I'm never going to replace anyone you lost, but I do want to be someone special to you." "I don't want marriage; I'm not over the one I got into yet." "I don't want to be called fiancé; I can't talk about you." "I don't want to be called a girlfriend; that makes me feel like I'm never going to go beyond being a girlfriend." "I can't accept the term lover, or my lady, or my partner."

"I thought you asked me not to bring in my thoughts when I entered the room?" I told her.

"This is different; I want to know where I fit in with you." "I know you, and I'm afraid you'll think that the best thing for me would be away from you." "Smith, don't come in one day and tell me that brain of yours got to working and the best thing for the both of us was to have me go about my own way." She said pleadingly.

"You've been talking to your mother, I see." I told her, "Jane, I don't know how to get your attention to show you; my intentions." "I'm not able to say the words that I want to say." "You can say I love you with ease; to me, I've never used them, and if you loved me, what would you call me?" "It's the same thing," I said to her.

I got ready to get up when she rolled over on me and stopped me. "Smith, you're a brittle man; I'm cranky because I couldn't go to sleep without you." "I wasn't being disrespectful or angry with you, I was being honest, and it's not if I was in love with you; there isn't any if." She stated.

"I don't feel comfortable using words that I never used." I told her, "They aren't easy for me, but if I was to introduce you to someone, I would tell them this is the woman that I love, and one day I wish she could look at me and not be like me, insecure in her life." "I would tell them that if she loved me only half as much as I love her, she would have peace." "To your mother, that's what a son-in-law means; to you, it's darling, honey, sweetie, or anything else you wish to call me." "Jane, I never had a bond with anyone." "You ask questions, but the answers are cloudy to you." "That's the way a relationship is to me; I can't see through the fog." "I've never been in the position that I'm in now," I told her.

"Then, I've found what I'm here for." She whispered in my ear, "I'm here to call out your name so you'll not have trouble finding me."

I tried to get up in the early morning hours, but the girl restrained me. "I need my sleep, Smith, and I can't get all I need when you're up and down." She said as she clung to me, "You laid down about an hour ago." She said, and I used the morning hours to think out my plans as I lay there.

"You're not asleep, are you?" Jane asked later without moving to speak.

"No," I told her.

"Smith, get up and go and work on your problems then." "I want you to be able to do whatever you had done before we met." "I'm not here for the purpose of changing your lifestyle but to learn how to live with it." "I love you, and that means leaving you alone when you have things on your mind that's bothering you."

I got up to put on a pot of coffee when I heard Jane following behind me; she noticed the yeast rolls on the table.

"I taught your mother how to make them before I came to bed last night," "taste one," "your mother made them," I told her.

She took one and put it in a microwave for a few seconds, and put some butter on it. She moaned like her mother.

"My mother, did this?" "My mother can't cook."

"I beg your pardon." I heard the lady comment as she snuck up on us.

I poured us all a cup of coffee, and when I sat down. I told Ellen that Jack would be home before dark.

"He's going to be tired, and he's going to be hungry." "When he eats, he likes to nap," I said to her.

"Is that why you're cooking tonight?" She asked.

"Jack's strange when it comes to food; that might have been where I began to taste food." I stated to her, "Ellen, for a while, when he wasn't with you twenty-four hours a day, he was with me for twenty-four hours a day." "I'd be cooking, and Jack would taste everything to make sure it was seasoned properly and to tell me when he thought my food was done." "It wasn't hard." "I would cook it and let it rest, and when Jack couldn't stand it anymore, he'd asked when was the food going to be done?" "It had been ready for thirty minutes or so, but I'd make him wait for a while, and then I'd fix his plate, I'd starve him until he said he was hungry." "When it came to eating, Jack's a dedicated man." "Even more so, when he's hungry."

I got up and poured us another cup of coffee.

"Ellen, a clock moves slowly while it's being watched." "Jack won't get here any quicker than when he walks out of that elevator." "It's been said that time flies when you're having fun, you and Jane need to go outside and have a look at what Jack built me."

"Computer; display photos of the resort and all the surrounding shops, and restaurants and other businesses," I ordered verbally.

When my screens came on, I told them to watch the pictures, and when they got ready, all that they had to do was walk over to the elevator and give it a command to open. "It will only respond to the voices that I let it recognize," I said to them.

"I thought I was more like a person that was here as a captive?" Ellen said to me.

"For the first hour, you were, for the first day, you were, on the second day you didn't see yourself as being held as a captive, and on the third day, you became like Jane." "You were happy here, and our encounters dissolved the thoughts you had about me." "I just needed a little time with you," I spoke my thoughts to her.

She took her eyes away from the screens and looked at me.

"You make it sound like you were playing me like a puppet." She stated.

"That's interpretation." I told her, "You were angry as soon as you met me." "Jane was lying in bed with me, and you didn't like seeing that; it came as a shock to you." "You are who you are because that's the person that you want to be." "Jane is who she is because that's the person she wants to be."

"When you're together, you both have each other, your close, but Ellen, I can also see a little bit of Jack in her too."

"So all I have to do is walk over to that elevator and say open, and I can leave, right?" Ellen said.

"Yes, ma'am."

"I'm missing something here." She replied. "Smith, are James and Ruby the only androids you built?" She asked.

"No, ma'am." "Computer open storage bay twenty-four," I commanded.

I started walking out of the kitchen, and the ladies jumped up and quickly came running to be by my side. When I rounded the hall, both of them stopped as I kept on walking.

"Holy smokes," Jane said as Ellen walked over and started looking at the humanoids real close.

"How many of these things do you have here?" Ellen asked as she looked around.

"In this bay, there are one hundred and ninety-five androids." "They were made for each country in the world." "James is programmed to build my prototypes without me," I told her.

"You said in this bay, are there more? Ellen asked.

"Yes, ma'am." "Computer, have all my androids meet us in my exercise room in fifteen minutes." "Initiate my commands now," I said, giving my verbal orders to the master computer.

I turned and started walking away when I heard Jane commenting. "No, no, I'm not seeing this, momma." They arrived a few minutes behind me.

When the humanoids began lining up, Ellen and Jane both were in a daze.

"What I build is not for use by any government." "Each one represents each country, so they're dressed and look like the people of that country." "They only have one function," I said.

Ellen looked over at me.

"Everyone, please go back and get undressed and wait for me to call upon you again." "Initiate my commands now," I ordered.

They turned and walked away.

"You said that they only have one function," Ellen commented when she looked over at me.

"Ellen, one country cannot dominate the world; there would be chaos until all beliefs are eliminated except one, and then that one would separate in half, and that half would separate, and then, they would start to turn on each other." "We live in a new age; it's an age where a man can kill all mankind just by starting one tiny little war; all it takes is a small spark to ignite a whole ocean of gasoline." "Cancer starts out the same way, it starts out as a small seed, and it grows into a tumor; it's undetectable until you suffer from a pain."

"All nuclear power plants are targets and will be destroyed, and man will walk around in radiation." "He won't die from cancer that he'll ail from, and he won't die from failure of his immune system; he'll die from starvation before he even knows he's dying." "Ellen, you just don't live in the life that others live; watch the news; it's happening now," I told her.

"So, what's their function?" She asked with a little worry.

"Their job is to protect all species that adapt after man is gone." "Man is the supreme being, without man; almost all species will perish from the disasters that man built." "To destroy the earth isn't my decision to make." "I can only try and save whatever remains." "We live in a perfect time," I told her.

"Then that's what you meant," Jane said. "You were talking about what you saw the future as, weren't you, when you said that about us living in a perfect time?"

"I need both of you to look through my eyes." I said to them, "We have robots to build our cars; we have robots to run an assembly line in all products that man can buy in a store." "We have robots to cook those products." "There isn't anything that man does that robots aren't used for." "All machinery and heavy equipment are robotic." "Vacuum cleaners, lawnmowers, anything that man can invent is done so where people aren't needed." "The time draws near where nothing that man built to operate will operate." "All oil wells in the oceans will end up breaking apart, and no one will be able to do anything to stop it." "No airplanes will fly, and no cars will travel down the highways, no computers will function, and none of the conveniences like electricity will be functional, and that means water will become contaminated." "That means that all food sources will be shut down." "So right now, we live in a perfect time. I can't promise you about tomorrow, or even thirty minutes from now." "Whether the destruction of the earth is manmade or by the intervention of an intergalactic force, all of these things will come to pass, and my humanoids will one day be released to walk the earth alone." "When man becomes extinct, they will begin to repair all systems that were damaged and dismantle what man-made."

"But if what you say was to happen, then your things wouldn't work either," Ellen said.

"Ellen, the reason I can't let them fall into the wrong hands is that each one carries a fuel cell that contains enriched uranium." "They'll survive for millions of years, but put ten of them together, and you have enough explosives to wipe out all of New York City."

"Smith, you scare me talking like that," Ellen said.

"Ma'am, I'm a pessimist, and I believe that all things are possible, and all accidents are preventable." "This earth is unstable, and all manmade structures will bow to the forces that she unleashes."

"Then what's the point in living anymore?" Ellen commented.

"Well, if my theory is correct, you won't be." I told her, "Right now, we live in a perfect time, and we should live each day as if the sun will come up tomorrow."

"You said that too," Jane said.

"Jane, life is short, and death is forever." "When you were born, and you took your first breaths, you defeated death and lived to the age you are now." "You didn't do that by accident; it was instinct-driven." "No matter what the outcome, we fight from our birth and to the death to survive; it's the last breath we take that stops us from fighting."

When I started walking away, I could hear Jane and Ellen behind me as they followed me into the kitchen.

I began dicing up my onions and the bell peppers, along with the celery. I was putting butter in a pan when Ellen made a comment that needed to be addressed.

"Smith, you preach gloom and doom." She said.

"That's interpretation." I told her, "Everybody knows that they're going to die, but when an angel of death, a doctor, meets with them and then tells them that death is coming for them, that's the gloom and doom you speak of." "Nothing matters anymore to that person; they have been told that it's their time, and one day soon, they'll fall asleep and not wake up." "But man ate the fruit from the tree of knowledge, and man is the only species that knows he'll die; why does it come as such a shock?" "I know I'm going to die, and I started dying the minute I was born." "Our life span is vulnerable." "It's how we live that we should be concerned with." "That question was answered for me recently when Jane came into my life." I looked over at Ellen. "You found Jack when you and he found each other." "You lived much of your life disliking your life." "But you tolerated that because to put an end to it meant that you would have to live without Jack." "Jane has a lot of you in her, and that's a good thing; it's going to take all the strength that she has to tolerate me as long as you've tolerated Jack."

Jane got up and came over and started kissing me. She walked back with tears in her eyes. I looked over at Ellen, and she had tears also.

I put the vegetables in the pan to sauté them and then took my chicken out of the refrigerator and started preheating the oven. I turned on the grill on the stove to give the chicken texture and began dressing the chicken breasts for the grill, and after I put them on, I started slicing the sausage and put it in the pan with the vegetables and then returned my attention to the chicken.

Jane and Ellen were silent as they watched me.

It was after I had turned the stove too low when a voice could be heard from down the hallway; Jane and Ellen both were startled.

"Hello," Jack said as he entered the room, and that prompted a glance from Ellen.

"I told you Jack would be here before dark." "I did so because you associated before dark as meaning late this afternoon; to expect him earlier would have had you pacing." "Time flies; Ellen and Jack are here; I had to mislead you for that purpose." "If you listen to all the things you hear, you'll be misled," I said.

"Smith, you have a touch of evil about you." She said, smiling at me.

She got up and told us to excuse them for a moment as they both departed from the room. When they walked out, a few minutes later, they returned, and Jack had a smile on his face. Jane looked over at me, and I gave her a smile. That's when her eyes met her mother's.

"That is so gross." She said.

"Honey, I'm not going to kiss him unless I know it's your father that I'm kissing." She uttered to her.

I got up and took the pan and started flipping the shrimp with one hand and flipping the sausage and vegetables with my other hand, and then set them back down to continue cooking.

I took out a pot and started heating water to boil my pasta in, and then unfolded a stick of butter, dropped it in the water, and stirred the pasta to keep it from sticking. Jack came over and gave the shrimp a little stir and then grabbed one in a spoon and tasted the shrimp and then did the same with the sausage.

"Where are you now?" Ellen commented to Jack.

"You mean James and Ruby?" Jack said to her as I was pouring my whipping cream into another pot.

"Yeah." She replied.

"Their back in storage waiting to be called on," Jack said to her.

I took a couple of handfuls of parmesan cheese and dropped it into the cream to melt, and took my chicken out of the oven after I grilled it and diced it up, and then put it in a bowl. I stirred my pasta and called for Jack. He got up and took out a noodle to test it. "It's ready," he said.

I took the pot off of the stove and poured the pasta into a colander to drain and then poured it into a bowl and poured a little olive oil on it and stirred the oil in.

When that was finished, I took some bowls out of the cabinet and gave Jack a double heaping of the sausage and shrimp and chicken I cut up along with some vegetables and then poured Alfredo sauce over the top, and added a little more cheese along with some salt and pepper to it. I put three rolls in his bowl and gave it to him. He didn't bother to wait for the rest of us.

I looked at Ellen and asked her how she liked hers, and then I asked Jane. I also gave them the same double heaping of meat and vegetables like I fixed Jack, but they liked butter on their rolls. When I sat down, Jane slid her bowl over next to mine and sat down next to me. She ate with her left hand and held my left hand with her right hand. I felt a gentle squeeze, and when I looked over at her, she smiled.

"What am I eating, about eight thousand calories?" She asked me.

"It was skinless chicken breasts, so you can subtract about ten calories from that if it'll make you feel better," I said to her.

She started laughing, and I put my fork down and watched her. I felt Ellen's hand on my wrist. "Smith, are you all right?" She asked me.

"Oh!" I mumbled as I was brought back from my thoughts. "I'm sorry, I was drifting."

"What were you thinking about?" She asked.

"I was listening to Jane laugh," I said as I sat my fork down. "I saw her happiness come out of her body." "I got caught and thought about the last time I saw my brother laugh like that; he laughed all the time." "Jane was telling me in her laughter that she was happy too."

"Smith," Jack said, "have you been able to work out?"

"It's all right, Jack; Jane's helped me to come to grips with my past," I said to him.

"Ellen, I loved my brother; he was laughing like that on the morning I walked him to school." "I never saw his face again after that." "I told you that I saw Jane's happiness coming out of her, and I felt something that I haven't felt in a long time." "My brother was dependent on me, and when Jane laughed, she told me that she was dependent on me too." "I thought I lost those feelings, but I guess I just misplaced them," I said.

I felt a tight squeeze on my hand.

"Smith," Jane said, "I want you to relax and breathe in slowly through your nose and exhale through your mouth."

"Jane"

"Smith, I need you to relax and close your eyes and focus for me." She repeated to me.

"Jane"

"Smith, close your eyes. I know what I'm doing." She said slowly.

After I had done what she asked of me, she began. "Breathe, breathe, breathe," she said in a low voice. "I want you to relax." "Smith, that was a long, long, long time ago; I told you I can't replace anybody, and what you said about me laughing was the biggest compliment that I ever got." "I am happy, I'm very happy, and with each day that goes by, I become happier and happier." "When you talk to me, I hear words that are said to me that no one's ever said to me." "A man can't build a man like you; I don't care how many of those things you have." She said.

"Smith, when we were back at the cabin." "I noticed your sketching pad over in the corner, and I think I did what I wasn't supposed to do." "I let my curiosity get the better part of me."

"I know," I said. "You did what was normal." "Anybody in your situation would have tried to find out what they were involved in and with whom," I told her.

"How did you know?" She asked.

"You didn't put it back the way I left it," I told her.

"See, Smith, that's the thing, knowing who you are now, back then I didn't know you knew I looked at them." She said.

"What were they?" I asked her.

She thought for a long time and looked into my eyes.

"I don't know." She said.

"We'll take this matter up later," I said as I looked over at Ellen.

"Jack, finish eating." She said as she poked him in his ribs, and then he looked up at me with a mouthful of food.

Jane twirled some noodles around on a fork and stuck a shrimp at the end of my fork, and put it up to my mouth; she forced me to open it, and when I did, she inserted the food.

She repeated her act, and then I took the fork away.

"Dad, did you know about those other things too." She said to him nonchalantly as she took a bite of her food.

"You have to be a little more specific, honey, when you describe anything around here; Smith has a lot of things."

"Those androids he built." She said.

"You mean James and Ruby?"

"No, the other ones." She said.

"Which other ones, Smith, has different prototypes?" He told her.

"What other ones are you talking about?" She asked as she looked at him strangely.

"Honey, that's what I'm asking you." He told her.

"Smith has prototypes in waiting." "He has a positive outlook." "He has androids that will seek out other life forms as it travels forever through universes." "He built them for one purpose; if they were to encounter other intelligent life forms, they would tell the story of man's doom that they brought among themselves, and they'll only be launched if Smith's prophecy comes to light."

When Jane and Ellen quickly looked over at me, Jack knew his answer.

"So, I'm assuming here that neither of you knows about the astronauts then?" He said to them. "How about the doctor's then?" He added.

Jane diverted her eyes from mine to his. "What doctor's?"

"Smith," he said.

"Go ahead; you're doing a good job," I told him.

"Honey, Smith wants to build hospitals and use androids as doctors." "All operations involving invasion of the body will be done in decontaminated vacuum chambers." "His androids don't breathe, and cancers can't come into contact with air."

"When did you think all that up?" Jane asked me.

"I was stitching some lace into a purse, back at my cabin." "I made four purses before I had my plans laid out." "Your father is working on getting me some land and a grant." "When the money is appropriated, and the land is given to me, your father will be responsible for building it, like he built my lab."

"Jack, they were referring to the protector's," I informed him.

"Oh, okay, what is it that you want to know about them." I'm sure if smith showed them to you, both of you got your answers, or he wouldn't have shown them to you." He said.

"Yeah, but we didn't know about the other's." Ellen followed his comment.

"There's more, he calls them imitators, and they can be anybody or anything he wants them to be." "I came here sometimes, and James was building his prototypes." "We had a lengthy conversation, and I found out more than once that you can sometimes forget that you're talking to a robot." He said. "But I haven't found a man or machine that can make a better pot of coffee than James or Ruby." "Ellen, what Smith has here can change the way that man goes about his business." "Honey, they've been among us for almost three years, and I haven't been able to identify any yet." He said to his wife. He changed the subject. "You seem to be healing pretty good." He said to me.

"Yeah, I had Ellen take my stitches out," I told him.

"Are you using your glue?" He asked.

"Yeah, and up to now, it's worked," I replied.

"Hello, knock, knock, who's in there." "You're treating us like we're a third party here," Ellen said to Jack.

"Ellen Smith was working with a chemical compound that resembled endorphins, but he wasn't satisfied; he had to go further; he had to find a way to turn a temporary pain reliever into a long-time pain reliever." "He came up with his glue." "It's an anesthetic compound that was intended to be poured into a wound and seal off the bleeding and provide combat soldiers relief." "That's one prototype that he didn't know that he'd be testing out on himself." "Smith, pull your shirt off so I can see." He said to me.

I crossed my arms and took off my shirt.

Jack got up and walked over to give me his inspection. "James did good work." He said as he easily felt along the top of my scars. He gently pressed an area. "Did you feel that?" He asked.

"I felt pressure, but no pain." I told him, "I did a little thinking and designed a quick solution to my problem, Ellen tested it out, and Jack, I don't think you would be able to handle a right cross from her, so beware."

"Stop it; you scared you know what out of me," Ellen said.

"Give me a minute, and I'll be right back," I told him.

When I brought it back to show him, he scooted back from the table and felt of the material and hit it with the flat of his hand on the back, and then did the same to the front.

I told him to put it on and then told him to hold it at the bottom.

"How does it fit?" I asked him and then threw a punch into his abdomen. He reacted normally and fell backward, not from the thrust, but in defense of the thrust.

I gave him a smile as I helped him up and addressed my actions. "There isn't any way to convince someone but to show someone what you're talking about." I said to him, "Right, Ellen?" She sensed that I was referring to the first time she reacted when she saw her alter ego.

"You could have warned me." He said, chuckling.

"I've been working with some padding that I intend to put between my skin and the overlay." I said to him, "I'll be finished tomorrow night."

He took off the overlay and went back to eating. When he finished that bowl, he went back and got some more. Ellen gave him a stare.

"What?" He said to Ellen.

"Are you starving?" She asked him as he poured Alfredo sauce over the chicken, sausage and shrimp, and linguini.

"As a matter of fact, I am." "Smith always had something special waiting for me when I came walking through that elevator; it helped me to unwind."

When Jack finished, he didn't waste time. He excused himself and went to lay down, leaving me alone with the ladies. They both returned their eyes to mine, and I got up from the table and started walking away. I gave a command to the computer to raise the doors that entered into my control room. When I walked in, I was once again followed by Jane and Ellen.

After I sat down in my chair, I commanded my computer to initiate the retrieval of James and Ruby's information. We watched as the plane circled over an airport and landed and then watched as they got into a transport truck and were taken across the border. Their travel lasted for nearly four hours before I finally started to see what I needed to see.

Jane awoke from her sleep on the sofa that offered the tired no escape and came over and quietly sat down in my lap. When I eased back in my chair, she was uncomfortable. She took my arm, wrapped it around the small of her back, and held it tight; it was her way of informing me that she wanted me to hold her. When I squeezed her by putting my other arm around her waist and clasping it in my other hand, only then did she lay her head down on my shoulder.

"Jane, there are reasons behind all the things that I do." "Computer; retrieve data on the travelers, and give me full display viewing," I ordered.

Jane looked up, and then she sat up. She started rubbing the sleep from her eyes. "What is that?" She asked.

"That shot was taken in nineteen eighty-two, the film wasn't stored properly, and most of it was damaged." I had to digitally restore it." I whispered to her, "The next segment is pictures that were taken ten years later in Nebraska." "Jane, do you believe in aliens?" I asked her.

"Those are the pictures I saw on your drawings." She said

"Let me show you something." "Computer show the actual speed of the aircraft," I commanded.

"Are those things real?" She asked.

"Yeah, they're too real." I said, "We only have one way to travel outside our atmosphere; they can do it in less than ten seconds." "They don't leave a vapor trail, so there's no heat source." "Watch the tree's underneath them. They're motionless; there's not any movement of the air." "How can they hover without an energy source?" "Imagine beings that can possess that kind of knowledge." "I'm not worried about their travels." "My worry is that if they possess that knowledge to travel, what knowledge do they possess to defend themselves, and even more important, what can I learn from them?" "Right now, I'm fifty years too young." "My androids can only react and reach as far as its program, and none of them are equal to the intelligence of any being that can achieve that kind of velocity, I know, I programmed them." "In all religions that date back as far as when man first looked up to the sky, there was a common link. They all worshipped and believed in a supreme being." "Cave drawings depicted space travelers, but in times of ignorance, kings would call themselves gods and wear clothing that resembled that of a god." "A meteorite to them was a way that a god brought himself here, and in some cultures, a human sacrifice was offered." "Jane, back then, you would have been chosen first." "Emperors and kings were afraid of the lightning and thunder." "To them, it meant that they were angry with them." "I don't know what they saw, so I can't dispute their drawings, and I can't dispute anyone's theories." "I can't deny them either; you can see the same as what I see." I said, "What I'm attracted to is the individuals that claim that they were examined." "I listen and watch, and I read." "Just because I haven't been on the inside; doesn't mean that someone else hasn't either, and after all, who would believe them?"

"Jane take a good look at the screen and ask yourself, how would you be able to talk to someone and not be thought of as having a few loose screws in the cranium?" "Man can only handle just so much, and in the case of man, this would be too much for them."

"Is this the reason for the astronauts?" She asked.

I looked up at my screens. "If they were aggressive, they would be here instead of us, and if they wanted us for slaves, there would be nothing that man could do to stop it." "What puzzles me is that these are two separate incidents, and if history was truthful when it foretold the past, we might be talking about more than one intelligent life form." "All accounts have portrayed different shapes and sizes of spacecraft and of the aliens themselves." "Man can't accept knowledge of the existence of one, let alone two or more; he has his own belief."

"Smith, I wish you would have said hello or something to me at the party; you would have made a great friend." She said as she began practicing her rule on me.

She got up from the chair, helped me up, and held my hand as we walked over to her mother. She woke her up and told her that we were going to sleep and that she should do the same. She didn't resist.

When we got in bed, Jane rolled over next to me and laid her head down on my chest easily as if she was listening to my heart, then she raised her head and put her lips up against mine.

"Smith, I wish I didn't see that." She said as she pulled her lips away. "And I'm glad that you didn't show that to my mother." "But to be honest with you, in a way, I'm glad you did show it to me." "It tells me that you won't hold anything back from me, and that's what makes me feel happy when I'm with you."

I took a deep breath and exhaled. "Jane, your father and I lived by rules all of our life, and now those rules have collapsed." "I didn't expect for you to come visiting me, I didn't expect the cat to attack, and I didn't expect to be picked up and brought here." "How can all the things that I didn't expect come to happen all at once?"

"Smith, when you work out and drill yourself to the point of exhaustion, remember this." "I love you, and you love me; I know that, deep down inside, I know that." "I don't want you to be cooped up in this place working and me walking around afraid to talk to you because of a worry that I'll disturb you." "This stuff is way beyond what I thought was normal, and when it comes to first impressions, I had you misconfigured." She stated. I looked over at her, and she put her finger to my lips. "Why can't you be like everyone else, go to work, come home and read the paper, and fall asleep on the couch?" I was about to talk when she had done as she had done before, putting her finger to my lips to quiet me. "When I gave my vows," "I said for better or worse."

"I, unfortunately, found out what the worse part consisted of." "I'm willing to repeat those vows to you of better or worse, right now, in private, if that's what you want to hear." "But, there's something more important to me right now." "Smith, you have to come home to me, and I don't want it to be in a box." "Now, let's get on with our lives and see what the future holds for us." The next morning, I was sliding out of the bed when she woke up and put her arm around me. "What time is it?" She asked.

"I don't know," I told her.

"Computer; what time is it?" Jane commanded.

Zero three fifty-four, the computer replied.

She got up and walked around to my side, and helped me get up.

"What's first on your list?" She asked.

"I need to walk," I told her. I put my warm-up suit on and walked out of the room. I was walking at a slow pace when she walked in front of me and held my hand as we walked around the track.

"I know when something's bothering you." She said to me, "You've got a look on your face like you're a thousand miles away." "It helps to think sometimes when you talk out loud."

"I was just wondering why people have to die because they can't afford to live." I said to her, "I can't watch a child die because a parent can't afford the medicine or the treatment that child needs. I can give them that."

"So, you're thinking about your doctors and hospitals then?" She replied. "You said that my dad was working on getting you a grant and some land; do you always get what you want?"

"Well, I get what I want because they get what they want, only sometimes they want to play a game of pied piper with me." "I don't like to play games with politicians, and I make them hurt where they feel it the most, their pocketbook." "I send a message, and if my grant is given, their money is replaced, minus a few billion, and that's the simple end of the story."

"And if they don't, you hack into their computer and destroy their lives?" She said.

"Jane, these are people that cherish power, and they use it for leverage for their own personal advantage." "They don't worry about money or the people that they serve; they're more interested in interpreting a law to put that money into their own pocket." "I just let them know that I'm watching them, and if they make a wrong move, I make a correction in their account to reflect the amount that they embezzled." "As for hacking into their computer and destroying their lives, I don't see it that way. I see it more like righting a wrong." "Jane, you don't have to kill a man, sometimes all you have to do is merely give away everything that he worships." "There are hundreds of billions of dollars that can't be found in the Pentagon; there are people that know where it's at." "I don't socialize, so your father does it for me." "He talks to these people and asks them for their help." "If he's shown the door, I release their past back on them." "I don't like playing pied piper and not being paid my ransom for doing their work; it's not mine; it all belongs to all those people that that money can help." "I told you, not all enemies live in other countries; some of them are elected by our own people because those people can't tell the difference between a lie and the truth; they hear the untruth and believe what they hear." "This man's taken, hostages." "The agent risked the lives of her children and her husband for the freedom of what we believe in." "It seems strange to me that people take freedom for granted. They forget about family members that died so that we can enjoy it." "Jane, people are trying to take away that freedom you have now, and they do it all by the stroke of a pen." "How can I let these people be executed?" "I only have one answer; I can't." "I have to deliver my message so all can see." "You knew when you saw the President, it wasn't what you expected; it also told you he came to talk to me for a purpose." "Will you stand in front of me and block me from what I'm being asked to do?" "If I don't take this man out, many more people will die; that's another message I have to send to the people." "This launch cannot take place; if it does, others will follow from other countries." "I wish I could tell you that this would be my last job." "I thought that it was a while back, but I was wrong; more troubles are building, and more tensions are mounting." "Jane, we came together from different times in the world and different places." "This is my universe here." "My computers tell me everything I want to know without leaving." "But, that's not what I use them for." I told her, "Let's take you" "Computer open the doors to my command center." I said as we walked over to the control room. I typed in her name and then entered some codes. I found a picture of her and zoomed in on her face. "I bet you were a good volleyball player," I told her.

"That picture is from my tenth grade in high school." She said.

I zoomed in closer and looked at her mouth.

"You try to cover them and keep them closed." "I see a small puffiness on the bottom of your nose, you wore braces, and you were embarrassed by them." I began searching deeper into her life. "I see you only attended three semesters of college, oh, and you did take a course on psychology." "That must be when you got married." I said, "You're twenty-four, and you've been married for four years, so I would imagine that you dropped out of college when you married." I then looked at her. "You've got to be kidding me?" "Your last name is Smith?" I said to her.

"I do know one thing." She chuckled. "I can tell anybody my name is Jane Smith." "They'll think I'm married to you, so you can do your best at trying to explain why my name is not the same as yours." "I asked you what you would call me last night, remember." "Now, what are you going to call me?"

"I'd have to say that you're the woman of my heart, and I hope I never have a heart attack."

"That's not fair; do you know how sweet that sounded to me?" She said, "You're doing it again, aren't you, changing the subject?"

"Jane, my mother would sit for hours and never move from her chair." "She sat and knitted, and then she unraveled the knitting and rolled it back up into a ball, and then she would start her knitting all over again." "Whenever I talked to her, it was a one-sided conversation." "I spoke my comments to empty ears." "Your father and I never minced family and business, so when I spoke to your father, he was receiving my commands."

"Smith, am I smothering you?" She asked.

"No"

"Then tell me what's bothering you; I'd like to hear it." She continued.

"Jane, it's boring to people like you."

"Are you characterizing me now?" She asked.

I turned and began working on my computer. "Watch this," I told her, "These are solar sunbursts; see how the shock waves travel, they begin as an explosion, and as they expel outward, they broaden." "This is a force of matter." "It's like a wave of water that pounds against a cliff; their power is strong, and they'll wipe out any satellites that are on when it hits." "Right now, there are a little over three hundred satellites circulating the earth as we speak." "Weather, communications, and spy satellites, only the interpretation has changed from spy satellites to relay observatories." "In ten years, the names will change, but the meaning will remain."

"I've got a launch that's planned in two years." "It's going to be carrying a satellite that's infected with my program." "It's designed to destroy any satellite or satellites that I target." "I've built an artificial sunburst that blast shock waves and bombards their circuitry, and the result is I disrupt their communications." "I've performed three tests, and each one has proven my theories to be correct." "No one knows of this, except your father and now you." "I trust you, and if I'm wrong in my trust, it will mean my life and possibly the lives of all of the unborn." "So, one way or the other, I'm faced with the uncertainty of how my life is to go forward." "I'm the only person with the knowledge that can operate the satellite." "As long as I'm alive, no one will create world war three." "When I'm dead, the satellites will be left up to mankind to do with as they wish." "My computer will be forbidden to interfere with man's decisions, and man will be responsible for the remainder of his own making." "Jane, as long as someone makes money from a war, there will be wars."

"How long do these episodes last?" She asked.

I smiled at her. "They come, and they go." "Some last for a long time, and sometimes they seem to last forever." "Maybe that's what my mother felt; I don't know, but something in her life had to be so traumatic that it destroyed her." "For a time, I thought I was going to join her, but you pulled me out of my pit." "Jane, I had long thoughts that my brother and I could have been her last straw." "I can't give you the life you deserve, I'm not the kind of man you can depend on, and I think you've been here long enough to see that," I told her.

"Does that computer have an ignore button on it?" She asked.

"What?"

"Does it have an ignore button on it?" She repeated.

"No," I told her.

"Then, I want one put on it, and when you start speaking like that, I'm going to push it and do what I plan on doing anyway." "I told you I don't want to hear that kind of talk, yet you keep bringing it up, over and over again." "I want you to put a button on your computer to push where I can ignore whatever you're saying when it comes to talking in that tone of voice." "We had this discussion before, remember." She said, "Are you going on this mission to die?" She asked.

"I may not have that choice," I told her.

"There you go again." She said, "Yes, you do." "I want you doing whatever it takes for you to come back home." "Smith, I think you're having about one of your disorders right now." "Your mind is starting to get cloudy, and you're rambling in your thoughts." "If you don't focus and get it out of your head, you might not be able to think the way you should." "A successful man doesn't use doubt."

I closed my eyes. "Did you learn that in school? I asked her.

"No" "That one's mine; I'll give it to you." She said to me, "Smith, relax and listen to me." "I loved my husband, and I tried everything I could to make our relationship work, and I want you to know that." "I fell in love with you almost from the first time I set my eyes on you; I didn't want to." "At first, I was in denial, there I was lucky to be alive, and now you tell me that I'm going to lose you too." "I've been a loser all of my life, and it's not fair; I'm not going to let you go without a fight." She said as she started crying.

At that point, her mother and father came and sat down next to us.

"Jack, you'll have to help me. I can't tell her I have no way of knowing my outcome."

"Oh!" "That is a problem." He stated.

I sat her down in a chair and left to go put on a pot of coffee. Ellen followed me as I heard Jack beginning in his lecture.

"You don't think small, do you?" She said to me. "Some people think how much a vacation is going to set them back." "You don't think like that." "You think further, and I'm not talking about money; there's nothing that escapes that train of thought you have once it catches your attention."

"Ma'am, do you know what led to Einstein's creation of the weapon of mass destruction?" "It wasn't anything more than a thought of how fast a bus could get from point A to point B." "That theory evolved the theory of relativity." "Light travels at one hundred and eighty-six thousand miles a second." "A light year involves light traveling over six billion miles if I was able to harness that energy; imagine what it would mean if I can find a way to pound a tumor by saturating it with rays that are harmful to that tumor and not harmful to the body of man." "Ellen, it could mean the end to any more surgeries to remove a malignancy." "Look outside after a rain; sometimes you'll see a rainbow." "The only reason why you see it is because the humidity in the air allows the light to bend and penetrate through, showing the color that succeeded, and that's with the human eye." "Put lenses on cameras, and you see hundreds of different shades of light, and each of those shades of light represents good and bad." "Too much exposure and the body receives burns and cancers, but the sun's rays also give the body vitamin D." "Too much vitamin D and you can get melanoma." "Put a lens on a telescope, and you'll see that the moon is one big ball of titanium, with trace amounts of chemicals, even water." "Oil is found by taking pictures of the inner core of the earth, and man has the technology to locate it now without drilling unnecessarily." "What if one of them, or if all of them can benefit man in some way, we just haven't thought of it. It was designed with a different purpose in mind."

Ellen looked over at me. "Smith, are you all, right?"

I took a deep breath and exhaled. "No, ma'am, I don't think I am; everyone else seems to think something is wrong with me." "Your husband did, your daughter does, and you do too."

"Smith, that's not what I meant; I'm worried about your welfare; you don't relax, you're up and down, moving here, wandering there."

"Ma'am, there's a lot of things that bother me; for one thing, our genetics are fouled up, and I believe I may know why, but trying to convince others would waste my time."

"What is the problem with our genetics?" She asked abruptly.

"You don't want to hear what I have to say?" I told her.

"If it comes from you, I find it interesting." "Now, what about our genetics." Ellen returned my comment with one of her own.

"Ellen, incest was common in the youth of man." "It was practiced by all people of all faiths long before Jesus Christ was sat upon his cross, and it's still in existence today; you just can't see it." "In poor countries, they leave the babies that are born with these genetic abnormalities in the desert to die or buried at birth on the side of a hill; Ellen, it happens here too."

"Brothers were with sisters, and fathers with daughters, and mothers were with sons, Pharaohs had beliefs, kings and Vikings had beliefs, Attila the Hun, Nero, Claudius, all of them had their own beliefs." "Lott had two sons by his daughters." "All races of man have certain genes that interrupt their body's ability to function." We are born with an inferior gene that is bonded in with our DNA, and that gene sometimes becomes the dominant gene." "Man in his quest to bare children of his blood sentenced all man to a fate worse than hell, and all those that bare the children of these children one day meet and become united." "See, there was the Old Testament, and there is the New Testament." "One of them is censored, so not everything you read in the New Testament was worded the way it was worded in the Old Testament, so you might find that some of the Old Testament's material has been modified and rewritten or omitted entirely from the New Testament." "The bible is being censored and filtered to make the story sound better," I said to her.

"Are you saying that Jane may be the daughter of a man and woman that had the same ancestor?" She said.

"Ellen, you were taught as a child to believe in Adam and Eve, and somewhere, somehow, Jane was born." "Both of you could have been five foot, and Jane would still be seven foot one," I told her.

I got up and excused myself. "I'll be right back." I left and returned with a book.

"Are you familiar with Doctor Frankenstein?" I asked her.

"Sure, everyone knows that story; I saw all the movies when I was younger," Ellen stated, looking at me confused.

"Then maybe what you don't know was back then they had gravediggers, and it was against the law for a doctor to practice dissecting a corpse, so they dug up fresh graves and delivered the body to doctors to examine; this was the only way a doctor knew what man looked like on the inside." "Up until then, animals were the only source of intelligence." "If surgery was required at that time, you were out of luck." "Torture can come to you in many forms, intentional or unintentional." "The pain that was delivered in surgery was enough to kill a person." "All things that are against the law at one time become a law later." "Some people are born before their time, and some people are born too late." "Of course, you have to wade through the opinions, or theory, or someone who thinks he knows about something because he read part of a sentence in a book." I said to her, "The real Doctor Frankenstein was an Italian Doctor by the name of Galvani." "He used electricity on dead animals, and when he touched a nerve, the muscle jerked." "People were shocked, and his Nephew Doctor Alvini was given the authority to use electricity on men that were executed, with the same results." "You have to understand that back then, to see something like that terrified people, so they started building mausoleums because people were afraid of being buried alive." "I'm willing to bet that none of the movies you saw or any of the articles you read had any of their names in them." "Ma'am, penicillin was discovered by mistake, so inventions may not be what you started with, but what you end up with may be the foundation of a whole new beginning." "Televisions weren't in households, and no one had air conditioning." "Now, what conveniences does man have today, and if you take them away, how do they act." "They act as if the world is coming to an end." "Thousands of tests are performed on hopeful serums." "We may fail on all of them, but it might be the next test we run that gives us our breakthrough that we're looking for; that's the way a scientist has to look at what he does." "Ellen, there is a side effect; everything that is done for the sake of good can be used for the sake of bad." "Jack knows this, and now you and your daughter know this." "No one knows anything I do or for what purpose it's done for." "If I die, and someone tries to open my vaults, all my material will be destroyed, and the computers will order my androids to disperse." "I won't let anything fall into the wrong hands." "I don't trust anyone; I told you that."

"Smith, I need you to relax." She said.

I looked at her. "There's something that's bothering you," I told her.

"Smith, I don't want to know that my daughter is here and I'm living in another place."

"Are you feeling that if your daughter stays with me, you may be losing a part of your life that you're not ready to give up yet?" I asked her.

"I may be wrong in all that I think." She said, "But one thing is certainly clear; this experience is new to me." "I'm trying to relive my life and look back at the mistakes I made and correct what I did wrong."

Jane came into the kitchen and reached out for me as she stood there crying. I sat with her in my lap and began to rock her back and forth when Jack walked in.

"Ellen, I want to ask you a personal question if I can, and Jack, no help," I told him.

"Ellen, what is Jacks's favorite food?"

"What kind of offbeat question is that?" She asked me, "We were talking about genetics and Frankenstein, and you come up with a question like that."

"You're delaying and evading the answer." I told her, "Would you like for me to speak my question slowly for you to hear and understand?"

"I heard the question." She stated

"Then, I'm waiting for an answer," I told her.

"I can't, and I don't know."

Paulie J. Johnson

"Ellen, its lasagna, heavy on the meat sauce and broiled slightly on top to crisp the cheese, then served hot with toasted French bread and a glass of iced tea without sugar." "To involve yourself with someone, you need to know everything you can." "Jack's weakness was exposed, and I took advantage of it." "The rest is history, and you two ladies are nowhere and caught up in all of this." "That's something that Jack and I discussed and came to terms with." "We kept our involvement private, one reason is, and Ellen, you're familiar with this; politics doesn't make for an enjoyable conversation." "Most people take the point of what good does it do to talk about it, you can't do anything, and another, the conversation is repetitious, it becomes rhetorical, and it doesn't make for a good relationship to speak of it, and you bear witness to that." I told her, "Ellen, whether I'm here, or whether I'm at my home, you and Jack will always be wherever you want to be, I'll not stand between you and your daughter, I don't wish to control her life, she will also be wherever she wants to be, I never expected to be a part of it, to begin with." "Jack, I want to show you something," I said to him.

"Smith, there's one thing I don't like," Ellen said before I began to get up. "You have things you don't like, and I have things that I don't like either." "I know this is something that's for those with the need to know, but I don't like it when you treat my daughter and me as if we're a third party."

"Do you play chess?" I asked her.

"No"

"Do you play checkers then?"

"No"

"Do you play cards or bingo or any games at all?"

"Not really." She said.

"Well, Ellen, you and I will have a lengthy conversation when you and Jack return."

"I'm not going with him." "We discussed this years ago, and he's better off without me." She said.

"Are you both set in your ways?" I asked her.

"What do you think, Smith?" She asked.

I stopped rocking Jane.

Jane stood up, and when she did, I stood and walked into my computer room, took a look at some of my pictures, and was greeted by the rest of the troop. I looked at all of them.

"Smith, we need to know what's going on," Ellen said.

"You do understand when I leave, you'll not be permitted to leave this place until I return, or I'm dead," I said to her.

"I understand." She said.

"Take a look at my screens." "The first picture shows the dam." "There's one road in, and one road back out, and the next picture shows that the road that goes to the camp where he keeps my cargo is connected to that same road." "Everything is connected to that one road in and out." "The camp is going to flood when I blow up the dam." "Anything downstream of that road will be swept out to sea." "The next picture shows the dam's frontal view." "That's where I set up my gifts." I saw Ellen withdrawing. "Ellen, you said you wanted to be a part of my life, this is my life, and this is Jack's life." "Neither one of us wanted this, but we've got no way out," I said to her.

"You're talking gibberish to me," Ellen said.

"Ellen," Jack said, "Smith is talking about rescuing hostages and destroying the dam.

"Can you promise me that no innocent people will get hurt?" She said to me.

I turned to her. "No, ma'am, I can't." "I can only promise you that it won't be by my hands." "I told you, I don't like wars; wars destroy every person that's involved in it, one way or another." "Very few can avoid the emotional destruction; it leaves you lifeless." "Is that the right way to look at a man that fights for his country and loses?" "I can only hope that the people that won were the right people." "If not, then a country will be purged of its problems by means of nothing less than murdering those that lost." "What do I do, Ellen?" "It's too late to buy flood insurance on a home once it's been flooded."

Ellen looked at me and gave a rebuttal. "You don't care what I think, do you?"

"You have hostility in your voice." I told her, "And in response to your comment, I do care; that's why I'm going on this mission." "Jack will tell you the same thing I tell you; you can't live in my life without living my life." "It's not me that's going to keep you away from your daughter, but you."

"Smith, momma, stop it, both of you." The girl interrupted us, "Momma, I told you to leave him alone." "Smith," Jane said, looking at me, "I don't like hearing you two getting worked up." "For one thing, Smith, you take it out on me" "and momma" "I told you Smith wasn't like any other man, you can't get flustered when you don't hear what you don't want to hear."

"No, Jane, this is something that needs to be brought to the surface and cleared up now," I told her. I turned around and typed on my computer, and an image showed up.

"This is my man here." I zoomed closer in on his eyes. "He rules by fear." I zoomed closer still. "Now, ma'am, tell me what you see."

"He has a crazed look about him; his eyes are glassy, almost like he doesn't know where he's at."

I switched to another image, exposing the eyes. "Now, tell me what you see in these eyes."

"He's angry; he has the same look as the other man."

I reduced the zoom and showed her a picture of Adolf Hitler.

I put up another pair of eyes and asked her to tell me what she saw in them.

"She looks depressed and lonely." She said.

I reduced the zoom to normal and exposed the picture; it was a picture of her.

"That's a mean and rotten thing to do." She stated to me.

"That may be, but a self-diagnosis is given to every doctor that you see." "All they do is give you a prescription to fill; they treat the symptom and not the cure."

"Ma'am, there are many things a person can learn if they want to learn something, all you need is the yearning for knowledge, and one thing I know is, we all suffer from bouts of depression or loneliness, or both, at some point or points in our life." "It's just that some people suffer from it longer than others," I told her.

"If you choose to stay here, Jack can work without bother." "If you choose to go with him, Jack can work with the knowledge that he'll be sleeping in bed with his wife. I remember the days that went by when Jack slept where I stayed." "You don't have to be a genius to know that when a woman doesn't want you around, the best place to be is somewhere else." "Between Jack's job and with the committee's he was on." "I suppose you had a good life."

"What's that supposed to mean?" She said.

"I've watched you since the first time that I saw you." I told her, "Ellen, you have the same barrier between you and the people that I have." "There's a reason for that, and I know what it is." "Ma'am, you know when people are trying to take advantage of you, and they do it because of your husband being who he is." "They don't want your help except to talk to your husband." "So, you don't associate with outside interest, and you don't socialize." "You and Jane are like me." She put her hand up to her mouth in one quick action. "Ellen, you can stay here, or you can go with your husband wherever he goes, and you can come and go as you like." "No one is forcing you to do anything except what you want to do." "The same as your daughter; she's free to do whatever she wants." "You have a good life," I said to her.

"What do you mean a good life?" She asked.

I turned around so that I didn't have to face her.

"What do you see when you look at your life?" I asked her, "Are you fulfilled?"

"Yes, I'm very happy." She quickly said.

"I don't believe you." I told her, "You put a lot of blame on Jack for not being home when he was with me. That's one reason you and he had problems when Jane was young." "How do you think I got to where I am?" I said, "He gave up part of his family life for my benefit." "I told you I recruited Jack, and he's been my liaison since we met." "When an important job came up, he had to choose his job over his family. I didn't have one, so, to me, it wasn't a question." "Jack saw me as a young boy, and he was frightened that I took on too much too fast; he thought I was out of control." "I admit I was lost then, and I didn't know it." "When I first saw you, I knew then what I had done." "I guess I've aged some; maturity makes you see things with clarity." "If you feel the need to blame someone for those years you lost, then that blame should be placed on me and not Jack." "I've told you that many times, but you still find anger in your past." I turned around to face her. "Ellen, Jack's taught me so many things, and I'm sorry for taking those years away from you, and I'm sorry for taking those years away from Jane." "If I had to do it all over again, knowing what I know today, I'd do it without Jack." "But Ellen, he didn't complain one time." "That told me a lot of things about you and him." "So, if you stay here, I'd like for you to remove that barrier of being anti-social and replace it with a look of being where you're wanted and where you want to be." "It's hard to talk to people if they're not happy, and I found it hard to talk to Jack then, and I find it hard to talk to you now." "I can't go back in time and undo what I've done."

"Smith, I keep asking myself who am I talking to?" She stated.

"That's the problem I have." "You'll see many sides of me." "I'm not one or two people, and I have multiple personalities." "Ask Jack." "One day, if we're having a conversation, that issue may come up again." "Maybe then you'll be able to give me an answer to your question." "If not, then your question should be directed to Jack," I told her.

"Jack, who's handling the trawler?" I asked him.

"His code name is Ramon." He said.

"Watch the screen." I told him, "This is a three-dimensional view of the terrain." I said as I removed the trees and the shrubbery that surrounded the hillside from the picture. I took my mouse and had my pointer appear. "Right here." I said to him, "We're dealing with a thousand-foot drop."

"What happened between you two?" Ellen asked.

Jack turned to face her and reported, "Ellen, it was politics; Smith tried to tell me that the wrong man was elected into power." "I disagreed with him, and after four years, I retired, I didn't seek reelection." "Everything unfolded just the way he told me it would, and I couldn't be a part of what was happening anymore." "He needed his grants, and I became his lobbyist." "We stayed apart because that's what he wanted, and we didn't intervene with each other's lives."

"Smith, I made one hell of a mistake, and I want you to know that won't ever happen again." He said to me. "I was wrong."

CHAPTER FIVE

Late morning I awoke to a pair of eyes looking at me.

"Do you know when you sleep, you constantly move?" Jane whispered to me, "It's almost like you were fighting something even in your sleep." "Do you know what the hard part was? I couldn't reach over and wake you to stop you." Even when you sleep, there's something that's going on in there." "Ever since I was a little girl" "I always had reminders wherever I went." "Being seven foot one, people stare and follow you around wherever you go in public." "The kids were the worst; wherever you went, there they were, staring." "You go to the mall, and everyone that passes would turn their head for a look at you, so I pretty much had to have most of my clothes made by special order." "After a while, I began thinking, what good does it do to look good." "I didn't really have any girlfriends, and I pretty much never got to meet many boys, so I had problems, and I didn't have anyone to tell them to." "It's odd to think that all that I have to do is tell the computer to deliver me whatever garment I want, and Ruby would alter them for me." "Smith, I'm still having problems excepting all of this." "I've only been here for a little while, and this is a dream world to me." "I got to noticing that where ever I went, there isn't anyone following me, asking me questions, or having to listen to someone trying to act cute." "You don't make me feel like I'm a freak." "I thought no one else had problems as tough as I did, and when I laid here watching you sleep, I knew I was way off base." "Mine is more of a physical distraction, and I can't even begin to identify all of the problems that you face inside that brain of yours."

"I'm not fighting anyone. I work in my sleep." I said to her, "When I wake up sometimes, I sketch my dreams out on paper, and they stay hidden until one day while I'm thinking about something else, something else pops into my mind, and I put two and two together, and a thought takes on the form of possibility." "The difficult part is overcoming the obstacles that stand before you, and you can't proceed on an invention until you overcome that obstacle and move on to the next one." "I just have a little problem there. I don't quit just because something stalls me." "I just put whatever I'm working on, on hold until I find a solution."

"You see things that other people can't, and you build it." Jane said, "Is there a Smith inside that mind of yours that takes time to be with me?" "Or, is the Smith that's inside of you afraid of me?" She whispered.

I put my arm around her neck and held her tight.

"From the first day you came to, there were known sacrifices that I was bound to." I acknowledged, "I can't ask you to understand how much it means to me to have you next to me; no one except my brother has been where you're at now." "But, now is now, tomorrow you may not be with those feelings that you speak of me."

"Is there something bothering you?" She asked.

"Yes"

"Were you dreaming about it, just then?"

"Yes"

"Then get up and go and do what you need to do, then." She said.

I looked into her eyes. "Jane, I had a dream you left me," I told her.

"Smith, I have those dreams about you too." "Sometimes I have two or three a night, and sometimes I wake up in my dream, and I scream and holler to the top of my lungs, but you never turn around." "No matter how fast I run after you, you keep slipping further away from me." "I'm tired of waking up crying." She announced, "My mother has a problem too. That's why she acted the way she did yesterday." "It's not her fault, she has the same feelings about you that I do, but when you talk about getting killed, it frightens her." "She doesn't mean what she says to you; she doesn't like to hear you speak about things like that." "Now, get up and go on and work on whatever you got on your mind." "Don't be surprised to see me pop in on you now and then." She said.

"You won't bother me." I told her, "Now, you made mention of you being a freak." "I wish you wouldn't use that term when you talk about yourself because you're talking about the woman I love." "I don't like that kind of language; you only used it because someone said it to you." "No one is perfect; I can vouch for that; when it comes to heaven and hell, then you may find that heaven doesn't contain anyone except children." "There are none that walk among us without the taste of sin."

"You're a man that can slay me with his words, and you can overcome my strength with your wit." She said." "You should have been a lawyer."

I smiled. "Can you see me in an office all day and talking to people."

"So, what's on the agenda?" She asked.

"I don't make plans, my time is not allotted, and perfection involves double-checking, and then you check it one more time." "Planning something doesn't come to me when I sit and think; it comes to me when I'm working on something else." "When something comes in my mind, I stop and work on the foundation of my plan that I was thinking about." "I don't work on one thing at a time, I have dozens of projects, and I proceed with each one only after knowing that I'm taking the right path." "Failure is not an option that I can accept," I said to her.

"I know it's not in my power to ask you to stop." She stated, "What do you want me to do?" "Stay out of your way, or what?"

"You can do whatever you wish," I answered, "but I prefer you to be with me or near me." "If I seem as if I'm not listening, don't be misled. I am." "If I recall, your mother and father went through this same lifestyle once your father met me." "Now, I'm causing his daughter the same nightmare that her mother went through." "You saw how she acted as you grew up, I didn't, and your father and I never spoke of it." "You'll be living in the same world that your mother did."

"Smith, my mother, and father had their moments just like every couple, but my mother was happy with my father, and I'm happy with you." "The difference between my mother and me is I want to be with you; Smith, listen real good to me; I want to be wherever you are." "You said that in your dream, I left you." "That leaves me to believe rule number one hasn't been getting the proper practice you need. That means neglect to me." "Now, we've accepted each other as two people that love one another, so, when you kiss, kiss me slowly and when you kiss me, let your kiss tell me that you love me, I don't need to hear the words, I need to feel the words." "Now, let's begin again." She said.

It was late morning before I came out of my room. I walked into my kitchen and saw that coffee had already been made. I poured myself a cup and sat down across the table from Jack and Ellen.

I took a sip of my coffee, and Ellen began a conversation.

"I'm not going with Jack when he leaves tonight." She stated, "It seems that I don't exude an elegant portrayal of a person that emits a greeting of the feeling of a warm welcome when I talk to a guest." She was taking a jab at me with her comment. I was beginning to see why Jack lost so much of his willingness to argue with her. She was relentless. "I want to apologize for my actions yesterday." "Smith" "you're not an easy man to talk to, and I get bitchy sometimes."

Jack's eyes quickly shot a glance over to her.

"Ellen, I come from country settings, and I never saw many people where I lived." I said to her, "You don't like talking to people." "I understand why, and I don't like talking to people either." "It's difficult for me to explain, the same way it's difficult for you to explain." "You were being used, and you knew it." "It's hard for you to tell people that there's a door; get up and get out." "Look at me, I can't talk to people, and you can see how I react." "You said so yourself, and I behave as if I was a person with multiple personalities." "You found out that it's not easy talking to someone that has multiple personalities." "So, you speak to others, and they see you as the person they see, or maybe sometimes, they look at you and see a person like me." "But Ellen, it doesn't matter how they see you as." "Chances are they see the same person in everyone else that they look at." "You see a person, and you see them as pretending to act the way they do, and you call this a plastic expression." "What you don't see is a person that doesn't care anything about you. They only care about themselves." "Jack shows everyone the same smile that he shows everyone else." "He's portraying himself to be a lobbyist that works for a corporation." "The ones that show him this plastic expression are the ones that give me my information; they are not without flaws." "You don't have to go with Jack; you can stay here and go wherever you want to go; no one is going to tell you what to do, except you." "So, drink your coffee, and then maybe a thought will come to you." "You don't have to look at me and ask permission to do anything." "Ruby will take your place, just like she's always done."

"I just wanted to say that I wanted to stay here and learn more about what you want to build." She said.

"If that is your decision, then it's a decision you made, and it's a decision you'll have to live with, but you can quit at any given time." "If you're not enjoying what you're doing, then your help wouldn't be any good to anyone." I told her, "Jack, it appears that we're going to have to change the way we did business." I told him. "Tonight, you'll be taking six imitators with you." "I have to protect my cargo."

I stood up and told them that the time had come for me to stop resting. I left, entered my workout room, and put on a warm-up suit. I began moving my body slowly and purposefully. I breathed air in and exhaled with control.

Several hours had gone by. I was still meditating and working my body for exercise and to remove my soreness.

I had my eyes closed.

"Hello Ellen, come in. You wouldn't be here unless something was bothering you."

"How did you know I was here?" "You never saw me." She asked.

"It was your perfume." "It's imported from France, and that fragrance pays you a compliment." "It's not strong, so you spray the wrist and then rub it into the neck."

"Smith," "I'm trying real hard, but I feel like you don't like me, and what are you doing?" She asked.

I moved slowly and answered her with the same speed I was using to practice my techniques.

"Ellen, you feel as if I don't accept you because I don't show you what you seek with my emotions. That's a part of having multiple personalities." "I only saw my father once." "I took care of my brother, and my father took him away from me." "Now, all three of them are gone." I moved and kicked slowly and then continued talking to her. "Do you want to know what it feels like to be temporarily insane; I think maybe I've been there?" "I was alone, and it felt like I was on the inside of a mirror looking out." "Ellen, I lived on a parallel universe where I could see out, but no could see in." "I taught myself at the age of four how to read and how to write, and I've been learning more and more every day." "And, it's not true that I don't like you." "Jane said I was a know it, and being "a know it all," people become offended when they find out that they were wrong, I could show them the proof." "I was able to overcome that problem by living in seclusion." "But there's been a change made." "Now, the second part of your question pertains to what I'm doing." "All body points have nerves and muscles to control offensive and defensive maneuvers." "Each move is for a purpose, so therefore, nothing is to be ignored."

I stopped and walked over and took out a movie on my shelf and inserted it into the television and then put the sound on mute." When the movie came on, I slowed the picture down to the actors moving in slow motion and went back to my exercises. I began explaining what she was watching as I went through my forms. "Pay close attention to the actor as he attacks," I told her. "Pay the same attention to the moves that their enemy uses for their defense." "Notice how the blades are passing without touching anyone." "I'll leave you alone to watch the movie." I told her, "But notice how a reaction follows each action." "The ultimate goal is to win; to lose means death." I began moving faster, and my workout began to get the better part of me; when I stopped and walked over to the chalkboard, I began drawing a picture. I went to my computer and zoomed down as low as I could to see the missile that was my target.

"Is something wrong?" "Ellen asked.

"No, something's right." "That perfume you use; you wear it to attract a man to excitement." I used my imagery to isolate and propel a three-dimensional picture onto the screen. "They use a portable air conditioning unit to keep the computers cool." "Insects are driven solely to propagate and assure that their species survives."

"So, what are you saying?" She said.

"Ellen, I found my way in." I said to her as I looked at her, "Insects and animals attract their mates by using pheromones and their scent glands." "Much like that perfume you're wearing." "My target can be killed by releasing sulfuric acid gas into the air conditioning units, and when it gets sucked up to the computers, it'll kill their communications."

"How did you come up with sulfuric acid and perfume," She asked.

"I was thinking about using insects coated with a corrosive pheromone, but the acid entered into my mind," I said to her. I left and returned to my workout. "Keep watching the movie" "and do as I say, pay attention to the force of the strike and watch the defense from a blow." "The Chinese are excellent martial artists." "The Japanese are also excellent fighters." "Boxers are difficult foes to defeat, as well as the extreme cage fighter, all of them are trained forces to be dealt with." "The ulterior goal is not to encounter them whenever possible." "But that's not always the way it turns out." I stated, "We're fortunate; we're not dealing with men trained in the art of self-defense."

"We're dealing with men that only learned how to fire a weapon into the air."
"When the element of surprise is lost, then one must depend on his ability to defeat his enemy the old fashion way." "Ellen, never underestimate an enemy; it'll get you killed." I walked over, picked up a bamboo pole, began working out, and delivered my thrusts with my sweeps and downward motions. I stopped and saw that Ellen was watching me and not the movie.

"How did you learn those things?" She asked.

"By watching those movies, just the way you are now, and doing exactly what they're doing." "To defeat an enemy, you need to know what he's weak in." "Any part of the body that is weak is your target, and all men that stand in front of you that want to kill you are the enemy." "Your objective is not to let them." "Knowledge of the art of self-defense is only useful when you are the victor," I told her as I thrust my bamboo into a pretend adversary.

"Can I come in here and work out with you?" She asked.

"You mean with the movies?" I asked her.

"They would make for some good exercise videos." She said.

"I'll be here every day, sometimes all day long." I told her, "You're welcome to come and work out anytime you wish, and Ellen, you need to stop worrying if I like you are not." "I do, but I get to thinking, and soon, I begin to annoy people."

"Smith, I like hugs, and I want one."

She walked over to me and squeezed me like Jane. She then kissed me on my forehead.

"Do you feel better?" I asked her.

"No, that hug didn't tell me exactly what I wanted to know." She stated, "My husband said that you never were a child, and to me, that tells me that you were never told that you were loved." "I told Jane that every day, that I loved her, and Smith, she'll tell you that every day, that she loves you, she's insecure." "I don't think that I have ever seen Jane as happy with her husband as I see her now when she's with you." "I don't think she married because she was happy. I think she might have gotten married because she thought I was worried she would never find anyone." "So I blamed myself when they got married. I thought I pushed her away." "Somewhere in the back of my mind, I had thoughts that what happened to her was my fault." "I know I'm a brash person, and I know that I become bossy at times." "That's something I didn't realize until someone pointed that out to me." "Then it fell on me like a ton of bricks." "I thought I knew everything about my husband, and I see you and learn that I know nothing about him at all." "You know more about him than I do, and I've been married to the man for twenty-seven years."

"Ma'am, I think the first thing that we need to clear up is your daughter's husband." "He married her solely to kill her for money. He saw her weakness and moved in on her; she became his victim when she fell in love with him; that's when he was able to carry out the plan he formulated." "There never was love involved. It was an act." "He had to have a woman that came from a respectable background, or he couldn't have been able to get an insurance package of the amount they had." "Secondly, I know nothing of what a mother has in the rights that she's entitled to." "I can only imagine that they are anything that she wishes to do, whenever she wishes to do it." "I won't put limitations or boundaries between me and you or your daughter." "That won't do Jane any good, and that won't do you any good either." "If I did, it would be laborious communicating with everyone." "Look around, and you'll see that there are four walls; I don't want people around me afraid to say anything to me." "If you wish for me to further explain to you how I feel for you, then understand my ways." "I wouldn't be having a conversation with you or answering anything you ask me." "I would tell you that it was classified material and walk away without further correspondence." "I won't have restraints put on anybody from doing as they wish." I told her, "I know what that mountain can do to a person, and if Jane decides to spend her time elsewhere, then I would be helpless to stop her." "I understand how difficult it is to live there, but that's my home."

"Hey," Jane interrupted us. "It's not polite to have a conversation about someone when that someone isn't there." She informed us as she bent over and kissed me.

"The conversation wasn't about you." I told her, "You just happened to walk in when your name came up."

I went back to working out and going through my forms. "Your mother is testing the limits of the person that her daughter is going to spend her time with, and she wants to know how I receive her." "Jane, your mother doesn't want you to be where she can't get to you." "She has to have your companionship, and she's worried that I might change the way you are," I said, summing up what Ellen's fears were.

"Don't stop now." Jane said, "You're on a roll."

I walked over and took a pair of swords down from the perch that they sat on and began using my swords to strengthen the muscles in my chest. As I worked out, I continued speaking, "We have a problem, and it's one that I have to put a lot of thought into." "It involves the both of you and Jack." "In time, I'm sure I'll come to the proper conclusion of what I must do, but for now, I have to be positive that I'm doing the right thing."

"What are you talking about?" Jane asked.

"Do you want to be happy?" I asked her.

"Well, duh, yeah." She said.

I looked at her mother. "Do you want to be happy?"

"Yes," She answered back.

"Then if I ask Jack, I would bet he would want to be happy too." "I have to figure out a way for everyone to be happy, and I don't know where to begin to start my work." I changed the topic "Ellen put the disc back on and put it on slow motion." "Watch and do as they do, try to achieve the same delivery and the blocks that they do." "Then restart the movie and watch it again, and once again watch it in slow motion and deliver your attacks as close to the positions they are in." "You have to learn to yield when the attacker becomes the aggressor, and you have to learn how to absorb the blows by yielding." "Defense is defying an enemy of his attempt to harm you without being harmed."

"An improper defense can be just as fatal as the offense, so you have to learn how to yield." "Keep doing this until you know each move by memory." "Perfect the positions of the hands and the feet and the body to that of the teachers." "They are the actors in the movie." "You couldn't find better teachers anywhere." I informed her, "When you have achieved the actions of the offense and the defense, you can then watch the movie again." "If you can master the movements with control, then I have a whole shelf full of a martial artist ready to teach you more." "That is unless you want to quit." "I saw all of those movies, and I trained my body hard to perform what was demanded of me." "I move a little slower now, but people don't realize fully how the body works." "A weightlifter can lift four hundred pounds maybe once." "A bodybuilder uses smaller weights and lifts twice as many pounds as the weightlifter lifted once." "Who was stronger of the two?" "In the art of defense, it doesn't matter how fast a person reacts." "A small movement can block a punch and cast the blows aside." "What does matter is a force of the blow that is delivered." "If you always remember one thing, to miss a target is a waste of energy, and a tired fighter is a dead fighter." I stopped my workout.

I looked and saw Ellen approaching me. When she was in front of me, I told her, "Try to hit me in the face." I said to her. When she did, I caught her hand, and then she punched me with her other hand, and I also caught it.

"You were slow." "You didn't want to hit me; I saw hesitation followed by a reaction." "But the second one was more of a test to see if I was ready to defend myself against a second attack." "The muscles in your body moved before you swung." "When you practice in the art of visual perception, you see into the mind of your enemy." "Ellen, you're not a very good enemy." "No one achieves perfection overnight, and no one maintains muscle tone unless they work at it." "Peace comes when the mind is in tune with the body, and when the body is tuned into what the mind requires from it." "Until then, you're not a student; you're letting your thoughts be somewhere else, other than where it should be." "Study the movie and learn from it; next week, we spar, and then we'll see if you enjoy the exercise or if you enjoy being able to defend yourself." "Ellen, I don't use excuses for being the person that I am, you are who you are, and no one can change you."

I started taking my weapons and began playing with them and recalling the purposes they were used for.

"Do any of you know where the fountain of youth is?" I asked with no reason as I was practicing my forms.

"Where did you come up with that?" Ellen asked as she threw her kick.

"Pick it up a little," I told her. I stopped to help her reach the right position. "You must concentrate on doing it right the first time, or you'll do it wrong every time." "Look into the mirror and see if you are identical to the person you are trying to imitate." "If you have to, pause the movie and work on that one part to do it; perfection is the key when using the art of self-defense." "There isn't any other way than the right way." "Now, I asked, do any of you know where the fountain of youth is?"

They both stopped their workout and looked at me.

"No, I guess I don't," Ellen said to me, thinking I was acting strangely.

I began explaining, "Everyone was misconceived into believing that the fountain of youth was a fountain of water that contained a potion that gave the person that drank it the gift of youth." "People heard stories as young children, or the story was told to them by teachers." "It doesn't matter; everybody envisions that magical fountain hidden someplace." "The truth is; the fountain of youth is in your mind." "For a long time, I was trapped in a young boy's body; I did my best to run away from almost all of my problems." I said while twisting my body for a sidekick and then followed up with a sweep to the feet, "One day, I grew up, and I became the man, you see." "I have aged in the body; I'm twenty-eight; I'm supposed to be at the beginning of my prime." "But my mind has always remained at the age of nineteen." "That's where the fountain of youth lies; you have to tell the body that you refuse to let it act the way it acts because of age." "A brain that thinks like a nineteen-year-old doesn't feel soreness or the aches that other people their age does." "Exercise is for the body, as well as the brain." "We punish ourselves if we don't work to keep our mind and our body in the shape that we want to stay, and for me, that's nineteen." I said, "Ellen, we did battle on overworking the body and how it does more damage than not working the body at all." "You said that we need our rest, but you can't get that rest when you force yourself to maintain a workout that pushes you hard every day." "You were right, and I was wrong; a rested body is quicker to respond to an attack faster than a tired body."

"Why do you think of things like that?" She asked.

I didn't answer. I stopped talking, walked over to my chalkboard, erased what I had drawn on it, and began working with some formulas. Several times I erased them and reconfigured my results. I still wasn't happy, and I erased it again. I went to my computers and began my design at the beginning. I started my thoughts off with the basics, and then I returned to work out with my weapons.

Soon, I was back at my computers and working out my ways to merge the compounds that I was engaged in my thoughts with.

That night, Jack left, and Jane and Ellen tired themselves from working out in the exercise room, and they fell asleep quickly. I was caught up in my projects, and Jane came and took my hand and led me away. "I need you, and I can't sleep," Jane said.

When I awoke, Jane was still asleep, and I eased myself up and out of bed and went into the kitchen and made a pot of coffee, and Ellen came walking in while I was on my second cup.

"Smith, I love my daughter, and I don't want to lose her. I'm at an impasse here." She said.

"In a little while, you may not have those worries anymore." I told her, "So until then understand, I'll not be myself when I speak; I speak to myself, and I answer questions with more questions to get the answers to the questions that I ask."

"You're talking in riddles to me." She said.

"Are you still at an impasse?" I asked her.

"Yes." She answered.

"Ma'am, when you and Jack argued, did you ever want to strike out in anger at him physically?"

"What are you getting at?" She asked.

"Nothing, ma'am, I was wondering if a person like you could experience a point in which she reached a level that she would want to harm someone that she loved," I said as I sat my cup down and went into my exercise room.

"Smith, are you mad at me, or do you want to be alone?" She said, sounding concerned as she followed me in.

I began going through my forms slowly to stretch my muscles.

"Ellen, I'm not mad at you, and I don't mind you being here." "If I were mad at you, I'd tell you to leave, or I would tell the computer to close the doors behind me after I entered." "You're trying too hard to be close to me when you shouldn't be trying at all." I put the movie in that she and Jane were working out the day before and told her to show me some of the kicks and punches she remembered. She began on offense, and I blocked her moves easily.

"How do you feel?" I asked her as we were battling.

"A lot better if I was connecting." She said.

"Remember, a blow that is missed is energy that is wasted," I told her.

I took the attack and stopped short of hitting her on each blow or kick I delivered. Each time I stopped, she could feel the palm of my hand or the ball of my foot, but no pain was given as it brushed the side of her face. "You've trained before." I said, "You react to defense better than you react in the offense."

"I took some classes, but I didn't take them seriously." "I quit after about six months or so." She said as she stopped fighting, "Smith, about me leaving you alone." She said.

"Ellen, your daughter is in love with a man that's half crazy, and I don't think you'll give me any arguments there." I told her, "She was going through a rough period when we met."

"Do you think you're crazy?" She asked me.

"Ma'am, that's a decision that is reserved for the observer." I said to her, "You've had problems with me because you don't understand someone like me." "All of this that you see only comes alive on television; this is where movies come from." "To you, there isn't anything happening like this in the real world." "It's just make-believe, and we're all on a movie set."

"Smith, are you picking my brain again?" She asked.

"Ma'am, have you woke up at night since you've been here and looked around thinking you were home and you had a bad dream?" I asked as I began going through the rest of my workout. I pushed myself by moving to a much greater speed. I felt the pain, and I used my thoughts to deaden the feelings. I watched as Ellen watched me. The power and the speed began flowing through my body. I felt alive and fighting the foes that stood before me. I walked over and took twelve star-shaped metal discs from the shelf. They were round and had six points that were one inch long protruding from them. I tossed the first one, followed by the second one, and so on. All delivered thirty feet away, and all were striking the neck of the mannequin that I used, the last star severed the head.

Now Ellen was staring at me with a great deal of awe.

I walked back over and grabbed a handful of knives. I looked at my target and began throwing one after the other less than three seconds apart. They all struck my heart, and I saw the lady staring at me again.

I then looked at her. "No man wants to be put in that kind of a situation, but sometimes it can't be avoided." "Ellen, if you knew of a man like me, and you found me to be doing what was right, but you kept silent about him, would that make you a sane person, or would that you an insane person?"

"Why ask me?" She said.

I walked away and began running on the track. Soon she was running with me.

I looked over at her and asked, "Are you pushing me, or am I pushing you?"

"Smith, what did you mean just then?" She asked.

"Ma'am, I gave a lot of thought into who I was." "For a long time, I didn't care about anything." "Now, I don't have those thoughts anymore, Jane believes in me, but ma'am, today is today. Do you seriously think Jane can tolerate someone like me?"

"Do you love Jane?" She asked me.

"This is not supposed to be," I said to her.

"That's not what I asked you." "Do you love Jane?" She asked again.

I took a deep breath and exhaled. "I think she's as beautiful now as when I saw her at the party," I said.

"Smith, do you know how much that meant to her to see that drawing you gave her?" "Jack couldn't tell me what I was wearing when he left." "Let alone what I was wearing when we met."

"That's not true," I said.

"What?" She looked at me, confused.

"He said when he first saw you, you were playing tennis with a girlfriend of yours." "Ellen, he admired those long legs you have." "It was the second time he saw you, he said, and it was the first time you saw him when he introduced himself to you." "It wasn't by accident; do you think those tickets that your girlfriend got to go to the football game where he happened to be the man sitting next to you was by chance?" "Do you think that the restaurant that you and you're parents went to the night he was sitting at the table next to you was by chance?" "Do you think that the mall where he happened to run into you was by chance?" "Ellen, you were set up each time, and you took the bait," I told her.

"All this time, and he never told me." As she looked over at me, "Smith, what drives someone like you to be this way?" She asked. "You're a very brilliant man."

"I don't think anyone grows up thinking that they would be involved in matters like this." I said to her, "Our mail lady would drop off books by mistake now and then, and I read them to my brother and showed him pictures in the magazines." "I was reading a story to my brother about Doc Holiday." "He was a man that had an education in his background." I said to her while running, "He had tuberculosis and knew he was dying." "He drank to help kill the pain he had, and I don't know if he had a thirst for alcohol. That's a part of history that's open for debate." "He was fast with a gun and took offense easily, so people were respectful when they were around him." "He had a death wish, though, and that was to find the man that could outdraw him and put him in his grave." "No one did. He died in pain, begging for the reaper." "In the end, he got his respect." "He was a notorious gunfighter that faced the young and the old with only one outcome." "The young were quick; they carried their pistols with triggers filed down, but he was quicker." "The old was smart, lacking quickness of the youth; they carried shotguns." "That's the way most of the problems were taken care of back then, no witnesses, and you didn't have to outdraw a gunslinger." "It didn't happen the way you see it in movies." "It was depicted as two men facing each other and the man wearing a white hat waiting on the bad guy to draw first."

"Most people were killed by ambush." "It's difficult to place fact with fiction." "Writers sold what was called dime novels; because they cost a dime." "They made legends out of the gunfighters and mountain men, and they sold their books fast." "People that lived in the North, South, and East couldn't get enough, they wanted more, and the writers gave them all they could read." "Ninety percent of the stories were made up." "Ellen, the gunfight at the O.K. Corral didn't happen at the corral, it was in the alley near the corral, and the gunfight only lasted for around fifteen seconds." "But people believed what they read then, the same as they do now." "He could have let someone kill him and put an end to his life, but he didn't." "He only killed those that tried to kill him; his instincts to survive were strong." "Ellen, I don't fear death, I saw what it looked like, and I accept it." "After all, I can't stop it," I told her.

"I did a little thinking about what you said last night." She said, "You were right; you mentioned the fountain of youth as being in your mind." "I had problems with that one at first, but I can feel a little age creeping in on me." "I looked in the mirror this morning, and I didn't like what I saw."

"Ma'am, a nineteen-year-old can jump from a porch, and he's going to feel the pain when he lands." "A person with age can jump from that porch, and he's going to feel the same pain that the nineteen-year-old did, except the man with age, walks over and walks down the steps because he knows he'll feel the pain that will be delivered once he hits the ground." "That doesn't mean he is an old man, he still feels nineteen, but he has the wisdom that a nineteen-year-old doesn't." "Mix both of them, and common sense over-rules and replaces intelligence." "You're looking out of breath if you don't mind me saying so," I told her.

"I can take it." She said, so we continued until she couldn't go anymore and had to stop.

When she did, I walked into my computer room, sat down at my control panel, and started work. Soon I could hear breathing coming from the back of my neck.

"What are you doing?" She asked.

"I have to drop from the air, unannounced." "I've been working on a project for four years, and I was thinking," I said to her without looking up at her. I fidgeted around with my computer, and soon, a video came on.

"Watch this," "this is an albatross," "he's not made for takeoffs or landings, but in the air, he floats on the currents, much like that of the eagle, or the vultures, or the condors." I changed the video to a pterodactyl. "He's a glider like an albatross." "His skin was thin, but he could fold up his wings," I said to her as she watched the video.

I began working on my computer and started my animation in progress. "I weigh two hundred, and with my equipment, I'll be looking at two-thirty, two thirty-five maybe," I said under my breath to myself.

"What do they have anything to do with you?" She asked.

"That's my ride down from the plane." I told her, "I can't use a parachute." "I can be spotted."

"What if it doesn't work?"

"Then the mission will be a failure from the beginning." I told her, "Like those rolls you made, if they didn't rise, then no rolls."

"So this is a place where you build these inventions of yours?"

"Their prototypes, they're not inventions." "Ellen, I come here to prepare myself to kill." "I design weapons to destroy weapons." "The invention of the Gatlin gun was the door opening on man building a weapon that gave him the upper hand, the same as the caveman that invented the wheel." "He probably didn't know at the time how many people that wheel was going to kill from that one simple idea." "So you have to ask yourself if mother necessity is the root to all inventions, did the caveman invent the wheel to move the meat he killed, back to camp, or did he create the wheel to use it for killing, and if not, then who was the first person that set those wheels in motion?" "Combine that wheel to the gun, and you had the Gatlin gun that had the force of a hundred men ready to fire in a pattern that mowed men down without mercy, and all it took was the turn of a handle." "We are limited only by our imagination in what we can achieve." "My lab is not a place I like to be, I'm here for a purpose, and I don't like to be here, but maybe one day you'll understand that I'm here because I have to be." "Just like it was back in the old west." "For every fifteen outlaws, you had one lawman." "I don't know who I am," I told her.

She turned around and left. I was alone for the rest of the night, and I went to work on my projects.

I worked long into the night and didn't notice Jane when she walked in.

"What are you building?" She said.

"I'm doing a little reconfiguring and making some changes," I said.

"What is it?" She asked.

"It's a prototype that I call the pterodactyl." "I'll make my jump at twenty-four thousand feet," I said to her.

"What's it for?" She asked.

"Computer: Display animation of the pterodactyl," I commanded, and Jane watched my screens.

"You're not serious?" She said.

I just looked at her with a smile.

"My mom was with you tonight, wasn't she?" She said as I was changing the length of some rods to change the support angle on the wings.

"What makes you think that?"

"You're acting strange." She said, "My mother doesn't talk to too many people." "Smith, she wants to make a good impression on you. You don't know what this means to her." She said as she bent down and kissed me. Her hand touched me on my chest, and she caught herself trying not to touch me, and then she gave me a closer inspection by opening my robe. "What is this?"

"Something didn't feel right with my other vest, so I molded this one into a modified version of my shield." "It's similar to my skin, but this one doesn't feel tight." "I've been wearing it since last night," I said to her.

"It feels and looks like real skin." She replied.

"Yeah, and all I had to do was go on the internet, and I got thousands of ideas." "I put two and two together and came up with this." "I built this one with an adjustable Freon cooling system." "The other one made me sweat inside." I crossed my arms and took hold of the bottom and peeled it off like a tee-shirt, and she became silent and looked at me again.

"Your unbelievable." She said, putting her hand on my scars and feeling them.

"Jane, remember when I told you, I'm not myself when I'm not at my place." "You wouldn't be able to recognize me beyond these walls; outside of my lab, I'm not the man I am here." "I studied some makeup artists training films, I envision a character in my mind and paint my portrayal, and become who I pretend to be." "I made your father mad one night." "It was a full moon shining down, and I dressed up like Quasi Moto, you know the hunchback of Notre dame." "I began running around and jumping from rooftop to rooftop swinging my arms, and I heard the cops coming because the sirens were wailing, and the dogs started making all kinds of a commotion." "Had it been Halloween, nobody would have paid me any attention." "I ended up back in my room, and soon, your father came running in, and I was sitting on my bed reading, and he was out of breath." "He looked hard at me and then said, that was you, wasn't it?" "I gave him a few seconds to catch his breath, and then he began to start smiling and then chuckled until he began laughing." "He looked over at me." "You know what you have done, he said." "Those people out there are all telling the police stories of what they saw." "They're all looking for you." "Do you feel better now, he asked me."

"Jane, your father never once tried to stop me from doing anything that I wanted to do, and he shielded me from everyone; he told me that everyone had to vent their frustrations or anger, or whatever hurt them, and what harm was I doing, he said." "Jane, if your father hadn't taken me away when he did, I don't know where I would be." "So, when he needed assistance, I was there for him; when I needed assistance, he was there for me." "He's here now. That should give you the testament that's needed to show you of his loyalty." "You should have seen him when I made your mother; he was like her." "Our meeting brought together two people in his life that was separated." "A daughter that he tried to raise and a boy that was not what he expected." "After that, I started working on him." "When he saw himself, he didn't know what to think." "Your father left me alone and let me train and workout and build my androids." "I'm self-taught in all that I do." "That's one of the things he understood about me." "I didn't need tutoring, and that eliminated leaks." "I preferred my solitude, and he gave me all that I needed."

I returned to my control panel and began typing.

"What are you doing now?" She asked.

"My contact" "Ramon" "has a girlfriend." "Ramon is the informer that the agent warned me about." "He's a double agent, and I'm not leaving any stones unturned." I looked over at her. "I've been working on something; I need a tester; will you volunteer?" I asked her.

"Not if it involves being thrown out of something or being shot?" She said, smiling.

"No, nothing like that; it's a simple sniff test." I walked over, took a piece of paper, squeezed a small fluid container onto it, and then asked her to sniff it. She eased her nose down and sniffed lightly, and quickly jolted her head upwards, holding her nose. "Ewww, that stuff stinks." She replied.

"I call it the essence of skunk," I told her. "I used a mixture of chemical compounds, and the result was my essence of skunk." "Imagine a pot of a mixture boiling, and when the mixture is cured and removed, only the thick molasses-like mixture remains." "Its power is ten times the smell you smell on the paper." "The goal is to catch an enemy off guard and make them believe they are under a gas attack and keep them at bay." "If three minutes is enough to get in and get out, my essence of skunk might be useful one day." "I had to wear a gas mask when I made it." "That was five years ago, and it's been fermenting since then."

"I thought you quit?" The girl said.

"I came for supplies and to drop off my work when I came here." "I did a little, but I didn't do too much," I told her.

"Lay down on the couch with your head in my lap." She said. "I want to talk about something."

She held my hand as we both walked over to the couch, and I did as she asked me to do. I felt her hand as she stroked my forehead slowly. She started speaking in a low voice, which became lower and lower. I awoke that evening to both of the ladies sitting in the hot tub. I walked into my room, put on my trunks, and joined them.

"That was a rotten thing you did to me this morning," I said to Jane.

"You were tired, and you needed rest; you were fighting it." "Smith, working two, three days without sleep, doesn't do anyone any good." "But, I know you better than you think I know you." "You can work tirelessly for days but sit still for a few moments, and you doze." She said as she smiled at me, "I told you, I know your weakness, and you needed more sleep than what you were getting."

"When did you discover this? I stated to her.

"In the sleeping bag, you fought me, but you always dozed off." She replied.

"I underestimated you." I told her, "I won't let that happen again."

This time it was her mother that commented.

"You're a tough nut to crack; you know that?" "A man is supposed to be predictable, but I don't find you to be like that at all."

"I never had anyone tell me to do anything," I said to her, "so I find it to be difficult when others tell me to do something." "I don't like it, and I react the best way I know-how. I turn and walk away and leave whoever thinks that they can tell me what I am to do." "If left alone, I achieve my goals of calming a situation." "No arguments can be argued if there's no one to argue with." "If they can't be achieved, I take offense." "I encountered a man one time that was getting cocky and carrying out an act of his manhood." "He was loaded in ammunition. He was invincible; the alcohol encouraged his boasts." "Three hits later." "He had each arm broken, and his nose was broken." "To make matters worse, I ripped his nose ring and his earrings out that he wore." "I can still hear his screams." "His friends opened their ring that they had formed around us for the fight, and as I walked towards them, I walked through that opening they give me, and I never bothered to look back." "He was a man that was around my age now, and he liked to show off his body." "The weather was around sixty or so, but he wore a tight shirt without sleeves to allow his abdomen and muscles to be seen easily in his arms." "I walked by, and he made a smart remark to me to impress the girls that were around him." "The problem was, I knew beforehand what he was going to do, I had seen him looking at me as I was walking up, and he commented on one word." "He called me a wimp." "I stopped and took a deep breath and then resumed walking." "He made a louder boast, and as I walked nearer, he got louder, and his friends began laughing." "I stopped and thought to myself for a moment, by the way he acted, he was going to fight someone that night, and I just happened to come along at the right time." "I thought I did wrong in what I did." "But then I thought, what if he was to hurt someone? After all, it seemed to me that he was going to have an altercation sooner or later."

"Me walking away might have boosted his ego some into thinking he was tougher than what he thought." "And then I got to thinking, what if he found someone that would accommodate him, only the person that accommodated him, could have had a knife or a gun." "I went back and calmly asked him to leave me alone and that he should go back to where he lived or where he was staying before he got hurt." "When I saw his friends beginning to form a ring around us, I could sense the excitement and tenseness in the crowd he drew." "I looked around, and all I could see was people that wanted to see me get hurt." "He was bigger than me." "I knew he was going to respond, there were too many people there for him not to, and when he did, he never finished his first word." "When it was over, I threw his nose ring, and his ear ring back on his chest and listened as I turned to walk away to hear that no one was laughing anymore, the silence told me that they weren't expecting what they had seen." "They expected me to be beaten to a pulp, and they wanted to see it come out that way." "I felt bad on my walk back for what I have done, and I didn't sleep for almost a week." "I let my anger overcome me, and I used force when I didn't have to. I could have walked away, but if I did, someone was going to be his victim."

"But the guy sounded as if he had it coming to him," Ellen responded.

"That may be, but when you train to prepare yourself for defense, it doesn't seem right when you take an offensive position and inflict damage to a person that you know you can beat by walking away from a conflict." "It makes you feel like you don't truly understand what you practice for." "I let rage overcome me and reacted like a Neanderthal; I lowered my intelligence level and acted like him." "He may have been a recipient of the injuries, but I was a loser too."

"Still, he sounded like he had it coming." She said. "And like you said, he could have hurt someone else."

"Well, he was going to have to find a different way to get his pecks and his six-pack abs to stay where they were." "His problem was by the way he looked and pumped his muscles to the girls, he was doing steroids, and he wasn't shy in the amount he used to get them that way." "As I said, he was bigger than me, and I didn't refrain in my attack. I meant to do what I did to him."

"You look like a man that has a body of his own," Ellen responded in turn.

"I first started building my house of stone by carrying rocks from the river to the house." "When I first started, I had to stop five or six, or even more times to take a break before I reached my little place." "I carried all the rocks from the river to my house and laid them in a pile." "It took me almost a month before I had enough to begin building my mansion of stone." "I spent more than a few nights sleeping under my dome while it rained."

"Your dome?" Ellen commented.

"Shh, momma," "I'll tell you later." Go ahead, Jane said.

"I was working one day, and a thought came to my mind." "I had read in a book about a man speaking to another man about carrying a calf every day up a hill. He said by the time that that calf gets full-grown, he would be able to carry the cow." "That's not a true statement; it was a figure of speech." "But, I worked until noontime, and when I stopped to rest, I looked at my stones and reached down and picked one of them up, and began to carry it to the river and then stop and carry it back." "It took me nine months before I could carry the stone from my place to the river and back without having to stop." "I did that every day, and I never stopped." "The following year, I found a larger stone and carried it the same way, back and forth to the river that was two hundred yards away." "I counted each step to remove the thought of the burden I was carrying, and like before, the added weight caused me to work until I tired, and then I would rest and then continue in my quest." "I knew the walk was sixty-six and two-thirds of a step to the river." "The stone being heavier now made my steps shorter." "I would start in the low nineties, and I struggled with my stone until I could carry it sixty-six and two-thirds of a step one way, and sixty-six and two-thirds of a step back, without stopping."

"I carried that stone like I had done the other stone, and the stone got lighter and lighter." "Today, I still carry that same stone." "I didn't challenge myself to a heavier weight. I don't need mass. I need strength," I said. "I carried that weight, but when I came in contact with your daughter, I didn't have much time of my own to do anything; she required all of my attention."

I saw Jane smiling.

"Is there something that I said?" I asked her.

"No, I was remembering when you were picking me up and carrying me when I needed to go to the bathroom." "I wasn't a chore for you; you never seemed to struggle when you carried me." "My husband couldn't do that, and back then, it crossed my mind, and now hearing the story you just told sheds some light." She told me and then continued, "A hundred and sixty pounds isn't a sack of flour."

"My daughter showed me the clothes you made for her." "Where did the skins come from?" Ellen asked.

"I was visited by the bears and the wolves and mountain lions trying to get at the meat that I had in the shed and the smokehouse." "I chased them off now and then, I wanted to persuade them not to come back, or they would eventually give me trouble." "Animals are pretty smart, and some of them are smarter than the rest." "I got to working, and one day I got a thought of my own, and on my next trip to get supplies, I ordered some firecrackers." "When they visited, I found out that a small pack, when lit and thrown out a small hole, did a better job." "After a while, they didn't come around anymore, and they allowed me my territory." "Ma'am, a person that milks a cow can milk that cow for a week, maybe two, but sooner or later, the cow is going to kick whoever is milking it." "It's like that when you live in bear country; you have to pack for bear confrontations." "I carry an elephant gun wherever I go." "My intentions were not to kill, but not be killed, and if threatened, I had to put an end to those that became aggressive, the quickest way that I could." "I would have been stalked every time I was seen." "I've only had to kill three of them. All the rest retreated upon my sight." "Two came into a cave that I visited uninvited and gave me notice to leave; they both greeted me with intentions of killing me." "I shot one when he reared up to show me his strength and size, and he went rolling backward." "I never had to use the other round." "The second one came in the same way, two months later, only he crouched low, I fired, and he was hit hard." "I fired again, and that put an end to him." "The third one came charging at me from across a bluff. He was running at me at full speed." "I didn't have time to think." "I fired, and he kept coming, I fired again, and he rolled down the embankment where I shot him at." "I came up with one of my thirty-thirty rifles that were on each of my shoulders and fired all six rounds." "My heart was pumping blood fast."

"The others considered me to be bad business and avoided me, the way I avoided them if I could." "Those three, I couldn't." "I was feared by the other predators and never really encountered any activity after that. I talked to myself out loud so that I could be heard coming." "The ones I saw either were curious, or they were to be dealt with." "After a few rounds that killed the aggressive ones, the other predators got to know me and lived with me." "I started carrying firecrackers wherever I went after that and gave notice I was in the area." "We had a mutual understanding; leave me alone, and I'll leave you alone." "I believe the cat was attacking your daughter because she was wearing those skins." "I don't have a big place, your daughter can tell you that, but it's big enough for me." I felt Jane turn her head. "And, I'll have to make it bigger; Jane has a problem sleeping when she can't extend her legs out far enough." I felt an arm come around me and squeeze me.

"What about me?" The lady asked.

"It's not a place for a woman like you; you're used to going to local restaurants or buying that French perfume you wear at the mall." "Where I live, you don't wear makeup or even shave your legs, there isn't anyone there to see them, and you won't be walking around bare-skinned anyway." "I don't want to sound rude, ma'am, but you won't need to dye your hair; there's not anyone there that will see you." "That's the place where I live, at the edge of nowhere, go too far, and you'll fall off the earth," I said.

"Then why live there?" She asked.

I hesitated momentarily. "That's a tough one," I said and then answered her. "Imagine the life of a person that lived fifty years ago. Could you live back then the way they did?" "Now, imagine living a hundred years ago; could you live the way they did?" "Now, imagine living two hundred years ago; could you live the way they did?" "They had to, they didn't know anything else, but your ancestors had to survive long enough for you to get here." "They had to survive Mother Nature in her maddest of moments." "To get to where they were going, they depended on guides to get them through the mountains." "They were immigrants on their way to somewhere from someplace, and the languages were many." "They didn't know much about how to drive a team of mules to pull their wagons, let alone how to get to where they were going." "That's why they hired trail bosses to guide them along." "The passes were the tough part; during wintertime, some passes were snowed in like your daughter was with me; she was trapped by winter." "Most of the people died of diseases and from the harshness of the weather, and very few survived once winter caught them off guard; they weren't prepared for what was to come." "The guides knew, and some lit out before the bad weather hit, leaving those people behind to die." "Who was going to turn you in? Some guides never intended on completing their part of the deal from the start, a month or two into the journey, and they would never come back from a scouting trip." "They knew if the horse couldn't walk in the snow, they were dead, and they would high tail it to a pass a week's ride away, but wagon trains moved slowly, and they couldn't navigate some of the terrains." "What took a horse a week, took a wagon a month, or more." "Two hundred years ago, mountain men roamed all of this and that area." "They were pioneers looking for gold and pelts of furs to trade for their goods, such as coffee and food." "They lived here because most of them were on the run for a crime, and this was the only place the law wouldn't come looking for them." "Back then, the only transportation you could depend on was a good horse or a sure-footed mule." "When they died or got killed by a bear, or a cougar or the wolves, you ate the meat and then set out on foot."

"That was the only choice you had." "Wintertime showed no mercy for the weak or the dim-witted; she was merciless in her delivery." "Nor easterner's came roaring through with winds blowing at ninety miles an hour and temperatures dropped to twenty to thirty degrees below zero, that is if you were lucky." "The snow-covered most of the evidence, and when morning time arrived, some areas would get up to ten to twenty feet of snow, or more burying all of the pioneers." "If you were lucky and you did survive the night, you may not survive the avalanche from the weight of the snowdrifts that piled up against the side of the mountain you were under." "Jane's husband wasn't a pioneer; he knew what he was doing." "But he made one mistake."

"He's somewhere up there in the pass that lies in between my place and here." "Mother winter claimed him the same way that the wagon trains found themselves to be in, caught in the middle of winter, in a storm." "He couldn't find the can of gas he left from all the snow covering everything up." "No one will be sent to look for him till winter slips into spring." "It won't matter anyway; he's bear meat." "Ellen, do you find that to be upsetting?" I asked her.

"My daughter would be dead if you hadn't have been there; he got what he had come to him." She blurted out, with an ugly tone to her voice.

"So, to you, he wasn't entitled to a fair trial then." I said, "Ellen he was someone's son, and if his parents are alive, they grieve for him." "I'm sure they would have feelings for your daughter, but they grieve for their son, and now they will carry a burden of what he did for the rest of their lives." "I feel sorry for them." "They will do battle with good and evil, and Ellen, it's a battle that no one can win." "You have to release the hostility that you hold for him, or you'll be trapped like me when I could have walked away and not vent my anger on that boy." "Anger is only a part of what causes those that are considered to be normal to engage in an act to be abnormal." "But to be truthful, I reached for my gun as soon as I saw what he did to your daughter, but by the time I reached my gun, he was out of sight." "As far as me living in my house of stone, I was on a scouting trip and looked down into the valley below; I wanted to set up camp and see the sight come morning." "The third bear stopped me from doing so." "By the time I skinned him to tan his hide, I saw four more bears that day."

"A few months later, I discovered why I seen so many bears." "The stretch where I wanted to set up camp only had about four hundred yards between the mountain and the cliffs that were on each side." "They had to come through there to get past the mountain or travel along the valley below." "Bears being cautious travel high ground, the scent from below is carried by an updraft, and they could tell if danger was near." "The bear that came charging me did just that." "Like the mountain men, I live there because it's the only place that man won't come looking for me, I had my privacy, and I was at peace with myself, at least that's what I thought." "That's all been changed, I'm here, and there's a reason I'm here." "You know that reason, and you know me, now you know why I wanted my privacy." "You want to share your life with me in a more definitive way; you want to be more than friends with me." "You talked to your husband about me, didn't you?" I said to her. She didn't answer.

"Come on, Ellen, it's human nature to ask questions about someone that you're with; you can ask Jane that." I told her, "I asked him about what you did, and he said that even when he was with you, he wasn't with you." "I asked him what he meant by that, and he said, Ellen and I don't like talking about my job, I'm not comfortable discussing the matter, and I left it at that."

"You were right; he won't talk about you." She stated, "So I started watching you more and talking to you more, and I found out more." "He didn't tell me anything; you told me everything." "Why?" She asked.

"That's difficult to answer," I said to her. "Jack's a loyal man." "Right now, there's been a threat of nuclear arms falling into the wrong hands, and no one is resting easy." "Jack and I have worked together on other areas that produced problematic hot spots. "If I'm successful, a threat will be dissolved, and if I'm not successful, then Ellen, you may get a front-row seat to see the world at war." "I won't know it; I'll be dead, and the one thing that hurts me the most is I was fighting for the people that didn't want to get involved in government, so they never knew, and for the most part, they didn't care."

"So, you have problems talking to people, and that's what makes you want to run away from them?" She said.

"Yes," I told her, "I'd be wasting my time." "Ellen, I find myself speaking bluntly and to the point." "I give commands, and I read people by their actions or by the lack of their actions." "Either one, I can see who I'm dealing with." "You know me only for one reason, and that's because of Jane."

"I didn't know how to approach her with the problem she was in when she woke up in her strange surroundings with a man that she didn't know." "If it had happened to you, you would have been scared just like her." "I wasn't willing to tell her things that she wanted to know, so I was hesitant in my responses." I continued, "I don't know what happened; when she said she loved me, I was caught off guard and unprepared." "I lacked the courage to tell her, and as the time went by." "I couldn't deceive her anymore, and my convictions forced me to release the reason why; I had to tell her, and I had to tell her the truth." "I'm sorry, Ellen; I found that I couldn't deceive you either; I choose to be involved, my way." "Ellen, do you know what the first signs of insanity are?" I asked her.

"No," She responded.

I then continued, "No doctor can tell you either; they can only evaluate a person, sane or insane, but only after giving you several tests." "Since you've been here, you've experienced several releases of the mental stresses that you carried with you for a long time." "You were teetering on the edge of the first signs of insanity." "You felt the pains of withdrawal that Jane did." "You fueled your depression with loneliness, and Jane did too." "Both of you now understand how much you both need each other." I changed the subject.

"Jack's going to be coming in tomorrow evening." I said as I looked down at the water and then continued." "Ma'am, I do have multiple personalities, but not the way you think. They're selective. I transform and mold myself into the character to be successful in my mission." "There were times in your life that when Jack came to spend his nights with me, I saw his problems as he slept." "I knew he was unhappy because he would wake up early and take naps as he sat down." "He never did that when he was happy, he could sleep till late morning, and I'd tease him a little by telling him good afternoon." "Ma'am" "In anger, you transformed from the person you are into a person that you're not." "Isn't that a person with more than one personality?" "So if you two had problems, you are concerned about your daughter and me when we have problems, and that's the problem you have, you know we're going to have problems, and you can't do anything about it." "You want what you can't have because time is a barrier, it blocks you from knowing the outcome of your daughter's future, and that's what frightens you the most." "Not knowing her future." "So, you pretty much made a vow of your own, and that vow was not to let go of your daughter again. You're here to protect her, but I pose to be an obstacle to you." "You've vented your anger with me more than several times." "Ma'am, if you'll forgive me, I told you that I speak bluntly and to the point, and I apologize, but I see a person that's tired; you're the one that's been running from her life, not me."

"Is he right, momma?" Jane asked her.

"Yes," She said. "So, what do I do now?" She questioned.

"Jane says she's happy, and she won't be if you live somewhere where you're not nearby; that point has been established." "You're not only her mother but her friend, so we wait, and we let the future unfold," I told her. "I'm not in a position to make guarantees, but it seems like you'll be a part of her life for a long, long, long, long time."

I saw the expression on her face manifest into a different expression.

"Ma'am, life is strange; it has a way of changing with a birth; it calls for calmer heads to prevail." "Without Jane, you and Jack could be divorced, and he might not have been there for me to help me find my way." "Do you find it strange that all these things came to pass because of Jane?" "I know I do." "Ellen, your life ended the day Jane got married." "You should be happy; she'll never leave you again," I told her.

CHAPTER SIX

"How do you do that?" Jane asked as I woke from my sleep. She had been watching me sleep again.

"Do what?"

"You were sleeping soundly, and when I started watching you, you started to get restless and woke up." "It's almost like you felt me watching you." She answered.

"It must be this mattress." I told her, "I'm used to my bedroll." I then leaned over to her and gave her a kiss.

"Wow." "I'm honored." She spoke with a sarcastic tone. "I didn't even have to beg for it." "We're making great progress." She said as she pulled herself to me. I returned her affection by putting my arm around her and gently holding her.

"Smith, do you ever wish you were back there at your place, and none of this ever happened?" She questioned.

I didn't answer her quickly. "I never gave it a second thought." I began, "I was caught up in a circumstance where I wasn't in any position to protest, one way or the other." "Jane, back at my stone house, I watched you as you slept, much like when I wake up and find you watching me." "I was frightened of you."

"What for?" She asked.

"I told you that I'm not a person that someone can live with." I told her, "I saw that assessment comes to reality many times over." "I never could stay anywhere; my house was my home." "Living in seclusion has its pitfalls." "All you have is time, and the only way you can kill time is to work it to death."

"Smith, what do you think I'm thinking when I watch you sleep?" She asked me. "You may be a brilliant man, but you're human." "You have felt the same as everyone else, you need to have someone to love, and you need to have someone that loves you." "I have a confession." "When you got into your bedroll to warm me back at your place, I could feel you shaking." "After a while, I knew it wasn't from the cold; we were both sweating." "I don't know what it was, but there was something about you." "I was like a little schoolgirl with a big crush on her teacher." "I started to fall in love with a man that I didn't know, and to make matters worse. I don't know how it happened." "I thought this couldn't be, but it happened." "When I woke up in the cave, I thought I was dreaming, Smith. I knew then and there. I was starting to fall in love with you." "I knew it too early, but after I got to thinking about my husband, I realized that he never was in love with me." "I thought I had enough love for the both of us to weather out any storms that came up." "But, I knew I was wrong." "No two people can survive in a relationship with a one-sided love." "I found that out on a firsthand experience." "Smith, I still feel like a little school girl when I'm around you, and when you kissed me this morning, I was assured that my worry about me being in a one-sided love affair was all in vain." "It told me everything that I needed to know, and all those worries that I had about you vanished." "And it was all because of that one little kiss."

"Jane." I stopped her from speaking any further. "I love you." She was startled and acted somewhat surprised. "You know a kiss is only part of what you need to tell you, everything that you need to know," I said to her. "I never said the words I love you to anyone other than you, and other than your parents and me, you've never heard those words spoken from anyone else either," I told her.

"You're speaking about my husband, aren't you?"

"Yes"

"How did you know?" She asked.

"When I pulled you out of the snow, I could see a girl out of place, and you had an emptiness about you." "When I was giving you a bath, and sewing you up, I held you in the water at healing waters, and I looked real hard at you, I could see you closer; you had the same look; you were a girl that was out of place, and you had an emptiness about you." "I was at a loss, and it's taken me until now to figure it out." "When I first told you, I loved you." "You wore a shine on your face then, and you have that same shine to your face now." "You don't have the face of a girl that's out of place when you talk to me; you wear a smile of happiness." "I didn't know he never said he loved you, not until you showed me by your smile. I was just trying to see if the pieces to the puzzle fit in." "Your mother told me that she didn't have a problem when she talked to your father." "She said she felt comfortable around him." "I think I know what she meant because I feel comfortable around you, and even with your father, I've never felt that way about anyone before."

"You talk too much," she said, "and when you're talking, that means you're not practicing on rule number one."

She then rolled over on top of me and began exercising her lips with her kisses. I gave her back all the reassurance she needed.

Later that morning, we walked out of our room to witness her mother sitting at the table. When she saw us coming, she got up and poured us a cup of coffee and set it down at the table when we arrived.

"You been up for long?" I asked her.

"A couple of hours or so." She remarked.

I took a sip of my coffee and then gave her a look.

"You're in a warm-up outfit, and you're wet with sweat. This coffee is a fresh pot; you just got through working out?" I said to her.

"I don't like sleeping alone." "When Jack was gone, I couldn't sleep." "I guess I got used to him being home when he retired." She stated.

"Ma'am, I can't ask him to move aside." "Not now. It'll kill him." "You saw what he became when he left office; he'll go back to being the man he was then." "You two may have your differences, but Jack has meaning for what he does, and no one can explain the good he feels knowing he's a player."

"I'm okay; I've learned to live with it, especially since I've learned what he was involved in." She said as she took a sip of coffee."

"Do the back of your legs hurt when you kick?" I asked her.

"They're sore, and I can hardly lift them." She said.

"Now is the time you have to make a decision." I told her, "The pain is unbearable, and most people quit after the soreness begins, but those that overcome the pain achieve their personal goals in all that they do." "I hope you can overcome the pain," I said.

I got up, walked over to my supply elevator, and opened the door to witness my order of a rib roast and other items. I took the trays one by one to my counter to prepare the meal for my guests.

"Who sends that food to you?" Ellen asked.

I gave her a smile. "I have contacts," I said.

"Do you have those things up there too?" She asked.

I gave her another smile and ignored her.

I set the double oven to preheat and then began applying my base to the roast. Both Jane and Ellen walked over to watch me.

"When we're happy, we dine," I told them. "When we're unhappy, we don't have an appetite." "To be merry is to celebrate good fortune." "Jack liked to celebrate by eating fried catfish and French fries on rainy days." "If it rained three days in a row, Jack ate fried catfish and French fries three days in a row," I said as I applied stone ground mustard to the rib roast. "So when it rained, I fried fish and French fries." "Then he would lie down on the couch and catch up on some rest, he would say." I cracked fresh black peppercorns completely covering the rib roast and sat it in the oven that I had preheated to three hundred and fifty degrees. I refilled my cup and sat back down after I refilled their cup. "A strange thing happened to me." "Now, when it rains, I crave fried fish." "When I'm here, I crave prime rib." "All people suffer the addiction of food the same as everyone else, it's a drug, and I do have a weakness for it." "You can always tell when someone isn't happy." "They don't have an appetite."

"So, you watch everyone when they eat?" Ellen asked, "Don't you ever lighten up and simply enjoy an evening with friends?"

"I didn't have friends, and Ellen, when was the last time you sat down to have a meal with friends?" I asked her.

She gave me a look of surprise.

"Am I going to be looking over my shoulder to see if you're watching me?" She asked me.

"A visual observation of an individual isn't the only identifiable means to see the person you're dealing with." I told her, "I listen to the tone of a voice." "I don't need my eyes."

"Are you reading me now?" She asked me.

"No, ma'am," I told her. "You're happy now; the thought of knowing that you'll never be separated from your family again has secured that."

"But what about your home?" She asked.

I smiled a small smile. "It's still my home." "I carry it up here." I tapped my head with my forefinger. "Ma'am, I've learned a lot of things in a short time." I told her, "One of them is not to take anything for granted." "You shy away from women because you've learned the same thing that I learned; you were being used, and when you realized it, you grew tired of it and wanted distance from Jack's acquaintances."

"It didn't take a smart man to see that you weren't in a relaxed atmosphere when you arrived, and given the circumstances, I think you were entitled." "There was nothing I could say or do to help you; no one is at ease until they are at ease," I told her.

"Smith, you're starting to scare me, and another thing, I thought about last night and what you said." "Smith, a mother doesn't move in with her daughter. That's not the way it's supposed to be done." She stated.

I stood up, walked over to the counter, and began washing potatoes.

"Are you ignoring me?" She said.

"No ma'am, I heard you."

I then began washing mushrooms to remove any dirt.

"Smith, we need to talk." She said.

"Ma'am, you weren't asking a question, and you weren't disputing what I said." "You were making a comment." "You wanted me to counter with a statement of my own." "I told you, I can't tell you what decision to make. This decision is to be made by you alone."

"Jane," she said, "maybe you can talk some sense into him."

"Momma, why not give it a rest and do what he says."

"You're just as crazy as he is." She told her.

"No, momma, look at me, in case you didn't notice when I was growing up, I didn't have any friends either," "momma, I'm happy here."

I turned back around and began cutting an onion to put in the mushrooms.

"Can I do something?" Ellen asked.

"You can do the rolls." "First off, we call them the rule of eight." I began the same way I had taught her before.

"I remember that part; I just can't remember the amount of stuff I'm supposed to use," Ellen said.

I gave her a smile and began telling her how many ounces of everything we needed, and she followed my directions as I began repeating each of the weights of tablespoons and cups. This time Jane got her hands involved. After the rolls were set aside to rise, both of the women looked at each other and began smiling at seeing them all covered in flour.

"When I cook, I cook to satisfy the most difficult of critics." I told them, "Now, you two are the critics, and you will judge your creation harshly and honestly; an artist is his worst critic." "Those rolls are the result of work that you two have shared in." "Will they meet up to your expectations?"

"You watched us. Did we mess up somewhere?" Ellen asked.

"Jane, I told your mother that baking is a formula, you follow the formula, and things can still go wrong." "If the bread doesn't rise, you check the yeast, and if the yeast blooms, check the water, too much iron in the water, and the bread doesn't rise." "The temperature of the water may have been too hot and killed the yeast." "When the rolls are taken out of the oven, then you'll see the real critic in you." "Until then, you'll have to have patience and wait."

"I don't get it, you spend all day and most of the nights on your computer and working on your inventions, but you like to cook," Ellen commented.

I looked over at Jane.

"Jane, do you feel good?"

"Yes"

I looked back at her mother.

"I feel good too." I said, "Jack will be tired and ready for rest; the flying takes its toll out on him." "After dinner, he'll sleep till morning; the sin of gluttony will overtake him, just like in the past when he ate his fill." "Ellen, Jack also has other weaknesses; he's predictable." "I told you, I had to appease the most difficult of critics." "That's me," I told her.

"So you're going to cook all this stuff, huh?" Ellen asked.

"Yes, ma'am, I have the easy part." "The rib roast, and baked potatoes, and the sautéed mushrooms with fried corn don't take much, just light a fire and add a little butter, that's all." "It was the rolls that were the hardest for me, and you and Jane got that out of my way." "That's a relief," I said to them. I looked up at the clock. "Your husband will be here in a few hours." "Are you going to greet him looking like that?"

"What's wrong with the way I look?" Ellen said.

"A man that's been gone for a few days probably wouldn't notice his wife wearing baggy clothes and not showing her figure, so why bother, right?" I said.

"What's your point?" She stated.

"Go look in the mirror, and it'll tell you no lies." I told her, "Would you prefer your husband to see the woman he married when he got married, or would you prefer him to see the woman he saw like he never left?"

"Again, what's your point?" She said.

"Ma'am, you've lost weight." "Jack won't notice that with you wearing those clothes." "You need to wear something that reflects the change that has occurred but not advertises subtleness." "Choose something soft in color, and I prefer jeans, and ma'am, your hair."

"What's wrong with my hair?" She again challenged me.

"If you want to show off the body, then you need to compliment the figure with the hair." "Ma'am, I'm sorry, but that style is definitely not you," I said to her.

"No, huh-uh, not my hair." She argued.

"Ma'am, it's outdated; it makes you look like an old woman." "And ma'am, everybody can tell that you dye your hair; it's way too dark," I told her.

"Not my hair." She said again.

"Computer: bring me my makeup kit and hairstyling instruments," I commanded.

Moments later, Ruby brought in my request. Jane and Ellen watched as she turned and left.

"I thought she was with my husband," Ellen said after she left.

"She is" "and Ellen, you don't have to be secretive around any of them; they are only here for you." "All you have to do is give the computer your command, and it will be granted." "The only reason I haven't released a toy version of my robots is that at one time, they didn't have remotes for appliances." "Now, no one gets up from the couch to turn anything on." "If I released even a toy version, it would be used to get someone a drink, do yard work, or any number of things that it was asked to do." "People are lazy." "And Ellen women don't like putting makeup on. Imagine having an android putting your makeup on every morning." "No one would go to a hairstylist anymore, and no one would cook a meal for their family."

"How many of those things do you have?" Ellen asked as I was brushing and cutting her hair.

"You mean Ruby, or are you referring to all my androids?" I asked her.

"Both," She said.

"Well, I call of them Ruby or James." I said as I cut her hair, "It's said that man can learn a lot by watching ants." "I gave them a lot of studies, and I'm studying them still; it's an exciting hobby for me." "Some are soldiers, and some are workers, and some never see the light of day." "Ant's have colonies that go as far down as forty to fifty feet." "You can kill the mound, but two mounds spring up next to the mound you kill." "You don't come close to killing the colony, and all you do is end up severing a line of supply to the colony by killing the mound." "One day, you notice another mound a hundred feet away from the mounds you killed, and then you start fighting the new mounds along with the original area that you were attacking." "Then one day you see other mounds a hundred feet from the new mounds you're fighting, now you're fighting three areas that are known to have trouble." "Then more and then more appear." "My robots are a lot like ants; they are a colony."

I brushed her hair down and then stepped back and observed my work, and then I started applying a light blend of rouge and continued her answer to her question. "The strange thing about ants is that they don't have a leader." "All of them know what they're responsible for, and they do it." I said as I backed up and looked at her again and finished my answer, "Ellen, each of my creations is programmed so that they can build another, and each of the androids that it builds can build others, just like him." "You'll never witness that; that'll only happen if a man becomes extinct or if I give an order for them to build me whatever I need to go on a mission." "So rest easy," I told her.

"Smith, what if something went wrong." She said.

"My programs are programmed with a virus; they would become deceased and brought back to be reprocessed." "Ellen, I thought about that too," I told her.

I stepped back and looked at her again.

"Well, how do I look?" She asked.

"Momma, you look beautiful," Jane said to her.

I gave her a smile. "Now go find a nice outfit that shows your features." I told her, "Remember, I like jeans," "they're comfort clothing."

I checked on my rib roast and covered it with tin foil; the top was the crispness I wanted.

I picked up my scissors and told Jane to have a seat.

"I don't believe you can work you're magic on me." She remarked.

I didn't say anything, and I just waited for her to get up and do as I asked. I brushed her hair and began cutting her hair to look a little like her mother's. When I was through, I stepped back and gave her a look.

Ellen came walking in, modeling her new look.

"Turn around," I told her as I was applying Jane's makeup.

I walked over to her, pressed the pants together, and then pulled down on her pants leg.

"Take them off and bring them back here." I told her, "I need to hem them an inch tighter, and that blouse won't do either." "I don't want to see you in buttons. I want something tight that says you're a woman but not flaunting her attributes, and Ellen, blue looks good on you." "Choose something that's light blue with no neckline."

When I finished with Jane, I gave her a kiss. "You're a beautiful girl," I told her. She ran off to look at herself in the mirror as Ellen returned with her pants, and as I sat there hemming Ellen's pants up, Jane walked in.

Ellen gasped when she caught sight of her.

"You look so different; you don't look like my baby girl anymore." She said to her.

"I like it," Jane said, fluffing her hand through her hair.

Ellen did the same "It feels funny, though." "Not having to do anything other than brushing it aside with your hand." "One thing I did notice, I won't be having any more bad hair days." She giggled.

I handed Ellen back her pants and told her to try them on.

I was checking the temperature of the rib roast when Ellen walked back in, once again modeling.

"Now, how do you feel?" I asked her.

"A whole lot different." She said to me.

"A good different, or a bad different?" I asked.

"I feel younger."

"Good, when you feel younger, you look younger." "They don't feel too tight in the crotch, do they?" I asked her.

"They feel snug." "I'm not used to tight jeans." She said.

"You have leg muscles that ease into the muscles of the butt." "Their firm, but the pants don't give distinction between the two." "I tightened the crotch a little, thus pulling the thigh muscles down and away from the butt." "Walk in front of me," I told her.

She walked past me, and I watched her as she passed.

"Stop," I told her. "This time, when you walk past me, walk slower, and let the natural movements of your walk tease the observer, in this case, Jack."

"I can't do that."

"Jane, will you show your mother how to tease someone?"

"I don't need that?" Ellen said, fighting me.

"Same old Ellen, huh?" "Ellen, a marriage should be lived as if every day was the day you got married."

She began walking slowly past me, trying her hardest in her act.

I pulled her pants up a little higher and then tucked in her shirt inside of her pants and tightened her belt one notch tighter.

"Now, walk by me again," I said to her.

Once more, she began her walk.

"We'll work on that a little more." I told her, "Maybe, you won't have to know how when Jack comes. Maybe your effort won't be as difficult for you."

"Sit down in the chair," I said to her.

I took her chin in the palm of my hand and tilted her head up a little. I brushed a light shade of light blue eye shadow above her eyelids and rubbed it in with my forefinger to where it was ever so slightly visible.

I then took my hands and fluffed her hair to let it lay naturally. "There, all done," I told her.

She left to go see what she looked like again, and I turned to Jane. "How do you feel?" I asked her.

"Smith," she said to me, "there's not a day that hasn't gone by that you haven't left me dumbfounded."

I walked over to the sink and washed my hands and checked the temperature on my rib roast, and then pulled it out and set it under a heat lamp, and then I turned up the heat to the oven to cook the rolls.

I turned to see Ellen looking at me.

"Did you like seeing what you saw?" I asked her.

"It feels odd, not using mascara." She said. "I don't look the same."

"Ma'am, mascara and lipstick was made from crushed insects at one time." "Mascara contained a crystalline form of quinine, a word that is Spanish meaning Guano." "Dung."

"You're kidding me?"

"No, ma'am." "That's one of the things they didn't advertise when they advertised their product." "If they did, no one would buy it." "Years ago, a lot of people bought products that contained lead, and formaldehyde and toxic chemicals that were in cosmetics."

I took a cake pan out and began layering my wafers for banana pudding.

"Women, as they age, don't want to look the age that they are." "The hair is dyed regularly, and they have drawers full of makeup, hand lotions, body gels, and every product that promises to make them look as pretty as the models that they show on the television." "It's deceptive advertisements, it's propaganda, but the interpretation is up to the consumer." "They wouldn't be in business if the consumer knew the truth." "None of those products works." "So, today, plastic surgeons are what the rich turn to." "Nothing's changed since the eighteen hundreds." "Men came in on wagons and started shouting that their magical elixir could cure baldness, gout, arthritis, and even blindness, and their claims drew crowds." "They sold bottle after bottle." "It was pure grain alcohol, that had opium mixed in with it, and some of the people that thought of it as a cure-all was killed by their belief." "Ellen, you have to understand, back in them days, man didn't have the luxury of pain killers or anesthesia." "Alcohol was drunk by the patient until he passed out." "Cocaine became a popular additive to these magical elixirs, the people still felt the pain, but they didn't care." "Soft drinks contained cocaine too, but they didn't have alcohol." "Children drank it as well as the adults." "I look at people in magazines, and they all look beautiful." "But, pictures are deceiving." "If a model has a bruise, that's not a problem; it's simply airbrushed out." "Acne, black eyes, busted lips, tattoos; all can be hidden from the viewer." "If the face is gorgeous, but the body isn't perfect, you simply remove the head and place it on a body that is perfect." "Computers have made it to where you don't even need a person to sell a product, you manifest an image, and you can't tell the difference." "Every woman has beauty, but it's in the eye of the beholder." "You've heard that said, but I don't think you listened when you heard it." "Women are more concerned with their appearance, while a man is concerned with the way a woman acts to him; that's the beauty he sees, the inner beauty." "Ellen, women who are more concerned with their appearance find themselves not looking the same as they did at twenty-one." "We all age; there's nothing we can do about it except accept it with grace."

I removed the pudding from the stove to cool and began slicing my bananas and placing them in my pan.

I then removed the rolls I had put in and turned my heat on the mushrooms and corn to simmer. I took out the potatoes and sat them under the heat lamp with the roast.

"Tell me, Ellen, when you thought about leaving Jack, how did you feel?"

"How do you know about that?" She responded quickly.

"It's no secret, every man and woman that is married has those thoughts, not once, not twice, but over and over again." "It surfaces in every dispute," I told her.

"I cried." She said.

"But you're still married; why?" I asked.

She didn't answer.

"Ellen Jack's had those thoughts too." "He's still with you, so that must mean that you have an inner beauty that he sees, and that inner beauty causes him to overlook all the faults that you may think you have." "The same as you overlook the faults that he thinks he has."

I went to the refrigerator and grabbed a can of whipped cream, sprayed some of its contents into my pudding and stirred it in, and then poured the mixture into the pan and set it aside.

"What are you doing now?" Ellen asked.

"I'm making fresh butter," I told her.

"You do everything from scratch?" She said.

"No" "I just like fresh butter," I responded. "Ellen, food is fuel for the body. It serves no other purpose." "But, if the body needs fuel, why not provide the body with the best of energy." "That's not to say I'm complete without hesitation when it comes to saving time." "After all, I did use canned whipped cream in my pudding when I could have whipped the cream and used fresh whipped cream."

I turned around and began running water into my sink of dirty dishes, and Ellen walked over and pushed me aside. "Sit down, take a break and relax for a few minutes." "I can do these."

I protested but to no avail.

When the elevator opened, Jack walked out and stopped when he noticed his wife.

She stood there looking at him.

"Have you lost weight?" He said.

She ran to him and started showering him with her kisses. He put down his briefcase and repaid her attention with his own.

When they both regained composure, he noticed his daughter and gave her a smile. "I see I left you two in good hands." He said.

He then lifted his head a little and began sniffing the odor in the air, and started to walk in the direction that his nose led him.

He looked around and opened all the lids on the pots to see what was cooking; he then took a knife to cut a small piece of meat from the roast. His wife took it away from him. He waited a short while, and when she was far enough away from him, he quickly cut off a piece and gobbled it down before she could get to him.

When she saw what he had done, she began to verbally abuse him telling him he could wait for dinner.

I smiled and then began fixing his plate for him. I sliced each of us a steak about two inches thick along with heaping helpings of the sautéed mushrooms and fried corn. I turned off the mixer and put a large spoonful of butter into each roll. I towered the potatoes in sour cream and cheese on a saucer and sat one down with each plate.

When I handed Jack's plate to him, he looked up at me. I smiled and handed him his horseradish sauce.

There was silence among us for a long period of time.

Jack looked back over at his wife.

"What made you cut your hair?" He asked her.

"Smith did it, he said he didn't like my hair the way it was, and he said it made me look old." She told him. "Jack, do I look old?"

He then looked at his daughter and back at his wife.

"I like it." He said, evading her question.

"Why?"

"You don't look like the woman I've slept with for twenty-seven years." "It gives me a feeling that I'm cheating." He said, smiling while chewing on his food.

Ellen smiled and got up and kissed her husband, and then walked over and kissed me. "Thanks for everything." She whispered in my ear.

"And Jane," he spoke to her, "I never really realized how close you resemble your mother until now." "It's been a long time since we've all been together like this."

I saw his eyes beginning to turn red and quickly stepped in.

"Jack, it's been a long day."

"Yeah, it has." "We hit some strong tailwinds, and it pushed us around a little." "It's hard to sleep when you drop two hundred feet and then struggle to level out." He said.

He stood and walked away. Ellen took one glance at each of us, and she, too, left, leaving Jane and me alone.

"You know you made my mother happy." She said to me.

"I got lucky," I said to her "my goal was to make you happy, and she got caught in the middle."

Jane grabbed me and began practicing rule number one. She stopped and stated, "You must have put something into that dessert you made." "I don't normally act like this."

"I warned you, remember." I told her, "But, you can bet that won't be the last time I prepare that dish for you, now that I know one of your weaknesses is banana pudding."

"Smith, I'm in love with you."

"Jane, I'm in love with you more than you're in love with me."

She resumed her practice of rule number one.

I gathered the dishes from the table, placed them into the sink, and turned the water on for them to soak before I washed them.

Ellen came walking back in, and she and Jane helped me clean up.

"Is that offer still open?" Ellen said without turning around from the table to look at me.

I stopped what I was doing and dried my hands.

"You knew when I knew, didn't you?" She told me when she turned to face me, "It was when you saw me looking at everyone, wasn't it?"

I smiled at her. "All I ask of you is never, never, ever, lie to me."

"Smith, I promise, I'll never do that to you."

I went back to washing the dishes and then setting them on the rack to dry.

"What am I going to say to Jack?"

"Jack knows that he doesn't need an offer." "He had two homes, not one." I said to her, "You're going to make Jack a happy man when you tell him."

"There's so much to do. I don't know what."

I interrupted her, "Ellen, listen to me." "There is nothing in that house other than pictures and keepsakes that is of any importance to you." "When the time comes, go home and get all the things you wish to keep, and you can give what isn't of value to you to charity." "Let it go, and it's all material things." "A fire or a storm would destroy it all, then what would you have?"

"But, I'm not supposed to be living with my kids." She said in a whining voice.

"You can do as you wish." "You can decide right now, tonight, tomorrow, next week, next month, next year, or whenever you decide." "I told you, I don't know what a mother's right is; I only think that she has the right to do whatever she wants to do when it pertains to her daughter."

"You don't forget a thing, do you?"

"No, ma'am, and I hope you remember that, and ma'am, you don't have to be frightened of me."

"I wasn't thinking that." She said.

"Weren't you?"

"Smith, I don't think I'm going to like living near you."

I gave her a smile and then stated, "There was a survey reported that because of inflation and underpaid jobs that twenty-five percent of parents were moving in with their children, and twenty-five percent of their children were moving in with their parents." "Social Security is cut in half when inflation doubles." "In twenty years, Social Security is only worth twenty-five percent." "But that pertains to people that are in need of help."

When we finished cleaning up the kitchen, we all were tired and went to our rooms to rest.

I pulled up the cover so I could get into the bed. When I did, Jane put her arm around my waist and pulled me to her.

"Computer:" "Lower the temperature to sixty degrees." She said.

I arose early morning and went into the kitchen to fix myself a pot of coffee.

I stopped scooping the coffee into the pot without looking around. I said, "Hello, Ellen." I turned and then looked her in the eyes. "You're up early."

"You already know what I'm thinking, don't you?" She said to me.

"I think I know; that's why you couldn't sleep," I told her.

I turned around and took some flour out of the pantry and poured some in a bowl, and then went to the refrigerator for butter and milk, and then started working on my biscuits.

"Smith, I need you to tell me that I don't have anything to worry about." She said.

"I can't do that." "You're the only one that can answer that question." "You've allowed yourself to become too close to me." "I'm not important; life is short no matter how long a person lives; it's over within a blink of an eye." "Jane doesn't like to hear me speak of such things." I said to her, "Ellen, you don't either." "So I can't tell you the words that you wish to hear."

I put my biscuits in the oven and then went and got some ground meat and pan sausage and started frying them up in a large pot.

Ellen poured us a cup of coffee and sat it down at the table for me when I was ready. I walked over and took a sip. When I did, I sat down to let the meat brown slowly.

"Why you?" She asked.

"I told you, your husband was going to be assassinated by a dictator, and that put the blame on the people that wanted him out." "Your husband was used as a mediator; some people call him a negotiator." "He was involved in several negotiations in which he was successful." "He became known as a person that when he was called on, he took care of the business he was asked to take off." "He was a go-to person." "No one asked him questions; he gave no answers." "There wasn't any problem; only one man gave him his orders." "That was me. "Nothing was left behind giving evidence of any countries involvement." "So, no one knew anything except that a problem was temporarily resolved." "That's the reason for my lab." "Ellen, it only takes one man of ignorance to come into power, and war will be waged." "A lot of countries will spend a lot of time talking about ways to deal with a problem." "I have a quicker way of resolving a problem." "I've eliminated three situations that arose in that region in the past, and now I'm going back again in five to ten years. Someone will be called on to eliminate another problem." "It's been that way for four thousand years." "When men of power use Gods in their speeches, they inherit the support of half of the people in that country." "To speak against that man is viewed to speak against their God's will." "People are like a flock of sheep following Judah's goat; they have a mind, but they choose not to use it." "They'll follow anybody that thinks the same way as they do, especially after witnessing hangings and beheading by a group that's not responsible." "It's not hard to put the blame on the innocent when two groups oppose each other." "All you have to do is blame others for which you are guilty." "The ones that are responsible put out propaganda to incite those that believe they're hearing the truth." "Our government practices those tactics too." "One day soon, our country will turn into a Socialist Country."

I got up and went back to the refrigerator, took a bell pepper, celery, and onion out, and began cutting it up in the mixture with the meat.

"Smith, we need to talk," Jack said as he came walking into the kitchen and poured himself a cup of coffee.

"You can speak; there aren't secrets here," I told him.

He looked at his wife and then back at me.

"Word has it that he's dealing with drug kingpins, and Smith, he's at the top of the black market when dealing in organ trafficking." "All records of patients have been confiscated, and people have gone missing." "He detains all of his prisoners until he needs them." He reported.

I stirred my mixture to keep the meat from sticking.

I walked back to the table and sat down to finish my coffee.

"The drugs will be the downfall of the families." "I disrupt shipments and let the roaches scatter." "Jack, send our contacts envelopes and reward them well." "Doctors are involved, if we let them slide, they'll set up on their own somewhere else, and it starts all over again." "Computer: Research and locate the doctors that are involved in transplantations and release imitators to keep an eye on them," I commanded.

"Then what?" Ellen asked.

"They become the hazards of war." "When I find out who they are, their organs will be donated.'

"You mean you're going to kill them?" She responded.

"Ellen, these people harvested organs from healthy specimens." "The victims didn't have a choice in the matter." "And in answer to your question, yes ma'am, if they're involved with murder, I'll eliminate them without prejudice." "The slaughter of children is something that doesn't fit well with me." "Ellen, this man has medical records of everyone in the schools, the prisons, anything having to do with any medical facility." "You don't allow a man with that type of access to use it for any purpose like that." "Jack, there's something your wife wants to tell you," I said, getting up and looking at my biscuits and then pulling them out of the oven.

As I was stirring the pot of meat and vegetables, she found her voice.

"Smith asked me to move in with him and Jane." She said.

I put the leftover mushrooms from the night before into the pot, added one large can of cream of mushroom and one large can of cream of celery, and began stirring the mixture.

"And I've decided to accept his offer." She said slowly.

"You've only been here a little over two weeks." He said, "I thought it would take you a little longer."

"You mean you're okay with this?" She said, seeming to be surprised.

"Ellen, here we don't have neighbors living ten feet on each side of us." "Here, we don't need to lock our doors when we leave to go somewhere, and here, we don't have cars, no traffic jams, no horns, and no accidents."

While they talked, I broke up two biscuits into each bowl, scooped the mixture on top of the crumbled biscuits, and gave each one a bowl with a spoon.

Jane caught my eye as she came out of our room, so I started fixing her a bowl, along with mine.

When she sat down, her bowl was in front of her. I poured her a cup of coffee, and she took a sip immediately.

Jack didn't hesitate; he began eating as if he hadn't had anything to eat for three days. His wife watched him.

"Jack, you can't be that hungry after what you ate last night?" His wife said, toying with him.

"Take a bite, and see for yourself." He said, "If the military had served chipped beef that tasted like this, I'd still be in the service."

She did as he said, and she soon was scraping the last of the morsels from her bowl.

"I can see right now; this isn't going to work." She said, "I work out and gain everything back in one meal."

Jack got up and put some more into his bowl, along with another biscuit for good measure.

Jane ate half of hers, and so did I. I grabbed my chest.

"Are you in pain?" Jane asked.

"Pan Sausage is one of my enemies; remember the eggs and tomato sauce?" "Remember I told you I had three enemies, pan sausage, eggs, and tomato sauce?"

"Oh yeah, I forgot about that." She said.

"Well, I'm not going to be energetic today, that's for sure," I said to her.

I took the bowls up and sat them on the counter to be cleaned.

We sat drinking our coffee while Jack dined alone.

When he finished, he sat back and patted his stomach with both of his hands.

"It's been a long time, Smith, a long time." "I've eaten in a lot of restaurants while on the road, but none of them have ever compared or even came near to the taste of the foods that I've eaten here." "Yes, sir, it's been a long time."

"Ellen, what say you and I step out for a little bit of skiing, and then we can take in a movie and go on a snowmobile ride and do a little smooching?"

"Jack, hush, that's no way to talk." She scolded him.

"I'm serious; this is a place where people come to have fun." "I built it and never got to see what everything looks like." "Ellen, we need to live a little; come on, let's do it up, you and me." He said, "Today will be the first day of the rest of our lives."

"I don't have anything to wear." She contested.

"That's not a problem, and you know it," I told her.

"Are you asking me out on a date?" She said to Jack.

Jack got up and walked over to her, and held his hand out to help her up. "Come on; let's take that vacation that we've not had in a long time." "We can't keep passing up the opportunity of a lifetime."

She took his hand, and they both left hand in hand.

"What's on the agenda for today?" Jane asked.

"I have to become serious in my preparations," I told her.

"So you want me to stay out of the way then?"

"Quite the contrary, I prefer you with me in all that I do." "I find comfort in your voice, I am pleased by your presence, and I adore your company."

She got up and came and sat down in my lap.

"What would have happened to you if I hadn't come along?" She asked.

"If you're talking about another woman," I said, "I'd still be looking." "But fortunately, I found the one I was looking for without looking for her."

She eased her head down and practiced on her rule, and after a few minutes, she got up.

"Come on," she stated, "if I keep that up, you won't get anything done." "What are we going to do?"

"First, we sit in the hot tub; it helps me to let my food digest, and then I take about eight antacids, and then four hours of training, and then more antacids."

"Did you say four hours?" She said.

"I normally do eight, but that's with weights around my ankles and my wrists." "I can't go that far yet." "Four hours is pushing my limits." I told her, "I then run for ten miles and walk for five, to unwind, and then I eat more antacids." "My enemies are strong." "The foods I've been cooking are high in iron." "The red meat is protein." "I'd rather eat it than swallow raw eggs and whey, though." "That just doesn't appeal to me." "Eggs being my enemy and all, and I'm not fascinated with whey."

"Yuck, just the sound of it makes me not have an appetite." She said.

"Well, it's a good thing that we both have that in common." I said to her, "Jane, when a person eats too much, the calories that aren't burned off are stored in fat, you know that." "Exercise turns fat into muscle, muscle weighs more than fat, and you know that too." "You have muscle; no matter how hard you try to lose weight, you won't be able to do it." "You have muscle and no fat." "Being tall, your heart has to work harder to pump blood." "It takes forty-five seconds for your blood to return to your heart once it left." "You have a high metabolic reaction; you burn more calories by resting than what other people burn by working out two hours a day." "Jane working out two hours a day only burns around four hundred calories." "The problem with people who have muscle is, if they quit exercising, those muscles turn to fat, and you lose the muscle tone." "That's why men get beer bellies and women, well they change somewhat too." "When I was back at my stone house, I stayed active, and I didn't run. I walked everywhere." "I was physical in all that I have done." "I worked out in martial arts so that I maintained my reflexes, but knowing this, I also know that I'll be working out for the rest of my life." "But, it's the life I choose; it's my form of relaxing and unwinding." "I can't explain it, but I feel rewarded."

"Then we better get to it." She said, "I'm not going to let my man look fit, and I will be out of shape."

We went and put on our swimsuits and sat in the hot tub. She put her arm around me, and we sat back and relaxed.

"Does it bother you that I'm hanging all over you, like a young kid?" She asked me.

I pulled her over with one arm and sat her down in my lap.

She put her arm around my neck and squeezed me tight.

"Jane, I'll be leaving in a short while." "I want you to know that the time I've spent with you has been the best time of my life."

"You sound as if you aren't coming back, and I don't like to hear you talk like that, so stop it." "If it takes me poking you with an electric cattle prod to convince you to push yourself harder to where you'll come back to me, I'll poke you all night long, do you hear me?" "Smith, I said do you hear me?" She said louder.

"Jane."

"That's it, get up, and let's go start our work out."

"Jane."

"Smith, get up, and do as I say." She said, "I'm not going to sit here and listen to you talk with a defeatist attitude." "You're a brilliant man with brilliant ideas." "I've watched you while you work, and I'll be hanged if I sit here and let you tell me you love me and then go off and get killed because your mind was a thousand miles away." "I refuse to let that happen; now get up, and let's get on with it." She was forceful in her tongue.

She stood up and held her hand down to help me up.

When I stood, she grabbed me and started crying.

"Jane, I'm sorry." "I should have controlled my thoughts better."

"Smith," she said, crying, "I'm scared." I picked her up and cradled her in my arms and sat back down in the spa "Smith, when I told you that when you were with me, I wanted you to be only thinking of me, and not thinking of your inventions and planning; your battles." "I was wrong, and I was being selfish."

"Jane, that's not true." "You mistook what I said, and I liked being with you." "For years, I wandered through my life as if it had no meaning." "Since you came into my life, I've slept, whereas before, I dozed." "I've rested, whereas before, I was restless, and I've smiled, whereas before, I wore a frown." "I didn't have anything to be happy about." "That's all changed, and you're responsible for that." "You're the first girl I've kissed, and you're the first girl that's said she loved me, and you'll be my last," I told her.

"You say the most beautiful things to me." She said to me.

She laid her head down on my shoulder, and we sat for a long time.

She caught herself dozing off.

She slid off of my lap and submerged her whole body underwater, holding her nose with her finger and her thumb. When she came up, she purposely tossed her hair back and forth, slinging water all over me. Then she repeated it once again.

She eased up on me and kissed me.

"Get up, let's go to work." "We don't have time for play." She said as she stood and helped me up to get dressed for our workout.

I met her in my weapons room. She put a movie on and then turned to me, "let's see what you got, big boy." She said.

I watched as the movie began.

"Fast forward it until there's action," I told her. She hit the button, and we waited for a few minutes.

"Now, push play, the action is being worked up." "Get behind me, to where you can watch the television, and you can watch me at the same time." I turned around to face her and not see the television; I could only react to the sounds they made.

I moved every move on offense, and I moved every move on defense, the same as the actor, only I slowed down in offense and used defense to defray her attacks.

"Watch how the hands are on defense when I strike on offense," I said to her. "For every action, there's a reaction," I told her while mimicking the fighters.

"The art of self-defense is where your opponent is being hit and rendered inactive."

I stopped and told her to stand still and not move.

I walked close to her and then side kicked my foot to her face, stopping at the tip of her nose, holding it, and then tweaking it with my big toe.

"The ball of the foot is four times more powerful than the hands, the forearm, or the elbow." "It only takes seven pounds of pressure applied with the right force to break any bone in your body." "The neck is the easiest to break of all." "One kick to the chin, and the neck snaps like a twig." "The knee is the strongest part of the body, deliver it in a strike zone, and the breath is removed." "Your enemy is at your mercy." "Now, standstill." I told her, "I then swept my foot to the top of her shoulder in one quick and fluid motion and rested it there." "That's called a chop, done correctly; it's enough to bring a man to his knees to where he can be finished off." I then went and pulled some mats over to where we were at.

"I want you to try your best to hit me." "No playing around. I want you to do your best and try to hurt me."

She was quick in her thrust, and I was gentle when I flipped her onto the mat.

I looked down at her.

"Let's see you do that again." She said.

She got back up, and she swung with her other fist. I once again looked down at her.

She got back up and swung at me with a vengeance. This time, I ducked under her blow and pushed her away with my foot to her rib cage. She came back with a sidekick of her own, and I swept the floor, knocking her to the ground.

"Remember, for every action, there's a reaction. To defend yourself, you must be ready to react when the offender acts." "Offense is only used when an opening occurs." I lectured her.

"Now, once again, try to hit me," I said to her.

She did her best to strike as fast as she could. I had her hand turned to the side, guiding her in the direction I wanted her to go, and then I released my hold.

"How do you do that?" She said.

"You use the force of your opponent against him." "Swing at me, as you did, but in slow motion, and you'll see how it's done." As she swung, I came across my body with my thumb and middle finger and bent her hand in the opposite direction, and she once again was being driven in the direction I wanted her to go in. "Now, let me show you a few basic blocks." "This time, swing at me like you're fighting me, and swing as many times as you can, and as fast as you can."

She was fast, I gave her that. I ducked and bobbed and pushed her fist away with my forearm and came up with both forearms crossed to block her fists and her kicks.

She tired out quickly and was breathing hard.

"Take a break and breathe." I told her, "She didn't; she came at me swinging and kicking with everything that she had." I blocked and ducked like before until she couldn't go any longer. She put her hands on her sides and began walking around, trying to catch her breath.

"How long did you say you've been doing this?"

"Since I met your father, and I started the same way you did, by watching those movies." "You can't find better teachers," I repeated to her.

"Where did you get all of this equipment?"

"There movie props, when practicing, one mistake could end your life." I walked over and looked and grabbed one of my spears and began working out by thrusting in offense and swirling it around my head for defense, and as I was doing so, I worked myself closer to Jane, and in one move. I thrust it into her chest. She jumped back instantly. "Too late." "You're dead." "The spear went through your heart."

"Let me see that." She said, walking to me.

She took the spear and put her palm on the point and pushed it down, causing it to bend.

"You scared the living daylights out of me." "You could have told me you were going to do that."

"It was more effective this way." "Now you know how your mother felt after seeing her double, and your father when he took a blow to test my chest shield."

"It looks real." She said.

"It's supposed to, sometimes it takes two, three, four, or maybe a dozen takes before they get the right shot they're after." "Sometimes's the actors get stuck accidentally." "If the weapons were real, they'd have to find a new actor." "Pretty soon, you wouldn't have any actors left."

She glanced her eyes in my direction and began using the spear to try and strike me with it. Each time I moved out of its way. She fought a good fight, and when she thrust it to my body, I kicked it upward and caught it in the air.

She lunged at me with her fist flying. I put my hand up and caught each blow with my palm as she struck.

She once again put her hands to her sides and walked around breathing hard, and then commented. "You can't catch a fly by the wings with chopsticks by any chance, can you?"

"It's the altitude." I told her, "The air is thinner here." "Take a break, and relax." "If you enjoy what you do, you'll come back again and again." "If you find what you do is tedious and tiresome, you'll dread what you do for the physical exhaustion you receive." "The brain is in charge of the body, but the body tells the brain it doesn't want to do what it says, and the brain yields." "The body always fights the commands of the brain when it isn't happy." "We all have different lifestyles." "And we all have different metabolisms, and some people suffer medical conditions that prohibit strenuous workloads." "Heart conditions and depression play a large role in who we are." I gave her my opinion as I was going through my forms in slow motion "People give up on what they do to make the body healthier." "Boredom is usually the answer, or you wouldn't be able to stop that person from doing what they like." "Sex burns four hundred calories, and running three and a half miles, burns four hundred calories." "Walking at a fast pace for three and a half miles burns four hundred calories, so it doesn't matter if you run or walk. You still burn the same calories." "One cigarette smoked burns one hundred calories, so a person that smokes two packs a day burns four thousand calories, and they never broke a sweat." "A person that chooses to run, or walks, or participates in any physical exercise, increases his metabolism and it becomes more active, and they feel as if they have more energy." "If they were to exercise, by running, or walking, or doing whatever they enjoyed, and then stopped because of an injury, or some other purpose." "Their metabolism would still remain as active as it they never stopped, but it would begin to slow down eventually." "I felt the pain, the same as you and your mother." "I overcome my obstacle by telling my body that my brain is in charge." "My body fought me in every move I made." "I read that successful people don't use excuses; I might not be able to continue my fighting with the same intensity for a lengthy time, but that doesn't mean that I can't continue my exercising." "I've learned that to defeat an enemy, you don't have to hurt him with every blow, all you have to do is deliver the fatal blow." "I slow down, and move my body with deliberate movements and practice on perfect hand, feet, legs, and body positions so that my response is natural." "Like right now." "You're tired and worn out, you exhausted yourself from exertion, and you feel like all your energy has been drained." "If you quit now, your body wins; you've gained nothing except you're tired." "Now's the time that you have to tell the brain that it's up there for a purpose. You have to push yourself until the body no longer feels the pain." "Watch the movie in slow motion and try to follow every move they make, and try to extend your legs as they do." "One day, you will be as good as they are." "But you can't achieve that goal overnight, and I assure you, your body will put up a fight tomorrow." "That is if you're here," I said.

"You don't think I have what it takes, do you?" She answered back.

"The odds are stacked against you, and no one would criticize you for stopping," I told her.

She started the movie over, watched the actors, and began moving to their movements with new reasoning.

We worked out for most of the morning, and we once again found ourselves in the hot tub. I went there on purpose; the heat of the water was soothing to her muscles. I told her to lean across my lap, and I began giving her legs a massage. She moaned on every squeeze of my hand.

"You pushed yourself too hard." "You start out slow and work your way up." "You overdid it, and now you suffer for it."

"You said to push me." She shot back.

"That's me, I can do that, and you aren't me."

"Smith, I always thought of myself as being a loser." "When I grew up into a young teenager, and my girlfriends began dating, I lost my girlfriends because no one wanted to go out with me." "I kinda faded away, I guess." "When you're here or where ever you're at, I want to be there too, with you." "I don't have anyone else."

"Then, we start running now." "The muscles will begin cramping unless you stretch them before they do." "When you're tired, you walk, when you regain you're breathing, start running, and when you tire, walk." "You can't keep up a pace that you're not capable of." "I couldn't imagine when I first began, and it took me months."

We rose dripping wet and began a pace that was sustainable for her to begin. We didn't do much talking. She was concentrating on breathing, and talking would have made it too difficult to catch her breath.

"Can you pick up the pace?" I asked her.

She lunged ahead of me.

"I tried out for track in school," she said, "my legs were long, and the coach's tried me out in the long-distance and relay races."

I caught up to her easily.

"Yeah, but the important part is, did you win any races?" "It's not how fast you run. It's how much you can endure before you slow the pace." "Ten miles is a hundred and sixty laps around my track." "We've got a hundred and fifty-nine to go," I told her.

After eighteen laps, she stopped and walked with her hands on her hips, breathing hard. I left her and continued, only quickening my pace to double the pace I was running. Then after ten more laps, I was running all out and passing her over and over again.

I finished the last lap, stopped next to Jane, and began walking; only this time, I was the one out of breath. I didn't waste time in my walk. I spoke as I eased ahead of her.

"It takes twenty minutes for the heart rate to build up for any good to be done to the cardiovascular system." "You can walk for two hours and not achieve anything." "Walk faster, and you'll find that it'll be hard for you to slow down once you've found the pace you can maintain."

She had to run a little to catch up to me; when she did, I looked over at her. "You can stop and rest, and you've done more than you should have."

"I'm not a runner." "I told you the coach's tried me out." "I didn't make the team." "It seems I was clumsy." She said, laughing.

"Running only gets you there faster," I told her.

"Why do you run then?" She said.

"Back home, after my mother died, I ran a lot." "I loved to run." "Every time I did, I found myself not thinking of anything. I was free, and I wanted to go further and further." "I found out, though, that I had my limitations." "Thirty-five miles was all I could go, my legs locked up, and I spent the night out in the woods." "I couldn't move my legs, and they hurt really bad." "I crawled to a stream and laid my legs in the cool water, and that night, I watched the stars." "I could hear armadillo's digging under the brush, and they kept me awake all night." "I made a vow that night to always have a pack of matches on me, no matter where I went." "There's a lot of strange sounds that go on in those woods at night." "The next day, it took all I could to walk back home, it was one of the hardest days of my life, but I didn't give up, I walked all day and night and made it back late that next morning; I slept in a chair because it hurt to sleep in my bed." "That next week, I ran for a little way, and I walked for a little way." "I went five miles further that time." "So walking, combined with running, can get you further, and you won't be in as much pain."

"Is that why you run and then walk? She said.

"No, I run because I like running, it helps me not to think of anything, and I like walking because it works in reverse. It helps me to think." "My mind is clear, and my answers to all my questions come to me." "I have to be moving," I told her.

"Are you thinking of anything right now?" She asked.

"No, all my attention is focused on you." "You want to please me and help me in my workout." "That's not going to work." "You have to work out to your own level of endurance, and you have to know when to stop." "I've got thirteen years behind me." "You've only got a few days." "That's a big difference." You're going to hurt yourself trying to help me by trying to keep up with me; you'll help me more by walking and not running just because I'm doing it." "There's another thing." "If you're not enjoying what you're doing, you're wasting your time." "You don't have to do something just because I do it." "That's one reason why you see so many treadmills in garage sales."

"Smith, there's only one way I can understand who you are, and that's to follow you around and do everything you do." "That way, I can answer questions I need to know without asking you." She said.

"I'm okay with that part," I told her. "It's the part that you think you need to show me that you won't be in my way." "Jane, you don't have to prove anything to me." "If you want to prove something to yourself, and this is what you want to do, to do it, then you need to start off slowly." "If one mile of walking is taxing, then stop, and then walk one mile whenever you feel like walking." "One day, you'll want to walk two miles, and if you walk those two miles, and it's all you can walk." "Then you know your limitations, and that's two miles." "Walk those two miles until you feel you can walk three, and so on, and so on."

She walked over, sat down in a chair, and laid her head back. She was not going anywhere. I picked up my pace to where I was walking about as fast as most joggers jog. I noticed Jane watching me as I walked.

When I was through, I stopped and put the palms of my hands on my knees so that I could take deeper breaths, and then I walked to the spa and sat down; she was right behind me.

"Jane," I said as we sat together, "my time is going to be spent preparing to leave." "There's going to be times that I'm going to be involved in my work." "I want to be with you more than life itself, but more than one life is at stake here." "There are children involved." "I can't think about my pleasures and knowing what their future holds."

"Are you saying that you're going to have to turn into one of your characters?" I didn't answer her. "When you turn into your character, does he let Smith out, now and then?" She asked.

"I won't be myself anymore." "That's the hard part about loving someone, and I don't have a job where I come home and hang my hat and ask what's for dinner." "I feel wedged between two boulders, and not being able to call out for fear that when my breath leaves, I'll slip deeper, and that'll be my last breath." "I get sidetracked easily, and I get to working on something else that I have to do." "The reason is if I work on a project and my attention is not on that project, then I could make a mistake."

"You knew all along you were going to have to face this moment, didn't you?" She said. "This is what you've been telling me ever since I met you." "You did all you could to protect me, but you made one tiny mistake." "How long have you been worried about this?" She asked. I turned and looked her in her eyes, "Smith, when I came to at the stone house, it was a whole different story. I had no way of knowing that my life would turn out to be anything like this, but there's been a lot of things that's happened to us since then." "We've run into problems, and we've been able to talk them out." "That's the good point about us; we can talk." "Now that brings up something that my mother asked you?" "For my sake, do you have multiple personalities?"

"It depends on your interpretation," I told her. "But your question poses suspicion." "You still don't know me the way you want to know me." "You listen, and you hear what is said, but I become guilty by that one suspicion." "You repeated what your mother thought of me." "That means you question what you see in me about what she saw." "You said you have to follow me in order to understand me." "Come with me," I told her. We changed clothes, and then we entered my makeup room, and I sat down at my computer. I soon had a picture of the man on the screen. "The name's not important," I told her. "I don't invite them to my house." I took a computer image of him and transferred all of his contours and all the other outstanding marks that he had and broke it down to one ten thousandths on the computer. "This is a composite of his features, and we all have them, and we're all different." "Each side of our face and head is not the same; they're separate from each other." "The eyebrow droops a little more on one side, and the sideburns are not the same." "Injuries are common, and small details are a major concern, for example, the indentations on your forehead from being hit by the fans." I walked over to my press and inserted a small sheet of plastic. I pushed enter on my computer, and tiny pieces of metal began protruding from the press until a face formed, and then it slowly began pressing against the plastic. A small amount of smoke drifted out of the imprint, and my press began rising slowly.

"Plaster used to be the mold that was used." "But, with plaster, you had to put it on the face and allow it to dry." "Take a look at the mask used during Halloween; it's not that difficult of a task to accomplish a realistic face." "I just have better equipment." "That's all." I took a screwdriver and worked the side up until the mold broke free. I lifted it up to show Jane the front of the face. I put it side by side with the picture on the screen of my computer.

"This is a mold of my enemy." I took two contacts and inserted them into my eyes, and placed the mask on the front of my face, "makeup does the rest," I said to her, "I become my enemy to confuse my enemy's men." "Five seconds is all I need."

"What made you become like this?" She said.

"Trouble was brewing, and it was easier to stop a problem before it turned into a bigger problem." "Your father spent several nights trying to put water on a fire." "I took a trip and returned without your father knowing I was gone." "He received word of their outcome the next day."

"What happened to them? She asked.

"They committed suicide," I told her.

You mean you killed them?" She said.

"Money makes people keep on doing what they do until they get caught." "The hard part is trying to figure out first if they really committed suicide, or out of fifty people that were associated with them, who was without reason?" "I don't take orders from anyone, so I wasn't obligated to follow any protocol." "No investigations were launched, and they were ruled a suicide; the handwritten letters that they left behind didn't hurt." I told her, "But, everyone wanted answers, and none could be found." "Your father was suspicious of me, but he didn't ask any questions; that way, he wasn't able to give any answers." "Jane, your father's a good man, and he didn't have anything to do with anybody getting hurt." "He hunts peace, and so do I, only he hunts differently than me." "He wanted me to stop and not become involved any further." "That wasn't an option, and he knew it." "He was worried, like you, that I would be killed." "I told him that I knew what I was doing, and I don't need interference from a friend or a foe, and I asked him to step aside." "He didn't do it; that's when he listened to me." "The simplest way of eliminating security problems was for your father to take orders from only one man." "You were safe, your mother was safe, and no one knew anything about anyone." "Your father came to me and delivered the concerns that brought problems that seemed to have no answers." "But the problem to a problem is there are always a common denominator; guns and ammunition." "But, you can't buy guns and planes and missiles except when you have someone supplying the money, or the arsenal, or both." "As of now, we don't know who our suppliers are. When I find out, someone's going to receive a message." "Jane, you've heard that all roads are paved with good intentions." "Countries that are poor travel mostly down the wrong roads." "Some Government protects gun runners and sex slave trafficking and drugs." "They receive offers that they can't refuse." "Do as we say, or you and all of your family members will die."

"So, just because a government is causing problems with their people doesn't mean the government is to blame; they may be forced by an extremist cult." "I have to know the story behind the story." "When you sever supplies of an offense, the enemy takes defense, and you halt an advance, and if a truce is called, a retreat is soon to follow." "All wars are like the body." "Blood flows to the heart, sever the artery, and the heart weakens." "War's the same; severe supplies and battalions are defenseless." "I don't look for fights; I do my best to avoid any at all costs." "Your father was worried about me, and he bestowed upon himself to become my personal attendant." "He was afraid I was too young." "That's not quite the way it worked out, though." "Several months went by, and your father found out that he wasn't the teacher. He was the student." "That was the day he divided himself from you and your mother." "After your father built my lab, I began working on my tools of the trade." "He was a lot like you and your mother." "He began by asking." "What are you building?" "What does it do? What's it for?" "And so on." "His imagination was whetted, and he paid close attention to my prototypes." "Like before, your father was called in for some advice." "He listened and brought the message back to me, but he didn't know. I already knew what was said." "I left that night." "I crossed mountains and traveled the jungle." "Smugglers were dealing in kidnapping, and these people weren't ordinary people, so a large sum of money was demanded to pay for their safe return." "They meant business because, in the past, they killed twenty hostages when their ransom wasn't paid." "They weren't expecting me, plastic explosives were planted and detonated while they slept, and my androids took care of the rest until we were able to escape." "They were in it for the money; they needed guns and ammunition to supply their attempted coup to overthrow their Government." "Their leadership wasn't knowledgeable in the field of battle." "I counted on our movements to be hindered by the darkness of the night, and I set booby traps and detonated them to delay them." "They dispersed, and I was able to find a clear path." "A plan that works well is a plan where no one gets hurt." "That night, my plan worked well." "When I left, no one knew I was even there, and that's the way it was supposed to be." "The prisoners were British, and naturally, they denied any involvement." "No one came forth to take responsibility." "Your father was never talked to harshly again by anyone; his status was elevated and not questioned anymore." "Not even the Vice President had access to him."

"So you play chess with the people that you go after then?" She asked.

"I have to know their move, Jane." "I sent imitator's with your father to keep a watch on my cargo and let me know every move that is made." "If the wrong move is made, I won't have much time. I'll have to leave, so I have to be prepared for today, tomorrow, or next week." "To win in a fight is always to be on the offense. To take defense is allowing an opponent the opportunity to give him the advantage to have the upper hand." "So when in defense, you still use offensive delivery to defend yourself." "You have to make him hurt for trying to hurt you." "Find the weakness and attack that weakness vigorously." "He's not there to test his manhood." "Your father is my messenger, he listens, and he relates to me what he hears." "People don't leave paper trails behind them." "They feel they have privacy in all transactions that they do over the computer." "Big mistake on their part." "Someone, somewhere, uses a computer for the work that they do, and they give me the information I need." "I check records, and soon I have names, and they lead me to more names." "My satellites think a lot as I do. After all, I did program them. I monitor any transmissions of my suspects and decide to whom they are sent too, and where they come from." "Even though people are afraid of cell phones, some people still use them, so we still have to listen in on private conversations." "After I'm through reading their files, I know how much money they have and where every penny comes from and what it's spent on." "I know every conversation that takes place whether it is for business or for pleasure." "I know if they plan to attend a meeting and what it's for." "I know what restaurant, what movie, or what tire they put on their cars." "I read what isn't written." "All enemies write the book about their lives." "The way they move, the way they walk, the way they talk, the way they act, all of those are clues." "That could be the chink in their armor that I need." I poured the mixture of latex into the mold, pressed against it mildly, and held it firm.

"Smith, remember when you and your brother used to play when you were young kids?" Jane asked.

"Yeah?"

"You haven't grown up; you're still fighting the bad guys." She said, "Everybody out there thinks they're safe and secure; like my mother and me, we think someone is on guard protecting us so we can sleep soundly through the night." "Smith, some people never stop fighting for what they believe in." "My father is your servant; I don't see my father as the person that you describe him as." "I never thought my father was involved with anything like this, and I know my mother; she didn't either." "But, I don't see my father as the man you described him as." "My father wouldn't help anyone do anything to hurt anybody unless he was forced to." "Those men you killed and my father knew about them forced him to make his decisions in doing what you wanted him to do, and you know that that's why he's your servant." "I know what he does now is not ordinary, or for that matter what I've seen, you're far from ordinary, but I've had a lot of time to do a lot of thinking." "I watched police videos chasing men that were driving over a hundred miles an hour, and when he was finally caught and cuffed, everyone began to calm down and asked him questions, but they were polite." "They knew they were being lied to." "But, they still kept their temper and explained that they didn't appreciate dishonest answers." "I heard one of them say." "You're going to jail, and you and I both know you're looking at twenty if you're lucky." "Answer our questions, and it might help you by helping us." "Those cops were in shape, and they didn't take any chances." "That made me think of you." "I thought of you like one of those cops, they risked their lives, and their family could have lost someone they loved, either by accident or on purpose that night." "But, the next day, they get behind the wheel, and a new day is about to begin. They might have to go through the same thing all over again." "They're not fighters, but if the need arises, they put themselves in the middle of it." "They do it for one reason, and the bad guys can't win." She said. "You're one of the good guys." "You know what will happen if no one does anything about anything." "Smith, what happens today, can't keep happening, and I know that." "I see you as a man that tries to stop the bad guys from winning." "You don't want to fight, but you put yourself in the middle of one." "My father must have seen something in you." She said.

"Come with me, and I've got something I want to show you," I said to her.

We walked down the hall, and I spoke aloud, computer: open bay twelve. I commanded. After a few moments, we walked into the room.

"Test it out," I told her. She walked over and sat down on her bed.

"Layout on it," I said.

Even with her length, there was still several feet clearance to the end.

"Jane, you ever jump on a bed when you were young?" I asked her.

"No, I was too big."

"You can jump on this one." "I reinforced the frame with seven three-inch stainless steel square tubing," "you," "me," "you're father, and mother," "can jump on that bed, and it still wouldn't bend." "Go ahead, do something you've always wanted to," I said.

"I can't." She blushed.

I ran and began jumping up and down on the bed as high as I could, and did several backflips as I was jumping and told Jane of my beliefs.

"Jane, the best way to test anything you build is to let a seven-year-old play with it." "If it breaks, the product isn't any good." "If it survived the seven-year-olds roughness, then that toy will be played with by their children." "Come on, Jane, be a seven-year-old and see what you missed out on," I said to her.

She was a little tentative at first, and then she began to put a little more pep to her jumps, and then she started laughing.

She sat down at the edge of the bed, and so did I.

"I feel silly." She said, "What made you do that?" She asked.

"You needed a bed to sleep on that fitted you, so I had James build you one." "You won't have any problems with your legs hanging over the rails any longer or having to tuck your feet in," I told her.

"What made you think of that?" She said to me.

"I told you I enjoy your company, and I don't like it when you're not with me." "I feel like you think I don't want you around, and that's the furthest from the truth. It's a form of paranoia that affects me as well as others. I was safe from it until I met you, though." "I had James build it because; I'm going to be occupied with my time." "This is the only way I can tell you that I want you to know. I want you with me."

I bent down and pushed a button.

"The hydraulics is driven by a motor that pumps the pressure up enough to lift the bed." "The pieces you see on the side that are sliding out are the wheels that hold up the bed and allow it to be moved wherever you want me to take it."

"Where are you going to be?" She asked.

"My control room; the imitators that I sent with your father are sending information that they see back to my master computer." "I'll be reviewing documents and photos tonight," I told her.

"Roll it in our room then," she said to me. "I don't need to follow you around and be with you on everything you do." "I'd get in your way, sooner or later." "Nothing's changed since I've been here." "If I want to know where you're at, I'll come looking for you, and if you're worried about what I think, then you don't have your mind on your job, you're thinking of me, I don't want that." "When you think of me, come to me, when you're clear-minded, you concentrate on how to accomplish your mission, and then I want you to put every drop of that brain of yours on that goal." "Now, the bed" "I think that was the sweetest thing anyone has ever done for me." "It tells me that you're thinking of me, and you have no idea how much that means to me." "After you finish rolling the bed into the room, I need another massage on my legs, I can hardly move them, and they hurt so bad." "No wonder people quit; it hurts."

I lowered the bed and installed some headboards I had built. After bolting both the headboards and the toe boards, I went and got the sheets Ruby had cut and resewn and the blankets that she made and made the bed.

"When did you have time to do all this?" She said.

"James and Ruby," I told her. "They're the ones that did the work." "They cut pieces until I had all the pieces I needed, and then they started sewing all of that together and finished it off by sewing the two pieces together outside of the inner blankets to make the quilt." "I found that four army blankets were the best filler to put in between the bottom and the top of the quilt."

"If you notice, the quilts are two quilts sewn together to make one; the size of the bed dictated that." "Look at the top; the design is all facing the same way." "The bottom half of the quilt is not of the same pattern as the top, and you will also notice that the bottom half of the quilt is upside down." "One day, the quilt is positioned one way, and the next day, you turn it around, and it becomes a different quilt." "When you turn it over, it's a different quilt than what is sewn in on the other side." "It also has four different patterns, so there are four quilts in one." "More is being made as we speak," I told her.

"Can you teach me?" She asked me.

"Jane, making quilts isn't that easy." "It's not that difficult to do, but when you start working, you become obsessed, and each new piece you add only increases your desire to do more." "One quilt leads to two, then another, and then another; there's no cure for the quilt maker, but there's one thing you'll learn about making quilts." "No one can offer you enough money to buy it; it can only be given away." "We have four kids here." "Their parents were exceptional people." "They had fairly good jobs, but tragedy struck." "A tumor was removed from one of them, and a blood clot in the brain caused a problem in another." "The other two are mentally challenged, and they won't develop past the age of fourteen." "I was doing research and brought them here with their parents; it wasn't easy to get their attention at first." "I was perplexed." "I knew there had to be a way to reach them, but I was failing." "I looked around and saw one of the kids." "He was the only one that was paying attention to me." "I didn't worry anymore about the other kids; I found a key; I paid all my attention to that one kid." "A lot of mistakes were made, and I showed him the right way, and I showed him how he made his mistake." "He learned both ways, the right way, and the wrong way." "Kids who have problems learn better when you put them with the kids that know what they're doing." "They don't feel intimidated." "One day, when you're out with your mother and father, wander into the stores, and you'll find their quilts wherever you go; in every restaurant, in every hotel, and in every establishment that operates here." "They're a work of art, and we put the picture of the artist that made it next to it." "None of them are sold for less than two hundred apiece; the money doesn't mean anything to any of these kids; they don't have a concept of what it is." "We've had offers to buy every quilt we make, but profits would be made off of children." "I don't want that. I want people to have to come here to buy a quilt if they want a quilt."

"Every day, come rain or shine, those kids are working on making their quilts together, and they have fun talking to one another." "You can't make them stop and take a day off; they're doing what they like doing." "You can't pay those kinds of employees enough." "Their parents went back to their jobs, and they left them knowing that they were able to take care of themselves."

"Through them, we've gotten people here that couldn't leave their children; they had to be with them." "They work here, and they're with their children too." "If the people that work for you are happy, then no one has problems." "Jane, I just want to be able to offer a solution to people that think they don't have anywhere to turn." "I have to build my city of hope." "This is in me; there's nothing I can do. I can't turn the people away and tell them I can't help you, I can't." "If I taught those kids how to make a quilt, I should be able to teach you." "Maybe you'll see what I'm saying to you that way, and you'll have a better understanding of what I mean." "We'll start with the basics." "Come with me, and we begin." When we entered the room, I showed her all the material that she needed "The best tool we have is our imagination." "It's up to the painter or the sculptor." "Cut out small pieces and sew them together to show the flowers, add some green petals, and a little girl with an apron and a bonnet." "Or a little boy was wearing a straw hat that's barefooted." "Maybe he's wearing a patch to cover up a hole in his pants." "You choose the right fabric you want and sew it on." "Then take a bed sheet and sew the completed picture onto it and do the next one the same way until you have a top of a quilt completed." "It's time-consuming, but, as I said, it's a work of art that you find hard to put a price on." "But most of all, I find it to be gratifying." "Jane, I find it to feel good to feel good." "Go slow, and follow your pattern, and I'll have Ruby help you after you get all the pieces cut." "She'll help sew each piece until you get the hang of it, and then you're on your own." "You won't need anyone anymore." "Have the computer print out some patterns, or choose the patterns that I have. I never used them; I just looked at the pictures." I brought out a folder and showed her patterns that all she had to do was put it on the fabric, pin it together, and then cut it out. I did several pieces, and then she took over. "Computer; send Ruby in bay twenty-four." "Ruby will help, and when you don't need her anymore, you can tell her that." "It's easier if someone can show you how to do the first one."

"Go on," she said, "Leave me alone; I'm working here; don't you have something you need to be doing?"

When I left her, I turned around to see that she was involved in what she was doing.

I did as I had said. I went to my control room, sat down at my computer, and began searching for information. I had to think, and the best place I found was as I was taking a walk around my track. After several laps, I went back to my computer and looked for all the names that visited my subject, and then I brought up their passports. I spotted their generals in command, and through them, I found the men I was after.

I initiated an anti-locking download to track their computers. Someone knew something, and I wanted to know what it was. Orders had to be given.

I was working on my prototypes when Jane came walking in and showed me what she had done.

"You're hooked, aren't you?" I said.

"I didn't think it was this easy." "But you're right; it is a lot of fun." "I struggled at first, but Ruby made it look easy." She mumbled and then walked off and left me alone.

I continued to work on the prototype of my pterodactyl, checking each gear, and each line for any signs of a leak, while I pressured up the lines to test its weight capacity.

I then went to my wardrobe room and worked on my mask, it was meticulous in what I was doing, but I had to be; no mistakes went unnoticed.

That night, I made several faces; all different; one person would be noticed if he had been seen before. With different people, no one suspects that each person is the same.

I was viewing my pictures when I heard Jack and Ellen coming down on the elevator. When they got off, Ellen was talking ninety miles an hour and trying to tell me what all she saw.

"So, you're going to do everything again tomorrow?" I said.

"Smith, why do I even talk to you?"

"Ellen, Jack hasn't shown you everything. One day isn't enough, or one week, or one month, or one year." "You're caught out in the middle of a wilderness, and you'll be trapped in a place where you won't be able to leave." "There are two seasons here, winter and spring; the others are not even noticed." "I warn you, don't go with him tomorrow. He's saving the best for last; he's going to take you up to see the valley come sunrise, and you'll discover the answers to all the questions you have or will ever have." "I warn you, Ellen, for your own good, don't go with him," I said to her.

"There's one question that I'd like to have an answer to." She said bluntly. "My husband wouldn't answer them." "I noticed something." "My husband uses one card for everything." "I looked in his wallet, and he doesn't have cash, just that one credit card."

"Ellen, Jack set this resort up as a charity organization" "anything and everything that Jack purchases or that requires money is used on the card, and it's charged off as charity work." "All of the people that work here have a card that they use." "They leave here to visit loved ones that live somewhere else, they use the card, and it's charged to charity." "No one gets paid for anything they do." "All monies that they would be paid is put into a savings plan for them." "Loyalty doesn't come cheap." "They want to leave; a check is written out to them." "It's that simple." "The only recourse is, once they leave, there's no coming back." "Ellen, your house was bought by my corporation, and every month a certain amount is written off because Jack is a lobbyist for my corporation." "He lives in that house because it's an offer towards his benefits for working with this corporation." "That includes his electricity, water, telephone, his car, and anything else that requires an expense, it's all written off as charity, and we don't pay taxes." "Jack doesn't receive compensation for what he does, like a paycheck." "Ellen, there's a lot of things that you don't know; Jack was caught up in listening to a young kid and trying to think rationally." "That's not an easy thing to do." "You had your troubles too, and you still do." "Jack was pessimistic." "No one invests his life savings in what a kid says." "He went against his own beliefs, and he gave me access to every penny he had in his savings plan."

"Ellen, you're worth a little over seventeen million dollars right now" "and each year, you get a return on your investments of a little over three million." "All of which is reinvested, and every month, your worth increases." "In seven more years, you'll receive seven million a year." "But, if you get sick, that money won't mean anything to you." "That sounds like a lot of money." "I can write you out a check for the full amount. Right now, you can enjoy life the way you've always wanted to live it." "But, if you choose to do so, you can't live here anymore once you do." "That's the same offer I offer everyone that comes to live here." "Sometimes, you have to think real hard. Money does a lot of things to a lot of people, not all of them are happy here, and they find it best that they move on." "Those that choose the money always end up running out and seeking more." "There's never enough." "Those that choose to stay here are loyal, and they do what they do because a lot of them have reached the bottom of their pit, and nearly all of them know where they'll end up at again." "We have a lot of handicapped people employed here." "No one wants to hire the handicapped." "But Ellen, the handicapped are the hardest workers I have; they love their job." "For many of these people that live and work here, this is the only home some of them have ever had." "Some are runaways, except not all of them are kids." "I'll not release any information on anyone until after an investigation has been completed." "They came here for a purpose, and it might be helpful to give them the benefit of the doubt. It could be enough to save someone's life." "We have our rules, and if the rules are broken, then they came here with an intentional act of deception in their mind." "I have ways of keeping an eye on them." "Like James and Ruby." "For instance." "Some are invited to leave because drugs and alcohol are easy to come by." "There's one thing for sure; everybody here is here because they want to be here; no one's holding them back." "You have to ask that same question, the same as they did." "They know the rules, and they know if they break the rules, they're gone." "No questions asked." "I have surveillance to backup proof."

We were interrupted by Jane walking in.

"How did everything go?" She asked her mother.

"We had fun," "and I learned some things that I didn't know." She said.

"Come with me, momma, and I want to show you what Smith built me," Jane said, urging her.

They both left, leaving me and Jack alone.

"Jack, I don't want to sound offensive, but I find it complicated when dealing with women." "They get sensitive when you talk to them."

"Smith, there's been changes made, that's for certain." He said.

"It was a little rough going for me and your wife and Jane at first." "They seem to be taking this well, though," I said.

"It's you, Smith," he replied, "women like to throw their weight around, and they tend to be a little bossy sometimes." "It's our own fault; we spoil them." "I noticed my daughter, Smith. You aren't any different than anyone else; you're spoiling her." "That's our job, though," "we feel better when they're nice to us, but when they're angry, you can be on the other side of the world, and they still seem to find a way to reach you." "Some people think the telephone was one of the best inventions of the world, but it isn't." "Turn it off, and your wife can't reach you, and she claims you did it on purpose just so you didn't have to talk to her." "Son, you're going to be out working late on a lot of your projects, a woman has her moods, and they have a way of twisting an argument around to where you're always under attack." "I found that the best way to deal with Ellen was to sleep a few nights on the couch; she couldn't stand it when she slept alone, and I was on the couch." "It makes them start thinking the fight was all their fault." "Don't give in quickly; let them think that maybe the couch is going to give you better comfort." He told me.

"I'm telling you this because Jane is a lot like her mother." "If the time comes, and it works for you, then I can help you out some more; that is if you seek out my advice." He said.

Ellen came back in and started telling her husband to follow her. She led us to our room.

I knew what was coming. She showed Jack our bed.

Jack walked over and felt and looked at the headboard and ran his fingers across it.

"It's cedar." I told him, "James took a router and drew an outline of flowers." "He sanded everything smooth and put on two coats of varnish to conserve the beauty of the wood." "Can you smell the cedar?" I asked him, "The mattress was simple" "The bottom and the sides have inner layers of stainless steel slats welded to each row of springs."

"Did you make the quilt too?" Ellen asked.

"Ruby did," I told her.

"She did a good job." She said.

"Watch this, momma." Jane removed the quilt and put it on the opposite way.

"I'm impressed; that's a bit creative." She stated, "I didn't notice that."

"That would depend on how you look at it." "There's not another one like it in the world, and we have it here with us." "Besides, I would need eight of those to keep me warm at night back at my shack, and when you're cold, you don't really care how a quilt looks. You can't see it in the dark anyway."

She plopped down and then laid out like she was sleeping.

"Smith, would it be too much to ask if you could make ours a little bit longer too?"

"No problem," I replied. "Computer; tell James and Ruby that Ellen would like to have a bed and a quilt like they made Jane's. "

"I keep forgetting that I'm living in the twilight zone." She commented.

I then walked back to my computer room and began studying messages from people that I thought were people of interest. Nothing went unnoticed. Jack walked into the room.

"You see anything, Smith?" He said.

I turned around to face him. "Have a seat Jack?" I told him.

"When you look up into the sky at night, you see what seems to be an endless amount of stars; you can't tell me how they got there. You can only tell me what you were told." "A hundred years ago, if you were to have told someone that we would put a man on the moon, you would have been laughed at and labeled a lunatic." "When computers were born, you had to house them in a room as big as two bedrooms; now I can carry one in the palm of my hand and control all ten computers in the control room from the one I put in my pocket." I said to him, "You've heard of living by the sword and dying by the sword." I said to him, "The meaning doesn't apply to the sword itself; it was used as a parable." "It means no one gets away with everything, one day they get caught, and it won't matter whether they're innocent or not, they'll be condemned." "It was their past that convicted them." "That's why they have prisons and cemeteries." "There's the plain talker." "I'll be bringing in a load Monday, don't be late. I don't like waiting around." "Those are the guys that I like the most." "It leaves me little to look into." "Then there's the person that creates his own dialect." "He's the easiest of all to trap." "What did you see in me, Jack?" I asked him bluntly.

"I don't understand?" He said.

"That first day when I showed you on the computer about the congressman, you took me away." "Why?" I asked him.

"Smith, you were young, and you were brilliant." "Not everybody in politics plays fair, and I believe you would have been deemed as too dangerous to let live." "There are a lot of people that get killed because they know too much." "You're an honest kid; you said things that a lot of people didn't like." "I wanted to give you a little more time to grow up, that's all." "But, I didn't know you could take care of yourself, better than I could." "I only saw a kid that had one way of dealing with people." "You said what was on your mind." "I didn't have any idea; what any of this was going to lead to." "I thought a mind like yours could lead to a lot of breakthroughs in fifteen or twenty years with good guidance." "But, Smith, you've exceeded my expectations a hundred percent." "Smith, I thought someone would have killed you." I turned back around to watch my messages as they raced by. "What are we going to do, Smith?" He asked me.

"Davy and Goliath met on a battlefield." "A deal was struck to send the mightiest of soldiers of both armies to fight, instead of everyone." "Goliath was reared as the most fearless of all soldiers. His height towered well above little Davy." "No one really actually knew the height that he was." "There was a moral to the story, but most people don't see it unless someone tells them what it means, and even then, they may be given the wrong answer." "Anyway, Goliath held his sword high to strike down at Davy, thinking he wasn't a threat." "Davy hurled his stone and knocked Goliath to his knees before everyone that witnessed it." "At least that's one version of the story." I said to him, "There are other versions." "One was only that Davy knocked him down, and he ran over and killed Goliath with his own sword." "Another version says that it wasn't David at all, it was another person, but a point was trying to be made." "It all depends on who the listener is and what story is told to them." I turned back around to face him. "I'm like David." "There's no turning back now, and you knew that when you showed the president where I was at, or you wouldn't have sought an interview with him." "The only thing is you didn't know was your daughter was with me, and you didn't know your daughter was in love with me." "So now, after all these years, you're worried more about something happening to me."

"I'm worried about Jane, that's all." He said.

"Jack, tomorrow I'll have a picnic basket full of sandwiches sitting on the counter for you." "Don't come back till the sun sets down below that mountain." "The moon will be at its fullest." "Don't leave until the wolves begin to howl. That's a memory that no one forgets. It leaves a lasting impression." "Let's go into the den, I need a fire," I told him.

We walked down the hall, and I ordered my computer to raise the door that entered my den. I put seven logs into the fireplace and ordered for my computer to light the propane igniter under the logs. Jane brought in a box of fabric that she was putting pins in so that she could sew them up. She looked over at me. "How many rooms do you have in this place?" "It's a shame when I have to ask the computer to show me what room you're in." "I keep finding myself in places that I haven't been." "I take a walk around and look over and say wait a minute, that wasn't there yesterday." She exclaimed.

"Jane, what you see on the outside perimeters is the beginnings of a maze of rooms." "All doors are sealed unless a command is ordered to open them." "Some are for testing chemicals and protons, and neutrons and some are for some other scientific purposes. Atoms were a big thing at one time." "Now, the atom bomb is worthless." "I don't believe that we've fully discovered the use it has for man." "Have you ever heard of a black hole?" I asked her.

"Sure," she answered.

"A black hole has enough intensity to bend light rays." "It's sort of like a vacuum hose consuming everything in its path." "They do exist; over thirty-six have been located and documented." "Fortunately, none are headed in the path of earth, that is if you judge time by light years." "Its strength is so strong that it tears a planet or a sun apart and pulverizes the remains into dust, and a new life begins to form anew." "A trillion years and a new star is born." "Lightning is caused by friction in the air, the current is visible, and the rush of air racing back to where the lighting struck causes the thunder." "There's a lot of other planets out there that resemble ours, but they're millions to trillions of light-years away." "Light travels at one hundred eighty-six thousand miles a second." "Multiply that at sixty seconds, and multiple."

"Okay, I get the picture." Make your point." She said to me.

"Imagine, if a man had that kind of power, what would he do?" "My belief is, whatever I think, someone else has already thought of it." "So if I think of something, then I work on what I'm thinking." "I counteract an act by being prepared for what could be." "A man once said." "Whatever can happen will happen." "Those that don't have a belief in that saying have an accident, and then they start to understand." "All pessimists were once optimists." "Jane, it's true" "it's evident that accidents will happen again. People ignore the lessons of the past." "I have many rooms in my lab, and I have many projects that are in infancy, and some of them are ready for my command."

"Then it seems you have your hands full." She said to me, "You told my mother; James would have her bed built by tomorrow night." "I'll be working all night, so the quilt will be ready by then." "You're building her a bed. I'll sew her a quilt." She said.

"Jane, you can tell Ruby to do it, and she'll have it ready in an hour," I told her.

"It wouldn't be the same." She said.

"That's the way I see it too, but you need to sew two sheets together that's one-third the length from the bottom of one and one-third the length at the top of another one to get the right measurement for the bed." "I never ask for anything that I can do myself either." "The bed was different." "I thought if I did, I eventually would begin to ask my computer to do everything, and where would that get me?" I only asked James and Ruby to do it for me because I had things on my mind that needed tending to."

She listened to my comment, knowing what I was talking about, and then started putting her pins into pieces to be sewn while Jack and I discussed other matters.

"Jack, hospitals, research facilities, rehab centers, and therapeutic services don't come with a cheap price." "Doctors gave the oath to treat anyone and everyone with or without financial capabilities. That's not the way business is done anymore." "You get into an ambulance, and on the way to a hospital, they are checking out who you are and when they find out you don't have insurance, they tell you to drive on by, their full to capacity." "Doctors may have given that oath, but hospitals didn't." "Do you remember when you first won the election to the senate?" I asked him, "You were jubilant, and you wanted to go out to the highest mountain and shout to the world." "I've got ideas, and I keep getting more ideas." "We can build a hundred-acre indoor hydroponic garden, ten stories tall, capable of growing anything as long as the right environment is offered."

"Smith, you do realize how big one hundred acres is, not to mention, a building that's ten stories high?" "You would end up with one thousand acres. He commented.

"We'll get a grant," I told him.

"You don't just go around and say give me money to build me a one thousand acre farm." He relinquished his thought.

"Jack, this environment is harsh, and nothing can grow here." We're dependent on other countries for our food." "One hundred acres times ten is one thousand acres, not to mention that it's all compacted in a harsh environment that's unsuitable for the growth of edible vegetation." "We'll get our grant, and we'll build our dome, along with our hospitals; it'll be the beginning of our future," I told him.

"Smith, are you wanting more labs?" He said.

"Jack, every scientist that can call him or her a scientist will not argue that's there's a possibility of other life forms, in other universes, that exist." "You of all people should know that. You've seen them." "We'll get our grant."

He got up and said he was going to call it a night. Riding the snowmobile jarred his bones.

"Smith, why are you wanting to build this?" Jane asked.

"Do you remember doing very much with your father and mother while you were young?" I asked her.

She thought for a while.

"I was mostly with my mother." She said.

"Did anything occur to highlight any moments while you were with your mother?" I asked her.

"No, people stared at me a lot." "So we didn't go to many places."

"That's my goal; I want children and adults to remember the fun they had here." "I don't want them to see the misery of hospital staff." "I want people dressed up in costumes, with bright colors, and clowns carrying balloons." "It takes the hurt away from kids." "I want shows, all kinds of shows." "There'll be gunfights, union and confederate soldiers, Native Americans and characters will be wearing what was worn in the eighteen hundreds." "I want some of my characters seven feet tall, and soon no one will even look at those people anymore." "In case you're wondering, they'll be androids." "Jane, you'll be able to walk around, and no one will look at you twice," I told her.

She put down the pieces that she was working on in her lap.

"Smith, if you keep saying things the way you do every time I talk to you, I'm not going to get much done, and neither will you." "Now quit bothering me, and let me work on my quilt, and Smith, that was sweet of you."

I got up and walked back into my control room and began filtering the messages I had missed while I wasn't there, and after, I walked to my workout room and began going through my forms.

I worked up a sweat with nothing to show for my actions except for the exercise. I went and took a shower and then began working on making my sandwiches for Jack and Ellen's picnic.

Jane came into the kitchen to make a pot of coffee.

"It's going to be a long night." She said, "I didn't realize how much time each piece took." "What are you doing?" She asked.

"Tomorrow, your father is going to take your mother up to the land of Noah's Ark." "There's a lookout point that looks down into the valley below."

"Why is it called Noah's ark?" She asked.

"No special reason," I said to her. "I looked out one day and thought to myself that Noah must have seen the same thing when the Ark landed." "So I named it Noah's ark."

"There are picnic tables there that line the edge of the mountain." "It's a popular spot, and most of the time, people wait for hours to view the sun as it sets." "The glow from the sun hits the side of the mountain at the top as it rises and at the top of the opposite side as it sets, and you can see the shadow of time as it climbs to the top." "Your mother will discover that time moves faster than she thought it did." "I'm making a picnic basket for your father and mother." "They'll be there before sunrise, and they'll be there after sunset; it's not easy to leave." "They get hungry, they'll have food, they get thirsty, and they have a drink." "Memories are going to be made between your mother and father tomorrow?" I told her.

"What are you cooking?" She asked.

"In the cold air, you consume more calories than you normally consume." "You burn more energy shivering from the cold." "You have a bigger appetite, and your father has a big appetite even in spring," I informed her. "I'm making Muffuletta sandwiches." "Normally, people make them from a loaf of French bread." "But, to me, that's a variation of a hero sandwich, so it's not a Muffuletta sandwich unless it's made with Muffuletta bread." "Go get your pattern, and we'll sit in here to talk," I told her. "It'll take me a while."

She left and soon returned, and we both sat sipping on our coffee, and then she started working on her quilt as we waited for the bread to rise.

I turned the oven on to preheat it.

Jane was watching me closely as I sat sipping on my coffee. "Is there something that's bothering you?" She said.

I looked over at the dough and saw that it was ready to be put in the oven. I got up and carefully inserted it to keep the dough from falling.

"No, I've got my mind busy right now," I said to her.

She went back to putting her pins in her pieces of fabric.

I went to the refrigerator and began taking out packages of cold cuts and cheeses, along with a jar of pearl onions and green olives.

The girl watched me as I pulled everything out.

I took a look at my bread, put on a mitt, and brought them out to cool down. I turned it upside down with my mitt. "You can tell when the bread is done by thumping on the bottom; it should make a hollow sound." I thumped, and it sounded resonant, "success I said," and then walked over and poured her and me another cup of coffee while the bread cooled down.

I took a sip of coffee and then went back to my computer room and sat down. I reread the messages that I read earlier in case I missed something. Jane walked in, looked over my shoulder, and watched what I was doing. "I don't see how I overlooked this before," I said, thinking aloud. I got up and walked back and forth and then went to work on my sandwiches once again.

I sliced the loaves to make two circular halves and buttered each side.

"I like to brown the bread a little," I told her as I placed it in a cast-iron skillet. I then put one half on a pan-seared the butter and did the same to all of them.

I then put onto the sandwich an ample amount of sliced ham and salami, and hand crushed the pearl onions and the olives and put that on top of the cold cuts and finished by putting Swiss Cheese and Provolone Cheese on top of the olive dressing and then put the half of bread I sliced on top. With the other, I put on sliced roast beef. "This one's ours. I informed her.

She got up and walked over to me.

"Those are big sandwiches." She said.

"Those two there will be enough to feed eight people when I'm through."
"Your father has always looked at the food with his eyes and not with his stomach. That explains what I said earlier about him having a big appetite and putting on a few pounds." I chuckled. "I like roast beef; what do you like?" I asked her.

"I like ham." She said.

"Okay, let's put it on." She took a handful and sprinkled it on the bread.

"Jane." "The palate cannot be fooled, put some ham on there, and don't be shy with it."

I saw the way she was looking at me, and I smiled. "A little testy, are we?" I said to her, "Now, we take the mixture of crushed olives and pearl onions and put on top of the meat and put some Swiss Cheese and Provolone Cheese on it as I did with your parents." I then put the top of the bread back on and stuck them back into the oven.

I turned to Jane; "this is another variation of the recipe." "I like to melt the cheese over the olive dressing to hold the dressing together." After a few minutes, I took them out and let them cool.

Jane walked over and gave them a serious look. She then diverted her eyes toward mine.

I went and got some milk and cocoa and turned the coffee pot off. After I finished, I poured the thermos full of cocoa and sealed it off.

I saw Jane looking at me. "It's for your father; he likes cocoa when it's cold," I stated to her.

"I didn't know that." She sounded surprised.

I cut the sandwich in quarters, put one on her plate, and set it down in front of her.

"I can't eat all of this, it's late, and it's too big." She argued.

"I'm not asking you to eat it." "I'm asking you to taste it, then we put the rest in the icebox and eat it tomorrow; that's why I made it for tomorrow." "We made this sandwich together, and we should celebrate."

Jane pushed her empty plate towards me.

"Would you like some more?" I asked her, "We can make another one tomorrow." I said to her.

"Smith, I can see why you said the food was a drug." She unbuttoned her pants and took in a deep breath.

"I didn't have anything to do with it" "love was involved, and we both wanted everything to turn out right, and judging by your empty plate, I would say we both built a great sandwich together, wouldn't you?"

CHAPTER SEVEN

I was sitting down in my control room, reviewing records, when Jack and Ellen came walking in. They still had their coats on.

"We've got to talk, Jack, when you can give me some time," I told him. It was Ellen that spoke for him.

"You can speak in front of me; I know what's going on." "I don't like being treated like a third party anymore." She restated a statement she had made before.

I looked at Jack.

"I found these in the CIA's secret documents." I told him, "Watch the screen." "Notice the car right here being parked just beyond its legal parking spot." "There's a reason for that." "It's to keep a school bus from pulling in from the roadway." I ran the tape until a man got out wearing sunglasses, and I then paused the tape. I zoomed in, and my clarity began losing its focus, so I ran a profile on every person in my files. "Jack and Ellen," "all animals and all birds have a distinctive way of walking." "Man is no exception." "Watch what happens when I digitize and reduce the frames back to normal." The picture became clearer, and the face was still distorted again. I zoomed in closer and did what I had done before. "Now we zoom in on the highlight of his facial features and add a little touch of a three-dimensional imagery; and when we match the way he walks with the way he looks, and we have our man." "That picture was taken at fourteen hundred hours, three months ago, in Juarez, Mexico." I fast-forwarded it to fifteen-thirty hours. "Notice the school bus coming down the road and turning." "It has to stop exactly where it was supposed to." "The car was blocking the bus." The car blew up, and I left the film running. "Jack, it was a diversion; take a look around. How many cops are at the scene?" "My report said that it was suspected that over thirty million in heroin and cocaine got through." "That's a lot of money, Jack. The shipments were being escorted." "The surveillance video was taken from a camera they used because riots were frequent there." "Nine children died in that explosion; eighteen ended up with severe third-degree burns to the upper part of their body." "The rest were lucky; the ones that were in front escaped with lacerations from broken glass and broken bones." "It was in retaliation for the military giving them problems." "His name is Miguel Angel Vasquez; he is the general to Carlos Alvarez, who controls seventy percent of all the drugs that enter South America." "Miguel is his commander, and he isn't shy in the way he carries out the orders that Carlos gives him." "When entering or leaving any country, you need a passport." "I ran passport checks on all people from all countries that were allowed to leave and enter the country." "Carlos Alvarez visited our man three times under false names." "In one week, there's going to be a major distributor of a large proportion of drugs." "The money is going to buy weapons." "The lieutenants of his gangs that are causing his

215

diversions are going to be there." "That means the Messiah is preparing his missile for a short trip. He wants the war to expand his territory," I said to him.

"I know this sounds silly, but how do you know that?" She asked.

"They have police that works for them, Ellen." "The police shield them from capture."

"Are they your androids? She asked.

"No, Ellen."

Jack interrupted me. "So when does all this take place?"

"The distribution is going to be in an abandoned warehouse where there aren't any witnesses." "That's my destination," I told him.

I heard Jane's voice from behind.

"Whoa, what destination?" She spoke.

"I have to leave; there's something I have to do." I said to her, "It appears that there's less that's known to this story than what we were told."

"You're not ready." She answered.

"Jane, it doesn't seem like I have that much of choice in the matter." "This is what I meant when I told you that sometimes you're plans changes." "What I had hoped for didn't happen; other situations have come into the picture." "I have to go in and prepare to put an end to a problem." "In one week's time, someone else will try and take over the spots that I eliminate," I said as I returned back to my computer. "Take a look, Jack." "Does he look familiar?"

"No, I've never seen him."

"He's not a social man." I stated, "He maintains a private life and keeps a low profile, but he likes to let people know he's the boss." "He's got a reputation that precedes him." "When he's seen in public, someone's going to be whacked." "He's making a move, and I think I know how he's getting his backing." "His name is Francois Alvarone." "He also visited the Messiah." "He's been contributed to thirty-seven kills." "Number two is this man here." I showed him walking with his briefcase. "He's a well-groomed man and highly educated in the field of law, so he knows a little about procedures." "Do you know him?" I asked Jack.

"No, I can't say I've seen him." He responded.

"You should; he's the secretary to the secretary of the Attorney General." "He knows every move that's made, and he's knowledgeable of all of the moves that everyone makes." "He's our informer; he's not as slick as he thinks he is, he left his password exposed, and I retrieved it." "I told you earlier there was a reason, and he's part of the reason." "Going after the other two would be dangerous with him in the way." "Take one out, and he knows someone is on to him." "He delivers what's told to him." "The problem is who is he tied to?" I got up and walked around thinking out loud, "I need to know what's going on, and when, and how do I do it?" I stopped walking and then looked over at Jack and stated, "In the days of the buffalo hunters" "they killed the lead bull, and all the rest waited until the bullet was fired that had their name on it." I turned around to face my guest. "So, how did your day go today?" I asked them.

"How can you do that?" "One minute, you're talking about leaving, and in the next minute, you're talking about how our day went," Ellen commented.

"I just told you about mine." I told her, "I was wondering if you enjoyed yours."

"I did until the wolves started howling." "The hair on the back of my neck began to stand up." "I told my husband then, it's time to go; I never heard anything so spooky in all my life." "They sounded like they were down in the valley." She said.

"They were telling each other where they were," "Ellen, wolves position themselves to tire out their prey from running to escape to make a kill." "They were letting the others know where they were." "That's pretty smart for an animal if you ask me." "Follow me." We walked into her room, and I pointed to her bed. "Try it out, and see if it fits," I stated to her.

She sat down and then laid down on the bed and then grabbed a pillow to put under her head.

Jane walked over and pulled out the quilt that she had made, put it on the bed, and straightened it out.

"You made that?" She asked her.

"It took all night, but it was worth it." She said as she held up her swollen fingers to show her that a needle makes you practice better sewing.

"It's beautiful." She replied.

The lady then looked back at me.

"You did it again." "You're good at sidetracking issues." She said.

"I'm not sidetracking," I told her, "And I'm not trying to hide anything from anyone." "I had hoped for a longer period of time before I engaged in any actions." "I learned that changes occur at any given time." "I was fortunate that I didn't have to go the day after I came here." "You can plan all you want for whatever you are attempting to accomplish, but when unexpected circumstances arise, you are obligated to deal with them." "The problem we have is, is one of the men that works for them is also working for us." "Now, do you understand why no one knows about me?" "If they did, then he would too?" "Due to circumstances that have occurred, Jane is here, and that's the only reason why you're here." I told her mother, "If she wasn't, you wouldn't be here either." "I'm sorry, but that's the way this event would have to happen played out." "Now you know everything about what I do." "Do you think I expected that?" "I was uneasy being forced to change the way I did things, I wasn't pleased with it, but I had no other option." "It would have been impossible to live two separate lives, so I chose to take the only road I could take and not deceive you or Jane." "I hope I didn't take the wrong road; it's impossible to turn back now." "Ellen, I want you to think of what our lives would have been like after I gave you a shot to make you think everything you have been through seemed as if you were living a dream." "I told you one time when you find out who you are; then you'll know more about yourself." "I don't know if you ever gave it any thought, but I am who I am because this is who I choose to be." "I try to resolve moments when tempers are not pleasant, and I'm not good at trying to talk to women and telling them why I have to leave; that's something that I never had to do before." "Jack and I never had this kind of a problem."

"When are you coming back?" Jane said.

"Both of you have known for some time that I would have to leave; you were forewarned, and you were told repeatedly of what to expect, so there shouldn't be any surprises." "When an opportunity presents itself, you have to be ready to take full advantage of it." "If I don't take these people out, can you give me an estimate on how many people will be killed if I don't?" I said to everyone there, but it was for Jane and Ellen's knowledge. I then proceeded, "The sale of vital organs comes at a high price, and rich people pay those prices, so someone has to die so that they can live." "You didn't know about that, did you?" I said to Ellen, "It's hard to have everyone in the room when conversations arise." "This guy sells organs on the black market to finance his operations." "Babies, kids, young women or young men; if the shoe fits, then someone wants to wear it." "Another problem I have is if I don't stop the doctors, I don't stop the sales of organs in the black market." "Now, everything is out in the open." I said to them, "There aren't any secrets, and they'll be no lies among us." "Jane, I can't promise you the days I'll be here or the days I'll be gone." "I can't promise you time; I may not have any." "That was one of the things that I found difficult to tell you when we talked at my shack." "No matter the conversation, you can't give answers to questions that you don't know." "I'm still without the proper words to tell you how I feel." "Your father will tell you all the reasons why I couldn't." "Jack" "there's going to be an investigation into the death of John Hammel." "You're going to be sent for; I want you to deliver a message for me." "Tell him; John Hammel was the number two man."

"Hold on." Ellen said, "Who are you telling my husband to tell this to?"

"The president." I told her, "I don't know of any other way to tell him so that we understood each other." "He's going to want to know what happened." "That way, he has answers to questions he's going to be asked." "He'll be forced to give someone the authority to run a full investigation, but no answers will be found." "Let's say that you're faced with a situation like this." "Are you going to call someone and tell them to tell someone else to tell someone else?" "I'd have half a dozen men waiting on me." "Ellen, I don't need to ask for anyone's permission?" "When Jack is sent for, my message will be told to him that John Hammel was involved with the Messiah." "The sale of the organs was only part of the finances that he accrued." "Mister Hammel set up the transplants and collected the money for them." "He'll be told that for now, that's all he needs to know and not answer any questions with any knowledge about him." "Ellen, Hammel isn't our lead man. Someone else is involved." "When I begin," "they'll be people that will come to the president with a lot of anger; they'll talk of gang wars and drug cartel retaliation." "They'll be telling lies" "I need you to understand this; the ones that do are the ones that I'll investigate; they're the ones that are having someone putting heat on them." "I find out who puts pressure on ambassadors or prime ministers, and I deal with it." "It's easier when they come to me instead of me going to them." "Ellen, you and Jack have had a long day, call it a night, tomorrow will bring a different day," I said to her.

"I can't sleep now." "I'm worried, and I'm scared." She said.

"I don't take chances, you should know that by now, and I use the odds when they're in my favor." I told her, "Whether you're against me or not, there's nothing you can do about it, so go to bed, and when you wake up tomorrow, try to find a way to realize that the man you thought you wanted to be friends with, for your daughter's sake, didn't turn out to be the man that you were hoping you would find."

She was going to talk some more when Jack started pulling her away. She resisted him, and he told her, "We need to have a talk in private." She then resisted him no more.

"Your mother seems to be a little more excited than you," I told Jane when she began leaving.

She stopped and turned around and reported her reasoning to me "I know a little more about you than my mother does." "I admit I was surprised when I first found out things I didn't know." "But nothing about you surprises me anymore." "All the things I've seen from you have shown me that." "I found out a man that I thought loved me didn't." "You, you're different." "You can't lie." "I waited a long time to hear those words," she said. "I knew that one day like today, you were going to say I have to leave." "Smith, my mother doesn't want this." "When the time does come, I still have problems too." "But I knew one day, this day would come."

I picked her up, carried her into the den, and sat her down on the couch; she acted as if she enjoyed the ride. I lit the fireplace and watched the flames as they took on all shapes and forms; I then sprinkled some flakes of metal on the logs, and they gave off-color, and then went and sat next to her.

I laid down and put my head in her lap. She began stroking my hair, and I looked up at her.

"What is it that makes a man turn into a man like you?" She asked, "Are you angry, and this is your way of lashing out in vengeance?" "Most children I hear say that they want to be a teacher, or a fireman, or a policeman." "I never heard any of them say they wanted to grow up being a," she hesitated a moment, "a problem solver." She finally said.

"Jane, when my brother was killed, and I lost my mother, I died too." "I lost my feeling for emotions." "I never gave it any thought about killing anyone." I said to her, "The first kill didn't bother me; it was either him or your father, and as far as being a problem solver." "I try to think of myself as more of a keeper of the peace." "The second person I killed didn't bring me any concern either." "He lined up a village full of men and shot them all; they were the recipients of an old fashion firing squad." "He and his men raped and sodomized the young girls and women, two of the girls were ten. He then had them lined up and shot too." "Jane, I felt sick for the way I felt." "I felt good for what I done." "Since time began, someone, in some country has always wanted to be the king of the world." "Death is witnessed as a pleasure to the men I kill, and I don't find a problem ending their pleasure." I said, "I may be, but I don't see myself as a murderer, but as I said, I do kill, so I can call myself whatever I want, or someone else can call me whatever they want, but the simple truth is, I am a murderer." "Once again, it's open to the interpretation on how one sees things." "Hundreds of years B. C., there were hundreds of millions of slaves that died building monuments and temples to glorify kings and emperors as being Gods, they were nothing more than lunatics, but they had power." "Conquerors captured their enemies and used them for whatever purpose they chose." "Nothing's changed." "Dictators still overthrow a government of the people, and then trouble is born." "Like now, people come up missing, and bombs are blown, and threats are made by the wrong people." "Nothing has changed, and nothing will change, people will always come up missing somewhere, for whatever cause, and bombs will continue to be blown, and threats will always be cast; uprisings offer the perfect opportunity to divide the pros and the cons." "They'll be no peace." "I can't sit back and watch the crimes of hatred against humanity go unpunished."

"I have absolutely no idea of what you were trying to explain to me." She said.

"Jane, you fell in love with the wrong man," I told her.

"No, I fell in love with the right man; it was you that fell in love with the wrong woman." "I'm not a pushover when it comes to someone telling me that there's the door in front of me, and now the time has come for me to use it." "I can read between the lines too." She said, "Besides, I'm bigger than you are." "Just promise me, no heroics." "I asked you when you came to me to come thinking only of me." "Now, the role is completely reversed, I don't want to be responsible for a mistake, so I don't want you thinking of me." "Do I make myself understood?" She said and then spoke, "You were wrong when you said no one gives you orders." "You will obey anything and everything I tell you." "Tell me I'm wrong, and I'll walk out that door, right now, and never look back." "Smith, I'm waiting." "You can't, can you?" "See Smith; a woman hangs around a man long enough to set her hooks in him." "Then the man can fight all he wants, but when he's hooked good, it's not that hard to get you in the boat and on the stringer." "You're not as tough as you think you are, mister." "Smith, you just told me that you loved me again."

She pulled me up to her lips and began kissing me. I felt her tear fall on my cheek.

I got up and turned everything off, carried her into our room, and sat her on her bed, and I laid down next to her.

"Smith, what am I going to do without you?" She remarked.

"You're pretty good at making quilts." I tried to console her.

"I'm serious." She said, crying.

"I am too." "Doing something you enjoy occupies your time and your thoughts." "I saw a hint of satisfaction in your expression when you handed your mother her quilt." "Trust me; I know what kind of work goes into making one, and to finish it as quick as you did, you pushed yourself pretty hard." "I'm proud of you." "As I said, it's a work of art, and a work of art always seems to be missing that little something," I stated to her.

"How did you feel when you finished making the quilt?" I asked her.

"Satisfaction." She answered.

"By the way," "how do your fingers feel?" I asked.

"I bet I stuck myself a hundred times, and each time I wanted to quit and go to bed, they hurt so badly."

"Ah!" "Jane, that's where wisdom is taught." "That's why you take your time and work slow; I don't have to tell you what you thought of yourself when you stuck yourself." "The problem was after doing it over a dozen times. You would think that you would learn after the first time." "Besides, maybe the next time, you'll tell the computer to send you some thimbles in to put on your fingers to keep you from sticking yourself." "It didn't take me long before I started wearing them," I told her.

"I keep forgetting where I'm at." She said.

"There's a lot to see around here," I responded, "if you get bored, you can go take in a movie, or do some skiing, or go for a walk." "You can't stay here locked away inside my lab for long; cabin fever sets in and plays tricks with your mind." "Besides, no one likes to walk anywhere anymore; they'd rather ride, so you would have plenty of peace on one of those snowmobiles."

"It wouldn't be the same without you," she said, "and why are you so concerned about my welfare?"

"Having a hobby is important; it's how much you become involved in that hobby that's more important." "When you have nothing to do, it causes you to search for something to do; only, you find that there's nothing to do." "That's because you're bored." "You need something to give you some kind of a lift in your spirit, and that's the part I'm concerned with," I said to her.

"Smith, I'm having a little problem trying to understand what you're saying right now." "Are you going somewhere with this?" She asked.

"We have three workshops here where people gather and help each other out, mainly by listening as they vent an experience that traumatized them!" I informed her, "I don't promote pity. I promote opportunities for them to have a new life if they so choose." "I'll give them that life, but only if they work for it." "I believe in teaching a man to fish instead of giving him one." "Jane, not many of them qualify." "I don't need foxes waiting for the right opportunity for a fat hen to get too close to him; I help them along their way quickly." "No one can help anybody stop doing whatever they choose as a vice." "Like drugs and alcohol, I was telling you about" "The only person that can change them is them themselves." "When they find this out, they can look at their watch and discover that the road to their recovery began at that time." "One out of twenty will succeed; the others will be buried or cremated. They'll find out the answer to how much the body can take before it can't take any more." "Take a tour of the handicapped making their quilts or the wallets and purses." "Some of them make some fine furniture, but watch them as they work. None of them are unhappy. You'll always see them wearing a smile." "Check out some of the shops that line along the row to the ski lifts." "All of those people that are working were taught that this job was a field of hospitality, and we cater hospitality by being as hospitable as it takes." "We teach those that want to be taught, but some of them aren't ready to learn yet. It may be too late for them." "I thought about building a college." "And Jane, in case you're wondering, all of those people that you see that are wearing those smiles, they came here without hope." "All of them are here because they want to be here." "They know the rules, and if they don't abide by them, then the people that work here decide their fate." "We don't run a commune, but everyone knows that they can feel safe when they sleep." "I have guards that can guarantee that," I said to her.

"You've got other things to worry about, without worrying about this place." She said.

"I've got no other place I can call home." "And for that matter, neither do the people that come here." "All of them come looking for hope." "Those who have personal goals, we don't need. It only takes one person to disrupt a group of fifty." "I'm just saying that while I'm gone, listen to what some of them have to say, and ask yourself whether that person is lying or telling the truth." "Some people are good at lying," I told her.

"I really do love this bed." "She grabbed hold of me and started practicing her rules and surprised me by teaching me a few others."

I think she got tired of me talking.

She fell asleep that night, holding onto me tightly. Each move, she stopped me from getting away from her. I saw her eyes open slightly. "You owe me a little bit longer." "I need more sleep, and I can't get it when you get up, so squeeze me, then tell me you love me, and go back to sleep." "Obey my commands." She said and then made certain by wrapping her arm around me and holding onto me. I yielded and followed her orders; she was true to her word, she fell back to sleep quickly.

Late that morning, I awoke to the smell of coffee. I got ready to rise when Jane said kiss me. I did, and she released me, and then she went back to sleep.

Both of my guests were waiting when I arrived. Ellen got up and poured me a cup of coffee and sat it down on the table, in front of my chair, waiting for me.

I took a sip and declared a victory for the person that made it. I then said, "Jack, I can tell your coffee any day or any time." "You didn't make this pot," I said to him.

"Do you always do that?" Ellen asked.

"I try to make myself clear in my statements so there will be no misunderstandings if that's what you mean," I said to Ellen.

"No, I'm talking about being analytical in everything." She followed.

"It's a habit." I told her, "Let's take you" "every morning when you wake up, you take a shower." "I can smell the fresh scent of the soap on your body." "Then you shampoo your hair." "I can smell the scent of the shampoo." "Then you have to brush your teeth and use mouth wash." "Baby powder is applied on you everywhere." "I smell it on Jack, too, when you're not around." "So, I know you two snuggle when you sleep." "Ellen" "you've been here for only a short while, but you sit in the same place at the table, as do Jack and Jane." "To sit anywhere else would give you a feeling of being out of place." "So being the person that I am, you spoke of me as being analytical; I would think that you sit at the same spot at your table, at your house." "By looking at you, I can see you slept good last night," I said, "your eyes aren't puffy, and they have a certain sparkle; that tells me two things, one is last night was the best sleep you've had in a long time."

"Smith, you're starting to really bother me." "What's the second?" She quickly asserted.

"You've made up your mind," I told her.

"Where are we going to stay?" She asked.

"I'd like for you to stay here." "Jack and I will be gone for periods of time." "Jane will be alone, and there will be times that you will be alone also." I told her, "So with the both of you here, you can keep each other company."

"This is a hard pill to swallow," Ellen stated.

"Ma'am, you made mention of the way your life was before we met. Has it changed?" I asked her.

"Well yeah." She said.

"That's because you are amongst those that are related to you by blood and marriage." "You can't talk to anyone like the two that you talk to here." "I lost all the people that I talked to, and I went through some changes in my life." "I didn't have anyone anymore, and I couldn't tell anyone about anything. I chose to run away from my life." I told her, "Jack paid a high price to help me." "Another reason why you chose to stay is you saw the valley of Noah's Ark." "Last night, you watched the full moon as it crept up over the mountain." "Its view was encapsulating. At least that was the sight I saw when I built my fire and stayed there till morning." "I knew then, and this was where I was supposed to be." "Did you look at the moon from one of the telescopes?" I asked her. "You could almost see a person if he was to stand there." "That's when you came to terms and made your decision at that moment to stay." "I want people to remember the fun and the sights that they see here." "I want people to be able to come here sick and go home well." "Not all of my wishes can come true, I know that I want a lot of things, but I want to build a memory that no one will forget." "Come as a child, and you'll remember this place as you age into an adult." "Come as an adult, and I want you to be a child again." "My goal is laughter and happiness and relief." "My thoughts are that laughter can heal the wounds that doctors can't." "Ellen, the body needs a strong immune system to fight the fight of its life." "I want people when they come here to have a placation, not a place to be visited were more pain is going to be given."

I went silent.

"Go on, and I'm listening." She said.

"I'm starting to rant," I told her.

"No, Smith, I hear what you're saying." She stated and added, "And it sounds good."

"Ma'am, what sound brings excitement to kids?" I asked her.

"I don't know." She said.

"Have you ever been to a carnival?" I then asked her.

"Sure," She said.

"That's what I was thinking about." "I was thinking that I could build it in the center of the hospitals," I said.

She looked over at her husband. "Did he talk like this when you and he met?" Ellen said.

"Ellen, this is the most that I've heard him speak since I met him." "He never confided in me." He stated.

She looked at me and asked, "Why not?"

"I didn't have those kinds of thoughts then," I told her. I didn't speak quickly, and then I looked at her eyes and crossed my arms "Now Jack," "back to John Hammel," "he's a jogger." "He jogs on the same path every morning, and he's meticulous. He begins his morning jog at ten hundred hours." "I plan on stealing an air compressor and setting it up in the path, and arrow will detour joggers away from the road and eyewitnesses." "When he passes me, I hit him in his temple with a two hundred pound thrust of air that is compressed into a cylinder that is held in the palm of my hand." "His brain will become liquefied, a hose is blown, and it looks like the force of the air that was held in the hose caused a freak accident."

Ellen started pushing her hands toward me. "That's too much information, it's too graphic, and it sounds disgusting."

"Then you need to make up your mind." I told her, "When Jack's around me, we discuss matters like this." "Do you want me to tell you to leave?" "You said so yourself." "You didn't want to be a third party." "I'm about to say something that will offend you." "If that's the case, then when Jack walks into the room, you should excuse yourself." "Jane asked me to come to her only as myself." "She didn't want me with her if I had other things on my mind." "Ellen, Jack's known me for a long time, and he knows me better than anyone, and he knows that's not something I find easy to do." "I can't say that didn't happen between you and Jack." "It did. When he was with you and Jane, he still let his mind slip and wonder, back to me." "He led a conflicting life, but that's all behind him now." "Both of you are born again."

I saw her lips gently twist, and then I looked at Jack and back at Ellen.

"You renewed your wedding vows last night at the lookout, didn't you?" I said to her.

They both gave into a large smile. "I want a house that's completely on the other side of the property from where you and my daughter live." Ellen said, "I don't want you to know every time my husband and I decide to have a little hanky panky, and when I look at you, I'll think you know." She scolded me.

I took another sip of coffee and then spoke.

"Ellen, I need help," I told her.

"You need my help?" She started laughing.

"I walked over to the control panel and began typing my commands, and then grabbed a remote and came and sat back down at the table and took another sip of my coffee.

The screen came on showing a party with kids at school.

"Watch the film," I told her.

When it was over, I stopped the film and asked her if she had noticed anything that was unusual. She didn't answer. I started the tape over again and let her watch it. Still, she acted as if she was not noticing anything.

I restarted the tape and paused it. "Watch this kid here." I pointed to the one I wanted her to show interest in. I then restarted the tape. When it was over, I once again asked her, "did you notice anything unusual?" I asked her.

"He was looking at everyone else." She said.

"Yes." I said to her, "Why was he looking at everyone else?"

"The rest of the kids had people around them." She said.

"Schools are often a place that parents send their children to, to get rid of them." I stated, "Poor parenting is passed along to their children." I pushed another button to fast forward the film and stopped it from playing when the new film came on. "Watch this one."

After it ran, I pushed pause. "Now tell me what you saw."

"I saw kids acting the same way." She said.

"I told your daughter what she needs to do while I'm gone." "You can talk and answer all of your own questions." "Now, I'm going to tell you what I told her." "You can't stay in this place day in and day out." "It becomes a prison; you can only go so far one way, and you can only go so far another way." "Those kids you saw in the film were eight to ten years old." I backed up the film to let her see the children, and then I enlarged the picture of their faces.

"What do you see?" I asked her.

"Help me, Smith. I'm not with you." She answered.

"Abuse doesn't have to be physical, and mental abuse is just as destructive." "Now, watch this." I skipped to the last end of the film and then ran it at normal speed. "In the first film, a lady came in and watched everyone doing what they were doing in the classroom." I increased the volume.

"She walked over and knelt next to the little boy." "I don't have anyone to see the work that they do." "My grandson doesn't go to school anymore, and I miss him. I was wondering if you would maybe show me some of your stuff and do some of the things with me." The boy's face became excited, and the rest of the film was shown as he enjoyed himself along with the others. The next film was the same way, empty parents or grandparents needing someone to share their moments with.

I turned off the tape.

"Those are just four of the kids we found abandoned here." "We know who the parent was that dropped them off; I have them on tape when they got on the train." "We don't ask questions, we can only hope that all of them find their way back, someday, but we can't do anything else." "Some of them are in their twenties now, but we're lucky, so far, none of them have shown signs of having wrong in their hearts." "Ellen, all of those women you saw were androids." "I don't care what you do; I just think being here all day is too much for you." "Children and adults that lie in beds in hospitals lead a life of restriction." "Give them a place to go to and meet people, and you'll see that their body strengthens because it has a will to fight." "Loneliness only leads to boredom, and boredom is a drug that I can't fight with another drug." "That's when I thought of the carnival." "No one loses. Everyone's a winner." "Kids love, they don't care if you've had a stroke, and all they'll do is be honest and ask how come you walk funny?" "Tell them, and they ask more questions. They have a unique ability to force people to pay attention to them." "Children bond quickly together, and they brighten the spirits of the ones that are frightened," "Ellen adults are frightened of hospitals, just like kids are, and they fear the pain they know that's to come." "The children that will come here will feel that way too." "I'm hoping I can change the way both of them feel about this place when they leave." "A child is fragile," I said, "If you see one having to go through chemotherapy, you'll see the child frightened." "How would you feel being stuck with needles and wearing bags attached to your arms and slowly seeing yourself go bald? How do you fight that kind of a feeling?" "These children make friends easily, and there are special kids." "Especially when some of them are with my androids." "You can go to any hospital, in any state, county, or city, and you will find someone that doesn't have anyone that comes to see them." "There are reasons, and they are many." "When I build my hospitals here, I don't want an atmosphere of a hospital." "I want an atmosphere of a place to stay while attending to their medical needs." "I want roommates to help cope with the problems we all have." "The children are good with other children, and they are good with adults." "They're the best medicine for all people that are sick." "I want a game room with pool tables and video games and movies." "Ellen, a four-year-old, thinks they are fifteen; we can't deny them their will." "I want a black light putting golf course, and I want a maze of mirrors that they can travel through." "I'm telling you of these things because when you find yourself feeling bored." "The only cure is to become involved in whatever makes you feel the happiest."

"So you thought a carnival would do that, huh?" She announced.

"I don't know," I said. "But I do know that none of them will be with a companion that suffers a different problem." "Ellen, you have to be delicate in answering a question," I said to her as I smiled.

"I never had anyone talk to me the way you do." She said.

"Ma'am, you wouldn't have heard a word I said two weeks ago." I told her, "Do you find offense in my comments?" "Ma'am, I watched you now for a while, and I've spoken to you, and I've listened." "You suffer the same as many others suffer." "You have an inactive lifestyle; you have to change that; you have to become more active." "You may not see it now." "It may take you a week, or it may take you a month, or it may take you the rest of your life." "But, one day, you'll take a walk, and you'll watch something, then you may take a dose of advice and become involved." "That's an area that no one can push anyone into."

"Why bring all this up?" She asked.

I took a deep breath and then tried to explain.

"When Jane came up missing, the first night you had hope, the second night you had hope." "The third-night mourning was a part of your life that lasted all day and night." "Your tears flowed heavily; they lasted longer, and they came and went." "The dishes didn't need to be washed, but the bills still needed to be paid." "They went unattended and ignored; there was worry that was heavy on your mind, and that was to be understood, a dagger had pierced your heart." "They became lifted after you received the call from Jack; this time, you cried for a different reason." "That train that brought you here didn't travel fast enough." "I know how that kind of pain feels." "Children need someone to hold their hand sometimes, and sometimes they need someone to talk to." "I provide that care with my androids when they have no parents with them." "When you thought you lost Jane, you hurt." "Try telling a child where their mother or father went." "Ellen, how old does a child have to be to tell them that they died?" "I can't program an android to do that." "Jack built my lab so I could work." "This resort was what changed my life." "I needed people to run it." "I found those that came here, came here because they were running away from a past." "I gave them a good future, and some of them have worked out." "I ran background checks, and contacted every one of them and told them of what I found, and thus began their one chance program." "Everyone here received the same letter." "No one here knows of anyone's past, and that's the way I left it," I informed her.

"So you've got those things up there watching people?" Ellen asked.

"You've got it all wrong," I told her. "The only reason why they put locks on cars is to keep the honest people honest." "Remember what I told you when we first met?" I asked her.

"You'll have to refresh my memory." She said.

"I told you that I don't trust anyone." "You've heard almost everything I said to everyone else." "I'm just telling you when you get bored. There are others out there that could use a little help." "They could be five months old and needs someone to rock them to sleep, or they could be five years old, and a good story would cheer them up, or they could be fifteen years old or even fifty." "I devoted my life to these people and people like them." "Had it not have been for the people like the Chief, the Judge, the Counselor, or Jack. reaching their hand down to pull me up." "I think I would have gone to be with my mother and brother." "Ellen, no one can save everyone, but with a kid, there's a chance."

"So, you're basically telling me that I need to find something to do, then?" She responded.

"In a sense, yes, but only when you're ready, and not until then." "You'll know when the time comes." I told her, "There's a cliché; a working man is a happy man." "Do you know what that means?" I asked her.

"I guess if he's working, he's paying his bills." "Right?"

"If that's your idea of a working man." I said, "To me, it means a working man to me is a man looking for a job to call a future." "A working man clocks in and clocks out." "A working man dresses for his job." "It also means something else." "A working man is a man that's always looking for another job somewhere else where he gets a better paycheck." "The one he's working on now is either about to be finished, or he doesn't get paid enough, and he's looking for another job that pays better to be able to spend time with his family." "Jack had to be elected for him to keep his job." "So he was a working man too." I said to her, "A working man is a man that's feeding and clothing and raising a family; that's what makes a happy man." "A non-working man is a man that's not a happy man." "To me, that's not acceptable." "I have to build this, Ellen; it can help a lot of people; it's my legacy." "I'm going to need all the help I can get." "But I only want those that want to help me." "You're a woman of wisdom," I told her.

"My daughter doesn't stand a chance against a man that can talk like you." She said, "I think I know a little about how she felt being alone with you."

"Ellen," Jack said to her, "Who do you think wrote my speeches?"

"What did I get myself into? This isn't an ordinary family." She stated.

"When did you ever have an ordinary family?" I asked her.

She took a sip of coffee and looked at me.

"What's that supposed to mean?"

"Whose house did you ever go to just to visit and not go there for business?" "Jack was in demand." "His endorsements were sought by all." "Jane's husband wasn't in love with her, and that meant he thought very little of you or Jack." "You said you never went to too many place. I'm assuming you were alone most of the time when you did." "This didn't turn out to be anything of what you thought it was going to be, but you're happy the way it turned out just the same." "All that matters to you is that your daughter is safe, and most of all, she's happy."

She smiled her smile. "I think my husband and I made the right decision." She said.

"I don't really think that your husband had too much involvement in the decision at all. I think you did most of the talking," I said back to her.

I got up, got the coffee pot, and refilled all of our cups.

As I refilled the cups, I spoke to Jack.

"I'll be leaving after dark; I should return by tomorrow afternoon." "When I return, I'll stay for one day, and then I'll be traveling to Monterrey and from there to Juarez."

"According to the latest blueprints, there's an underground drainage system that leads to the warehouse." "That'll be my point of entry." I told him while pointing to a spot on the blueprint "Computer:" "Start assembly of the bobcat imitators." I instructed.

I took my coffee and walked into my lab while I was being followed by Jack and his wife. I looked over at Ellen, and then I spoke to Jack.

"Tomorrow, with luck, there's going to be breaking news of Hammel getting killed." "He was good, and only he left behind evidence." "Jack, every agent that was killed had roots going back to him." "Every death had a stamp on it; Carlos, Miguel, Hammel, and Alvarone."

"So, you're going to kill them all?" She said.

"You tell me," I said, looking at her. "You said you didn't want to be treated as a third party, and you tell me that you don't like me to talk of someone's future ending." "Ellen, you know what they've done, and you know what they do." "As of this moment, you are my commander, and I take my orders from you." "Do they have a right to do as they please, or do their rights override the rights of others?" "The question is simple, life or death." "It's your decision alone." "But what will the outcome be if you make the wrong decision?" I said.

"I can't do that." She replied softly.

"Ma'am, these people don't think twice about killing someone and then ordering breakfast after they leave." "This is one of those grey areas that you don't have anything to add to a conversation." "It sounds ugly to hear that someone is going to die." "What sounds even uglier is to know that I'm the one that's going to do it." "All of this could have been avoided; they could have traveled down a different path." "That didn't happen, though, did it?" "Ellen, they chose their own path that sealed their fate?" I told her.

I got up and began making dough for biscuits. I turned on the oven to preheat it, took out some sausage links and cut them about four inches long, and then sliced them in half and began frying them. I took out a cast-iron skillet and poured a little oil inside it to heat it up to where my biscuits would begin to cook as soon as they touched the oil.

They listened to the sounds of the links frying and the butter bubbling, and I knew it was cooking at the right temperature. I cracked three eggs one at a time into a small bowl and then slid them into the pan.

"How come you do that?" The lady asked.

"Eggshells happen." I said to her, "Crack them one at a time, and you can get the eggshell out easier if it breaks loose."

"That's not what I mean, and you know it." She said.

I ignored her, and when the butter began heating hotter, I pulled the pan off and slid my spatula underneath to where the omelet could slide with the slightest movement and then added some ham and cheese and folded one half over the other and slid the omelet off onto a plate. I added two pieces of sliced fried link sausage along the side and then sat it down in front of Jack. I looked at my biscuits, and they were slightly golden in color. I pulled them out and put two on his plate.

"What, no butter on my biscuits?" He said.

I put honey in front of him, went to my pantry, and grabbed some peach preserves.

"Now, that leaves you." I told Ellen, "How do you like your eggs?"

"Scrambled." She said and stated, "You seem to know more about my husband than I do.

I took four eggs, cracked them like before, and scrambled them up. The butter was bubbling perfectly. A few minutes later, she, too, received two slices of link sausage and two biscuits.

"What about you?" She said.

"Jane won't eat alone." "I'll wait for her." "Besides, eggs are one of my enemies." "I'll eat them all day long." "Don't be misguided. I love them, and I love them cooked any way that they can be cooked." "But, my digestive system suffers." "The pan sausage in the chipped beef was also one of my enemies, and I fought him all day long too." I told her, "Now, I question, do I want to eat eggs and suffer, or do I skip the eggs and just eat a biscuit sandwich." I said to her.

"Do you always act this way?" She asked.

"I'm sorry," I said. "I've never noticed myself in the way that you notice me."

"I don't want to sound rude" "but you seem to be talking to two people sometimes, and they're both you." She was honest in her opinion.

"In a person's mind," I said to her, "thoughts are sometimes better observed if listened to." "The problem that I face is that there is a right and a wrong in everything that I do, and I don't want to do the wrong thing."

Jack interrupted and answered, beef liver. He laughed. "That's her enemy."

"Ah, I see." "Have you ever heard of Foie gras?" I asked her, "It's a pate that's spread on small slices of toast or crackers." "The middle class can't afford it, but in social circles, it's a display of a sign of wealth, much like caviar, and there are different caviar, so there are different prices." "The problem lies in that Foie gras isn't allowed in the United States." "See, a goose is diabetic, and in order to enlarge the liver, they force-feed figs into the goose, and it makes it's liver about four times the size it should be." "We have organizations that frown on that type of act." "So we use ducks instead, for the same purpose; they are also diabetic." "The point I'm trying to make is someone may not like beef liver, but as not to offend other guests, they find out that the flavor may have changed." "Our taste buds sometimes change from what we don't like into something that we do like." "I don't like Foie gras, and I don't like caviar, but I do love liver and onions with rice and gravy."

"You really love to cook, don't you?" Ellen said.

"How were your eggs?" I asked her.

"They were good." She replied.

"The link sausage and the biscuit you ate, was it good also?" I asked her.

"Yeah, it hit the spot." She said.

"Then you have already judged me, only you judged me in a different way." I told her, "You judged me by whether I satisfied the hunger you developed from the odor of the food." "Or is there something else out there that you seek?"

"See, there you go again," she scolded me; "you're talking in riddles and sounding like you're not talking to anyone at all." "I know you're talking to me, but you're not making any sense." She said.

Jack spoke.

"Ellen, leave him alone," Jack stated.

"Smith, are you all right?" She asked me when she looked back over to me.

I turned my head slowly over to look at her. "No, ma'am, I'm not." I said to her, "I have to go away and do something that I don't want to do." "I need to be alone for a while." "This is a happening that I don't find pleasure in." "They all have families." "Wives, sisters, brothers, children, and the lineage continue on." "Ellen, there's a big difference between them and me, at least. I hope there is." "If not, then I'm no different." "I don't like what I do, and they don't have a problem with it." "You don't let wrong continue to doing what is wrong." "Jack and I discussed this matter earlier." "It pertained to you and Jane; we never ever had anyone with us when we spoke." "Our conversations were always private and between us, and that's the way all of our conversations stayed, between us." "You know our operations, and you know why I have to leave here." "The discussion came up that neither of you was supposed to be here." "We ended our conversation there; we didn't know what the outcome of our future held." "We could only let it unfold and handle it as it came up." "As in the past, Jack held his silence and let me think of what I thought was the best for all of us." "I asked myself why people argue if there isn't a need to argue." "I thought If I didn't make a decision to Jack's liking, he would have voiced his opposition." "I would have listened, and then we would have conversed more on the positive and the negative outcomes." "In the end, he knew as well as I that only one decision could be cast." "He never questioned my orders." "I may be acting like a fool for allowing myself to let a girl come into my life," I said.

"Hey, I heard that." Jane's voice could be heard coming from beyond the kitchen and into the hall.

I got up and made a fresh pot of coffee for her.

"I heard my name, and I don't like it when it's mentioned, and I'm not in the room." She said angrily.

Jack interrupted her to calm her down.

"Your name wasn't mentioned until just now; Smith was talking to your mother," Jack said.

I looked over at Jane.

"Computer activate all verbal communication." "It's a good thing you're up." I said to her, "What I have to say concerns all of you."

"I told your mother that Jack and I had a talk about you and her." "I told her only to catch her up to our conversation that we were having before she came in." "That's because back then, our operations consisted of only two members." "Only your father and I knew of what went on down here." "Now there are more, and you two are a part of them, and I'm not certain of whether I did the right thing or the wrong thing." I poured Jane a cup of coffee, handed it to her, and then went on to speak, "What I did was private." "I lead a life of seclusion for a purpose." "My life changed by accident; I was forced to attend to matters that needed attending to at the time." I then went on, "Ellen," "I gave it a lot of thought and came to the conclusion that without you here, Jane would be alone, and I do mean that in a harmful way." "That wasn't the only reason I asked you to stay." "You both know what it is, but you have to be told what doesn't need to be told." "Jane," I looked at her, "you need your mother" "and ma'am," I looked over at her and then said, "you need your daughter." "What you see here" "has never been seen or spoken about to anyone." "I can only hope my trust was given wisely." "I think of myself as a man as having realistic values," I spoke, pacing back and forth, "and I believe all things can change or be changed, whether by accident or by a reason." "I find myself not being able to part company with those that I feel the warmth from." I said, "So, I suffer from a feeling that I never thought could happen; after all, my belief is whatever can happen will happen." "This is a prime example." "Ellen, you say I speak in riddles; Jane had a rough time understanding me also." "Jack doesn't really pay attention to me other than when I give him an order."

I walked over and poured Jane another cup of coffee and refilled mine and the others.

"You're awful young to have the wisdom of a wise man," Ellen said.

"Ellen, wise men are as many as those stars that shine in the night." "I would think that a wise man would tell you that you should eat, drink, and enjoy what little life you have; we are not gods." "Ellen, we know more about the moon than what we know about what lies under the water of our earth." "Knowledge is not yet accessible to people that don't know where to look or how to know what they are looking for, and I think we should be thankful for that." "I know I am." "I've never met a wise man," "but I have met a lot of men that thought that they were wise men." "Funny thing about wise men, we change the name of an airport to honor him, and when he dies, they change the name of the airport to honor another man that thinks of himself as being a wise man." "Some of them even get a street or a building named in their honor." "Strange thing about those men, some of them betrayed the people and lied to get us into a police action."

"So, what are we supposed to do then?" She said. "We can't sit around wondering where you're at or what you're doing."

"I guess that's one of those things that you and Jack will have to talk about, what I know, others know too, there's other people out there like me, and so I don't disclose my intentions once I'm gone." "Silence is golden in my business." "But, if you really want to know what is happening, watch the news, and maybe you'll see the story that's behind the story." "Or maybe you'll hear a lie being spoken." "There's a lot of people that believe a lie that's said."

"You don't seem to worry about something going wrong," Ellen said.

"Ma'am, when you hear a hose blow with a great deal of pressure on it, what would your reaction be?"

"I'd probably duck." She answered.

"Yes, ma'am," "that's just what I'm expecting him to do, and when he does, I hit him in the temple with the air and keep on jogging and not look back." "That is if my plan goes as planned," I said to her. "Can I do a test on you?"

"What kind?" She responded.

"I need to show you something," I said.

"Go ahead then." She said hesitantly.

I gave her a big smile, and in return, she then smiled at me.

"See there," "you reacted to my actions." "I expect him to do the same." "When the hose blows, I'll duck, and he'll react the same way; it's spontaneous, and that's when I pop him." "If I don't, onlookers will see and give notice, so if my plan doesn't go as planned, then I have to abort that plan and come up with another one." "I won't chance to warn the others that I'm on to them." "I don't think I'll have that to worry about, though." I told her, "He visits a young lady now and then, and from my reports, he likes to go for a nice jog when he's in town." "His schedule has him leaving in three days, so I don't think he'll break his routine; he's methodical."

"What can we do?" She asked.

"Ellen, I won't be alone." I told her, "Our first president said that in order to have peace, you must be prepared for war." "He was right, but he lived over two hundred years ago, and Ellen, he wasn't without his sins; he owned slaves." "But back then, no one had a problem with that. After all, it was a way of life that they lived at the time. In reality, it's still the same today; all men are servants to the public servants."

"Every time you watch the news, you'll wonder if I had anything to do with anything involved in killing someone." "One day, you won't be able to hold your tongue, and you'll have to ask questions." "How can I give you what you want?" "You have to look at me like I'm a penny. On one side of the penny, I'm one way." "And, on the other side of the penny, I'm a side that you don't want to see." "Are you willing to see who I am?" I said to her. I then went back to talking, "Ellen, what do you honestly think of me?"

"I'm frightened of you somewhat." She said.

"That's acceptable," I told her.

"Jane," I said, looking over at her, "since you've known me, tell your mother how you feel."

"I think you're a genius." She said.

"Ellen" "do you know what it means to love someone?" I asked her.

"Smith, you're asking me a question that I can't understand the answer you want from me." She said.

"Well, I guess that would be a tough one to answer." I commented to her, "I had trouble with it too when Jane first said I love you." "I thought she was suffering from delirium, and she said it to me again, only that time she didn't have a fever." "I didn't know those words, and I tried to find a way to explain them." "Ellen, it's hard for me to explain it to you, you've been married a while, and you may have a different explanation that you can give."

"What do those words mean to you?" Jane asked me.

"I can only offer you an analogy," I said.

"I don't care; I'd like to hear it." She stated.

"My conclusion was that a woman loves a man when he can do no wrong." "And, when she's not in love with a man, he can do no right," I said and then looked back over at Ellen. "You and Jack renewed your vows to each other." "You put your past behind you and spoke of the future."

Ellen looked over at Jack. "How come you don't talk like that?" She said to him.

"He wrote my speeches, but we never talked of my personal life; you can, believe me, I would have used that one more than a few times." He said to her.

"Smith, I don't worry about my daughter the way I used to anymore." Ellen said, "And you're right. That's what being in love means." "I'm glad you pointed that out to me."

"Computer," I said. "Activate all bays open."

Soon, Jane and her mother were standing up looking around.

"I didn't know none of that stuff was there," Ellen said.

"Let's all do some walking, and I'll do some talking," I said to them. Jane and Ellen were more interested in watching my androids working. "Ellen, what you see are my imitators." "Old people die alone."

"But there must be hundreds of them." She stated.

I stopped one of the prototypes as she was walking by.

"Do you remember these young ladies?" I asked her.

"Yes, sir" "On my first encounter with Misses Morgan, she fainted." It said.

"That'll be fine." I said, "You can continue." Ellen was looking at me strangely.

"Ellen, all of these things as you call them, know everything about you, and all of them are assigned to you and Jane for your protection." "If any of them had to, my master computer would call all androids that are near to come to your defense." "Trust me, from now on, you or Jane can't leave this facility without being guarded."

"Was someone watching us the other night?" Ellen asked.

Jack answered her question.

"Ellen, I was always guarded and never knew by whom or by what." "You were with me, so that means the computer observed every movement or sound that was made and recognized it as to whether it was a threat or not." "I think you'll understand a lot more as time passes." He explained.

I entered a small room and showed them some pictures. "We encounter barometric pressure changes in our atmosphere." I said, "For example, high pressure, and the cows lie down to chew their cud." "The fish don't bite, and forest animals lie down and rest." "Man's a little different; he tends to become irritable and agitated." "I began bombarding rats with a dome of concentrated barometric pressures and found out that the first trigger under a heavier than normal pressure is that they go into an agitated and aggressive state of mind." "I put them under a heavier pressure, and they fought each other until only one rat was left, and it died from its wounds." "Watch" "Computer: display rat experiment one twenty-four," I ordered.

"Ewwwww," "that's disgusting," Jane said, turning her head away.

"No, that's not the disgusting part." I continued, "Rats and humans have a lot more in common other than cohabitating on the same planet." "They both react the same way when a dome of high pressure is pounding them."

We walked out of that area and continued down into others. Jane and Ellen watched my androids with more of a serious note, and Jane noticed an android standing at attention.

"What's with him?" Jane asked.

"That prototype is a supercharged atom laser," I said. "This little baby will never leave this lab." "It's for my hands only." "She's handheld, and she can sever the hull of an aircraft carrier and sink it in less than three minutes or slice a jet fighter into two parts, for that matter." "Can you fathom what it could do if it was ten times larger and controlled by my computer?" I said and looked up at Jane. "I hope I never have to use it."

She understood more than her mother about my comment.

"What's that thing on the counter?" Ellen asked.

"Computer run Tsunami program." I ordered.

I watched as Jane and Ellen witnessed the powers of the water. When they turned to me, I began answering Ellen's question.

"It takes a motion to create a motion." I told them, "A Tsunami is caused by a collapse of a shelf from a mountain underneath the ocean." "It pushes the water away as it slides down, and thus a force is created that's capable of wiping out anything that is manmade in its path for miles, all the while killing thousands of people." "It's not that hard to cause a Tsunami." "Ellen, I can be five hundred miles away from my target, and within two hours, it'll be demolished."

"How"

"Elephants can hear a frequency from another elephant thirty miles away, and it's a low frequency that man can't hear?" I said to her, "Earthquakes happen all over the world; I send low pulsing frequencies to cause a vibration in the tectonic plates, and I cause an underwater avalanche that activates a wave that can get up; to thirty to forty feet high." "Ellen, ships can't get out of the harbor, and they sink."

She looked hard at me. "Why do you build these things?" She said.

"Because whatever I think, someone else is thinking of it too." "What if a Tsunami was headed towards Florida," I said to her as I continued to walk. "I think we both know that the outcome would be catastrophic." "But what if I could trigger a Tsunami to counteract and confront that tsunami, and the effects could be minimal." "Ellen, I have six of these in place now, with plans of installing six more."

When we walked down further, Ellen caught her attention to one of my rooms.

"What's all this?" She asked.

"This has been a work in progress since the time I built it." I stated, "I run a program of every plane, jet, helicopter, or anything that flies and learn to fly it." "Get in, Ellen, and let's see how you do." "It works like a flight simulator of any plane you want to fly." "It'll let you know when you make a mistake, and hopefully, you won't make the same mistake twice."

"Jack, have a seat and get ready for a ride," I told him.

"She'll be all right." He said quickly.

"Come on, Jack, let's take a little ride." She said.

Jack begged me not to make him go.

"Ellen, a baby has to learn to crawl to get to where it wants to go" "it has a yearning, and the yearning forces the baby to find a way to get there, so it learns to crawl." "One day, the baby has a desire to get to where it wants to go quicker. It stands and begins to try and walk." "The first attempt gives it a few steps, and the balance is lost, and the baby falls, and the baby cries because it received pain from the fall." "The next time the baby builds up its courage, it does so knowing that it will receive pain if it falls, so it plans to protect itself by landing on its butt, instead of the head." "The baby must learn to crawl before it can walk, and the baby must fall before it can walk without falling anymore." "You will learn that you're a baby in this program." "You will have to learn to crawl. I'll set the program on a beginner, and as you feel more comfortable." "You tell the computer that you want to go to the next level." "Do whatever the computer tells you to do." "It will explain the purpose for each function." "Listen to the simulator; let it guide you through the flight." I told her, "I was fortunate; I got to read the instructions before I flew."

When Jane and I exited the door, Jack said he was getting too old, and I heard Ellen comment about him acting strange. I stopped and turned around and told her that all she needed to do was tell the computer that she was ready to begin. "Ellen, enjoy your flight," I said, smiling at her and Jack as I closed the door.

When Jane and I turned, we watched the simulator begin tilting up slightly, and then jerked hard to the left, and then it jerked hard back to the right. I smiled.

"Jane, your mother is going to experience a virtual reality." "She's going to feel every mistake." "Now you know why your father didn't want to go with her." "She'll have her share of bumps and bruises, and the computer will tease her." "I outfitted the simulator with a language character that holds all the nasty things you can say to someone to humiliate them. I take pride in the way it challenges you to be argumentative with it," I told her.

"Smith, I'm beginning to see why you are the way that you are." She said. "You didn't have to show us all of this, but you did; why?"

"Jane, throughout history, conquerors of nations was betrayed by the woman he loved." "It turned out to be a false love, or the woman wouldn't have betrayed him." "You were betrayed by a false love, and you were a victim just like all the other people that were a victim of what you experienced." "Contrary to beliefs, man does get away with murder, and some of them have gotten away with it over and over again and never got caught." "Like Jack the Ripper." "He was only one of many." "I tried talking to my mother when I was young." "I wanted to know if I could reach her, and I asked her one time how old was she." "She began to chuckle a little and said, I'm as old as Methuselah, and then she'd start laughing." "No matter what effort I gave, she never spoke to me in a way that I understood what she was telling me." "Jane, I aged with people that thought I was like my mother." "I had to show you these things for you to see that when I speak, I'm not speaking to you like a crazed man." "If a man wants to get married, the best wife he can choose is to go to a divorce court because that's the real woman that he's going to marry." "This laboratory took me years to build." "You need to turn around and see who I am and what I am." "This is the real me." "I'm everything you didn't imagine."

"Computer: close all doors of security," I said out loud.

The doors closed within moments of initiating my command.

"Your father knows that the computer has his voice code to open any bay. You can tell your mother that the computer has her voice code analyzed, along with yours." "If you want to enter a room or bay, simply tell the computer to open the door." "That's why I had the data recorded in our conversation." "It has your mother and your voiceprints coded." "Jane, I'm just as scared of you now as I was when I first slept in the sleeping bag with you." "I'm afraid I'll lose the person that gave me feelings."

I turned around and walked away, and I had business to attend to. She didn't stand long before she came running to me, swung me around, and bent down to give me a long kiss.

I wiped away the tears that ran down her eyes.

"Smith, the only problem that we have in front of us is that you're a genius, and I'm not." She responded.

"I wouldn't say that," I told her. "That would be insulting to my intelligence. Look who I picked to fall in love with." "I want to tell you something else before I leave tonight." "Several nights ago, I began writing a letter." I said to her, "It contains my thoughts on what you mean to me and how I feel about you." "I hope you don't take what I say in the letter the wrong way." "I'm confused with how I'm supposed to know what to do, and when I'm not sure of myself, I'm compelled to say what I feel."

"Where did you find time to write a letter?" She asked.

"I was assembling my explosives, and I ordered my computer to take down everything I dictated and have it printed out so that I could give it to you." I answered her, "Jane, please follow me."

We walked into the control room.

"Have a seat," I told her.

"Computer; please turn out the lights in the control room," I ordered.

The room went dark.

"Computer; initiate a three-dimensional hologram of the solar system." Jane quickly responded by jerking back and grabbing my arm, and then released her hold that she had on me.

"That's amazing." She sounded thrilled.

"You do it." I said to her, "Simply say computer; show me the hologram of the top of Pike's Peak."

The hologram came up, and once again, she responded in the same way. I then told her, "Sometimes you have to be careful about what you say." I said as she walked over to look down from the top, "I won't let this information out of this room either." "Computer; have the hologram show me where our defense missiles are housed in their silos, and give me each compartment of the facilities," I said.

Jane looked at the hologram and then back at me.

"See what I mean, I didn't give it orders to show a particular missile; had I, you would have received only the information you requested." I said to her, "What you see is a composite of all the defense missiles and what's associated with each one." "That's why you have to be careful of what you ask for." "There's a cliché that says that you can't see the trees because of the forest." "In this situation, you can't see the missile without seeing all the missiles."

"Do we really have that many?" She asked.

"Yeah, that and submarines that are armed and ready to be fired." "Can you imagine the results if a person could gain access to the command center?"

"If all of those missiles were fired, that would be the end of the world, wouldn't it?" She asked me.

"Jane, that's not the worry of these people." "Those missiles are the ones that we have, and other countries have more." "Right now, they are being used for peaceful purposes, and everyone is prepared for war." "Everyone knows there will be no winners."

She gave command of her own. "Computer: show me where all of China's defense missiles are based." She said.

When they came up, it covered a larger area than ours. She once again looked over at me.

"Now do you understand why my prototypes are sealed," I said to her?

"Computer: show me Russia's locations of its defense missiles." She ordered. When she saw the hologram, she looked back over to me again. "I can see why you preach a doomsday." "Smith, you said."

I stopped her from continuing with my answer, and I knew what her question was. "My master computer will override any commands of any country in less than a second." "That's why I told you that they'll be no nuclear war as long as I'm alive," I told her.

"Computer," she said, "Show me a hologram of two people making love." She looked at me when nothing happened.

"I didn't program it for that," I told her.

"Computer; show me the anatomy of a man and woman," I said, and they both appeared anatomically correct.

"Computer; remove the epidermis away from each person." I ordered, "Now you can see each muscle, tendon, and leader and what it's attached to." "Computer; remove the muscles from the people." She said.

"Notice the arteries and veins," I told her.

"Computer; remove each vital organ, one by one, and tell me what its function is used for." She said.

She watched and listened in amazement.

"I wasn't thinking about programming it for entertainment when I designed it." I told her, "Be careful of what you ask of the computer." I said, "Your answer is given to you by a machine. It won't lie to you."

"Computer: display hologram of Smith." She said, and to her surprise, nothing came up.

"My hologram is a prototype." I told her, "Man won't use it for what I intended it to be used for."

"And what was that?" She asked.

"When the elderly go to nursing homes; some of them suffer from neglect, it can be used as a friend to talk to, and a friend that listens and talks back, but the hologram was just a thought." "The androids were given birth from that thought." I said to her, "With the hologram, I wanted kids to see the event that took place at that moment in time, so they could watch and see how history unfolded." "I thought it would be a good tool to teach someone that was troubled in math or reading or maybe even be able to give someone a little psychological help." "Not all people are capable of learning a lesson as quickly as others." "When I'm gone, you can play games, or you can sit and talk and ask all the questions you still have of me."

We were interrupted by Ellen and Jack walking in, and the hologram disappeared.

"That was an experience that I'll never forget." Ellen said, "And, that voice on the simulator needs to be changed."

Jane gave her a smile.

"Did you have any crashes, momma?" She said.

"That's another thing I want to talk to you about." Ellen said, "Do you know that thing feels like you're really crashing?"

"Momma, did you have fun?" Jane prodded her.

"It was fantastic." She replied, "I really felt like I was doing the flying."

That evening I was getting ready to put some of my needs into my backpack when Jane came into the room. I took a hooded warm-up sweatshirt and pants down from my closet and put them into my backpack along with my uniform.

She looked at my gear.

"I don't know what to say?" She said.

"This isn't something that someone should discuss." I stated, "I have a job to do, and that's all it is, and now the time has come to where I have to leave." "Jane, what's taking place now will unfold over and over." "I should be back tomorrow, and then I'll leave again." "Jane, this man is a secretary of an organization that's transferring billions of dollars into the hands of known mafia and drug kingpins." "I do what I have to do."

Jack came in, and I gave Jane a kiss goodbye, and we departed. On the ride up the elevator, Jack looked over at me.

"Five years ago, you would never have let that happen." "I'm glad the way things worked out." "Smith, you keep your mind on what you're doing; you hear me?" "I don't want to lose a son that I've known as a son before he was my son."

"Jack, they're going to keep you up late tonight, asking you a lot of questions." "Remind them of the hologram or tell them to call James or Ruby."

When we exited, we took a short ride on a snowmobile, and then I lifted off in my helicopter. I saluted him when I turned around to give him one last look before I departed. Thirty minutes later, I was landing in my private airport and leaving in my jet. My destination was almost three hours away.

I arrived later and stole a truck to pull an air compressor to the location I needed and then used a piece of heavy equipment to lift it in place.

I had it started and rigged to blow with a detonator that I had concealed inside the seam of my pants. The air pressure was set at two hundred and fifty pounds. I needed a loud noise to distract attention away from me.

I watched and waited to see if my target had changed his itinerary. He didn't, and he was right on time. When he got out of his car, I watched him as he began exercising and stretching his legs and the muscles in his body. When he finished, he started off slow. That's when I began, only coming from the opposite direction.

I kept my eyes on him without looking his way. I had to time my arrival to be at the exact time that the compressor was detonated.

He looked around with suspicion at seeing the air compressor going without anyone around, but he saw other joggers as they jogged by, and then he looked over and saw two men wearing an orange vest that was stepping out of a truck. That's all he needed for assurance. My mission was still a go.

When I grew nearer to him and the compressor, I blew the hose and ducked at the sound of the hose exploding. He reacted as I had hoped, and I was back to continue on my way. I saw people running over to him, but I didn't look back or act as if I knew anything had happened.

When I walked into my lab that evening, all eyes were staring at me. Ellen walked over and poured me a cup of coffee, and Jane pulled her chair over and sat next to me.

"It's been on the news on every channel." Ellen said, "They're going to perform an autopsy." "So far, everyone says they heard a loud pop and saw the man on the ground." "You thought that through pretty good." She then said.

"Computer: replay news media about Hammel," I ordered.

"Ellen, I want you to watch the interviews." I told her, "That man there giving his account is an android." "Notice the jogger that's jogging by him while the interview is taking place." "She's there for a visual distraction." "Her breasts are bobbing up and down as she jogs." "No man hears anything that's said." "Their eyes are on something else." "She's an android too." I told her, "A man's dead because of me." "Doesn't that make you feel a little uncomfortable?" I asked her.

"While you were gone, we sat down, and we had a discussion." "By the way, Jane introduced me to your hologram." Ellen said, "I have to admit, when I first met you, I found you to be a man that got on the wrong side of me." "Jack told me why, and he said you were good at being able to make someone tell you what you wanted to know." "My daughter also told me that." "Jane came out of her room this morning crying." "I didn't know what happened." "She gave me the letter you wrote to her and left it on the desk before you left." "Smith, first off, no one writes a letter of love that's three hundred and forty-two pages long." "I read that letter, and you talked about me sweetly and gracefully." "I always thought you didn't like me, but now I find out you were just getting the answers you wanted to know about me."

I looked at Ellen and then turned to Jack. "Someone's going to ask what that compressor was doing there, and why was it running?" "Computer: rerun the news media coverage of John Hammel." "Those two men wearing the safety vest came to get the compressor." "Somebody is going to be looking for some answers. That compressor wasn't supposed to be there." "Computer: run search engine virus and send it to the President of the United States office computer," I ordered.

"What is it?" Ellen asked.

"It's nothing more than a virus," I said to her. "Someone is on the inside," "I have to triangulate all messages to and from John Hammel from top officials and reform them, and since the president is at the top, it just seems natural for me to know what he's doing." "This way, I can tell who is playing games with whom; somebody had to give information to somebody." "I protect myself from everybody, ma'am. The president is human, and all humans are similar in characteristics. There are good people, and there are bad people." "I found that if you pull a weed before it has a chance to root, then the plant receives all the nutrients," I told her.

"I don't have a clue to what you're saying." She said.

"In movies, you see people being teleported to other places." "It's something like that, but a little bit different." I stated, "Whenever anyone uses their computer to communicate with the president, my virus is delivered to that computer, and whoever uses that computer to communicate with him is going to be invaded with my software, and so on, and so on." "Information I receive is instrumental in who is telling whom the truth." I tried to explain it to her "You heard me tell you that I don't trust anyone, especially people in our government, or any other government." "Crime is only committed by people that think that they'll get away with it." "In three days, I'll have every computer in the Pentagon is on a three-way freeway, I like to call it." "That's why I triangulate all messages for clues that throw out red flags, and Ellen, you can trust me on this. When it comes to our government, you can build a whole new prison and still not have enough cells to house them all."

"You don't seem to hold a high opinion of our government?" She said.

"I love our government." I told her, "It's the people that betray their country by selling their vote I don't like." "The problem is half of the people believe what they hear and keep voting those people into office that take away their jobs." "They only vote for a person because they don't like the other person." "Ellen, I'd love to stay and chat some more, but I can't. You don't like talking politics, and I came in to get some supplies and then leave."

"Do you have any idea when you'll be back?" Jane asked.

I bowed my head. "Give me a minute." I said, and then I looked up at her, "Somewhere between sixty-eight and seventy-two hours." I said to her.

I then turned to Jack. "I'm going to need you for return transport," I told him.

He got up and headed towards his room.

"What's going on?" Ellen asked.

"I have a job to do." I said, "Jack is dropping me off in Monterrey, there's going to be trouble in Juarez, and I don't want to land there." "He'll stay for one night to rest, and then he'll return home."

"How?"

"My jet?" I said.

"Jack knows how to fly a jet?" She asked.

"Ellen, didn't you learn anything in that simulator?" I said to her, "It's not the flying of a jet that one should be concerned with." "It's the landing of the jet that you should be worried about." I smiled and then told her, "Jack was a lot like you when he started out; he flew by the seat of his pants." "He was scared of everything; his problem was he didn't like to fly by instruments." "His landings demanded that he had to go back to the simulator for more training." "You should remember, he got three broken ribs from it." I told her, "When he got to where he could land in a fifty-mile hour crosswind." "I told him he was ready for solo." "Ellen, he stole my jet from me and didn't return till it was out of fuel." "What kind of a man steals your jet and not even refuel it?" "What kind of man does that?" I asked her.

She scratched her head. "I didn't know Jack could fly?" She said, shaking her head back and forth.

"Ellen, I move at night." "That's why I fly at night, and I do everything under the cloak of darkness. I move easier that way." "When we get to Monterrey, it'll be close to morning." "I'm going to have to wait till nightfall before I make my way to Juarez." "Have you ever been to Monterrey in winter?" I asked her.

"You mean like Monterrey, as in Mexico, Monterrey?" She asked.

"There's a restaurant there that serves the best tamales one could ever eat." "I tried to imitate the recipe, but I can't." "Ellen, this is your chance."

"You mean, go with you?" She said.

"Jack and Jane will need company on the return," I told her. Jane looked over at me quickly.

They both left running, and I went to my lab and started gathering my supplies when Jack walked in.

"Are you sure about this?" He said.

I went and sat down on the couch and asked him to sit with me.

"You and I don't play by the same rules that we used to play by anymore." "Espionage, assassinations, and explosives have advanced over the years." "It would be easy for me to fly a drone over and signal a missile strike." "But, that would show the involvement of a country, and you know that the first ones to be suspected would be us, and you know we can't afford to damage a relationship with a bordering country." "We give them a taste of what we do, and they'll come back with a better overview." "You've seen Ellen; she can't accept what I do as being right. It just doesn't fit well with her." "Besides, my friend, you are going to have a co-pilot that's going to keep you up all night asking about all the gauges and what do they do." "Jack, how do you feel about flying with Ellen?"

"I don't have a problem with that." He said.

"No, I mean, how do you feel about flying with Ellen?" I asked again.

"No, no, wait a minute, you don't mean Ellen, as in the pilot, Ellen?" He said.

Ellen walked in before he could give an answer and asked what we were talking about.

Jack quickly intercepted her question.

"We were talking man stuff, that's all." He said.

I gave him a smile when he turned and looked at me.

I looked over at Ellen with her suitcase in hand.

"That's not going to work," I told her.

"Here, the weather is in the teens. In Monterrey, the weather is in the eighties." "You'll have to act like tourists and buy new clothes; it's one of those small details that get overlooked when flying on an overnight trip," I told her.

Then Jane came in with her suitcase.

"Have you ever been to Monterrey Jane?" I asked.

"No," she answered.

I smiled and then gave her the same speech as I gave her mother.

"Bring only what you intend to wear on the ride back from the plane to the lab." "That's the only time you'll need cold-weather clothes."

"We're ready, she said after looking at her mother."

"You're just going to be there one day," I said.

"We know, we packed lightly." She said to me, "You men can pack two weeks of clothes in your backpack; women don't work that way."

I shook my head back and forth and told Jack that all of this was his fault. and then everyone was putting in words of their own as we prepared to enter the elevator. I stopped and said.

"Computer; send me my cats and initiate closure of all rooms," I commanded and then ordered the doors to the elevator to open.

I knelt down and waited, and while I waited, I opened my bag. My bobcats came running in, and Jane and Ellen both jumped back. I then zipped up my bag.

When we all got in, Ellen looked over at me, and once again, Jack intercepted her thoughts.

"Ellen, you asked if we were being watched that night we went out." "We had guardians, like rabbits, or spiders or any animal or insect you see." "They surround the resort and feed information to the computer." "If all is not well, his androids move in and remove whoever or whatever is causing trouble." He told her. He unzipped the bag, took out one of the cats, and started stroking it like it was a kitten. "Honey, I told you I couldn't even identify any of his androids." "This is one of the reasons why." "I was always looking for a humanoid, not an animal." He said, stroking the cat one last time and then putting it back in the bag.

When she looked at me, I simply explained.

"I don't like rats," I said, "and these bobcats send them on their way." "Plus, they're my eyes and ears," I told her without going into a full detailed explanation.

"Computer; prepare the helicopter and ready the jet," I commanded to it.

Our trip to the helicopter on the snowmobile was a good one for Jane. She held onto me tightly. She gave me the feeling that it wasn't because it was cold.

When everyone was in, I began warming up the engine and going through my routine of checking all my gauges, pressures, and movements of my helicopter. I looked around to make sure everyone was strapped in, and then I began to ascend and move forward with haste. I heard some sounds that sounded a bit weak.

I spoke into my helmet. "Is everyone all right back there?"

"I never rode roller coasters or fast rides, and I definitely never rode in one of these contraptions." Ellen said, "I don't like it."

"Then we need to train you to fly a helicopter in the flight simulator," I told her.

"No," she replied.

"How are you feeling back there, Jane?" I asked her.

"I'm on cloud nine." She said.

Ellen was curious, and it showed.

"Smith, those people we saw," "was they androids too?" She asked.

"Yes, ma'am." "And in case you're wondering, the ones in the hangar pulling out my jet are androids too."

A little later, I was in the cockpit going through the same routine as the helicopter. I eased out on the runway, and a few moments later, I was pulling up my landing gears. I tripped a switch above my head, and everything became silent.

"What did you do?" Jane asked.

"This is a prototype fitted with silent running, and I built the plane to reflect any source of radar or sonar or lasers or echo sounders." "It's shielded for high and low flying stealth." "This is another prototype that I won't release."

"Do you release anything?" She asked.

"No, man isn't ready for the knowledge he can control; good technology always seems to fall into the wrong hands, and its good intentions wind up being used for bad purposes instead of good." "You can buy anything you want if you have enough money to pay for it," I told her.

I put the plane on autopilot and got up from my seat. Jane didn't expect it when I reached for her hand. We walked into the back of the plane, and I began taking out my mask and applying my makeup and wig. I was putting on my last eyebrow when Ellen came in and became startled. When I finished, I looked over at her.

Jack came walking in about that time.

"Will someone please tell me what's going on?" Ellen said. "And who's flying this plane?

"Ellen, Jack said, "his master computer has control over everything he builds; it's being flown by it now. In case of an attack, the computer can respond in a millisecond for aversion." He said to her, "You're safer on this plane than taking a walk in the park."

She looked back over at me and asked, "Who are you supposed to be anyway?"

"I'm Pedro Gonzalez," I told her, with a heavy accent. "I am the special envoy to El Presidente Eduardo de Fernandez." I said.

I walked over to the side of the panel, tapped it lightly, and began typing, and soon a small booklet came out as I was working on another one. Ellen picked it up.

"This is a passport, she said, and it's mine." "It has the presidential seal embedded on it." Soon Jane had hers in her hand, and I had identification. I began working, and soon, their visas were in their hands.

"Jack has his already," I told them.

"With that presidential seal, you are protected from any agency." "Every cartel knows to harm either of you will bring the war that they don't want to fight." "I'll be with you at all times till you leave tomorrow." "You should know that anything out of the ordinary can be expected." "You're entering areas where gangs are bold; they prey on tourists by attacking them from the front, the sides, and from behind, they only have one goal, and that's to beat you until you don't have any more fight in you, and then they run off like the rats, with their bounty in hand." "You can try as hard as you may, but you can't blame them for what they have become." "The young as well as the old need money to live on." "Not everybody commits a crime because he wants to. Some of them don't have much choice." "Look at Jane as a young child, hungry; how far would you go to bring a smile to her face?" I asked.

"How will those people know we're there?" She asked.

"When we land, we're going to be greeted by customs." "Someone in security will tell someone, and then the whole town will know before we even get out of the airport." "Trust me; you'll draw plenty of attention." "That's one of the reasons that we're here." "They know who you are, but they don't see me." "It's a magician's trick." "You provide an illusion accomplishing a sleight of hand."

"So, we're more or less decoys then?" She spoke.

"I think I would call that an interpretation." I told her, "You're going to have dinner in Monterrey; you're getting to do something that you've never done before." "I was hoping to embed a memory of having a dinner in

Monterrey, that's all." I told her, "But for now, the best thing is for you and Jack and Jane to get some sleep." "Tomorrow night will be a long ride home, and Ellen, don't worry if Jack falls asleep; he's done it before." "The plane is designed to override manual control if proper procedures are not executed." "So don't ride him too hard tomorrow, on the flight home." "Maybe, you'll pay more attention to the flight simulator now," I said to her.

I got up and went into my cockpit; soon, I heard the door open and close behind me. I could tell it was Jane by the way she shut the door.

Without looking, I told her. "I thought I told you to get some sleep."

She sat down next to me, looking out the front windows at the clouds as we flew just over them.

She then asked if I wanted to be alone.

"No, it's a long day tomorrow, and you'll need your rest," I told her.

"How do you do those things so easily?" She asked.

"What things?"

"Well, you access all the documents you need, and no one is the wiser, for one thing." She said.

"Can you spot a counterfeit bill?" I asked her.

"No." She responded.

"Well, they had that trouble in seventeen seventy-six too." "Benjamin Franklin was only in politics because he wanted the contract to print all government paperwork." "He owned a company that had a printing press, and he was the author of Poor Richard's Almanac." "He was also the first person to come up with a way to tell if the paper money that people took was counterfeit or not." "He pressed a leaf into the paper with the ink, and the veins of the leaf were too hard to counterfeit." "He helped give birth to paper money, and he, like all other contractors, wanted a contract with the government." "That's what we have here." "We are entering a country where supervisors are afraid of their superiors, and they don't want to jeopardize their rank by not doing as they are instructed." "They won't be able to identify the counterfeit passports or visas." "But, I already thought about that and instructed their security to accept the seal with approval; I like to play it safe," I stated.

"You're a cocky, confident sort of man; you know that?" She said.

"Good, it's my character," I responded.

"No, it's not; you act like you know what's going to happen." She said.

"Okay then, let's look on the other side." "We get arrested for illegal entry and thrown in jail, and all kinds of charges will be levied against us." "Which do you prefer?" I asked her.

"Are you sure this plan is going to work?" She asked.

"No, I'd be lying to you," I said to her "nothing can be taken for granted, but if I tell you to duck, then you duck."

"Jane, you're too tight. You need to loosen up and let me worry about what needs to be taken care of." "In all governments and military, there is always someone that is your boss." "Are you going to stand up and question your boss's orders?" I didn't wait for her to answer, "They won't either." "If I create a scene, it'll catch someone's attention, and action will be taken." "Trust me. I've been here before."

"Let's just say, what if it doesn't?" She questioned.

"Then Jane, you better duck." "Are you having second thoughts?" I asked her.

"No, I was just thinking that I liked it better when we were alone." She said.

"I don't spend enough time with you, do I?" I asked her.

"All girls want the person they love to be with them at all times." "It's a girl thing," "we want to squeeze the man we love, and we want to be kissed by the man we love." "I'm not going to press this relationship, and you told me back at the cabin a lot of the things that I asked was privileged information." "At the time, I didn't have any idea what world you lived in." "I had thoughts of my own." She said.

"I know you thought of me as being neurotic," I said.

"Smith, I didn't know you." She said apologetically, "When I saw the hologram and talked to it.

"You went back after I left, didn't you?" I interrupted her.

"After I read your letter, I did" "and when I talked to it, it talked to me like me and you are talking to each other right now, but it responded like it was trying to be gentle to me." "Not like we were in love." She said. "And that scares me."

"You aren't recording all that, are you?" She asked as she lifted her head a little to one side to give me the eye.

"Everything is processed and recalled when needed," I responded.

"You mean, like you?" She asked.

"It's in the memory banks." "It's building a closer bond with you; the goal is for you to accept the conversation as being with the person you want to be with." "I use a more idealistic approach." "All the questions you asked of it, they were about me." I told her, "Those questions you asked were honest questions, and as I told you, you have to be careful of what you ask. You will only be given honest answers." "When I programmed the computer, I didn't know you this way."

"That's what I'm saying," "you kept saying I can't afford to be involved in a relationship, or I can't take a chance, or I can't do this, or I can't do that." She said as she became a little miffed, "If you programmed the hologram to only speak the truth, then I feel something is wrong."

I took her hand, "you're here with me, and we are a couple that finds comfort from being with each other." "That hologram was programmed before I met you. I didn't have feelings for you then." "Now I have to do a bit of reprogramming so that the answer it gives has the opportunity to have a better connection with the questions that you pose to it from now on." "When you use it again, and you will, you'll receive a different reception." "Jane, I wasn't exposed to others after your father began to take care of me, and I had a lot of time to think."

"Smith, I don't think I'm going to be able to be comfortable sitting in a man's lap that doesn't look like the man that I love."

"We'll see." I told her, "A week from now, you'll be bored with me and see someone in a magazine or on television, and then one day you'll say, can you make yourself look like this guy here?"

"You better be trying to be a comedian, mister." She quipped, "Because, I done told you once, and you had a photographic memory and all, should remember, I got you on the stringer and in the boat." "If I have to put my foot on you to keep you down, then I'll do it." "You aren't getting away from me, at least not without a fight." "It's you that I worry about; I don't want to be boring to you."

"Oh!" "So that's the problem," I said to her.

"What problem?"

"You've seen a lot of things that occur to appear to be futuristic to you, and a lot of those things you saw, you thought never could materialize." "You see me, and you see yourself, and you see yourself as not quite capable of measuring up to what you think I might think of you, if not now, then someday." "You are encased in a cocoon of low self-esteem." I notified her of what I thought.

"Wait a minute; give me a little time here." She said, "I have to rehear what I heard and cycle it in today's way of speaking." "Is that what you think?" "That I'm not intelligent enough for you?"

"No," I didn't say that." I said to her, "remember, I said I would never question your intelligence; you chose me over all those other guys out there."

"What other guys?" "No one wanted a date with an Amazon." She said.

I pulled on her hand to sit in my lap. I pulled on a switch, and my chair began to ease back slowly. "Say when," I told her.

"When," she said after she could lay her head down on my shoulder, "Am I uncomfortable for you?" She asked me.

I put my arms around her and held her tight. "I asked you not to speak of yourself that way." "If you were smaller, I might not have fallen in love with you." "It so happens that I'm extremely attracted to tall women, and the taller the woman, the more attracted I am to her, so you best be watching out because if I see a taller woman than you." "I might turn my head." "Jane," I whispered, "That hologram was a prototype and nothing more." "I had problems dealing with problems, and one thing led to another." "I dabbled with fiber optics, worked with mirrors, and installed a program that offered a personality that delivered a differing point of view." "It didn't help me." "I programmed it, so I knew all the answers that it was going to give me." "But it does do a good job of analyzing the comparisons of my characters."

"But how can you do that?" She asked softly.

"I've been working on being able to bend light since I started studying black holes; the hologram turned out to be a small side effect, on what it can do." "There's a downside of that prototype; I can control the weather with it." "Let's say a nuclear attack was underway from any country to any country." "I can create an antimatter magnetic fog, and a solar vortex erupts, and the electric field that the vortex generates disturbs and releases negative electrons and discharges electricity directly to the warhead as it passes through it." "Nothing can penetrate it." "You'll only see that if the world goes to war, but if I'm not here when it does, you won't see it come into play." "This plane is carrying another example of the success that my hologram led to." "When someone points a laser beam at you, it bounces back, and an object can be detected." "It's a lot of big word explanations I could use, but the best way to explain it is to say it simply, it's a force field that allows any device used to travel over or under my plane, and in the end, it bends around it." "We don't exist on any radar until we want to exist, such as landing this plane." "If I don't let them see me, they'll try and wreck my plane looking for the reason why, and that would ruin your dinner."

"So you won't release what you know because you believe that all good things are used for bad things." "You're a brilliant man; you know that, don't you?" She said.

"I listen better." I told her, "As I said, I read where it said that all roads are paved with good intentions, but sometimes there's a story behind a story." "It basically describes that when the roads are paved with the good intentions, the price a person is willing to take to change the direction of the road requires that the road be changed in many different directions." "Not all people take the same amount of money to change the road, some of them want more, and it takes a lot of people to build a road." "Jane," "my views are realistic." "The day you become angry with me is the day that you'll begin to lose what you see in me, and I'm a man with a lot of things that go through his head, and all of them show that the odds are stacked; up against me." "My hologram gave you that same answer, too," I told her.

"My mom and dad are still happy," she said softly, "and you can't go by what the hologram told you, you programmed it to say that, and Smith, this is one time you're wrong." "You've been right about everything in the past, I'll give you that, but this is one time. You're wrong."

"Maybe that's because they have you," I said to her. "You're a common bond between them." "Besides, your mother is a dedicated woman, but don't tell your father that your mother will lose her strength against him."

"I take after my mother's side of the family." She told me, "Smith, we've been together for only a short time, but that letter you wrote me had a lot of mystery to it."

"Jane, you've been in love many times." "You see a movie, and you get a crush on a young man." "You see a man waiting at a counter for a drink, and you think of him as being cute." "You fell in love with your husband." "You felt love, and you lived love." "I never felt those feelings about anyone, so every day that I'm with you only teaches me more." "You brought up the suggestion about me getting bored with you." "We have something in common." "You can see I'm not a man that goes out in public unless there are intentions, and when I do go out, I don't go out as the man you sleep with."

"Why did you bring us along with you?" She asked with a curious misunderstanding.

"Up until now, all you've heard about me was words spoken without action." "I've shown you a lot of the prototypes that you've seen, and it's helped change a lot of things that you had questions about." "Each day, you have less and fewer doubts of what I say, and so does your mother." "There is only one final solution to help you to understand who I am, and when you return to the lab, you and your mother will talk." "This is how I get into a country without being seen, and when you return, you'll be with the same problems that plagued me." "Take your mother into the control room, and both of you can ask the hologram any question's that you have about me, or if you like, you can ask the computer to send in an android." "It's going to help your mother more than it will you." "The hologram offers an image to my computer." "It analyzed your voice, and now you and your mother can activate it." "Don't be afraid to experiment, and it won't do anything you're not authorized." "It's like when you asked to see two people making love." "Jane, all you have to do is ask, and it will obey your commands."

"You don't trust me?" She said, smiling.

"Ask the hologram that question," I told her. "And remember that it was programmed a long time before you arrived in my life."

"Smith" "you're going to laugh," "but I feel awful funny kissing you when you look like that." She said, smiling. She reached up with her lips and started kissing me, and then she began laughing. "I'm sorry, Smith." She resumed kissing me, and she started laughing again.

"I'm sorry." She said again.

"Smith," she said, as she stopped kissing me, "Do you understand how difficult it is to have a flight to Monterrey in a private jet to eat dinner and not be able to tell anyone anything about it?" She then took on a more serious nature "I asked the hologram about my husband." "Why did you answer it the way you did?"

"I don't think I want to reply to that." I told her, "Ask the hologram. That's why I built it."

"I did," "and it gave me an answer I sought." She said, "I want to talk to you, a live man, not a hologram." "I want to come to you for answers, not a hologram, or call for James or Ruby." "I want to know why you answered my question that way."

"Marriage was once a contract between two people to live with one another." "It was supposed to be a marriage that nothing could separate." "And then for the sake of man, a divorce was granted to the men that no longer wanted their wives." "So, in order to calm the people in their religion, they were granted their freedom from each other." "In reality, the contract was broken when either of the two could no longer live harmoniously with one another." "I answered that question knowing that all people that enter into a contract of marriage will be tested at some point in the stability of the marriage, whether it's the first test or a test of many, somewhere the contract was broken." "I find that to be true in all marriages."

"That's your interpretation." She said, "All people have fights or some sort of disagreements, but that doesn't mean that all of those people that have a fight end up in a divorce." "Smith," "I started crying from the very beginning of your letter." "You said" "and I'll never forget this," "you said the only way you would know if you were in heaven or hell as if I was with you, then you knew you were in heaven." "I burst out in tears, and Ruby came in to talk to me." "My dad was right; sometimes you forget you're talking to an android."

"How long does it take?" I asked her.

"What?" She answered me.

"When people fight, how long does it take them to heal a wound that cuts deep?"

She looked at me strangely.

"Smith," "will you marry me?" She said.

"You've already asked that question, so you know what the answer was that I gave." "Isn't that what this conversation is about?" I asked her.

"I'm not asking you in a way that the computer answered me." "I would marry you by a contract of a vow only." "No paperwork, no church, no dress with bridesmaids dressed in white." "I went through all of that, and it didn't have the meaning I thought it had." "I would tell you that our marriage would be a marriage that only existed as long as you wanted me." "When the day came, and you felt tested, then that's the day, as you say, our marriage will be dissolved." "Your computer told me to expect that day to come." "So, I'm in a dryer being tumbled around as it turns." "Smith, I don't want that to happen to the man I'm in love with, and I don't know where I stand in your life." "In my dream, you kept getting further and further away as I ran for you." "Sometimes it hurts, you know?" She concluded as her reddened eyes said it all.

"Jane, you and I both are weighted down with insecurity." "No matter how many times I tell you I love you, and no matter how many times you tell me you love me, we both wonder sometimes about making mistakes." "What does being married mean to you?" I asked her.

"Nothing, it's exactly the way you described it. Every day I woke up to another lie." "At least that's what happened to me." Her words were breaking up.

"Jane," "commitment between two people were sharing a common feeling for one another in marriage." "I watched as you moved around back at my stone house, and I find marriage to be very painful." "I'm not much of a man that can offer anybody much of anything, but as to your marriage contract of vows, my hopes of finding the person that I would make those vows to grow old with is being held in my arms." "I hope I die proving that what I thought was right was wrong." "I was a different person then, and I'm a different person now because of you."

"So, you're saying that you would marry me?" She said.

"Jane, you and I were married when you put your arms around me and held me," "when we were in the sleeping bag back at my stone house; you had your hand on my heart, and it hurt." "I never felt anything like I felt then, and I knew that come spring, I would have had to take you away and leave you at the resort." "I know what it feels like when you fall in love with a person and not be able to tell them. That's a strong learning experience." "Somehow, I slipped up."

"You're wrong again, Smith. If you only knew how bad I feel right now, you'd know."

"Jane, as far as the marriage vows are concerned, there's a lot that we would have to work on."

"Give me a for instance," she said, "and I'll stop."

A light came on, and the plane began to tilt and turn south a few degrees.

"What's going on?" She asked.

"We're over water;" "we've reached the closest point of land before we reach the point of no return."

"What's that supposed to mean?"

"The point of no return is when you reach the point to where it's closer to try to make it to land one way and not try to go back the other way, it's further." "But that's only if we have engine trouble," I told her.

"I don't really like flying that much." She said.

"I designed and built the engines," I told her.

"Don't tell me; they're prototyped too, right?" She said.

"Yep, aerodynamically correct to utilize all currents of wind flows." "We fly at different altitudes to take advantage of the quickest currents, and we silently drift along." "As the fuel draws down from the tanks, I developed a gas that floats on the fuel, and as the fuel is used, the gas lightens the weight of the plane, and thereby requiring less fuel." "So the longer we fly, the less fuel we use." "A small airline operates airplanes that weigh seventy tons or more." "A large airline operates planes that weigh around three hundred tons." "They have to push that weight all the way to where ever it's going." "Mine doesn't; the less fuel, the lighter the plane, and the less the engines have to produce." "But there's more." "The weight of a plane is constant, and you can't change a constant." "But, the angle of the wings automatically begins to contract and lift to capture those hundred and sixty miles an hour tailwinds, and we use them to help push us along." "You might look at it as if we were a kite being held up by the wind," I told her.

She looked into my eyes.

"My mother was right; you're good at diverting attention away from an answer."

"Jane, can you get up for a moment?" I asked her.

I reached down and took a dollar bill out of the drawer, started rolling it, and fashioned a ring that I slid on her finger.

"Where did you learn to do that?" She asked.

"Shanghai," "I watched as a man bet another man that he could turn it into a ring." "I paid for both of their drinks and then disposed of their bodies." "I drugged their drinks, but that man taught me how to make a ring before he died."

"What did they do?" She asked.

"They were in the business of stealing babies and selling them." "I came upon them by accident." "I was involved in something else, and they got caught in the crossfire." "The problem was trying to find where all of them went to." "No records were kept, and there were very poor samples taken to identify anyone." "How can you know you were stolen and sold if you grew up with a family that has papers to show them that you were born to them?" "One thing was certain; they left the country," I said. "They were adopted or sold as sex slaves."

"So," she said, "you felt you were better off taking the option you chose then?"

"There were over three hundred abductions in two months after they were disposed of; the numbers retreated by almost a hundred children."

"You did the right thing." She said, "I can only imagine what a mother goes through when she finds out that her baby has been stolen." "I see stuff like that on TV." "And in this case, you did the right thing."

"But it didn't have anything to do with my mission" "I made it personal," I told her.

"Smith, right is always right." "Sometimes you can't kill roaches by spraying them; they don't die quick enough, they lay there kicking and running around, the only way to kill them is if you stomp on them, and that way you know that they're dead; and I hate roaches with a passion." "Smith, I'm not much of a help to you, I'm awestruck with what I'm around, and like I said, intelligence isn't one of my strongest attributes." "But I read too," "and I read that a rose by any other name is still a rose, you said that too" "the same goes for roaches in my books." "A roach by any other name is still a roach, and those men were roaches of the worst kind." "You can't spray them; you have to stomp on them." She lectured me.

"You don't find my actions as being ugly?" I asked her.

"Smith, the only way I learned was from you. I watched a lot of movies that were supposed to have been based on true stories." "And up until now, that's all that they were, actors and actresses telling a story." "Besides," "this isn't a dinner in Monterrey anymore" "now it's a honeymoon and dinner in Monterrey." She said, laughing, "So when it comes to making memories, you've got a patented delivery to your proposal."

I walked back into the small kitchen area, made a pot of coffee, and then went back to the cockpit. Jane sat in the copilot's seat and gazed out the window upon the horizon.

"It never gets old," I said.

"What?" She asked.

"Up here, you see the sun and moon from a different perspective; you can leave in the morning from somewhere and arrive in the morning to where you're going." "You gain time, and you lose time, depending on where you're going or coming from." "Do you remember when I was telling you about the covered wagons with the pioneers?" I asked her, and without hesitation, I continued, "Now look at how far we've come." "That was over two hundred years ago."

I once again got up and went and poured us a cup of coffee. I pushed a button, and Jane asked what I was doing.

"Your father likes to have a little time to wake up." I responded, "We passed the point of no return a while back, and I need to give instructions on our landing to the tower." "So, I pushed an alarm to wake him" "I found out, he likes his coffee waiting for him when he awakes." "He growls loud if you don't." I turned off my stealth mode."

"You two were close, weren't you?" She stated.

"We got along for a while, and then we went our separate ways." I told her, "That was in the past; those issues that we had were political." "And a wise man once said that there are three arguments that you can't win." "That's politics, religion, and your wife." "Stay away from those topics, and a conversation can be held in good taste." "Discuss any of those three issues, and an argument is going to develop."

"Morning," Jack growled as he walked into the cockpit with a cup of coffee in his hand. He was followed by Ellen. She was also carrying a cup.

"Have you notified the tower yet?" Jack asked.

"No, I was getting ready." I told him, "But I did turn off our stealth mode,"

"Go ahead and get the cats ready; I'll take over from here." He said, yawning, and then took a sip of his coffee and set it down in a holder as he took my place.

I listened as he readjusted his seat, and then I heard his wife start asking him all sorts of questions.

I sat down at the computer and began giving orders to the tower to accept our flight without interruptions and that our clearance was authorized. I put a danger sign that dignitaries were aboard and that all interruptions would be inhospitable and consequences would be dealt with severely.

"It's that easy?" Jane said as I began putting chutes on the bobcats.

"Those without authority don't question those with authority." "But in all situations, I take precautions." "I intercept calls made to upper echelons, and my computer copies verbal tones and then initiates verbal responses that are identical in speech. If they use a computer, they are already infected with my virus. I just sent it to them." "All contacts are blocked, and my computer issues their orders." "By the time we arrive, affidavits will be in their computer," I told her.

"So, you give orders to those that give orders?" She queried.

"Jane, a computer is the mainstream of an avenue that the brain can control." "The brain is the most complex computer of them all." "It's a friend if you have friends that belong to you." "The computers at the airport; they all belong to me." "I capture a message that's sent, and that message infects all computers that it has contact with; that's why it's called a virus." "Think of it as veins that feed all extremities of the body and then return back to the arteries to go to your heart." "Jane, when we leave this plane, I want you to know that I'll no longer be smith; I will become Pedro Gonzalez, in body and in mind." "So when we exit, our relationship as a couple."

"A married couple." She quickly inserted.

I smiled again.

"What are you thinking about?" She asked.

"Your husband hasn't been found yet, and legally you're still married to him." "You're breaking the laws in some states," I said, grinning.

"You know what gives here." She stated.

"It doesn't matter; you're still breaking the law, according to the interpretation of the law, and in this matter, the law is clear, you're guilty of polygamy," I said to her.

"But, we're not really married." She said.

"Aren't we?" I responded.

"Smith, I'm a grown girl, and I know my place; you're a man that needs a lot of space."

"Are you saying my vows were worthless?" I asked her.

"No, I've never been so happy in my life." "But your hologram."

"Jane, that hologram is going to be changed; I won't take back my commitment that I made to you."

She threw herself at me and started practicing her rules.

She pushed herself back and tried to straighten out her hair and her clothes. When we entered the cockpit, we both had a fresh cup of coffee in our hands.

"What's the temperature, Jack?" I asked him.

"Eighty-six and the sun's just starting to rise." He reported.

"Computer; open doors and eject the cats," I ordered.

Jack and I watched as a red light came on and then turned to green. I turned to Jane and Ellen.

"Alright ladies, listen up." "Nothing to drink unless it comes from a bottle; the water is impure, that means no ice." "The German's drank beer, and the Italians drank wine; for that very reason, the water wasn't pure." "You stand out in the crowd wearing those warm-weather clothing." "So that's a matter that we'll have to attend to first, and that means we have to go to a marketplace, Jane." I said, looking at her." "Jack doesn't eat till we eat at a restaurant a little ways away from the tourist areas." "They make the best tamales, and Jack stuff's himself to the gills." "He used to be able to handle three dozen and then order three more dozen to go." "Time has ticked by since we visited it last." "I don't even know if it's still there or if it has changed ownership." "So if any of you are hungry, we could eat breakfast, or a brunch, or lunch. This is your day, so you do the deciding," I told them.

The lady looked at her husband and then back at me.

"I can wait." She said.

"Jane, I'm afraid that leaves you out; whether you're hungry or not, the majority rules."

"I wasn't hungry until you mentioned tamales; now I'm starving." She said.

Jack spoke up.

"If they're still there, you'll remember that place for the rest of your life." He started laughing. "I remember when we were here not quite three days." "I ate tamales for breakfast, dinner, and supper." "I couldn't stop eating them." "They put this chili over the top and talk about eating; I kept on ordering a dozen at a time." "I'm going to take my chances and hope that they're still there." He concluded.

"Then," I said, "first the marketplace, and then we eat." "That is if Jack can hold off a little."

"Buckle up," Jack said, "We're starting our descent."

I sat across from Jane and watched Ellen tense her muscles.

"Ellen relax; Jack wasn't the best pilot when it came to a landing." "Now that he's flown all over the world, he's learned a few things since he first began," I said to her to calm her.

When we finally landed, we walked towards customs and were greeted by an agent. He looked at our passports and then asked some questions. I answered him in his language, and he responded with an attitude. I became irritated, and it caught the attention of one of his supervisors.

I could tell he was automatically beginning to choose his side that he was going to support, and it wasn't mine.

He walked up and began to use his power to dominate control. I gave him a smile when he reached for my papers. I told him that I didn't like traveling for hours every day and receiving treatment like I'm receiving now in my own country. I can expect treatment of this nature from other countries that I visit. I get angry easily when I encounter those that push me too hard. Show me your papers. I told him. I looked up and saw a man pushing a broom, cleaning the floors. I then looked around and saw other people doing janitor work. "If you had read the information that was sent to you, we would have avoided this confrontation."

Jane walked up to me and then began asking if there was a problem. She then went on to add that she was tired and that she only had a little time to spend here. "Tell those people, Pablo," she said, "to get on with whatever they need from us." "If not, I'm ready to get back on the plane and go on to Cancun." "I'll file my report in flight."

"Senorita, that's Pedro, not Pablo," I said to her.

"Whatever" "I get bored with these people." She stated with an attitude, "Eduardo promised me there wouldn't be any delays."

"Si senorita" "I'll take care of this immediately." I bowed to her and then returned my attention back to the officials.

"If I have to return to the plane, the president is not going to be pleased." "Those janitors over there will be doing your job tomorrow, and I promise you that you'll be the one pushing the broom." "You have three minutes." I told him, "And if you have doubts as to what my authority extends to, you can call the President; I don't like people to push me around, especially those that are my inferior officers."

He gave the passports back to the women and Jack, and he handed me my papers.

"I'm sorry for the inconvenience." He said to all of us.

I handed him an envelope. "Tomorrow, you'll be receiving a promotion." "It's a gift to you for any of my future arrivals." "I don't want to go through this again." "It makes officials of other countries upset." He looked into the envelope. "It draws attention from people that report what they see if you know what I mean." I told him, "But understand this; you'll be buried the next time we meet if you give me any more problems." "Do I make myself clear?" I asked him.

"Si," He replied quickly.

"I'd like the plane to be fueled and ready to depart tonight." I told him, "No one is allowed inside; it's not accessible." "The fuel cells are equipped with gauges that determine if any foreign substance has been added to cause problems while in flight and will shut down all fueling; if this happens, I'll hold you personally responsible." "Accidents don't just happen; they are caused." "Capitan, if anything happens to my guest." "Blame will be given to our President."

"Si," He said.

"Bueno," I told him. "I see you are moving up quickly," I added.

He saluted me and then began giving orders to not give us any problems, and he personally escorted us through the gates.

A taxi pulled up and asked us where we were headed, and I spoke to him. Soon we arrived at the marketplace and were talking to women that were looking at Jane and Ellen.

I told them we had changed our flight plans, and they weren't prepared for the heat.

"How much?" I asked the ladies.

They were giving me an amount that was too high. I then responded. "If you can deliver our goods in one hour, I'll give you ten times that of what you ask," I told them.

They quickly began and started using tape measures to get their sizes. "Muy Grande." One of the ladies spoke of Jane.

My mind was on other things.

"Jack," I said to him, "we have observers," I said, laughing and tapping him on the left shoulder. It was a signal to show him where to look without making eye contact.

"There are three on your left side, standing against the wall," I told him so that he was aware of their locations. "They have a way of identification; all the buttons on their shirts are unbuttoned." "Twenty feet to their left are four more. The ones smoking the cigarettes are for the frontal assault." "They'll move past their counterparts and get in position."

"Are you sure of an attack?" He asked.

"When they saw us, they began their preparations; I'm certain of this, the women are a mark."

I turned around as if I was looking at all of the items that were for sale. Jack also did the same.

"Look over at the fruit stand, and there's four more." I told him, "They'll make a move when the others move." "See that clearing over by the water fountain." "That's where we'll have our encounter; a small opening gives them the opportunity to deliver full power with their punches or kicks or their weapons." "Jack, this is something we don't need to tell the women. It'll only make them nervous."

Purses were bought, shoes were selected, and bracelets and necklaces were purchased. As we began walking through the marketplace, I saw Jack looking out of the corner of his eyes at our assailants.

I walked over to Jack and spoke to him in a jubilant way, "When I tell you now, grab the women around the waist and pull them down." "The window of opportunity is small, and they can vanish into the crowd that's in front of them, the people will get out of their way so that they can make their escape." "They won't want to get hurt by them." "I don't want anyone hurt," I told him.

The group of men began pushing past their counterparts, and I shouted to Jack, now. They were not expecting what had taken place. I grabbed an umbrella off of a stand and began using it to apply pain by stabbing the solar plexus of several of the men with the pointed end and following through with a sidekick to the jaw and a back kick to the sternum of another. A blow came my way, and I blocked it with the curved end of the umbrella, twisted his arm with it, and forced him down so that I could give him a front kick to the face. When I did, the force knocked him out and ended my threat from him. I gave a roundhouse kick and caught three men unprepared and then finished them off with a sidekick to the jaw to each one.

Immediately after, two came at me with knives. I began backflips and put myself in front of the women, only to see them staring at me and then running away.

I walked back over and paid for the umbrella and thanked the man for letting me use it. Then I walked over and looked down at the men lying on the ground, moaning and groaning in pain. I gave each one a hard knock to his head and went through each of their pockets. One of the men wasn't the way he was supposed to be, I gave him a punch to his nose, and when his head hit the pavement, I no longer found him to be uncooperative, and I proceeded in doing what I was doing. I took everything that they had of value and threw everything that they owned into the air, and all the people began scrambling around trying to get as much of it as they could.

I turned around and looked at Jack. "Are you hungry?" I asked him. And then I turned to the women that were looking at me like I had done something that they didn't expect.

"What just happened?" Ellen asked.

Jack spoke for me, "Both of you were an easy target. They were going to grab your purses and run." "Smith and I were going to receive the brunt of the attack, and while you were doing the best that you could, that's when you were going to take a hit so that they could steal your purse." He said, "Or maybe there was another reason." "Right now, I don't have any reason to believe we were a target for a hit; I think we were involved with petty thieves." He said.

"When did you know they were there?" She asked.

"When Smith told me." He said, smiling at her.

She then looked over at me.

I gave her her explanation "When we got out of the taxi, the group of men was gathered in one area; they split up and positioned themselves so that they could attack." "That was my first clue; you don't separate from friends unless you had something planned." "If they had stayed where they were at, then they wouldn't have been a threat." "But, they didn't, and I knew then that we were the mark." "The second was they had identification." "They were the only ones with their shirts unbuttoned." "Let's go; Jack's been waiting all morning."

We traveled by foot, and the women stopped now and then to explore the differences of the culture. They didn't like seeing the goats skinned and hanging in the open, though.

I turned my head now and then to look at all the products that were available, but I was really surveying my surroundings to see if we were being followed, and when I did, a young man made a rush to grab a ladies purse in a crowd of people as they passed about twenty feet up from where we were walking. As soon as he neared, he came running towards us, and before I could act, Ellen caught him in the groin with a knee, and when he gave way to pain, Jane gave him a kick to his jaw. He was out cold.

I walked over and looked down at the man and then looked back at the woman. I spoke to them in a heavy accent. "I don't really think you needed me back there, and it seems like you could have handled yourself on your own," I said as I went through his pants and took what little he had, and like before, I threw it into the air. People were rushing in to pick what few coins fell.

"I just reacted," Ellen commented.

"Yes, ma'am," "the art of self-defense is a reaction to an action, and I would say that you both reacted nicely." I then looked up at Jane. "You have good form," I said, smiling at her.

After the lady that was the source of the crime came over and took her purse, she couldn't thank them enough for what they had done for her. Ellen turned to me.

"Do all tourists that come here go through this kind of thing?" She asked.

"This area isn't recommended for tourists." "We're not in the protected areas." "They wander in and out along the edges of security." "They prey upon those that wander too close, and those that don't expect anything to occur, find themselves to be a victim of a pipe or a knife, or a fist." "A sucker punch to a woman is all that is needed to grab hold of what is targeted and make a quick exit."

"Do you come here all the time?" She continued in her question.

"No ma'am," "I travel to all countries." "I don't socialize and inhabit many areas where suits are required." "I don't have those kinds of clothes, but in this, I'm an official, I have to wear a suit of distinction." "To find a rat, you have to go where the rats live." "This area here is in the outskirts of the city, and we're starting to travel through the slums now." "They see very few tourists here, so you can understand the risk is often worth the chance," I said to them.

"You could have warned us, you know?" Ellen expressed her concerns with an agitated way of speaking.

"I did. I said for you to expect anything out of the ordinary." I told her, "You weren't listening, that's all."

"Yeah, but you could have been a little more specific, and you also said that we would be protected; I didn't see anyone around except you." She added.

"That's because Jack likes to let me take care of the small fish." I told her, "He was ready and waiting to spring into action, but I told him to stand down." I gave her a smile. "Ellen, no one knows what to expect from anyone, not even in our own country." "In this country, what you have in your purse may be a year's income for most of these people." "Now, if you'll excuse me, I see Jack's in a hurry." "He only has one thing on his mind, and that's to see if the restaurant is still there, and more importantly, do they still make the tamales that he craves? He's a man that's been deprived for too long." "Jack is not without his faults," I told them.

We left with people gathering around and watching as we departed, and I noticed several hundred feet up the road; Jack began to quicken his pace.

"What's gotten into him?" Ellen asked.

"He sees the restaurant." I said to her, "He's a hungry man with a mission." I added, "And judging by his movements, it's still there." "I told you Jack has his faults."

"I wasn't hungry until I smelled the food. Now I'm a little hungry too."
Jane said, "They don't cook those goats there, do they?"

"They're called Cabrito." "So don't order Cabrito," I stated to her.

When we sat down at a table, chips were brought with salsa, and everyone
didn't waste any time beginning the feast. When the waiter came, I ordered
three orders of tamales, heavy on the chili for Jack. The waiter looked at me
strangely, and I told him the story of how he always ordered one at a time
when we came here a long time ago. "He has much admiration for your
tamales, so, I say why wait when I know what is to come," I told him.

I then continued by ordering separate orders of tamales for each of the
rest of us and then ordered one of all of the other items that were listed on
the menu.

Once again, the waiter looked at me strangely.

"I want my guest to sample all of the food you have available." "And I
don't want a sampler platter, and there are reasons for everything." I then said
to him and slipped a wad of money into his pocket. "My friend, these people
are important people." "I need special attention for my guests," I told him.

He left and constantly returned with food, and he had to pull up extra
tables to hold it all and to see that everyone was being taken care of in the
manner that I requested. He took on the role of becoming our personal
attendant and remained by our side.

As usual, Jack ignored everything except the tamales. The women were
different; they had to take a bite of everything that they hadn't tasted, but
their decisions were not that easy to make on what to taste.

Later on, after everyone had eaten all, they could.

I told the waiter that I needed nine dozen tamales to go, and I needed a
lot of to-go boxes. He returned and began to put the rest of the food away,
and by the time he finished, the tamales were ready for Jack.

After leaving the restaurant, we entered a taxi, and I took my guests away
from the city and into the countryside.

Along the way, we passed some of the local inhabitants. The children
chased us as we drove by. "These people are the poorest of the poor." I told
them, "They don't have a dime." "That restaurant you ate at, these people
won't ever eat there."

We passed a small place and watched as the kids ran along with us,
holding out their hands and watching us as we drove down.

Jane shouted, stop. I instructed the driver to do as she asked.

"Back up," she said. Once again, I instructed the driver to do as she asked.

"Stop," she commanded. She got out of the car, and all the kids and
people that lived there began running towards her. They were amazed to see
her height.

She gave them all the boxes of food that we didn't eat, minus Jacks tamales, and that was because he kept a firm grip on them, and the kids didn't waste time eating it. When she got back into the taxi, the driver turned to her and spoke to her.

She looked over at me. "He said that you are a woman with a heart as big as your size."

We then traveled to other places, and more clothes were made for the women. No other problems were encountered. I told the ladies that visitors don't come out here because there's nothing here to attract them. "They stay where the nightlife is active, and they don't take home what the real city of Monterrey consists of. They could stay at home and see any Spanish rows of shops and see the same thing." "But, this is the real Monterrey." I said to them, "Take notice that none of the people here poses themselves as a threat." "When in poor neighborhoods, police aren't around; here, a thief isn't tolerated." "These people take care of their own, and when it comes to safety, I'd rather be here than in the city." "The city is money to those that have evil intentions on their mind; there isn't any money here, so there aren't any thieves," I told them.

As nighttime grew close, I instructed the driver to return us back to the airport. I paid him what he would have earned in three months. When he thanked me for the tip, I spoke to him.

"If I contact you again, can I trust you to be there for me?" I asked him.

He looked at the money, and then he looked at me.

"My country is a country of good and bad." He chose his words well as he looked at me.

"What is your name?" I asked him.

He was reluctant to answer.

"My friend, there is a number on the side of your car, I can find you easily, and if I wish to harm your family, it wouldn't be difficult." "Once again, I ask you what your name is, and tell me no lies."

"Raul Martinez." He said in Spanish.

"Raul, many men here will do anything for money, you included." "I didn't come here looking for those that break the law." "In my travels, I saw prostitutes, dealers, and I encountered other controversies with petty thieves." "Is this the country you wish for your children to grow up in?" "I don't see a future for them other than crime."

"Where do you stand?" I asked him.

"I see nothing, and I hear nothing." He told me, "I mind my own business and not stick my nose in places that will get it cut off."

I gave him a smile. "Good answer," I told him, "Now, we need to talk" "You can speak English better than any of us; my guests are with me." "Who do you work for?" "And don't give me any of this. I am a poor taxi driver bull." "Which country are you with?" I demanded.

He began hesitating and acting as if he didn't understand what I was talking about.

I stuck a knife to his throat. Jane and Ellen both became startled. "Do as I tell you and do it now if you get foolish; this taxi will be saturated with the blood that will flow from me, cutting your throat." "I want answers, and I'd be careful. I'm a man that doesn't like liars, and at this time, you're not on my friend's list." "Start talking, and I'd start now. I don't like wasting my time counting," I told him.

"I'm assigned to Congressman McNally." He said in a choking voice. "I observe and report any abnormal activity."

I took my laptop and told him to put his thumb on the square that I ordered him.

Within moments, I pulled the knife away, and he began rubbing his neck, checking with his fingers to see if he had any blood on it.

"How did you recognize me?" He asked.

"I saw you three times, once in the marketplace, and once before we went into the restaurant, and each time you were unoccupied and parked; a taxi doesn't make money when it's parked, and on the third time, you happen to be conveniently available when we came out of the restaurant and ready to leave." "But do you really want to know what gave you away?" I asked him.

He looked back at me in his rearview mirror.

"You have an American dialect, and there aren't any taxis that enter that part of the city. There isn't any money there." "The tip I gave you was three months' wages, yet you didn't seem impressed." "You're a rookie at this game, kid, and why would someone like McNally give you this job, knowing you knew very little about surveillance?" I asked him and then asked him another question without waiting for an answer. "Why are you here?"

"I was sent to observe." He said.

"Observe what?" I asked him.

"The activity in drugs is beginning to carry over into the U.S. has increased three hundred percent, and the violence is beginning to hit the border towns." "I saw you with Senator Morgan and wanted to see if I could come up with anything that was out of the ordinary." "One thing I do know about Pedro." "Pedro doesn't know martial arts." "So, I know you aren't Pedro." "Who are you, CIA, FBI, SS?" He asked.

"First off, your name isn't Raul Martinez; it's Jose." I told him, "And secondly, you don't have the clearance to ask me anything, and I don't have the opportunity or the time to let you know anything about me." "I ask the questions, and you give me the answers. That way, you and I will get along fine. If you choose not to give truthful answers, we'll end our relationship now." I said to him in a soft voice.

"McNally requested you personally." "Why?" I asked him.

"I busted a load of heroin with a street value of close to half a million." He said.

"Huh!" I chuckled.

"Did I say something funny?" He asked.

"Let me guess." I told him, "You're going to be in Juarez at the end of the week, aren't you?"

He looked up at me. "How did you know?"

"McNally's coming here, isn't he?" I said to him.

He didn't answer me.

"You're being set up, kid." I said to him, "First off, a gunfight will erupt; only it's staged." "The purpose is to draw all the law enforcement to that one area; it's nothing more than a diversion, the Police Chief is bought and paid for." "Secondly, you were chosen personally, and I'm guessing here, probably because the bust you made could have been McNally's load, and he may have you in his sights." "Ask yourself this one little question, what are you doing here, and why did he send for you?" "The question I have now is, what am I going to do with you?" "I can't kill you, and I can't let you go," I said.

"Jack, take Jane and Ellen back to the lab," I told him.

I got into the taxi. "Drive," I said.

"Where to?"

"Juarez," I told him.

As we were driving along outside of the city, I noticed a car parked off the side of the road. Its lights came on when we passed. Soon, red lights came on, and we pulled over; I took off my shoe and turned my heel around. The officer asked me for my papers, and I showed them to him, and then he walked back to his car.

When he started to come back out of his car, I saw in the side mirror that he was bringing out a shotgun with him.

I tossed my shoe out of the window back and hit the car, and it exploded.

"What happened?" Jose said as we sped away.

"I was a target of a hit." I told him, "It appears that our friend Pedro isn't liked by the cartels." "When I entered Monterrey, I encountered a little problem with one of the customs agents." "I have a friend in Mexico." I told him, "Jose," "all cops," "no matter what country, will ask a driver for papers first without asking the passenger for his second."

"Who are you?" "And how did you kill them?" He said.

"The heel of my shoe has plastic explosives inside." I gave him my explanation.

"Are you a spy?" He asked.

I once again chuckled and told him, "You've been watching too many movies." "Now, let's get moving. We don't want any more cops on our tails."

As we were driving along, I spoke to him.

"When I read who you were, I noticed that your brothers were killed along with your father." "They were all gang members, but you didn't go that route," I said, looking over at him.

"I came to that crossroad a long time ago." He said, "My mother was paralyzed that day, and she took a while before she died, but she made me promise not to get involved with any gangs." "She said I would wake up dead." "I heard the gunshots that day when I was across the street playing with my friends, but I didn't think it involved my family." "Those guys were gone before anyone got a glimpse of anything. All the witnesses said that they were in fear of their lives and ducked." "No one said they saw anything." "Even I didn't see them, and I was across the road."

"Jose, a gang operates, by fear," I told him.

"Well, after that, I went to stay with my aunt and uncle." "It wasn't much different there either. There were gangs there too." "Every city I've been to, they all have gangs." "So I figured the people that killed my family got killed the same way. If they didn't, then they were killed somehow. That's the only way out of these slums." He said to me, "I figure, this is where I belong, and it's my way of fighting back."

"You're wasting your time." I told him, "You can drain the water out of a ditch, but when it rains, it fills up again."

"What are you going to do with me?" He asked.

"I have a job to do, but I can't afford to take a chance and let you foul it up." I told him, "This is too important."

"So what now?" He said.

"Give me your arm." He was reluctant. "I said, give me your arm." When he slowly held it out to me, I stuck a band around it and attached it to a magnetic strip. "This is a movement locator." "If you leave the spot where I tell you to stay, I'm going to have to activate a small pin inside the band that will kill you." "On the tip of the pin is a flesh-eating virus that double's in size every second. It'll be injected directly into a vein in your wrist." "In less than thirty seconds, blood will begin to reach your heart, but that won't be what will kill you." "Your heart will look like jelly in five minutes." "It's that simple, and in case you're wondering?" "If you try and remove the band yourself, you'll be committing suicide." "Let's look at it from my point of view." "If you're an honest man, you've got nothing to worry about." "With me, it's the liars that get themselves killed." "Or you can think of it this way." I told him,

"If I'm right, I'm not keeping you from being killed by me; I'm keeping you from being killed by someone else."

"Who do you work for?" He asked.

I didn't answer his question.

"What's going down?" He once again asked.

"You don't listen very well, do you?" "You work for McNally." "I told you, you don't have the clearance. You'll know what you want to know when everyone else does, but heed my advice. You've come to a path that travels in two different directions." "You won't live if you go down the wrong road. It won't be one of the gangs that'll kill you; it'll be one of the cops."

I received a message from my computer and spoke to Jose, "Pull over." I told him, "There's a hotel in Juarez called Lupe's; remember that, Lupe's. Find it, ditch the taxi, and get a room and stay there until I come and get you."

"What makes you think you can trust me to do this?" He asked.

"I don't." "The band on your arm has a transmitter." "You can think of it as a lie detector, but with a lot more accuracy." "It reads your nervous system." "It's sort of like when you touch two magnets together, when they repel, you know something is up." "Everything you say and do is being monitored." "I'll know within three seconds if you betray me." "Jose, I don't want to kill you, but if I have to, I wouldn't think twice." "I've learned that no one can be trusted." "You will, too, if you live long enough." "And Jose, there's one other thing you should know, you stand out like a sore thumb, no gang member walks around without identification, and you don't have any." I said as I smiled at him, "You're a good kid, but you've got a lot to learn, this isn't where you can show a badge, and everyone throws down their weapons." "Jose, a gang member, is riddled with tattoos that tell his story of his life, his way." "You've got Fed written all over you." I got out of the car, walked to the driver's side, and knelt down. "Follow my orders and get rid of the car, and you'll find Lupe's Hotel is catered to a guest of the wealthy, so come morning, dress for success, and stay put, whether you know it or not, as soon as you check-in they'll know exactly where you are, and you can trust me on this, someone will be watching you until you make the call.

"How do you know about that?" He asked.

"I didn't." "But, now I do." "You were to call McNally and notify him that nothing was suspicious in the area, weren't you?"

"Yes." He answered.

"That was the signal for gunfire to start an all-out war." "No one would have survived." "They'll give proof of the raid being a success by showing pictures of bodies." "It's a simple way to dispose of people that get in the way." "They'll show pictures of the drugs that they confiscated." "You can wrap sugar or salt up in plastic, and it looks identical to cocaine." "People read and believe what they read, especially if you have a picture for the eyes to verify what was read." "It fools the brain." "You, my friend, are their signal for them to begin to move the drugs; you would have been the only victim in the melee, that is, except for the other people that were executed and planted." "You will be hailed as a hero." "Jose, you stopped one shipment while ten to twenty others got through?" "You were requested for one reason, and he wants you dead." I told him, "Oh yeah, there's one other thing," I said to him, "Drugs that have a street value of half a million isn't anything when you're talking about thirty to forty million." "Think about that while I'm gone." "You're being played like a puppet."

"When you made the busts, there were other agents involved, weren't they?" I asked him.

"Yes, sir."

"How many?"

"There was four, sir." He responded.

"Then that's another question you should ask yourself, where were those men supposed to be, and how come you were the only one to make a bust." "Jose, there's only one reason for McNally to come here this Saturday. Unfortunately for you, I think you're going to be involved in a diversion." "Honest cops trust their superiors and do what they are told to do, without question." "Jose, McNally needed someone, and he's fulfilled his quest." "You can't kill the enemy unless you destroy a vital organ. That's the only way it's going to die." "You're in a tough spot here." I told him, "You betray me, and you die." "Don't make me kill you," I repeated to him as I ran and concealed myself in tall grass.

I worked over to where my computer guided me. I needed to pick up my clothes and my explosives.

The sun found me resting with a camouflaged blanket that resembled my surroundings. I took advantage of the quiet and dozed.

A whiff of cool air alerted me to the change in the temperature, and I eased up from my blanket to see that the sun was beginning to set. I then closed the blanket and waited.

Nightfall was only minutes away. I was rested and resumed my travel until I found my point of entry. "Computer: is there any human activity in the area?" When I received my response, I looked up ahead of me and saw rats running everywhere, and that told me that my cats were active, and it also told me that no one else was around before the computer answered. When I arrived, I asked the computer if I had clearance, and my authorization was given immediately. I couldn't hear any sounds through my audible enhancer inside my ear, it was clear, so I worked my way out of the sewer.

I asked my computer to analyze all surveillance and scan my surroundings quickly. I set up my camera so that I could observe the people that attended the meeting, and then I spotted a hundred-gallon propane tank.

I put a one-way signal acceptor on a vial of my explosives. I then went back into the sewer and began setting the other explosives under the building. I also triggered them with a one-way acceptor. By morning, I was finished and rested as the day went by.

Nighttime found me watching the hotel for any signs of anybody watching their surroundings. I entered through the back door and hid as I saw a young lady walk out of a room and go into a bathroom. I quickly opened the door and when I saw that no one was around. I found Jose's room through her book of guests, exited the door, and hid behind the wall as she went back inside.

I sent a signal to my computer to create a block on all transmissions on their security cameras; they saw nothing except empty halls. I shot an anchor into the side of the building and recoiled myself to the room where Jose was supposed to be. I took out a thin piece of metal from my sock and opened the locked window of the bathroom. It was quiet, and I listened by putting my ear up to the door, and with my audible enhancer, I heard his snoring.

I eased open the door and saw that he was asleep, and then stepped lightly and sat down in a chair by the door and waited for him to awake.

Morning came, and he wasn't prepared for the unpleasant sight that sat in his chair before him. It was me.

"How did you get to live this long?" I asked him, "No wonder McNally requested you." "You're a walking dead man."

He became angry and retaliated by attacking me. I shot a sidekick and popped him in his sternum, sending him flying backward. He became enraged and only grew angrier. I ducked under two of his blows and then gave him a roundhouse kick, and once again, my foot to his sternum sent him flying backward. When he came at me, I flipped over him and popped him in his sternum with my fist. He was breathing hard and heavily.

I extended my leg pushed his neck up against the wall with my foot, and held him there.

"We can go through this all day, and you'll be in a lot of pain." I told him, "You can put away all of that hand-to-hand combat training that you think you can do." "You're not the killing machine you think you are." "Guns don't train; they just kill if they hit what they are aimed at." "In this line of work, guns bring attention to where you are, and if they know where you are, you're a dead man." "I'm just teaching you how to live." "I only know of one way to deliver a message, and that's by impacting a memory."

"Who are you?" He asked.

"Let's just say, I'm Pedro Gonzales," I said to him. I didn't waste my time explaining the way I looked to him. He couldn't see my face.

"Give me your hand." I told him, "When he did, I took off the bracelet." "You're free to go." "I don't need you anymore."

"Wait a minute, first I'm a threat, and now I'm free to go?" "What gives here?" He blasted me with his words.

"I can't help you," I told him. "You don't have any idea of what kind of mess that you're involved in here." "Do you think that McNally is the only man involved?" "If not McNally, then someone else will kill you." "Fear makes powerful men take care of their problems before they become a problem, and you have clearly shown yourself to be just that, a problem."

"So, what happens to me?" He said.

"You're going to die." "Jose, after this weekend, if you show up alive, someone will know you had some kind of a hand in the cookie jar." "There are other people that knew you were being set up." "It won't be hard; you being a man that does what he's told to do will be an easy hit," I informed him.

"I can't run." He said. "I'm not a coward."

"Jose, every man in every agency is in my books; no one goes unidentified; why do you think it was so easy for me to find out who you are?" "Everywhere you go, someone will know you." "You were given an award, and a picture of you was posted in the paper." "That's great publicity come election time for congressmen." I told him, "The only reason why you're still alive today is that he had something else in mind for you." "And that's Saturday" "there's only one way to put a stop to this, and that's to kill you."

He looked at me quickly.

"Relax," I told him. "When this is over, you'll be given a new name and a new identity."

"Then what?" "I go to work in some hamburger joint or digging a hole somewhere?" "No thanks, I joined to fight, and I'll do what I joined to do." He said.

"Do you know what your enemy looks like?" I asked him, "Well, he knows what his looks like; he has your face to put to it." "You can be riding the bus, and the man behind you pulls a gun." "You can be picking up a loaf of bread at a supermarket, and the lady asking you if you could help her by reaching for an item on the top shelf sticks a knife in your heart as you reach up." "That's what you weren't taught by the SEALs." "Now I've got a problem." I told him, "You look like you might try and take out McNally by what information you've heard, and you seem to agree with me on the issue of you being set up." "What if I'm wrong?" "There could be numerous other reasons why he's coming here."

"Then why are you telling me all these things? He said.

I walked around and began thinking, "Jose, I find it strange that McNally is coming here Saturday, I have my reasons, and they coincide with each other, so there are too many arrows that are pointing at McNally as being the piece in the puzzle that I'm looking for, and if he's a piece then he'll be with the rest of the pieces." "I won't know anything until later." "Right now, I don't have all the answers."

"What's happening later?" He asked.

"Jose, my job is to take care of problems, and you've gotten mixed up in one of my problems, and now that makes you a problem," I said to him.

"You were telling me that I was free to go a minute ago." He stated.

"Yeah, you're still free to go, just open the door and leave." "I'll read about you in the obituaries." "Do you think that matters to people that don't even know your name?"

"What's your point?" He asked.

"Jose, there are four kinds of cops." "One kind finds that his form of pleasure is received by bullying, as a cop; he can hide behind a badge to protect his pleasure." "He's a racist that doesn't like Mexicans." "The second kind of cop is the ones that have been bullied, and they hide behind the badge to protect themselves from being bullied." "Fear these cops; they can become bullies like the bullies that become a cop." "The third kind is a hero." "That's you." "He joins for the sake of protecting good citizens." "Then there's the fourth kind of cop, a man that uses the badge to conduct himself like the criminals that he puts behind bars." "One of the rules, before you engage in battle, is knowing who your enemy is, and you don't." "Another point of interest is never going into a battle without having the upper hand, and again, you don't," I told him. "Patience rewards the cat with the mouse." "Next, never take a chance that involves putting your trust in someone." "It could be a friend that destroys the life you live."

"Does that involve you, sir?" He asked.

"Jose, there was a Statesman." "He sat around and spoke his wisdom with other men that thought of themselves as being wise men." "One day, he came to work, and every man there stabbed him with their knife." "The man looked up and saw his best friend holding a knife, he said as he clutched his forearm; you too." "His friend was in a terrible fix, he didn't want to, but he was forced to; if he didn't, all those there would have done the same to him." "See, they wouldn't have been able to trust him unless he stabbed him too." "That made him part of the murder, and to implicate others would implicate him too." "Whose side are you on?"

"Sir?"

"It's a simple question," I said. "Whose side are you on?"

He sat down on the bed and took a deep breath. "When I was growing up, I saw ten-year-old kids selling dope on the streets." "Some of them made good money working for gangs; that sure beats minimum wage." He said, "Most all of the girls were raped or pregnant or on crack by the time they were fourteen." "There isn't any way out of the hood unless you get killed, or you get lucky, and get sent to prison." "One day, a young kid was being beaten up, and I tried to stop those guys from hurting him." "His crime was he was wearing the wrong color of a shirt where I lived." "We both ended up on the ground; they kicked our butts good." "What you just said hit home to me." He stopped talking and then bent his neck down to look at the floor. "To make a long story short, I saw that kid now and then, and when he became a man, I saw him wearing a badge." "He stopped and pulled over one time when he saw me, and I walked over, and he reached out and shook my hand." "Jose, he said, I was raised in this neighborhood right along with you, and I got my butt whipped all the time." "I don't think I ever won any of those fights, but that didn't mean that I didn't get my licks in too." "I got tough; these streets made me tough." "Now I'm back on the streets I left." "You take my advice; there aren't any jobs a man can do around here; you join the military and make something out of yourself." "Get out of this hood; this isn't any place for you." "These streets, they're not the same streets we grew up in; everyone here is on probation or wanted on a warrant." "Take my advice and get out; the military is the only way for you to escape from this prison." "The next week, I read where a twelve-year-old punk kid shot him in the face." "After I left his burial, I went and joined the Navy and ended up training to be a SEAL." But I was a SEAL out of water. I didn't see any action; all I did was to train." "What you said about not knowing who your enemy is, makes a lot of sense to me." "Dan was a good cop, he was a hero, but he didn't expect a twelve year to be the one that had his name on the bullet that killed him." He looked up at me. "Dan died trying to make the hell hole we lived in safer." "I don't expect you to understand my reasons, but I think that death isn't about dying; it's how you go out that counts." "Dan got out and became a cop, but he came back to the place he wanted to get away from." He said.

He got up from the bed and started to walk towards the door.

"Where are you going?" I asked him.

"I need time to think." He said.

"Wait a minute." I got up and put my hand on his shoulder.

CHAPTER EIGHT

"Jose," "Jose," "wake up," "Jose," "do you hear me," I said, shaking him mildly.

"He's out," Jane said.

Ellen was gently shaking him and wiping his face with cold water when he slowly began coming around, and she gave him some water with a straw. "You hungry," she said, "we have grilled Salmon tonight, with rice pilaf and steamed broccoli and cauliflower."

"Where am I?" He stated with a voice of confusion.

I walked over to him, looked down at him, and gave him a smile. "Jose, I'm sorry" "but I couldn't leave and let you go out and get yourself killed." "For your protection, I injected you with a knockout drug and brought you to a safe place."

"Who are you," He said as he eased up from the bed and looked around, "You're Jack Morgan," he said to Jack rubbing his eyes.

"We've met," he said to him, "and you are Jose Espinoza." "It's an honor to make your acquaintance." He stated." "And for the record," "I'm just as confused about you being here as you are," Jack said.

When he looked at Jane, she identified herself a Jack's daughter, and then he looked at Ellen.

"I'm Ellen," "Jack's wife." She told him.

"I saw all of you in Monterrey." He said as he looked at me and once again asked, "Who are you?"

"When you saw me, I was Pedro." I told him, "My name is Smith, just Smith, no first name, no middle name, just Smith." "I'm sorry I had to knock you out." "There's this little thing I have about trust." "If you recall, we had a small conversation on the subject." "These people here have all earned it."

We left him and went into the kitchen, and I began preparing our plates for dinner. We watched as Jose entered the room and looked around, and then sat down. I gave him a cup of coffee and started plating the Salmon and handing each of them their plates.

After fixing my plate, I sat down and looked at Jose. "I suppose that an explanation would be in order."

"Computer: display Juarez on the screen."

A view of the warehouse came on.

"Have you ever seen this warehouse?" I asked him.

"No, sir."

"Jose, there's going to be a meeting there Saturday." I said with a mouth full of food, "Money is going to be transacted, and drugs are going to be dispersed."

I looked over at Jose, and he still wasn't eating. "Jose," "I know you're hungry," "you're making me feel like you don't want to dine with us."

He took a bite and then another, and then another. Soon he was like the rest. I proceeded in my analogy.

"John Hammel was a swing man" "he picked up and dropped off money whenever he was ordered." I told him, "I'm sure you heard about his death from the news agencies or from some other source." "You can't believe everything you hear." "I killed him." "Carlos Alvarez and Miguel Angel Vasquez are both going to be present in that warehouse this Saturday." "Those two alone are worth the time I invested in arming the bottom of the warehouse with enough explosives to level that section to the ground." "Do you know any of them? I asked him.

He looked me in the eyes, and he sensed that I knew the answer.

"Yes, sir." "I heard of them."

"Through McNally or from the bureau?" I asked him.

"Through the bureau, I know that their operators in the cartels." He said.

"Computer switch to camera one and activate." "Zoom to two hundred and fifty percent." "See that propane bottle in the corner; that's what will be reported as destroying the warehouse." "None of the people there will be left to be identified." "You could have done a lot of damage to my plans and gave notice that I was on to them, so I had to take action to avoid any discrepancies." "That's why I brought you here." "There's no way in and no way out unless I know of it," I said, talking to him with another mouth full of food. "Have you ever heard the term that big brother is watching you?" I said to him.

"Yes, sir." He replied.

"Well, here it applies," I said, taking another bite of the Salmon. "My computer lets me know every move you make, so if you have any thoughts about anything, remember, I'm watching you."

"Computer give me a three-dimensional overhead view of the river," I commanded.

I got up and walked closer to the screen and gave my computer another order "Zoom view two hundred percent of section three." Another view came on "Go to autofocus." I ordered it. "See here?" "To you, they look like submarines, but that's how they move their stuff." "From what I've observed, traffic is slow at zero three hundred hours to zero five hundred hours." I looked at Jane and Ellen, "that's three o'clock to five o'clock in the morning." I told them, "The River is too shallow in some parts, so they have to surface and use crawlers to go over the sand bars." "Computer" "initiate animation of the salamander." "Judging by visual perception, this animation you see is probably the most accurate way it travels." "The problem is they can be going five thousand yards up or downstream of the river, or they can be going five miles up or down the river, and then return when they're ready to take another load." "That vessel can reach thirty knots in ten minutes and travel in less than ten feet of water." "That means transport time of fifteen to thirty minutes in the best of conditions." "We don't have the option to wait." "We spray the wasp nest and kill the wasp that's on the nest." "It's going to take time to build them a new nest, and by then, we'll have all the information that we'll need to do this all over again." "Computer give me an update on Francois," I ordered.

"Francois Alvarone?" Jose asked.

"You know of him?" I said, turning to him.

"McNally is supposed to meet Francois in the Bahamas Sunday," "he was going to leave from Juarez Saturday and fly there." "I heard him on the phone." "But sir, he refers to him as Big Al when he talks to him."

"Do you know where?" I asked.

"There's only one place he goes to when he goes to the Bahamas." He said. "He sees a doctor there."

I turned in and canceled my last order. "Computer research and access all medical files of Francois Alvarone." I ordered.

I sat back down, continued my meal, and read the files on Francois. "The man's a diabetic and suffers from anxiety attacks, hypertension, and high blood pressure, tachycardia, and there was a triple bypass performed on him two years ago, go figure." "He's going to die in less than three months even if I don't kill him." "Give me your hand," I told Jose. I looked at it and turned it palm side up. "If this is the hand that brings me my death, I hope it heals the wound that festers in your heart." "Jose, all of us here in this room, has lived with our own life of regret; no one is any different than you." "Your story is like everyone else that comes here, except the life you have seen, has been seen through your eyes only, and these other people have seen their life only through their eyes." "When you can look and see the lives that others live, you might find others to be worse off than you." "That's when you'll learn the real reason why you chose this profession." I told him, "But, for now, you should eat; we'll know more later."

"Sir, I'm confused."

I pushed my plate away and sat back against my chair. Jack was savoring each mouth full, and I saw Ellen was beginning to have a better appetite than she had when I first met her. She was more relaxed and had a calmness about her, and her smile reassured me that when she looked at me, I was awarded her seal of approval. My thoughts began to drift, and my attention was taken to another dimension. I was snapped back by Jane shaking me.

"Smith, are you all right?" She asked.

"Yeah, I was thinking." "I have to be in the Bahamas Sunday," I told her when my eyes met hers. "We leave Saturday night," I told her.

"Sir, may I ask why?" Jose asked.

"Francois is one of my hits; he visited the Messiah, along with Carlos and Miguel and Hammel." "I have the advantage in my favor." "I know my target, but he doesn't know his." "Do you know anything about the Messiah?" I asked him.

"Yes, sir." "Sir Hammel came to McNally's office and dropped off two briefcases' and then left." "I was told to wait outside when he came in."

"That's interesting." I said to him, "Computer format all vital organ transplant recipients from every country beginning one year back, and give me the location of the surgeries and the surgeons that were involved." "I want the hospitals, the donor's names, and their ages." "Activate program." I gave my command and watched as the screen passed the information. "Computer increase speed of delivery," I commanded.

I stood up and walked closer to observe the information "Computer; increase speed again," I waited shortly and issued an order to increase the delivery speed again "Computer; give me January seventh, and January twenty-second." "Notice the doctor's names and the hospital, Jose." "Computer; give me March eleventh." "Notice that we have the same doctors in a different hospital." "They all travel to perform their surgeries." "Computer; give me May fifth," and once again, their names came up. "Computer; what was the average worth of each patient, and give me the length of time that they waited for a donor on those transplants that I asked information on." I watched as the figures came up, but I wasn't alarmed to see what I saw. "One point two billion for a liver is a little extreme, don't you think; no insurance company will handle that." "He was never on a list to receive a transplant; I find that to be amazing." I pointed to another man. "This next man needed a heart; he too never was on a donor's list." "He paid three billion." "This one here," I put my finger on the name to show them who I was talking about, "was on dialysis for two months" "he had a rare blood type, so when a donor was found, he paid a billion; for each kidney." "Nothing was collected on the deceased." "They died while they were still alive and well." I told them, "Jose," you said you were confused a little while ago." "This makes me confused also, but not as confused as I was earlier." "Let me explain something to you." I told him, "John Hammel collected the money from each recipient and transferred the money into stocks and bonds, and the stocks and bonds were transported to McNally, and no money is traced to him." "McNally purchases the drugs with them and disperses the drugs." "He's working for Alvarone, and Alvarone is working for the Messiah. It appears our friend McNally has amassed a nice sum of money for his efforts." "I have a quandary; do I kill the men that paid the money for the transplants, knowing that people died for them to have that right?" "Or do I let them live?" "If I choose to kill them, then do I kill the children that benefited too?" "That question plays a heavy toll on my mind," I said. I looked over at Jane.

"What?" She asked.

"I was visualizing how you would look in a bikini." I told her, "We leave Saturday night for the Bahamas." "Jose, tell me, how do you feel about this?" I asked him.

"When you say this, are you speaking about killing Mister Alvarone?"

"That's my intention," I told him.

He looked down, and then he looked back up at me. "I've never been on a mission like this." He said.

"You mean an assassination?" I corrected him.

"Yes, sir."

"I know" "I read your files." I told him, "Jose" Francois Alvarone has a wife and two sons." "Both of the sons are grown men, and they are both involved with their father." "They aren't any different than the situation that your father and brothers were in." "You have outlaws and lawmen." "You have terrorists and military to combat the terrorist." "You have good gangs and bad gangs." "I don't look at myself or anybody that's with me as a member of a gang." "I see myself the same way you saw yourself when you went to help the boy that was getting beat up." "You knew what to expect, and it turned out to be the way that you expected it." "But," "you still went and stood your ground," "you did so because you knew it was the right thing to do, and you've been fighting back the only way you know, however, since then." "Interpretation is a tool everyone uses to answer all questions that are posed to them." "When you joined the military, you joined a gang, when you trained to be a SEAL; you joined a different and tougher gang." "If you had seen action, you would have done the best you could to kill the gang that you were attacking or attacking you." "I don't do what I do for pleasure, but the people I will do." "You have a problem, and it's not hard to see what it is." " You can't see the good because you're too busy looking for the bad." "Give me a number," I told him.

"Sir?"

"A number, give me a number," I told him again.

He still looked at me confused, and Jane said. "Twenty-two."

"Computer: run film twenty-two in section one," I commanded.

A picture came on with a convenience store being robbed, and I began telling them what was taking place "Computer, lighten image of the offender and the defender." "That man is six foot two, weighing at two hundred and seventy pounds." "Now watch," "see the old woman beginning to walk towards him, she weighs ninety pounds, and she's four foot two, and one hundred years old." The lady raised her cane and struck the man squarely on the head, and when he went down, she struck again and again. "She was seventy years older than him and two-foot smaller." "What made her think to act like that?" "Now, give me a number," I said to Jose again.

"How about thirty-five?" He said.

"Computer; initiate activation number thirty-five, section three." I ordered, "Notice the man at the counter is waiting for the clerk to come wait on him." "Now, notice the man behind him." "Computer zoom to sixty percent and increase the squares twenty through twenty-five, thirty through thirty-five and forty through forty-five, and reduce the speed of action to seventy-five percent." "That man is ninety years old," I said as they watched. "He feels uneasy because the man is closer to him than what he is comfortable with." "He senses something and reaches to touch his wallet, now there," I said to him. He turned and began beating the man with his fists pounding him hard with each blow. He held him with one hand by his shirt and had him pulled into his body with that hand.

They all watched as the pickpocket was subdued by other bystanders.

I turned to Jose and addressed him. "You think you could still fight like that if you made it to ninety?" "It looks like the pickpocket picked the wrong pocket to pick, and if the pickpocket picked the wrong pocket to pick, then he'll find there aren't any pockets to pick in jail." I said to him and smiled at him, "I guess that was an ill attempt at humor." "Give me another number," I told him with a serious face.

"Seventy," he responded.

"Computer: initiate number seventy, section two."

They once again began watching the screen.

"This is a purse snatching that was caught on a surveillance camera at a mall." "Computer lighten subjects and increase speed to normal speed," I commanded it. "Watch this guy pacing back and forth." "He marked his target when she went into a store, he knows she'll come back out the same door, and when she comes out, that's when he's going to make his attack." A few minutes went by when the attack occurred. The man took off and was almost ten feet away when a boy tackled him at his knees. Men were on him quickly. I once again turned around. "That boy was only eleven, and he just started playing football." "He tackled him the way he was taught to tackle him." "When asked why he did it, his answer was, he hurt the lady."

"Are you going somewhere with this?" He asked.

"No," I said to him, "I was hoping to show you that I'm fighting back the only way I know how" "just like you" "and just like the people in the film you saw."

"Are you going to kill his sons too?" He asked.

"No" "they'll lead us to the next drug lord. We need bait." "We'll leave the underwater vessels alone, and they won't go to waste. Someone will use them again." I told him.

Jack finally pushed his plate away from him and wiped his mouth.

"Young man," he said to him as he leaned back in his chair and put his hands on his stomach, "I really don't understand why Smith brought you here, or for that matter, what he sees in you." "But he's given me the task that I undertook thirteen years ago that's he giving you." "Why I accepted it, I don't know, maybe I'm getting too old and soft, and this is his way of keeping me young."

"Why me, sir" "there are all kinds of people out there with far more experienced at this sort of thing."

"That's true" "You're what I call a learner." "A learner listens and learns the way that he listens. The problem I face is I have to first teach you to learn how to listen." "I can't teach a man that thinks he knows what he's doing." "It's like the adage that you can't teach old dog's new tricks." "It applies to humans more than it does dogs." "I don't put my trust in many people." "As you can see, I have very few guests."

"You said you don't trust me, but you bring me to a place that you say is a secret place, and I wake up to a dinner." He said as he got up from his seat and looked at me. "You didn't implant some kind of microchip that will kill me if you find out I'm not the man you thought I was, did you?" He asked with honesty.

Ellen walked over to him and put her hand up to his chin and pressed it firmly, moved his head a little each way, and then reported back to me.

"I see a man that doesn't want to be on the side of wrong." She stated to me, "I see loyalty." She looked back at him and then back at me and then back at him and calmly said to him, "He doesn't have to put a microchip in you to kill you. He can do that with his bare hands."

I gave her a smile. "You see too much of yourself in him." I told her, "Jose, Ellen, and I clashed most of the time we were together." "Her problem was dealing with my problems; I wasn't the man she liked for her daughter, I was dominant in my deliveries of speaking, and she wasn't used to my way of communicating." "She had difficulty adapting to my life in my laboratory." "You can see, I'm constantly giving orders to my computer, and I had difficulty in being able to talk to Jane or Ellen." "Jose, no one is without fallacies." "We all have our problems, and I'm no different." "Computer: initiate voice recording and analyze," I ordered.

"Can I ask a question?" He said.

"Sure, if you wish, all of us here will answer anything you ask." "But, I have a better way of telling you what you wish to know," I said.

"Sir, I'm curious. What if I turn out not to be the person you thought of me to be?"

"When you woke up, did you have any recollection of what happened?" I asked him.

"Yes, sir," "I remember everything."

"Well, the next time, you wouldn't." I told him, "You'll be back in Mexico and waking up behind the wheel of a cab." "You'd have a little trouble with the loss of memory, but that would pass."

"I'd go take my position and make the phone call, wouldn't I?" He said.

"Yes, I think McNally set you up for a diversion, and if you show up somewhere alive, you won't live long." I told him, "Jose, I told you once before," "there are two roads you can take" "one road leads to a dead-end, and the other road will hopefully lead you to a life more rewarding than what you envision it to be now." "You'll know more Saturday if I'm right or if I'm wrong." "Tomorrow, you can go outside and get some air." "Take a walk, and you can get a better understanding of what's going on." "Money isn't any good here." "You'll be issued a card to get what you want." "People will know by the card that you work here. Tell them you're in training if you're asked questions." "If it turns out that McNally is a piece to the puzzle, there won't be a Jose Espinoza anymore." "He'll be dead; he was killed in a gun battle between the police and a drug cartel in Juarez, Mexico."

I looked at him, thought for a moment or two, and scratched my head. "Computer; give me a picture of Jose Espinoza." His picture appeared on the screen. "Computer: increase facial orientation one hundred percent," I ordered.

"What do you see, Jose?"

"Sir?" He responded.

"What do you see?" "Tom, Ignacio, Richard, Caesar, Johnny, Juan, who do you see in that picture, other than Jose?"

"I see Dan, sir."

"Then Dan is your name from now on." "You were born to a Spanish father and a Spanish woman."

"Computer; put a short mustache and a beard on Jose; make it black." I watched and stepped closer to the screen. "Put a beard on him and thicken the beard." "Stop," I ordered. "Change the color of the beard and mustache and the hair to light grey and black," I ordered. I looked back at Jose. "Some things aren't as simple as they appear, are they?" "Computer; include the eyebrows too," I said, disgusted. "What do you think?" I asked him. "Do you think you could be this man?" "I see him as a quiet man, straight and to the point." "He says what he has to say and listens to the responses, and leaves." "This man earns his respect." Computer: give me all information on the blood work and all medical information on Doctor Messina, Doctor Rogers, and

Doctor Clemens, and search for patients on the list to receive transplants that are compatible with all vital organs of Doctor Messina, Doctor Rogers, and Doctor Clemens." I commanded.

"What are you going to do?" He asked.

"Jose, or should I say, Dan," "the Doctor is in the business of harvesting organs for transplants for wealthy clients from non-consenting healthy donors." "These doctors know the patients are kidnapped or brought to them from prisons." "They have to die, but not before I harvest all the vital organs and disperse them to people waiting to receive them."

"Are you a Doctor?" He asked.

"I read a book on it once." I told him, and he looked at me sort of funny like, "But," "that's going to have to wait till I return." I said.

"Where are you going?" Jane asked.

"When I finish dealing with Francois, I have to prepare for the Messiah; he's the nucleus of my problem." I said to her, "The Messiah will know something is up when the warehouse is demolished. That's a supply line." "I'll have to act fast and move faster."

I looked over at Jose. "I can't call you Dan. I know you as Jose, and so does everyone else in the room." "So outside of this resort, you are Dan Gomez." "You are two people that are the same person." "One is not real and one that is." "You'll be given complete access to everything in my lab, but, not without someone with you, I have rules." "Computer: send in James and Ruby." I ordered, "This is the only way you'll be satisfied in the questions you have." I told him.

"Sir, how come I've never heard of you?" He asked.

"Jose, it's simple." "I don't draw attention to myself unless warranted, and you've already seen that I don't leave any evidence behind."

"Do I work for someone?" "Yes, I do." "I work for Jack, and Jane, and Ellen, and I work for all the people that come here to help me build my legacy." "So it may be that I might be working for you too." "Our future is nothing more than a vision that's in someone's mind, and in this matter, you'll see what you see through your eyes, the same things that Jane and Ellen saw through their eyes." "Where we've come from today was started from a conception of a theory that was born in the past." "All inventions are taken for granted, like the telephone, the television, the radio, cars, planes, everything started out as a vision that someone had, and they believed in their belief so strongly that they showed the world that they were right." "Back then, they were all considered to be breakthroughs in technology."

"Today," "we're moving ahead at a faster pace," "and we have one hundred times the knowledge in technology than what our ancestors theorized in their inventions of yesteryear."

James and Ruby entered the room.

"Jose, this is James, James, this is Jose Espinoza."

"Mister Espinoza, it's an honor to meet you." He said.

"Jose, I'd like for you to meet Ruby."

"Mister Espinoza," she said as she bowed her head a little.

"James and Ruby," "Jose is going to be staying with us for a little while." "He's going to need a lot of help trying to sort out the real from the unreal." "Please assist him when needed," I told them.

"Jose," I returned my comment back to him. "Imagination is limited only by an individual." "I don't watch movies for entertainment; I could care less about the dialogue." "I do watch them to pay attention to the machines of war; one day, you or your children may witness these machines in action." "I hope not, and they're weapons of mass destruction." "Comic books depict crime fighters as good citizens battling evil oppositions with superpowers that were generated by accidents." "You've got villains that they fight with superpowers that were achieved by accident too." "In the end, the good always conquers evil." "In truth," "you can only stop a crime if you get a tip that one is going to occur." "We don't possess anti-gravity yet, although I am working on that project, and we don't have capabilities to run at the speed of light or lift a train without messing up the locks of the hair." "That parts a fantasy, but if you take a little of this part out of the picture, and add another part from another picture, and reconfigure a little of this and a little of that, you'll begin to see that reality. Might have potentiality." "Imagination comes at you in small ways, and it's up to the person to accomplish what he sees and transmits his idea into reality."

He looked over at Jane and then Ellen and then Jack.

Jane spoke for all of them. "Jose," "he's telling you not to freak out at the things you'll see." She said to him, "My mother and I did."

"Sir, you could have killed me." He said.

"How many friends do you have in this world?" I asked him.

"Sir?"

"It's another simple question." I said, "How many friends do you have in this world?"

"I'm sorry, sir" "I don't understand the question." He sounded embarrassed.

"At one time in my life, I could look at my hand, and I saw a fist." I told him, "That's how many friends I could count on." "I couldn't count to one." "Then one day I looked and saw one finger, and then there were two, and then three." "Life has a way of changing without you knowing it." "Jose, friendship is earned, not appointed, or given." "And as far as killing you, I can still kill you, anytime, or anywhere, and there's only one way that will ever happen." I took his hand and balled it up into a fist. "That's how many friends you have now." I then unfolded his forefinger. "If you can't find anyone you can call a friend, you can always remember, the next time someone asks you if you have any friends." "You can hold that one finger up." "I'm probably the only friend you have, and you don't even know it." "If you don't trust me, then you'll understand why my trust is earned and not given." "There's one other small thing, and I don't like liars." "If you ever tell me a lie, you'll be on your own, and I won't have to kill you; someone else will do that for me." "The person that brings my identity to the surface will be responsible for putting all my work and everyone that has ever had contact with me in jeopardy" "no innocent people socialize with the guilty, or they come under scrutiny." I told him, "You want to know the reason why I didn't kill you?" "I see you as a man that doesn't go looking for a fight." "I don't need a man that thinks of himself as being invincible." "That's why I called you a learner." "I need a man that will listen and carry out his mission exactly as I tell him to." "It's important to me, for every action a man takes tells me the answers that I need to know, and the body language tells me more than what the mouth does." "When on a mission, one tiny mistake and your mission is a failure." I pushed myself away from the table. "I'm sorry, but I've got things I need to do." "Jose, feel free to wander." "Computer: open all bays," I commanded.

"I'll take care of this, Smith," Jack said. "You go on and take care of business; I'll show the young man around." James and Ruby followed behind them.

"Young man," "one time me and Smith;" their voice was fading as they walked away.

I looked at the ladies. "I've got some work to do." "I need some company to help keep me busy, and if you two don't have anything planned, then I'd like for you to join me in the control room." I turned and walked away and heard two sets of feet running to catch up with me.

I sat down at my control panel and began typing in my orders of what I wanted it to do. I didn't use an audible command for worries of someone making a comment; wrong messages filter wrong commands, and then I would have to go back and delete that part out and then have to go back and redo what I had done up until then. To me, it meant double work, and I felt that double work was a waste of time.

Ellen was the first to speak. Jane was too busy with her arm around my neck, squeezing me.

"I didn't want to say anything earlier, but you mentioned Doctors and transplants." She said.

"Could you be more specific on the question you ask so I can answer the question properly?" I said to her, "I wouldn't want to waste time on a subject not related to your question."

"Jane, are you like your mother? Do you have a non-understanding on anything about this?" I asked her.

"No," "I know what's happening." She said.

"Ellen, it all started in Brazil, over twenty years ago," I began "kids that lived on the street came up missing, and then more than a handful came up missing an organ, and the police didn't have anything to give them any leads." "What sounded the alarm was the kids that were kept alive had uncommon blood types, so they were worth letting them live." "The Messiah has gotten his hands on all medical records in various countries, and Francois Alvarone sets up a kidnapping." "No one misses an abandoned kid or a homeless person." "This country is one of the countries that keep records of all patients." "I can tell you everything involving medical history about anyone you know since they were born." "That's one of the reasons why I've got to take out Francois." "His people have what I have." I told her, "Those three Doctors have done seven improper transplants in this year alone" "I guess not all Doctors are in the practice of medicine for healing. It seems that money can even affect them too." "It's just à matter of how much you're willing to accept to persuade you," I answered her as I was typing in my commands.

"What are you going to do to them?" Ellen asked.

"I don't think you really want to hear that?" I said to her.

"Smith, I know what's happening; I just want to know if you've got a plan?"

"I had a plan the first minute I found out what was taking place." I told her, "These people are inhuman, and they walk the streets and are admired, all because of the money they have." "I'm going to let them keep all the money that they've accumulated."

"I don't understand. If these people are killing people, and they get away with it, why let them get to keep everything." She said, frustrated.

"I said I was going to let them keep all that they accumulated." "They're not going to get to keep everything; I'm taking their livers, their hearts, their lungs, their kidneys, the platelets from their blood, cornea's, bone marrow, and other things for those that are in need of them to live." "Ellen, when you watch the movie of Doctor Frankenstein again, then maybe you'll see where transplants were born. That's the story behind the story." "These doctors are Frankenstein's, their monsters of the worse kind." "That's the reason why I gave orders to my computer to give me information on the waiting list." "The recipients that qualify will be given a new life." "They can save a lot of lives in their deaths," I said to her.

"And who's going to do this?" She asked.

"My staff and I." "I have to keep them alive long enough to harvest their organs and disperse them to the hospitals that will be waiting; in transplants, the fresher the harvest, the better the success." "You can keep a person on life support for twenty-four hours before the internal organs begin to deteriorate slightly." "I'll only need a few hours," I told her.

"You mean you're going to perform the operation?"

"Ma'am, these questions are not what a woman needs answers to," I said as I was programming the computer.

"I need to know." She said.

"Ellen, that's not a question, you already know the answer, but they'll have to wait." "I'm taking out Alvarone, and then I have to go after the Messiah." "With Hammel and Francois out of the picture, he'll have suspicions; you don't lose your generals and not be curious." "I have to make my move on him while he's still trying to figure things out."

I walked my chair back around with Jane in my lap, still clinging onto me, and finished giving my final orders. I then gave the computer an order to switch to audible "Computer; give me the hologram." "Computer; give me a picture of Ellen in a Bikini."

When it appeared, she became red-faced, and then I said. "Computer; show me what she looks like in a thong."

She quickly inserted, "Don't you dare?" "Smith, that's not funny."

"You're going to the Bahamas Saturday." "I need both of you dressed as two women on a trip enjoying themselves." "You need to shop." I told them, "Computer: we're headed to the Bahamas; please show Jane and Ellen the tourist fashions of that area." Jane watched as the different clothes came on and off of her body with a different pair every three seconds. She was fixed on the pictures as they flashed on and off with a different types of pants that showed her wearing the clothes. After that, I ordered for the computer to analyze her features and dress her in blouses and shoes that went with outfits that made her look like a model. "I don't ever want to hear either one of you complain about not having a thing to wear again." "You've got a catalog full of clothes; all you have to do is tell the computer which ones you like, and like before, Ruby will have the clothes ready for you the next morning." I smiled at them when I told them.

"Department stores could sell a lot more clothes if they had one of these," Ellen said.

"I thought about that too." I told her, "Ellen, I caught myself laughing one day, and it felt good." "I was thinking of using it to tease puppies with, they like to play when young, and they could tire themselves out trying to catch the pants legs, or the rabbits or squirrels as they ran from them." "I thought people could look through recipe books, and the hologram could either tell them they were out or where it was located." "It could even place an order for you." "But then I thought a little further, and I came up with my shields, and that put a stop to any further thinking I had of its use for good."

"You know Einstein was a brilliant man, but not all questions can be answered," Ellen commented. "Are you understanding of what I'm saying?" She asked.

"Yes, ma'am, that's true, but Einstein couldn't remember where any of his bathrooms were either, so they built seven of them for him." "I have a problem with that, though." "My belief is that failure is only accepted because I gave up trying, and as far as you beginning to understand what I'm saying, it could be that you're beginning to listen to what I say." "Einstein's theory ended the thoughts of war." "No country would be able to amass an army to attack or defend itself with the arsenal that man possesses." "But it depends on the person you're talking to; they may have a different opinion than mine," I said.

She shook her head back and forth and started smiling. "It's time for me to find Jack and talk to someone that's down on the same level that I am." She said.

As soon as she left, Jane stuck her head out to see her leave and then began her practicing her rule.

"I missed you." She said.

"I need to ask you a serious question?" I said to her.

"Go ahead, silly."

"Does being in love make you sick?" I said.

"What kind of sick, do you mean?" She asked.

"My abdomen hurts when I'm with you, and I want to hold my arms around you like a captive, worried that you'll try and break away."

She gave me a strange look and then began giving me a little smile.

"You're good, you're really good, and you're a quick learner too?" She told me, "For a minute, you had me going, but you're good at telling me the things I want to hear."

"Then if I was to say I love you, would that be included in with the rest of the words that I said?" I played my words of wit with her.

"No, that's reserved for a special place because it has a special meaning to me, and Smith, you're doing it again, aren't you?" "You know the hard part about you is that you're probably the smartest man alive on this earth today." "So when it comes to being the person that you are, I have to take a backseat and leave you alone." "Back when we first met, it took a few days for me to realize you weren't concerned with me." "I never crossed your mind, except when I needed you." "I was more than curious; I didn't expect you in all my wildest dreams." "You don't think like me, or my mother, or my father, but I was fortunate." "When you held me at the cabin, I felt that same sickness that you feel in your stomach." "It's strange that you asked me if being in love makes you sick." "I felt that way a few times myself, but no one ever told me that they felt the way I did and do now." "Then you tell me what I want to hear, and you tell me that you love me." "I must be a total jerk." She said.

"You say things that aren't true." "I'm not a brilliant man; I know nothing." "It wasn't in my life." "But, one thing I believe is two people that have feelings for each other have difficulty talking to each other." "We don't want to say something to offend each other." "You know me; I wasn't the best person to be around at my shack." "So, I get sick wanting to hold you, and when I talk to you or kiss you."

"Smith, the best time I ever had in my life was when I was alone with you back at the cabin." "I was fully prepared to spend the rest of the winter there." "But it didn't work out that way." "I met another part of you, and like when I had first met you, I didn't expect the you that I saw in all of my wildest dreams." "I gave marriage vows to my husband that said for better or worse." "You know about those meanings more than I do." "They were just words, weren't they?" She asked.

"Yes, I think the vows were made by one person; it didn't mean anything to your husband." "In other cases where two people give vows of love to one another, the first fight they had changed the meaning of the vows that they made and the commitment to each other faltered and didn't last." "A vow of forever is a promise made, but vows and promises mean very little when anger dominates a conversation. That's when vows are forgotten." I told her.

"Smith, I know you. If you ever get to feeling like you want to leave, I want you to come to tell me first." "I deserve that."

"I have problems that I can't fight." "Jane."

"That's what I'm here for; you couldn't talk to my father like you can talk to me." "You can't talk to my mother like you can to me." "And, you can't say you love me and tell me a lie." "I need you in my life, and my mother needs you, and my father needs you, and all the people here need you." "Smith, we can talk, and you'll see that I can help you." "You'll never be alone as long as I'm around, and if I have anything to say about it, you wouldn't be able to leave me." "That man I saw flying the helicopter when my father came and got you, that was one of the androids, wasn't it?"

"Yes"

"Well, that ends that, if you ever leave me, I'll tell the computer to send James in and fly me to where you're at." She said, "Smith, while you were gone, my father took us to one of the workshops that you told us that we should attend." "My mother and I listened in, and then a lady stood up and began reading rules that pertained to the actions of all the people that were there." "She started off with the first person by asking her what she was doing here." "She was shy, and she didn't answer." "A man stood up and asked if he could say a few words." "He had four children and very little training." "He held mostly temporary jobs and moved his family wherever he found something that looked like it could last." "That was three years ago, and now he and his family don't worry about him finding work anymore." "He just wanted everyone to know he sat in the chair where they're sitting, at one time." "And then he left."

"Jane, the people here decide who stays here." "If one of those people is a problem, he or she is ordered to leave by the people." "No one needs to lock their doors here, and they know it."

"What if children are involved?" She asked.

"When you fall asleep at night," I said, "do you remember what time it was when you fell asleep?"

"No, no one does." She answered.

"Then if a person commits themselves to engage in matters that could get them removed from here and if that person knew what would happen to their children if they were forced to leave, then it's a possibility that the person isn't concerned for the welfare of the children." "We have problems here, the same as anywhere else." "Temptation is too hard to resist to some people, and they relapse back into a person that is totally opposite of the person that they were before they relapsed." "Jane, it's like a person falling asleep. You know you're going to bed for that purpose." "Some of these people do what they do for a purpose."

"I can't help anyone, Jane. Some of them didn't come here for the purpose that they said they came here for." I said to her.

"But, what about the children? What'll happen to them?" She said.

"They'll pay for the sins of their parents."

"That's not right." She said.

"No, it's not; seventy-five percent of the kids that left here because of their parent or parents were abused." "I fixed that. I send a guardian on every person that is asked to leave." "Any mistakes, and I bring the children back here." "Everyone that comes here is told of this, and if it ever occurs, we will do our best to remove the child from that environment." "Jane, sometimes kids are killed by a parent." "No one that comes here is without this knowledge that you have." "They have to prove to themselves and no one else that they are responsible for themselves." "I can't help someone if they don't need it." "Give a man one chance, and if he needs two, then he'll need three, and then four, and then more and more."

"We've gotten some of the kids now, they're runaways, and they came here because this was the only place that they could call home, just like you do." I said to her, "Only, we don't have any problems out of them."

"What's that supposed to mean?" She asked.

"You were abused as a child too; you grew up quickly and taller than anyone in your peer group, a laugh here and a snicker there, and my guess that was not having a father around to talk to for half of your life, didn't help any either." "You never really felt close to your friends, and no matter where you went, you said you were always at the center of attention." "It's not hard to see why you're happy here." "You grew up alone too."

"So that's what you think?" She asked.

"It doesn't matter what I think, I'm not the one with the answers to my thoughts, and you're the only person that can concur or dispute what I say, that is if you choose to object to my comment." "I offer all that come here the same as I offer you, a new beginning in life." "The future is written by them alone." "Jane, in marriage, how many chances does a man have with you if you get a divorce from him?"

She looked at me quickly.

"Once," she said.

"Why not twice?" I shot back.

"I don't think I'll be able to argue with you." She said.

"Then you'll obey me?" I asked her.

"Are you serious?" "You're asking me to obey you?"

"Jane, you just said that you wouldn't be able to argue with me, and now you're arguing."

She began acting upset, and then she stopped fidgeting and looked at me.

"How did I let myself get caught up like that?" "Smith, if you don't stop playing me like a toy, I'm going to."

"You're going to do what?" "I've got you trapped in my arms, and you're nothing more than a helpless damsel in distress." "You're afraid to call out for help because someone might come and pull me away from you." "Who is the captive here, the spider or the fly?" I asked her.

"I love you." She said.

"We had that discussion earlier, didn't we?" I told her.

She was practicing her rules when her father and Jose let their presence be known by clearing their throats. She got up, kissed me, and left us alone.

"Sit down, Jose," I told him.

I watched as he sat, and then he looked at me, waiting for me to talk. I kept silent for a period of time, and then I opened our conversation.

"Computer: engage detection service," I ordered.

"Jose, this is my control chamber. Jack showed you some of the other chambers, but not all of them." "I'm going to ask you some questions, and my computer will let me know if I'm not being told what I need to hear." "You're being read by heat sensors."

"I thought we went over that earlier?" He said.

"We did, but if you remember," "I don't trust anyone; I can't afford a mistake on my part." "You're an agent of the FBI, and you think like an agent."

"Computer: activate hologram," I said; the hologram appeared, and he was in shock.

"I didn't believe those things actually existed," Jose mumbled.

"They don't, well they do, but not like this one." "Jose, the hologram is nothing more than a projection of an image, all you have to do is command the computer to activate the hologram, or you can simply talk to the computer and receive the answers you request, within certain restraints, of course." "If you have problems, ask the computer how to do what you want it to do," I added. "It's simplified, so you don't really need any kind of experience." "Just ask the computer for anything you want it to do or what information you request." "The hologram helps by acting out the behavior pattern of my subject, but that's only part of what its purpose is used for." "If you remember, I told the computer to record your voice." "You can open any bay simply by saying Computer open this bay." "It might not open because you might not have the authority to do so." "That's when you tell the computer to send James or Ruby to you." "They'll make sure you won't touch anything that'll kill you." "Jack told you that what is here will remain here; these prototypes are for defense purposes only, in the wrong hands, a million people wouldn't know what hit them." "You can ask the computer anything you want to know about me." "You may not want to hear what you hear." "But I don't know how to tell others what I have to say without speaking frankly." "You have question after question about everything that you can't answer." "This way, you get answers, and I get peace," I said.

"Sir, you called me a learner; what did you mean by that?" He asked.

"Computer; answer that question," I ordered.

"If Smith dies in an accident, no one will be left that's qualified to avoid or avert an action that needs to be controlled." It replied.

"I'm not your man, sir." He said.

"Don't tell me; tell the hologram." I told him, "You'll hear no lies; a computer is for knowledge, not to give false witness."

"Sir, I saw some things, and."

"Jose, ask the computer," I told him.

"Computer; he spoke." "I'm not that man, and he thinks I am."

As the computer was answering him, I grabbed Jack by his arm, led him out of the room, and walked with him to the kitchen to make us a fresh pot of coffee.

"I hope you know what you're doing?" He said.

"Jack, when you first met me, did you know what you were getting into?" "Besides, did you want me to let the kid die?" I answered, "And Jack, I see something in him, I don't know what, but he has a will that's not bendable."

"You didn't have to bring him here." He said.

"He's a sitting duck in a shooting gallery, and you know it." "I didn't have much choice in the matter; he would have been killed, and you know that," I told him." "But don't you think that you're being a little too risky?" He asked.

"That may be, but I look at him, and I see a young man with strong convictions." "Even your wife said he showed loyalty." "He's incorruptible, and that's a very rare quality to let it pass. In due time, he'll find out that he's like everyone else that has a story." "Jack, I chose you for the very same reasons." "You were incorruptible, I wasn't wrong about you, and I don't think I'm wrong about Jose." "He just needs a little fine-tuning," I said.

I poured us a cup of coffee and sat Jack's cup down in front of him, and after he took a sip, he started a conversation.

"I was a lot like Jose when I was young," he said. "I was lucky; I found a young man that took care of me." "When you made your first kill, you saved my life, and you did it all without anyone knowing anything about it." "It was a perfectly executed mission, and even I didn't know what happened until we had that talk on the plane." "Son, we had experts that couldn't have pulled that off, I think that's the day I started watching you closer, and the closer I watched you, it became clear I wasn't the one that was in charge of anything." "You built all this stuff in here, and I couldn't even begin to tell you what's where and what's what." "Smith, I never killed anyone." He said.

"Jack, you ought to be thankful for that." "Only a monster can kill a person." Jose entered the room and sat down at the table.

I poured him a cup of coffee and sat it down in front of him.

"You were only in there for a short while, and you have a lot more questions that you want to ask me." "I'm sure you didn't get all the answer's that you wanted," I told him.

"I got my answer." He said, "Sir, I don't have the qualifications that you seek," "I'm not the man you are."

"What was the question?" I sighed.

"I asked if something was wrong with you." He said.

"Jose, everybody has something wrong with them. We're not perfect." I commented, "You don't talk much, and you don't answer a question with anything except the answer to the question that was asked." "You have to be deprogrammed from the programming that the military fed to you." "We don't play this game the way they do, and a simple answer is the only way to answer a question; you were taught to be a killer and nothing else." "Your missions were given to you by men that were given assignments by another man, and he was given that assignment by another man, and none of them ever went on a mission or even fought in a fight." "How many men in the positions that are held in the military, and the CIA, and the FBI, and all the other agencies that are under the government control, can you trust with your life if they expect a certain amount of casualties?" "One person killed is a plan that wasn't well planned." "I don't take orders from anyone that sits behind a desk."

"Sir?" He replied.

"Jose" "when I leave my lab, I dress as an officer or a government official from every country in the world." "Are you familiar with a children's book about an emperor and his new clothes?" I said.

"Sir, I'm not understanding?" He said.

"Well, being an emperor, his tailors were frightened that they couldn't satisfy the emperor with anything that they made, so they gave him a pair of pajama's and said that the clothes that he wore were only seen by those that could see real beauty; so all the people were told of this and when they saw the emperor they thought that they were lowly because they only saw him in his pajamas." "But the people applauded and threw pebbles of flowers and praised him for being the most handsome of all emperors because he looked admirable in his new clothes." "A child was heard, but mommy he's wearing his pajamas, and the emperor saw that he was wearing pajamas." "The moral of the story was a child's honesty can't be silenced." "But everyone else held their tongue." "In a government that has a military, rank has privilege, and the higher rank you have, the more the privileges." "All officers and non-officers never question what they're told, and they're like the people that praised the emperor." "In the military, you did exactly what I just told you." "You obeyed all orders given to you by a superior in charge." "Jose, there's only one person responsible for you in living or dying, and that person is you." "If you trust anyone else, you won't die of old age." "Come Saturday, when you make the phone call, we'll know more," I said to him.

"You can destroy the world, can't you?" He stated.

"You asked my computer that already, so I won't waste time repeating the answer that my computer already gave you." "I assume you asked if I could or if I would, and you received your answer to your question or questions." "Jose, the most powerful weapons in the world don't come near to the hostility that the universe can unleash." "One simple fraction of a wobble will cause the earth to have oceans where deserts once were, and deserts where oceans once were." "This has happened already." "You can't stop an action that the universe creates. The only good thing about that is you'll never know about it." "The weapons I'm concerned with are overdoses of rays that are harmful to the human race." "These can be built, I know, I built them." "It's the person that can build a gamma-ray or an x-ray, or lasers of destruction, and use them for that purpose is what I worry about." "Millions of people will die instantly, and millions will die in a week, and millions will die each day after until mankind joins all their ancestors before them." "That sounds like a lot of people dying, but when you talk about seven billion people on earth today, a million a day will take years before man found himself to be extinct." "You told me that it's how you die that matters." I told him, "Dan told you that." "He died believing he could make the place where he grew up in a better place for the other kids that were growing up there." "Dan might not have helped very many kids escape from their community, but he did help one, and to me, that's better than none at all." "Jose, where you came from, is a place like any other place in the world." "We can't choose our parents, and we can't choose our environment where we were raised." "We can't change anything that happened in the past, but we do have the ability to choose whether we want to do what is right or what is wrong in our future." "And Jose, I already know what you decided." "So all I can say is welcome."

"How did you know?" He asked.

"You didn't sit in my control room very long, so I'm thinking that you asked the computer a question, and the response was blunt; I think you realize that you're being played for as a pawn, and besides, you don't have any options." I said, "We have one problem, though." "Jack isn't happy bringing you here." "You can jeopardize everything we've achieved." "There's not really that much he knows about you, so he's scared of you." "He has a good reason for that. Everything we've done in the past has remained between us." "Jose, what he doesn't know is to betray us is like putting the gun in your hand and killing your parents yourself." "I don't have that fear. I know your enemy, but you don't, and that makes everyone confused, except me." "Jose, this is a safe haven; no one knows anyone here except Jack." "He's our lobbyist, and everyone knows he asks for money to build what I envision." "Computer; display an overall view of my plans."

A screen came on showing everything that I wanted to build and a few other things that came to my mind.

"Jose, charity is a nasty word that many people with money avoid those that ask for it because they worship what they have." "They won't put a car up for sale, they won't put a house up for sale, and they won't touch their retirement, they worship these possessions, so they look for assistance to take a family member to." "You work hard for thirty years, and one operation will take away everything you saved." "That's the way some people are, and there's nothing that can be done. I've seen them let their children die." "They try to console themselves by saying it was God's will." "Some people don't have money, and they don't have a house for sale, and the car isn't worth much, and they don't have anything in savings, and some people have sold everything they have in searching for anyone that can help their children." "It's a sad thing to see people turned away from good Doctors because of money." "In the health field, money does matter." "Today, in all cities, we have drive-by ambulances because the hospital knows the patient doesn't have insurance, so they report that all beds are full." "The visitors and vacationers will bring in the money to give medical treatment to those that were passed by or turned away." "This is the legacy I want to leave behind." "Jack, get's me the money and the land to build my vision." "He's my liaison, and when he delivers my messages, he leaves knowing that he's going to get what he was sent for." "I make sure of that." "We all work together in what we do, and not a single penny of it is for our own personal gain." "Go out and look around, rent a snowmobile, see what lies beyond the mountains." "You're not a captive; I'll not hold you against your will." "I didn't bring you here for that."

"Sir."

"Jose, you won't know anything of what to believe in until Saturday has come, and then you'll know what I say to be true." "Until then, we have to wait."

I got up and then proceeded to leave.

I heard footsteps following me, and they weren't the same sound that Jack's feet gave as they landed on the floor. I ignored them, for I knew what the purpose they were for. Jose wanted to know the real me, not the hologram he talked to.

I walked into my weapons room and turned to see him looking at all of the equipment that was around.

"You'll never master one percent of all these weapons to defend yourself." I told him, "You were trained differently." "Guns are out; they give away your position, and then the enemy will converge on you, and you'll end up being captured or killed." "Pick a weapon," I said, "anyone that you feel stronger in."

He looked around and then picked out a knife.

I smiled at him. "You've carried one since you were old enough to know what it was used for." I said to him, "And you thought of it as protection."

He started twisting and turning it in his hand and then began quickly folding and unfolding it to make it look like he was knowledgeable in its use.

"I guess that's supposed to impress me, huh." I said to him, "Now, I'll choose my weapon." I told him.

I reached on the back of the chair and grabbed a towel. "How do you want this?" "Do you want me to attack, or do you attack thinking you have an advantage? I'd think carefully. I've already got you wrapped up, and only you don't know it." "Make your move," I told him. He charged, and when he lunged, I wrapped the towel around his wrist and then turned his arm around to where the knife was sticking at the edge of his neck while he held it in his hand." "I thrust my palm at the back of it and stopped." "You're dead," I said. "You're carotid artery was sliced when I thrust it into your throat and pulled down on your wrist with the towel." "The blood pumps out of your

300

body as long as the heart beats." "Given the energy that was put out during the fracas, I estimate that your expectancy to be around a little more than a minute." "At first, you'll feel weak, and then you'll feel warm, and then you won't feel anything anymore." "The problem you have is you'll pass out from the loss of blood to the brain before the heart stops." "Would you like another weapon?" I asked him, "It seems clear that you're not as good with a knife as you think you are."

He looked around and chose a sword.

I gave him a smile. Then I saw the ladies walk in to watch.

"A sword was used by many people of many different cultures." "Guns weren't invented, and swords were used to chop off hands, arms and heads in battles." "If guns were available, swords would have been worthless." "Men practiced every day so that when needed, they were a powerful foe for any army to contend with." "Spears put an end to a life before a man could swing his sword." "My friend, you don't have any knowledge in the art of using a sword." "I choose my body against your sword." I took my stance and then smiled. "Make your move, or I will," I said to him.

Within moments I had flipped over the top of him and had my foot shoved hard against his groin, lifting him off of the floor.

He wasn't breathing naturally, and the grunts of pain he had were evident by the way he held his mouth open.

"Jose, use the sword." "Swing it and kill your enemy, you have a weapon, and I don't."

I flipped up and stood behind him. When he was able to regain his breath, he turned towards me.

Jane walked over and turned on the television, and inserted a disc. She muted the sound and started talking "Jose" "Smith told my mother and me to follow the moves of the actors, on defense and offense." "My mother and I both work out every morning; we do it for our own reasons." "You can watch the movie to stay in shape and work out with us, or you can practice in private and kick Smith's butt one day." "I've tried, and he loves to play his games with me too." "But I'm going to surprise him one day." "Smith has a way of telling people what he thinks of them by showing them." Jane said to him, "What he showed you was that you need training and a lot of it." "You won't ever be anybody until you work to become the person you want to be." "That's what I saw when you fought." "You're slow to react, and you don't think before you act; you just react." "I did the same." "He uses all the moves you make to weaken your body, and then he attacks." "You're predictable to him, and he uses it against you." She took the controller and slowed the action down. "This is the way he showed us so that we used the correct techniques in defense and offense." "We were told that if we learn the wrong way, we'll always use the wrong way to protect ourselves." "You can hear what I say and ignore it, or you can listen and learn." "I was shown what he meant, the hard way when I used an improper position on my forearm." "He made me pay the price, and I still have the bruise to prove it." "Smith had a talk with my mother and me." "While he was gone, we took him up on his advice." "Tonight, you and I are going someplace; I want you to see what Smith wanted us to see." She said. "It helped me a lot, and maybe you can begin to see the Smith that we see." "When I came here, I didn't know where to begin." "I was confused, so I would think that you have a lot of things on your mind that don't quite add up." "I say that because I did too, so, some of the things that you think were the same things that I thought." "You should have seen my mother when Smith began talking to her." "She wasn't used to being talked to the way Smith talked to her." "It took her three days to calm down and not get excited when she and Smith talked; she'd be flustered and walked around as if no one was there." "I had a whole lot of explaining to do on my own, and so did my father." She then turned to me, "Smith, I asked the computer a question that came to my mind." "There's one thing to look at a hologram or talk to a program to deliver answers it's programmed for." "But I won't accept the answer it gave." "I won't tolerate self-annihilation as a reason for not spending a little time with me."

She and her mother then turned and left without making any further comments.

I looked over at Jose.

"Have you ever been in love, Jose?"

"Oh!" "Many times." He said, "Women have a way of telling the person that they love, how they feel."

"I don't know anything about women," I confessed to him.

"Sir, she was telling you that she has affections for you, love is blind, and I can see you are too." "If I found a girl like her" "I'd be going to her now and telling her why I couldn't live without her."

"Jose, I think you're not telling me everything." "You learned a lot living on the streets," I told him.

"Sir, I had three girl friends that I felt really close to." "My relationships were short, two died of an overdose of heroin that I didn't know they were doing, and one died in a shootout." "She was riding with two men I didn't know, and they held up a bank." "When they caught up with them, she was hit four times." "I fell for all of them, and all of them failed me." "I think you're making a mistake now." He said.

"In what way?" I asked him.

"You're here talking to me when you should be in there with your girlfriend, talking to her." "Judging by some of the things I saw, I've got a feeling that whatever happens, I'm pretty sure I won't remember anything anyway, so I'm going to speak my mind." "I think the most precious item you have here is her." "Besides, I've got business with the computer." He said.

I left and met Jane lying on the bed. She had tears in her eyes, and I rolled her over to face me and then took my thumb and erased the wetness from the bottom of her eyes.

"Hey," I told her in a soft voice, "I was told that I was not too smart when it came to talking to someone."

"Smith, that's not it." "I know you're not interested in anything except your work."

"I had a lot of problems when I was young," I told her. "I wasn't able to talk to anyone that was my age when I met your father, and for that matter, I didn't talk to too many people after that." "When I see you, I don't see you as a threat, so I don't pay attention to you the way I should, and I'm sorry for that, but I'm twenty-eight, and when it comes to a girl, I don't have the brain of a twelve-year-old." "When I got sick, back at the cabin, I didn't know what I was supposed to do until you showed me."

"Smith, that may sound silly to some people, but it doesn't to me. I know you all too well, and when it comes to kissing, it's not something that someone has to show you. It's supposed to come naturally." "Kiss me." She said.

I pulled her in close and kissed her.

"See, that kiss felt like you were kissing an aunt or a cousin. That wasn't a kiss; this is a kiss." She said.

She grabbed me and smothered me with her affection, and then stopped, "I don't expect that kind of affection from you, but I'm hoping that one day, you and I will be able to have better communication between us when we hold each other." "A kiss is where you can't let go of the person you're kissing." "It's a way of saying I need you." "I'm your first love, and I don't think you're capable of loving me back, or anyone else for that matter like I love you." "I was feeling down, that's all." She said.

"Jane"

"Smith," she stopped me, "all women go through what I'm going through."

"I don't think I understand," I said.

"I'm possessed with the curse of being a woman." "I started today." She said, "And I really feel miserable right now."

I put my hand on her stomach, and she lowered it a little so that the heat from my hand could be applied directly to the spot where she felt her discomfort.

"You know," she said, "you've got one thing going for you?"

"And that would be?" I asked.

"Your body is hot, and if it was cold, you wouldn't be here with your hand on my stomach, easing my cramps."

"Jane, I don't know how or what to do to show you that you mean a lot to me, and I've never said those things that I've said to you, to anyone else." "A book won't do me any good; love to me is difficult to understand; it hurts."

"I know," she said, "but it's the small things that catch a woman's attention." "When you came in here to be with me, that showed me what I meant to you." "Smith" "I know when your mind is on something else, but here you are, and that's important to me." "The ring you made me, I wouldn't take any amount of money for it, to me it's priceless, and the letter you wrote and gave me was about me and you, that's a treasure that I'll read over and over; again." "The ring cost a dollar, and the letter didn't cost anything except for the paper that was used." She started laughing at me. "Smith," "I was depressed when I came in here, and now, I'm not." "How can anyone show anger with a man that's never been with a woman, especially a man that talks and tells you what he feels, and not what you want to hear, and when you tell me the things I want to hear, I melt like ice cream on a hot sunny day?" "That's what the magic of love does to you."

"I can't take the credit." I told her, "Jose was the one that told me I wasn't paying attention to you."

"How did he know?" She asked.

"He said there were three girls that he was in love with." "Two killed themselves with drugs, and one was killed in a bank holdup." "Jane, I could see the pain in his eyes."

"Jose said that?" She drew her head back and looked at me oddly. "Smith," "Jose may be afraid of women too." "Tonight, I'm going to take him to the workshop and let him listen in on what other people went through before they came here." "It helped me to understand a lot more than yesterday. It might help him too." "Maybe what Jose needs is a good dose of reality; I think he needs to hear that he's not the only one that has problems living in a life." She said.

"Jane, you have to be careful. You can't believe all that you hear; some people have gotten good at lying." "I know when they're doing it, but you don't." "I watch all new arrivals, and I'm aware that some of the people have warrants against them." "I don't turn them in unless they come here to scam the tourists, then I remove them." "But, you can't blame everyone for the actions of a few." "Earlier, I said that seventy percent of all criminals commit seventy percent of the crime." "That leaves thirty percent looking for help." "To a lot of people, all that matters to them is to have a roof over their head, and clothes for their children to wear, food to eat, and knowing that medical attention isn't one of their problems." "Provide that, and a lot of problems never occur." "Mistakes are made in life by everybody, and for some of them, it follows them to their grave." "The best help to give them is the people that need help too." "I guess the easiest way to say it is; it's like two people in a sack race, they lean on one another to make it to the finish line." "If they turn out to be worthy, they're visited and told that we know of their past." "They can rest assured, it's forgotten, and they can be at ease." I stated, "I choose to use the term that I'm giving someone the opportunity to have the opportunity to support them while discovering the career they choose when they choose it." "I ask you; how many will succeed?"

"Smith, with a man like you, I see a lot more succeeding than failing."

"Jane, that course you took in psychology is being used, and I'm your target," I said as I smiled at her.

"My mother's right; it's not easy talking to you," she said, "you always know when my mother or I am not telling you something that you know."

"You give it away." I told her, "You lift your left eyebrow a little when you're trying to whip me with wit." "When around me, you hold back on touching me; you fear that you're bothering me." "You never speak when I'm conversing with anyone else, except to explain my explanation." "That means that you're protective of me." "I can name a lot of things that I can see in you; very little escapes my eyes." "You do distract me when you're around, though." "I want to pick you up and sit down and hold you in my arms until you fall asleep, and then I want to watch you while you sleep." "You're very pretty."

"Is that reverse psychology you're using on me?" She asked, "Because if it is, it's working."

"You'll have to think about that and give me an answer, and when you think you know the answer, you can tell me what you think the answer is," I said to her.

"I have a quicker way; I'll ask the computer." She said, laughing.

Then silence overcame both of us. She rolled over, rested her elbows against my sides, and looked at me in the face.

"Smith, I know this may sound stupid to you, but I'm happy the way things turned out, you know, with you and me."

"I never believed in luck." I told her, "That's another matter that I'll have to ponder." "I'm lucky you love me."

"Okay, now I know you're using reverse psychology on me, and you're good, I mean, really, really, really, good." She responded, "Now, get up, you've done your job, and tell Jose we've got some shopping to do before we go to the workshop." She lowered her head down and kissed me. "I'd tell you how handsome you are, but you'd probably get a swelled head from it."

"Ah! I'm reminded of a fairy tale" "I'm the beast, and you are the beauty." I replied instantly.

"Smith," "you can say all the right words at the right time." "It's a good thing that you've never been around girls; you would have had a lot of trouble."

"You are a devil whenever you use those words of love, and the oddest part is you don't know what you're saying when you say it." "You can say what you feel, and that makes you extra special to me." "Now get, I've got to take a shower, and I need you to put on my makeup for me; I'll call you when I'm ready." "Go tell Jose my plans, so he won't be surprised."

She gave me a kiss and went into the bathroom. I walked into my control room and saw Jose lying down on the couch.

"Jose" "I was sent to you to tell you that Jane is taking you somewhere, and when she calls for me, you'll soon be taken out of the lab." "I don't have to remind you that this place isn't known to others." "Computer; execute closure of all security doors." I gave my order, and seconds later, everything looked like a long wall "Computer; execute opening of all secured doors." I ordered, and the doors began opening. "Jose, there is only one person outside of this lab that knows me." "You know enough to know that any exposure of my identity can be harmful or fatal to anyone I know."

"Yes, sir, understood." He said.

"And Jose," I said to him.

"Yes, sir."

"This isn't Mexico; it's a whole lot colder here, so no one is interested in showing off their six-pack abs." "Here, warmth is more important than what the body looks like." "You'll understand that shortly," I told him.

I heard Jane call for me, and I left Jose in the control room.

Later, when we returned, Jose looked at her and told her, "You look gorgeous."

"Don't get cute; I didn't do it; Smith did." She said.

"It is an honor to have you as an escort tonight." He remarked.

"Jose," I stated to him, "I may not have that hard of a time teaching you. It seems you may have picked up some good qualities along the way." "Hospitality is the key to respect, and the best way to handle any situation is to give respect when respect is given." "If respect isn't given, then hostility usually can be predicted."

I watched them as they left and saw Jane's eyes looking into mine. I gave her a smile, and it was contagious.

I turned and began working on testing the corrosives that I was going to use to burn out the hard drives on the computer in the missile. I didn't have time to watch the time. I was almost finished when I heard Jane's voice from the computer.

"I'm in bay thirty-two." I informed her, "If you need help, send for James." I said to her.

She and Jose walked in as I was loading the last vial into some pellets. When I finished, I turned to greet my guests.

"Did you enjoy your night out?" I asked them.

"Sir," "who are those people?" Jose said.

"Jose, I couldn't begin to tell you." "People watch the news and see refugees fleeing from poverty in other countries." "Those people you saw tonight are refugees themselves." "All cities and counties and states are cash restricted." "Yet I still hear how the economy is growing." "If that was the case, then why do the tax assessments on property keep going up and tax revenue that is generated by tourists keep going down." "That's called propaganda; it's another word for lying." "It's not a difficult task to achieve; over half of the people don't get involved in politics, and those that do, vote for a straight party ticket." "The strange thing about that is, is when you vote for a straight party ticket, you're voting for a one-party rule." "People don't like hearing the word communism or socialism, but that's what a one-party rule is." "Those people that you saw tonight lost their jobs because another country can do it cheaper." "Or they could be homeless, or ex-cons, or drug addicts, alcoholics, or anyone looking for a way out of where they came from." "Some of them could have come from your hometown, and I don't know." "Six months ago." "There were less than half that many, and six months from now, and there will be four times as many." "What has begun can't be stopped; our country was betrayed by the people that the people voted for." "Jose, the people are frustrated and angry, they are losing their jobs to slave labor in other countries, and they believe anything anyone tells them." "Hatred is spoken today by politicians that don't have the intelligence that the pet that they have has." "What does that tell you about the people that vote for them?" "My problem is," I said to him, "what I believe doesn't matter; the only thing that matters is what you believe." "You can disagree with my beliefs, and that would mean that one of us is wrong." "What would happen if the people that were wrong came into power?" "That's happening as we speak." "Jose, sit down for a minute, I want to explain something to you, and I want you to listen carefully." "World war one, and World war two, and the Korean conflict left the people devastated." "No one bought products from any country other than our own, and America prospered because people were buying American products. But, fifty years change what people believe in." "Today" "engineering in all products is tilted, they're not dependable." "So those people out there you saw are the beginning of what is to come. We can't compete with foreign labor." "But, as I said, you may disagree and see a whole different view of what I just explained to you." "I see you bought a new set of clothes." "I told you, this isn't Mexico." I chuckled. "Jose, take a look at the labels on the clothes you wore before you got those and tell me where they came from." "I bet none of them came from America." "The problem is these companies wouldn't be selling those products if people didn't buy them." "People complain of corporate greed, but it's the people's fault. They're the ones that are supporting every other country except ours by buying items that were made under slave labor."

I turned around and hung my vest up with some other explosives that I was going to take with me.

"Sir, can you tell me what you see?" He asked me.

"I'm sure that Jane has told you about me, and knowing Jane, I'm sure she already mentioned to you a few things for you to avoid around me." I smiled at her and then looked back at Jose. "No one can foretell the future until it becomes the past, and then it can be written." "The economy has outpaced the consumer; thirty years of savings is worth less than twenty-five percent of what it was worth ten years ago." "It takes two people to eke out a living today." "One person loses a job, and what was once a happy relationship; is now troubled," I asked Jane to show Jose the ring I made her. "That ring is made from a dollar bill." "Two hundred years ago, you could have bought ten acres of land for it." "One hundred years ago, you couldn't have bought one acre of land." "Today, that dollar bill will take a million of them to buy the land you paid that dollar for." "All money finds its way back into the government's hands by taxes." "Money has to be circulated, but it's being circulated in other countries, and in our country, we have stagnant job growth." "That means things will only get worse before it gets better, and when I say worse, how low can you go?" "Those people you saw tonight are the products of an economical downswing." "Computer: display project overlay," I ordered. It immediately came on the screen in a three-dimensional view. I then looked at Jose. "I can't help everyone; I know that's impossible. Not everyone that comes here is looking for help." "Jane took you out tonight to show you around and meet some of the people that work here." "She was trying to show you what she saw when I told her to take a visit and listen to what other people were going through." "Jose, she was trying to help me to help you see what she saw, and if you saw one person in a crowd of a thousand that you thought was worthy of our help, could you walk away knowing that you could provide that help?" "Dan didn't, and you can't either." "It's not in you," I told him. "That's the good I see in you, only you need to see it yourself." "You're ambitious and eager, but that'll get you killed in this business, and that's not my way of dealing with a problem." "Those people are going to build my legacy for me, and after that, they're going to be working here as long as they want." "They need a job and a place to call home." "If this is it, then they'll be a lot of happy people living and working here, and one happy worker works harder than three unhappy workers." "Two thousand people, then five thousand people, then ten, and then twenty aren't inconceivable." "I build my legacy, and then when I'm through, I'll build more if I need to."

"Sir, if I may make a suggestion?" Jose said.

"You have my attention," I told him.

"Sir, the train is slow," "You'll have to build an overhead railway system going and coming from the hospitals, not only do the tourists get there quicker and get to where they're going quicker, but you can transport more people, and the train you have now, just can't do it." "You can always leave the train for the people that want to see the scenery, going or coming, but that train can't carry all of the people that you're talking about, sir."

I folded my arms and gave my computer an order to show an overhead train, and then I looked over at Jane. She smiled at me.

"This thought that you have done it just popped into your head, or did you see something tonight?" I asked him, "There's something missing to this puzzle. The pieces aren't connecting as they should."

"Sir, when I asked you where those people came from, I noticed that nearly all of them were women with babies and small children."

"I wish I could answer that with one answer, Jose" "but I can't, everybody in all walks of life have trouble that comes their way, and no one is immune." "People vent anger in a different way." "A verbally abusive father or husband does just as much harm as a physically abusive father or husband." "It could be the woman that's to blame or the man." "Jose, I'm going to be personal with you." "Those girls you said that you fell in love with were using you." "Sure, they may have had a feeling of love for you." "But in truth, it would have been a short time when you would have discovered their secrets." "Could you have persuaded them to stop doing what they were doing just because you wanted them to?"

"No." He answered.

"That's the same problem we have here." I said to him, "We can't stop someone from doing something that they don't want to stop doing." "We have a chance with people that are here because they need us, not because we need them." "We don't provide a welfare service; everyone here works, and those that want to learn a trade are trained or schooled." "But they have to do this after they work."

"I can't stop someone from putting a bottle to their lips or putting something up their nose or in their arm." "Once a week, a council hears complaints that were alleged." "The complaint has a visual fact to back it up." "I told you, everyone is being watched." "It's the people that live here who say whether the individual can stay or not. If they disapprove, they will be removed." "They didn't own anything when they came, except personal items, and that's the way they'll leave." "In case you're wondering." "When it comes to alcohol or a drug-related incident, refusal of a test is an automatic dismissal, and the reason is always the same, they're lying, and I don't like liars." "One night doesn't tell you everything that you need to know, it's going to take a few more, and then you may choose to go to more meetings." "I don't want to control your life, Jose, or anyone else's, and I have trouble controlling mine." "Draw your own conclusions and talk to the hologram, or you can tell the computer to send in James or Ruby, and you might hear common sense plays a large role in the answer that you're looking for." "Now, that overhead train; what do you see as brakes, magnetic, or pneumatic?" I asked him.

"If I was building it, I would use both, that way. You always have some sort of a backup braking system." "I've heard about too many accidents at theme parks because safety issues were overridden." "Sir, this is way beyond anything I've ever seen." "The hospitals, and the housing units, the hotels, the parks, the dome, everything, can't be built without exposure, so you have to have someone that can act on your behalf." "When do you plan on beginning this project you wish to build?" He asked.

I took a deep breath and exhaled. "I might not," I said to him.

"Smith," Jane said to me, "don't start that kind of talk. If you want me to leave, just say so."

I looked at her and told her I was sorry.

"I can leave if I'm interrupting something," Jose said.

"No," Jane interfered, "I don't like it when he talks like he's not coming back." "Sir"

"I work alone," I told him before he finished his sentence.

"Then why do you want me to train if I'm not going to fight anyone, all I'm needed here for is to deliver messages and then wait until you need me again?" He challenged me.

"You have contempt in your voice," I told him.

"I'm sorry, sir," "Jane told me not to make you angry. She said you tend to want to find a place of solitude and be alone." "Sir, I can't be the person you want me to be without me being the person I want to be."

"Go ahead. I'm listening." I told him.

"Sir, your eyes are always looking for trouble. With me, you don't have to have eyes behind your back." "I went through a lot of hand-to-hand combat training, I never went on a mission, and you still want me to train. I think the fact is you don't want me on a mission."

"You think you're ready for action?" I asked him.

"Sir, I'd rather die in a fight than sit behind some desk and act like I'm somebody I'm not." He retorted with the same tone he had used earlier.

I handed him a pair of glasses. "Put these on," I told him.

"What do you see, Jose?"

"Sir, I'm sorry about saying that you don't have eyes in the back of your head." He said.

"There's a small button on the left side of the earpiece; push it," I said.

"I didn't believe this existed." He stated.

"What is it?" Jane asked.

"Xray vision," Jose replied.

"Keep your eyes to yourself." She told him.

"Now," I said to him, "in the upper right corner is a distance finder." "Computer; turn off the lights in this room," I ordered it. "Jose, push the button," I said.

"Night vision." He answered.

"Yeah, except it's outfitted with heat sensors and motion detectors." "I developed it for mountainous terrains," I said to him. "Push the nose piece up to fit your eyes better."

"I can't see, sir." He sounded somewhat confused.

"That's because this room is like a slide under a microscope." "That's because you're view is set for five thousand feet. Keep pushing the nose piece until the picture clears up. It's nothing more than a pair of binoculars, except stronger." I stated and went on with my lecture, "In all situations where the glasses are needed, I can't afford to lose them." "The metal band that wraps around your head holds the glasses from being knocked off accidentally." "By the way, that's where my cameras are so that I can see behind me and the cameras that are located in the earpieces make up the peripheral vision that I lose from the difference from the front and the back." "That gives me a three hundred and sixty-degree vision." "Everything that the glasses see and hear is also seen and heard by my computer." "The computer can spot the slightest movement that is easily missed by you." "It'll zero in on the target for you." That's when the binoculars come in handy." I told him.

"Sir, I feel like a fool." He said.

"Jose men sometimes do a lot of thinking." "Sometimes, a man thinks of something while conversing with a person, and speaks his thoughts out loud what he is thinking to the person that he's having a conversation with." "That's a conversation between two people." "You said you feel like a fool." "A man answered the person that made the same comment that you made with one of his own." "He said it was better for him to ask a question and be a fool for five minutes than to remain silent and be a fool for the rest of his life." "Now, those words are written on a piece of paper and put in frames and hung on walls." "Wise words are useless when not read." "There's a lesson to be learned there, but how many people pay attention to what is said." "It's forgotten as soon as something else catches the attention of that person, and what was written won't be remembered." "Why, I ask?" "Jose, one of the problems I cope with is that I have a negative view towards many of the people I meet." "The attention span of people is somewhere else other than on me when I talk to them." "I'm a non-diplomatic person, so I speak firmly; that doesn't play well when socializing with people," "I solve that by not socializing." "You saw me in Monterrey as Pedro, but you said that Pedro didn't know martial arts. You knew at that time, and I wasn't Pedro." "You were playing me for a fool." "When I spotted you, I had no way of knowing who you worked for, but when you picked us up, and we traveled, I heard you speak." "I had to know why you were watching us." "A fool is a person that doesn't pay attention," "Jose" "you're no fool." I told him, "There's a lot of questions that I ask myself; let's take Jane."

"I'd be careful if was you," she said, "very careful."

I giggled a little and went on to explain. "Jane's in love with me." "She wants to help me, and she has taken it upon herself to be my healer." "She listens while we talk, and later when we're alone, she isn't without ammunition when it comes to a conversation."

"Hey!" She quickly warned me.

"I don't accept any form of irritation to be displayed from those that I give my messages to." "I'm not afraid to sound like a fool. I'm going to ask the questions that I need to know." "I have records of every transaction that they've ever done." "It's all captured on their computers." "All movements made by the person that receives my messages are analyzed by me." "That's why Jack is always accompanied by James or Ruby, or both." "If I see anything that tells me the truth isn't complete and details are held back; a twitch of an eyelid, a scratch to the leg, or a foot-tapping are clues; it's a sign of nervousness." "I send Jack for a return visit, except he carries my message on a disc." "I don't like people playing games with me, I take offense easily, and I give them a warning that I know I'm being misled." "If Jack comes back without the answer I seek." "Then, I look further into the reason why, if I find corruption, I'm not a tolerant man." "I've seen fifty-year-old men that were set in their ways." "Their beliefs were misguided to be polite, and they responded with an attitude." "A person that would sit and argue with those men, to try and prove them wrong, would prove to be futile." "Yet, a child in the third grade goes and asks these outhouse wise men to help them with a school problem, and they tell the child to go to their mother." "I ask myself questions as you ask me questions, and like everyone else here, especially Jane." "She's invested her life in mine, and she likes to keep an eye on her investments," I said, smiling when I looked at her. I started chuckling. "There I go again, talking too much, and I forgot that no one cares what I say." "Strange how I seem to dominate a conversation; you mentioned that you thought you were a fool, and I wanted to correct your thoughts, and I found myself rambling on," I said to him.

"Sir, I'm not smart." He spoke, "I didn't do too well in school. That's one reason I enlisted." "I ask a question, and you give me an answer." "One that I can understand, you don't use big words that I don't know what they mean." "I call myself a name, and you criticize me and tell me everyone is a fool at some point in his life."

"Is that what you heard?" I asked him.

"No sir, what I heard was a man that tried to build my character back up from feeling pity." He said.

"You can only see one side of a story, and that's yours, Jose." "Everybody has a reason for doing what they do or not doing what they do."

"Sir, when I was young, I worked for a lot of men." "No matter what I have done or how hard I worked, it wasn't ever enough for them."

"I stood on my corner along with the rest of the men looking for work and waited for someone to stop and pick up a crew." "That was the only job I could get, so I did this every day." "Four times, immigration came out and arrested us all." "I was a citizen, and after they found that out, I was released, but some of the other people weren't." "To make a long story short, I believe they called authorities to keep from paying us what was owed." "I've seen my share of low life's, and I know why the people in the hood are in the hood." He said, sounding somewhat upset that he was used.

"Did you ever get paid from the people that owed you money?" I asked him.

"I came from a low-income housing project, I couldn't afford a lawyer, and I never had any kind of proof that I worked for them." "We were day workers, and we were picked up and promised a paycheck." "I filed charges with the police and when I went to small claims court to try and get my money." "Those men brought lawyers with them, and the case was ruled against me every time. I didn't have any proof that they hired me." "The third time I was labeled as a habitual seeker of monies not owed because I filed lawsuits against people I didn't work for, my past proved it." "The fourth was thrown out of court."

"Jose" "during your training, you had men that were squad leaders." "Most of them, if not all of them were like you; they never had a mission, they act tough but when a person encounters a situation to where it's kill; or be killed, some men find out really quick that a new career is in their future." "Actuality changes many men to question their wisdom." "That's why some of those men acted so tough; they were trained on how to train others." "Hand-to-hand combat is all right when you're up against one person, but two, three, four or more, and you're dead." "A bullet shatters hundreds of thousands of dollars that was used to train you by men that never went on a mission." "It's been forty years since intelligence found out that there was a lack of intelligence." "Techniques and training are outdated." "Technology today makes all military personnel easy targets." "The sad thing is I can sit behind a control center, like this one, and kill everything that moves with a joystick." "I don't even have to be there to do it." "We have that technology, but it's not being used, we still expose our men to an enemy, and we don't know who ours are." "Men don't learn the art of war unless they've been in war." "You don't use men; you use computers." "But I see men coming home hurt for no reason, and that angers me." "You can't fight an unconventional war using conventional training." "The revolutionary war proved that."

"Brave men or brave because all people praise bravery." "Would it surprise you to learn that soldiers were shot in the back by our soldiers?" "That's called friendly kills." "Look in any cemetery and look for the soldier that was killed in a war." "He's six feet under, and his children, or grandchildren, if he had any, buy products from the country that he fought against, so what does bravery have to do with anything?" "Time has a way of erasing wrong decisions, and what happened then is no longer brought up in a discussion." "The people are too young to remember what went on years ago, and they find it dull to read about it." "Bravery is for people that act foolish and live to do it again." "Not many in battle live to tell about it, only the ones that fought the battle a thousand miles away." "They'll be a grave dug for the soldiers that killed them, and words of praise reminding everyone of his bravery will be said." Three generations will pass, and nothing is remembered of the soldier that died a hero; no one will visit his grave." "He died from a lie."

"Yes, sir." He said.

"Computer; display files on Jose," I ordered, and a record of his files popped up. "Scroll down until I order you to stop," I commanded. I then gave my order to stop. "Samuel Edwards was the first person you filed charges against." I told him, "Computer; scroll down until I order you to stop." A few moments later, I ordered it to stop. "Joseph P. Jackson was the next person you filed against." "Computer; scroll down." "Stop," I ordered. "Randall Anderson." "Computer; scroll down." I waited, and then I ordered for it to stop "Aaron Spellings." I said to him, "Jose, these names were gotten from the immigration administration, and apparently, as you mentioned, they were raided the same day the men were to be paid." "I can see an occasional random investigation, but in this case, all raids were given information."

I turned around and began typing.

"What are you doing now?" He asked.

"Jose, in the Internal Revenue Service, a person is guilty by accusation alone; it's up to the taxpayer to prove them wrong." "These people are going to spend thousands of dollars in fines and back taxes." "They have to prove how they harvested their bounty, and the accusations support that they knew that they were hiring illegal aliens, and in this country, that's a no-no." "All of them have businesses, and the dollars and cents of their accounts don't add up according to my review." "There's money that's missing from their accounts, and they won't find it." "What they saved by calling the authorities is going to cost them all that they have." "Which is better, pay a man for a promise or betray him because he took advantage of the law." "In this case, they betrayed the wrong man because he knows a man that knows how to strike back." "A promise is a promise, and to break a promise is wrong." "It could be interpreted as a lie, and Jose, you know how I feel about liars." "I told you that I'm not a tolerant man." "I take great privilege in doing all that I can to anybody cheating anybody out of anything that they are due." "Sometimes vindication moves slowly." "But, it's rewarding when you finally see it was happening," I said to him.

"What did you just do?" He asked.

"I ordered the IRS to investigate these people?" "I brought charges against them, and tomorrow, they'll be picked up, and all papers will be confiscated and reviewed for evidence; Jose, proof on paper to allegations made, leads to a plea bargain." "They're guilty of the criminal charges that they have against them." "All I needed was to see where the money came from and how it got there." "They cut corners and installed inferior products." "That's why they used day laborers; they do what they're told, and they'll work seven days a week, sixteen hours a day." "The number one clue in any wrongdoing is keeping sloppy paperwork that doesn't show the same numbers that other papers show." "Everybody messes up somewhere." "Fifty thousand is a lot of money to some people, and some people spend that much on a party." "The real clue is, once someone thinks that his pilfering is fooling everyone, he ends up taking a little more and saving it somewhere else, and it becomes an obsession." "Get away with a small amount, and it's repeated every time after." "That's why our prisons are overcrowded." "Computer; initiate the names of the people that hired the contractors and give me the last twenty years of their financial records, along with any other contractors that they hired." When the records began appearing, I ordered the computer to collect all files and display inaccuracies. I watched as the files began coming up one by one.

"Computer; increase the speed of display."

I watched as the files appeared and disappeared. When I had seen enough, I gave the computer the order to cease with my previous order. "Send the IRS all documents.

"You read that, Sir?" Jose asked.

"I'm a speed reader Jose." I told him and then added, "Jose, I only found one man that all the records showed that he was the ringleader of the construction sites." "A total of twenty raids were performed at various jobs he worked on." "He's eighty-six now and dying of cancer." "One of buildings that were built by his contractor's; the same contractor's that you had worked for had a fire, and the water line was weak and broke when it was needed; they didn't have any pressure." "Six people died; four children and two adults." "The man I'm speaking of was the mayor at that time." "That's why you lost your cases." I told him, "That part of the story in your life is over, it was a long time ago, and the people that cheated you are going to Federal prison for income tax evasion, and they'll die behind bars." "The only other person is alive but dying." "Every breath he takes brings him pain." "He begs for the reaper." "I can finish it now, but which is worse?" "Kill someone for a crime he committed, or let him die a slow and painful death from his organs shutting down one by one." "So, to kill him will be rewarding him." "This is your call," I told him.

He walked away, sat down on the couch, and put his hand to his chin.

"Sir, how can people be like that?"

"Jose, man has never been at peace with one another, and since the dawn of man he has always been a slave to man, nations that were conquered were captured and enslaved to do the work that they were ordered to do, and it's still going on today." "I'll give you an example." "Years ago migrants worked jobs that no one would do over here." "Today, that's frowned upon." "My question is, why did they bring slaves over here." "Money enslaves all; it's worth less than half of what it was worth ten years ago." "When it's that easy to fool the people, then the only success you will achieve is a higher crime rate." "Gangs end up hiring almost all of the people that don't have a job." "That means that the sale of drugs and rape, alcoholism, burglary, prostitution and murders, and a lot more crimes are going to get away with what they do." "First off, you can't be everywhere at once, and prisons cost a hundred and twenty-five thousand dollars a year to house one inmate." "Once they are released, they all need money to eat and pay a probation officer, and they only have one solution; no money only means more robberies and more deaths." "So the answer to your question is greed." "You never have enough; you always want more." "There's a strange thing about prison; it's like a college, prisoners learn how not to get caught."

"Sir, I don't understand."

"Jose, I see anger and hatred, frustration and agitation, irritation and talk of annihilation." "I see, the same excuses being blamed on our problems being levied against other countries." "It was planned a long time ago." "This country has corporations that are for sale." "When it's sold, people end up out of work and losing their houses." "Let's say someone can make billions of dollars if an assassination was carried out." "It's not as difficult to achieve as what you might believe." "It only takes one order to the right person, and the ball starts rolling." "The end result is accomplished, and no one points the finger in the right direction." "People believe what they're told." "Our country is no longer the country it was twenty years ago." "Corporations sell out to other Countries; they make them an offer that they can't refuse." "The end result is all profits go to that country." "We don't own gas stations, department stores or auto parts stores, or hardware stores." "That's just to mention a few." "Auto manufacturers are building autos in other countries because labor is cheaper." "The same goes for food." "They get rid of Unions by having food made in other countries." "Man is ignorant." "One day" "man will have problems, but they'll put their blame on the wrong people instead of pointing the finger at themselves." "We buy whatever is the cheapest."

"Sir, you're talking in the tongue." He said.

"Yeah, but I have a problem." I told him, "You want to be a warrior that fights for what's right." "After all, you were trained to kill, yet you've never killed anyone; that's difficult for me to process." "Death is an end to a life; I kill because they were all deserving." "I'm sure a man like you has a reason for being the man he is and doing what he does for a purpose." "That's another one of those little things in life that all of us humans have in common, a reason for being the person that we are." "Computer; give a satellite display of all rivers coming out of all countries and highlight the pollution in yellow."

"Begin the sequence of pictures in alphabetical order." I commanded, "Jose, take a look." "Fifty years from now, ocean life is going to become extinct, one small organism at a time." "One animal feeds another animal, and that animal, may feed several animals, and so on." "It doesn't frighten anyone if a species or two or even three were killed because of the pollution into the rivers that flowed into the sea that these countries allowed." "What affects all ocean life affects everyone." "Food will become inedible; contamination breeds microorganisms that our body can't fight, and the organisms spread." "They'll be new diseases and new strains of viruses." "Man knows this, but money is being made, but when it ends, the villages die, and rats and snakes take back what was theirs in the first place." "We've been given warning signs of what's to come, yet, we choose to ignore them." "The earth is being reformed, and continents are being pulled apart or are being pushed together." "It's been going on like that since the earth was born." "Are you familiar with the lost city of Atlantis?" I asked him.

"Yes, sir."

"This earth is surrounded by a crust that contains a core that is so condensed that it generates enormous heat." "Periodically, the pressure becomes too great for the crust to contain the molten lava." "Volcanoes and hot spots all over the earth are proof of that." "Yellowstone National Park is a ticking time bomb, and when it blows, the earth will feel its concussion and its impact on the opposite side of the world within minutes." "Atlantis was one such city; the only reason Atlantis was cited was that at the time it was a major port of trade, there were hundreds of other cities that were wiped out as well." "Like everything that surrounds Yellowstone, Atlantis collapsed, and water covered up its history." "It sank hundreds of feet deep, and everything it had to offer was condensed into a powder that resembled dust." "Atlantis will never be found; it was totally destroyed in the blink of an eye." "There's pumice in other countries that have proven that an explosion took place that was one thousand times the explosion of Mount Saint Helens." "Every city for hundreds of miles was disintegrated." "Yellowstone will be ten thousand times that." "Jose, which one is going to kill all men first?"

"Sir!"

"Jose," Jane said, "the last Tsunami tilted the earth's axis three degrees, and Mother Nature gave states and cities storms as they've never experienced before." "Those three degrees caused a change to occur in the weather."

I looked over at Jane with a curious look.

"I talked to the hologram." She said, smiling.

"Sir, is that what you meant about not being able to stop a universal catastrophe?" Jose asked me.

"The Tsunami wasn't caused by a universal mishap; it was an act of Mother Nature, not an act of human participation, or a universal incident," I told him. "Jose, the earth is going to release the pressure from inside of itself." "It happened that way a hundred thousand times, and it predicts that it'll happen again and again, and it all started hundreds of millions of years ago."

"Computer, run program R sixty-five." I commanded, "I started working on this film seven years ago; it's an ongoing work in progress, Jose." "Right now, it's three hours long." "I'd like for both of you to watch it and see what you see through my eyes." "I narrated it myself, and I've sent this film to every country in the world."

I left them and went into my study and turned on the fireplace; its glow captured my thoughts, and I gave more thought to my thoughts. I moved over into the rocking chair, sat down, and then began moving to a pace that I found to be perfect, not rocking and not being still.

I closed my eyes and went back in my mind to the first time that I saw Jane falling from the ledge and how everything had come together. I had to fight off a part of me that plagued me with knowledge of the truth. Never put my trust in anyone, but I realized I had changed, and I came to the conclusion that the only thing about change was to change itself.

I opened my eyes and told the computer to run last night's meeting at the workshop. I zoomed in on everyone that was present and, like always, watched the moves that they made very closely. I had just finished watching it when I was interrupted by Jane and Jose.

Both of them were silent as they sat down. I got up and sat with Jane and tried to display to her that I needed her. Her immediate response was to put her arm around me and hold me tight. There was something wrong, and I felt uneasy. I stood up and told Jane to do the same. When she did, I sat in her spot and pulled her into my lap.

"Are you happy now?" She said.

"I'm sorry." I told her, "I thought." My sentence was interrupted as Jane was making herself comfortable in my lap.

"Smith," Jose said, "she's kidding. She's right where she wants to be, with you." "Now, sir, what was the response from these countries?" He asked.

"There wasn't any." "I told you, money gets in the way, and all monies end up in the government's pockets, and all monies, no matter if it's a penny, or a yen, or a Juan, or a dollar, or a euro is going to be lost because shutting down businesses stops the flow of these monies that go into their pockets." "Jose, man is doomed by our own actions." "All countries with weapons of mass destruction put on a show of force on a small scale." "Radiation and other forms of by-products from these tests disperse, and people and animals, and fish are bombarded with it." "Eventually, cancer will soon affect all people born on earth; and I'm helpless to stop it unless I assassinate every political leader, and then I'd have to do the same to the next ones that took their place." "People can't see what a hundred years from now will look like, and a large majority could care less." "Food has to be consumed in order for the body to survive, and all of our food comes from other countries; they're the ones that are polluting the top of the chain by allowing the low end of the chain to become contaminated." "Technology; you can only advance in technology so far before the technology evolves to where humans aren't needed to make the product." "I grow tired of a criminal getting off because they own a politician." "Back in the early twenty's, high profile gangsters openly attended clubs and restaurants, and socialized with Police Chiefs and Judge's, Mayor's, Governor's, and all of them had a smile on their face when their picture was taken." "These criminals have wanted men roaming around in the open." "There was prohibition, and alcohol was the drug of choice, revenuer's supplied gallons on the black market." "One of the suppliers had grandsons, all three of them became senators, and one became the president of the United States." "I think some answers don't need much explanation to what was going on and is still going on." "I'm here to find them and remove them from office." "You have to surgically remove cancer from the body, and you have to do the same to cancer that has affected a government. If allowed to persist, countries will be conquered from within, and greed will be their conqueror." "Jose, it doesn't take an army; they do as they're told." "You should know that." "It only takes one man, and millions will die because of him."

"George Washington said in order to have peace, you must be prepared for war." "But he also said that the plague would kill you faster than a sword." "But I heard a general say you don't have a military for defense; you have a military to control a populace." "That's two conflicting adage's." "What means will this country go to stop the aggression of its people?" "Perhaps, you can recall the War Between the States?" "It wasn't fought over slavery; it was fought because the South was going to break away from the North." "The North couldn't let this happen; they would lose revenue in taxes from the ports of the South, and commodities such as cotton and tobacco, not to mention the Louisiana Purchase from Napoleon." "If the South would have won, we would be British subjects."

"Jose, this country has a lot of educated people in charge that aren't using educated decisions." "That's why I was asked to help put a stop to it." "I know what's been on your mind since you've arrived this morning." "There's a time and a place for everything." "I am independent, but I do work for democracy. That's why this lab is secret; we are a divided nation, half republican and half democrat." "If the wrong side gains a dominant control, we'll have the Socialist Republic." "The wheels have been set in motion." "I hear talk of terrorism." "Jose, look back in your mind when you were a little boy." "You heard gunshots and looked to see your father and brothers on the ground." "That's terrorists; they were nothing more than people out to fight for control of a territory." "We don't need to go to foreign countries to fight terrorism; they're in every city and county and state in America." "And they buy assault weapons freely."

"What do you want me to do?" He asked.

"I need you to learn what needs to be learned." "Before you can understand the purpose you fight for, you must know why you fight." I told him, "First, I need information." "Computer; run the program of last night's meeting." When it appeared, I ordered it to shift its focal point over to the left, and when my subject appeared, I ordered for it to stop "Computer; zoom in fifty percent larger." I ordered, "Jose, do you notice the lady in the middle wearing jeans? Did you see her last night?"

"No, sir." He said.

"I need to know more about her." "I'll arrange a dinner, and I want you to talk to her."

"Yes, sir." "What is the information you need?" He said.

"I'll be watching you." I told him, "I don't need anything other than a small casual conversation." "You can tell her that in order to assign a caseworker to help her in getting settled, you need to know what she's interested in." "You said you were ready for an assignment." I said to him, "Let's see how good you think you are." "Computer: send Ruby into the exercise room, please."

"Follow me," I said. I took Jane's hand and led her into the exercise room where Ruby was waiting for us. "Jose, you said you were trained in hand-to-hand combat." "I'd like for you to test your skills against Ruby."

"I'm not going to fight a woman." He quickly asserted.

"You want to live?" I said to him.

"I can't hit a woman." He replied.

"I don't think you have to worry about that." "Ruby" "use defense only" "no offense."

She waited until Jose threw a sidekick with reluctance. He missed, and she easily pushed his leg aside.

"Jose, that wasn't a punch. If it was, whoever trained you didn't know squat." I stated to him, "Let me see what you got." I once again challenged him. He threw another sidekick with the same reluctance.

"Ruby put him down," I said to her.

Three hits later, Jose was flying backward.

"Jose," "Ruby can handle her own; now let me see what you got." I told him, "This time, use what you learned as best as you can." "Don't worry about Ruby. I can guarantee you; you won't touch her."

We watched as Ruby put him on the floor again and again. After he was out of breath, he put his hands on his knees to try and breathe deep to replenish his oxygen.

"I can see why you don't need me." He said.

"Jose, all I said was that you need more training." "You have a weak defense, that's obvious, and you have an even weaker offense. You didn't block any of her punches." "And as far as offense is concerned, I didn't see any." "Remember when I told you that the person that kills you might be the person that's asking you to get something from the top shelf at a grocery store?" "The art of self-defense requires that all moves that are made are done so for a purpose, whether it is for defense or offense." "You have to pay attention to all things, no matter how small." "A stiff body is slow, and kicks end up pulling muscles, and you'll die at the hands of someone that took advantage of an injury that was caused by your own actions." "So now, you've had a busy day, and tomorrow is another day." "I'll show you to your room, and when you're ready to retire, you'll know where to go," I told him.

We left with Jane following us.

When I opened the door, he took a good look around.

"It's nothing fancy, a bed, a bath or shower." "If you have any questions, ask the computer; your job will go easier knowing what to expect from the people you meet." "In case you're wondering, I have a speaker set up where all you need to do is ask your question, and the computer will give your answer."

"Sir, are you going to sleep?" He asked.

Jane interrupted him.

"He's going to put me to sleep." She told him, "I haven't had but a few hours here or a few hours there since he left." "I need my sleep, and the only way I can get it is when Smith is lying next to me." "He's getting ready to leave again, and he'll be gone from my life longer than I want, and then I'll be back to tossing and turning and waking up thinking he's been killed, and I won't be able to go back to sleep." "Jose, I need my sleep." She said with authority as she looked down at him.

"Jose," I said to him. "If you don't feel tired, feel free to wander around; just don't touch anything." If you want to know what you're looking at, simply ask the computer to display the hologram and then ask all the questions you want to know." "Or you order the computer to call for James." "It's a whole lot safer that way for you and the rest of us." "James will follow you everywhere. You can ask him what you want to know, don't be upset if he responds that you ask a restricted question."

"Is he going to stand guard outside of my room?" He asked.

"No, he won't have to." "My computer does that."

"Yes, sir." He said.

We left, and when we entered the bedroom, I turned the shower on to feel fresh. I heard the door open behind me, and when I turned, I saw Jane taking off her clothes.

"I need a shower too." She said.

That was the first time anyone had ever given me a shower. I learned from it and returned the attention that she gave me. When I finished, she took me in her arms and held me tight under the water. Her hair was taking the spray of the showerhead as she bent down to kiss me.

She stopped for a moment and nibbled on my ear, and whispered words.

"You were right; I do find myself wanting to be with you all day and all night." "I don't pay attention to anything; all I have on my mind is you." Then she returned to kissing me under the running water.

The next morning, I smelled coffee brewing when I came out of my room. When I walked into the kitchen, I was with everyone except Jane.

"Morning," they all replied.

I smiled as I poured myself a cup of coffee and took a sip.

I stopped and smacked my lips. "This is good coffee Ellen," I told her.

"How did you know I made it," Ellen asked.

I had to ease a smile. "You use a level scoop." "Jack scoops it up and ends up with half as much more."

"You think you're slick," she chided me, "but I had that pulled on me before." "I know what you're doing." "My mother used to tell me that I made the best tea she ever drank, so I made tea all the time thinking I had a knack for it." "Later on, she said she told me that because I would make the tea." "You're pulling the same stunt that my mother pulled on me, and I don't make the best coffee; you do; Jack never drank as much at home as what he does here." "How do you do it anyway?"

"It's not much." "When you use pepper, what kind do you use, powdered or peppercorns?" I asked her.

"Powdered," she answered.

"There you have it." "If you use peppercorns and grind it when needed, the oils of the pepper are still inside, and the flavor is stronger. The oils in the powdered pepper are dry." "Coffee beans are the same, grind them only when needed, and it gives the coffee a better flavor." "But that's only my opinion." "Now, every time you drink a cup of coffee, somewhere else other than the pot that's made here, you'll be judging the flavor for yourself." I told her, "Ask Jack."

I sat my coffee down and went and took my clippers out of a drawer, held Jose's head straight, and began cutting his hair. "Jose, you have a natural part, but you part it the other way. That's why this area here," I showed him in the mirror, "has a slight lift to it." "In days of old, it was referred to as a cowlick, and to make it conform to their standards, they used oil, or hair spray, to make it lay down perfect." After I finished cutting his hair, I showed it to him by putting a mirror in front of his face. "I cut it short on purpose." "When you deliver my packages, I have to dress you in disguise." "You'll have contacts in your eyes so no one can scan an optical trace on you." "If someone offers you a drink, don't take it, they want a DNA check performed on you, and you'll be wearing false fingertips at all times, and there's one other thing, no more hair oil." "When you're here, you won't be wearing any disguise. You'll be you, but when you're away from here, you'll become Dan Gomez." "When offered a casual conversation, give no comment; simply say you try to listen before you determine a decision." "When asked a question, give no comment; answer the same way as a casual conversation. This way, they get no direction to where you lean." "If someone pushes you." "Tell them you're a professional. You only came to do a job." "Deliver the message and leave." "After a few times out with Jack, you'll be going on trips by yourself." "In case you're wondering the messages you deliver, they carry nothing except confirmation that I'm on to them." "I offer all of them a chance to do right." "But Jose, I can't catch everyone in time, and those that I miss, shame on them." "Let's take tonight." "You'll meet up with someone you don't know, and people ask questions." "You have to be protective as not to say something harmful." "You can't be uncaring; that would show a sign of being rude and business only." "The answers you get will only consist of the questions you want to hear." "If you act too friendly and you show that the dinner may have been for a different reason other than to assign her a caseworker to help her." "She'll think that she's being played." "This is a woman that doesn't know whether she's going to be able to stay here or be sent packing." "She sees you, and she knows you're the man that is going to tell her what she wants to know." "You look at her straight-faced, and she will assume the worst." "You greet her with a smile," I said to him. "And the smile tells her that you have good news to offer her." "The men you meet, you won't greet them that way. That's when you use a straight face." "I read people, and other people can read people, you have to learn how to never show anybody anything, and one way is never comment on any comment." "Tonight will be a test of the basics."

"Sir, what do you mean, the basics?" He asked.

"Jose, when you come back tonight, you can ask that question again. I'll answer it then."

I went and poured myself another cup of coffee.

When I walked back over and sat down, I looked over at Jose.

"I can see Jane picked out the clothes you brought back." I said to him, smiling, "You look good in them." "Not flashy, not casual." "I think you should listen to her when she talks about clothes." "I don't dress for success; you can see that." "You're a different story, though." "You meet men of powerful corporations and dignitaries from countries all over the world. They dress to show others that they have power."

"Computer; dress Jose in dull gray suits, with coats and shoes until I order you to stop each item; initiate activation."

Almost a minute had gone by before I started stopping the computer on each item I chose. I increased the picture of Jose dressed in the suit and other apparel.

"You like hats, Jose?" I asked him.

"No, sir."

"Good," "no remnants for someone to rub and find out the hair type." "They'll know it's a wig." "What do you think, Jose?" "Is that you?" "Can you be that person and compose yourself to be him?" I asked him, "That means no smiles when someone tells a joke, no reply about your ethnic background, and no form of anger of any kind will be expressed when someone tries to push you into a corner." "That's the test that I'm going to see in you tonight." "Jose, I chose you because I think you'll make a good man one day." "Maybe you'll make it till you rust away in some rocking chair because you learned that we're all in this together."

I looked over at Ellen. "You said I treat you like a third party." "I'm sorry for that." I stood and walked over to her and noticed something about her "May I?" I asked her.

"Go ahead." She said.

I took her chin in my hand.

"There were tears that fell last night." I said, "They were tears of joy." "You look relieved and rested." "The puffiness around your eyes is gone, and I see a sparkle to them." "You have happiness upon you, and Ellen, I can see that you have your worries about me too."

She burst into tears and ran from the room.

I looked over at Jack and responded, "She's frightened of me, isn't she?" I said.

"She loves you, and yes, she is frightened of you, like I was when we met; only what took me a few days took her a little longer." He stated his mind about her.

"Sir, may I speak," Jose asked.

"You can interrupt a discussion anytime, Jose." "You don't need permission to speak here," I said.

"Sir, if it means anything, I'm scared of you too," Jose replied.

I looked over at Jack, and we both began smiling.

"Jose, I'm a man that has many problems, and I lose focus often." "I battle myself constantly and psychoanalyze the people that I talk to." "Ellen is easy is for me, and that makes her mad." "Jack has to go talk to her to settle her down, she's held her emotions to herself, and she needs to release those emotions she's had." "We've been together for a short while, and Jack can testify that she wouldn't be here at all if circumstances were different." "Ellen has to be sent a message, and Jack has to deliver the message for me." "I can't do it myself, it's not proper." "People say things that are heard, but they don't hear the words that are said." "Jack has to go to Ellen, and he has to tell her that I love her." "That's the words she's been waiting for me to say, but I couldn't; she wants a family, and by me telling her that I love her, tells her what she needs to hear." "Now, Jack has to go and listen to her cry for the rest of the day." "She won't come out of her room." "Her eyes will be puffy and red again." "Then after a while, she'll calm down, and then she'll start crying all over again."

I gave Jack a smile, and he left.

"Thanks a lot, buddy." He commented as he was leaving.

Jane walked in when her father had just left, and walked over and poured herself a cup of coffee, and scooted her chair next to me and sat down.

"Where's everyone at?" She asked.

"I talked too much, and they left," I told her.

"Smith, did you get mad?" She asked.

"I don't know." "I said what was on my mind, and I don't know if I offend someone when I do." "I find that giving honest answers don't always get nice results."

"Smith, which one did you talk to my mother or father?" Jane asked.

"Your mother was happy, and I told her what I saw in her eyes; that's when she ran off crying."

"Then what'd you do?" Jane said.

"I sent your father in to tell her that I loved her."

She took a sip of her coffee. "Smith, you've done nothing wrong," she began "my guess is you better get ready for a woman with a strong grip on her." "You have given her what you gave me; she knows what the word love means to you, and to hear you say it means that you and she are more than friends."

I looked over at Jose.

"You entered an organization after I met Jane and her mother." "You don't have any idea of what's going on, and it's not easy for you to follow our conversation." I told him, "You don't know what started the life of Jane and me or her mother." "You look around and see my lab, and you have a clear picture of me, but not anyone else, except for Jack." "I don't think it's wise for you not to know what has happened from the start." "Not knowing everything only confuses you." "You should ask the computer to tell you about how our lives came to be."

"What are you going to do?" Jane asked.

"I've got to take a long run, or you up to it?" I asked her.

"I'll tell you what." She said, "You begin, and when I'm dressed, I'll catch up to you."

She gave me a kiss, and she left to change clothes. I looked over at Jose.

"Enjoy the lecture," I told him as I walked out the door and walked down the hall to my track. I began walking at a pace and built the pace up as I felt the muscles in my body starting to loosen. I took on a gait that had me trotting, and then my gait increased after the first mile. I felt good. My mind was clear, and I watched as each foot hit the track. Jane began running next to me.

"You're going to hurt." I told her, "You didn't stretch and relax the muscles before you began."

"Did I tell you that I love you today?" She said.

"Jane, how come people didn't like me when I was young?" I asked her.

"Oh Smith, people who are intelligent can't talk with people that aren't up to the level that you possess." "People want to boast and brag about things they know, and when you correct them and shame them in front of others, they don't get the respect that they are trying to impress on other people." "Smith, you make people feel uneducated when you're around them." "You don't bother me, and that's all you should care about." "Smith, you can see what others can't, and that's why people treated you the way they did."

"In case you're wondering, that's how I was able to answer your question so quickly. That's the way I felt when we met." "I told you before," she said, "I stay out of your business because your business isn't any of my business." "But it's hard for me to sit back and watch you battle questions trying to find the right answers. You beat yourself up over little things."

"I exercise." I told her, "I feel good when I do it."

"I'm not talking about running and walking or working out in your room." She had concern in her voice. "I'm talking about that brain inside of your head." "You fight senseless questions that don't have answers, and I'm worried that you can take this too far."

"From what I hear, you're telling me that you're thinking that I could become insane?" I smiled and then started talking to her "Jane when you and your husband had a fight, how did you feel?"

"What do you mean?" She asked.

"Your emotions, what were your emotions like?" I asked.

"I cried." She said.

"Insanity is not being able to identify the action one needs to take to rectify a wrong. You cried because you were hurt and confused" "Jane confusion is a form of sanity that allows insanity to be questioned." I said to her, "Insanity is punishing a child too severely for being a child." "Insanity is when someone commits a crime and pleads his innocence as being insane at the time." "Insanity is a tightrope that we walk; those that fall off will never land; it's a bottomless pit." "That's where those that are really insane end up." "Don't worry, if they're truly insane, they won't know where they're at anyway." "My mother didn't." "Those tears you cried, you cried because you were hurt, you lived the last four years of your life in a lie, but you didn't know that until he tried to kill you." "So that tells me that there had to be a time when you started to feel unappreciated."

"It was about six months after we were married," Jane commented, "he never acted as if I was around; it was all about him."

"There's your answer." I said, "Sanity and insanity are the same as doing what is right or doing what is wrong, there's good or bad, and there's being happy or unhappy." "Six months after you married, you encountered the act of being unhappy, and you asked yourself many times if you were right or wrong." "The fault wasn't yours, it never was, but you still pondered those thoughts of sanity and insanity." I said to her and then continued, "I fought that battle, and I woke up not knowing where I was, and I found it to be a very lonely place." "I found my key, and my door was opened."

"What was your key?" She asked.

"You," I answered.

She stopped, and I continued on running, leaving her behind. She was like her mother. She ran off crying.

I was met by Jose as he caught up to me.

"You're going to hurt, not warming up before running," I told him.

"You seem to chase off everybody you talk to." He said to me, "I saw Jane crying as she was leaving."

"Does it fit in with what you listened to about me?" I asked him.

"Sir, you can't do this alone." He said, "You said the weakest point of your defense was coming from your back." "I think you're worried about this mission." "Why did you bring me here?" "I won't be taught anything after you leave."

"You're not ready, Jose."

"Sir, if not being ready means being equal to you, then I'll never be ready." "I don't come close to matching you in wits or fighting with you. I know my place, and it's taking orders." "But, you called me a learner, and it if takes me sixteen hours out of the day to practice, then I'll practice seventeen hours out of the day."

I slowed to a walk and breathed deep to catch my breath. When I did, I looked over at Jose.

Before I could talk any further, he stopped me by finishing his comment.

"Sir, you said your life ended at ten when you lost your brother; mine ended at six when I lost my whole family." "What problems could you possibly have that I don't have?" "I hurt too, and I can't do anything to stop it." "You want me to act out a character that you want me to be." "I can't be that man without being able to help fight." "I have to know what I'm up against."

"I've always been a one-man show." I told him, "I moved a lot easier that way, and I only had one person to worry about." "Technology today demands even better technology in order to override a system, and then that system becomes outdated almost as soon as it's applied, and a new system is put into effect."

"Jose, I can't be everywhere I need to be." "Tonight, don't be so formal; lighten up and make her feel easy being with you. It helps when they feel like they can talk to you." "They tell you more about what they wish they could do, and that's the person we encourage them to become." "You'll only wear a disguise when away from here, so she'll be seeing the real person that you are." "You're a well-mannered young man, and I expect nothing but more of the same from you." "Go take a shower and shave, and Jose, I like seeing you in light blue. It tells a person that you aren't wild and rambunctious; it gives you the look of being calm and settled." I told him

I walked over to my hot tub, sat down in it, and bowed my head. I felt a breeze flow along the bottom of the floor.

"Hello Jane," I said without looking up to see if it was her. "How did you know I was coming?" "I felt the air currents as you walked." "Your parents would have moved without concern of making a noise, and Jose just left to take a shower. He has a meeting tonight." "So that leaves you," I said.

"Smith, you've got to quit saying things that sound spooky." "You catch me off guard, and I lose control." She said as she entered the hot tub.

"That's the part that I don't understand," I told her. "I read books that said that women sometimes wanted to be alone, and I've read books that said that women sometimes need company." "Jane, when you cry, I don't know what I'm supposed to do." "I don't want to make things worse for you." "I can't read a woman when she's crying."

"Well, first off," she said, "You made me feel good when you said I was the person you needed." "Secondly, you opened my eyes when you told me that I was living a lie, and for a long time, I blamed myself." "I was remembering when I was at the cabin, and I first held you in my arms." "You were right, I found the key to open my door, and you gave it to me when you laid down next to me." "When you said you found your key, and it was me." "In case you haven't noticed, I'm a little moody right now, and I lost control, that's all." She said.

"I'm thinking about taking Jose with me." I told her, "I informed him that I work alone, and he gave me a good reason." "To leave him behind will do him more harm than good."

"This girl that he's going to meet tonight." She asked, "What is it that you see that's so special about her?"

"Jose has to learn a lesson. Not all things are as they seem." "He'll go expecting to pretend he's trying to find the right caseworker for her and that he needed to ask her a few questions." "Jane, the girl is a deaf-mute." "He'll be caught off guard."

"How did you know?" She asked.

"Computer: display last night's workshop starting from the beginning." "Notice how people are talking, and she never looks to where the voices are coming from, she's gazing around, and she's positioning herself in the rear of the building, so she can watch the reaction of the people." "Computer: end transmission," I said.

"He's not going to like this," Jane commented.

"I had to give him a message." I told her, "The impact will explain the meeting." "This is his first lesson; to always expect the unexpected."

"Smith back at the cabin. We were together every night." She said, "And what's odd is, when I woke up, I did that too; I didn't expect the unexpected."

"You're a man I can look up to, figuratively speaking." "In your letter, I didn't like the way you leaned on some subjects, and I was bothered."

"You have to be direct. I can't guess what you need to say," I told her.

"It's sensitive, all right?" She said, "And you can't just come out and say something that's sensitive."

I bowed my head and closed my eyes.

"Now, what are you doing?" She said.

"I'm encountering an immovable object." I told her, "I have to enter the center of the universe through meditation."

"So, now you're saying I'm the immovable object, and this is how you deal with your life." She responded, irritated.

"Jane, let's go dry off. I need to change into my workout uniform. I have something I want to show you." "Then I want the answer that you asked earlier about how I deal with my life." "I need to hear true feelings to give true answers," I told her.

Later, Jane and I walked into my workout room, and moments later, Jose, Ellen, and Jack did too.

"Well, since we're all here." I said, "Jane and I had a discussion, and my comment was that through meditation, I was encountering an immovable object." "She took me wrong and thought something else."

I placed the fingertips of my two forefingers and my thumb of each hand onto the floor, lifted my legs outward, and wrapped them around my forearms while supporting my body with my two forefingers and thumb on the fingertips. I then slowly began unwrapping my legs from around my forearms and went into a full handstand on my fingertips. A few seconds later, I had to yield. When I stood, I informed all of them that my attention span was lost, and I failed. "To achieve the level of Zen is to last a minute or longer." "Only one man has achieved that level; he did it when he was eighty-seven." "Now, Jane, you were going to ask a question earlier," I said.

"Smith, please."

"Jane, if it's about me, no questions should be held back." "I have nothing to fear that I haven't confronted."

"Smith, you kept referring to yourself as being a person that's mentally unstable in your letter." "I don't find that to be true, and I don't think anyone here can find that to be true."

"Jane, I was beginning to encounter a mental block." "To me, it's an immovable object that seals me in a barrier." "When they hit me, I often went into a severe depression." "I had to focus my thoughts to keep from losing my control." "It's a form of mental instability." "Your father saw me go through days of where I didn't know where I was at." "I had to find a way to control my mental lapses." I looked over at Jose.

"You look distinguished." I said to him, "Pick up your shoulder's a little, no slouching."

I walked around him and adjusted his belt and the bottom of his pants. I then picked up his collar a little.

I walked over to a drawer, pulled out a briefcase, and carried it over to him.

"This will tell her that you come to her as an agent of the resort." "I've got confidence in you," I told him. "You'll be all right." "Just remember, you're having a dinner to find the right caseworker to help her get adjusted here."

"Yes, sir."

"You feel all right, Jose?" I asked.

"I feel like I'm going on a blind date that someone set up for me." He said.

"Jose, she's special, and I need her." "Tell her tomorrow, and you'll come back and pick her up and take her to meet the person that's going to help her get settled."

"Sir, anyone can do this." He said.

"I'm not testing just anyone, I'm testing you." I told him, "You have to carry yourself as the person you are." "Tonight, you go as Jose Espinoza, and you'll display a character of who you are as Jose Espinoza." "When you leave this resort, you'll leave as Dan Gomez." "You'll carry yourself as Dan Gomez and not show the side of Jose to others when you do." "As far as testing is concerned, I'll always be testing you; there may come a time that you and I won't agree." "If it does, our relationship will be compromised." "Ask Jack; we separated for over eight years because we differed in opinion." "Even when not testing you, our relationship could be compromised," I said while turning to look at Jane. "Sometimes words are said, and they're taken out of context." "The person didn't hear the real meaning that she heard." "The only way to convince her was showing her what I was thinking when I made a comment in our conversation." "I drifted in my thoughts, and I was trying to refocus." "I never had to explain myself or my reasons to anyone, so I spoke my thoughts out loud without explaining what I meant." "The ability to reach my mind's inner circle and focus on my mental stability; is only able to focus for about fifteen seconds, and it drifts, that was shown to you just then." "That's why I mentioned myself as being mentally unstable to you," I said to Jane. "I then looked around at all of them." "You all came in, in the middle of the conversation that we had." "So you didn't know what had gone on before you walked in, so you drew your own conclusions at that time." "When we don't hear the whole story, we form false beliefs," I said.

I walked over to Ellen.

"You are so much like Jane." I told her, "She doesn't realize what she's gotten herself into, and neither do you."

She immediately grabbed me and started hugging and kissing me, and her crying began again.

I squeezed her back to show her that I had feelings for her too. As I was hugging her, I spoke gently to her.

"Ellen, I grew up without a family, and I grew up alone." "I don't know what it's like living with other people, and you don't realize how hard it is for me." "When I met your daughter, she saw a man that looked repulsive." "Here in my lab, I'm not the man I was to her when she first saw me." "I'm involved in many areas that pertain to many other areas that catch my attention." "You might say I'm a man working on a thousand ideas at once." "Do you think you can learn to cope with a madman?" I asked her.

"Smith, I don't know whether I should laugh or whether I should cry." She said.

"See, I told you, you were just like Jane." "She feels the same way."

That's when I was hit from behind by Jane hugging and squeezing me. "Ladies, I can't breathe." I told them, "All right, there won't be any more crying from either of you." I said to them, "We all know I have problems that I have troubles dealing with, and one of the problems in dealing with my problems is someone being silent to me, thinking that I don't want interference from them." "On the contrary, I talk to myself all the time; I enjoy talking to others now and then."

Jane stepped back and stared at me.

"You're doing it again." She said.

"What?" Her mother said to her.

"Nothing, mother, it's between Smith and me; it's a private understanding, you might say." She chuckled.

"Jose, before you pick this girl up." Jane stated, "You need to bring her a gift to show her that you come as a friend." "One long red rose." "A dozen isn't appropriate."

"Yes, ma'am."

He then turned and left, and we all walked into the study, and everyone sat down on the couch. I lit the fireplace, sat in between Jane and Ellen, and watched the fire.

We heard Jose shout out. "Would someone tell me how to get out of here?"

Jane shouted to him that all he had to do was say, computer open the elevator. I had to smile.

"What are you looking at?" Ellen said.

"The fire." I told her, "Fire has been around for a long time, long before man came into existence." "The fire never took care of itself, and at some point, it always went out." "When a man came and discovered fire, someone had to develop reasoning for the fire to go out." "That required an imagination, so someone stumbled upon adding more wood, and low and behold, the fire increased in strength, and it gave out more warmth." "That was the day that man's imagination gave birth to knowledge, and this knowledge led man to sit and use his imagination to create skills in increasing his odds of achieving success in hunting to feed his family." "He built his weapons by the fire, and with his knowledge, he formulated his language skills so that he could explain a plan to others." "Knowledge and imagination together created the wheel, so the wheel wasn't the mother of all inventions, it was fire, and then imagination, and then knowledge, the wheel was the fourth in line, not the first." "Have you heard of area fifty-one?" I asked Ellen.

"Sure, some people think an alien crashed, and they have it there."

"Do you believe in aliens?" I asked her.

"No, if it was true, then why haven't we seen any, and I never have?" She said sarcastically.

"That may be, but area fifty-one came about after a report was that there were five men involved with the research, and one alien, thus the name of area five one came to life, and then it was called area fifty-one." "You hear what you hear, and you take what you hear for granted." "Sometimes even when the fact is introduced, the nonbelievers think the film or photos were doctored," I stated to her, and I saw Jane with a grin. "So now what do we got?" "I've got a fire in front of us, we've got our imagination working, and we have knowledge that aliens don't exist because you've never seen any." "How would you react if you did?" I asked her, and I saw Jane's head as it turned towards me quickly. She was worried. "Back in the days of radio, a broadcaster introduced the birth of acting out a story on the radio." "He told everyone that it was only a story before it began." "People tuned in late and actually believed the story was real and chaos developed." "People killed themselves and others over the fear of aliens attacking them." "The radio announcer apologized to the people for what he has done, but he didn't do anything wrong." "He told everyone before the show started it was only a story." "People believe in what they want to believe in." "See what I mean about people believing in something that they want to believe in. "The wheel set in motion man's imagination and triggered man's knowledge of wondering if he could build the image that entered into his thoughts with his knowledge." "I look at the fire, and I see a vision of my future legacy, and when the flames dance, they divert my attention to another thought." "You see fire, and I see ideas that I can work on and maybe alter the future or contribute to mankind in some small way." "Is there reasoning for life, or are we here only because we are nothing but organisms that feed off of a dying planet?" "Now look at the fire again." I told Ellen, "When was the youngest time that you remember a fire?"

She thought for a while, and then a smile came to her lips.

"I was twelve, and we were swinging on a rope and diving into the water." She answered, "There were two girls with us, and we did the wienies and marshmallows thing." "It's funny, I can't remember their names, but night time came, and we all had our flashlights on to keep the animals away, we always worried about that, we always thought something would come in and eat us, so we tried to stay awake all night." "But, we never made it, we'd fall asleep, and come morning, the flashlights would still be on, but the batteries were dead."

"Ellen, a fire offers a poor man a way to focus his attention on what bothers him." "Judging by the way you spoke, you never saw the girls much after that, so a fire doesn't have any meaning to you the way it has to me."

"You want to hear what I think about a fire?" Jane asked, and without waiting for anyone to give her an answer, she started telling everyone her thought of the fire.

"That first night at Smith's cabin, I woke up to a warm place." "I never acted like I was awake because I was scared." "I watched Smith keep the stove hot and draw his pictures." "Now and then, he had to go out and get more wood, and then he would continue drawing in his pad."

"I had to go to the bathroom real bad, and finally Smith noticed my moving around, and then he told me that I had been out for a while and that he knew that I had to go." "That was the answer to my worries." "Those fears that I had were no longer my concerns anymore." "He picked me up gently and carried me to the sled and then carried me back to the cabin and put me back into the bed, and then he sat down and put more wood on the stove and began drawing his pictures again." "So now when I look at a fire, I'll always remember the first night I met Smith and what he was doing." She then kissed me.

"Smith, what does a fire have to do with anything?" Ellen asked.

"When my brother died, they burned him, when mother died, they burned her, I ran away and came home, and my home was burned." "We all have memories of fire, only every time I see fire, I have a battle that rages inside of me, and it's awful hard to contain it, it's invisible to others, but I can see it like it was yesterday." I replied, "The truth is I didn't want Jane back at the cabin, and I didn't want Jane here, and I didn't want you here either, for that matter." I said to Ellen, "I didn't want Jack here, and I didn't want to be here either." "I wish that Jane and her husband would have found themselves to be happy and had a good time while they vacationed." "That didn't happen, and everyone knows the story up until now." "I think one of the problems we've had is living with me." "That's what got all of this day's event started." "Jane and I had a conversation, and everyone didn't know the story that led up to the story." "Living alone meant that I didn't have interaction with anyone, so I didn't have conversations like we're having now." "I never explained my actions. Now I find myself being followed and watched." "You saw what happened in Mexico." I said, "It happens here in this country too." "Crime is everywhere, and all jails are over-occupied."

"Smith, calm down." Jane said, "We're all by the fire having a casual conversation."

I looked over at her.

"I need to practice more on achieving the inner level of Zen," I told her.

"You can go do that later, right now; we need to learn how to talk when other people are with us." "So I want to speak my piece, and then I'll keep quiet." She said, "Smith, this isn't aimed at you." "Momma, Smith makes me happy." "I don't get any fancy answer when I talk to him, he's straight forward, and he says exactly what he means." "Momma, I've learned that dad double talked to you when you talked to him, and you believed everything he said." "Smith, you're right, I did take you wrong, and I'm sorry."

"Ellen, are you waking up in night sweats?" I asked her.

She was slow with her response.

"Yes."

"You can take medication for that," I told her.

"Whoa, wait a minute, what's this talk about medication?" Jack asked.

"Jack, you're wife is going through hormonal changes." I told him, "The problem is these changes can affect someone for years, and they become irritable and hard to talk to." "Jane, it's better that you take your mother to the hologram; an inanimate object delivers answers to questions that aren't sugared down." "You're mother needs to know that what she feels is normal."

"Smith, you're doing it again. You're dominating a conversation." "You can't keep doing that," Jane said.

Jack began talking about some of the problems that we had in the past after they left. He talked for a long time. The night grew long, and he still was talking.

Ellen came in and told Jack that it was time to call it a night. "For some reason, I didn't get much sleep." She said while looking at me. As they began walking off, she let go of his hand, came over to me, and whispered into my ear. "Smith, I don't care what Jane says; I like it when you talk." "You know how to put someone in their place." "Thanks." She said.

She then walked off and caught up with her husband.

"What did she say?" Jane asked.

"I suffer from short-term dementia sometimes," I said to her.

"You're not going to tell me, are you?" She said, testing me.

We were interrupted by a noise that I heard coming from the kitchen.

I activated the intercom and told Jose that we were in the study.

Jane commented about never having any time alone with me.

"You know why it's so hard for you to talk to someone?" She said to me, "You have to explain everything that will happen in full detail to answer anybody, and you find it worthless because somewhere after those fifteen seconds, no one is paying attention to you." "It's not you that loses focus, but the people you talk to." "Those messages that you send, I bet it's over within fifteen seconds." "Am I right?"

"Yes"

"So, all we have to do now is to figure out the other nine hundred and ninety-nine reasons why you have the problems that you give a name to." "Smith, I'm starting to see a lot of things a whole lot different than when we first met." "I don't know which one I love the most, but my problem is that I love you both." "No matter who you are or where your mind is." "I know more today about you than what I knew about you yesterday, and yesterday I learned more about you than the day before."

Jose walked into the room and looked at us both sitting on the couch.

I immediately asked him to have a seat and enjoy the night before he went to sleep.

He was silent as he watched the flames of the fire, and Jane watched him.

I kept silent, I knew what he was thinking, and I wasn't going to be the first to speak. It was my way of getting the point across.

Jane opened up his thinking by asking him politely how his night went. It was a simple question and one that was appropriate. I thought.

"It turns out that she's a deaf-mute, and our entire night was spent writing questions and answers." He answered.

I put my hand to my chin and looked down at the floor.

"So, did you tell her that you would get someone to help her get set up?" I stated.

"Sir, she didn't understand what's going on here."

"I'm sure you explained all that in the answer's that you gave." "Didn't you tell her she had a job and she would be given a caseworker?"

"I tried to tell her like you said, sir." "It was her decision, and she said she doesn't know anything except cleaning hotel rooms or washing dishes." "Then she wrote down that she got fired from her last job because she couldn't hear the people that were in the room, and she walked in on them naked." "Sir, she said washing dishes and mopping floors and vacuuming the carpet is the only training she's had."

"Well, Jose, we do need people to do that kind of work." I said to him and continued, "Did you ask her about her age, or schooling, or where she came from, or if she had a family?"

"Sir, it was a quiet evening, and when we ate, we didn't do anything." "After we left the restaurant, I wrote in her book that she would be contacted and told what to do."

Jane spoke her thoughts, and it concerned Jose.

"Jose, look at the flames that the fire forms as it dances." "What do you see in those flames?" She asked.

"Ma'am!"

"I ask myself, what if I was a deaf-mute and I was the only person there that couldn't speak or hear?" "I would feel alone." She told him, "I bet she's crying right now because just like all of her life, she can't live in a world where people can't communicate with her." "She has to read her orders." "You think your dinner wasn't enjoyed because it was just a dinner, no pleasantries in talking and being able to get what you needed by having a casual meeting." "Put yourself in her place, and tell me how you could say or do anything to make her understand." "Did you offer her hope, or did you offer her another miss in finding the place she wants to be."

"Sir, did you know about her?" He asked, looking over at me.

"Jose learning is a process of constantly studying, I watch people, and I watch the people that I need to watch closely." "Did you want to talk to her like you and me and Jane?" "Is she a girl that you feel nice when you're with?" "If the answer to that is yes, then the questions that Jane was asking you were the questions that you couldn't tell her." "Her language is slow when talking to a person that can't speak her language." "She's not like the rest of us." "Her problems affect her in a different way than the problems that you and I and Jane face." "And yes, I did know she was deaf-mute."

He took a deep breath and began talking, "What's going to happen to her?"

"I wouldn't be concerned. I'm sure she'll be happy wherever she goes to, we'll take care of her, and we'll try to help her the best way we can, Jose." "But there's a reason that I wanted her," I told him.

"Sir!"

"Jose, every day is a day that we learn something new." "I was told that earlier and thought it fit in with what I want you to hear." "The girl is going to be your assignment." "You're going to be her caseworker," I said to him.

"Sir!"

"Jose, I want her to teach you how to sign, and I want others to learn how to sign, and I want you to help her feel welcomed. Other than you, she's only seen one person here." "You pass this assignment, and the rest gets easier." "Neither of you are capable of transmitting anything other than what's on the paper that you write." "Go back and tell her I wish to see her." I told him, "And Jose, when you want out, simply say computer open the elevator door as Jane told you."

"Yes, sir."

He left, and then Jane attacked me. I was being kissed repeatedly.

"Now, that's better." She said.

I smiled at her.

"You used the flames of the fire to your advantage when you were speaking to Jose," I stated.

"Yeah, and you did the same to my mother, so we're even." She replied.

"Jane, are you learning the game of chess?" I asked.

"No, I've got you wrapped around my little finger, and I like it." "I told you, you had a weakness, and I found out what that was a long time ago." "You want to know when?" She asked.

"Yes"

"It was the first time that I slept against your body." "I felt it then." "You were under my control as soon as we touched." "You know the strangest thing came to my mind then" "I should have felt like I was doing something wrong, but I didn't." She said smiling, "You really felt warm." "And that wasn't a nice thing to say when you said that you didn't want me at the cabin or here, earlier."

"I thought people didn't listen to me that much." I gave her my excuse "I said that because what I do is not considered to be accepted by people." "I really do wish you and your husband could have lived a good life, and I wish he could have been the man that gave you what you wanted." "You don't meet a girl, and she asks what do you do for a living, and then tell her that you blow things up." "So, I had to say it was restricted information, and that made you even more curious." "Jane, I don't restrict any of my thoughts from you anymore." "If I anger you, I have to know what I said to have angered you; that's the only way; I'll know what not to do." "Did I speak demandingly, or did I not say something that I should have?" "There are a lot of reasons why two people want to be apart." "I don't want to be the reason for you to want to be apart from me, and I know how easy that would be for me to make you feel that way."

"Smith, first things first," she said, "a mistake was made in my life," "and I almost paid for it with my life." "It's true; I wanted to have a good life when I got married; every girl feels that way." "I can't say that anymore. That's a memory that I can't forget." "But, as far as being happy, I can also remember the happiest day of my life was when you laid down in the bedroll next to me." "Now, we need to learn how to control the way you talk to me." She said, "It's not from something that you said wrong, but the words you speak to me make me cry, I love you, and when I hear you talk, you say things that tell me how much you love me, I can't help it." "Now pass me the tissues. I need to blow my nose and dry my eyes."

"Computer; secure rooms," I ordered.

"What's wrong?"

"Jose's coming," I said to her.

I watched as Jose and the girl came walking into the room. I got up, along with Jane, and waited till they stood in front of us.

I signed for her to have a seat.

She looked at me strangely.

I started speaking as I signed to her.

"In order for everyone to understand what we are saying, I'm telling them what I'm telling you, and in order for others to understand what you're saying, I'm telling them what you're saying."

"Are you the person I'm told that would contact me?" She asked.

"No, Jose is. I want you to teach him how to sign," I told her.

She looked at him.

"I can't teach him." "He needs someone else," I told everyone what she said.

Jose grabbed a pencil and wrote why quickly. I told Jose that all he had to do was ask me, and I would translate to her what he said.

She started signing. I began telling everyone what she was saying "She says her heart has many wounds, and she felt another one tonight, Jose." "She says she would be better at being a maid or doing janitorial work." After she finished, she was emotionless.

"Tell her that." "I." I stopped him before he went any further.

"Jose take her into the controd room and activate the hologram and let the hologram tell her for you; tell her that what you do is restricted information and that you work for me, and I keep myself secret from others for a purpose." "She'll calm down, and you and she can see each other differently." "Now go, take her hand and lead her into the control room and activate the hologram and tell the computer to respond."

He reached for her hand, and she jerked it back.

"Give her a while and not fight her, just tell the hologram to respond to what you want to say in sign language, and the computer will tell you what she says." "Try to understand; she's feeling like you felt when you woke up here." "Jose, I need her."

I signed to Maria, asking her if she would please follow Jose.

Jane laid down on the couch and put her head on my lap.

"Smith, I don't get you, you're brilliant, and yet you are so loving." She said.

"I had a lot of problems after my mother died," I told her. "I could hear whispers in my head." "That's when I started having troubles sleeping, they weren't real, but I thought they were." "You remember when you said you had cooties, it was a game of teasing, but other kids went around jokingly telling everyone you had them." "You were so frightened that you probably had to ask your parents what they were." "Jane, teasing lowers self-esteem in children and adults." "You grew up, and your so-called friends stayed behind. I think that's why you got married." "You were hungry for love." "The girl in there with Jose grew up being called a dummy, only she didn't know she was being called names, because she couldn't hear them, but she could sense what was going on by the way the people laughed; you can tell when someone's laughing at you, they make eye contact." "When I first saw her looking around the night of the meeting, she was protective, and she had the same look on her face when she came in here." "She knows what people think of her." "She came here for only one reason, she needed work." "That makes her like everybody here." "She's hardened into a defiant young lady; I never once saw her let her guard down." I said to her, "Being a maid isn't what someone wants to grow up to be." "When it's the only thing you can do, you're forced to take whatever you can get."

I looked down at Jane, and she had fallen asleep. I smiled.

I watched the fire as it glowed, and soon Jose and the girl came out of the control room. I put my finger up to my mouth to signal them to be quiet.

I started signing to the girl and asked her if she was getting all the answers that she wanted.

"This place is big." She said, "You'll need a lot of maids, and that's the only thing that she knew how to do." She answered.

"Oh! I'm sorry." I told her.

"Jose, you can take her back to her place." "She's happy doing what she's doing," I said as I signed.

"Yes, sir."

He took her arm and began walking away when she jerked it back and then stopped and turned to look at me. She started signing.

"Why am I important to you anyway? There are many people you can get to do the job." She said.

"I didn't want just anybody." I signed to her, "I thought I had the right person chosen when I chose you."

"Why me, what makes me so special to you?"

"We'll keep this between us." I signed, "This conversation will be private." "Jose" "there's something that I need to say to her, and it's private." "I'm sorry, but I need to make her understand some things." I then began signing to her, "Jose is not knowledgeable in areas that he needs to be trained in." "The fighting skills he learned are useless; he needs to learn how not to draw attention to himself." "He's loyal and trusting, and for those very reasons alone, I want to protect him." "If I don't, he's a dead man." "I chose him for the same reasons I chose you, loyalty, and trust." "His family was murdered." "There's more to the story, but he's just a young man set out on wanting revenge, and he doesn't have someone to guide him, and for that reason, I fear the worst for him."

"You are his boss." She said.

"Of who," I asked her. "How can you train a man that wants to get killed?" "You've had hatred all of your life, and I can see it written all over your face." I told her, "Last night at the meeting. You didn't understand anything that was going on." "All you were concerned with was were you going to get hired or were you going to be sent away." "I think both of you deserve to be together with one another. Both of you have enough hatred to fill this room." "I'm beginning to think I was wrong," I said to her.

"You don't know me or anything about me." She signed angrily.

I signed to her, "I see a person over in this country illegally and taking any job she can." "There has to be a purpose for that." "You're not married, and you don't go anywhere, so that means you're in hiding." "You knew you were taking a chance coming here." "Is it the fear of being caught and reported?" "No, you've been deported before, so you know how to handle yourself when it comes to making your way back." "Maria, you know anything about chickens?" I asked her.

"Chickens," she signed.

"Yeah, chickens; see, a chicken will roost in its house at night." "But, if it finds a hole, it'll head for the hole every time you let them out of the hen house." "You don't have to worry about the chicken as long as it's fed in pen; it will return to its roost." "Come morning when you let the chickens out, that chicken will head for the hole he escaped from, only to find that the hole has been fixed." "He becomes bewildered, and he paces back and forth looking for the hole that he knew was there." "You can learn a lot by watching. You should know. That was the only way you learned." I told her, "I see a girl that has anger, and being pretty, I assume you were raped, and being an illegal alien, you were deported to keep you quiet?" "How many times did it happen to you?" I asked her.

"Twice," she said.

"So, the incidents were never reported." "You left at night." I signed to her, "It must be hard to hold the thought of vengeance back." "I can give Jose orders to go and find them for you." "You want them dead for the pain they gave you." "I'll tell him now, and he'll go without question, but that's not the way I work." "I may be his boss, but that won't protect him from being killed." "He doesn't know how to see through a man that's lying to him." "I can see what others are thinking, and I take care of men that don't follow my wishes." I told her, "I look at you, and I see a woman with only one way to judge a person." "You have a disadvantage, and Jose isn't without his problems either, men used you, and the girls he thought were his girlfriend's, used him."

"His problem is that he can't think clearly, and for that reason, he doesn't have what he needs to fit into my plans."

"Are you a gangster?" She asked.

"Maria."

"How did you know my name was Maria?"

"You've gone by three names, Mary, Maria, and Gloria." I told her, "The last time you were deported was three years ago." "You've gotten smart at not getting caught." "So I assume when you were deported, that's when you were raped by the first man." "I knew about you before you walked into the room. I did a background check on you." "Did Jose say anything to you about me?"

"All he said was that I was asking restricted information." She replied.

"Is that why you're angry, you can't get answers?" I asked her. She didn't reply, "In your country a long time ago, a man by the name of Poncho Villa fought men that stole precious items of gold and silver from the poor." "They were soldiers that used their uniform to do what they wanted to do, rape, rob, and steal in the name of Mexico." "The problem was Poncho Villa was similar to the soldiers he killed; the land was a lawless land." "But people chose Poncho Villa as a man that fought for them." "He was glorified everywhere he went, but he made one mistake, he didn't have concern on keeping his whereabouts unknown hidden." "That led to his demise." "The reason why he gave you the answer of the questions as being restricted information was that I told him not to tell you anything about me." "I see you think I'm a lot like the rest of the people you've worked for, and you find yourself with no way out." "You're drawing the wrong conclusion." I told her, "Jose has shown me to be an honest man, and I told him that I don't like liars, and if he ever told me one, I would cast him away and never have contact with him again." "The simplest way I can explain his demise is he would be killed by the other men he worked for, he's called a pigeon, but in his eyes, he thinks of himself as being more of a hawk." "I can assure you. He's not a hawk." "He's one of my agents, but he has a lesson he needs to learn." "Tonight, Jose was given a test, and that test was to have dinner with you. The test was to show him that he needs to learn to expect the unexpected." "He didn't know you were a deaf-mute, and he believes he failed." "I'm sorry for using you, but I was hoping that you could help him, and in return, he could help you." "I wanted him to be your caseworker to help you get settled, but I don't think you'll have to worry about that anymore." "And you don't have to worry about immigration either." "When I return, I'll go and get your parents and bring them to you myself." "You can be with your family and be happy too."

"If you knew this, then why did you bring me here?" She signed.

"I have my reasons," I told her.

"What about Jose?" She asked.

"He's not your concern anymore," I told her.

"Did you have someone in your family that was like me, and that's where you learned to sign?" She asked.

"Maria, I speak seventeen languages fluently, and I know how to sign in all seventeen languages."

"Jose didn't fail; it was me." She said, "He was nice to me."

"Maria, I didn't say Jose failed. I said he thinks he failed." "I told him whenever he meets anyone I send him to, to respond cordially, I'll take care of the ones that give him a problem." "He did as I instructed him to." "You've been through quite a bit in the last few days." "You're tired, and a lot of things out of the ordinary have appeared before you." "Right now, you feel like you don't know what you can believe from anyone anymore." "Jose has learned a lesson today as well. Now I have to deal with that lesson," I told her.

"I told you, it wasn't his fault." She signed in anger, "This is my blame."

"Maria, I know exactly what happened, I have it all on tape, and you don't have to explain anything." "You can go now, and I'll have my talk to Jose."

She put her hand to her forehead and walked back and forth, and then stopped and looked over at me.

"You don't need me to teach him. You never did; you've got some sort of thing in there that can teach him everything I can." She signed.

"What's changed with you since you came in earlier?" I asked her, "You were bitter and irritable." "Now you're quick to shift your position and stand up for someone you don't even know." "Did he not tell you he came to help you?" "Did he not tell you that he had a job for you?" "Why the change of attitude?" I said to her, "Maria, it's all right for you to feel the way you do. Everyone that's here has the same feeling you feel, only no one has ever seen me like you, and I must ask that you keep it that way."

"Can Jose still be my caseworker?" She asked.

"We'll be gone the day after tomorrow." I told her, "And, I don't know when we'll be back." "Jane and two others that live here will return Monday morning." "I can't promise you anything else. It's not foreseeable."

"Jane is your friend?" She asked.

"Maria, you have a whole lot of different questions you want to ask." "Take Jose back into the control room and point to the computer, and he'll know what you want." "Ask anything and everything you wish." "When you sign, and you want Jose to hear what you ask." Sign to the computer and tell it to do so. When you wish to speak in private, tell the computer that you wish to speak in silence so that only the computer can answer your questions without Jose listening to the answers." "It does what you ask, that is, unless you ask the wrong question." I said to her, "And then its response will be that you asked a restricted question." "Maria, there are very few people that know of this place, and I have to keep it that way."

"If I left earlier, would you have killed me?" She asked.

"That's the same thing Jose asked me when he woke up in my lab when I drugged him." "He was like you, scared and confused." "I'll tell you the same as I told him." "No, I wouldn't kill you. I would have drugged you, though, the same as I told Jose." "You would have woken up in your room, and you wouldn't have remembered anything about tonight; you would have thought that all of this was a dream and you would be assigned your rooms to clean." "Maria, I'm fighting a losing battle." "Jose wants to help me, but I don't want him to get killed in the process." "He needs something I can't give, someone that can coach him and push him to become the man that he wants to be." "I can only do what I do and not tell others what they should do unless it's a message I want delivered by him," I said to her.

"Then what is it you want from me?" She asked.

"I want you to tell him that the people that come here depend on him, and I want you to tell him that some of them want his help, but they don't know how to ask him, and I want you to tell him that sometimes we can't always achieve our goals, but that doesn't mean we stop trying," I told her.

"How come you don't tell him?" She said.

"I tried to, but the woman that I sent him to help me didn't want to help me. She just wanted to work." "That's what I was going to tell him in our talk before you stopped and turned back around." "Somehow, I think hearing it was coming from you would paint the picture better for him; it'll be one that he'll remember."

"How?" She asked.

"His life isn't in my hands. It's in his. He has to learn the reason why he fights, or he'll be defeated by his own bravery." "Maria, you can see with your eyes what's happening in the world." "Sometimes you can't deploy a military, it would mean war, and countless lives would be destroyed over nothing." "I've always done my work alone, but two men with the same goal working apart interfere in each other plans, and someone will end up getting killed." "Jose's destiny is written; he will die." "Destiny can be postponed if you're adversary is weaker than you." "Jose has to train harder and learn faster." "He needs someone to help him learn, and right now, I don't see him having the right coach." "When I talked to him about the dinner, he was just as upset as you were." "He came back and saw himself as a failure." "How long would he last if he went as a defeated warrior before he even went into battle?" "He's weak when it comes to facing an enemy; he needs what you have." "He needs to see his enemy with his eyes and not his ears." "You've got two choices; each one of them involves Jose." I told her, "You can take him into the control room and ask the questions that now have changed, or you can tell Jose to open the elevator to let you out." "But as I said, you won't remember anything about tonight." "Sorry, I didn't plan on automatic open and close doors in the elevator." "No one gets in without approval."

"No, we're not through yet." She said, "You said you were testing Jose by taking me to dinner." "I'm here, so you were testing me too, weren't you?"

"Do you trust me?" I asked her.

"No," she said quickly.

"I don't trust you either." I told her, "Just because I see good qualities in you doesn't mean that you don't have bad ones too."

She looked down at Jane.

"Is Jane your friend?"

"Ask the computer if you're interested or choose the door; the choice is yours," I answered.

She put her hands on her hips and then turned and grabbed Jose by his arm and led him down the hall into the control room. Jose didn't have much to say about it; he was being drugged all the way.

I sat back against the couch and reaffixed my eyes back on the flames. I didn't want to tell Maria that she was right; I was testing her.

I carefully slid my arms under Jane, picked her up, and went and laid her down on the bed easily. She helped me by putting her arm around my neck.

I then went and opened the security door to the lab that contained the prototype of my pterodactyl. I began reconfiguring its design. I don't know how much time had passed when I saw Maria walk in. She took her time looking around and then began to sign.

"I don't remember this room." She said.

I smiled at her and told her that I have secrets that I keep, and if I tell everyone, then my secrets wouldn't be secret anymore.

"Are you keeping more from me?"

"Yes, a lot more." I told her, "Where's Jose?"

"Asleep on the couch, and I didn't want to wake him." She said.

"What is that?" She signed and then pointed her finger at it.

"I have to go away, and I can't waste time getting to where I'm going; with Jose aboard, I need to reinforce and modify my transportation.

"You said Jose wasn't ready." She said.

"He's not, but he's steadfast in his beliefs." "I gave it some thought while you and Jose were in my control room." "If I don't take him with me, he won't train the way he should, and then there's the possibility that he may not live through this anyway." "What do I do," I told her.

She walked up to the board I was drawing on and looked it over real good.

"You're making this?" She asked.

"I build everything I use." I said, "Computer; open all doors," I ordered.

"Take a walk." I signed, "You need to see that I'm not sure." "Be warned, touch anything, and today may be the last day you'll see." "Not by my hand, but from the material you touch."

It was late in the night, and I made a pot of coffee. I was concentrating on my calculations when Maria came walking into the kitchen.

After the coffee was made, I poured myself a cup and asked her if she wanted one. She drank hers black like mine.

"I'm sorry for the way I acted earlier." She signed, "I wasn't trying to be rude when I was asking if the girl in your lap was a friend."

"You still know very little." I replied, "Besides, there wasn't any harm done." "You had every right."

"But," she said, "I was hostile towards you, and Jose asked me not to do that again." "Sir," She began, but I stopped her.

"My name's Smith, just Smith," I told her.

"I know, I asked that, and I got the information I didn't want to hear." "I acted disrespectful to you, and I want to apologize for that."

"Forget about it," I signed. "I'm treated that way by everyone, and I would think that under the circumstances, you're entitled."

"Computer; activate all of Maria's employers."

"Look at the screen." "Do you remember the men responsible for raping you?" I asked her.

She gave me the names, and I ordered the computer to activate and disperse all monies that they owned.

I then looked back at her and began signing, "In the morning, they'll find that their checking, savings, and retirement accounts will be gone, they'll be victims of an identity theft, and worst of all, they'll be broke." "They hurt you; I hurt them." "I transferred all their money and sold their stocks and put it all into an account that I transferred into your parent's account in Mexico." "You won't need money here." "You'll never have to work again, you have a little over three million in your parent's name, and no one can trace anything back to you; hackers will be blamed in Russia for it." "But, you won't know any of that until you wake up in the morning, and a message will be delivered to you telling you of your good fortune." "Does that right what they did wrong?" I said to her.

"No," she said.

"Maria, there's nothing that can change history; it's already been written." I notified her.

"Smith, what is all this in here?" She asked.

"Their thoughts that came to my mind," I told her.

"I asked that thing about you, and it said that you were a whisper of the wind in time." "Why?" She asked.

"Maria, I'm not even going to make a dent in what decisions that man makes." "For every good person in the world, there are a hundred bad people."

"So you lock yourself away in here?" She stated.

"Do you feel safe walking the streets at night?" I asked her, "You can here."

"Computer; initiate blueprints of my legacy." "Look at the screen," I said to her. She did and studied it and then looked back at me. "I'm going to build it." "In the days of kings, there were beliefs that you took your wealth with you when you died." "Tombs were robbed, and some were discovered that contained billions of dollars in gold and jewels, so much for the theory of being able to take it with you." "It is said that heaven is paved with streets of gold." "It also is said that money is the root of all evil." "God is pure, tempt him with evil, and vengeance is hell." "I wish to see my legacy come to life before I die." "I'm not going where everyone else thinks they're going; I'll be with all of them." "I want a future for those that are without hope, like you. That's the reason you came here." "You had a feeling of emptiness when you came here. Need I remind you that your parents now have three million in the bank." "I told you I could have sent Jose to take care of those men for you, but I didn't work that way." "Your parents now have what they had; that's how I work." I signed to her, "Man has the knowledge for curing many problems, but its use is only available for those that can afford it." "Those that pay dearly for the best doctors may die older, but they still die." "It is said that only the good die young. Maybe that's the reason that some people live a long life." "Here, it doesn't work that way, no money, no problem." "One day, everything I build will be destroyed." "Nothing will be left; I have no control over anything that Mother Nature wishes to throw at me, so that's why I said I was a whisper of the wind in time." "Nothing survives eternity." "Mountains erodes, and farmland remains millions of years later." "Rivers are diverted, and forests catch fire and are destroyed along with all the inhabitants that lived there." "Maria, I'm a dreamer, I walk at night when the moon is full, and my only reward for my dreams is to see the sunrise; some people can't see it, even if they are looking at it." "I find myself to be with great discomfort when among people." "You see me, but you don't see the battle that rages within my mind."

"What do you see in me then?" She asked.

I took a sip of my coffee and thought for the best way I could tell her.

"I think if anything gets in your way, you won't let it stop you from achieving the goals that you set on yourself." "You've overcome everything in your life, and you did it without the help of anyone." "Have you ever seen a woodpecker?" I asked.

"Sir?"

"A woodpecker, have you ever seen one?" I said again.

"Yes, sir."

"Did you know that the woodpecker never stops pecking the wood until he receives the meal he's after; that's persistence?" "You have that." "Jose needs to learn that those that have everything to lose fight the hardest." I told her, "He can hear it from me, but he can learn it better from you." I said to her.

"Why me?" She asked.

"You asked about Jane earlier if she was my friend. She's more than that to me." "But there can only be one person that makes a final decision; there can't be two kings in one castle." "You dominate Jose's strength, and he obeys you with a little urging." "Maria, you have to show him that the door to knowledge stays open twenty-four hours in a day." "Without you pushing him, he'll never open it and enter the room." "He thinks he's ready, but he's not, he'll fight the only way he knows how, and he'll die that way too."

I got up and refilled our cups, and she took a sip, as well as I.

"What's behind those walls you keep hidden?" She asked.

"I only keep them closed when people I don't want to know what I do, come here." I signed, "You keep referring to my hologram as that thing in there." "In the wrong hands, its use in war is limitless." "I didn't invent it for that purpose, but be that as it may, someone would." "I can't let any of my projects fall into the wrong hands." "That won't happen." "My computer monitors my vital signs, and if I die, everything in here will undergo a different direction." "But with three million in the bank, your parents won't need to work anymore either." "Go to the hologram and tell it to open the door." "Tomorrow, you'll wake up to good news," I told her.

CHAPTER NINE

orning broke with the sounds of doors being opened and the aroma of coffee drifting through the air. Maria noticed it too. We were in the room where I was modifying my transportation when Jane walked in and noticed Maria.

The conversation between them forced me to sign questions and return answers. I told Maria to take Jane into the control room and have their talk.

"Jane," I said to her, "use the hologram, and both of you can benefit."

When they left, Jose walked in.

"Sorry, sir" "I dozed off."

"Jose, dozing off is waking up a few minutes later" "you fell asleep, and you've been asleep all night." I told him, "We'll be busy today." "Watch, and listen, and then we'll do everything all over again." "Jose, picture yourself as a cheerleader; all of them move in the same step, and this is what we have to do."

"First off, we need weapons," I told him.

I reached up and turned on a small machine and waited for it to turn off automatically, and then repeated the process seven times.

After the last container was filled, I turned my eyes to Jose and held onto the container.

"Jose, when up against men that carry weapons, you need to stop them from using them." "These vials contain roughly five hundred red wasps each. I've been raising them for a little over two years, for just this sort of reason." "Right now, they are at peace; they have nowhere to move." "You shake the container, and they become angry, you throw them where your enemy is, and you've accomplished a platoon of men running in every different direction." "Their weapons are useless when feeling the venom of the sting." "These are for their control rooms; it'll clear a building quicker than fire." "These are nothing more than fireworks here. I showed him by holding one up for him to see, they look like real grenades, and they serve the same results, but they weigh four ounces, compared to a four-pound grenade." "I insert the grenade with a compound of a small amount of nitroglycerin and rock salt." "The noise from the nitro exploding, and the screams that come from the men being hit by the rock salt causes disarray." "Are you with me so far?" I asked.

"Yes, sir."

I picked up some backpacks that I had loaded earlier off of the counter. "Come with me," I told him.

After reaching our destination, my explosive room, I ordered the security door to be closed. I told Jose it was soundproof.

I took out what looked like a rock and told him to throw it at the wall. The explosion caused his reaction to duck.

"The outside is volcanic pumice; I pulverized it into a fine dust." "I compressed the pumice with a bonding compound to firm the pumice around the explosive." These were first made for testing; the ones you'll be using will be about the size of a softball." "They're used to stun my enemy; the concussion causes loss of hearing, and the pumice dust is blown into the eyes, causing dryness and temporary blindness." "You asked me if I could destroy the world. You're getting the answers you wanted to know."

"This here is a fusion explosive," I showed him "it contains a small amount of nitration toluene." "That's what they make dynamite from, and the shell is nothing more than coral that's been crushed and put under seventy tons of compression." "It may look small, but one of these will take care of a hundred men." "Its reaction occurs when mixed, so you turn and push the top button down." "Sit down on the floor with your feet sticking out," I told him. "I told you that guns draw attention; all of these explosives can be delivered from a hundred yards away." "This here is nothing more than heavy-duty rubber." "It's a water balloon launcher, and it will fire everything I've shown you from that distance." "They all have the same triggering mechanism." "Turn and push the button down." "Don't worry if the top button is accidentally pushed. Nothing will happen; the only way to engage the power is to turn the top button and then push it down." "That way, you won't kill yourself by dropping it." "Everything in a hundred-foot radius will be affected, so I hope you can throw a weight of four ounces at least fifty yards. If not, use the launcher, or you may be a victim of your own weapon." "This weapon here slips up through your hand around your forearm and past your elbow to hold the weapon in place." "These two straps are one that goes around you're midsection and one around your neck." "You can't lose the weapon accidentally when engaging in a fight or when avoiding a fight. When fired this piece here," I showed him, "flips up and fires small needles that are filled with a poison that injects and immobilizes whoever it hits." "The needles are made of sugar and dissolve in the body when warmed; it takes effect almost immediately, if hit, the subject dies a slow and painful death." "It's small, but it contains one thousand rounds." "When shot, fire short bursts, each burst fire twenty to one hundred rounds depending on the amount of time you hold the trigger, or the number of men your shooting at." its use is to spray the enemy with the needles, so don't waste your shots." "One hit is all it takes." "You have a dozen cartridges on top, and each one will eject after it's no longer usable." "The undercarriage of the weapon also has a dozen cartridges, and they also have needles in them too, that gives you twenty-four cartridges with one thousand needles." "You seem to have a stronger confidence using a gun; that weapon can kill more than two to five thousand men, twenty-four cartridges times' one thousand needles give you twenty-four thousand rounds of ammunition, and not one sound can be heard when it's fired." "Jose, your body makeup has everything that oil has." "So it's not as difficult to disguise a chemical that can kill you that impersonates the chemical that your body has in it." "That's how cancer grows in the body; it disguises itself as a sugar to keep the immune system from attacking it." "Now, that brings us to the dam." I said, "James and Ruby will be going with us. When we're clear of the dam, two hours later, the dam will be blown, and nothing will remain downstream of the dam." "If I die, nothing will happen; man's fate will be in the hands of man." "Jose, I worked alone because I don't like to work with heroes. They get you killed; as soon as someone knows something is going on, our presence will be known, our cover will be blown, follow my orders, or you'll compromise our security." "Are we clear?"

"Yes, sir." He said.

"Good then, let's go over our plan again, and then again, and then again." "As I said, I worked alone." "I need to know we work as one." "Oh, and there's one little thing I didn't find time to talk to you about, so I guess maybe now would be a good time to bring it up." "You didn't fall asleep." "I drugged you, and I took the liberty of planting a cochlear implant inside your ear." "Everything you've said and heard up to the moment we've been talking has been recorded." "I didn't do it because I wanted to spy on you. I did it because not only do I hear a conversation you have with one of my clients, I can also talk to you, and you can talk to me." "Radios are useless today." "That way, no guessing is taken place." Computer; activate Jose's implant, and perform a communication test." "Jose, I'm sorry, but you're an agent, and sometimes's an agent doesn't know which side of the game he's being played for."

"Yes, sir," was all he said.

"Computer; give me a readout on Ramon for the last two weeks," I ordered.

I then went back to working with Jose, and when we finished, we both sat down to enjoy a cup of coffee.

I took two sips and then told Jose that I needed to think. I walked to my track and began running. I was on my second lap when Jane came jogging along beside me.

She didn't speak; all she did was try to keep up with me, so I slowed down a little to give her a pace to where she could.

After circling around another lap, I opened the conversation.

"I need to know if you are mad at me for something?" I asked her.

"No, Maria and I had a talk, and she's struggling to accept what's happening to her." "You know she thinks of you as a smart man, and because of that, she doesn't understand why she's here." "Then our conversation shifted to me, and we had our girl talk, she thinks you're trying to find Jose a girl, and she thinks it's her." "I think so too." Jane said, "She told me about her being raped and you transferring the money the men that raped her into her parents' account."

I looked over at her and responded, "No." "You can tell her that she may think of me as being smart, but when it comes to women, I haven't got the intelligence it takes to talk to the girl I love." "Secondly, the money I put into her parent's account was for revenge." "She lightened up on me after that." "I merely punished the men that took advantage of her."

"Smith, you keep talking like that, and I'll have to leave here for you to finish your exercise." She said smiling, "You always seem to make me listen instead of talking."

"Jane, there's going to be times that I won't be able to be with you, I'm sorry, but I can't help it." "I feel like I'm cheating you out of a life."

"Yeah, I know." She began, "But, you have to look at it in a reasonable way. When my husband knocked me over the cliff, I died from the fall, and you revived me." "If I'm going to be cheated out of my life, I want you to be the one that does it. After all, you saved me." "Smith, I learned a lot after I came here, and you could have walked away from me easily, and no one would have been the wiser." "I know you kill people, and I know why you kill people,, I know it seems odd saying this, but I'm comfortable with it." "You told me that you didn't have feelings or emotions. I can't buy that." "You may not act like other men, but you are a very caring person, or you wouldn't want to build those hospitals." "Maria talked to me about Jose and the test you were giving him." She stated, "I told her you see things in people that other people don't." "She told me that she knew that I loved you." "Smith, I told her you were an honest man and a sincere man." "I told her I loved you because you taught me that lesson, I didn't expect what happened to me, and when I woke up and saw you, I instructed the hologram to show her what you looked like then and told her; imagine waking up and seeing that a few feet away from you." "Smith, are you trying to set them up?" She asked me.

"Jane, Jose looked sad when I saw him talking about what transpired." "He would have been of no use to me in that kind of condition. Now she is possessed with that knowledge of what I was doing and why."

"She told me that." She said, "I just wanted to know if you were trying to bring two people together that you thought would make a good couple, that's all." "I mean, you did something to me, and I kind of thought that maybe you saw something in her like that." "After all, you did send Jose knowing what was wrong with her."

"Why are we having this conversation?" I asked her.

"Because I know you, you think only of others, at least that's what I told Maria when she asked me that question." She said.

I started walking, for she was beginning to wear down.

I chuckled, and she picked up on it.

"What's so funny?" She asked.

"I was just thinking, that's all," I said.

"Smith, that's all you do, is think; your mind might be on the planet of Neptune, or mars, or in another galaxy in outer space." "What's so funny?" She asked again.

"I was thinking about baby sea turtles being hatched and calories being burned." "One in ten thousand sea turtles makes it to adulthood. I said to her.

"Where did that come from?" She seemed bewildered.

"Did you know that?" I asked.

"No," she said.

"Now you do." "Jane, the odds of you and I meeting each other were one in three hundred and fifty million." "That's how many people live in America, according to the last census." "And yet, you ended up in my stone house," I said to her as I took off jogging and left her behind.

She soon caught up with me.

"What's wrong with you?" She asked.

"Watch Jose and Maria. You tell me what you see and if it's different than what I see." "I'll continue this conversation later." "She asked me if you and I were friends, and I told her that we were more than friends." "She told me that I should talk to you more. Not all people are blessed with being able to do so." "We talked, and I told her it wasn't that simple for me, and you knew a lot of things about me that others didn't." "Jane, I've gone for so long being the man that I am, that I don't think about you when I'm thinking, and that worries me." "She's right; I should talk to you more."

"Smith, you and I are going to have different moods with each other, like the one I'm in now." "To you, they may seem like we're having an argument, or you may see my face and read the wrong thing." "I think you have a fear of disappointing me, and that might have something to do with it." She stated, "And I do see both Maria and Jose wanting to open up to each other." "I didn't tell her that, though."

"I think I got that figured out," I told her.

"Is it secret?" She asked.

"No, a laptop is all that's needed for them to talk to each other when away from the hologram." "I'll format a program with animation and audio to help Jose learn to sign correctly." "I'm taking her with us to the Bahamas," I told her.

I turned my head a little, and she seemed to notice my thoughts were drifting.

"What's bothering you." She said, concerned.

"What do you think it feels like to remember everything in your life?" "What day it was on a certain date and what the weather was like." "Seeing you for the first time and then seeing you again under different circumstances."

"What do you think it feels like to remember every conversation that we've ever had, along with every other conversation that I have with others?" I had a hint of pain in my voice.

"I don't have that worry." She said to me, "I would think that if I had that sort of a brain, I would think that I would have a lot of problems sorting out a lot of things." "I happen to be one of the things that you have to sort out." "I can get like you, you know. I can leave and go do my own thing, and let you go through whatever you're going through." "That's the only answer I can give you." "What worries me is two weeks can go by and still no Smith in my bed." "I won't let that happen, but you'll have moments that I need to be away from you, and I'll have moments where you need to be away from me." "I'll know when I'm around you whether you want me around you or not." "Smith, you've never said anything to hurt me; you may have problems talking to people in a normal way, but when you talk to me, I only hear nice things from you." "You're a man of authority; you give reasons for your actions because we're all confused about what you're doing, everyone that is except my father." "We all ask questions, and you're not used to this. What's happening to you had happened to all of us when we were young kids playing on the playground." "Smith, have you ever sat in a swing or on a see-saw?" She said.

"No"

"See, we're different, your brain is analytical, you see the real person that's inside, and you're good at it." "You scare my mother, and you scared Maria, and you scare me." "Now you mentioned calories. What brought that on?" She said, "What about them."

I told her, "I was just thinking that you can run ten miles and then eat a bowl of ice cream, and you consume more calories than what you took off by running the ten miles." "I just thought it was funny, that's all."

She grabbed me, stopped me from running, and kissed me.

"Smith, you're doing it again, aren't you?" She sounded mad.

I smiled at her and then continued running.

She soon caught up with me.

"You asked me if I knew what it felt like to remember everything." "I have problems remembering what I went to buy at the store." She chuckled. "So I end up shopping, and when I get home, I have several bags of groceries, and then I remember what I went to the store for."

I stopped and then began a pace to where we could walk by. "That's called a temporary memory loss, associated with your thoughts being on something that's bothering you." "You don't have to worry about that here." "You simply tell the computer what you want, and it's delivered to you." "You need something you forgot, tell the computer, and it's delivered to you."

"Then you and I will make a good couple." She said, "I can't remember anything, and you can't forget anything." "We won't have any arguments because whatever you say, I'll have to take your word for it." She sounded as if she was being playful with what she was saying. "Besides, I never liked putting on my makeup, and with you around, all I have to do is sit back, snap my fingers and let you work."

"You can always call for James or Ruby," I told her.

"It's not the same, they may be good, but you're better." She informed me.

"I'm fully aware when someone is using psychology on me," I told her.

She took my hand and held it up to look at the difference in size that mine was from hers.

"I don't know what it's like to remember everything that ever happened in your life." She said, "But look at my hand; it's not hard to see that mine is larger." "I had an awful time growing up, and I can only imagine the feelings you had and still have." "In a way, I guess I'm no different from you. I still feel out of place." "I don't like it when people stare at me." She said sadly.

"I noticed that." I said to her, "You always sat in my lap or in a chair when we were together."

Jose came walking into the room and started walking with us.

"Let me guess." I said to him, "Maria is asleep."

"Yes, sir." "She sat down, and I noticed her eyes were starting to get a little heavy." "I led her into the study, and she sat down in the chair, and I sat across from her on the couch, and the next thing I knew, she was out." "I got up and came in here to do what you're doing, taking a little walk."

"Jose, you remember when we first met?"

"Yes, sir."

"And do you remember when you woke up?" "You didn't know where you were at or what was going on." "When you and she talked to my computer, she had a temper to her." "How did you react to her temper?"

"Sir, I couldn't; I don't think that she listened too much of what I said." "Because the questions she asked were questions I couldn't answer." "It involved you and what this place was, and I told her that I wasn't at liberty to discuss your work." "She told me to go sit on the couch; she wanted to be alone."

"What do you think of her?" I asked him.

"I don't know how I can answer that, sir." He responded.

"Jose," Jane interrupted, "when you and she went to dinner." "Did she have a smile on her face when you handed her the rose?"

"No ma'am, when she opened the door, I told her that I was here to find out what she wanted to do." "She didn't answer me, she took out a note pad and began writing down what was wrong with her."

"Jose, she's illegal, and she hasn't had a life without trouble." "We had a talk last night while you slept, and your name was mentioned." "I want you to work with her," I said to him.

"Sir, I don't understand?" He replied.

"Jose, it's difficult for me to answer." "She had the opportunity to leave, but she chose not to. I feel like I'm trapped in a place I don't want to be." "She's been deported once, and when she came back, sometimes she left a job when money was owed to her because she thought someone reported her." "She's been living a life of acute paranoia." "You know a little about that." I told him, "When I sent for you to get her last night, I noticed by the look on her face that she thought she was caught again." "I told her the things that I knew about her." "But, my intentions were not related to her." "I had a job for her, and that I was testing you, and you thought you failed, when in fact you succeeded, you learned a lesson that all things are not as they appear, you must learn to expect the unexpected, I told her." "When I told you to take her back, I told her that we were going to have a talk." "She took the blame for she thought I was angry with you for not being successful in your test." "She argued with me still because she thought you were in trouble." "I signed to her that our conversation would be between us, and it would remain private." "I'm sorry, Jose, but I gave my word to her." "If she wants to tell you what was said between us, then she'll have to be the one that'll tell you."

"But sir?" He protested.

"Jose, all I can say is I have my reasons, and I want you to trust me on this."

"Yes, sir." He said while walking away.

"You are trying to set them up, aren't you?" Jane said when he left.

"Did you want me when you first met me?" I asked her.

"No, I didn't even know you." She stated.

"Maria didn't want Jose either when she first saw him." "How long did it take for you to see me differently?" I asked her.

"You weren't like everyone else." She said. "I don't know, really, and that confused me."

"The first time that you meet someone, you don't really meet them." "It's more like two people looking at each other and then walking away into the mist that rises from the warm air that touches the cool ground, and the person vanishes as the mist thickens. Nothing is astray." "The next time you see each other, you watch as each vanishes into the mist, and this time, you turn to see each walk away." "The third time a word is said, and some words are said back, and soon more words are exchanged." "Unification of two people that I know is not my goal." "I have difficulty in that area, so I'm not someone that anyone should follow as an example," I said to her.

"You want to hear something stupid?" She commented.

"When you're in bed with me, I tell the computer to lower the air conditioner onto its lowest setting and cover-up." "Sometime later, I'm kicking the cover off because you're burning me out, then you leave, and I have to put all the cover back on and tell the computer to turn on the heater." "Smith, if you and I ever move to a warm climate, I'm going to have to have my own bed." "I won't be able to sleep with you; you're too hot."

"When you were sick at the cabin, you held me tight; I wondered if it was because you were cold or if you liked holding me." I told her, "Jane, you made me hurt bad inside." "You said that you told Maria that you're my weakness and my strength." "I've been thinking about what you said, and your right." "I had no control over you, and I, in turn, went against all that I believed, and I found that I lost my will and desired you." "Today, life is different, marriage is cohabitating your life with another life for a period of time until you longer have those desires that you once had, and that marriage is no longer." "My father and mother separated before we were born; when he found out that my brother had Down's syndrome, he was going to have to support him for the rest of his life." "I believed he was forced to sign up in the military so that he had insurance and a job." "I think that might have had a lot to do with him being an alcoholic, and I believe it eventually let him use it like a trigger on a gun." "I believe that's why he picked my brother up that day, he was pointing his finger at someone, and he might have blamed my brother for his life." "I don't have facts to verify any of that." "I never saw my father's face before he picked him up, so I can't see what he was thinking, I have to accept that I can't answer all my questions, and that's one of the answers that I really want to know." "Jose and Maria will bond in friendship; being around each other requires interaction." "One is a positive person, and one is a negative person." "Their life together began at the time that they saw each other, even though the evening didn't have a good outcome." "Where their life takes them is the same as you and me. You can't tell the future until it becomes the past." "They've each had others, as well as you, and those relationships didn't last." "I can't force two people to cohabitate, and I can't stop two people from going about their life in their own way." "It's not under my control."

"Smith, sometimes I have to listen hard to everything you say." "You aren't exactly a good conversationalist, you know?" "You don't speak to others; you teach." "You have a gift, and you just wanted to have a normal life like everyone else." "It didn't happen that way, and you were cheated out of one." "I think I prefer you the way you are now because everything you do is mature, you never act childish, and you never say anything that's hurtful to anyone." "What's hurtful is the truth they hear." "I told my mother that." "The strange part about you is you don't let yourself go; you don't laugh, you smile; you don't play, and you are very positive in what you set out to do." She said to me, "Smith, we'll be leaving tomorrow night." "You may not think so, but you need some rest. Without it, I think you're at your weakest before you go and do what you have in mind." "You do have a plan, right?" She asked.

"He takes nitroglycerin to dilate his arteries. If not, he doesn't get enough blood to the heart, and to complicate matters, his high blood pressure gives him lightheadedness." "He can only take the maximum of three pills a day, or his arteries would burst." I told her, "He has to take two shots a day of insulin to live." "I'm going to replace his insulin with my own, and when he takes his shot, it'll hit him as if he took ten times the amount of nitro that's he's taking now, and I'll lace it with a heavy dose of adrenalin." "If a heart attack doesn't kill him, then he'll bleed to death internally." "Once the shot has entered his body, he'll have less than five to ten minutes to live."

"When did you plan this out?" She asked.

"The moment I saw his medical records, I knew how to dispose of him." "There won't be an autopsy; his body is going to be cremated at the morgue." "I'll be there to make sure of that."

"Smith put me to sleep." She said.

We walked into our room, and we both took our showers, and it was her that put me to sleep.

I awoke with her gone.

I got up and went into the kitchen and saw everyone at the table eating; it was breakfast.

"Morning," Jack said.

I gave them all a look, and Jack spoke.

"Son, you've slept longer than I've ever seen you sleep." "Personally, I think you needed it." He stated.

"Computer; turn on camera's one twenty-two and one twenty-three," I ordered

I poured myself a cup of coffee and sat down. Maria asked me if I wanted some breakfast. I began to sign, and I spoke aloud so others could hear what I said.

"I fast before I leave here." "My body can't function properly, and it slows me down or causes me to become drowsy." I then took another sip of my coffee. When I sat it down, I once again began signing to her, "Maria, we're going to the Bahamas, and I need you to go with us." "Jose draws less attention when he's not by himself," I told her. I saw Jane give a little smile as she moved her chair over to be with mine.

Maria told me that she didn't have beautiful clothes to go to.

I crossed my arms and looked at her.

"Jane," I said to her, "I have to marry Maria to Jose."

Jose jumped up and nearly choked on his breakfast, which caused Maria to wonder what was happening.

Jane gave orders to my computer to display what Maria would look like in a wedding gown. Then Maria was the one that looked red-faced.

"What do you think?" She asked.

"I don't know." "Computer; lighten the hair color and show me a series of wedding rings." I soon stopped the computer, backed it up, and selected her ring. "Computer; show me a series of earrings on Maria." Soon I stopped it again, and then I asked the computer for a necklace. After I finished, I looked at Maria. She had her hand over her mouth "Computer; give me a golden diamond tiara and center it on her head."

"I like that," Jane said, "it adds a special touch, but she doesn't have the smile of a woman in love." "Computer," she said, "give Maria a smile and stop when I command." Soon she gave her order and looked hard. "Computer; back up a little on the smile," and again she ordered for it to stop. "What do you think?" She asked me.

"Computer; show me the picture of Dan Gomez in a white tuxedo." "Nice" "Now, put Maria with her wedding attire next to Dan." After my commands were completed, I ordered the computer to give me a picture and a marriage certificate. "Maria," I said out loud for others to hear as well as signing for her to understand. "Jose's safety depends on his ability to remain a mystery." "He'll remain here at this resort for the rest of his life until I send him to deliver a message for me." "Cameras are everywhere, and if I have control over all of them, then you can believe that other people out there have the same technology, and they use it for the same reasons that I do." "Now, you said that you didn't have clothes." I said out loud while signing, "All three of you ladies will have packages that will be waiting for you when you arrive at the hotel, in your rooms." "Bathing suits and casual wear; I don't know what kind of clothes any of you like to feel good in, so expect different colors and styles of bikini's, or one-piece bathing suits, and also different styles of shorts or pants, and blouses, as well as shoes for you." "Supper will be at Jack's favorite place, and I'll meet you there later." "Jane, I need your help," "Maria needs clothes, and I need you to show her how to order them," I said.

"Smith," Ellen said smiling, "I'm not going to be surprised, am I?" I also had to give her a smile. I started signing my answer.

"If I was to make a comment, all of you here would hear what I say." "I don't think that's right to exclude Maria out of our conversation." "I'd like to change that." "Whatever is spoken by her or any of us, I would like to let Maria hear the conversation too." "That means I would have to explain what I had told you earlier," I said to all of them, referring to Ellen.

Ellen's face became red.

"I'd like to hear what the surprise was," Jack said.

"No," Ellen retaliated quickly. I was signing to Maria while they talked. I finished my cup of coffee and then told them that I had work to do. I left and was soon met in my control room by everyone from the kitchen.

They sat down and were silent as they watched me.

I walked my chair around with my feet to look at all of them.

"Something's up?" I said.

"We didn't want to bother you," Jane spoke for them all. "We like to be with you." She said.

I smiled, put my head down, and ordered for the hologram to sign for Maria.

"When I was young, I never knew what it felt like to be needed." "I've aged a little now, and I find that everyone at this resort is dependent on everyone here," I said as I turned back around to download a program on one of my laptops. I started talking, and the hologram was signing for Maria as I talked. "I find myself with a difficult dilemma." "Jose, I want you to hear this the most." "Failure in my missions isn't an option that I can accept." "Any hesitation in my orders could mean death."

After I started running my program, I turned back around to face them and began signing while I ordered the hologram off.

"I didn't ask to do this, but I find myself in a position where I can't refuse." "Jack was the only person that had any knowledge of me." "I want you all to understand that this isn't my way of doing things." "But, there comes a time when you're faced with only one way to dissolve a matter." "I'm dealing with a killer that has power, and I have other complications that make this mission even more complicated." "Jose, that's where you come in, I can't stop an army, but I can distract them while I work." "Jane, you remember when I looked at the letter, I said the agent told me the name of the traitor."

"Yes," she said.

"Ramon is the agent that turned her in when she gave him information to be given to her contact here." "Ramon is my contact." "So, Ramon knows I'm coming, and that means that the Messiah also knows that I'm coming." "What he doesn't know is where I'll hit first, and that puts the odds in my favor." "Jose," I said, looking over at him, "this isn't a mission for one man, and it's not a mission for two men, but I don't have any choice in this matter." "The Messiah likes to inflict fear in his people by beheading or hanging his victims and let the people watch as the head is decapitated from the body, by the rope being too long." "He likes to stick the head up on a pole and let it be seen by all that oppose him." "It's his way of inflicting fear." "Everyone is afraid to say anything to anyone for fear that they would be talking to one of his men."

"My plans have changed, and my primary targets are now my only concerns." "According to my pictures, there's three locations of a buildup in armor, the Messiah's palace, the control room, and the missile." "In front of the control room stands the dam, and down below the dam is where he keeps his prisoners." "I've only seen four trucks; that means my cargo is at the palace." "If he had them at the prison camp, there'd be a lot more guards than what's there."

"Sir, how did you get those pictures?" Jose asked.

I looked over at Jack and then at Ellen and Jane.

"Computer: send in my serpents and initiate hologram," I ordered.

When they started slithering in, even Jane and Ellen reacted the same as Jose and Maria.

I picked up a cobra after they stopped by my feet. "He's frightening to anyone that see's him," I said to Jose and then looked at Maria. She had backed up and away from the rest of us. "Show Jose your mean, look," I said to it, and his head became swollen. "Your first reaction would be to either run or back up quickly." "Realistically, you would never see them unless they were needed." "These are how I get my pictures," I told him.

"Smith, you're going to have to stop doing that," Ellen said.

"They're my eyes and ears." I told her, "I see what they see, and I hear what they hear."

I put it back down and ordered the computer to recall them and to send in James and Ruby.

They soon were standing in front of us.

"Jose, I told you that James and Ruby will be accompanying us." I told him, "Do you remember that?" I asked him.

"Yes, sir."

Both of them stood in front of Maria and Jose. They were confused.

"Computer; send in James and Ruby," I ordered again to Jose's surprise. When they entered, we were looking at a pair of James and Ruby. Now Jose and Maria were surprised.

I once again ordered for the computer to send in James and Ruby. Another set appeared in front of us.

When Jose stared into my eyes, he didn't have any words. "Jose, they're androids, and the serpents were imitators," I said.

I then turned back around and dislodged my program from the laptop and handed it to Maria, and signed for her to open it up and push the on switch and watch the screen as I said out loud to the others, and began continuing my conversation without signing anymore.

I informed everyone that now Maria is able to use the laptop to listen to what everyone says, "It signs to her when you speak." I said, "It has a camera the size of a pen point that will cipher her sign and either speaks audible or it types out what she signs, so no one can hear her except for the person she's speaking to."

She looked at me and signed, asking me how this was possible. Everyone smiled at her when the voice on the laptop translated what she signed, and Jane spoke to her. "Maria," she said as Maria looked down at the screen of the laptop. "When I met Smith, I felt the same way you do; how do you that?" "I kept asking him." "My mother and Jose are like you too." "We still ask how do you that." "Last week, we traveled on a trip, and Jose awoke and found himself here." "You can talk to him, and he'll tell you what he thought." "He's been here a week now, and like us, we woke up to a new surprise, honey; we all had and still have those same thoughts that we have, and you will still have them until you learn to accept Smith as who he is." "You and I have a lot to talk about." She said to her, "You won't get the answers you're looking for unless you ask the rest of us."

"But, this is amazing," the computer began replying. "I can tell what people are saying, and I can speak to others and see what they are saying; this is a gift."

"Maria," I said, "it's yours to take with you anywhere you go; you'll no longer have to worry about writing things down on paper," I told her.

Her face had a smile, and I, in turn, smiled back at her.

"That's the first time I've seen a smile on you," I said to Maria. "That's a good sign that you're beginning to accept the company you're with." "No one here had a smile on their face when they first met me," I told her, "But they did when they began to accept their company, just like you."

Tears were coming from her eyes, and Ellen got up and went over to console her by putting her arm around her. Ellen's eyes were red too. I dismissed the androids.

"Hon," she said to her, "like my daughter said, we're here for you."

"How do know he's crossed?" Jack asked, referring to Ramon.

"Computer; display the past two weeks of Ramon's activity," I commanded. "This picture here shows him with three known henchmen of the Messiah." "My guess is the men he's with are going to try and kill me." "Computer; next picture," I commanded. "This is his girlfriend with the same men, but that's not important" "What is important is the figure in the background." "Computer enlarge quadrant two to two hundred percent."

"That's Alvarone," Jack said.

"That's not all." "Compute decease quadrant two and enlarge quadrant four," I commanded.

"Who's that?" Jack asked.

"He's Doctor Messina, he's one of the doctors that does the transplants, and according to his records, they'll be performing another surgery in three weeks." "The problem is my cargo; he took them away from the prison and protected them in his palace." "The question I ask is why?" "Why would he take them to his palace and not hold them in his prisons?" "He knows I'm coming for them, so he takes them from the place where I believe them to be and removes the guards with them." I walked around a little more and then began pacing back and forth. "His first priority has to be the missile; he wants a successful launch, so he protects his missile," I said, thinking out loud. Then I looked up to all of them staring at me.

"He's using them as a human shield," I told them. I walked around a little more. "The air conditioners have dehumidifiers; the water is removed from the air, and there's no way to damage the computer," I said, thinking as I walked.

I squeezed my lips a little, and Jack said to me, "I've seen that look before, Smith." "What's on your mind?"

"Jack, that's my way in." "The dehumidifiers, I plug the drain valve on the dehumidifiers, and that's where I drop my acid capsules, every component will be corroded that the air conditioners are used to keep cool," I stated to him. I looked at Jose "we have to change our plans; after planting the capsules, we need to have a distraction." "We want them to know we're there." I began pacing again. "We need several small explosions to concentrate their men and then change our attack to a different target."

"Yes, sir, understood."

"Are you playing chess, Smith?" Jane asked.

I looked at her and spoke, "He's the king, and his prisoners are the queen; he doesn't want to lose the queen, so he guards them with his rooks and knights, his fighters, and uses his pawns; on the missile." I'm not interested in the queen right now, he'll think I'll come for them, and he'll move them, right to where we're at."

"Where?" She asked.

"He'll take them back to the prison camp; if I blow the dam, my cargo will be killed, and he's counting on that stopping me."

We were interrupted by an alarm. I ordered my computer to display the warehouse on my screens.

"We've got movement at the warehouse." I said to everyone, "Computer; activate camera one twenty-three, and magnify two hundred percent," I commanded. When the screen cleared, we saw four men looking around. "Three of those men are scouts. They are making sure the area is clear," I explained.

Everyone sat around the table watching the men. It was several hours later when four cars entered.

When lights came on, I ordered for my computer to switch to the camera that was inside the warehouse and then ordered the magnification of the camera to the front car; we saw four men get out.

"That's Miguel, and there's Carlos; the other two men must be their bodyguards," I stated. I then ordered the computer to move the camera until the second car could be seen.

"That's McNally," Jose said, standing up and walking over to the screen "those two guys with him are the agents I was with, sir." He said to me.

"Computer" "focus on the next car," we saw more bodyguards, as well as the fourth car "Computer; switch to camera one twenty-three." I commanded, "I expect the trucks that are loaded with drugs to be arriving soon." I said, "Judging by McNally's movement, I get a feeling that he doesn't like to be in a part of town that he doesn't feel protected." I spotted movement down the road and gave my computer an order to enlarge the movement. "There they are, right on time." I said softly, "Four trucks, that's broken down into twelve to twenty different loads of transportation." "Small amounts are distributed, you lose one, and you don't lose twenty-five percent of a load." I told them, "That brings new questions to the table." "Who are they going to, and that also means that McNally has other men involved that are working with him?" "My next question is who are they?" I said, "Ahh, just as I expected, the cops are their protection as escorts." "Jose" "come here" "I need you to see something." "You're looking at the minimum of twelve loads to be delivered in at least twelve different cities." Someone on the other side is being set up as we speak to stop a load, and all attention will be diverted so that the rest get through." "He can be an agent like you or a cop on patrol, or they can choose an easier way, call the police and tell them that a bomb was planted in a school or at a sports event, and they drive through without any trouble." "That's how you got rewarded," I told him.

When they entered, the agents walked with McNally, and we watched as he waited for one of the men to bring a package out, and then we saw McNally make a small slice in the package and snort some up his nose and then put a little into a vial. We watched as he added a chemical and shook it, and saw it turn blue.

"It appears McNally likes his nose candy, cocaine." I said, without talking to anyone in particular, "He's checking it for its purity."

We saw the transfer of four briefcases and watched as they opened them.

"Computer: zoom in on the briefcases until I tell you to stop." "Stop." "I was right; they buy the drugs with bonds and stocks, and it's all done legally like," I said.

I then ordered the computer to switch to my outside camera.

"Jose, they've completed the transaction; now they're waiting for you to make the call to tell him that you're in position, they'll be ready to move when you do."

I got up, and Jane asked me where I was going?

"To get a cup of coffee, they're waiting for Jose to call. I can't call without making them wait a few minutes; McNally is in his world, he'll wait and pace around, and he'll walk over and take another snort or two, or three, or four." "They won't make a move until he gives them the command." "He's our ringleader; he's our distributor."

When I returned, I saw everyone with their eyes glued on the screen watching.

"Relax, we've still got some time until it's dark. They won't move until then." I then looked at Jose. "That's when you were supposed to make the call."

"Yes, sir." He responded.

"You're not my servant, you know?" I said to him, "You can lighten up on that yes sir, and no sir, my name is Smith." "No first name, no middle name, just Smith."

"That's not easy for me." He said, "I thought of myself as being tough. I was trained to kill and ready to die." "That was what I was taught." "What I wasn't taught was that one man, like you, can dispose of five hundred men that are tougher than me with one flip of a switch." "Sir, I'm not smart like you." He said, "You knew about McNally, didn't you?"

"When you told me that Hammel brought him the briefcases, I knew he was involved somehow, but I didn't know how I could speculate." "When you said he was going to be in Juarez today, that's when I knew he had to have something to do with the shipment." "When you have briefcases, and you have McNally in Juarez on the same day that Miguel and Carlos are going to be in Juarez, it doesn't take much to tie the two together." "What put the final touch to the puzzle was when you told me that McNally was going to meet Alvarone in the Bahamas." "That left me with only one problem; even though he met all of my suspicions, I didn't have one hundred percent certainty, so I had to wait to make sure." "I had to tell you of my plans because I had to put together my weapons." "I was going to have to leave and take you with me to keep you from coming in contact with McNally if he didn't turn out to be who he was." "And then, I don't know what my next move would have been." "We all share the same goals" "and I believe in what I do is right, and so does Jack." "I can only say that loyalty bonds our friendship, but as you can see, loyalty comes at a high price; take a look at McNally on the screen; the price wasn't high enough to keep him honest." "His greed is his downfall, and with the evidence before you, I find him guilty as charged." "Jose, we don't have a democratic rule here." "I make all the decisions; that way, no one can blame themselves for a mistake."

I took several sips of coffee and then ordered the computer to place the call for Jose. "Computer; switch to camera one twenty-two and magnify McNally."

He reached into his pocket and pulled out his cell phone. "Computer show overhead view in quadrant seven, and reduce visual to section one zero two to one twenty-two. "That's you right there, Jose," I said, pointing at a warehouse. "Your inside with a pair of binoculars waiting for a shipment. You're making the call to let him know that you're in position." "Computer; switch to camera one twenty-three." "Look at the screen, Jose" "computer magnify three hundred percent." "That's a lot of explosions taking place, wouldn't you think." "What you don't know is that there are probably twenty corpses in that warehouse that were killed the night before." I said, looking at him "it looks like there's a war going on, and that's where you were supposed to be," I said to him. "You must have pissed him off." "Computer: increase decibel audio." When it did, Jose could hear that he was caught in the middle. "Now, we have the fire," "that's to cover up all remains of a gang that was trapped inside, but they'll say it was started from within." "They'll have plenty of pictures to show the press." "Computer; activate annihilation." The explosives leveled the warehouse and shattered the buildings with debris.

After the dust cleared, everyone watched as they saw that nothing was left, no cars, no trucks, and nobody.

I looked at Jose and took a deep breath. "Now there's no more maybe this, or am I being fooled." "You know the truth behind the question of why I brought you here, if you go anywhere away from this resort as Jose Espinoza, you can be spotted, and if you are, you're dead, but not until you're tortured to find out what they want to know." "You don't have to worry here." "Everyone that gets on the train is screened." "I'll know within one minute who comes here that I need to watch." "And now I also know who I'll be going as when we leave," I said.

"Sir!" Jose seemed lost.

"You said that Alvarone was supposed to meet McNally in the Bahamas. I'll be going as McNally, and we don't want to disappoint our guest, do we?" I said to him.

"Everyone, we leave in two hours." "Dress light, you won't need anything except your bathing suits and your evening gowns." "Jose, me, and you have a business to attend to." We left our companions, and Jane told Maria to come with her; she'll explain things to her.

I gathered my equipment along with a few other items, and I went in and poured some latex into a mold and then fed my computer the image of

McNally. Soon, I was pulling the latex skin from the mold. Jose was watching intensely.

I opened a drawer, pulled out a small voice box the size of a camera's battery, and ordered my computer to adjust my voice box to McNally's voice. I put it up to my throat and spoke some words, and my voice soon sounded like his.

"So that's how you looked and sounded like Pedro." He said.

"It's not perfect, but when you work at night as I do, nothing has to be perfect; a few moments of uncertainty are all I need." I told him, "You'll be wearing one too; we don't want a matching voice pattern." "All agencies inside the Secret Service have computers that have nothing but voice codes of all agents, good or bad." "This way, the only voice pattern they have is Dan Gomez. If you speak as Jose Espinoza, they'll know Dan Gomez, and Jose Espinoza is one and the same." "You'll be given top-secret clearance, and you won't converse with anyone other than the person I send you to see." "Don't worry if you have problems; walk away. The next time you leave to go where you're sent, you won't have the problems you had the last time." "Jose, when I send you somewhere, you won't be going alone." "You'll be under guard by Jack and Ruby, and no one will put a hand on you." "That's why I tell you, respect others, and let me take care of the problems," I told him.

I then went into my lab and began disassembling my glider, the prototype I called the pterodactyl.

"What is this?" Jose asked.

"We need a ride," I told him. "I call this the pterodactyl."

"It looks more like a bat." He responded. "How does it work?"

"I don't know; I'm going to find out, though." I told him, "You can relax, Jose." "A person that reaches maximum velocity can't fall any faster than six hundred feet a second." "If fifty feet a second is enough to kill you, then why worry about a few more feet faster." "I had to modify it; I wasn't planning on more than one person riding on it." I told him, "But there are three hundred rotating discs underneath the body and the wings." "Half is rotating one way, and half is rotating the other way." "Both are channeled to vent to allow air to be trapped on one side and let air escape on the other side." "That allows the wing to tip to the left or to the right, depending on which way we want to go." "The speed of my jet propels us forward, the same as someone throwing a flying disc, and the air that's trapped underneath the disc as it rotates keeps the disc flying in a straight pattern." "Hopefully, our descent will be slow, but I can't predict updrafts or downdrafts." After I disassembled it, we began carrying it to the elevator. I collapsed the wings and folded them, and we stored them into my chopper.

Before we got back on the snowmobiles, Jose looked over at me. "Sir, I'm curious?" He stated.

"If you're talking about my copter, I had help." "James and Ruby are pretty handy to have around sometimes," I told him. "It would have taken me better than a year without their help." "But, it ended up being built in less than ten days."

"Sir, about them."

I stopped him from continuing.

"Jose, in answer to your question, I have more; in fact, I had a total of thirty working on my helicopter, twenty-four hours a day." "No lunch breaks, no coffee breaks, no sleep." "That's why it was finished in ten days." "It's a hundred and seventy-four feet to the bottom of the dam where the turbines operate." "My androids, James and Ruby are going to attach themselves to the bottom; they have enough explosives inside their energy cells to more than do what needs to be done." "The force of the water escaping will demolish everything in its path." "There won't be any evidence to be found; everything will be washed out to sea, along with the side of the mountain." I told him, "Now, does that answer one of your questions?"

"Yes, sir."

Twenty minutes later, we were back at my lab.

"I mentioned to you about the Messiah congregating his men in three areas." I told him, "The most men we'll be dealing with by my estimate is around eight to ten thousand; one bomb would destroy this entire area." "But, if we did that, we would turn allies into hostiles." "That's the reason we can't leave evidence behind; we can't give any clues as to what occurred." "The only result is speculations." I told him, "That is unless there's an intervention of an unknown source."

"Sir"

"Jose, how do you stop ten thousand men?" I asked him.

"Sir, I never know what you're thinking." He said.

"In order to promote chaos, we need fear, and in order to promote fear, we need chaos." I stated, "We're dealing with people of serious convictions when their religion is questioned." "In Mexico, they have a festival called Hallows eve. In this country, it's called Halloween." "You were raised in California; do you know what Hallows eve was?" I asked him.

"Yes, sir, it was a festival to celebrate the day of the dead." "People dressed up as corpses, and that way their ancestor's wouldn't be recognized, and they could walk with the living." He said.

"If you were congregating you're men in three locations, wouldn't you have men on patrol all over the area to watch for anything out of the ordinary?" I said to him.

"Yes, sir."

"Computer; send in three corpses," I said.

About five minutes had gone by when Jose became startled. "Give me the living dead program." I ordered, and each one began approaching us with their arms extended." "Stop," I commanded. "Jose, no one, and I do mean no one stands their ground when all their bullets are gone, and the dead keep coming." "We promote the fear, and the chaos follows." I told him, "Computer; send two hundred corpses to the palace and two hundred corpses to the control room, have them dig in and cover themselves up, and prepare for my orders." I told it.

"Sir, this is way beyond me." He said.

"Jose, a man, has eyes, but they can't see." "I was reviewing my recordings, and I had fifty pictures flashing in thirty-second intervals." "I look for the obvious." "As an agent, whenever you made a report, you put down whatever happened, just the way it happened." "Movies give my imagination a lot of time for thought." "That's how my zombie androids were born." "Jose, no one is looking for me when they are running from a zombie." "It's in all the movies, watch one, and you'll see what I mean." "I'm sure at some point you'll have more questions." "Never be afraid to ask me anything. If you're bothered about a question, and you don't feel comfortable talking to me, then you can talk to the hologram or James or Ruby." "All my androids and humanoids receive their commands from me or my computer." "Those Bobcats I dropped off in Juarez, they sent back information for me to destroy the warehouse." "They'll find their way back in a week or two."

When we walked back into my lab, I headed straight for the backpacks and the other items that I selected for my mission.

I handed Jose my makeup kit and a couple of the backpacks, James and Ruby helped share the burden of our load, and I looked and gave my lab one last look around and gave the order for all security doors to be closed. I looked around at everyone and said. "I guess we're about as ready as we'll ever be." I gave the computer an order to open the door on the elevator, and we left.

When we got to the snowmobiles, I signed to Maria that it was time that she acted like a married woman and rode with Jose. I didn't have to say anything to the others. They knew without me telling them when they saw Maria getting on the back of the snowmobile with Jose.

"Computer; ready my helicopter and jet," I commanded.

Once we arrived at the helicopter, Maria was acting a little squeamish; I could tell that she had never ridden in one. Jose took over and took her hand and urged her a little bit. When she defied him, he took control and picked her up, and carried her. She didn't like him acting dominant and putting up a fight; Jose was taking a beating.

"You want me to knock her out?" I asked him.

"No sir, she's scared, that's all." He commented, "I'll talk to her."

I looked over at Jane and shook my head at her to tell her not to interfere. He used authority when he buckled her in and when we took off, Maria wasn't beating Jose anymore; she was now clinging onto him. I saw a smile coming from Jane's face when I gave her a look, and I returned hers with my own.

She then pointed to herself and then pointed two fingers at her eyes and then pointed her forefinger at me. That was her way of signing and letting me know that she had her eyes on me.

"We'll arrive around five in the morning," I said. "It's best that everyone get some sleep tonight. You don't want to be tired when we arrive; it takes the fun out of traveling."

"What about you? Don't you get lonely flying without someone to talk to?" Jane asked.

"That depends on what you define lonely as." I said, "Your father was my only companion on trips." "He usually laid down and took a nap most of the time, and that left me with nothing but the clear skies." "Sometimes you could look out and see the horizon; up here, it's different; you can see daylight while it's still dark." "When you're alone, you have a lot of time to think," I told her while everyone else was listening. Maria had calmed down, but she still clung to Jose for security. "When I think, I think about a lot of things." I said, "Us, for example, and how we all met, we all have a lot in common, we've all had moments of being alone, and we all had our misfortunes along the way." "What separates us is I can remember all of those things that I thought about while thinking." "They bother me until I download those thoughts on my computer." "If you think about it, we're all writing our own story in the book of life," I said. "Some never got a chance to write a word on the first page; babies don't always survive their births." "I've seen books that were written in prison; young men get foolish when there's a full moon, they end up spending life behind bars, paying for being young and foolish, they chose a life that had a dead end." "I've seen rich men die poor, and I've seen poor men die rich." "The problem with me is I see a lot of people writing their book, but they're not writing a book about themselves; it's fiction." "Jane, your book reads that you were alone when your husband was with you and when he wasn't with you." "That chapter has already been written." I said to her, "Now, Ellen, your book reads that you were alone when Jack was away with me or delivering a message for me. I told Jane that I cheated her out of her life, and I did the same to you." "That too is a chapter in a book that can't be rewritten." "Maria, I see a book that reads that you've always been alone; you don't meet too many people while trying to avoid contact with people, I read your book, and it's filled with fear." "You don't have that to worry about anymore, and one day you'll come to realize that that chapter has been written in your book also." "Jose, you're book reads that you joined the military because I didn't see you with any friends that didn't have something to do with trouble; everyone you knew fell to being victims and landed into a pit of crime." "So, our books all have a beginning, a middle, and an end." "No matter how you see it, our life is an open book, and we are the writers." "As long as we live, there'll be a new page added to the book each day, and one day two words that say the end will be written, and the book can be put up on a shelf where it'll be forgotten."

"That's not what I meant, though," Jane commented.

"I know," I told her, "But; when someone is angry with you, that person doesn't want you around them." "I've watched a lot of people, and they all want to be somewhere else other than with the person that they're angry with." "Maria didn't want Jose around her, and I'm sorry Ellen, but there were times that I'm sure you were happy when Jack had to go away for a few days." "From what I've read, there's nothing I can do to avoid someone being angry at me." "Jane, everyone here has been angry at me." "I couldn't explain anything to you back at the cabin, and Ellen, when you and I first met, we had conflicts." "Jose, when you woke up in my lab, I told you why you were there, but tonight, you saw the truth in what I was telling you." "Maria, you had a lot of anger inside of you that needed to be vented." "You're not the same girl that entered my lab with Jose," I said.

"Smith," Jane commented, "you're a man with some very strange feelings, and they sometimes get in the way of a relationship." "You put too much thought into being analytical." "The only reason you and I are together is that I know everything about you, and I can live with that."

"You don't know as much as you think you know about me?" I told her.

"You have feelings for me," she said, "and that's all I care about." "You know what the hard part about you is?" She asked.

I looked over at her.

"I thought I was in love when I married my husband, but now I know I wasn't." "After being with you, I know what love really feels like, and Smith, for the record, I wasn't in love with my husband, like I love you."

I was interrupted by Jack as we neared the airfield where I kept my plane. He was diverting Jane's comment away from me answering her. He knew my odds.

"Smith," he said, "I need to know the mode of transport."

"We'll talk on that issue as soon as we depart," I told him as I began approaching my landing site.

When we landed, James and Ruby unloaded our gear and loaded them into the plane while I went through my checklist and warmed my turbines. Right before takeoff, Maria once again began to become on edge. Jose held her hand and told her to close her eyes and think of good things, but it did very little to help settle her down. He put his arm around her to hold her tight. Once in the air, I flipped a switch to initiate the silencers on the turbines and put the plane on autopilot.

Jack walked into the cockpit, bringing me a cup of coffee.

"You're going to want the Nautilus, right?" He stated.

"Yeah" "that reminds me." "Jack, he's got Jets, and he's got gunboats." "Computer build me a dozen seagulls with six ounces of C fours in them and six dolphins with explosives to destroy the Messiah's gunboats and have them readied on board the Nautilus for departure." "What do you think, Jack?" "If I leave the women behind, they won't have any idea of what we do." "It's your call," I said to him.

"I think they'll be safe, but I don't think it's a good idea." He announced, "But if you don't let them go, then they'll never know anything about what you do."

"I don't know the exact time of drop off, so you may be in waiting." "We'll know more later." "The sub is rigged for silent running, and Jack, there's one other thing." "I think the Messiah is getting help from another country." "You don't have six gunboats and four jets without help." "I don't have the details on when the launch is supposed to take place, so I don't have a timeline that I can give you.

"What about Ramon and the boat? I'm sure they know it's rigged for action." He said.

"I have to destroy the boat and steal another." "Jack, the Nautilus is not the sub that you used to be in. I made modifications." "I don't expect any problems to occur, but I don't underestimate my foe either." "If I tell you to prepare for action." "Tell the girls to strap themselves in and get ready for a ride."

"I don't like you taking me out of this." He said in a way that let me know that he knew he wasn't the man he used to be.

I thought for a moment and then gave him an answer.

"Jack, in this game, you're an old man after forty." I told him, "I don't look at you as retiring. I look and see you changing jobs; you've been promoted to other commands since we've been together, and it's the same thing now." "You're still active; Jack the mule pulls the wagon, but someone still has to tell it where to go." "Besides, the computer will take over if any threats are detected," I said, smiling at him.

"I think Jane has a lot to do with me being here." He said.

"I asked myself thirteen years ago, what am I doing here?" I told him, "Since then, you've been asking yourself that same question." "You know why you're here, and Jane feels the same way." "I'm being guarded by people that want to spoil me, and you can tell your wife that I'm wise to her too."

"You knew the people that took care of me." I said to him, "If any of them had done what they were supposed to do, you and I would never have met, and I wouldn't be here, and for that matter, neither would you." "All of them wanted me to live with them, but if you're not part of a family, you always have a feeling as you don't belong there." "We were together for a short period of time; before we parted, I was hurt." "But, I came to realize that I can't control the fate of anyone that crosses my path as a friend." "The truth is, I expected our paths to have crossed again someday, but I didn't expect it to cross this way." I said to him, "You're here now, and you'll be here for as long as you wish, just like before."

He got up with tears in his eyes and gave me a couple of slaps on my back. "I wish I could take back those years." "I missed you, kid." He said and then left.

Jane got up and sat where he sat. When he closed the door, Jane looked down with tears in her eyes and asked. "What happened with you and my father?"

"It was a little thing, but I told him that I didn't want to be a part of what I don't believe in, and your father and I saw things differently." "I didn't support a man that your father supported, and he asked me not to take matters into my own hands; he was frightened of me and afraid I would cause a problem." "But, that's in the past, and like I always said." "I can't convince someone that they're wrong when they think they're right." "When your father got out of politics, he quit being a part of the party." "It's money that attracts the votes they give, not the people." "Your father became a changed man; he has seen what I saw." "Jane, he looked and saw that he didn't have any friends; that's why he didn't run for office anymore." "He became like me; he didn't want to have a part in it."

"I never saw my father cry before." She said as tears fell from her eyes.

"Your father's been struggling with himself for years." I told her, "It's not easy to hear a man tell you something and you disagree with him, and then you find out later that that man was right and you were wrong, especially when that man isn't even a man." "Your father released a heavy burden that he bore for a long time."

"Is he right; is he here because of me?" She asked.

"That's not the question you want to ask," I told her. "The question you want to ask is, are you here because of your father?" "Jane, when I look at you, I always see the eleven-year-old girl I saw at that party." "I'll never forget the look on your face." "You were a girl that stood alone; you knew why you were invited, you didn't even know the girl, so it wasn't because of the girl inviting you, it was because of your father was a senator, and that girl's father wanted his endorsement." "It's always been your father in your life." "He's always had influential people that catered to him, and they used you and your mother like at the party, the congressman needed your father's endorsement." "I think you knew that then, so like your father, you've been carrying a heavy burden on your shoulders too. You were always introduced as Senator Morgan's daughter instead of Jane Morgan." "Jane, I'm in love with you, not your father," I told her.

She began crying again and laid her head down on my shoulder, I leaned the chair back a little, and held her tight in my arms.

"Smith, why does the truth hurt so much?" She said with a broken sentence.

"I don't know that answer," I told her. "If our lives had an active role with each other, when we were younger, I might have grown up different, and you might have grown up different." "But it didn't; it ended up the way it is now." "One day, you'll blink, and you'll be at the age of your mother and father, then you'll blink again, and you'll be older." "You'll have the wisdom to answer that question then." I said as I rubbed her eyes dry of tears with my thumb, "You remember when you were sitting in my lap, at healing waters?" I asked her.

"How can I forget?" She said, smiling.

"Do you remember what I was wearing?" I said.

She thought for a few moments and answered. "Thermal underwear, and I was too." She said, laughing. "I'd give anything to be sitting in that water right now and sleeping in the sleeping bag next to that hot body of yours." She said as she began kissing me again, and I squeezed her harder. She then stopped and picked up her head from my shoulders. "Smith, somewhere inside that mind of yours, there's a point you want to make." "You don't just say something without it entering your mind."

"What do you remember?" I asked her.

She looked at me hard. "Smith, I remember everything, from the time that I first met you till now."

"And do you know why?" I asked her.

"Because I've been with you since the first day we met." She said, "What's your point?"

"I don't want to do this." I said, "I don't want to leave."

"Then why are you going?" She asked in a soft voice.

"I didn't start out doing any of this," I said. "I ended up this way because I couldn't stop others from doing what they were going to do, so I had to make a decision." "I trained all my life to be prepared for anything that these men were capable of, and with all my training, I can't stop what happens after I'm dead." "When I met your father, my life was complicated, and I focused all my energy into putting a stop to these men that used their power for personal reasons." "I never made a dent in stopping innocent people from being victimized."

"Today, drugs and alcohol are responsible for killing more people than all the wars that man has ever fought since the birth of our independence." "If people didn't desire these things, then these people wouldn't be in this line of work." "I can't stop the people that need it to survive.

"Smith, I want you to listen to me." "Do you think you saved lives by killing people like McNally and those other men?" "You're a fighter for a cause; the president came to you to ask you for your help, himself." "My father has faith in you, or we wouldn't be here, and you know it." "When I was in college, there were people that drank and did drugs; no one forced them to indulge in what they did; they studied hard and long to graduate and get a good job." "People aren't like you; they have minds that listen to excuses, and I saw a lot of those people graduate, but what started as an innocent party to relieve stress carried over, and those people became dependant on those things long after they graduated." "Children, women, and men are all victims of an excuse, and believe me; you can't write a book that big when it comes to excuses." "I thought I knew all of them." She said.

"Your husband used cocaine, didn't he?" I said to her.

She laid her head back on my shoulder.

"I found some hidden in his shaving kit." "We were married a little over two years before I found out." "We had a fight, and that's when I found out that he was doing it before we were married." "I didn't say anything to my father; I couldn't." "He said he only did some every now and then and that it helped him to prepare him for court." "He got to acting worse after that, and then he changed and started acting nice. I thought he had stopped doing it because he was good to me and treated me better." "That's when we went on vacation here, and I fell into your arms, literally." She said.

"I think what happened to you entered into his mind before he met you," I told her. "Anyone with an idea is capable of carrying out that idea."

"But Smith, that's where you come in." "All of that stuff destroys people's lives, those that do it, and those that don't." "That's one reason I don't find you to be who you think you are, a murderer." "You're a good man, and I believe in you." "People do things that are right for the wrong reasons; you do what's wrong for the right reasons." "Without you, what would this world be like?" "You won't be able to rid the world of all the bad people." "It's like you say, someone will be born; yesterday, today or tomorrow, and trouble will be here or elsewhere." "But, I do know one thing; you give hope to a lot of people that are depending on you back at the resort." "Without you, none of those hospitals are going to be built, and people are going to continue to die because they are poor." "Smith, you're a man with a vision, and without you, none of these things you see will come to life." "This trip that we're on, this man is responsible for the deaths of some of those innocent children, women, and men, right?" She said.

"He's a kidnapper that's involved in human trafficking," I told her.

"Then there's your answer if you don't do anything, more people will come up missing." She replied, "You said that if you don't succeed, we may get to see World War Three." "Smith, if that happens, I won't live long enough to see peace again, and you know that." "That's why I'm behind you; I'm not standing in your way, we all believe in you, and even those that don't know you, and never will know you, because everyone is like my mother, we all believe our government is out there protecting us when it turns out that there are members of Government trying to overthrow this country." "It so happens that I was given the opportunity to meet one of the people that does what he does to protect us." "I'm lucky, I'm married to him, and I got a ring to prove it. He made it for me himself." "You've got a job to do, and the whole world will start caving in unless you do something to stop it." "All I ask from you is do what you need to do and come home to me." "I need you too." She pulled my head over to kiss her.

CHAPTER TEN

J ane had fallen asleep along the way, and the rest of the trip had silence. The sky was clear on a moonless night, and my thoughts stretched far and wide. Time was peaceful to me as I gazed at the stars. It was all too soon before I reached up and signaled for the others to awake; we were approaching the point where I needed to call the airport for permission to land. Jack came walking in with a cup of coffee for me.

"Has she been there all night?" He asked.

I gave him a smile.

"Honey," he said, shaking her gently, and when she opened her eyes, he told her. "We're getting ready to land in a little while." "You need to wake up." He said.

She then looked at me. "I don't remember falling asleep; why didn't you wake me? I would have sat in the chair?" She said to me.

"There wasn't a need; I was comfortable," I told her.

She got up and left us to go and wash her face to get the sleep out of her eyes.

Jack watched her as she bent down to go out the door, and then he looked over at me.

"My wife asked me how come you always tell everyone that we're going to be dining at my favorite restaurant." He said.

"Jack, your wife, doesn't know you as well as she thinks she knows you; that's got her to thinking about the other side of you that you never presented to her." "It's like talking to a different man than you never talked to in all the years of her marriage." "You had secrets that couldn't be exposed, and you knew the reason why, but she didn't, but now she does." "She's never realized what you went through, so now she has a little spirit to her life, and that makes her feel young again." "She's not married to the old Jack anymore, she's in love with a new Jack, and he's totally opposite from the old Jack."

"Are you saying that I'm not as boring to her as I was before?" He said.

"No, both of you blamed yourselves for the arguments that you encountered along the way, only she was right most of the time; you had secrets." "Now, she knows why you had secrets, and she knows if I asked her to keep a secret from you, Jack, let's just say that she knows you better now, that's all." "You made it this far, so there must be a connection between you two." "Now she finds out that she's married to a man, that she's never seen him behave like the man she sees now." "I'd like for you to understand; Ellen is impressed with the man that you are; those years of keeping secrets are not needed any longer."

"Isn't that why you renewed your vows at the top of the lookout point at Noah's Ark? I said to him, "Now, I've said what I want to say." "What did you tell her?" I asked him.

"I told her it was a long story, and she said she had a lot of time to listen." "We never discussed things like that, so I had to do a lot of thinking before

I could find the words I needed to say." "I don't have the resources you do." He said, laughing "I told her that whenever we had stopovers in countries, we would wind up in different areas, and in all these areas we ate at the restaurants that were nearby, and whenever we went back, I always found myself wanting to go back to the restaurants that I liked the best." "I told her I found myself tasting food before we even got there, and so every time we went to this country or that country, we always ended up where I liked to eat." He said, laughing louder. Then he toned it down to a smile and said, "My wife talks a lot about you, and Smith, I think she's worried."

"When you speak to her again, you can tell her that worries are always a part of living a life; we can't wake up without encountering something that makes us worry." "These worries can last for weeks or months or even years, but in the end, worries are not good for what ails the soul." "Tell her that she has to stay strong; Jane has these worries also, and to see her mother with the same worries only gives misery the company that it needs." "Jack, let her know that time is an enemy when you think hurtful thoughts," I said.

"If I talk like that, she'll know you told me to tell her that." He confessed.

"Jack, she uses you, you know that and she knows that, and you let her," I said, smiling at him.

"Smith, is it any different between Ellen and me and you and Jane?" He asked with a straight face.

I turned my head to gaze back at the stars.

"Son, you were brilliant, but you didn't have control, and for that matter, I can't see where much has changed about you." "But I think Jane has the same effect on you as what Ellen has on me; the only thing is I know it, and you don't." "So, when that time comes, and it affects you the way I'm telling you, then this time, you'll find out that I'm right, and you'll be the one that's wrong." "Go on; I'll take over from here; you've got to get dressed." He said "Smith" "Jane had a lot of problems growing up." "I couldn't help her." "You've changed the way she feels, and now she doesn't think the way she used to think." "Do you know what I'm saying?"

"Thanks, dad." I chuckled and then got up to leave when he stopped me.

"You were right about my wife and me, I've noticed the change in her too, and Smith, I don't see the same Ellen I used to know either."

"That's not a bad thing, Jack." "Sometimes we feel better when we've been hiding in a closet, and one day, it's opened, and you're breathing is easier." I told him, "You've been in hiding for a long time."

I turned away and was met by the others waiting outside. "Come with me, I told them."

I sat down at my desk, began putting on my mask and makeup, and began telling them of my plans.

"When we land, they'll be a limo waiting to take you to the hotel," I said while positioning my voice box. "Your morning will be breakfast, a trip to the spa, and then the beach." "A nice stroll will do you good." "Your afternoon will be aboard a yacht, and when you return, dinner will be at Tony's; it's a five-star restaurant that Jack discovered." "There are some things he is good at," I said, putting on my wig.

I then began applying my makeup as they watched.

When I finished, I told Jose to sit where I sat, and I began applying his beard and mustache and his gray wig. After I colored his eyebrows, I lightened his olive skin somewhat and handed him a pair of sunglasses. "These will keep others from getting a good look at you." I told him, "Jose, you may meet people along the way that you may know; the sunglasses will shield wandering eyes." "None of them are friends, they learn to kill, and they get paid for it, at one time they were called mercenaries, now they prefer to be called security guards, and they'll kill you whether they know you are not, so remember, you don't have any friends, anywhere." "You said four men worked for McNally; only two of them were present with him. I have to know if the other men were involved in this too." "That's why you have to become Dan Gomez, in voice, and in person." I placed a voice box against the bottom of his beard.

"All it does is highlight the accent to represent Spanish in your Spanish ancestry and distorts your voice to a raspier voice." "Now get up; I've got more to do," I told him.

When he got up, I signed for Maria to sit down, and I began applying her makeup.

"Maria, you're heavy on red lipstick," I said as her laptop was signing in animation. "Red looks good on you, but not that much red, we'll tone it down about seven shades lighter and Maria, no more lipstick, you look better with gloss, and you need to leave your facial skin alone; you're too heavy on the blush, and I don't think it does you justice." "You want your best features displayed and not distracted by what you think is your worst." After I finished with her, I told her to listen to what I had to say; this is important. I told her. "The time has come to where Jose is not Jose." "He is now Dan Gomez, and you are his bride, Maria Gomez." "If you and he have differences, then keep them here, in the plane, or in the lab, but when together, you two are newlyweds and are enjoying a honeymoon." I then signed for her to get up because I had others that required my attention. When she did, I told Ellen to sit, and then Jane was the last.

When I finished with Jane, she stood up and gave me a smile, and then motioned with her head for me to look at Maria. She was standing in front of a mirror, looking at herself with Jose standing close to her.

"Jane, she might need a little help in choosing the clothes that look good on her," I told her. "Fashion isn't one of her best attributes."

"Don't worry." She said. "I think you've accomplished in what you set out to do." "She's not fighting him anymore, and as far as clothes are concerned, you leave that up to my mom and me." "What about you?" She asked.

"Alvarone is staying at a hotel next door to where you'll be staying." "So I'll be signing in as McNally, and I have to switch the medicine bottles before breakfast."

"How are you going to do that?" She asked.

"I'll be a waiter." "I deliver a knockout drug in his coffee." "Three minutes later, I'm out his door, and his coffee is still hot." "He'll think he dozed off, and then I'll switch his coffee and let him eat his breakfast and take his shot." "I'll be waiting for him outside the hotel on the beach." "I'll be the last person he'll ever see again." "But I need confirmation." "Do me a favor." I asked her, "I want you to have fun today; you're building memories that will last a lifetime." "Most people don't get to see what you'll see." "Life is too short; it's reserved for the living."

Jack came over the speaker that we had roughly thirty minutes.

Ellen went and took her seat in the co-pilot's seat next to Jack. I saw Jack's hand reach over and hold Ellen's. Jane saw it too and immediately shifted her thoughts on me verbally.

"Are you some kind of cupid that hides behind a human's body?" She said, toying with me.

"No, but I can visualize what a person thinks about another person." I told her, "Like you." "If I wanted to know what you really thought of something, I would make you mad enough to where you would tell me everything you want to get off of your chest." "I would hear everything about how you really felt about me." "I don't see anyone with anger on their face, I see everyone here with desire, and that includes you," I told her.

"Is this the kind of work my father, has done?" She asked.

"He was used as a distraction only; your father can't defend himself; he's a diplomat, not a fighter." "I don't want him killed, so I'm replacing him." "When we had our talk, he knew that I wasn't pushing him aside." I stated to her, "I think he got that impression when I brought Jose in." "To be honest, I think he was ready to retire."

"Smith, I can't kiss you; that face bothers me." She said, laughing.

Jack came over the loudspeaker that we were on our descent to approach the runway.

Maria closed her eyes, and Jose pulled her close to him. She accepted him by putting her arms around him.

"I told you." "Jane said." "You're cupid." "This is it, huh?" "I'll see you again when we leave." She said sadly.

"Oh! I don't know," "a person like me shows up here and there, and then gone again." "Jane have a good time; you're building memories," I said right before we landed. As they departed, I handed them special envoy papers. I watched as they went through customs without interference. A man wearing a hat held their names high in the air, and I watched as they entered the limo and waited to see if anyone was following them before I departed the craft. When I exited, I signaled the doors to seal. I showed my papers and was given the special treatment that I ordered. When I ordered for my plane to be refueled, I signed for the payment using McNally's name.

I caught a taxi and was soon opening the doors to the hotel and entering my room. I quickly undressed and began putting on my uniform. When my computer warned me that an order had been placed from Alvarone's room, I was waiting at the door, listening for the elevator door to open. Moments later, I eased open my door and saw an empty hallway, and without hesitation, I gave the waiter a knockout drug with my ring and hurriedly took him into my room. A rough-looking individual opened the door that I knocked on and stared back at me.

"Your breakfast, sir. Would you like for me to set it up, or would you prefer your privacy?" I asked him.

"No, bring it in." He said, and when I entered, I noticed that he looked both ways down the hall before he shut the door. I put his coffee on the dresser next to him and eased the table over to where he could sit on the side of the bed and eat his food.

He took a sip of his coffee as I was removing the lids on his plates and waited until he fell backward. I switched the vials, pulling out the insulin and refilling it with the adrenaline that was mixed with nitroglycerin. I knew he would finish that one off first. I then poured the coffee into the commode, flushed it, and refilled his cup.

"Will that be all, sir?" I said.

"What?" He said drowsily.

"I said." "Will that be all, sir?" I repeated once again.

"What happened?" He asked.

"I'm sorry, sir, you were talking to me, and then you fell back asleep." "I can come back later if you wish, sir," I said.

"No," "I must have, never mind, that'll be all." He told me.

"Yes, sir," I replied as I left.

I went back into my room, got undressed, and woke the waiter from his drug-induced sleep.

"You all right," I said to him.

"What happened?" He asked.

"I was coming out of my room, and I looked over and saw you coming out of that room, over there." I pointed it out to him. "Man, you were stumbling, and you looked like you were out of it." "Have you had a tooth pulled or something? You look pale; that's a sign of anemia, you know?" "Because man, you passed out, you went plop right where you were standing." "Maybe you're not getting enough red meat, or maybe you could have low blood sugar." "I'd have that checked out if I were you."

I helped him to his feet, and he walked away, pushing his cart and scratching his head.

I turned around and went back into my room, and reappeared as McNally. I exited the elevator and told the desk attendant to tell Mister Alvarone when he came down that McNally was on the patio, enjoying the view of the beach.

A few minutes later, he was being helped by his sons to sit down.

"Big Al, you seem to be breathing a little heavy today." I told him, "You don't look so good."

"Yeah, and from what I heard, you're not supposed to be breathing at all." He said sarcastically.

"Big Al, I've been asking myself why the Benitez family would tip me off." I told him, "That makes me wonder if someone wants me out of their way or if someone wants to expand his operations." "Al, I'm not a very happy man today, I lost four cases of stocks and bonds, not to mention the drugs, and then I find out that I shouldn't go to the warehouse. I want you to know that I'm going to get to the bottom of this." "Big Al, Miguel, and Carlos are dead, not to mention some of my best agents, but you could have known that information Friday." I said to him, "That makes me think, who will benefit the most with me out of the way?" "I'd keep my eyes open if I were you," I told him as I got up to leave.

"Mac, you talking to me like you're thinking I would sell you out?" He rebuked.

"Al, right now, I don't know what to think. All I know is that the Benitez family tipped me off, and someone cost me a lot of money and a lot of drugs?" "Right now, I don't know who to trust, especially the people I work with," I said and then turned to leave when his sons stepped in front of me. "Big Al, maybe you should give your sons here a lesson in how to live. It seems that their testosterone level is raging." "Maybe you should tell them that I have marksmen waiting to shoot anyone that so much as lays a hand on me, and right now they're in their sights, and your sons are pushing my envelope."

"Let him go." He ordered his sons.

"Boys, your father doesn't look so good." "Has he had his shot?" "He looks a little pale."

When I got to the doorway that entered the hotel, I turned and watched him as he began walking and then stopped; when he fell backward, I could see blood soaking into the sand.

I went back into my room and got dressed to go and greet Al at the Morgue. I signed for his delivery and signed for his cremation by his oldest son. After flipping the ignition on the gas, I began my work as a janitor. Two men came in and requested his body; they were his sons.

"Who's in charge here," the youngest said.

"Janitor," I said smiling, "janitor." "I'm a good janitor." "The doctor said I was a good janitor." "He said a good janitor keeps everything clean, and he said I'm a good janitor."

"Where's the person in charge," he asked again?

"I'm a good janitor," "I keep the floors mopped, and the walls wiped; the doctor said I was a good janitor." I started mopping the area where they walked in and around them. "I'm a good janitor." "I keep the floors clean."

"Get away from me, moron." He said, pushing me back and leaving. I went into the office where the attendant was and gave him a shot to revive him and quickly exited out the back door.

I inserted my card into the lock of the door and opened it entering Jane's room, and when I did, I saw clothes strewn all over the bed. After I finished, I slid my makeup kit under the bed and left.

I walked my way along the pier, worked my way up and into the boat, and waited. They arrived pretty much to the schedule that I gave them.

Jack shouted, "Ahoy, Captain." I looked down and told them, "Permission to come aboard."

I let loose the moorings, climbed up to the cabin, and eased the yacht out into the channel. I was visited by Jack and the rest of the group.

He knocked on the cabin door and asked for permission to enter.

I gave them permission.

"Where are we headed?" Jack asked.

"I was told to take your guests out to let them bathe along the sandy beaches away from the crowds," I told him.

Jane walked over to view the scenery, and then she looked at me.

"Does this boat belong to you?" She asked.

"No, ma'am, I'm the Captain." "Mister Alexander is the owner," I answered.

"Where is he at?" She continued.

"He's in New York, ma'am," I told her.

"Who told you to take us out?" She asked.

"I only obey my orders, ma'am." "I don't question Mister Alexander."

I saw that she was upset.

"Ma'am, you should relax and enjoy the view; it's a rare sight to see." I told her, "You're building memories today, and not many people get a chance to see it." I said.

"What did you just say?" She asked me.

"I said you should learn to relax; you're building memories." "You seem tense," I told her.

She looked confused, and Jack intervened. "Jane, it's Smith." He said.

She bent down and looked at me harder. "I wish you wouldn't lead me along like that." She said, and then she wrapped her arms around me and squeezed me tight.

"I didn't think we'd be together." She said while taking a breath from kissing me.

"My work is finished here." I told her, "Here, take over for a minute." I said.

I pulled off my mask, washed my face, and then returned to the wheel.

I looked at the rest of the group and told Ellen to turn around.

"Funny, ha, ha." She said, "You think you're cute." "My husband saw that thing and asked me to try it on."

"How did he say you looked?" I asked her.

"That's personal." "Smith, that was like waving candy in front of a kid." "Jack wouldn't leave me alone."

Ellen looked around and saw that everyone was listening and didn't have a clue about what she was talking about. Her face became blushed, and she stated. "I was looking at the hologram for clothes, and Smith asked the hologram to display what I looked like in a thong bikini." She said to them, "I blasted him and told the computer to stop." "He sent me a pair of thongs with my other clothes, and Jack wanted to see what I looked like." "Okay, is everybody happy now?" She said, looking around.

"Ellen, the truth is I think you wanted to see what you looked like in it too, or you would have never tried them on," I said, giving her a smile. "Ellen, I know you looked in the mirror. I think it was to see how much you've changed," I told her.

"You're a mean man; you know that?" She said, smiling.

"Momma, I think Smith is trying to tell you something?" Jane commented. Jane looked at me. "Smith, are you?"

My mind shifted, and Jane's question caused me to focus back on the topic that we were conversing about.

"I find that everyone looks at themselves in the mirror, and they see their faults." I said to her, "I find time is wasted on trying to find the blame; I find that time is better spent on working to be the person you're pleased with." "Me; I don't look in the mirror and see a life of glamour, I can't socialize very well, and because of that, I find it difficult to apologize for the truth." "I can't tell you what I looked like when I was younger; I'm face blind, and I can't see my face," I said.

"You're kidding?" Ellen commented.

"No, ma'am." I said, "I can't see myself in the mirror." I reiterated, "I know it's psychological." I told her, "I can see you and everyone else, but there's a block that I can't see through; it's fuzzy to me."

"But, I don't think I understand?" Ellen stated.

"Ellen, let's take a rest on the deck and enjoy the sun," Jack said. "Maybe we can have a little talk."

"I think I'll join you," Jose quickly commented, and when he turned to follow them, Maria clapped her hands together to get his attention and began signing to him. The laptop was in audible, and it stated. "Smith said we were newlyweds; he told us to act like newlyweds. Is this how you treat your wife; you just walk away?"

He looked over at me and then at Jane, and then he took Maria's hand and led her away. Jane and I watched as Jose sat down in a lounge chair. Maria gave him a slap on his hand and ordered for him to pick one up and sit it close to his, and then she sat down and held his hand. He looked over at her, and her smile took on a different look than when she had first met him.

"I don't care; I still think you set them up." Jane said, "Look at them, their laughing and oblivious to their surroundings." She stopped talking and put her hand to her mouth. "Oh, there it is, isn't that sweet, their first kiss."

"I think that's beautiful." She looked over at me again and took my arm.

"See that island over there, in the distance?" "That's where we're headed," I told her.

We came to within one hundred feet of the beach, and I let the anchor fall. We all got into the rowboat, and I began rowing our way to shore.

"How deep is it here?" Jane asked.

I looked over the side. "It's about ten feet," I told her.

"It looks so clear." She said.

I gave her a mask and told her, "Hit the water."

She was reluctant until Jose asked if I had another one. I handed him one and Maria one also. He went overboard without question and dove to the bottom. The girls watched him from the boat as he swam around, picking up the shells and inspecting them. Then fear was overcome by them both, and overboard they went. I gave Jack the oar's and followed them until we were wading out of the water.

"This place is beautiful," Jane said.

"This isn't the place," I told her. "We're going to a lagoon about a half-mile into the island." We walked a little way, leaving the women wondering how far we had left to go.

"It's right over the hill," I said to give them a renewed inspiration to keep on going.

When we reached the top, everyone was breathing hard, and then they noticed that they were looking down at a small waterfall.

"That's freshwater." I told them, "The sand is white as snow and covers the bottom of the pool." "The water's only six feet deep at its deepest." "It's small in comparison to other rivers, but it's an underground river nonetheless."

"How did you find this place?" Jane asked.

"I was doing some geological test to see if this area was sinking or rising, and I spent three days trying to set up my equipment in the right spot." "That's when I found this place." "I set up my equipment and programmed all of them into my computer." "You can't learn everything from books. Sometimes the book has to be written." I told her.

"What's the prediction?" She asked.

I turned to her and told her, "It's a book that will never be read." "The difference between the Antarctic and the Arctic is that the Arctic is a sea that's surrounded by land and the Antarctic is land that's surrounded by sea." "The Antarctic has thinner ice than the Artic." "If all the ice in the Arctic melts one day, this waterfall will be two hundred feet below the top of the ocean." "This river, although it may be small, has an effect on the existence of this island." "This sand isn't the same sand that's on the beach." "So, where does it originate from, and how does it get here?" "Is it a small branch of a larger underground river? If so, what role does it play to the inhabitants of the island?" "And if it is a small branch, then there may be thousands of these small branches that are seeping into the sea?" "A lot of questions have yet been unanswered."

"Smith, are you okay?" She asked.

"I don't like it when I can't put the pieces together." I told her, "It leaves me with questions that have more questions."

"Smith, you once told me that thoughts come to you when you aren't thinking; so, I don't want you thinking when I'm around you making memories." "Can you do that?" Jane said.

"I got sidetracked again." "I'm sorry," I said apologetically.

"It's all right, I know you, and when you drift off like that, I can't help but wonder what you're thinking too." "Smith, sometimes I get to thinking that life is a riddle to you, and you told me that no one would listen anyway, so the key to life would rust away in a drawer somewhere, and no one would use it."

"Jane, I highly underestimated you." I told her, "You take my words and use them against me."

"I told you once, Smith, and with you, that's all I need to tell you. I listen to what you say." "I may not understand what you said until I think about it for a while, but, regardless, I got you wrapped around my finger." "Now, it's your turn to listen to me." She informed me, "I've always wanted to stand underneath a waterfall and let the water give me a shower." "I don't think I'll ever get this chance again." She said, running towards the water.

I walked and dove into the middle. I scooped some sand from the bottom and was looking at it under the water. I felt a tap on my shoulder and turned to see Jane shaking her finger at me sideways. I let the sand fall to the bottom and swam with her under the waterfall.

She pulled me to her and held me in her arms tightly.

"Smith, I've spent more time with you in the last six weeks than I ever spent with my husband in the four years that we were married."

"I understand," I told her compassionately.

"No, Smith, let me finish. I have to say this; it's been bothering me." She said. "After I found out that he was doing coke, we didn't do too much together, we were married, but he seemed to stay gone a lot."

"He never stopped doing it," I told her.

"That's what I'm talking about." She said, "The difference between you and him is like night and day." "You're there for me when I need you, and he never was." "You work, but you spend the time that you're with me, being with me." "I have to fight myself from running over and grabbing you and showing you all my affections." "I never felt that way with my husband." "The odd thing about all of this is my husband brought me to you."

She bent down and kissed me as the water fell onto her head. When she stopped, she looked at me in the eyes and said, "I'll never forget this day," and then she kissed me again, and we then went and laid down on the sand along the shoreline of the pool to capture the rays of the sun. She leaned over, put her hand to her head, and rested her elbow on the sand. "You know I never saw my mother in a bathing suit until she met you." "Now, she's out here with the rest of us, and she's having the best time of her life." "Look at her over there acting like a kid in the pool with my father." She said and then looked back at me. "You do know we'll never live alone, don't you?"

"Jane, that's for a purpose." I told her, "When I'm gone, you can't live alone, and it'll be just as hard on your mother; your father will be a part of my operations in one way or another." "He's doing what he believes in, and for that reason alone, his loyalty to me is like your mother, and Maria, and Jose." "You, you're a different person." "You have another reason for being with me, and it would be devastating to me if you weren't," I said.

"Smith, when you told my mother you're face blind, what did you mean?" She asked.

"It's psychological." I told her, "People that are face blind can only see outstanding features of a face." "It may be your lips or your eyes, or the nose, or whatever, but that's all they see, just those outstanding features." "They can't see the whole face." "I don't want to see myself in the mirror." "I read books after books after books, and not one of them ever refer to being face blind to only yourself, so that means it's got to be psychological." "I guess the key to my problem was what I just said." "I don't want to see myself."

"What about a picture?" She asked.

"When you asked the hologram to talk to the image of me, what did you see?" I asked her.

"You know my mother was right; you are scary." She said, "I saw a body, but there wasn't a face, just a cloud." "When I asked to see your face, the computer told me that I was asking an invalid question." "Smith, when I woke up in your bedroll and saw you, you were everything that I imagined when I came to my senses and found out what happened." "You fit the part." She said, "When I found myself in your lab, I was even more scared than when we first met." "But, you had James give you a haircut and a shave." "That's when I saw what you looked like for the first time." "I looked at you for a long time after that, and every time we passed or talked, I couldn't take my eyes off of you." "It was like meeting someone you loved but didn't recognize." "Smith, I thought you were handsome even when you had all that hair, but now that you don't, I still find you to be that way." "You are quite a looker, with or without hair and beard." "Smith, I love you both, you were a good man when I met you, and you're a good man now."

"But when you put on your mask, and you put on makeup, you change from the man I know and become a different person." She went on.

"Those people that I become aren't me." I told her, "When I lived at my stone house, I was always covered from head to toe." "My hair was long, and my beard was unshapely and shaggy." "When I came for my supplies, I'd stay and tinker, and then I would leave again." "But when I was out in public, I was a vagabond, and I didn't have any problem avoiding people. It was them that avoided me."

"So you hide the real Smith then?" She concluded.

"The real Smith is dead; he died at the age of ten." I told her, "I never had any interactions with my mother, I was my brother's brother, and I took care of him because I loved him." "I was all he had, and I didn't expect my father to do what he done; I guess for a long time, I blamed myself for his death." "So I killed Smith for not expecting the unexpected," I told her with tears in my eyes.

"Calm down, calm down," she tried to console me, "I'm with you, and I'll always be with you." "Smith, it's hard on someone to lose someone they love. It's even harder to lose someone you love when you're young." "What if I was to lose you?" She asked, "My life would be over too." "I would be just as you were, lost, confused, and angry." "I don't want to see what you went through. I can see what it's done to you." "Smith, I missed my grandparents for a long time." "We all had good times sitting around the table, and my grandmother always told my grandfather to hush; nobody cares what an old coot thinks." "She did it to make him mad; it was her way of picking on him." "I miss them both, and I know you miss your mother and brother too." "But, you once told me that all things must die." She said, "Smith, you protected Jose from being killed; you do have feelings even if you don't think so." "Do you see Jose as a brother?" She asked.

"No, I see Jose as a person willing to risk his life to protect people he doesn't even know, and the problem I see with him is common sense is ignored when engaged in a situation; he's a bear that rushes into battle, and a bullet that's fired doesn't have to hit the target it was aimed at." "His weakness is the person that he is, he was brainwashed and reprogrammed to carry out all orders, and he was a puppet being controlled by the puppeteer." "I took him out because; I see a lot of me in him when I was a boy." "But, I can't make him learn the art of survival unless he's willing to learn." "He thinks he's ready, but I have to show him he's not." "He'll be a different man for it if he lives through it." "Jose has street smarts, so he knows how to recognize and deal with trouble; that's one thing that gives him an advantage over others."

"So, that's where Maria comes in, huh?" She said.

"Maria was an only child; she doesn't even have a third-grade education." "She's had a lot of different jobs in her life to survive, and she's never had a chance to live." "I want Jose to teach Maria how to live, and I want Maria to teach Jose how to live." "Two halves make a whole," I said to her.

"So you did set them up?" Jane commented.

"No, I introduced two people together; the rest is up to them."

"You mean, like us?" Jane commented once again.

"No, it was all you when we met." I told her, "I didn't want you involved with what I do; I thought you would find me to be despicable and repugnant." "Somewhere along the line, I began to have feelings for you." "I never quite understood those feelings because I had never had them before." "I felt the sickness when you first kissed me; I didn't know how to kiss," I told her.

"I remember that." She said, "You've made some big improvements since then, and Smith, I have a confession to make, you've got a lot more training to do before you become the kisser, I want you to be, and the training begins; now." She said as she leaned over and kissed me again.

When she leaned back on her hand, she looked at Maria and Jose. "Look, they're kissing again," "Smith, that's not a pretend kiss she's giving him."

I watched as Maria sat up and hit Jose in his stomach with her fist and pointed her finger to her mouth. Jane smiled.

"See, she's telling him that he's not putting any effort into the kiss; that's the same thing I told you when I first kissed you," Jane said.

The rest of the day was spent swimming and lying on the beach. The evening was upon us, and I told everyone that they had reservations at the restaurant at eight. We needed to get back.

I lifted the rowboat and secured it to the rails and then hoisted anchor and departed. We approached the harbor, and I slowed down. I saw the harbor marine division patrolling the area and went another direction and unloaded my guests on the shore.

"Walk up the hill and catch a taxi to the hotel." "Enjoy the food, and have a good time," I stated.

"What about you?" Jane asked.

I looked over at the harbor police as they approached us with their lights and sirens on. I turned and smiled at them. "Go, you don't want to be caught here," I told them.

I backed away and then gave the boat full throttle. I secured the wheel and went overboard.

I walked into the restaurant that night, sat down at the piano, and began playing.

Several people came up and put five's and tens into the tip jar and asked if I knew a song that they wanted played. Several were on their honeymoon, and some wanted to hear the song that they remembered from a time ago.

Jane walked up and put a penny in the jar.

"Is that for my thoughts are or you unhappy with my performance?" I asked her.

"I'm looking for somebody." She said, "My friend says you have crying eyes, and she says she's only seen those eyes on one man before."

"Then you should beware." "A man with crying eyes always has loneliness for his companion."

"Not this man." She said, "He's a character."

"And you want to find this man?" I said while putting feeling into the music.

"He's not that kind of character." She responded, "A person doesn't recognize the characters that make up the scenery in a movie." "They go about their performance while the main focus is on the main actors and actresses."

A lady interrupted us and put a large bill into the jar, and asked for her favorite song. I nodded my head once and told her her wish was granted.

After she left, I finished the music I was playing and began playing hers with a great feel of emotion.

"This character you're looking for, what does he look like? Maybe I've seen him in here?" I asked her.

"I don't know. I look around at everyone and wonder if that's him, or if that's him, see, he's a mystery, so I don't know him." She said.

"Ah, so you don't know what he looks like then?" I said.

"That's not what I meant." She replied.

"The lady that came up here and requested a song, did you see where she came from and where she sat?" I asked.

She looked up and said yes, I see her.

"She's crying, isn't she?"

"How do you know?" She asked.

"Her eyes were red when she put the money in the jar, so she must have a fond memory of this song." "Judging by her reaction, I'd say someone died and that someone was someone she loved." "Did you notice her age?" I said.

"Yeah," she replied.

"The song she requested was from the sixties, and a lot of people lost their lives back then in a Police Action." "I would guess that maybe the song reminds her of him." "The goal of a musician is to play his music and bring the pain out of the body and into the open; you have to reach the heart." "Crying is the only vent we have to unleash our pain." "We hurt." I told her, "She looks for the person she loves too." "Only, he's gone, and she'll never meet him again."

"Do you play here, every night?" She asked.

"No, tonight's a special night," I told her.

"How long did it take you to learn to play like that?" She asked.

"Three weeks," I told her.

"Smith, is that you?" She said.

I looked at her. "Tell Maria to come to sit down at the piano," I told her.

She walked over and began speaking to her, and soon they were both next to me.

"Maria, I knew a girl that was deaf, mute, and blind." "She was wild in her ways until she met a special lady." "She was knowledgeable in dealing with special cases, but nothing is as easy as it seems." "She was a teacher and her patience one day began to pay off; the girl she was teaching was learning what everything was by signing." "The teacher put a name to everything the girl touched, and that opened a door for the girl." "She learned by feeling, and she learned how to sign by touch."

"Beethoven was a musician, but he had a problem, he was tone-deaf, he couldn't tell the difference from a G flat to an A minor, all notes sounded the same to him, yet he wrote symphonies that are still being performed today, he did it by feeling also." "Put your hands on the piano and feel the music," I told her.

After, she closed her eyes and began to move to the feelings she received.

I looked at Jane. "I'll have to be a little more careful." I told her, smiling, "I'll be joining you later." "I have something that I need to take care of first," I told her.

"Is something wrong?" She asked.

"It's a minor thing," I said, "but someone's taking pictures of all of you at the table." "I believe your father has caught the interest of some agents." "I don't want those pictures dispersed to others." "When you and Maria leave, walk away and don't look back, and Jane, did you receive your money's worth?"

"Smith, you stole that boat, didn't you?"

"No, my interpretation of stealing is to keep or sell what was taken. I tend to lean a little towards borrowing; you saw that I was bringing it back," I said.

"It doesn't matter, she whispered to me; you stole that boat."

"Are you mad at me?" I whispered back.

She gave out a sigh.

"Don't say anything to your father or Jose about the pictures; they might give suspicion to warn whoever's doing it."

"How do you know?" She asked.

"Your waiter waits on the same men that are sitting next to you." "He works for me, and later on, their drinks will be drugged, and tomorrow they will wake to a different day," I said to her.

"Is he an android?" She asked.

"Yeah"

"I wish I could put my arms around you and give you a kiss." She said.

"Now, that would be the best tip any man could ever receive." I told her, "The last time you told me you would give me a penny for my thoughts was back at my stone house; you never gave me that penny." I said, smiling.

"You have a way with words; you know that?" She remarked.

She pulled Maria away, and both of them walked to where their table was. I played one more song and then left.

When I came back a short time later, I was dressed and caught Jane's attention right away. I walked by her, stopped, and backed up to see her face. "How tall are you?" I asked her.

"What kind of question is that?" She stated as everyone there listened in.

"I was just curious; most women say that they're two or three inches smaller than what they really are," I told her.

She had an odd look to her.

"How tall are you?" She asked.

"Why you ask?"

"Because I was told that men say that they're taller than what they really are." She responded.

"I'm seven foot three," I told her. She stood up next to me and saw that she was the same size as me.

"Would you care to dance?" I asked her, "I'm a little clumsy when it comes to dancing and holding someone as beautiful as you, but I promise you; I'll do my best."

"Please tell me your name is Smith." She said.

"If that's the man you wish for, then yes, my name is Smith," I told her.

"What's your first name? She asked.

"I don't have one; my name is Smith, that's all, just Smith."

When I took her in my arms, she had a confused look to her. "Something's not right." She said. "I stood toe to toe with you, and we were looking at each other eye to eye; now you're taller."

"I read where women like to dance with men that's taller than them." "You know you should really learn how to relax; not many people get to come here; you're building memories," I said as we slowed danced for several dances.

"You really do become the character you portray." She said while we danced, "And Smith, this is one of the best days of my life." "What are you going to do when someone walks by me and says something that makes me feel like I'm talking to you and I won't know who I'm talking to?" "I'll be thinking that I'm talking to you when I may be talking to a total stranger?"

We were interrupted by the waiter delivering food to the table.

Jane looked at me.

"I took the liberty of ordering everything on the menu." "That way, everyone could try a sample of what they had to offer," I told her.

"Do you mind if I join you and you're guests?" I asked her.

When I sat down, Maria stared at me, as well as Jose.

I smiled at both of them. "Do you like lobsters?" I asked him.

"Yes, sir." He said.

"How many can you eat?" I said.

"Sir, one is enough for me." He said.

"Well, my friend here likes lobsters too, only he likes to eat until he can't eat another bite." I can personally vouch to you that there won't be any left." I told him.

"Bring us six plates, James," I said. That's when Jose and Maria stopped doing what they were doing and then looked at me. "I told Jane earlier that I took the liberty of ordering everything on the menu; you feel like taking a bite of this or that, don't be shy, or it may be gone by the time you want to take a bite." "I don't think we'll have that worry, though; they serve large portions here." "I want all of you to remember; you're here to have fun." "A little sun, a nice dinner, and laughter make you forget the past."

A few minutes had gone by when a man dressed in a suit came walking over.

"Good evening." He said to everyone. "I understand you've asked to try out everything on the menu."

"Yes, sir." I told him, "Food attracts travelers that come here, and we get to taste different foods from different countries and different restaurants."

"That's a lot of food." He said, "May I ask what you do, sir?"

I gave him a smile. "I'm sorry, but that's privileged information; if I was to tell you, my guest and I would receive preferential treatment." "That's not the way we like to do things." "We want to eat the same foods as everyone else does." I said as I smiled at him, "That way when we write our articles, we can write with an honest and unbiased opinion."

He bowed and told us to enjoy our meal and then left.

"What was that all about?" Ellen asked.

Jack responded to her, "Smith has whetted the curiosity of the number one person in this restaurant, and he's going back in the kitchen and informing all of the chefs that are preparing our food that he wants special treatment, he thinks; we're VIP's." "Ellen, I hope you're ready to eat because when you leave tonight, you'll be miserable," Jack said.

We weren't through with the first meals when the next arrived. We did the same to them as we had done with the first ones. We were less than halfway through when they brought another item on the menu, and we did the same as we had done before. Our plates were starting to take the shape of a twelve-course meal.

The waiter came out with the lobsters, and Jack sliced a large piece and dipped it in butter, and shoved it in his mouth. He began smiling with his eyes closed and chewing slowly. He took a napkin, wiped his mouth, and stated, "You don't know how long it's been since I've had lobster-like that, I'm in heaven." He said.

I watched as the last man at the table that James had drugged their drinks leaned backward and were out. I got up and quickly walked over to them and rifled through their clothes. The people around me watched me suspiciously. I pulled out my wallet and waved it high in the air for all to see my badge.

"I apologize for my behavior." "We've been alerted by the authorities of possible criminal conspiracy." "Please continue to enjoy yourself." "I have everything under control," I said.

I walked back and handed their papers and their wallets to Jack while I ate. "KGB." He said.

"I think they spotted you and got a little curious." I said to him, "I took their cameras and put them in my pocket to download on my computer as Jane watched me.

I whispered to her that they might have other pictures of value in them. When downloaded, they give me the purpose of them being here. I explained.

"What are we going to do with them?" She asked

"Nothing, they won't remember what hotel they're staying at." "They don't have any money, or visas, or passports; it's going to take them a while before they sort anything out." "Jane, have you ever had a brain freeze from eating something cold too fast?" "That's what they'll be experiencing in the morning, a mental brain freeze; only it's going to last for a long time."

After we finished talking, the waiter brought out more food, and everyone began looking around at each other.

"Come on; you're not through yet; the night is young," Jack said.

We acted as if nothing occurred and continued on in our dinner.

The waiter came over and asked if he could refill our water.

"Yes, please." I told him, "How many more items are left on the menu?"

"Twelve, sir." He replied.

"Start bringing out dessert and package the rest of the food in boxes to take with us." "I'm not pleased with the company I'm around," I said.

"Yes, sir." He said.

The manager came out walking fast and asked me if we were given any trouble.

"We've encountered these men before." I told him, "They tried to poison us in Spain, and because of that, they wrote bad reviews on the restaurant and used us as their examples." "The problem you have is that they never intended on paying for their food." "They know who we are, but they didn't think we knew them." "Their plan was to create a commotion, and during that commotion, they were going to split; we had that same problem in the past with them, that's when we found out we were poisoned." "Go ahead, check them out." "They don't have any money or any form of identification on them; they came here to make a scene." "They work for the tabloids, and they make their money off of telling lies." "This isn't anything unusual with us." "The competition always wants to get a leg up and make it to the top at all costs." "Call the police and tell them that they drank too much and passed out." "Leave us out of this; tell the police nothing other than what I said." "They drank too much and passed out." "We write about the taste of the food, we don't want to lower the standards of our articles to the level of reporting the name of restaurants that we ran into trouble at, so we only write about the food we ate." "What did you serve them anyway?" I asked the waiter.

"Vodka, straight vodka," he said.

"How many did they have to drink?" I asked.

"Three each," he answered.

I put my hand to my chin.

"Is something wrong, sir?" The manager asked.

"Have you ever had vodka?" I asked him.

"I tried it, but I don't drink it." He stated.

"These men were raised on Vodka; three glasses wouldn't affect them at all."

"I'm going to let you in on a little matter that the people at this table already know." "Those men are only a part of four international cuisine magazines that follow us around." "They print what we dined on and where we dined at." "Their goal is to put out their articles on dining where we dined at first, and when our magazine comes out with the same foods as theirs, needless to say, they try to embarrass us." "We have one team over there, at that table, and as you can see, they're out cold." "That tells me that someone's here watching us now, and if I was to guess, it appears that they wanted them out of the way and that someone must have drugged their drinks." "We're dealing with cuisine piracy here, punishable by international law." I told him, "As you can see, they'll go to any extremes necessary." "I need you to act as you normally do," I told the manager. "And try not to let anyone know what we know." "We're being watched as we speak." "I've got men outside waiting to follow anyone that comes out after we do." "Now, smile, and please start bringing out our desserts, as if nothing happened." "I don't want them to think that I know they're here."

"Yes, sir." He answered.

The manager reached his hand out to shake mine. "It seems that I owe you a debt of gratitude." He said.

"No sir, it's people like those over there that give bad names wherever they go." "I'll file a police report, and we'll mention the tactics that they use, and we've got our proof, the magazine will be charged with pirating, and those men there will lose their jobs."

He turned and left.

After he was out of earshot, Jane commented, "You ought to be ashamed of yourself." "You had that man believing everything you said."

"It gives us a little more time to be together, and besides, everyone needs a little adventure and excitement in their lives," I told her.

"But come on, waving a badge and telling everyone that you're the international cuisine police, that's a little bit too much, isn't it?" She whispered as she leaned over to speak.

"Take a look around; does anyone act as if something wrong has happened?" I whispered back.

She slowly surveyed her surroundings. "No," she said.

I looked at the rest of them. "People believe what they're told," I said, looking at Ellen.

"Does anyone have anything on their mind that they want to add?" I said. Maria was slow to answer.

"I was looking at the menu, and these prices that they charge are more than I made in a week." She spoke.

"Maria, have you forgotten about your bank account." I said to her, "You've made your parents very happy."

I gave her a smile. "Jack, hand me those wallets I gave you."

I took a credit card out of each wallet and gave the wallets back to Jack. I put the credit cards in my shirt pocket as the first of our desserts were getting ready to be served.

On the second serving, the police arrived and began trying to wake the men at the table; they were unresponsive, and then they looked for identification; they didn't find anything and escorted them out by carrying them.

Our waiter came by and asked if he could get us anything?

"I think we've had more than our fill." I told him, "Tell the manager I'd like to see him."

When he came walking over at a brisk pace. I handed him the credit cards and told him we enjoyed our meal beyond belief. "You'll receive a commendation at the top of our list on the restaurants that are a must-see restaurant." "I apologize for what happened earlier, but in our line of work, we meet the bad along with the good."

"I'm sorry, sir." "I can't take your money." He said.

"I insist," I told him. "If I take gratuity from a restaurant and write my reviews, then people like those you met earlier would find out and have a field day, at our and your expense."

"Yes, sir, I can see a problem there." He said.

"I want ten thousand dollars divided up and given to all the chefs that cooked for us, we thoroughly enjoyed ourselves, and I can't say that about every place we've been to." I expressed, "I personally would like for you to receive ten thousand for your intervention in seeing to it that we were able to dine without publicity." "I'm sure someone had a hand in meeting those obligations, and I believe I'm talking to him now." "Sir, don't worry, the money is charged off to the magazine," I said to him.

"Sir"

"I insist," I told him.

"Yes, sir." He bowed and left.

"You just spent what?" "Twenty thousand dollars and that's not including the food," Jane commented as Maria watched us.

The manager walked back and handed me the cards and the checks to sign. I scribbled the check, and he handed me back my cards and left. After he departed, I looked back at Jane and all the others that listened to my response.

"No, those agents spent twenty thousand; I didn't spend a penny," I told her.

There were six boxes filled with more boxes at the counter waiting on us. Jane grabbed one, Jose grabbed one, and Maria and Ellen grabbed one. That left Jack and me carrying the others.

When we grew nearer the door, I stopped and gave my surroundings a full view before I proceeded. We caught a taxi back to our hotel, and the women inspected and tasted foods out of each box of its contents, and several times Jack, Jose and I, heard moaning coming from the women.

I put my laptop in my lap and began commanding my master computer to access the restaurant's surveillance cameras. Jack and Jose watched as I erased all of us and the men from the film and replaced the people with other people from the nights before.

I started to work on the hotel's surveillance when Jane came over with a fork full of cake, and without any word, she stuck it up and into my mouth.

"Can you make me this?" She asked.

I smacked my lips. "They over whipped the topping; too much air was incorporated in it." "But, that could be from the trip in the taxi here." I told her, "Yes, I can make you that cake or any other cake you have a taste for."

Jack and Jose were attacked and were being force-fed desserts. The women kept coming back with different spoonfuls of this and that, and we were caught in taste this or be treated like a baby and have the spoon shoved in our mouths. That made my work difficult, so I set my laptop aside for the time being; the women needed their attention.

"I told you that Jack knew how to pick out restaurants," I said to Ellen as she took a bite of dessert.

Jane stopped eating and watched as Maria knelt down and gave Jose a kiss. Her eyes immediately took on a red glow to them, and she walked over and put the dessert into my mouth.

"Smith," Jane reached her hand out to me, "Take that stuff off of your face; I feel uneasy looking at you dressed that way."

I got up from our bed and went into the bathroom to take off my mask. Jane helped me in every way that she could. I didn't know that she wanted to practice her rule.

She stretched out her blouse and wiped her clothes free of residue from my makeup. We walked out to a chorus of that looks better. They all said as I unattached the extension from around my waist that made it easier for me to walk normally with my lifts in my feet and thighs. I had everyone's attention.

"Jane, what stands out the most to you on this trip?" I asked her.

"You stole a boat; we could have been thrown in jail." She said.

"Ellen, what stands out the most to you?" I asked her.

"I haven't ever seen a man do what you did tonight." "Not only was our food free, but those men paid for it." "I'll remember that for the rest of my life."

"Maria, do you have anything that stands out the most?" She began crying and signing. "I dreamed my dreams like all little girls dreamed." "Tonight, my dreams were real, and I'm scared." She said. Jose pulled her into his lap and held her like a child. That only made Jane's and Ellen's eyes more saddened.

"Jack," I smiled, "did you get your fill of lobsters?"

"Son, I gained twenty pounds since you've been back." "Something's got to give." He said.

"You can always buy a bigger belt," I told him.

"Jose, you don't have to tell me anything that I don't already know." "It hurts to have someone in your lap crying and not be able to help or know what to do." "There's only one way through to her, and that's for you to learn to sign." "But, that's up to you; you can't keep using the laptop or the hologram," I told him. "She only needs that when she wants to talk to someone that can't sign." "She needs a friend," I said to him.

"What about you?" Ellen asked.

I put my hands to my lips, stroked them, and gave my thought a few moments. I then looked at her.

"In the past, I didn't concern myself with self-satisfaction; I found it to be unnecessary. I guess it was because of my lack of feelings." I said, "I didn't take the time to stop and smell the flowers; there were other things that were on my mind, and I never gave it any thought until you asked that question." "So my answer is I look at all of you and see through your eyes that you had a good time, and that makes me feel good seeing you feeling good. I like it when I see people happy." "I chose not to mix business with pleasure." "But I can't make that claim anymore." "Jane changed that; she's dominant in her ways." "But, I can see that all of you women have dominated ways to deal with problems, and I can see that you don't have any problems when dealing with your problem; that's confusing to me." "You women are wicked; you play with us as a cat plays with a mouse," I said to them, smiling.

"Oh! And what about you?" Ellen said, "I never heard such a crock as I heard from you tonight in all of my life."

"Ellen, Jack interrupted, that wasn't Smith you heard tonight." "First off, Smith never goes out in public, and secondly, Smith is the person you saw, except he wasn't Smith."

She looked at him strangely. "I'll have this conversation with you later, now's not the time or the place; it's a private matter." He said.

"We'll be leaving at five in the morning." I told them, "Everyone is ready thirty minutes prior to takeoff." "That means a three A.M. wake up." "Dress comfortable for departure, and then you can change later into something that's comfortable for the flight; it's going to be a long one." "Jack, you'll have to refuel for the remainder of the trip back." "You have clearance to refuel in flight." "I don't want the plane landing anywhere to give anyone suspicion." "After refueling," "I've given the computer orders to change the aircraft call letters and the destination of the trip." "Now," I said smiling, "I can smell some more desserts that need to be critiqued."

The women got up and began tasting food out of one box and bringing each one of us a taste for ourselves. They went through all the boxes and set aside the food they didn't care for.

Everyone soon departed complaining of overstuffing themselves, leaving Jane and me alone.

"Now, it's just you and me." She said, "She stripped and had me stripped faster than I could do it myself." "I've got you all alone now, and I have you in my arms." She said as we lay down in the bed and covered ourselves up. "This is the most memorable part of the trip I remember." "Smith"

"Yes"

"I can feel that you have strong feelings for me." She said, smiling.

The next morning I was applying makeup when Jane arose from the bed. "What time is it?" She asked.

I looked up at the clock and told her, "It's about two-thirty." I told her.

"You can't sleep?" She asked as she got up and pulled a chair facing me.

"I had dreams, and I woke up," I stated.

"Do you have these dreams often?" She asked.

"I was having them every night until I put you in my sleeping bag, then I didn't have them anymore, until tonight." "Why now, I don't know."

"You're the smart one here." She said, "Do you have any reasoning for them?"

"They're always the same, I wake up quickly, and then I can't sleep." "It's childish, I know, but when something affects you every night, you tend to become prone to all kinds of forms of schizophrenia and phobias." I said to her, "I didn't fight it, I couldn't; I accepted my problem and took advantage of it." "I got a lot of things I wanted to do started or completed." "Depending on what I'm working on." "The computer opened my world, and it allows me to travel anywhere I want to go." "It tells me about the person I study." "Jane, it wasn't simple for me to be with you," I told her.

I stopped applying my adhesive for my wig, looked at her, and stated to her, "I manifested my fears; they were of my own making." "According to some people, dreams are a sign of insecurity." "I find that statement hard to argue with."

"You know what my worst dream was when I was young?" She said, laughing. "I would always be slipping into the water and sinking deeper." "No matter how hard I tried grabbing the bank or screaming my lungs out." "I kept sinking further and further until I went under." "Sometimes, I couldn't go back to sleep either." "I had forgotten about it until now." "I had that dream for a long time, and then a man came and grabbed my hand and pulled me from the depths that I was sinking into." "I looked up and saw his face, and now in all my dreams, I see that man's face, and I wake up wondering where he's at, or what's he's doing." "Now I dream that I'm having a dream while I'm sleeping." "I think we have fears that we see in our dreams, and those fears materialize when we can do the least to fight our fears." "Does that make any sense to you?" She asked, "Smith, sometimes we need someone to talk to when we feel our worst." "That's what I'm here for." She remarked, "If you can't talk to me, you can't talk to anyone, and Smith, who are you going to be this time?"

"I'm going to be a little old man with a cane," I told her.

"We need to work something out." She said. "I can't go around looking and watching everyone wondering if it's you underneath some disguise." "Give me a peace sign or something I can go on."

"It's not quite that easy," I told her as I turned my head to look at her. "Your father is a public figure, and he's known by many." "By now, it's possible that you and your mother are known to others as well." "In a matter of time, Jose will be known, as well as Maria." "Jane, if my cover is blown at any time, you and everyone associated with me would be put at risk." "So my anonymity must be sealed." "I have to be a face in the crowd for a purpose, and that purpose is to protect those I know and love." "Before, it was only for the purpose of not being recognized, but that's changed now." "You asked if I knew the reason for my dreams; those that seek retribution or retaliation have one thing in common." "They'll stop at nothing to get the answers that they want." "My dreams tell me to be careful of being watched." "I'd appreciate it if you wouldn't tell your mother that, though; I don't think she would enjoy herself if she worried about little things; she's happy, and why ruin it." "This way, no one knows where we come from or where we're going to." "My lab is secret, and that's the only place that I can take you and protect you and the others without worry." "If I make it back." I began.

"Smith, you're talking like that again, and you know I don't like it."

"It's time to wake the others." I told her, "You should be getting dressed."

"Not until you change the tone in your voice." She said.

"I'll yield." I told her, "But Jane, you've always known that I can't give promises; you have to know that." "When we come back, maybe things will be better for you."

"That sounds better." She said, "It's going to be hard without you around, though."

"You haven't been listening." I told her, "You can make quilts, you can work out, you can go to the workshops, or you can go for a walk." "Sit still at the lab, and time drags slowly by." "The only way to kill time is to work it to death."

"Now, give Jose and your mother and father a call to wake them up," I told her.

I finished preparing for my departure as everyone met in our room. Their attention was focused on me as I was sitting my makeup kit aside.

"What's the matter, you got no respect for an old man?" "You got to stare." "I may be old, but I can still take all of you young whippersnappers down a peg or two," I said to them all.

I reached down, grabbed my bags, and began to walk out. Jose took them from me.

"Where I come from, old men don't carry anything." He said.

I grabbed a cane that I had picked up in the lobby. "Well, we're all set," I said.

We caught a limo and arrived at the airport; when we entered the plane, I began removing my mask, and then I went into the cockpit and began checking my instruments and analyzing my fuel to see if anything appeared abnormal.

Jack came in and asked if I wanted him to take the first watch.

"No, it's going to be a long ride; try to get as much rest as you can, if you can," I told him. "I need to do a lot of double thinking." "Besides, you've got a long flight ahead of you tonight." "Jack, how'd it feel having Ellen sit next to you having dinner?"

"We just got through talking about that." He said, "You don't want me to repeat the things she said to me." "But Smith, that was her way of telling me that she's had a good time." "As soon as we get in the air, I'll bring you a cup of coffee."

Jane sat down in the co-pilot's seat and watched my every move. I taxied out to the runway for takeoff and took the mic in my hand.

"Can I do that?" She asked.

"Be my guest," I told her.

"Ladies and gentlemen," "welcome aboard Smith airlines; we're preparing for takeoff; please fasten your seat belts and make sure that all items are secured, and thank you for flying Smith airlines; we hope you enjoy your flight."

She handed me back the mic and said, "How was that?"

"You'd have a good career as a flight attendant," I told her.

"I've always wanted to do that." "And as far as me being a flight attendant, I don't think so; it's hard walking around and having to duck under all the doors."

I leveled off at thirty-five thousand feet; the air currents were pushing us. I flipped the silencers on my turbines, gave the computer my coordinates, and then put it on autopilot.

When Jack came in carrying my coffee, Jane got up from her seat and sat in my lap while Jack sat in the seat she got up from.

"I've been talking to Jose." He said, "Smith, what on earth possessed you to take a greenhorn along with you?"

"When you talked to him" "his response was yes sir or no sir." "Jack, you know he's not ready, and I know he's not ready, the person that knows that most of all though is him." "After McNally, he won't live an hour after he's been identified; he's already been confirmed as deceased." "I believe he joined the SEAL's because he thought no matter where he went to, he would always end up where he came from, but an opportunity came along, and he took it." "Jack, I've watched him since he arrived. Have you ever noticed his conduct?" "McNally took advantage of his personality and set him up, and you know as well as I do, he was an easy mark." "Outside of my control, he's a dead man walking." "He's a lot like one of my androids; he's a machine that's been programmed to do as he's told." "I don't plan on putting him in the middle of the action, but I can use him as a source of diversion." "Jack, he's a fighter that's never had a fight."

"You can use any of your androids for that." He said.

"I know, but there's something about this kid that I can't shut down." I told him, "The only thing that I know about him now is; I can't let him be seen as Jose." "What do I do, give him induced amnesia?" "If I got rid of Jose, then I'd have to do the same to Maria too."

"Smith, you and I both know you don't need him." He said.

"No, I guess not, but Jack, you have to ask yourself this." "If I don't need them, then why do I need you?"

Ellen interrupted our conversation by opening the cabin's door and sitting in Jack's lap. "Maria's in there crying." She said, "I think it's over Jose leaving."

"Cupid," Jane said, teasing me.

I took a sip of my coffee, and a green light came on overhead.

"What's happening?" Jane asked.

I looked over at my instruments and then gave her an answer. "The computer has located a stronger wind current two thousand feet below, and the wings are adjusting to the speed of the current to allow the plane to float along without using excessive fuel."

I took another sip of coffee to give the women confidence in that there was no cause for alarm.

"Smith," Ellen began, "I don't think I quite know how to say what I want to say."

"Ellen, I find that I don't know how to say what I want to say either" "so I say what I'm thinking at the time, and usually I'm misunderstood when I do say anything." "You of all people have a clear understanding of that." "So, if you've got something you wish to say and it concerns me, then I appreciate a person being straightforward and not being political in their conversation with me." "I'm not interested in anyone sweet-talking me while cursing me under their lips." "I have nothing else left to hide from you."

"That's what I want to talk about, right there." She spoke, "I didn't like you talking to me the way you did when we met." "I thought you might have been some sort of a psychic or something." "I felt uncomfortable being around you because you seemed to know what I was thinking and what I was feeling." "You're not a normal man by any means, and I had a lot of problems with that, but I wanted to tell you, you were right; I didn't understand you because I didn't know you then." "I talked with my daughter, and she explained a lot of things to me about you that I didn't think about." "I misjudged you." "It seems I do that a lot." Ellen said, "My husband never spoke to me about you, and when he did, he always told me that I'd find out everything I wanted to know when I needed to know it." "He told me you knew how to solve problems better than he did." "I noticed a couple of weeks back; you no longer treated me as an outsider." "At first, I thought you were a horrible man, and once again, my daughter and I would have a talk." "I said some things that I shouldn't have, and I wanted you to know that I'm sorry." She said with remorse in her tone.

"You shouldn't be," I told her. "The truth only hurts people that don't want other people to know the truth." "I don't concern myself with the truth; if those are your feelings then, it helps me to know when I'm being a bother to someone, and I try to act more pleasant towards them or leave them at peace." "It depends on the way I feel at the time." "Ellen, never be afraid to tell anyone the truth." "I'm not."

"Momma," Jane said, "I tried to figure out why Smith acts the way he does when he becomes another person." "This is Smith; this is how Smith is when he's himself." "Remember back at the lab, both of us were scared half to death when we saw his androids, especially the ones that looked like you and dad." "You didn't know them from the real you or dad." "We went Mexico, and we had dinner." Smith wasn't Smith." "We went to the Bahamas and had dinner." "Smith wasn't Smith." "All of those people we have seen were make-believe." "Momma, this is Smith." "This is the way Smith is when he's relaxed."

"That may be," she said, "but still, I was wrong. I said some things that I didn't mean to say."

"Ellen, human nature is not easily understood; my life has its complexities, and so does yours." "When you and Jack fought, it was from anger being able to penetrate your thoughts, and when you released those thoughts, you said things to win that argument." "You were sorry for what you said later when you calmed down, but you said what you felt at the time, or you wouldn't have said it." "You spoke the truth, and it hurt as soon as you and Jack parted." "Think back a long time ago," I told her. "How many fights have you had?"

"More than I can count." She said.

"And out of all of those fights you had, how many did you win?" "Or should I say, how many did you lose?" I asked.

"What are you saying?" She looked confused when she asked me.

"I'm just saying that those fights that you and Jack had, there weren't any winners, you both lost, every single fight you fought, you lost, both of you." "You allowed anger to change the person you are into the person you aren't." "You have multiple personalities too, and so does everyone else in the world." "You just don't know it until someone points it out to you." "There is always an alter ego that we become for whatever reason we choose." "We are good and bad, and sad, and happy, and mean, and nice, and ugly and warm." "We all become a different person, for whatever reason we choose," I said, giving her a smile.

"You're not making this easy on me at all." She said, "Smith, Jack, and I had a talk, and we both agree that we want to live as close as we can to both of you; we want to be a part of your lives." "But, we think it's best for everyone to live in our own place."

"Momma, that's not how we feel," Jane said.

"Honey, me and your father like our privacy, and we don't get it living with the both of you." "Besides, it's not like we're moving to the other side of the states; we'll be up the road a little, that's all." "I like to wake up and look outside the window and see what the day looks like." "There aren't any windows at the lab." She said. "But somehow, I think Smith knew what we had on our minds anyway, didn't you?" She said, looking at me.

"Yes, ma'am, Jose and Maria are becoming inseparable; they'll make the same decision when the time is right." "They'll want their privacy, too," I told her.

"So, you "were" setting them up!" Jane commented.

"The first time they met was a sour moment for them both." I answered, "Neither of them had feelings for each other; that was clearly understood." "Jane, you saw me the way I looked when we met." "I just didn't want them to go different paths without offering an explanation for my actions, and because of that explanation, they were told that it was my fault, and they formed a friendship."

"I'd say they're a little past friendship." Ellen commented, "While you two were under the waterfall, they were kissing on the beach, and I'd say by the way they were kissing; they were enjoying their honeymoon because if they were pretending, they both should go into acting, it looked like a real honeymoon to me." "And I had something I wanted to ask you too." She said, "How did you know those guys were taking pictures of us? I never saw anything?" Ellen asked.

"That's because you weren't looking." I told her, "There were twenty-eight tables; three were vacated and being cleaned for the next patrons." "Nine pictures hung above the windows that overlooked the beach; they were scenic views from different places of the Bahamas." "Of those twenty-eight

Paulie J. Johnson

tables, twenty-four of them had a woman or women with them; wine and other spirits were at every table." "There was a lot of love in that restaurant that night." "There were seven waiters; none of them were women." "There were two bartenders and three young men that cleaned the tables." "There was only one way in and one way out." I stated, "Our waiter was an android." I told her, "My computer identified them." "James, my android, drugged their drinks, and I got their cameras with the photos that they took." "Not to mention their credit cards."

"Is this what you meant when you said I was always guarded?" Ellen asked.
"Yes, ma'am"
"You really can't relax and enjoy a quiet evening, can you?" Ellen said.
"I don't have that luxury; my enemies don't play fair." I stated to her, "Besides, I can cook the same foods they cook, and when I rest, I sit by my fire and let the glow of the embers carry my thoughts to wherever thoughts are born." "I close my eyes and listen and hear nothing."

"Then, that poses a problem for us," Jane reported her thoughts. "From the way I see things since we've been together. I've learned that you lived in a place of solitude all of your life, and you've lived the lives of other people in your own little way." "Can you live with someone like me after living in that world you've lived in all of your life?" She asked.

I leaned back and smiled. "You're asking me to predict the future." "I can't do that." "You may wake up one day and leave." "I can tell you about the past, and I can tell you about the present, but I can't predict the future until it becomes the present and then the past." "Every day is a new day, and with each new day, new problems are encountered and forced to be dealt with."

Ellen interrupted, "That reminds me; my grandmother said something a lot like that when I was a little girl." "I asked her what she meant, and she answered that I would understand someday." "I understood what you just said; now I understand what my grandmother meant." "All wisdom comes with age." "Why didn't you tell me I was getting old?"

Jack was stalling and didn't give her an answer, so I answered her question for him.

"Ellen, a man that has admiration for his wife, like Jack, doesn't see you as other people see you." "I see Jane, and I see an eleven-year-old girl, she sees me, and she sees a twenty-eight-year-old man that was a sight to see." "When you look at Jack, you see the man you saw when you first met him, and he sees the girl he saw when he first met you." "No one that's in love sees age or imperfection; they only see the beauty they saw when they first saw that person."

"I think that I'm beginning to think that I've been around you for too long." Ellen said, "I used to think you spoke in the tongue by the way you talked, but now I think you've learned to come down to my level." "That was sweet." "Can you teach my husband to say things like that?"

"Ellen, it's not hard to read, people." "Jane has been absent from your life for the last four years." "Your room at the lab will remain the way it is; they'll be days that you'll live in the lab, and they'll be days you'll live in your house." "As I said, I can't predict the future, but I can see some things clearly."

"You're a tough nut to crack, Smith." Ellen looked down at Jack and asked, "How did you deal with him?"

"Simple, I just followed his orders." He said.

"Smith, you want us to take control so you can do whatever you have to do to get ready for this thing you're going to do?" Ellen asked.

"That sounds like a good idea." I said, "Jane, I need you to get up for a moment."

When she did, I got up too.

"Here you go, Ellen, have a seat," I told her.

When she sat down, I asked if she was comfortable.

When she returned my question with a favorable response, I told her to put her hand on the wheel. I then disengaged the autopilot.

"It's all yours." I said, "Steer it like a car and keep that gauge there." I tapped it to show her. "Keep it in the crosshairs." "The plane tilts down left, ease the wheel right, the plane tilts right, ease the wheel left." "If the nose drops a little, pull up on the wheel, and if the nose edges up, push down on the wheel." "After a while, you'll get the hang of it." "It's all yours," I said as we were leaving.

"Wait a minute; I can't fly this plane." She said nervously.

I stopped and turned to her "Ellen, the plane you were flying in the flight simulator was like a lot similar to this one; maybe the next time you fly in the simulator, you'll make it a little more serious." "I have faith in you; our lives are in your hands" "so fly carefully," I said as I shut the door.

"She doesn't really have the controls, does she?" Jane whispered to me.

"Yes, but the computer will override all errors and correct them automatically," I told her in a soft voice. "I had to do that because your father had problems when he first got into the simulator." "I decided the best thing I could do was to protect him and my plane by programming it with a program that automatically corrects an error."

"Does my father know that?" She asked.

"No, I never told him; he always thought he had control," I said.

"So my mother thinks she's flying the plane when she really isn't?"

"Your mother is having a good time in there, and knowing your father the way I do, I'm sure he's going to be trying to do a lot of coaching." I said to her, "What your mother is going through right now is what I call a confidence builder." "I don't think it's going to take a lot of coaxing to get her in the flight simulator anymore."

We sat down across from Jose and Maria. They were both holding hands. "Maria, you don't look nervous anymore." "Are you starting to feel better about flying?" I asked her. She pushed a button on the laptop and began signing to me. The laptop was in audible for the others to hear what she said.

"I don't have too much of a problem in the air; it's the landing and the takeoffs that bother me." She said.

"Maria, which would you rather fall from, one hundred feet, or thirty-three thousand feet?" I asked her.

"I don't understand." She said, "Both would kill you."

"I was trying to make a point." I told her, "This plane is equipped with four parachutes capable of lowering three hundred tons in case of engine failure; that's three times the weight of this plane." "I have four turbines and use only one at a time." "That leaves me with three turbines as a backup if one was to fail for whatever purpose." "I have sensors in all the turbines that are programmed into the computer, and every fifteen seconds, the computer receives information as to the condition of the turbine that's in use." "Any infraction and the computer identifies the problem, and if needed, it automatically switches to another turbine." "The fact is this plane cannot crash, even if I was to fly it straight towards a cliff." "I designed it, and I built it to think of self-preservation." "So, rest easy, and don't think of the what if's; there aren't any, I can assure you of that," I said to her. I then watched her as she took some deep breaths. She had the appearance of looking somewhat less tense. "Maria, the time has come for me and you to have a talk," I said to her. "I need you to swear allegiance to me, and that allegiance is simple. I only need to hear the words sworn to me that you'll never ever lie to me." "My request has merits, they may not mean anything to the person that's saying it, but they mean something to me." "I don't like liars, and I distance myself from one." "I told Jose the same thing." "I want you to think long before you give me what I ask because everyone here would be affected." "They've all sworn the same allegiance that I ask of you."

"I don't have to take time." She said, "I wouldn't do that to you." "You've never been unkind to me like others were, and you've treated me with dignity and respect." "No one ever did that." "I have no ears, and I have no voice." "No one expected for me to be anything other than a dishwasher or a maid, and neither did I, and here I am flying in a private plane, and leaving a country that I would never have been able to see, it's a place that only rich people get to go to." She said. "I'll never lie to you; I couldn't." "It would bring me shame for the faith that you have in me; you have my word."

"Maria, I dealt with a lot of people that have given their word to other people, and then they betrayed them." "Time is our only barometer that can be used to gauge our actions." "Have you asked Jose about his history?" "Yes, sir."

"And have you spoken about your history to him?" I asked her.

"Yes, sir."

I looked at them both.

"You both know now what has transpired in your lives up until today, and it only took one week to learn all you need to know about each other." "What you don't know is what has transpired in my life," I said. "That's one area that will remain a mystery; I don't know the things I want to know about myself. I can only give diagnoses that are based on symptoms that I've observed." "By now, you should know that there are restrictions in my day-to-day actions, I have limitations; you both have your opinion of me, and you'll have more, good or bad." "There'll be times that you won't understand my intention; that's to be expected." "Much like when I sent Jose to see you, Maria." "You didn't understand my intention then." "And if I told you, it wouldn't mean what it meant to find out the way you did."

I diverted my eyes to Jose. "You woke up and found yourself in a totally different part of the world, and like Maria, you were confused too." "Now, both of you know about each other's lives, and that's a start." "Jane has accused me of being a cupid and bringing you two together." "She was right; I was the one responsible for you two meetings." "But, the rest was out of my control. I wasn't responsible for what transpired along the way." "What was meant to be was meant to be." "Time will pass, and moments will occur where bitterness will cause friction between you." "No one is impervious to a release of verbal tension." "To me, it causes a distraction in what I do, and I can't afford distractions." "If you two are happy with one another, the way that you appear to be now." "I'd like for you to think of this moment, and when the day comes that that friction is encountered, I'd like for you to remember that friction could kill the one you love." "Jose, I need you to listen to me. I don't want you mixing it up in hand-to-hand combat." "It's got nothing to do with you personally, but you're still a long way away from taking care of yourself when your opposition is twenty or thirty to one." "You've been trained for a different purpose, but you do have training." "The equipment you'll carry only has one purpose, and that's to avoid any hand-to-hand combat at all cost." "That means if at all possible, avoid being seen." "You follow my orders; you get in, unload the explosives and get out." "Don't give them any time to find you in the spot where they are looking for you." "I don't want you thinking about me. I'll have my hands full on that matter." I told him, "Your job is to draw them away from me; without you, I can't move around without drawing attention." "It's like shooting a gun." I told him, "You can't fire the bullet unless you pull the trigger." "In this matter, you're the finger on the trigger, and I'm the bullet." "Jose, I know a lot about men like you, eager to participate in the action. The sad thing is that they're all dead." "They charged in with a devil may care approach, and that's where they wound up." "Explosives killed them all, and not one shot was fired by them." "No action is achieved without a plan, so no heroics. I need you to be where you're told to be, at all times. I don't want to end up accidentally killing you in the process." "This isn't going to be easy." I said to him, "Do you have feelings for Maria?" I asked him.

He had problems swallowing and then answered me. "Yes, sir."

"Maria, do you have feelings for Jose?" I asked her.

She took a breath and answered. "Yes, sir, I do."

"Jose, knowing this, does it affect this mission?" I asked him.

"No, sir."

"Are you seeking vengeance for the outcome of your life?" I asked.

"No, sir."

"You should." I told him, "It's people like this that have kept the poor in oppression." "Drugs are only for a supply of money." "Behind the scenes, there are people dying for others to become rich, like the people that are working for the Messiah." "You were raised where drugs were a common way of life, and so was Maria." "I don't know what experiences took place between either of you when you were young." "Everyone wants to be a part of a group or a gang, some don't, and that's what separates them from others." "But whether it is from friends or from a gang, some form of crime will occur, and it affects them for rest of their life." "The young don't pay attention." I said, "They don't possess a concern for tomorrow, so there's very little that can be done to teach someone that isn't old enough to understand what you have to say to them." "Let's take you and Maria; if you two were to have children, would you want them growing up in the same environment as you did, and if they did, what would keep them from experimenting with their friends?" I said to them. I gave them a moment to reflect on what I had told them and then continued my thoughts, "I think we all have reasons for what we do, but we can't find that reason, no matter how hard we look." "I believe it is embedded deep within our inner selves." "You two should know about poverty and what it can do to people, and you should also know that the largest employer in the world is the people that manufacture drugs, legal and illegal." "Which ones are the enemies?" I asked them, "If something goes into the mouth, it could contain a harmful element whether by nature, by accident, or on purpose." "Maria. I apologize if I sound offensive, but you wouldn't be here if I didn't have to bring Jose here." "Outside of my lab, he can never exist as Jose." "Jose is dead; he was killed in a gun battle." "He was set up to be murdered, but he wasn't. He found himself in my lab watching what went down on the screen; he's now living on borrowed time." "That means he cheated death, and death doesn't like to be outwitted." "That's where you come in," I told Maria.

"You say you have feelings for Jose." I said, "As much as I disliked what I had to say to Jane, I had to be honest." "Now, you have to hear the words I said to Jane." "Jose is aware of his possible outcome, yet he doesn't show his true feelings of being frightened. If he felt otherwise, he will die quickly." "Maria, no promises can be made today," I said to her.

"Maria." Jane interrupted me, "You know how Smith talks, and he didn't mean that the way it sounded, he can't help it, he says what he feels without feelings or emotions, sometimes I think he's like one of his robots." "Honey, he set you and Jose up from the beginning." "I'm a little wiser to how he does things now, so let's get this said and done." "He saw something in you that he wanted to see if what he saw was what he wanted to see." "That's why you're here; look where you're at now, side by side, with a man you recently met." "He sent Jose on a trumped-up mission to meet you, and he succeeded in what he saw in the both of you." "He's only saying that if you're upset with him for what he has done, then ask yourself if you're happier now, or would you have been happier before you met Jose." "He can't answer any questions about you until you two met." "So don't let that cold heart of his scare you." "He's all bark around me, and he's the same way with my mother, just as he is with you." "So when he speaks, don't take offense in what he says. He doesn't know how to deliver an answer without saying what he feels." She told her.

Then Jane turned to me.

"Smith, we've discussed this matter more than a few times now." "I don't want to hear negative responses whenever you speak of traveling." "From now on, it's when we return, nothing else." "Do you understand me?" She said.

I looked at her.

"Smith, I'm waiting." She stated.

"Jane." I began.

"Smith, this is got to stop." "It's beginning to hurt me when you say things that scare me, and I'm sure Maria doesn't like to hear things like that either." "Yes, the fact to the matter is, truth does hurt." She said. "But sometimes we have to be optimistic in our thinking." "Or Maria and I would start our mourning as soon as you and Jose left, if not this time then the next, if not the next, then the next." "But being optimistic is hoping that this will be the last time you'll leave too." "In that regard, I think I would be being too optimistic." "But Smith, please, I don't want to hear you and death mentioned in the same sentence anymore." "I worry every day about you, and it's hurtful wondering if I'll someday be waiting for that door on the elevator to open, and then after a while wondering if it ever will."

She then looked at Jose.

"Jose, whatever you have on your mind, at any time, you best be leaving it outside the door when you enter your room with Maria, you can take it from me; we girls don't like it when our men are with us, but their mind is concentrating on something somewhere else." "Did you hear what I just said to Smith?" She asked him.

"Yes, ma'am." He said.

"Then I don't need to tell you the same thing that I told him then, do I?" She told him.

"No, ma'am."

"Good then" "I see the spider has spun her web and has trapped her man. Maria owns you now; only you don't know it." "You shouldn't feel bad about that, though; I've got Smith held captive too." "The difference is, Smith knows that, and you don't." She informed him.

"Do you have a dollar?" She asked.

"Excuse me." He said.

"Do you have a dollar?" She asked once again.

"No, ma'am, all I have is the card Smith gave me to use." He told her.

She looked over at me. "Smith, I need a dollar."

I walked over to the cabinet, pulled out some bills, and returned to her.

"Make me a ring." She said.

I began rolling and folding until it was a perfect circle and gave it to her.

"Jose, do you see this ring on my finger?" She put her hand out for him to see. "Smith made it for me, and then he put it on my finger." "Its real value is only worth one dollar, but the ring to me is priceless because it has a special meaning only to me." "It tells me that I'm better than special to him." "We may not be married on paper, but that's not important to me, I've been married on paper before, and it turned out not to be worth the paper it was written on." "I learned that from Smith." "All marriages have a document to prove that they are legally married." "You get a divorce, and they'll give you a document that says you're no longer married." "You don't need a piece of paper to be married; you just need someone that needs you." "I have more than strong feelings that Smith loves me, no one ever said that to me with meaning, and when he gave me this ring, it told me everything I wanted to know without asking him anything." "I was looking for assurance; you'll find out that women always wonder if we're still wanted, or has the romance ended." "This ring was the assurance I needed from him." She gave him a ring that I had made for her. "Look at it." He did as he was told, and then Jane continued, "Jose, it's not gold or silver, but that ring has magic powers."

416

"Whoever you give it to will return the same love that you give." "I hope you give it to the right person one day." She told him.

Jose held the ring in his hand and stared at it for a long time; he then looked up at Jane, and without being able to say anything to her. Maria took the ring from his hand and put it on. She looked at it on her finger and then took it off and placed it back into his hand. Jane commented again to Jose, "I see you're a lot like Smith." She said, "You don't know anything about a woman." "I don't read sign language, but it seems to me like she just said that she wanted to wear your ring."

Jose looked at the ring again, and then reached for Maria's hand and motioned to her; he wanted to know if she would wear it. She didn't hesitate; she slid her finger into the ring and gave him a long kiss.

"Come on," Jane said, "we need to leave these two love birds alone." She told me.

We got up and went into the middle of the plane and lay down in the bed. "You're a woman to be dealt with," I told her.

"Hey, don't look at me; you're the one that brought them together." She argued, "Besides, the ring does mean a lot to me, it does have magic powers, and I do try to show you I love you anyway I can." "Smith, you're a simple man, you ask for nothing, but when you're with me, you do as I ask, you only think of me, and that's more than I can ever ask for." "That may not seem like much to anyone else, but I know how hard it is for you." "I'm twenty-four, and I was married for four years." "I find out that I wasn't loved by the man that said he loved me." "That leaves me with you." "It took me twenty-four years to find the man that said he loved me." "But right now, I want you to relax." She said, "I got up early, and I'm not an early riser." "I need you to put me to sleep, and I need you to get some sleep also." "Smith, you've got bags under your eyes."

She pulled me tight against her body and had me wrapped up in her arms. I don't recall how long it was before I was asleep, but I do know it was quick.

A little while later, I entered the lobby of the plane, poured myself a cup of coffee, and sat down next to Jane. I looked up at the clock. "We've got five hours left." I said, "Where are Jose and Maria?" I asked.

"They're asleep on the couch in the back." She answered.

"Has your mother been in the cockpit since we left?" I asked her.

"I checked on them earlier, and momma's still at the controls." "Smith, you have to tell her that she's not really flying the plane."

"If I did, your father would know too." "Somehow, I believe that this way, they both benefit. If he knew, he would have already told her, and that would ruin a good night." I said to her.

"I thought you needed sleep," I said to her.

"It was you that needed the sleep, or I wouldn't have been able to sneak out of bed without you waking up." She replied.

"What are you doing up?" I asked.

"Worrying, it's what most girls do when the person that they're in love with leaves for a destination unknown." "I had trouble sleeping; you know, bad dreams and all." "You're not the only one that has the market cornered on bad dreams." "So I got up and made a pot of coffee and sat here thinking." "Smith, I have a problem; no matter how hard I try to think about something else, you always come back into the picture, and I had a problem with that." "When my husband first started taking his trips, I didn't feel the way I feel now." "I asked myself why, but I can't come up with the answer."

"Jane, it was difficult for me to talk to you." "I still find it uneasy, but, given this situation, I'm powerless to avoid an interaction. This is one job that I can't walk away from." "All is not right with the world, and if I turn my head and try to ignore it, it won't go away." "I suspect it was the same with you and your husband." "Sometime along the way, you lost interest in him; I can't be for certain, but I believe it was about the same time when you realized that he didn't have the same interest in you as what you had in him." "You told Jose the ring was magical, and the girl he gave it to would give him back the love he gave." "The ring that your husband gave you was a ring of deceit; he never loved you." "It may have cost a lot of money, but it was worthless. His words meant nothing."

"I had a rough time sorting all of this out when I came to the lab." She said, "You were knocked out, and I had been crying when my father told me that I should take a walk, he said it would be a while before you would come out of it when I did, I saw a lot of things that really set me back, and I have to admit, it shook me up." "The sauna, the swimming pool, the track, I never imagined all that." "There I was in the middle of nowhere, and I was a prisoner." "Then I heard the sounds of a helicopter, and all of a sudden, I found myself with my father in the lab." "It took me a long time to get over the shock of finding out you owned all of that stuff as you told me." "But being boxed up out in the middle of nowhere, I didn't have a lot of belief about you." "You can imagine what I thought when I found myself in a private hotel." "I have to admit I was quite overwhelmed." "What really threw me off, though, was when you came to, and I began to see the rest of the place and what was in it." "That's when I started to see the reality of what I was involved in." "I would have never known anything was behind those walls." "Come to find out; there are walls behind walls and more walls behind the walls that are behind the walls." "Smith, billionaires, don't live in small stone buildings, and they don't live miles away from civilization." I took a sip of my coffee and then another. "Smith, for a long time before I met you, I wondered to myself, what would make me feel the happiest." "It wasn't my thing. It was more about knowing me as a person and what I wanted out of life." "It never came to me." "I guess it was like my mother finding out what her grandmother meant." "But I was taking my time thinking about you, and then I looked around and realized that I didn't see anybody around." "Not one person was staring at me." "I went and walked around the track, and the more I walked, the more I began to see that I felt good not feeling the eyes staring at me in the back of my head." "Smith, I told you I have problems socializing too." "I asked myself why a man that has everything would leave it all behind and live the life of a hermit." "I walked for a long time, and then I stopped. I realized that you were happy, and I wanted you to know that I'm happy being with you." "Last night, when you came by the table and asked me to dance, I wanted to cry." "So I realized that being happy can be sitting by the fire, working on my quilts, and wearing my reading glasses, and rocking in my rocking chair." "I want to hear you tell me that you want to grow old with me, or all of that stuff I just said was trash." She said as she looked over at me.

I took her by the hand, with both of mine.

"I read where first impressions were the correct ones, most of the time." I stated to her, "When you first saw me, you were scared." "You had your reasons, and they were good ones." "I was at my stone house for my own reasons; I liked being alone, just like you said." "The only way I could calm those fears that I saw in you was to stay away from you." "So, I piddled with this and with that." "I never really got into anything heavy, you might have needed me, so I took walks and scoped out the trees I was going to cut down for my totem poles and surveyed my surroundings for future needs. I tried to stay busy, all the while trying to stay close in case you called out." "I had to stay away from you on purpose; your first impression of me wasn't a good one, and I knew I couldn't change anything of what you saw in me." "There was nothing else I could do." I said, looking her in her eyes, "I lived my life, thinking my thoughts and drawing my illustrations of them." "I did a lot of reading, working on odds and ends, and chopping wood for the stove, and I was happy with that. I got good thoughts that way." "The day would turn into night, and the night would turn into day." "I lost all time of the hours, the days, and the months. I only knew two seasons, warm and cold." "Jane, I've always been alone in my life, and one day I wasn't anymore; that was when I found you, at the base of the cliff." "I didn't think of anything except taking care of you and seeing to it that you got back home, so the man that did that to you would be put away for the rest of his life." "When I pulled the hood off of your head, you weren't breathing," "Jane, I've never been so scared of anything in my life, but that day, I was scared, I knew who you were right away, and I didn't want to have to go to your father with the news." "If you had died, I was going to kill whoever was responsible, but Mother Nature took care of that for me." "Your father isn't an assassin, but I would have given your father the only justice he wanted." "It wouldn't have been hard; his name was on the rental receipt of the snowmobile." I told her, "I ask myself many questions, and the answers are there, but I can't hold one without grabbing for another." "You said you were twenty-four when you met the man you love; I was twenty-eight before I met the girl I love." "You can tell I'm not a romantic person, and I never ever gave any thought as to me being with someone, especially you." "Not after the way you looked at me when you first saw me." I said to her, "Jane, when I look at you, I feel very fortunate." "You're a very beautiful girl, and you just asked me to grow old with you." "I never heard those words, and I didn't think that words could hurt as much as they do."

"A simple yes or no will do." She said.

"Jane, look at your ring." I told her, "I'll be with you as long as that ring stays on your finger. If you ever take it off, then I won't need to ask any questions."

"Smith, you do have a way with words." She said.

"Then, your wish will be granted," I told her.

She got up from her chair and sat in my lap.

"Smith, about that first impression." "You shouldn't hold that against me."

"I don't." I told her, "I didn't have feelings for you, and you didn't have feelings for me."

"Smith, I had my problems back then trying to understand you." "You weren't an emotional guy, and I couldn't quite put a handle on the way you acted; you seemed protective of every word you said and everything that you did." "You're still not an emotional person, and you still seem to protect everything you say and do." "You don't give me information unless I ask for it, so I know you don't like talking too much about what you're thinking about." "I understand more and more about you every day." She replied, "But still, knowing all that I know today, I still have problems sometimes trying to understand you."

I took in a breath and released it.

"It's hard to discuss my operations with you." "If I was talking to your father or Jose, then that would be a whole different matter." "They understand what I have to say perfectly."

"I don't find comfort in telling you that if I'm successful, it'll cost five hundred, or a thousand, or five thousand men their lives." I told her, "I wish all of them were somewhere else and doing something else, but they're not." "So when the time comes where those that are standing in front of me, are standing against me, it'll be too late for me to ask them to stop what they're doing and leave peacefully, they'll be there for only one purpose, and that's to stop me from carrying out what I went to do."

"I see your point." She said, "But Smith, you have to know that I'm at peace with you, and to me, I don't see the man that you think I see when I see you." "My mother said that the congressman got what he deserved, and my father told us that if he would have been captured, he'd be out on the streets as we speak, and you knew that, not to mention, what would have happened to Jose." "You said the man you came to see yesterday was responsible for the kidnapping." She remarked.

"There's more, but that was the main reason I killed him." "He was the henchman for the doctors that performed the organ transplants; he was told by Messina who to take, and he gave orders to his sons, and they gave orders to others." "Whether he killed them or not, he was responsible for those deaths, and others not attributed to the Messiah, he was a man that was a lot like me in a way, he didn't like people getting in his way, and he has seen to it that they didn't do it anymore." "I imagine his sons will step forward and try to fit in their father's shoes, and I'm counting on it." "When they do, rumors will surface, and other gangs will fill the vacancies that were left behind by Miguel and Carlos." "I told you that McNally had to have someone working with him. With a little luck, I'll find him without looking for him." "That gives me the upper hand." First, I'll know the people that are involved, and secondly, drugs will once again be distributed by the subs." "What I did will repeat itself; only different players will be involved." "I had an imitator, one of the bobcats, attach a tracker to the salamanders, and I can follow them anywhere." "As long as I don't destroy their mode of transportation, it'll be used again and again." "Let me show you something," I said to her; I poured a small amount of salt into my hand.

"This salt represents a group of men that has a leader." "They all grouped together, and they offer many men to fight." "It represents a small army." I hit my wrist, and the salt flew everywhere. "An attack has dispersed all the men." "Now they're scattered, and as soon as the attack is over, they will start to regroup." "They aren't a group of many anymore, they're alone, and that's when they're most vulnerable."

"Smith, do you think you started doing this because of what you're father did to your brother? Do you think there's some kind of hatred that exists somewhere in the back of your mind?"

"You're being psychoanalytical." I told her, "But, it's a fair and sound question." "It came into my thoughts, but I dismissed that assessment." "No one knows why people do what they do." "My father was sick, like my mother; he needed medicine, and the medicine he chose was self-medicated, and he abused his medication." He let it kill him, and along with him, my brother." "My mother was dead in mind, I never ever heard her call my name, but her body still lived." "After I met your father, I began to see people taking advantage of other people, and I found that to be distasteful." "Jane, I was a boy, and I had to make a decision." "Let these people get away with what they are doing, or do them the same way that they were doing to others, and destroy them financially." "I leave the little problems alone and eliminate the big problems." "Most of the time, turmoil ended the little problems, so I didn't have to intervene." "That's when I began to feel feelings." "When people get away with stealing or killing someone, they celebrate their victory." "But, I received satisfaction at seeing their faces when they came into their office and found agents or they were a victim of identity theft." "That was the beginning of where I stand now." "What started out as one thing ended up another." "He, who laughs last, laughs loudest." "That was the game that they were playing." "My game was to the victor goes the spoils."

"Okay, now it's my turn." She said, "There comes a time when some people go too far and cross a line, and when they do, someone has to put a stop to those kinds of people, and you're that someone." "That's the man I see when I look at you, not all first impressions are correct; you even said that in so many words yourself." "I know in that mind of yours you're analyzing everything I say, but I hope you hear me and pay attention." "You're not a killer." "A killer finds some weird fascination in what he's doing." "You're not a murderer." "A murderer doesn't use discretion in the people he kills. She lifted my chin with her thumb and forefinger, gave me a kiss, and stated, "I need you to have a clear mind when you leave." "But somehow, I don't think that's going to be a problem to you at all." "Now, I don't like talking about this subject." She commented, "I was sitting here thinking about your vision." "Jose said you were going to need to build an overhead train to and from the park." "He's right, you know." "That train is too slow, and it won't carry the number of people that you'll need to transport." "Believe me, and that brings me to my question." "Smith, a place that big is going to need a park, and it needs to be big." "What if we build a train around the park and the hospitals and the ski resort? That way, people can get off where they want and when they want?" "It'll give everyone a complete view of the park; the hospitals, the schools, and the biodome, and you can make it out to be a ride all in itself." "Then you have to take into consideration walking or taking a tram wherever you're going to." "I believe it'll cut down on the traffic and reduce the threat of anyone getting hurt." "No one can walk to wherever they have to go." "The snow will put a stop to that." "But it won't be the skier's none."

"That's not a question," I told her. "It's a must." "I'll include that into my blueprints when I get back."

"You said when you get back." She said, "Now you're starting to give me the confidence I need."

Jose and Maria came walking into the chambers, and when Jose sat down, Maria sat in his lap, and she put her arm around him. Jane looked at me and gave me a small smile. I knew exactly what she was telling me with it. She then mouthed the word cupid to confirm my suspicion.

I looked up at the clock. "We've got a little more than four hours until we depart." I told Jose, "I want to tell you a little story." I said, "Throughout time, man has always used an art to fight in his wars." "Men marched in squads or legions and battled in formations." "If an arrow or spear, or bullet felled the man in front, the man to the rear of him, stepped up to take his place." "Many battles were fought and won, and lost this way." "Depending on the era of the battles or the continents, and whatever reasons they had to fight." "When outnumbered, battles that occurred were fought on the run." "Hide behind anything for protection and then shoot the arrow, or throw the spear, or fire the bullet." "This was utilized by men without the knowledge to the art of war; it was from fear of being hit by something that could kill them that made them better soldiers." "Hundreds of men that deployed this type of exercise killed thousands of their enemy, and thus began the reeducation to the art of war." "Jose, you were taught to engage in conflicts as a member of a team of assault specialists." "If one person dies in an assault, then poor planning was responsible in my eyes, and I've seen a lot of men die because an officer was more interested in his political career." "That's one reason I don't take orders from anyone." "Another is because one gun fired lets the enemy know where the attack was coming from."

"Jose, many thoughts have come to my mind on the plans I have made." "I don't have to tell you that all plans are subjected to change from time to time." "That's why I told you not to be caught where you're expected to be." "Our goal is to concentrate the enemy and incapacitate them."

"You mean kill them, right?" Jane asked.

"Jose, would you tell Jane what you heard from me?" I asked him.

"Ma'am, some of them are going to be killed, that's for sure, that's the hazards of war, men die, but most of them won't, they'll be knocked out from the concussion, and if we're lucky, they'll be a lot of them that's going to have broken bones." "Not to mention the brain damage and loss of hearing, and blindness." "That means just about every man that comes into the danger zone won't be shooting a gun." "They'll be useless, and that's the ultimate goal of defeat, rid the enemy of the ability to fight, whether by death or by wounding him. You don't have to kill them to remove them." "That's the number one rule of war." He said.

"I'm surprised," I told him. "Jose, the Messiah isn't a warrior, he's not a thinker, and he's not a leader. He got to where he's at by assassinating those that opposed him." "My contact," "Ramon," "turned in his parents when he was younger," "that's how they were identified, and they were subsequently executed." "But, when the Messiah started his operations to offer vital organs on the black market, he had his doctors ready to remove what they needed, and they were gone." "His power escalated quickly."

"He installs a curfew to keep his people under control." "That gives us the freedom to move after dark." "All those we see are our enemy."

I asked Jane to get up for me. When she did, I walked over to a drawer, pulled out a knife, and gave it to Jose.

"You remember this?" I asked him.

"Yes, sir, it's the Navy SEAL survival knife." "It has a cartridge in the handle that delivers five hundred pounds of air in the victim when stabbed; it literally blows them up internally." He said. "The blade repairs itself if cracked." He said, looking up at me.

"It sounds impressive; it's rated as the number two most deadly of knives, not only for the sharpness of the blade but the serrated top." "It's not worth a hoot if you don't know how to use one." "I don't use the grenades when not needed; it only gives our enemy awareness of our location." "We try and avoid all confrontations and concentrate on our targets." "My main objective is my cargo; they are my priority; an agent and her family, two kids, a boy, and a girl, and her husband." "I'm going to draw the Messiah out into the open." I told him, "Here, it's a present for you; it's yours." I said as I handed the knife to him, "Guns are worthless; you can't kill everyone with one. They're like the explosives; they bring the enemy to where you're at." "That knife represents stealth, that's what you were taught, but back then, you probably didn't understand that stealth allows you to penetrate a fortress without being noticed, and that's exactly what we're going to have to do."

"What's your plan, sir?" Jose asked.

I put my hands on my hips and walked several steps and turned and walked back and then repeated the process several times, and then walked over to my computer and sat down at the desk. I thought for a moment and then asked everyone to join me.

I typed in my commands, and a picture came on the screen, I explained as I was typing. "This is his palace." I zoomed in so all could see the surrounding area. I then switched to the dam and then to the prison camp. "The problem that I see is, if I make any attacks, I think he'll execute them then in front of me." "I think he'll reverse my intention and use them to get to me." "I'm not positive, so I can't afford to risk their lives on a guess." "I'll go one better; I'll wire my targets with explosives before we make any moves." "Then, the advantage will be with us, one entry into my computer and everything goes up at once, or when the time is right, one at a time." "That means Ramon has to be put on hold for now." "I don't want them to know that I've arrived."

"Ramon's the key." "Once we make contact with Ramon, then they'll know we're here." "So Ramon is our shield, and as long as Ramon isn't contacted, no one knows that we've arrived." "Do I have anyone with any thoughts of their own?" I asked them. When none answered, I continued, "There's a mountain ridge above his palace and the dam." I switched the picture back to the palace and its surrounding terrain." I then looked at Jose. "Our living dead surround the palace, and they are concealed under the earth." I told him, "That brings us to the dam," I said as I typed on the computer, "the prison camp is two miles below the dam." "Notice that there's one road in, and one road out, we can destroy the road when necessary, and there won't be any reinforcements that will be arriving too quick; they'll be blocked access by their own vehicles being disabled." "When we move, we'll move along the mountain ridge." "It'll be easier to lock onto any surveillance equipment, cameras, infrared, microphones, etc., and knock them out." "The ridge also shields us by day." "This is the control room here." I said, "It's there for a purpose; he doesn't want it and the missile to be a target that can be destroyed by one attack." "Jose, that's where our other living dead are concealed."

"What's this living dead?" Jane said.

"My androids, they're corpses," I told her without looking at her. "These people are extreme in their religion, and the sight of the dead are omens." I turned around to face her. "In one thousand A.D., it became a common practice to put stones in the cavities of the mouth and abdomen of the deceased. They didn't want the dead to come back to life and seek vengeance." I then turned back to my computer. "All along the top of the ridge and down below will have guards patrolling the area." "My plan is to corral them towards the control room with the living dead androids." I looked up at the clock, and by doing so, it caused the same reaction from Jose.

"You ever get used to going on a mission, sir?" He asked me.

"Everything has to be perfect." I told him, "I've been fortunate in the past. I try to put myself in the shoes of my adversary and look through his eyes." "You have to second guess what someone will do if this or that was to happen with him." "The Messiah isn't happy with me right now." "He's aware that something has happened to his generals, and his supply lines have been severed." "Jose, you can't ever get used to doing anything by the book, and what you were taught was taken from the book of war that I was talking about earlier." "In reality, it's kill or be killed. That's the real book of war." "So, the answer would be no, no one can ever get used to going on a mission, no matter how well you prepare yourself, you're always unprepared." "Time has a way of catching up to you if you follow your plans without a plan of evasion, you can't let ignorance be a part of a battle; it kills thousands of men." I looked over at Jane and then at Maria, and then back at Jose. "The only thing that separates me from this mission, and the other missions that I've been on, is now I've got a lot more to lose." "Take a look at you." I said to Jose, "A week ago, you never knew Maria existed." "Jose, I can recall seven times that I should have been killed." "But, I'm still here." "Jane fell and died from her fall." "Good fortune was upon her, and I was able to revive her." "You can ask Maria, and she'll tell you that she too suffered near-fatal incidences, and you know all too well of what I'm talking about. You've experienced those close encounters of your own." I said to him, "Our efforts are against a dictator, and because of what we do, this region will become infected, and the whole country is going to be affected." "This man is a catalyst for all the other countries that surround him." "Dictators don't last long without making a lot of enemies, and our Messiah is not without his." "When he falls, they'll be other that will fall with him." "I'm on this mission for one reason, I was asked to." "The messiah is going to be eliminated, and if others choose the same path as the Messiah, then they too will be dealt with and eliminated; if possible." "That's the word the people are going to hear, and the Messiah's death is the best message I can deliver to prove that."

I looked around at them all, and when I spoke, I spoke to them all, "This altercation is being watched all over the world." "Bring down a regime and revolts in other countries are predictable." "Innocent people will form marches for civil rights and will die, and they'll be more uprisings." "I can make these claims because that's all I've seen since I was four." "Murders, kidnappings, torture, and assassinations, they all go hand in hand." "You can find this form of terrorism in every country, ours included." "I found out a long time ago that countries couldn't get involved with foreign countries' problems; they were viewed as a threat to other countries that surround other countries, and continents that border other continents." "I didn't have much choice the first time I assassinated a man." "Then there was a call for a second time, and then a third." "This is another situation where no country can show involvement, and I'm getting ready to assassinate him."

"Sir, if I may?" Jose said.

"Be my guest," I told him.

"Sir, we're on the side of the right, and that's important to me." "I wouldn't be doing this if I didn't think we weren't."

Maria signed that she agreed with what Jose said.

"It seems your outnumbered, Smith," Jane commented.

I turned off my computer and stood up and poured myself another cup of coffee, and then went and sat down in a lounge chair with Jane molding herself into my lap to get comfortable.

CHAPTER ELEVEN

"Computer; deploy James and Ruby." I commanded, "Jane, it's time for Jose and me to prepare ourselves." Jane got up and held out her hand to help me up. When I arose, she grabbed me and held me tight. I noticed Maria was doing the same to Jose. I gave Jane a smile and said to her, "We've come a long way since you opened your eyes and saw me at my stone house." "The time has come to show you why my answers were so difficult to give to you."

When she released me, I went to the closet and handed Jose a suit to wear. "What is this?" He asked.

"It's a ninja outfit with a bodysuit underneath to conceal thermal imagery." "The only part of the body that can be seen is the eyes." "The glasses take care of that." I said to him, "Boots and shoes are noisemakers." "These here are like moccasins, but they soften the step." I told him, "You move as if walking on cactus." "Put everything on."

I took mine out of the closet and went into the next room to change, with Jane following me.

"I know this is silly of me to ask, but are you really a ninja?" She said.

"No" "I dress this way for concealment," I told her. I then went and took out my swords and my longbow with my quiver of arrows and strapped them on, crossing each one of my swords in the back and positioning my bow for comfort. I strapped my quiver of arrows to each side for easy access and then covered the arrows to protect them from falling out.

I wrapped three belts full of throwing stars-shaped knives to my waist.

"You are a ninja, aren't you?" She said as I was putting on my hood and adjusting it to my face.

"Looks are deceiving." I said, "It depends on an interpretation of what you think a Ninja is." "Ninjas were once the protectors of the royalty; they were guards trained in combat every day like the Secret Service protects the president and his family, but it went one step further." "They became known as assassins, and they became hunted killers because emperors didn't know who their enemy was and feared everyone." "There were constant battles, and it was a classic example of the good versus the bad." "Ninjas were warriors of honor, much like the marines that boast of having the toughest soldiers; the army also boasts the same, as well as the navy and others." "Ninjas didn't have what I have available to them at the time. If they did, they would have learned that no amount of training can protect them from technology." "I don't see myself as a ninja, I just dress like one, but I did study them for their secrets," I said while applying shoe polish to darken my eyes and the skin that surrounded them. "Folklore has it that the Shogun, a commander of the emperor's forces, was so afraid of the ninjas that he had a master builder come in and install cured wood so that a rat couldn't walk across it without the boards creaking from the movement he made." "Paranoia kills many of those that fear death from all angles."

"But, the swords and the bow and arrows." She said.

"The bow is silent when released, and arrows glide through the air from a safe distance." "My five-bladed knives are to assure me of striking my target. I don't have to be perfect in my aim; my swords will do the rest." "Twenty men grouped together can't fire their weapons without striking each other." I told her, "I told you that there were two types of ninjas, the protectors and the assassins." "The Japanese were an honorable people, and they believed in that honor, and they still live by honor." "It's much like someone who shakes your hand." "A short time ago, that meant something to people." "Today, you're being embezzled." "Jane, a person that will lie to you, is a dishonorable person; they'll do it again and again." "You were there when I told Jose that his Navy SEAL survival knife was the second most dangerous knife in the world." "The number one on the list is the Samurai sword." "I'm not Ninja, a Ninja is only a title, and I don't find reward in being one. Titles mean nothing to me, but I use ninja's techniques because I consider those techniques to be the most cunning. I use nine kung fu forms that I mix with tae kwon do as well, defense and offense, when used at the proper time, find a weakness, and the quicker you do so, the better off you are."

We walked outside the room, and I applied the shoe polish to Jose and then put on his grenade belts that crossed his shoulders.

"Jose, watch here." I told him, "I took one of the grenades off of the belt, and it automatically advanced to the next grenade." "I did this so you wouldn't be wasting time trying to reach or rotate the belt to get another grenade." "Time is of the utmost importance." "When the last one is used, discard the belt. It no longer serves a purpose, and then do the same to the other belt." "Fire no more than three grenades and move to a location above from where you were at." "By the time that they located the position you were in, they'll be congregated in one spot, and one grenade takes care of them." "Jose, you have to put guessing out of your mind and watch where they go to seek cover." "You see the enemy, avoid him." "If you don't see the enemy, use patience as you proceed; it might be him that's watching you." "Move like a chameleon, and stop to survey your surroundings, then move slowly only after assuring yourself that nothing is near." "Never take more than three steps at a time without repeating everything all over again, and never take anything for granted." I said to him, "You have your glasses for night vision and thermal imagery, and all you have to do is ask the computer for verification." "It can see things a lot better than you." "In situations where a small squad is in front of you, and an altercation is unavoidable, spray them with the poison needles, and remember no noise." "Listen to the sounds of the night." "There's a proverb." I said, "Birds don't fly at night. If you hear one, you're not alone." "You may be the prey and not the predator." "If you hear insects, nothing is around." "When possible, travel downwind, man has many odors, and the smell of man directs you to where he's at." "You'll not have the opportunity of color when using night vision." "Everything will be dark gray or light gray." "If you see anything other than that, then it's human; the heat of the body glows red."

I then went to the closet and opened a chamber that concealed what I had below.

I brought it over to Jose and slid it up onto his arm so that his hand was exposed and holding onto a trigger. When he looked up at me, I began explaining the weapon to him.

"Throughout wars, all weapons were tested for their usefulness." "Hunters bought weapons to kill their quarry for food or sport, and children used weapons to kill birds." "Our instincts travel far back in time," I said. "You have grenades, and you have needles of poison." "Combined, you have the capability of killing five to ten thousand men, but it won't do you any good if you get hit by the first bullet that was fired at you." "Avoid contact." I reiterated, "Jose, I told you we would be up against an army of maybe ten thousand." "I was wrong." "Sometimes, we're at a crossroad where we know our outcome." "When you pull the trigger, start spraying those that are charging you, there are fifty magazines in the casing, and each magazine contains one hundred soft-headed pellets, designed to flatten out to three-eights of an inch upon impact." "Like your knife, it also discharges air." "The pellet explodes upon impact and leaves a hole in you the size of a musket ball." "There's one canister pressurized to ten thousand pounds in the middle of the casing." "It's like a paint gun." "After each casing is empty, it's ejected, and the next is in use." "Jose, a weapon is only as good as the person that's using it." "Wasted ammunition on the dead doesn't do anyone any good." "Why do men build bigger guns when a bullet the size of a pellet is all that's needed?" I said, "I've had that prototype for seven years. I never even thought about using it; the truth is, I never felt I needed it. It felt cumbersome." "You trained with guns, so you feel confident having one." "I told you that guns alarm the enemy to where you are." "That weapon there is like the weapon with the needles; it doesn't make a sound." "There's a muffler outside the canister that suppresses the release of the compressed air." "Jose, you point that weapon and fire, five hundred men will fall in less than ten seconds." "Guns are burdensome," I added, "they jam, and they have to be reloaded." "That's when men are killed." "That weapon contains five thousand rounds of ammunition that will perforate any man shot anywhere." "You wanted a gun; now you have fifty of them at your disposal."

He got up, walked over to the mirror, and looked deep within himself.
"Jose, there are two missions you perform." I said to him, "One mission,
you dress like this, and the other mission, you'll be wearing a suit and tie."
"This mission requires you to be a man of action, it requires you to use all the
knowledge you possess for only one purpose, and that's survival." "The other
missions require you to be a man of distinction." "Remember my number one
rule, never reveal your whereabouts."

I walked over, pulled the weapon off of his hand, and attached it to the
rear of his belt behind him.

I took his shoulders and turned him to me. "Jose, I need your attention."
"Everything you have on is a weapon of death, and it won't do you one bit
of good if you're killed." "That's one of the reasons I asked you if you had
vengeance on your mind." "I need a clear head and not an angry one." I patted
him on the shoulder. "All I ask of you is please don't make me shovel the dirt
over you're grave." "Obey my commands to the fullest."

"Yes, sir." He said.

I turned and walked towards the cockpit with Jane behind me. When I
opened it up, Ellen gasped, while Jack said, "I figured you'd be coming in soon."

"How much time we got Jack?"

"Twenty minutes." He said.

I then looked at Ellen. "Have you been flying this whole trip?" I asked her.

"Jack's been helping me." "Smith, I've been having a good time." "I didn't
know it was this easy."

I saw Jane smiling.

"Ellen, you remember the simulator back at the lab?" I asked her.

"I'm still sore from it." She said.

"The code name for this plane is JASON." "If you want to learn how
to fly this plane, you can learn the same way that Jack did, and it took him
almost three years." "Type in the code word JASON into the computer and
begin your lesson." "No one is ever too old to learn," I told her.

"Hey, I'm only forty-seven. I'm not old yet." She said.

"Ellen, you started to become old when young people began saying yes
ma'am and no ma'am to you," I said, smiling. "Jack, on your way back, three
hundred miles out, the plane will make contact to be refueled." "I had to
change plans, so what I thought would be a few days will be longer."

"You know you're motto." He said, "No chances." "So don't start taking
any now." He warned me.

I took Jane's hand, and we both walked out, and I told Jose and Maria to
follow us. We entered the back of the plane, and I put more gear on Jose and
strapped my explosives on me.

I turned around and strapped Jane and Maria in a seat. "When we drop, there's going to be suction, and it'll pull you with us." "Don't get up until the doors close," I said.

After I saw that they were secure, I looked at Jane as I spoke out loud. "Jack, the girls are strapped in, and we're in position."

My computer relayed my message to him.

"Thirty seconds, Smith." I heard him say as Jose turned his head to look at me. He heard Jack's transmission through his implant.

"Sir, are you sure this thing will work?" Jose asked.

"No one ever knows if anything will work until it's tested." I told him, "You can trust me on this one, Jose; if it doesn't, you will be one of the first ones to know about it."

"Ten seconds, Smith," Jack said.

The doors dropped, and we fell. I deployed my wings and locked them in place, and the wing began to take the force of the updraft.

"You can relax, Jose." I told him, "Jack, you get a reading." I asked.

"You're coming in loud and clear." He said, "Break a leg, kid." He said.

"Sir, I can't help it." Jose asked, "This is impossible."

"It started out as my model." I told him as we descended, "I didn't design it for the load of two people." "I needed something to hold more weight, and I wasn't comfortable with the discs I installed; the air has to pass through them, but you need resistance to control the power of the wind to float along on its currents." "I stuffed ten rolls of toilet paper into the wings to be used as filters; that's why the wings came out so quickly." "The toilet paper allows the craft to float, and it allows the air to escape on a controlled leakage; it's the pores in the paper that give me the control I need," I stated.

"Sir, I made a lot of jumps in training, but we had shoots." He said, "I was scared."

"That makes two of us." I told him, "Any man that says he's not frightened of something going wrong doesn't understand that anything that can go wrong will go wrong." "Fortunately, everything has been in our favor, but I can't guarantee a few seconds from now."

"You're not making this easy on me, you know?" He said.

"Jose, you remember repelling from cliffs?" I asked him as we flew along. "Yes, sir."

"Which repel scared you the most?" I asked.

"The first one, I was leaning over and hanging with my feet upside down." "When I let go," "I found out there was nothing to be scared of." He said.

"Lean to the right a little." I told him, "Now, learn a little left."

I turned around and turned his night vision on.

"Zoom in up ahead." I told him, "See the cliff jutting above the others?"

"Yes, sir."

"We're landing on this side of it." "When I tell you to, bend your legs forward, that'll cause the tail to push down; we're coming in too fast," I said.

"Okay, now, push Jose, push." The craft slowly descended and landed gently.

We got off, and I buried my craft.

"Sir, do we make this kind of an entrance on every mission?" He whispered.

I whispered back, "No two missions are the same."

We made our way above the Messiah's fortress and watched from above. His men changed guards every four hours. I looked at my watch and then at Jose. I began searching for any surveillance equipment.

I spoke softly to Jose. "It's too late in the morning to work now." "Dig a foxhole and cover yourself with a brush, and tomorrow night we do what we came to do." I told him and then stated, "Get some rest; I'll keep watch."

"He began digging, and I held my hand down to the ground to signal him to soften the sounds of his digging." I signed to him to go slow and easy.

When daylight came, I heard helicopters over the ridge and the sounds of machinery. I left Jose asleep and crawled to be able to see over the ridge. I heard a twig snap and looked to see Jose almost next to me.

"You learn quickly," I told him.

"What's going on, sir?" He asked.

"They are building up their forces over at the site of the missile." I said to him, "That only means one thing; he has a launch date set." "It appears we've arrived right on schedule." "Jose, zoom in on the large building over to the right." "That's the control room for his missile guidance, and in front of that is the dam." "Take a look where we're at." "There aren't any walls to shield the control room." "The ridges are too steep to climb to worry about a full attack." "We're right smack on top of a defense line; there's another one about a hundred feet above the road." "Look, you can see that trail over to your right. It stops in the ditch." "I'm betting that we have a nest in there." "When the time comes, we'll have to take those men out."

I scanned the surrounding terrain and then stopped. I nodded with my head for Jose to look at what I was looking at. I let him know that was our point of attack when we attacked.

Then I told him to look down at the palace. "It's molded along the bottom of the mountain." "The bottom supports everything above it, collapse the bottom, and everything above comes tumbling down." "Destroying the palace serves no purpose except to distract our enemy and give them the feeling that there are more attacks taking place." "Take a look up the road and down the road." "We have to set up explosives for an ambush; we can expect to attract others."

We eased back over and slid under the brush and waited till the night fell. I woke Jose from his slumber and signaled for him to follow me.

We worked our way down to the palace slowly, careful not to disturb anything that might cause alarm, and waited for the changing of the guards. When they passed, we passed behind them, and I began planting the explosives while Jose kept watching.

Several squads came by, and a guard stuck his rifle in through the brush to ease it aside to have a better look. Jose had his knife out, ready to strike if he ventured further. He held his position, and a voice was heard. The guard backed up and left. Jose looked over at me; I gave him a thumbs-up signal to let him know that he let patience be his guide.

I installed a receiver, and we were ready to do the next one.

We eased over about fifteen feet when a guard came over to where we were going and stopped to relieve his bladder against the wall. We waited until he left and eased along to finish what I started and planted another explosive with another receiver.

We planted one more before we left and proceeded to booby trap the road. Nighttime was close to ending, and we sought refuge under a rocky canopy. I pulled some brush over the top of us to shield us.

"Congratulations, your first day went well." I whispered, "You're still alive, and if you had killed that guard, they would be alerted to us."

"Sir, I came close, real close." He said.

"You did the right thing, Jose; you waited." "What you did wasn't that easy to control, but you did, and that allowed us to continue in our work uninterrupted." "Tomorrow, we infiltrate his defenses and install the capsules into the dehumidifier."

"How are we going to do that?" He asked.

"By observation, how many men do you think we're up against?" I asked him.

"I don't know, sir." "I didn't count them." He replied.

"Then one more soldier won't be given a second look, would he?" I said.

"No, sir, I see your point." He said, smiling.

I sat watching the road while Jose dozed. The traffic was light, which comforted me. If it was heavy, then that meant that they were looking for us.

One of the envoys didn't appear like the rest. I zoomed in with my glasses to get a closer look. It was the agent and her family. I watched as they drove by, entered the prison compound, and took them to a barrack. That told me where the prisoners were being housed and where the soldier's quarters were stationed.

I watched as men that took them in came back out and locked the door behind them.

Jose stirred and began to survey his surroundings.

"They brought my cargo earlier." I told him, "They're in the prison compound now." "That confirms my suspicion that he's set a launch date." "We don't have the luxury of knowing when, so we're going to have to move fast on this one," I told him.

"Sir, I got your back." He said.

"Jose, one man moves quieter than two." "I have to install my capsules, and then I have to set up a transmitter to jam their frequency, and I can't move while waiting on you." "This is one of those times that you'll have to trust me." I told him, "Look over at the prison compound." I said to him, "I need you to keep an eye on those barracks in front, especially the second one from the end." "That's where my cargo is, and prisoners are housed in all the rest." "Those buildings behind them are the quarters for the soldiers." "That one building over there that sits by itself; I believe that's the torture chamber." "I need you to keep the surveillance to make sure they don't move my cargo before I get back; it's imperative." "You may think of it as me trying to keep you back, but if they move my cargo, and I don't know about it, it could be me that kill them and not my enemy."

"Yes, sir, I understand." He said reluctantly.

I looked at my watch. "Jack needs one more day," I said. "He's not halfway in position yet." "The Messiah has moved his hostages for a purpose, and that makes me wonder why?" I asked myself out loud.

"Sir, are you talking to me?" Jose asked.

"No," I said, "when someone does something, such as moving my cargo, I need to know his intentions." "I was going over a few things in my mind, that's all." I told him, "Jose, we're faced with a man that knows that his actions have upset people." "He's fighting his paranoia." "When he acts, you have to ask why, and then you can either wait for the man to act again to find out what he has or had on his mind, or you prepare for the worst." I sat back for a moment and then looked over at Jose. "Fact; he knows that we're coming for them, but he doesn't know when, and he puts them in a barracks that's not well manned." "The only thing that we have in our favor is that we haven't lost our advantage of being discovered." "That doesn't sound right, though. It sounds too easy to me." "Fact; he knows if I make a move, he'll know we're here and publicly display his act of aggression out on his hostages, first the children, then her husband, and then her." I looked over at Jose; that doesn't sound right, does it; I think it's a bluff?" I told him, "He's got the barracks rigged to blow if I go anywhere near the compound." "Everything is designed with protection from three sides, leaving the only line of attack from the top; his palace, the control room, and this prison." "That means he'll deploy nearly all of his men above our targets; he's thinking ambush." I said, "Computer; inform Ramon that he'll be visited in seven days."

"I thought you didn't want them to know we're here." He said.

"I'm trying to buy a little time." I told him, "I'm hoping he believes what he hears." "Jose, if you watch an animal go from one place to the other, he always uses the same path and that path forms a visible trail, and he'll use that trail every time that it's coming or going, a man isn't any different; he follows the path of the least resistant." "We know one location in front of the control room already." "While I'm gone, ease your way around to the end of the compound over there." I nodded with my head to show him his direction. "Do as I instructed earlier, move slow, stop and survey your surroundings and then when you know everything is safe, move some more." "If any movement is monitored, your glasses will warn you; they have audible motion sensors." "You might think of it as having the ears of a dog." "Like before, if you encounter an enemy, avoid them. If you are detected, kill them all." I told him, "One of the first lessons in the rule of living is not to take chances." "I need to know where the compound is being watched, and the easiest way is to see if there's a trail leading to the observers."

"I can handle it, sir?" He said.

"I know you can." "I wouldn't send you if I didn't." "Jose, my main concern is my cargo; you have to have your eyes open on them and on yourself."

I flipped a small switch in the nosepiece of his glasses.

"Those red dots are mines." I told him, "I don't think I have to give you a lecture on avoiding them."

"Sir, what if I find someone?" He asked.

I put my hand to my eyes and rubbed them gently to remove the dust. I then looked over at him.

"For now, observe," "but if your life is threatened, don't think twice." "I don't know what my time period is going to involve. You can't get in a hurry to do another job until you finish the first job." "A job that's done in a rush leaves room for errors."

I pulled one of the backpacks that he was carrying from him off of his shoulder.

"Jose, you have to take the advantage when the advantage is on your side." "One push of this finger here," I showed him my forefinger, "and this place will look like that warehouse when I'm finished." "That's how I like to do my fighting, with one finger." "Besides, the more explosions that occur when we're not around, giving them the impression of attacks that are taking place somewhere else." "They'll send squads to search for those that were responsible; only no one will be around." "That's what we want." "We have to separate his army from his army."

"Jose, as strange as it may sound, we're not here to kill his army. They're not our objective; the Messiah is." "You've heard the cliché to kill the serpent; you have to cut off his head?"

"Yes, sir." He replied.

"That's his method of intimidation; he loves his public executions." "His army will disperse, and the end to this mission will only be done when his head is hanging on a pole for all of his followers to see; they know they'll be next if caught." "People in our country are repulsed by seeing those kinds of sights, so they're censored." "But here, it's not viewed that way; dismemberment of a body is more of a closure for those that have vengeance on their minds."

I flipped on my night vision and thermal imagery and got up to depart. "Remember, if you're threatened, all bets are off, kill all those who stand in front of you." I then left and began making my way to the missile base.

When I reached my destination, I could see the dehumidifier. I waited and surveyed my surroundings, and when a guard came walking by, I popped him with a kick to his jaw and twisted his head in one movement, breaking his neck. After putting on his clothes, I walked in like I was part of his army. I kept a close watch as I blocked in the valve that allowed the filter to catch the condensate; I caught movement out of the corner of my eye to the right of me. I acted like I was relieving myself next to the air conditioner, and the men passed without incident. I went back to removing the cartridge and inserting my own; I then opened the valve back up and left the way I came in like I was part of the army.

I went back and retrieved my weapons that I had hidden in the brush, and ten minutes later, I was looking for a vantage point to set up my transmitter. My plan was to aim a field of positive and negative energy to agitate and encourage the acid to attach itself to any object and react quicker. When I finished, I looked at my watch. It was three o'clock. I didn't waste time.

I made haste back to the compound and looked around to find Jose. He was sitting behind some bushes. The only bad thing was there were three men above him easing their way down to him.

I didn't waste time getting to him. They were about twenty feet away when I took off my longbow, and they fell at his feet. He jumped up, ready to fight. I came up behind him. "Relax, they're dead," I said to him.

He bent down and looked at the arrows in their hearts.

"I didn't see or hear anything." He said.

"You let yourself become complacent." I told him, "You should have heard them twenty feet up the hill."

"What do you hear, Jose?" I asked him.

He listened and then said. "Nothing, sir."

"Exactly." I told him, "The night gives off many sounds, and when those sounds are absent, then something is out there that's not supposed to be there. They're quiet right now because we're here." "That was you're the first clue," I told him.

"I'm sorry, sir."

"You were thinking about Maria," "that'll get you killed." I said, "Besides, they weren't here to kill you, their mercenaries; they wanted to capture you to find out what you knew." "Or they would have taken you out with one shot when they noticed you." "Do you believe in luck?" I asked him.

"No, sir." He said.

"You should, or you'd be dead now." I told him, "Did you see anything?" "Yes, sir." "Right below us is three men in a bunker."

"Let's go then." I told him, "We need to introduce ourselves."

"What about these guys?" He asked.

"By the time they find out they're dead, they'll be dead," I said.

"What's your plan?" He asked.

"I thought I'd walk up and knock on the door, and when they answered it, I figured you could get a little on-the-job training with the poisoned needles or the gas pellets." "These men here are their replacements."

We knocked on the door, and a voice came from inside. I spoke to him, and the door began to open slowly. Jose was down on one knee when I kicked the door open out of his hand. Seconds later, I was telling Jose to take deep breaths and to relax.

We pulled them out of the bunker and tossed them down the ravine.

"How about my cargo?" I asked him.

"I didn't see anything about them, but they came and took some of the other men and drug them off to that building over there." "Sir, I could hear them screaming."

"They're political prisoners." I said to him, "Come on, we're too easy of a target to stay here." "Tonight is hell night."

We found a good hiding place that had sight of the compound below. I watched the road for activity and watched the men see when the guards changed shifts. They weren't a very well-organized group of men. It was clear that they were rebels that supported the Messiah for only one reason. They were able to get away with anything. To me, they were nothing more than scavengers.

"Sir, you need to get some sleep." "I can keep watch," Jose said, interrupting my thoughts.

"It doesn't work that way, Jose." "See their barracks over there?" "We've got to make our way around and into the back of the compound." "We have to sneak under the barracks to set our explosives, and when they go to sleep, we give them a wake-up call." "Come nightfall; the guards will have to be killed." "Jose, the Messiah is going to be greeted with his Armageddon." "Tonight, if all goes as planned, we get what we came here for."

"I thought you said that we only work at night?" He responded.

"I also said that all plans are subject to change too." "Right now, there's no one in the barracks. We have to take advantage of that."

"Yes, sir." He said.

I could sense something was amiss with Jose.

"Were those the first men you killed?" I asked him.

"Yes, sir."

"How does it make you feel?" I said.

"I thought it wouldn't be that bad, but sir, I feel sick." He said.

"Then you've learned a lesson today. The day that killing someone doesn't make you feel sick is the day that you become like them." "What separates us from them is we kill them to stop them from killing others." "We do that; we're through here, we move on to another page in our life." "These men here, their violence won't stop until they're stopped." "You have to come with the grip of there being a right and a wrong in life; they happened to choose a different path than you did, and now isn't the time to question yourself on the difference between right and wrong," I told him.

"Yes, sir." "Sir, in training, you're taught to kill." "But to actually do what you're taught, they couldn't have prepared me for that."

"That may be so," I said, "but unless you want to end up like them, you better get your mind focused on what we're here for, and I mean now." "Jose, there's going to be more, a lot more, so if these men bother you that much, then what will it feel like when a thousand of them come charging up that hill after you?" "You hesitate three seconds, and you're dead." "I asked you not to let me shovel the dirt in you're grave." I told him, "This is reality, not a mission of training." "You have to focus." "Come on; we've got to move." "I've got work that needs to be done." By that evening, we were near some brush that was close to the barracks. After several minutes we were crawling through the brush, and we quickly went under the first barrack and scoped out the prison compound. I applied some putty onto the floor bottom and inserted a detonator into the putty next to my grenades. After arming it, we then went to the next barrack and did the same.

Three men came by, and I took out three of my stars and waited. They left after hearing orders for them to fall in.

As we were working, I noticed trucks beginning to pull in. Jose and I both watched as they unloaded.

"Ramon's let them know we're coming," I said to him. "They're strengthening their reinforcements."

After rigging all the barracks, we eased ourselves back out and waited till night.

I looked over at Jose. "It's time that we make our move." I told him, "Stay close behind me."

The first guard went down without a sound from a well-placed throwing star to his forehead. I bent down to retrieve it, wipe the blood from its blade, and look over, and Jose had the mouth of another cupped with his hand as he sliced his throat.

If anything about killing someone affected him earlier, I cast it all aside then.

I opened the door on the first barrack, and one of the men began to call out. I was prepared and silenced him.

"Quiet, or you'll all join him," I told everyone.

I looked around and saw the key to the cells by the door and then helped Jose pull the guards inside. When I released the men, they made quick work in retrieving their weapons.

"Stop, silence," I commanded them. "We either work as a team in this, or you'll all die."

"Who are you?" A man's voice came from the back.

"I'm here to kill the Messiah," I stated in his language, "and one thing that I don't need is a bunch of men shouting and shooting. We won't get anywhere that way." "If I were you, I'd take to the hills and not look back," I told them all.

"If you came here to kill the Messiah, you'll need my help." He said.

He walked out into the light of the moon from the window. He had burn marks all over him. "They killed my son, and they killed our friends." "We came to kill the Messiah too but were betrayed."

"You had a traitor amongst you here." I told him, "He's lying dead over there."

"You have a name," I asked him.

"Abdul Muhammad Muhammad." He said.

"Abdul, this compound is going to be underwater." "I'm blowing the dam, and everything in its path will be destroyed." "That means his control room and this prison." "I'm not asking you to run from a fight. I'm asking you to run from death."

A half a dozen footsteps could be heard walking on the wooden platforms. "Quiet," I ordered.

I waited by the door, and when I saw them arming their weapons, my throwing stars made quick work of the men. After pulling them inside, I turned back to Abdul. "I need all of you to listen to me," "these barracks are wired to blow, one wrong move, or noise, and it's over with, everyone here will die before you can fight." "Follow me, and we attack one barrack at a time." "But, we have to have silence to succeed." "If you die, then nothing has been achieved."

"Abdul" "that man there was planted; he heard what you said and repeated it to others." "He's dead, and you will be too if you don't do the same to a man that sounds out. You have no friends here, be prepared to silence anyone."

The men took their weapons, and I went to the next set of barracks. Abdul told them all to follow him and to be quiet doing so. As they worked their way down, releasing all the men, I went after the agent and her family. I eased to the side and peered into the barracks through a window that was slightly open. Three men stood in my way. Jose came up behind me, and he, too, saw the men.

"Do we knock on the door, or do we kick the door down?" He whispered.

I took his gun from the back of his belt and slid it on. When I stood up, I fired a short burst through the window and then handed his gun back to him.

"Or we could just shoot them." He then stated.

I opened the door and found the keys on the desk that opened their cells. When we exited, Abdul had everyone standing before me.

"Do we attack the men master?" Abdul said.

I told them all to get down and initiated my signal to my computer to blow the barracks. It went up with one big bang. I looked at Abdul and told him, "No man needs to die fighting when it's not necessary."

I told everyone to sit tight. My computer warned me that it was tracking ten moving objects. "We've got trucks headed our way; they heard the explosions," I told Abdul and told him to remain calm.

When they came in range, my computer detonated my explosives on the road that we planted, and when the other trucks tried to go around the first truck. It was a mistake. I expected that, and it detonated my next set of explosives, and the road was blocked.

Abdul looked over at me.

"You are truly our master." He said.

"No, you're the master of your own lives," "Abdul," "I came to retrieve an agent and her family." "Now I have to deliver them, and when I return, I'm going after the Messiah." "I warn you, do not go past the ridge down into the compound, they're waiting for you; the man that betrayed you and your son also betrayed me." "If you go against my orders, all of your men will be slaughtered." "It's a death trap." "Wait until my return, and then we'll attack." "You've got about ten minutes to make up your mind." "That's how long it'll be before his men are here," I told him.

"I will do as you wish, master." He said, making a motion with his hand from his head to his chest and then to his feet. He was telling me that he was at my disposal.

"If it makes you feel any better, I'm going to find and kill the man that betrayed us." "Abdul, people of many nations are watching." "Your people need you, now more than ever; they follow you." "They need a leader that will think only of the people's needs." "Are you that man, or are you like all the rest that came before the Messiah?"

I grabbed one of the trucks, loaded my cargo up, and was about to depart down the road when I saw Abdul and stopped.

"Tell your men to retreat to the other side of the ridge and wait for my return." "They know they're under attack, and they'll be ready." "Abdul, I need someone that the people will follow. I'm not here for the purpose of bloodshed of women and children." "A good leader thinks only of the safety of others before he turns to fight." "Warn others to seek safety into the mountains." "Nothing can withstand the force of the water when the dam is blown," I told him.

"May Allah be by your side, master?" He said as I left.

I took off for the port, stopped short of it, and zoomed in on Ramon's boat. Jose eased up beside me.

"Over to your left, sir, is a man waiting behind a building." "There's a man inside the building across from him."

"I see them." I told him, "There's two more on the boat at the start of the pier." "Give me a few minutes and bring my cargo with you." I stopped for a moment and then told my computer to release my porpoises and seagulls, and then I notified Jack to tell the girls to strap themselves in; there were three unidentified objects closing in, five thousand yards behind them. "Tell them to hurry," I told him.

After a few seconds, I received a transmission that James and Ruby were ready. "Computer, activate evasion and destroy the vessels." "Jack" "tell the girls it's going to be a wild ride."

I then took off my longbow and worked my way down. When they showed themselves, my arrows found their mark.

I slowly worked my way around the boat, looking and moving silently in search of Ramon. He was a confident person when I woke him. He reached for his gun, and his hand fell with the gun still attached to it. I wiped the blood from my sword with his sheet.

"That's not nice, Ramon." I told him, "Why are you waiting for me?"

He was difficult to understand as he held his arm without a hand.

"Ramon, you jeopardized my mission; now I'm asking you politely, why did you betray me?"

He made a move for a knife and was rewarded by losing his other hand. He gritted his teeth and screamed as I once again wiped the blood from my sword.

"Ramon, you turned your own parents into the Messiah, for what?" "Was it money, or did he offer you a slice of his kingdom?" "No, wait, it had to be for the love of an agent?" "Why is it that all men think of themselves as being irresistible to a woman?" "Ramon, I need to know before I kill you." "It's one of those things that really bug's me when I can't come up with the answer." "You know what I mean?" I said to him.

"Americans are pigs." He had hostility in his voice.

"Ramon, there's no need to use words of hatred here; I thought we were having a gentleman's conversation." "You're a fool, Ramon."

I wiped the blood from my sword with his shirt, lit a flare, threw it into his fuel tank, and walked away.

Jose was at the dock when I came walking to the end. They were all watching the flames from the boat as it burned. I found one of the biggest boats that were there and told them all to get in. I hotwired the engine, and we took off with the engines at top speed. Soon we could hear the gunboats being attacked. Jose looked at me confused, and I answered him, "I ordered my computer to send dolphins loaded with explosives to take them out."

About two miles from the shore, I was warned that four jet fighters were approaching us fast.

"Take hold of the wheel; I told the lady."

"Where are you going?" She asked.

"I need to stall for time," I told her.

I took the launcher, loaded a grenade with my signal device, and waited.

When I first saw them, they were coming in low. I launched a grenade and ordered my computer to detonate on its call. They veered off before their bullets found their mark. On their second pass, we weren't as lucky, they came in from different angles, and my grenades couldn't handle more than one; their bullets were finding their way to their target. Jose was hit in the leg and shoulder and knocked back into the cabin wall.

He was trying to get back up when the planes disintegrated. He looked up at me, holding his arm.

"What happened?" He asked weakly.

I ran over and started tending to him, "What happened?" He asked again.

"Jose, do you know what brings down six hundred million dollars worth of jets?" I asked him.

"No, sir," he answered in pain.

"One flock of seagulls." I answered, "Birds cost the airline industries billions of dollars every year." "They get sucked up into an engine, and flights are put at risk; delays occur and all because of one bird that took on a three hundred ton airliner, and it occurs over a dozen times a year." "You don't need rockets to destroy a jet; all you need is a bird with a tiny bit of explosives inside of it." "I ordered my computer to install some seagulls loaded with explosives before we came." "His gunboats are worthless; they are sunk in the harbor." "Jack's not far away." "Hold on, and you'll be in safe hands soon."

"What happened?" He said again.

"I have a tracking chip in my ear, the same as you." "I ordered my computer to release my porpoises and seagulls." "I had to stall for time."

"I failed you again, sir." He said as I leaned him against the cabin wall.

"No, Jose, if anything, you proved that I was right," I said as I finished examining him. "You're going to be all right." I told him, "You'll be a little sore, and with some much-needed bed rest, and one day you'll be the way you were before this happened." "That's what a fighter does, he licks his wounds, and he struggles to get back to the man he was." "That's who you are." I'm lucky to have you."

"I didn't want this to happen, sir, I promised you; I wanted us to be like batman and robin."

"Jose, we are Batman and Robin." "We're a team, you and I, and a couple of bullets won't do anything to change that."

"But sir, I'm no good to you now?"

"Jose, it was me that let you down, and you can trust me. I've got all the parts I need to make you good as new." "I knew before we went on this mission that my chances weren't good." "There were way too many objectives that stood in my way." "Besides, none of your vital organs were hit."

"And having a punk kid like me around didn't help you any at all, did it, sir?" He said apologetically.

"No, that's not true." "I took you on for one reason." "I liked you, and I wanted you to learn how to live." "At the rate, you were headed, you didn't have the knowledge that an enemy doesn't play fair. They shoot first and answer questions later." "We did what we weren't supposed to do." "We let the enemy know where we were," I said.

"I guess you have to live it to learn it, right sir." He said.

"I really wish you would call me Smith," I told him.

"You didn't really need me, did you, sir?" Jose said.

"Let's say you didn't join the FBI or teamed up with McNally." "Do you know where you'd be at right night now?" I asked him.

"No, sir."

"You'd be like Dan; you'd be a cop patrolling the streets where you came from." "You'd be fighting the fights where he left off." "There are two ways to fight, a smart way and the wrong way. I was hoping you would slow down and learn the smart way to fight your enemy." "Jose, you learned a lot today, and tomorrow, you learn more, and the next day after that, you'll know more than the day before." "Besides that man's throat, you cut." "I didn't see him." "You proved to me that you had my back." "I owe you my life." "That means eight times now that I should have been killed, but I got lucky. I had a man to watch my back." I told him.

I was interrupted by the husband of the woman. He was telling me that they could see something up ahead.

"You'll be safe soon," I told Jose and then left him.

I took control of the wheel and headed towards my sub. Its beam guided me in. I cut the engine, and Jack came out, and then I noticed the rest of the crew that were with him, the women.

"Jane, Ellen, help everyone get down below." "James, I need your help; Jose's been shot."

He ran and jumped over into the boat, gently picked Jose up, and carried him into the sub. Maria began crying as she stepped out of James' way. I walked back to the boat and heard Jack's voice.

"Where are you going?"

"My job's not done yet." "How did the girls react to the sub," I asked him.

"They were all screaming when the torpedos started going off." "What did you do to the sub?" He asked.

"Have you ever watched a seal?" I asked him, "I put fin in the middle and rutters on the back tail." "There's one thing that we know." "Our enemies received a message that they aren't equipped to do battle with us." "Take good care of Jose; Jack, the kids got a lot of potentials," I said.

I then turned around and headed up into the cabin to leave.

My mind was occupied on my mission when the door opened on the cabin.

"What are you doing here?" I asked Jane, "You're supposed to be back at the Nautilus."

"Jose said you needed these." She said, "And me being not so bright, took them and jumped on the boat." "Smith, I didn't think. I just grabbed them and jumped." "Are you mad at me?"

"Jane, you don't belong here," I told her.

"That's a little late to be telling me that now, don't you think?" "And as far as us being here." "My father lost his battle when he was telling us to stay at the lab."

"Jane, you're not supposed to be here."

"You've already said that." She said.

"Why are you here?" I asked her again.

"I don't know; I just jumped." "Smith, I don't know what happened. I wasn't thinking; I just grabbed the stuff and ran and jumped."

I took the grenade belts and the guns and sat them on the floor. The door opened again with Ruby's hair and clothes dripping wet.

"What are you doing here?" I asked her.

"Sir, the order you gave me was to protect Jane." She said.

"I must be losing my mind," I said out loud.

"I'm sorry, sir, but you are my creator." Ruby said, "It is my duty to do as you command. I couldn't abort your command without your command to abort your previous command."

"Are you playing a game with me?" I asked her.

"No sir, no one can compete with the creator." She said.

"I didn't program you for this type of response."

"No sir, but under the circumstances, the master computer thought it was best to do so."

"Put on the vest," I told Ruby. "Computer initiate training on my weapons to Ruby."

Near morning I was back where I started from. I could see a squad of men down below in the ravine. I zoomed my lens in and saw Abdul.

I put my finger up to my mouth to signal Jane to be quiet and follow me and to move slowly. When we were above them, I ran and flew into the air and landed in the middle of them. I caught them by surprise, and when they raised their guns instinctively. Ruby ordered them in their language to put down their guns while she held hers on them. When they caught sight of Jane, they began bowing and chanting.

"What are they saying?" She asked.

"A prophecy was told that Allah, they're god, would send warriors to fight with them." "You're the tallest person they've ever seen, and you're a woman on top of that." "They call you Allah's warrior women." "It seems that you and Ruby are a good omen to them," I said.

We eased our way up the ridge, and I saw guards that had positioned themselves along the top. I stopped everyone and went alone. When I came back for them, they looked at the bodies as they crept low along the ridge. I stopped when I got to where Jose and I had spotted the first bunker.

"Wait here." I said, "They've got more men than I calculated."

"Computer; detonate the palace," I commanded, and the explosions could be heard. Abdul and his men thought the palace was being attacked, and it gave them a new spirit.

I turned to all the men and began speaking to them.

"Jane, get down on your knees and talk to the sky." "Remember the living dead?" I said, "I need you to raise them" "I told them that you're going to call their ancestors to help." "Computer raise the living dead."

She bowed down on the ground and started talking in an unknown language, and the androids began to rise up out of the graves that they had dug. The men wanted to run when Abdul shouted for them to stand and obey the warrior women. The androids were channeling the men into the control room area; they didn't have any other place to go. I ordered Ruby to start throwing the grenades. Men were being tossed everywhere, and they sought refuge in the only place they could, the control room. Ruby bombarded the control room to keep them housed.

Helicopters could be heard coming, and I ordered Ruby to take them out with the grenades.

I then took my weapons off of the belt and strapped them on Jane.

"Jane, sit here, and when the men begin to come out, start shooting at anything that moves and don't stop."

The helicopters came in low, and Ruby was pitching strikes.

"Take these vials and throw them in the windows on both floors," I told Ruby handing her the backpack.

When Ruby left, I told the men to seek shelter and gave the command for my computer to conceal my corpses. "Everyone down," I said to Abdul's men. I was warned of movement down the road and gave Ruby orders to wait. When the vehicles entered the compound, all my plans changed when I spotted the Messiah.

I gave Jane the order to start firing, and men were falling. When I ordered my computer to call upon the living dead, everyone ran as expected; no one knew where death was coming from. I told Abdul to tell his men to leave; they made their ancestors proud.

"I can't," he said. "I fight for my son, and I fight for my son's son."

I didn't hesitate. "Stay hidden and shoot." "Don't charge; let them look for you." "Few men can kill many if they don't know where you're at." "When the woman warrior fires her weapons of death, they will expose themselves to you." "Death to the Messiah comes now."

I gave orders for the men to position themselves in front of the control room and spread out every twenty feet, lying in a prone position. I was about to leave them when Abdul stopped me by grabbing my hand.

"You are not of my people, yet you fight for us."

"Abdul, I fight for all people that are prisoners in their own country," I said.

"I wish to fight with you, master."

"It is an honor to fight with such a brave man," I told him.

"As I master."

"Ruby, we're in position; release the vials," I commanded.

We crept beyond the compound and encountered men that were running out the back of the control room. Abdul opened fire, and men were falling over as they came running out. I stood ready. When he ran out of bullets, my swords were in play. I blocked the door with bodies and looked up to see Jane, and then we vanished behind the buildings. A minute later, men were running and screaming out the front. We could hear the gunfire as it erupted. My imitators held the soldiers at bay; they were caught in a firing squad. Ruby was throwing grenades while Jane held her trigger. We waited until the chaos settled down, and then Abdul and I stalked our way through the control room.

As we entered the hall, Abdul picked up another gun from a body that we passed. I checked each room, and then I heard a commotion at the end. I eased the tip of one of my swords around a door at the bottom to see what it was. Three soldiers were standing next to the Messiah with guns ready. I put my finger up to my mouth to signal Abdul to be quiet.

I took out my throwing stars and caught them in the back of the neck. The Messiah turned around quickly.

"You seem to be alone," I told him, walking in the door. "You're a king without a palace; you're a ruler without subjects," I said.

He eased his hand down on the control panel.

"Go ahead, fire the missile." "You know it's not ready." I told him, "The whole world is watching." "No country wants war, only the idiots that start them." "You and I both know that that missile isn't armed, but to fire, it would somehow give you the feeling of success."

I walked over to him, took the tip of my sword, put it up against his throat, and pushed him back.

"I won't give you that feeling; who's backing you?" I said to him, "We both know this country doesn't have the capability to defend itself; who wants this war." "Which country supports you?" He kept his silence, and I put my finger on the button and pushed it. The ground could be felt shaking, and the missile never got off the ground before it exploded.

"Now, the whole world knows you failed."

"Abdul, you have to ask yourself this question; compared to the world, this is a tiny nation." "What is to be gained by a man that preaches war when he doesn't have a military, and he calls himself a Messiah?" "Kneel down on your knees and bow your head, Angel of Satan," I told him.

He didn't do as I said, and I helped him. When he fell, he was screaming. I had kicked the side of his knee and broken it. I looked over at Abdul.

"Abdul, when I came for this man, it was because he had to be stopped." "But, you have a personal reason that is far above mine." "Men always want to be in control of others, but no one builds statues of those men, except those men themselves, and when they're dead, they're pulled down." "It's worthless unless the people build the statue because they thought of him as being a great man." "There are two kinds of leaders," I told him.

"This country needs a leader, not a ruler." "As long as you are a leader, I am your ally, you become a ruler, and I will come and deliver you the same message as I'm delivering to this man here."

I handed him my sword. "That blade is the sharpest blade ever made." "He'll not feel the cut, but he'll see your eyes before he dies." I said to him, "Release your pain."

He looked at the Messiah, and I saw his eyes begin to turn red, and with one swift blow, the Messiah was no more.

I took my sword from him, and reached down and grabbed the Messiah by his hair, and held his head up. "Hang his head high so all can see," I said to him. "Teach your people to live in peace."

"I will always be a servant to you, master." He told me.

"No, Abdul, a leader can only be a servant to his people." "Now, you have two hours, and this dam is going to be blown up." "I'm sorry, but it's for your own good." "Go into the mountains as high as you can." "All things will be destroyed when the dam blows." "All land will be washed away along with everything in its path."

I left him as he went out the front door with the head of the Messiah in his hand. Ruby was standing guard over Jane when I finally made my way to them.

I turned around and looked at all the bodies and debris that littered the ground and took the guns away from Jane.

"These will never be used by you again," I told her.

"Are you mad at me?" She said.

"Yes, and I don't have the words that I can tell you to make me feel better." "Come on; we need to quicken our pace." "Pick her up and carry her, Ruby." We began running to the shoreline down below. When we arrived at my destination, we waited for a few moments, and a submersible came rising out of the water. The door opened up, and we all got in, and I sealed the compartment. We began sinking, and soon we were off at a level of sixty feet.

"What is this?" Jane asked.

"When your father arrived, I ordered for the submersible to deploy and await further orders." "It's been lying on the bottom of the channel since it arrived here, waiting for me to activate it." "I thought if I made it this far, then I would need a ride home." "It's not a submarine, so to speak, but a parasite." "We'll attach ourselves to a ship that's heading in our direction, and my Nautilus Sub will intercept us, and we'll ride home in the Nautilus."

"You caused me a lot of problems back there." I told her, "It was hard to concentrate without wondering if something had happened to you."

"What if I was to tell you that I was feeling the same thing about you?" She argued, "Besides, Ruby was by my side the whole time."

"This is as far as the argument goes." I stated, "Jane, you won't ever surprise me like that again, or I'll put you in a cage until I return."

"You wouldn't dare." She pushed me.

"Computer, intercept tankers steered towards Miami," I said.

"Smith, you wouldn't put me in a cage, would you?" She asked.

"You violated my plans and put yourself in harm's way," I told her "I look at as if I was protecting myself." She commented.

"I couldn't ask for a woman with more devotion for someone like me to do what you did." "But you put yourself in harm's way by being there, Jane."

"Sir, she did stay concealed," Ruby said.

"Ruby, I don't want a debate right now," I told her.

"Sorry, sir, I apologize. I was only reacting to the program that you programmed."

We felt a slight movement, and my quarters turned to where we were level.

"We've attached ourselves to a tanker," I said to Jane.

"Smith, are you mad at me?" She said with puppy dog eyes.

"Jane, a lot of men died by your hand today. Doesn't that bother you?"

"I wasn't thinking about that at the time." She said, "They were all trying to kill you."

"You have no emotions, no feelings, no remorse?" I said to her, "That's not good."

"Smith, you always told me that you did what you had to do, and today, I know what you were trying to tell me, and where did you come up with this army of the living dead?" She asked.

"I was studying special effects on the movies that they make today." "I wasn't concerned with the movie, but the zombies did intrigue me. They've been idle for two years." "In our country, I never would use them, but in this country, they have different beliefs." "When you stood and turned to raise the dead, a story will be told of Allah's warrior women that called upon their ancestors to defeat their enemy," I told her.

"What's going to happen now?" She asked.

"His army is dispersing." "The missile was fired prematurely; his palace is dust, and what men he has that are loyal are going to be killed when the dam is blown."

"What happened back at the Sub?" She asked.

"You were going to be under attack." "I modified the sub to maneuver like that of a seal." "Did it frighten you?" I asked her.

"Yes, I was, but you're going to be asked a lot of questions from my mother and Maria."

She grabbed hold of me and started kissing me. I felt the tears run down her cheeks.

"Smith, I'm sorry for being stupid." She said, "You talking about dying and all, and after seeing Jose, I didn't think I just jumped."

"I don't like that word." I told her, "I prefer the interpretation of you not acting rationally." "And I meant it when I told you that I don't want you involved like that again." "Computer; initiate abduction of Doctor Messina, Doctor Rogers, and Doctor Clemons." "Alert the hospitals of transplants in four days, and inform them that our staff will be performing the operations." "Assemble my Doctors and deploy them to be ready when the organs are delivered." "Have the imitators amass twenty miles offshore and remain there until retrieved." I ordered "Computer; what is the condition of Jose." I said.

I listened for his condition and then spoke. "Jack, tell Ellen that Jane is unharmed." "We'll be arriving soon, and we'll all get some rest."

"What about Jose?" Jane asked.

"He's got a little bit of James in him now," I said.

"What do you mean?" She asked.

"His scapula was blown out along with the rotator cuff in his shoulder." "He had too many broken bones, and the only way was to replace part of his shoulder was with the parts I use to build my androids." "The bullet that him in the leg only hit muscle." "He'll be okay." I said to her, "Jane, I'm beginning to believe that Abdul's comment about Allah sending his warrior women has merit."

She whispered if we could turn out the lights.

I told her it didn't matter; Ruby could still see our bodies even in the dark.

"Ruby, initiate sleep mode," Jane commanded to her and then ordered for the lights to be turned off. "I keep forgetting who I'm with and where I'm at." She said.

We felt a slight shock wave, and it was over as soon as it started.

"That was the dam," I told her. "No more threats for twenty years."

"Smith, how long do you think it'll be before we get to the sub?" She asked.

"Two days, give or take," I answered.

"You mean we have two whole days alone with no one but me and you?" She said, "What about all of the other people that live inside that head of yours?"

"I asked them not to interrupt our privacy," I told her and took her into my arms, and tried to show her that her lessons didn't go unheeded.

The beginning of the end, but that's an interpretation